blue
rider
press

THE

FLIGHT

OF THE

SILVERS

ALSO BY DANIEL PRICE

SLICK

DANIEL PRICE

BLUE RIDER PRESS | A MEMBER OF PENGUIN GROUP (USA) | NEW YORK

THE
FLIGHT
OF THE
SILVERS

blue
rider
press

Published by the Penguin Group
Penguin Group (USA) LLC
375 Hudson Street
New York, New York 10014

USA · Canada · UK · Ireland · Australia
New Zealand · India · South Africa · China

penguin.com
A Penguin Random House Company

Copyright © 2014 by Daniel Price
Penguin supports copyright. Copyright fuels creativity, encourages diverse voices, promotes free
speech, and creates a vibrant culture. Thank you for buying an authorized edition of this book and for
complying with copyright laws by not reproducing, scanning, or distributing any part of it in any form
without permission. You are supporting writers and allowing Penguin to continue to publish books for
every reader.

"Whatever Lola Wants (Lola Gets)," from *Damn Yankees*. Words and music by Richard Adler and
Jerry Ross.
Copyright © 1955 Frank Music Corp. Copyright Renewed and Assigned to the J & J Ross Co. and
Lakshmi Puja Music Ltd.
All rights administered by the Songwriters Guild of America. All rights reserved. Used by permission
of Alfred Music Publishing Co., Inc.

Library of Congress Cataloging-in-Publication Data

Price, Daniel, date.
  The flight of the silvers / Daniel Price.
    p.   cm.
  ISBN 978-0-399-16498-9
  I. Title.
  PS3616.R526F55   2014   2013030273
  813'.6—dc23

Printed in the United States of America
1 3 5 7 9 10 8 6 4 2

Book design by Gretchen Achilles

This is a work of fiction. Names, characters, places, and incidents either are the product of the author's
imagination or are used fictitiously, and any resemblance to actual persons, living or dead, businesses,
companies, events, or locales is entirely coincidental.

PART ONE

SISTERS

PROLOGUE

Time rolled to a stop on the Massachusetts Turnpike. Construction and wet weather clogged the westbound lanes at Chicopee, turning a breezy Sunday flow into a snake of angry brake lights.

Robert Given puffed a surly breath as his Voyager merged with the congestion. Two long hours had passed since he hugged the last of his grieving siblings and herded his family into the minivan. The rain had followed them the whole way from Boston, coming down in buckets and thimbles by turns. Now the sky dribbled just enough to make the windshield wipers squeal at the slowest setting.

After five squeals and ten feet of progress, he pushed up his glasses and studied the speedy trucks on the overpass. He had no idea which highway he was looking at, aside from a better one.

"Don't," said Melanie, from the passenger seat.

"Don't what?"

"I see you putting on your explorer's hat. I'm saying don't. I'd rather be stuck than lost."

His wife had spoken the words gently, and with a small twinge of irony. Melanie was typically the flighty one of the duo, the titsy-ditzy actress who rarely reached noon without making some heedless blunder. Today's reigning gaffe was her choice of funeral dress, a clingy black number that was a little too little for the comfort of some. Worse than the sneers and leers of her stodgy in-laws was the scorn of her ten-year-old daughter, who chided her for disrespecting Grandpa with her "showy boobs." That hurt like hell. It wasn't so long ago that Amanda needed help buttoning her blouses. Now the girl had become the family's stern voice of propriety, the arbiter of right and wrong.

Melanie straightened her hem, then turned around to check on her other brown-haired progeny, the sweeter fruit of her womb.

"You all right, angel?"

Hannah warily chewed her hair, unsure if it was safe to be honest. At five years old, she was too young to understand the grim rituals she'd witnessed today. All she knew was that she had to be on her best behavior. No whining. No showboating. No wriggling out of her itchy black dress. She'd spent the morning on cold metal folding chairs, staring glumly at her feet while all the grown-ups sniffled. It was a strange and ugly day and she couldn't wait for it to be over.

"I want to go home."

"We'll be there soon," Melanie said, prompting a cynical snort from her husband. "You want to sing something?"

Hannah's chubby face lit up. "Can I?"

"Sure."

"No," said Amanda, her stringy arms crossed in austerity. "We said no songs today."

Her mother forced a clenched smile. "Sweetie, that was just for the funeral and wake."

"Daddy said it was for the day. Out of respect for Grandpa. Isn't that what you said, Daddy?"

Melanie winced at the buckling to come. She knew Robert would eat his own salted fingers before disappointing Amanda.

Right on cue, he bounced a sorry brow at Hannah in the rearview mirror. "Honey, when we get home, you can sing all you want. Just not now, okay?"

Friends often joked that Robert and Melanie Given didn't have two children, they each had one clone. Nearly all of Amanda's genetic coin flips had landed on her father's side. She bore his finely chiseled features, his willowy build, his keen green eyes and ferocious intelligence. The two of them doted on each other like an old married couple. Rarely an evening passed when they weren't found curled up on the sofa, devouring one heady book after another.

Hannah was Melanie's daughter through and through. While Robert and Amanda were made of sharp angles, the actress and her youngest were drawn in soft curves. They shared the same round face, the same brown doe eyes, the same scattered airs and theatrical temperament. Hannah had also been born with a gilded throat, a gift that came from neither parent. The child crooned like an angel and never missed a note. She could perform any song flawlessly just by hearing it twice. Her mother worked with her day and night, honing her talent like a fine iron blade. Hannah Given would carve her name in the world one day. Of this, Melanie had no doubt.

Sadly, the skews in parental attention—the balanced imbalance—were starting to bear bitter fruit. With each passing day, Amanda treated her mother more and more like a rival while Hannah increasingly saw her father as a stranger.

And the girls themselves weren't the tightest of sisters.

Magnanimous in victory, Amanda rummaged through her neatly packed bag of backseat boredom busters. "Look, why don't we do a puzzle out of my book?"

"Why don't you shut up?"

Both parents turned around. "Hannah . . ."

Amanda fell back into her seat, matching her sister's pouty scowl. "I was trying to be nice."

"You're not nice. You're bossy. And you don't want me singing, 'cause I'm better than you."

"That's enough," Melanie snapped. She rubbed her brow and blew a dismal sigh at the windshield. "This is our fault."

"No kidding." Robert rolled the Voyager another ten inches, tapping the wheel in busy thought. "Maybe next weekend, Hannah and I—"

The piercing screech of tires filled the air, far too close for anyone's comfort. The Givens spun their gazes all around but no one could see movement. Every vehicle was stuck on the flytrap of I-90.

The noise gave way to a thundering crunch. A long and twisted piece of metal rained down on the Camry in front of them, shattering the rear window.

Melanie covered her mouth. "Oh my God!"

Robert raised his wide stare at the overpass, where all the trouble was happening. A speeding tanker truck had flipped onto its side and skidded through the guardrail. Now the curved metal trailer teetered precariously over the edge. Robert barely had a chance to formulate his hot new worry before the Shell Oil logo bloomed into view like a mushroom cloud.

No . . .

The truck toppled over, plummeting toward the turnpike in a messy twirl. The parents froze, breathless, as their minds fell into an accelerated state of alarm. While Melanie forced a hundred regrets, Robert hissed a thousand curses at the invisible forces that brought them here, all the cruel odds and gods behind their senseless demise.

After an eternity of wincing dread, they heard the dry squawk of the wiper blades, the rustling scrapes of Amanda's black taffeta.

"Daddy?"

Robert and Melanie opened a leery eye, then stared at the fresh new madness in front of them.

The fuel truck hung immobile in the air, a scant nine feet from impact. Floating bits of debris twinkled all around it like stars in the night. In every other vehicle, silhouetted figures remained flash-frozen in terrified poses. Only the thin wisps of smoke from the cab's engine seemed to move in any fashion. They rippled in place with the lazy torpor of sea plants.

Amanda leaned forward, her face slack with bewilderment. At ten years old, her universe had settled into a firm and tidy construct. Everything fit together with mechanical precision, even the squeaky gears of her little sister. But now something had gone horribly wrong with the clockwork. Amanda was old enough to know that things like this simply didn't happen. Not to the living. Not to the sane.

"Daddy, what . . . what is this?"

Robert turned around as best he could, struggling to rediscover his voice. "I don't know. I don't know. Just stay where you are. Don't do anything."

Melanie unclasped her seat belt and reached a trembling hand for Hannah. "Sweetie, you okay?"

The child shook her head in misery. "I'm cold."

Now that Hannah mentioned it, the others noticed the sharp drop in temperature, enough to turn their breath visible. They glanced outside and saw a strange blue tint to the world, as if someone had wrapped their van in cellophane.

Amanda flinched at the new life outside the window.

"M-Mom. Dad . . ."

The others followed her gaze to the center of the freeway, where three tall and reedy strangers watched them with calm interest. The man on the left wore a thin gray windbreaker over jeans, his handsome face half-obscured by a low-slung Yankees cap. The woman on the right sported a stylish white longcoat and kinky brown hair that flowed in improbable directions, like Botticelli's Venus. Her deep black eyes locked on Amanda, holding the girl like tar.

Hannah and her parents kept their saucer stares on the man in the middle.

He was the tallest of the group, at least six and a half feet, with a trim Caesar haircut that lay as white as a snowcap. He wore a sharp charcoal business suit, eschewing a tie for a more casual open collar. Melanie found him beautiful to the point of unease. His skin was flawless, ageless, and preternaturally pale. His only color seemed to come from his irises, a fierce diamond-blue that cut through glass and Givens alike.

The trio stood with the formal poise of butlers, though Robert found nothing helpful or kind in their stony expressions. Melanie gripped his shoulder when he reached for the door.

"Don't. Don't go out there."

The white-haired man blew a curt puff of mist, then spoke in a cool honey bass that might have been soothing if it wasn't so testy.

"Calm yourselves. We just saved your lives. If you wish to keep living, then do as I say. Come out of the vehicle. All of you. Quickly."

He spoke with a slight foreign accent, a quasi-European twang that didn't register anywhere in Robert and Melanie's database. Despite all floating evidence in support of the man's good intentions, the elder Givens had a difficult time working their door handles.

The stranger shot an impatient glower through the driver's window. "I took you for a man of reasonable intelligence, Robert. Must I explain the danger of staying here?"

Robert once again eyed the fuel truck at the base of the bridge, now six feet from collision. Suddenly he understood why the smoke rippled slightly, why the hovering bits of metal sporadically twinkled. The clock hadn't stopped, just slowed. Their fate was still coming at the speed of a sunset.

Robert pushed his door open. "What's happening? How—"

"We're not here to educate," snarled the female of the trio, through the same odd inflections as her companion. "We came to save your pretty rose and songbird. Would you rather see them perish?"

"Of course not! But—"

"Then gather your daughters and come. Bring the cow if you must."

While Melanie and Robert scrambled outside, the white-haired man kept his sharp blue gaze on Hannah. She'd never seen anyone more beautiful or frightening in her life. He was a Siberian tiger on hind legs, a snowstorm in a suit.

Robert opened the side hatch and pulled her into his quivering arms. "Come on, hon."

"I don't like it here."

"I know."

"It's cold in the bubble and I want to go home."

Robert didn't know what she meant by "bubble." He didn't care. He clutched her against his chest, just as Amanda climbed out the door and wrapped herself around Melanie.

"Mom . . ."

Thick tears warmed Melanie's cheeks. "Stay with me, sweetie. Don't let go."

Soon the family stood gathered outside the minivan. Robert held his wary gaze on the strangers. "Can you please tell me what—"

They ignored him and split up. The man in the baseball cap turned around and moved a few yards ahead. The woman took a shepherding flank behind the Givens. The white-haired man stayed in place, bouncing his harsh blue stare between Robert and Melanie.

"We walk now," he said. "Tread carefully and stay within the field. If even a finger escapes, you won't enjoy the consequences."

They began traveling. Robert noticed that everything within thirty feet of them existed at normal speed and color, a pocket of sanity in the sluggish blue yonder. The field seemed to move at the whim of the man in the Yankees cap. He walked with strain, fingers extended, as if pushing an invisible boulder.

Battling his panic, Robert retreated into his head and imagined the analytical discussion he and Amanda might have in a calmer state of mind.

"Daddy, what did he mean about the finger and the field?"

"Not sure, hon. I'm guessing it's not healthy for a body to move at two different speeds."

"Did they slow down the world or did they speed us up?"

"Good question. I don't know. In either case, I figure we're just a blur to the people in the other cars."

"How is this happening?"

"I don't know, sweetie. It's entirely possible that I've lost my mind."

He looked up and saw exactly where the drizzling rain stopped, a perfect dome that extended all around them. A bubble.

Suddenly his inner Amanda posed a dark new stumper.

"Daddy, how did Hannah know the shape of the field?"

Robert's heart pounded with new dread, enough for Hannah to feel it through his blazer. She wrapped her shivering arms around his neck and buried her face in his shoulder. The air outside the dome carried a thick and smoky taste in her thoughts, like a million trees burning. She just wanted it to go away, along with the freezing cold and the scary white tiger-man.

Her mother and sister trailed five feet behind them, their arms locked together. Melanie's stomach lurched every time Amanda threw a backward glance at the fuel truck. For all she knew, one more peek would turn the girl into a pillar of salt.

"Honey, don't look. Just keep moving."

"But there are still people back there."

"Amanda . . ."

"We can't just leave them!"

Melanie bit her lip and winced new tears. Though her daughter often wielded her morality like a cudgel, there was no denying the depth of her virtue. The girl was good to the core.

Five feet behind them, the female stranger shined a soft smile at Amanda. "You're a noble one to worry, child, but little can be done. Even those who survive have short years ahead. I see the strings. I know the death that comes."

Amanda had been nervously avoiding eye contact with the woman, but now drew a second look. She was a shade over six feet tall, with an immaculate face that put her anywhere between a weathered thirty and a blessed sixty. Whatever her age, she was jarringly beautiful, at least on the outside. Her dark eyes twinkled with instability, like matches over oil.

"W-what do you mean?" Amanda asked.

Melanie tugged her forward. "Don't talk to her."

"It's no matter," the woman replied. "Just take comfort that you have a future, my pretty rose. I've seen you, tall and red."

"Leave her alone," Melanie hissed.

The stranger's smile vanished. Her stare turned cold and brutal.

"Be careful how you speak to me, cow. We spare you and your husband as a courtesy. Perhaps we should slay you both and rear the little ones ourselves."

"NO!" Amanda screamed.

The white-haired man sighed patiently at his companion. *"Sehmeer . . ."*

"Nu'a purtua shi'i kien Esis," said the other man, without turning around.

The madwoman pursed her lips in a childish pout, then narrowed her eyes at Melanie.

"My wealth and heart oppose the idea. Pity. Your flawed little gems would thrive in our care." She tossed Amanda another crooked smile. "We'd make them shine."

The Givens moved in tight-knuckled silence for the rest of their journey—past the turnpike, over the guardrail, and up a steep embankment.

The tall ones stopped at the peak and surveyed the falling truck in the distance. The fuel tank had just touched the concrete and was starting to come apart.

"Brace yourself," said the white-haired man, for all the good it did.

In the span of a gasp, the bubble of time vanished and a thunderous explosion rattled the Givens. Robert covered Hannah as a fireball rose sixty feet above the overpass. A searing blast of heat drove Melanie and Amanda screaming to the ground.

The strangers studied the swirling pillar of smoke with casual interest, as if it were art. Soon the madwoman swept her slender arm in a loop, summoning an eight-foot disc of fluorescent white light.

The family glanced up from the grass, eyeing the anomaly through cracked red stares. The circle hovered above the ground, as thin as a blanket and as round as a coin. Despite its perfect verticality, the surface shimmied like pond water.

Before any Given could form a thought, the quiet man in the windbreaker pulled down the lip of his baseball cap and brushed past the family with self-conscious haste. He plunged into the portal, the radiant white liquid rippling all around him. Robert watched his exit with mad rejection. It was the stuff of cartoons, a Roger Rabbit hole in the middle of nothing.

The dark-eyed woman gave Amanda a sly wink, then followed her companion into the breach. The surface swallowed her like thick white paint.

Alone among his rescuees, the white-haired man took a final glance at the Givens. Melanie saw his sharp blue eyes linger on Hannah.

"Just go," the mother implored him. "Please. We won't tell anyone."

The stranger squinted in cool umbrage, clearly displeased to be treated like a common mugger.

"Tell whoever you want."

Robert stammered chaotically, his throat clogged with a hundred burning questions. He thought of his minivan, which no doubt stood a charred and empty husk on the road. Suddenly the father who'd cursed the gods for his horrible fortune knew exactly what to ask.

"Why us?"

The stranger stopped at the portal. Robert threw a quick, nervous look at Amanda and Hannah.

"Why them?"

The white-haired man turned around now, his face an inscrutable wall of ice.

"Your daughters may one day learn. You will not. Accept that and embrace the rest of your time."

He stepped through the gateway, vanishing in liquid. Soon the circle shrank to a dime-size dot and then blinked out of existence.

One by one, the survivors on the freeway emerged from their vehicles—the injured and the lucky, the screaming and the stunned. In the smoky bedlam, no one noticed the family of mourners on the distant embankment.

The Givens huddled together on the grass, their brown and green gazes held firmly away from the turnpike. Only Hannah had the strength to stand. She was five years old and still new to the universe. She had no idea how many of its laws had been broken in front of her. All she knew was that today was a strange and ugly day and her sister was wrong.

Hannah moved behind her weeping mother and threw her arms around her shoulders. She took a deep breath. And she sang.

ONE

On a Friday night in dry July, in the Gaslamp Quarter of downtown San Diego, the Indian-dancers-who-weren't-quite-Indian twirled across the stage of the ninety-nine-seat playhouse. Five lily-white women in yellow sarees flowed arcs of georgette as they spun in measure to the musical intro. The orchestra, which had finished its job on Monday and was now represented by a six-ounce iPod, served a curious fusion of bouncy trumpets and sensual *shehnais*—Broadway bombast with a Bombay contrast. The music director was an insurance adjuster by day. He'd dreamed up his euphonious Frankenstein three years ago, and tonight, by the grace of God and regional theater, it was alive.

The curtain parted and a new performer prowled her way onto the stage. She was a raven-haired temptress in a fiery red *lehenga*. Her curvy figure—ably flaunted by a low-cut, belly-baring choli—brought half the jaded audience to full attention.

The spotlights converged. The dancers dispersed. All eyes were now fixed upon the brown-eyed leading lady: the young, the lovely, the up-and-coming Hannah Given.

With a well-rehearsed look of sexy self-assurance, she swayed her hips to the rhythm and sang.

> "*Whatever Lola wants, Lola gets.*
> *And little man, little Lola wants you . . .*"

She shot a sultry gaze at the actor sitting downstage right, a handsome young man in a cricket player's uniform. He was theatrically bewitched by her. In reality, he was mostly bothered. Her neurotic questioning of all creative decisions made rehearsals twice as long as they needed to be. Still, he was casually determined to sleep with her sometime before the production closed. He wouldn't.

"Make up your mind to have no regrets.
Recline yourself, resign yourself, you're through."

A sharp cough from the audience made her inner needle skip, throwing her Lola and dropping her into a sinkhole of Hannah concerns. She fished herself out on a gilded string of affirmations. *Your stomach looks fine. Your voice sounds great. Gwen Verdon isn't screaming from Heaven. And odds are only one in ninety-nine that the angry cough came from the* CityBeat *critic.*

You know damn well who it was, a harsher voice insisted.

She narrowed her eyes at the dark sea of heads, then fell back into character. The rest of the song proceeded without a hitch. At final-curtain applause, Hannah convinced herself that the whole premiere went swimmingly aside from that half-second skip. She figured the misstep would haunt her for days. It wouldn't.

She wriggled back into her halter top and jeans and then joined the congregation in the lobby, where half the audience lingered to heap praise on the performers they knew. Hannah had given out five comp tickets, including two to her roommates and one to the day job colleague she was kinda sorta a little involved with. None of them showed up. Lovely. That only left the great Amanda Ambridge, plus spouse.

Hannah had little trouble finding her sister in the crowd. Amanda was a stiletto pump away from being six feet tall, with an Irish red mane that made her stand out like a stop sign. She stood alone by the ticket booth, a stately figure even in her bargain blouse and skinny jeans. At twenty-seven, Amanda's sharp features had settled into hard elegance, a brand of uptight beauty that was catnip to so many artists. Hannah felt like a tavern wench in the presence of a queen.

Amanda spotted her and shined a taut smile. "Hey, there you are!"

"Here I am," Hannah said. "Thanks for coming."

After a clumsy half-start, the two women hugged. Hannah stood five inches shorter and twenty pounds heavier than her sister, though she'd squeezed it all into a buxom frame that drove numerous men to idiocy. Amanda felt hopelessly unsexy in her company, the Olive Oyl to her Betty

Boop. Her husband did a fine job fortifying her complex tonight. The only time Derek didn't writhe in agony during the awful show was when Hannah graced the stage with her grand and bouncy blessings. Amanda had hacked a sharp cough at him, just to throw sand in his bulging eyes.

Hannah scanned the lobby for her brother-in-law, a man she'd met six times at best. "Where's the doc?"

"He's getting the car. He's tired and we both have to be up early tomorrow."

"Okay. Hope he didn't suffer too much."

"Not too much." Her smile tightened. "He really enjoyed your performance."

"Oh good. Glad to hear it. And you?"

"I thought you were terrific. Better than . . ."

Amanda stopped herself. Hannah's brow rose in cynical query. "Better than what? Usual?"

"That's not what I was going to say."

"Then just say it."

"I thought you were better than the show deserved."

A frosty new leer bloomed across Hannah's face. Amanda glanced around, then leaned in for a furtive half whisper.

"Look, you know I like *Damn Yankees,* but this whole idea of turning it into a Bollywood pastiche was just . . . It was painful, like watching someone try to shove a Saint Bernard through a cat door. But despite that—"

Hannah cut her off with a jagged laugh. Amanda crossed her arms in umbrage.

"You asked me my opinion. Would you rather I lie?"

"I'd rather you say it instead of coughing it!"

A dozen glances turned their way. Amanda blinked at her sister. "I . . . don't know what you're talking about."

"Now you're lying."

"Hannah—"

"You just couldn't hold in your criticism. You had to let it out in the middle of my big number."

"That's not what happened."

"Bullshit. You know what you did."

"Hannah, I don't want to fight with you."

"Oh my God." The actress covered her face with both hands. "You do this every time."

"Well, I'm—"

"'—sorry you're upset,'" Hannah finished, in near-perfect synch with her sister. "Yeah. I'm well acquainted with your noble act by now. You might want to change it up a little. You know, for variety."

Amanda closed her eyes and pressed the dangling gold crucifix on her collarbone. This, Hannah knew all too well, was the standard Amanda retreat whenever her mothersome bother and sisterical hyster became too much for her. *Give me strength, O Lord. Give me strength.*

The lights in the lobby suddenly faltered for three seconds, an erratic flicker that stopped all chatter. Hannah furrowed her brow at the sputtering laptop in the ticket booth.

Amanda checked her watch and vented a somber breath at the exit. "He should be out front by now. I better go."

"Fine. Say hi for me."

"Yup."

The sisters spent a long, hot moment avoiding each other's gazes before Amanda turned around and pushed through the swinging glass doors.

Hannah leaned against the wall, muttering soft curses as she gently thumped her skull. Between all her regrets and frustrations, she found the space to wonder why a battery-powered laptop would flicker with the overhead lights. She pushed the concern to the back of her mind, in the dark little vault where strange things went.

Seventeen years had passed since the madness on the Massachusetts Turnpike. The Givens never spoke a public word about the bizarre circumstances of their rescue. With each passing year, a welcome fog grew over their collective memories, until the family embraced the cover story as the one true account. They saw the truck teetering. They fled before it fell. That was just how it happened. End of subject.

Eight years after the incident, death came for Robert a second time and won. His cancer and passing had shattered Amanda in ways even her mother couldn't divine. She spent her final summer at home like an apparition and then disappeared to college, coming home once a year with thoughtful gifts, a practiced smile, and at least one major change to her state of being. First she found God. Then Hippocrates. Then a credible shade of red. And finally, during her brief stint at medical school, she found Dr. Derek Ambridge, who was eleven years her senior. From there, the arc of her life went into gentle downgrade.

Hannah, meanwhile, had cratered early. A spectacular nervous breakdown at age thirteen ended both her and her mother's resolve to turn her into a child star. After a year of therapy, she landed comfortably on the civilian teenage track, where she became lost in a routine tsunami of highs and lows, LOLs and whoas, breakups, makeups, and adolescent shake-ups. Upon graduation, she went west to San Diego State, where she dyed her hair black and experimented with all-new mistakes. On the upside, she rediscovered her theatrical ambitions. She stayed in town after college, found an office job, and began the slow process of rebuilding her résumé.

Six months ago, fate reunited the sisters when Derek accepted a partnership at a private oncology practice in Chula Vista, California, nine miles south of San Diego. For Melanie, the move was a golden opportunity for her daughters to finally connect.

"I want you to see Amanda as often as you can," she ordered Hannah. "Because she's going to leave that guy sooner or later and she'll be the one who moves away."

Though Hannah promised to try, she'd only met with Amanda three times in the last half year. Their first two encounters had been brisk and cordial and as tender as a tax form. No doubt their mother would be even less pleased with how the Great Sisters Given fared tonight.

With a thorny glower, Amanda emerged from the theater onto J Street, where her hybrid chariot awaited. Cigarette smoke rose from the driver's side.

Amanda slung herself into the passenger seat. Her husband tensely tapped ashes out his window.

"In case you're keeping score, I lost five IQ points tonight. Plus my faith in man."

"I know," Amanda sighed. "I'm sorry."

Derek was two years shy of forty. Though nature stayed kind to his boyish good looks, he regarded his impending middle age like a Stage 3 carcinoma. He worked out every day, ate raw vegetables for lunch, and overtook the medicine cabinet with pricey creams and cleansers. Nicotine was his last remaining vice. He was never happier to have it.

"If you love me, hon, you won't make me go to her next musical."

"I don't even know if I'll go," Amanda admitted with a hot blush of shame.

"What's the matter? You two have a fight?"

"Yeah. I tried to tell her she was good tonight and somehow she took it as a personal attack."

"Well, you always said she was a minefield."

"I know, but there's something else behind it. I think she resents me for moving out here. Like I'm crashing the nice little world she built for herself."

Derek jerked a weary shrug. "I'm sure you gals will work it out."

He propped the cigarette in his mouth and merged into traffic. Two blocks passed in dreary silence.

"I'll say this for your sister, she's got quite a set of pipes on her. Quite a set of everything. Jesus."

"That was classy, Derek."

"I know. I'm a real charmer after ten. If it's any consolation, you have the better face."

Amanda snatched his cigarette and took a deep drag. She spat smoke out her window, at an illuminated bank sign. The digital clock had become hopelessly scrambled, forever stuck in crazy eights.

"Just drive."

The electricity continued to surge and dip throughout the night. Citywide power fluctuations were spotted in various pockets of the globe, from Guadalajara to Rotterdam. The night owls screeched and the utility workers scrambled, but most of the West slept through the muddle. In London, the morning commute was hamstrung by a chain of mini-blackouts. In central Osaka, the sun set on a flickering skyline.

And then at 4:41 A.M., Pacific Time, the entire world shut down for nine and a half minutes. Every light and every outlet. Every battery. Every generator. Even the lightning storms that had been swirling in 1,652 different parts of the world were extinguished by invisible hands. For nine and a half minutes, the Earth experienced a mechanical quiet that hadn't been felt in centuries.

At 4:50, the switch flipped again, and the modern world returned with confusion and damage.

The American power network was as complex and temperamental as the human psyche. In some areas, the electricity came back immediately. In other regions, the circuits stayed dead forever. On some streets, people struggled to help their neighbors out of stalled elevators and plane-wrecked buildings. In others, there was panic and violence. Accusations. Tribulation.

Throughout all the chaos, the sisters slept.

Amanda woke up an hour after sunrise, her alarm clock blinking confusedly at 12:00. She made a sleepy lurch to the shower and heard Derek's off-key crooning over the running water. She used the other bathroom.

"Power failure last night," he said twenty minutes later, as they both dressed.

"Yeah. I noticed."

"I'm not getting a signal on my phone either."

Her shirt still undone, Amanda turned on her smartphone and patiently waited for the little image of a radar dish to stop spinning. She gave up after a minute.

Derek crossed into the kitchen and nearly slipped on a pair of magnets. Yawning, he stuck them back on the refrigerator. Amanda flipped on the living room TV. Channel after channel of "No Signal" alert boxes. She peered out the front window and relaxed at the normal procession of cars and joggers, the comforting lack of screams and sirens. Aside from the all-encompassing power burp, life seemed fine in Chula Vista.

Soon her mind drifted back to the mundane—chores and cancer, Derek and Hannah. Her bleary thoughts kept her busy all the way to the medical office. She didn't notice the two separate plumes of black smoke in the distance, spreading like stains across the flat gray sky.

Two of the nurses failed to show up for their Saturday shift. From the moment she threw on her peach-colored coat, Amanda became a whirlwind of activity, spinning between the office's endless rooms and needs. Along the way, she picked up morsels of chatter about the blackout. Her fingers curled with tension when one of the patients mentioned something about a crashed Navy jet.

Tommy Berber eyed Amanda balefully from the far end of the hall. He was a barrel-chested biker with a bandana skullcap and a bushy gray beard that hung in knotted vines. Mechanical beeps emanated from inside the chamber.

"Yeah, hi. Remember us?"

She held up a bag of clear liquid. "I'm here. I have it."

Berber followed her into the treatment room, where his son Henry lounged in a plush recliner. The sweet and skinny twelve-year-old had already lost his left arm to osteosarcoma. Soon he'd lose his hair, his lunches, and any last semblance of a normal adolescence. But his long-term chances of survival were mercifully good. Out of all today's patients, Henry was the luckiest of the unlucky.

Amanda shined him a sunny smile, then adjusted his chemo dispenser until it stopped beeping.

Henry grinned weakly. "Thanks. That was getting old."

"Twenty minutes!" Berber yelled. "We've been waiting twenty minutes!"

Amanda nodded. "I know. I'm sorry. We're short staffed today and our computers are down."

"Is that supposed to make me feel better about this place?"

"Dad . . ."

Amanda replaced the empty bag of doxorubicin with a fresh dose of cisplatin. She reprogrammed the machine, then tapped the plastic tube until the liquid started to drip.

"You're going to feel a hot sensation," she warned Henry.

"Right. I remember."

She watched the liquid flow into his arm. "All right, my darling. You're all set. Anything you need?"

"Yeah, a sedative. For Dad."

"Oh, he's just mad because you and I are eloping. We're still on for that, right?"

Henry laughed. "Absolutely. Did you tell Dr. Ambridge yet?"

"Nah. I'll call him from the road."

The moment she left the room, she heard Berber's heavy footsteps trail her down the hall. He had to wait for a shrieking emergency vehicle to pass the building before he could speak.

"That can't happen again, nurse. You hear me?"

Amanda turned around to face him. "Mr. Berber—"

"I don't want his chances going down just 'cause you people don't have your shit together. You get him his doses on time. You understand?"

She understood all too well. In her two years as a cancer nurse, Amanda had seen every breed of desolate parent—the weepers, the shouters, the sputtering deniers. The tough dads were always the worst. They wore their helplessness like a coat of flames, scorching everything around them.

"I'm sorry, Mr. Berber. I'll do better next time."

"You're just giving me lip service now."

"I am," she admitted. "Ask me why."

"Why?"

"Because I can't fix computers and I can't conjure nurses out of thin air. All I can do is apologize and remind you that your beautiful son has a seventy-eight percent chance of outliving the both of us. Being twenty minutes late with the cisplatin won't affect those odds. Not one bit."

"You don't know that for—"

"Not one bit," she repeated. "You understand me?"

Berber recoiled like she'd just sprouted horns. Amanda had seen that look countless times before on others. *You can be a little intense,* Derek had told her. *You may not see it, but it's there.*

Soon the biker's heavy brow unfurled. He vented a sigh. "Got any kids of your own?"

Amanda's face remained impassive as a cold gust of grief blew through her. She once had a son for seventeen minutes. Those memories stayed locked in the cellar, along with her father's last days and the incident on the Massachusetts Turnpike.

"No," she said.

Berber eyed her golden cross necklace. "But you do have faith."

"Yes."

"How do you reconcile? How do you spend all day with sick, dying kids and then thank the God who lets it happen?"

Still fumbling in dark memories, Amanda lost hold of her usual response. *I thank Him for the ones who live. I thank Him for the ones who have loving parents like you.*

All she could do now was roll her shoulders in a feeble shrug. "I don't know, Mr. Berber. I guess I'd rather live in a world where bad things happen for some reason than no reason."

Her answer clearly didn't comfort him. He scratched his hairy cheek and threw a tense glare over his shoulder.

"I should get back to him."

"Okay."

Amanda heard a high young giggle. She turned her gaze to the reception desk, where Derek charmed the fetching young office clerk with his witty repartee. The moment he caught Amanda's gaze, his smile went flat. His eyes narrowed in a momentary flinch that filled her with unbearable dread and loathing.

Her fingers twitched in panic as the chorus in her head told her to run. Run. Run from the husband. Run from the house. Run from the sister and the sick little children. Don't even pack. Just pick a direction. Run.

The overhead lights flickered. A second, then a third chemo dispenser began to beep. Another wave of emergency vehicles screamed their way down the street. Things were falling apart at record speed. To Amanda, this seemed a perfect time to go outside for a smoke.

Three hours after her sister rolled out of bed, a half-dazed Hannah finally joined the world in egress. Her Salvador Dalí wall clock—now warped in more ways than one—told her it was 9:41. In actuality, it was nine and a half minutes short. But to Hannah and millions of other battery-powered-clock owners, 9:41 was the new 9:50. There was little reason to think otherwise.

She woke up in a foul mood carried over from last night. An hour after her spat with Amanda, she came home to an unscheduled hootenanny in the apartment. Her two flighty roommates had ditched her premiere in favor of barhopping and eventually stumbled back with a trio of frat boys from the alma mater.

Knowing she'd never sleep in this racket, the actress stayed up with them, brandishing a forced grin as she nursed a Sprite and suffered their drunken prattle. Sometime after the group blacked out, and shortly before the world did, Hannah retreated into her room and drifted off into uneasy sleep.

Now the apartment smelled like stale beer, and every device seemed nonfunctional. Hannah showered, dressed, and gathered her belongings. She had no intention of going back there before tonight's show. She'd just go to the office and enjoy the Saturday solitude. Maybe she'd update her acting résumé. Maybe she'd send some e-mails. Maybe she'd scan the local apartment listings. Or maybe not so local. In her mind, all the recent annoyances gathered into a clump, like tea leaves. They predicted a bleak future unless she made changes. Maybe it was finally time to consider Los Angeles.

By the time Hannah stepped outside, the sky had turned from misty gray to fluorescent white, a disturbingly uniform glaze that looked less like a mist sheet and more like an absence. To Hannah, it seemed as if God, Buddha, Xenu, whoever, simply forgot to load the next slide in the great heavenly projector. It didn't help her nerves that the temperature was ten degrees cooler than it should have been for Southern California in July.

She wasn't alone in her anxiety. As she walked down Commercial Street, an old man urgently fiddled with his radio, testing its many squeals and crackles. A teenage girl shook her cell phone as if it had overdosed on downers. A middle-aged woman tried to control her German shepherd, which hysterically barked at everything and nothing. A young jogger launched a futile cry at a fast-moving police car. "Hey. HEY! What's going on?"

Nearly three dozen people congregated at the train stop. Hannah opted to walk to work. Two lithe young women broke away from the crowd and nervously followed her.

"Excuse me," said one. "Can you help us? We're not from around here."

That much was obvious. One of the pair was dressed as Catwoman, whip and all. The other was decked out in a blond wig and white-leather corset ensemble, clearly some other super-antiheroine that Hannah didn't recognize. She did, however, know exactly where both women were going. All veteran San Diegans were familiar with Comic-Con, the annual gathering of sci-fi, fantasy, and funny-book enthusiasts that occurred downtown for four days in July. No doubt these gals were shooting for an easy surplus of leers from the geek contingent.

Hannah smirked at them. "Let me guess. You're trying to get to the convention center."

Catwoman snickered. "Yeah. Bingo."

"I don't know what's going on with the train. If you think your heels will hold up, you're probably better off walking. I'm going that way. You can come with me."

"Oh thank you," said the fake blonde, rubbing her arms for warmth. "The power went out at the place we're staying. Our phones don't work. We're totally screwed up right now."

After twelve blocks and twenty minutes, Hannah regretted her decision to serve as vanguard for the vixens. The women were maddeningly slow in their clacking heels, and their worried chatter made her increasingly tense. Not that they lacked cause for concern. As they moved closer downtown, they could see thick plumes of smoke rising up above the buildings. Soon Hannah spotted the edge of a vast rubbernecker pool, hundreds of people gathered at the base of some tumult.

They rounded the corner, turning north onto 13th Street. Just one block away, beyond all the cordons and emergency lights, stood the broken tail cone of a jumbo jet. The buildings around it were devastated with ash and debris. One apartment complex had crumbled to rubble.

Hannah covered her mouth. "Oh my God."

More than a hundred thousand planes, jets, and helicopters had been up in the air seven hours ago, when all the world's engines fell still. A third of them plummeted into water. Another third hit the hard empty spaces between human life. The final third just hit hard. San Diego had suffered twenty-two crashes within its borders.

Hannah gaped at the tall gray clock tower of the 12th & Imperial Transit Center, just a hundred yards away. It was a local landmark, one she'd passed a thousand times on her way to work. Now it had been de-clocked, decapitated. Every window on the south side of the building was shattered, with burn marks all over the frame.

All around her, people fretfully chattered. A stringy blond teenager brandished a transistor radio, declaring to anyone willing to listen that he'd heard voices through the static. People in other cities were talking about the same things.

"This is happening all over," he insisted. "Everywhere!"

Agitated bystanders shouted at him. Hannah took an anxious step back. Perhaps it was time to stop playing Sherpa for the Comic-Con chicks and move on to a much nicer elsewhere.

"Keep your head," said a cool voice from behind.

She turned around and lost her breath at the sight of the pale and handsome stranger, as tall as any she'd ever seen. He wore a sharp gray business suit without a tie and sported deep blue eyes that nearly blinded her with their intensity. Most striking of all was his neatly trimmed hair, which was chalk-white and achingly familiar. Hannah blinked at him in stupor.

"You remember me, child?" he calmly inquired.

She shook her head, even as old recollections came flooding back. She was just a little girl when she first laid eyes on the white-haired man. Seventeen years and the guy hadn't aged a day. Hannah was almost certain he was wearing the same suit.

"I don't . . . know you."

"Deny it if you will," he replied. "It doesn't matter. We saved your life once. Now I come to do it again."

Seeing the man through adult eyes triggered a disturbing new reaction in Hannah. She found him eerily scintillating now, like a housewife's vampire fantasy. God only knew what he could get her to do without saying a nice word. Fortunately, she couldn't sense a trace of desire in him. For all she knew, she stood as the same chubby-faced toddler in his eyes.

"W-what do you want with me?" she asked.

He spoke with a slight accent that she couldn't recognize. She spun her Wheel of Uninformed Guessing. The needle stopped at "Dutch."

"The answer would require more time than we have. All that matters now is that you—"

A sudden stillness gripped the area. All the car engines stopped. All the lights on the emergency vehicles went dark and still. All electrics great and small, all over the world, once again fell dead. This time, the power wasn't coming back.

Panicked voices rose all around her. Bystanders scurried and stumbled in all directions. A shoving match broke out between two teenage boys.

As Hannah watched the chaos, she felt cool fingers on her skin. Something smooth and hard snapped together on her forearm with a loud *clack*. She jerked her hand away. Her right wrist now sported a shiny metal bracelet, a half inch wide and utterly featureless. It felt cheap and dainty like plastic, but it gleamed in the light like silver.

"What did you do?" she said. "What is this thing?"

The white-haired man grabbed her other wrist, scowling at her with frigid disdain. There was nothing appealing about him now.

"This is the end. For them, not for you. Now listen—"

"Get away from me!"

He squeezed her wrist with cool, strong fingers. Pain shot up her arm like current.

"Don't test me, child. I've had a trying day. It pains me to see all my plans hinge on weak and simple creatures like yourself, but it seems we both have little choice in the matter. If you wish to endure, you'll keep your head. Stay where you arrive. Help will come."

"What are you talking about?"

"You'll be joined with your sister soon enough."

"Wait, what—"

The white-haired man pressed two fingers to her mouth. "I've saved your life twice now. Don't make me regret my decision. The strings favor you, but there are others who could just as easily serve our purpose."

He walked away, leaving Hannah shell-shocked, speechless. A shrill scream in the distance briefly turned her around. By the time she looked back, the stranger was gone.

Hannah scrambled to process all the new and urgent developments around her. Her left wrist throbbed. Her right wrist glimmered. The temperature had dropped low enough to turn all breath to mist. The crowd fell into chaotic distress. They screamed and shouted and scrambled into one another like bumper cars.

This is the end. For them, not for you.

A booming gunshot emerged from the police cordon. More screams. A large man grabbed at the girl dressed like Catwoman, and an even larger man knocked him down. Another gunshot.

Hannah felt a strong vibration at the base of her hand. She gaped with insanity at her new silver bracelet. Mere seconds ago, it was a fat and dangly bauble, wide enough for a bicep. Now it rested snugly on the thinnest part of her wrist. Whereas once it appeared featureless, now it was split down the middle by a bright blue band of light.

She glanced up to discover the biggest adjustment of all. A curved plane of silky white light loomed all around her, closing two feet above her head. The outside world took on a yellow gossamer haze.

Hannah tried to relocate but ended up walking into the wall of her new surroundings. The light was warm, steel hard, and utterly immobile. She was stuck here, just a hair north of Commercial Street, in an eight-foot egg of light. That was enough to send her mind into blue-screen failure. She was in full rejection of the events onstage. Suspension of suspension of disbelief.

Nearby strangers caught sight of Hannah's odd new enclosure. A befuddled young man rapped his knuckles against her light shell.

"What is this?" he asked, much louder than necessary. She could hear him just fine.

"I don't know . . ."

"How are you doing this?"

"I'm not."

"What's happening?!"

Not this, she thought. *This isn't happening at all.*

The Great Hannah Given: mental ward alumnus, habitual wrong person, and unreliable narrator. Ergo, no eggo. No crowd. No crash. No white-haired man.

Everyone froze as a thunderous noise seized the area—a great icy crackle, like a glacier breaking in half. Bystanders threw their frantic gazes left and right in search of the clamor until, one by one, they looked up. The eerie sound was coming from above. It was getting louder.

More screams from afar. More gunshots. As the crackling din grew to deafening levels, the sky above turned cold and bright.

A teary young redhead scratched at the wall of Hannah's light cage. The actress could see lines of frost on the tip of the woman's nose, though the air inside the enclosure was as warm as July.

"Please!" the stranger screeched. "Help me!"

"I can't! I don't know how!"

Suddenly the tallest buildings in the skyline began to splinter at the highest levels, as if they were being crushed from above. Metal curled. Stone cracked. Windows exploded. With a grinding howl, an ailing structure gave out at the middle, causing all floors above to topple and fall in one great piece. Hannah pressed her hands against the light as she watched the other buildings crumble. The sky wasn't just getting brighter and louder. It was getting closer. The sky was coming down.

Shrieks and cries rose from every throat in the mob. There wasn't an empty square inch around her egg now. More than a dozen people pounded at the wall, weeping and begging.

The skyline was gone. Now the great white sheet descended on the clockless clock tower, cracking the jagged neck of the structure and sending huge chunks of stone flying everywhere. One of them demolished a police car, along with everyone near it.

Hannah fell to the pavement—wincing, crying, desperately trying to shut out the horrible noises. In the final few seconds, the cruelest part of her mind forced her to open up and see the world one last time.

Everyone around her was at long last quiet. Frozen dead.

Then, with a shattering crunch that would haunt her for the rest of her life, the ceiling came down and smashed all the corpses into shards. It devoured the ground and just kept going.

The actress had no idea how long she existed there in the blank white void of existence, kneeling on a floating disc of concrete and sobbing at the nothingness all around her.

Soon the void swirled with smoky wisps of blue and the nothing became something. By the time Hannah's eyes adjusted, the glow of her bracelet had faded and the eggshell of light was gone. Beneath her feet and her fallen handbag lay the same round patch of 13th Street, but it was now fused into concrete of a lighter color.

She craned her neck and saw blue sky and white clouds, the distant gleam of several tall buildings. She didn't recognize a single one.

Her hands quaking wildly, Hannah smeared her eyes and sniffed the warm summer air. Her last few working neurons struggled to process her new state of existence but all they could tell her with any degree of confidence was that right now at this very moment, she was alive. And she was elsewhere.

PART TWO

SILVERS

TWO

It had been twenty-two years, three months, and seven days since Hannah Given last came screaming into a world. She'd emerged from her mother with little muss and zero fuss, the textbook model of a healthy childbirth. Growing up, she occasionally lorded that knowledge over her older sister, who'd formed a kneeling breach in the womb and had to be delivered by crash Caesarean. Hannah loved hurling that pebble, especially when Amanda was acting a little too cavalier in her role as the Impeccable One.

Unfortunately, there was nothing joyous or natural about Hannah's second nativity. This time she popped into the world as a five-foot-five adult, clothed in a navy blue T-shirt and stretch jeans and saddled with a ninety-dollar hobo bag filled with clutter from the previous life. This time her arrival caused an electrical disturbance for a thousand feet in every direction. And this time, in a baffling circumstance she would lord over no one, she emerged from an egg.

She struggled to absorb the strange new environment. What was once a plane-wrecked intersection was now a clean and expansive parking lot, peppered with ficus trees and flanked on all sides by jarringly unfamiliar businesses—Peerless Spins, Sunshine Speedery, Jubel's Juves & Shifters. Even more perplexing was the fact that every storefront was barricaded behind a smooth white wall of . . . something. At first glance, it looked like plastic. But the surface carried a faint shimmer, as if it were reflecting light from some nearby swimming pool. Protruding from the center of each barrier was a small placard that listed the store's hours of operation, plus a digital clock that was currently as blank-faced as Hannah herself.

Only one store stood open for business: the sprawling SmartFeast that stretched across the north edge of the lot. Hannah could see people—calm, living people—bustling about inside.

She mindlessly moved toward the supermarket, staggering ten clumsy steps before a painful tremor overtook her. Her muscles burned with acid. Her extremities flared with hot needle stings, as if her limbs had all just woken up with a vengeance.

Hannah dropped to her knees between two parked sedans, then sobbed into her fists.

"Stop it. Stop it. Stop. Please."

A shrill and tiny voice in her head urged her to stay perfectly still. It assured her that she'd gone quite insane, and that a single wrong move could turn her into steam or glass or a flock of small birds. Her knees could grow mouths that sang "Eleanor Rigby."

Four wretched minutes later, her panic and pain subsided enough for her to clamber back to her feet. She cleaned her face in a car's side mirror, then continued shambling toward the SmartFeast.

Now she could see the casual mayhem inside. Throngs of impatient shoppers congealed at every checkout stand while cashiers dawdled helplessly. Another blackout. Or perhaps the same blackout. Hannah exhaled with relief when the lights flickered back to life.

Just outside the entrance, a slender teenage girl kept a lazy vigil behind a cloth-covered table. Hannah reeled at her strange blond hair—short on the sides but ridiculously long in the back and front. She reminded Hannah of a Shetland pony.

Both her table and her sleeveless black turtleneck were covered with buttons, each one containing a photo of an adorable dog or cat, plus a bold-faced call to action. *Stop Pet Extensions.*

Hannah stared at the activist for a good long minute, trying to make sense out of her and her cause. Eventually the girl noticed Hannah. She studied the actress through a curtain of bangs, then took a long swig of bottled milk. It had a picture of a maniacally happy cow on the label. The brand name was Mommy Moo, and the drink was boastfully fortified with something called Casamine-4.

"Hi."

"Hi," said Hannah, in a parched rasp.

"You stretched?"

"Huh?"

"I'm asking if you're okay," the girl attested. "You look like you're not."

A bleak chuckle escaped Hannah's lips. She felt light-headed and horren-
dously fragile, as if a stiff breeze could crack her to pieces.

"No, I'm not okay. I can't even . . . Listen, my name is Hannah and I'd like
to ask you something. I know how crazy this'll sound, but I'm really screwed
up right now and I'd appreciate a straight answer. Am I . . ."

She took another shaky glance around the lot, then sucked a jagged breath.
"Is this Canada?"

The question earned her five seconds of stony silence from the girl.

"Are you rubbing me?"

"Excuse me?"

"Are you making some stupid joke at my expense?"

"No! I'm not! I'm really not, okay? If there's any joke going on right now,
it's at *my* expense. I'm lost. I'm scared. I'm sick to my stomach. And I don't
recognize a single thing around me."

The girl continued to eye her with doubt.

"I'm not 'rubbing' you," Hannah insisted. "I'm not making a joke. Please.
Just tell me where I am."

At long last, the blonde brushed away her bangs. She had radiant green
eyes, just like Amanda. Having grown up brown with envy, Hannah found
the strength to wonder why the hell anyone would hide eyes that pretty.

"You're in San Diego," the girl informed her. "Downtown. Just a few blocks
from the harbor."

Hannah pressed a fist against her forehead, as if struggling to hold her
brain in.

"Thank you."

"You want me to call someone for you? A doctor? A friend?"

"No. I appreciate it, but I think I just need to . . . uh . . ." She felt distracted
by all the girl's weird buttons and stickers. *Pet extensions?*

"I should just go."

"Okay. Keep walking."

Hannah cocked her head in fresh bafflement. Though the girl's words
were dismissive, she'd delivered them with cordial warmth, as if she were
merely wishing Hannah a pleasant weekend.

The actress slung her bag over her shoulder and made her wavering escape
from the lot. Five minutes after she turned a corner, the other stores began to

open. The waxy white barricades popped out of existence one by one, like soap bubbles.

Hannah drifted down the quiet avenue, praying to stumble back into some familiar part of the city. Signs informed her that she was on West Earl Boulevard, a street that didn't exist anywhere in her memory files. The area teemed with glassy office buildings, each one sporting a café or bistro at the ground level. One eatery brandished boastful signs about its "10× booths."

Her attention was captured by a twelve-foot street advertisement, a morbid image of a sheet-draped corpse on a coroner's slab. A thin female arm dangled out from under the covers, her dead hand clutching an unlabeled pill bottle. Grim black text flanked the bottom of the picture.

> ### SHE CERTAINLY DIDN'T SEE THAT COMING.
> ### PREDICTIVES: UNTESTED. UNLAWFUL. UNSAFE.

Under the tagline, a call to action urged citizens to contact the American Health Bureau at #99-17-18384.

Hannah stared at the poster for a long and restless minute before forcing herself onward. At the next corner, she mindlessly averted her gaze from the clear glass front of a newspaper box. She was overstocked on calamity at the moment. The last thing she needed was another dose of disruption in the form of a brain-busting headline. "Gelatinous Man Wins Congressional Nod," or "Tentative Accord Reached Between Humans, Apes."

A half block later, she suffered another pins-and-needles attack, forcing her to rest on a bus stop bench. She opened her handbag and was soothed by her familiar belongings—her wallet, her makeup, a Trader Joe's granola bar, a recent issue of *Entertainment Weekly*. Most cherished of all was her little pink iPod, which looked as dead as her cell phone.

As she idly nibbled her granola bar, a blue-and-white city ambulance came to a halt on the opposite side of the street. The driver, a stocky young man in a royal blue jumpsuit, stepped out of the vehicle and stretched. Hannah wondered what would happen if she went up to him and explained her predicament. He'd probably take her straight to the municipal nuthouse, where overworked clinicians would feed her big words and little tablets until she realized that her whole life up to this point was just a schizoid dream.

A tinny voice beckoned the paramedic from his belt radio. He rushed back to his seat and started up the ambulance. The rooftop lights spun bright and red. The motor sounded more like a hair dryer to Hannah than a gas engine.

With a steamy hiss, the vehicle floated to second-story altitude. The wheels folded inward until the hubcaps faced the pavement. The engine emitted a final roar, and then the ambulance shot down West Earl Boulevard like a cruise missile. Leaves and litter fluttered in its wake.

Hannah sat frozen in dead-faced torpor. A piece of granola fell out of her hanging mouth.

Inside her head, a stadium full of little Hannahs erupted in riot. They screamed, they sobbed, they pounded the floor. Only one managed to stay in her seat. Amidst all the chaos, she looked up at the sky and calmly suggested that she find a quiet place to gather her wits.

Hannah collected her belongings with shaky hands, then continued in the direction she believed to be west. Soon her sage little helper offered new advice. *The next time you see a newspaper stand, try to stop and look. You don't have to read the headline, sweetie. But you may want to check the date.*

The marina was a short hop away, just as the pony-haired girl had said. Hannah had to walk two more blocks before she caught the blue water of the bay between buildings.

Soon she found her nesting spot: a long granite bench at the base of the pier. The view was remarkably similar to the one she remembered from her coveted reality, her *terra sana*. Beyond all the docks and bobbing white yachts lay the long green shore of Coronado. The sky was blue, the air was warm, and nothing soared through the sky but seagulls.

The actress folded her legs in a calming lotus pose while she drank in passing strangers—three joggers, two lovers, one mother. Hannah did a double take at the woman's baby stroller, which was nothing but handlebar and chassis. Despite its missing parts, the carriage floated steadily along the walkway, as if rolling on invisible wheels. *That's not right,* Hannah's rational self insisted. *That is a crazy, sci-fi, future-world object, which makes no sense because this is not the future.* A newspaper and a digital bank sign had both confirmed the accuracy of Hannah's inner calendar. It was the same year, same month, same crazy Saturday as the one she woke up in.

A gangly young man entered Hannah's field of vision. From his wavy brown hair, his Dustin Hoffman proboscis, and the unsure way he carried himself, she reflexively filed him under *Nerd, Jewish.* He wore an untucked black button-down over jeans and carried a large spiral-bound book. Unlike the other amblers on the concrete strand, he shined his anxious stare in all directions. Soon it found Hannah and stayed there. She was close enough to see that he was focusing on her middle bits. Scowling, she crossed her arms over her chest. *Go away, go away, go away.*

Mercifully, he went away. Hannah returned to her thoughts.

Of all the dark and troubling aspects of the morning, the part she wanted to revisit the least involved the white-haired man who'd wrapped a bracelet around one wrist and a bruise around the other. Hannah knew it was crucial to revisit all the things he'd said, since he was the only one who seemed to know what was going on.

Tragically, the audio portion of her memory had been scrambled by trauma. His words hung in fragments, like poetry magnets. *Keep your head. Keep your head. This is the end. For them, not for you.* [Something something] *plans.* [Something something] *strings. Help will come.*

What help?

The skinny man with the notebook came back into view, once again eyeing Hannah from a short distance. His awkward attention bounced between her face and her torso.

Hannah glared, she glowered, she gloomed in his direction, until she was made of nothing but red lights and stop signs. She broadcast her dismissal so strongly that he took a clumsy step back.

As he departed, Hannah could see that his notebook was actually a drawing pad. For a moment, she was afraid she'd misjudged him. Maybe he only wanted to sketch her, not screw her. Who cared? She had bigger concerns.

You'll be joined with your sister soon enough.

That was it. Amanda. The white-haired man said that Amanda would be here, wherever "here" was. The thought made Hannah cautiously euphoric. Her sister was one of the most demanding and sanctimonious people Hannah had ever known, but she was also one of the sharpest. She could steam press this quandary into something a little more wearable.

But was Amanda really here? Did she pop up in an egg of light somewhere in Chula Vista? Or was it all just some—

"Excuse me . . ."

Hannah gasped and jumped in her seat. As soon as she saw the wavy-haired artist looming at the edge of her bench, her face flushed hot and red.

"Holy shit. You've got to be kidding me."

"I'm sorry?"

"No, no, no, no. You can't be this dense."

The artist tilted his head like a puzzled dog. "Uh, apparently so, because I'm not sure—"

"Do I look like I want to be bothered right now? Or sketched? Did you think I'd enjoy having some creepy guy stare at my breasts right now?"

"Wait, what?"

She pressed her palms together in a desperate plea. "I'm really sorry. I'm usually much nicer about it, but I'm on the verge of a complete meltdown and I need to be alone. So if you have even an ounce of goodness in you, I'm asking you to please, please, please just go away and don't come back. We have nothing to talk about."

His steely gray eyes grew wide with bewilderment, and suddenly Hannah felt the needle of judgment spin back toward her. From his current expression, she wouldn't be surprised if he had already filed her under *Nut, Skittish*.

"I wasn't . . ." He let out a shaky laugh. "Okay, this has taken a weird turn."

"Oh my God. You're still not going."

"I'm going! I'm leaving right now! Jesus."

"Thank you!"

"For the record, I wasn't going to hit on you. Or sketch you. I don't do life drawings."

"Fine! Whatever!"

"And I wasn't staring at your breasts, all right? I mean I see them now and they're very nice. Congrats. But prior to this, I was actually looking at your arm."

"I don't care!"

"Obviously not. Sorry to have bugged you. Enjoy your meltdown."

"Wait. What about my arm?"

With a frustrated scowl, he raised his right fist at eye level, as if he was declaring solidarity with the Socialist Youth Front. Hannah shook her head at him.

"I still don't get it . . ."

"Wow. Okay. And you called me dense. Look at my wrist."

She looked at his wrist. And now she saw it. The bracelet. The bangle. The same silver oddity she wore. Her mouth formed an O as perfect as their shared adornment.

"Well, look at that," the man huffed. "I guess we do have something to talk about."

THREE

The cartoonist joined Hannah on the bench, clutching his sketchbook against his chest as if he'd float away without it. At some point in the last half hour, the twelve-dollar pad had become an item of incalculable value. Each drawing was an anchor of stability, a snapshot reminder of the sane and rational existence that currently eluded him.

He was less sentimental about his other possessions. When Hannah asked his name, he surrendered the fat yellow lanyard that dangled around his neck. He didn't care if she lost his Comic-Con pass. He was fairly sure the convention was over.

She held the badge with fumbling fingers. "Zack Trillinger."

"Yup."

"Creator of *Meldweld*."

"That's me."

"What's *Meldweld*? A comic book?"

"Comic strip."

"Wow. How many newspapers?"

"None. It's a web comic. I self-publish online."

"Oh. Do you make a living from it?"

Zack kept his tense eyes locked on a woman's floating baby stroller. Hannah was darkly relieved to see the same confounded look that had no doubt become a permanent fixture on her face.

"I make some income off of ad revenue and donations. For the rest of it, I freelance."

"As what?"

"Commercial illustrator."

"Oh. That's not bad."

"I hate it," he retorted. "By the way, I'm sorry I got pissy with you before.

If you had a morning like mine, then you have every right to be freaked out by everything."

Hannah nearly cried with bittersweet emotions. Sharing her ordeal made her feel half as crazy as she did five minutes ago, which made the current nightmare twice as real.

"Thank you. I appreciate that. I'm sorry I went all psycho on you."

"No worries," he said, and then chuckled at his own choice of words. Hannah was too rattled to follow the humor.

"I'm an actress," she offered after an uncomfortable silence.

"Really? Like for a living?"

"No. I wish. During the day, I work as a traffic coordinator at a medical advertising agency. I run between the creatives and the executives and try to keep them all on schedule while they yell at each other through me."

"Huh. Interesting."

"Not really."

"No, I mean it's interesting that we both keep talking about this stuff in the present tense."

Hannah felt a cold squeeze around her heart. Zack was obviously five steps ahead of her on the road to acceptance. She didn't enjoy the dog-leash tug.

He nervously rotated the silver-colored band on his wrist. Despite its airy weight, the bracelet seemed undentable, unscuffable. He couldn't find the hint of a seam.

"The money's blue here," Zack announced after another silence.

"What?"

"I found a coffee stand while I was stumbling around. I tried to pay with one of my tens and the vendor stared at me like I was nuts. So I'm kicked out of line and I see the next guy pay with a shiny blue twenty. It had Theodore Roosevelt on it."

Hannah took another swig of her bottled water. She noticed small patches of ash on Zack's neck and a few more on his shirt and jeans.

"Where do you live?" she asked him.

"Brooklyn. I was supposed to fly back tomorrow morning."

"Oh. Wow. You have family there?"

"I do. At least I *did*. I can't imagine they're . . ."

He stroked his chin with trembling fingers, fixing his glassy stare at far-away shores.

"Did you notice that all the license plates here say South California? You guys usually refer to it as Southern California, am I right?"

Hannah sighed. "You are right."

"I also noticed that the cars are more rounded. Bubbly. Not like they were in the 1950s but—"

"I saw a flying ambulance," she blurted.

"I saw a flying taxi," he replied with an uneasy smirk. "I was building up to that."

"Zack, what the hell's going on?"

In addition to acceptance, Hannah's new friend was five steps ahead on the road to understanding. From the moment Zack ruled out the Rip van Winkle scenario—thanks to a discarded, date-stamped lottery ticket—the wheels in his mind kept spinning back to the words *alternate* and *parallel*. He wasn't ready to verbalize his hypothesis.

"I don't know," he said, his knees bouncing with anxious energy. "Until I saw you and your bracelet, I was pretty sure I'd lost my mind."

"Do you have a history of mental illness?"

Zack eyed her with furrowed perplexity. "Are you suggesting that I'm hallucinating all this? Because I think that'd be bad news for you."

"No. I only asked because I do have a history. I've been hospitalized."

"For what? Schizophrenia?"

"No. Just . . . emotional stuff."

"Well, that's a far cry from seeing flying ambulances."

"Look, I'm just going by that thing. I forget what it's called. Where the simplest explanation is usually the right one."

"Occam's razor."

"Yeah, Occam's razor. And right now the simplest explanation is that we're both having some kind of psychotic breakdown. It's either that or . . ." She pointed to the latest floating baby stroller to pass their bench. "What do you think's more likely?"

Zack pursed his lips, exhaling in frustrated sputters. "Denial."

"Who, you or me?"

"You."

"What, you think I *want* to be crazy?"

"I think it beats the alternative," he said. "I'd love to wake up in a rubber room right now. Because that would mean that nobody really died and everything has a chance of going back to normal. Unfortunately, I've never done well with rosy scenarios. After twenty-eight years of Jewish conditioning, I've come to believe the darkest explanation is usually the right one. Call it Menachem's razor."

Hannah scowled at him. "How can you even joke right now?"

The cartoonist jerked a listless shrug. "Just how I cope."

"If you're so convinced this is real, Zack, then help me. Tell me what's happening."

"I don't know!"

"At least tell me how you got your bracelet."

From the edgy look on his face, Hannah realized she was the one tugging the dog leash now. She also realized that Zack wasn't as nerdy as he first seemed. Up close, she could sense a thin layer of hardness behind his boyish features, the same uptight strength her sister always carried. Hannah would have killed for some of that now.

"It was pretty insane where I was," he attested.

"So a white-haired guy didn't come to talk to you."

"Someone did, but he didn't say much. I couldn't tell if he had white hair."

"You'd remember him if you saw him."

"I barely remember my own name after everything that happened. It was . . ."

"Insane," she repeated.

"Yeah," he said, with a grim expression. "Word of the day."

The opening crowd at Comic-Con had been only half the size of Friday's, thanks to all the fresh electrical mayhem. By 10 A.M., the exhibition hall once again bustled with thousands.

Zack manned his rented table in Artist's Alley, the back-corner mini-bazaar where professionals hawked their works. He'd surpassed his wildest expectations the day before: six sales and ten handshakes from gushing fans of *Meldweld*. One of his admirers, a statuesque Goth with spiderweb tattoos on her arms, scrawled her hotel information in Zack's sketchbook. He'd made a note to pin it up on his corkboard when he got home, as collateral against future ego losses.

Ultimately he'd spent Friday night alone in his hotel, text-messaging into the wee hours with his ex-girlfriend Libby. When she mocked him for passing up the chance to bang his first groupie, Zack merely shrugged and chalked it up to arachnophobia. But by 3 A.M., he'd come around to Libby's way of thinking, as usual. Another non-experience for the King of Missed Opportunities.

The next morning, Zack yawned and doodled from behind his table as the local crowd ignored him. Everyone seemed glaringly tense now, hopelessly thrown by their faltering technology.

Halfway through his latest bored doodle, the convention hall plummeted into darkness.

Zack shot to his feet as countless conventioneers squawked in blind worry. Dozens, then hundreds of cigarette lighters pierced tiny pinholes in the darkness. Though Zack was relieved to learn that he hadn't gone blind, the preponderance of flames created a new concern. He looked to the artist next to him, a portly man with a Fu Manchu mustache who waved his Zippo like a torch.

"I don't think that's a good idea," Zack cautioned.

"What the hell do you want me to do?"

"There are posters, banners, all sorts of flammable—"

"I just wanna get out of here in one piece. You want the same, then shut up and follow me."

Reluctantly, Zack grabbed his sketchbook and followed. He knew it wasn't entirely wise to trail the guy with the open flame, but then Zack feared that things were about to get very bad here, very soon.

A hundred yards away, a new crescendo of screams arose as a publisher's booth became engulfed in fire. Two shrieking exhibitors emerged from inside, both sporting a fresh coat of flames. They crashed into a neighboring stall, setting it ablaze.

Panic seized the hall as the fire spread. Every exit was visible now, and every route became choked by throngs of squealing evacuees. Zack joined the thinnest clog and was quickly shoved aside like a coatrack. He huddled into a protective crouch against a folding wall, away from the flames and mobs. *Wait it out,* his inner strategist demanded. *Better late than trampled.*

Soon someone sat down beside him, a tall and slender man in a black T-shirt and slacks. Tucked beneath his New York Yankees cap was a smooth white mask made of some oddly reflective plastic. Zack could spy only a hint of the stranger's face through the eyeholes. He had fair skin, sandy brows, and the scariest blue eyes Zack had ever seen. They glistened in the firelight, dancing with wild amusement despite the suffering of thousands.

Before the cartoonist could indulge his flight reflex, the stranger grabbed his arm. Zack couldn't hear the clacking sound in the din, nor did he register the cool silver bracelet as it sealed around his wrist. All he could process were those ferocious eyes. They weren't just amused, they were contemptuous. Mocking.

The man muttered something brief and incomprehensible before jumping to his feet. He waved his hand in a brusque loop. A puddle of radiant white liquid appeared by his shoes, as round as a manhole and as bright as a glowstick. Zack watched, bug-eyed, as the man plunged feet first into the pool's hidden depths. He disappeared beneath the rippling surface. The portal shrank away to concrete.

For Rose Trillinger's second son, this was the end of reason. The end of acceptance. Screaming, Zack rushed to join the stragglers in a fevered dash for the exit. He'd made it all the way to the doors when his new bracelet vibrated and he became sealed inside an egg-shaped prison of light. Within moments—

Hannah cut him off with a tense wave of the hand. "It's all right. I . . . know the rest."

Zack was all too happy to stop. From the moment the sky came down on the convention center, he'd retreated to his own private cineplex. He watched himself from the front row, confident that the hero would survive and all would be explained by the end of Act I. It wasn't until he encountered Hannah that the fourth wall crumbled and he fell into the messy reality of his predicament.

"I don't know what's happening," Zack said. "I don't know why we were singled out for bracelets. If your guy was as scary as mine, then . . . I don't know. I don't think they're in a hurry to bring us into the loop." He darkly eyed his silver band. "So to speak."

Hannah sucked a sharp breath as she suffered her third and worst attack of hot needle stings. She huddled forward on the bench, wincing. "So what did . . . what did this guy say when he gave you your bracelet?"

Zack jerked a nervous shrug. "It didn't make any sense. I don't even know if I heard it right."

"What was it?"

"He said, 'Any other weekend, you'd be one of the Golds.'"

Hannah eyed him in dim bewilderment. "One of the Golds."

"Yeah."

"That makes no sense."

"No kidding."

"Jesus, Zack. What are we going to do?"

"That's the question, isn't it? I don't rightly know. I guess sticking together is the first step, if you can tolerate my company a little while longer. We're going to need cash, or whatever passes for—"

The world fell abruptly silent as Hannah flinched in agony. Her skin stung like she was covered in firecrackers. Her heart rate doubled. Her vision took on a deep blue shade.

She pressed her palms to her face. "Oh God. I think I need a doctor."

Oddly, Zack didn't reply. She caught him staring ahead at the ocean, perfectly still and expressionless. He didn't even blink.

"Zack, did you hear me? I feel like I'm dying!"

She jerked his sleeve, tearing a three-inch hole in the shoulder seam. The fabric felt tough somehow, like Zack had over-starched it. And he still didn't acknowledge her.

Hannah struggled to her feet and moved directly in front of him. "Zack! Snap out of it! Please! I need you!"

Now his head tilted upward with all the speed of a sunrise, his eyes blooming wide in bother. A small voice in Hannah's head insisted that she'd seen all this before as a child—the slowness, the blue haze, the odd taste of burning ash.

"What . . . who's doing this?"

She frantically scanned the area. All over the marina, people moved at an absurdly lethargic pace, as if they all colluded on a silly pantomime. A middle-aged jogger creaked through a bounding stride. An Irish setter charged after a tennis ball with slow-motion pomp. A trio of seagulls spun in the air like a nursery mobile.

"WHO'S DOING THIS?"

Hannah turned back to Zack, who now watched her in rigid horror. She wanted to grab him and pull him into the bubble. Maybe he could explain it. Except . . . except . . .

Except there was no bubble this time, no white-haired man with his finger on the clock. It was just Hannah and the world moving at two different speeds.

It's you, her higher functions insisted. *You're the one doing this.*

"No . . ."

The last working piston in her mind told her to run, and so she ran. She ran over the grass and out of the marina, through the alley and all the way back to the business district. Wherever she went, she couldn't escape the smoky blue haze. Everywhere she looked, cars moved like pedestrians and pedestrians moved like turtles. Litter scraps fluttered in the wind like lazy bumblebees.

Suddenly a large shadow enveloped her. She turned around and looked up.

A massive metal saucer, the size of a Little League field, emerged over the building tops. It floated hundreds of feet above the asphalt, slowly spinning on its own axis.

Unlike everything else in Hannah's trudging blue world, the ship moved at a decent pace, at least twenty miles an hour. From below, it looked like a giant metal wagon wheel. Each wedge was filled with a fluorescent white light.

Once the silver hub came into view, Hannah saw a tableau of man-size letters.

ALBEE'S AERSTRAUNT

ALL-AMERICAN CUISINE

2-HOUR BRUNCH ROUNDS @ 8X

FOR RESERVATIONS CALL #49-95-ALBEE

Her last thread of perseverance snapped. A shriek rose up from the core of her being. She ran again, her frantic gaze fixed on the high-flying bistro. Her wind sprint lasted fifteen feet, ending smack at the side of a parked Metro bus. A crunch. A crack. A wall of pain. And then Hannah's whole crazy world, her *terra insana*, went from blue to black.

She opened her eyes to white clouds. The heads of a dozen bystanders formed a popcorn string around the edge of her vision. She could feel the cold, hard sidewalk beneath her aching body. The deep blue madness had ended, thank God. Her onlookers moved and talked at normal speed.

As soon as Hannah tried to get up, a sharp agony seized her left shoulder. She cried out.

A new head eclipsed her view—a stout, middle-aged man with beady brown eyes and a thick walrus mustache. He wore an authoritative green uniform that Hannah didn't recognize. A cop? A guard? A forest ranger?

"Try not to move," he told her. "You wrenched yourself pretty good."

"It hurts . . ."

"Yeah. I fig you dislocated your shoulder. I can pop it back in but we have to get you better situated. Just try to stay still, okay? What's your name?"

"I can't do this . . ."

"Yes you can. You'll be okay. Listen, I couldn't find cards on you. What's your name?"

"H-Hannah."

"Hi, Hannah. I'm Martin Salgado. I want you to relax now, all right? I'm here to help."

The man directed his voice at someone she couldn't see. "Turn her on three. Ready? One . . . two . . . three."

Hannah sensed three different hands on her body. They tilted her two inches to the right, triggering another sharp jolt in her shoulder. She squealed in agony.

"Sorry," said Martin. "No avoiding that. But the good news is that I got an epallay right here with your name on it. Just stay easy."

He slid a smooth board beneath her before rolling her flat again. With a soft electric whirr, Hannah rose three feet off the sidewalk.

Martin stood at her side with an adhesive bandage in his grip—fire-red, with a white "E" in the middle. He peeled it off and pressed it against Hannah's injured shoulder.

"What is that? What did you put on me?"

"That's the epallay," he told her. "In a few minutes, you won't feel the pain."

Just outside her view, Martin's partner gently pushed Hannah forward. She rode with eerie steadiness, like she was riding an oiled track. She thought about the baby stroller and wondered if she now had to add herself to the ever-growing list of things that shouldn't be floating.

The wall of bystanders opened up. A middle-aged woman crunched her brow at Hannah's two handlers.

"Hey, shouldn't you fellas wait for the police?"

"Mind your own," said Martin.

Hannah grabbed his wrist. "Wait, you guys aren't cops?"

Martin laughed amicably. He hadn't heard that word in decades. "No, we're Salgado Security, a private contract firm. I'm the proprietor. The one pushing you is my son Gerry. We're gonna take good care of you."

"No, no. Wait. Stop. Stop. I don't want this."

"Listen, Hannah, I don't mean to be quick with you, but we're on a bite here—"

"No, you don't understand. I need to wake up. None of this is happening. I need to wake up."

Martin raised his palm. The floating stretcher stopped. While he rummaged through his shoulder bag, Hannah craned her head at Martin's young and burly son. Tears flowed up her temples.

"I can't take it anymore. Help me. Please."

"Dad . . ."

"I got it," said Martin, while unwrapping another adhesive. This one was black and square, the size of a fingernail. He peeled it from the paper and then affixed it to Hannah's neck.

"What was that? What—"

"Baby spot. It's a mood-lifter. In two minutes, you'll feel a whole lot better."

The stretcher moved again. She floated thirty feet to the edge of a parked green van.

"Wait. Wait. Where are you taking me?"

"It's all right. I'm bringing you to folks who'll be able to help you."

"Who?"

"Nice people," said Martin. "Smart people. They hired us to find you all and bring you back to safety. You'll be okay. Trust me."

The Salgados loaded her into the van. Once inside, Martin sat Hannah up in her stretcher and popped her arm back into its socket. All the pain fled her body in a quick and glorious instant.

"Wow. That's . . ."

Martin smiled. "Told you."

By the time he finished wrapping her arm in a cozy black sling, the baby spot on her neck had opened every dark curtain in her head, flooding her with sunshine. Suddenly she could see the overwhelming positives of her situation. Maybe these clients of Martin's were as smart and nice as he said they were. Maybe they'd make perfect sense of everything. And if they could find Hannah, maybe they could also find Amanda and Mom and everyone else she knew and cared about. All the good people of Earth, gathered up like pilgrims to start a happy new society. It had the potential to be wonderful. Hannah could run the theater.

As the engine started, the actress found herself smiling for the first time today. She smiled at the people on the street. She smiled at the floating cars she couldn't see. She smiled at the flying saucer that served brunch on weekends. She smiled at the thought of mimosas over San Diego.

Soon the van pulled a U-turn. Hannah turned her head and smiled at the bus she'd collided with. She could see through the window, to the sprawling web of cracks on the opposite glass. She was pretty sure she caused that damage, but she wasn't remotely bothered. It was a brave new world with strange new rules, and Hannah smiled at the possibilities.

FOUR

Twelve miles east of the San Diego Harbor, and seven feet down, a writhing young figure came awake in darkness. For the first few breaths of her new existence, the girl in the bracelet lived in a near-perfect state of incomprehension, the kind she hadn't experienced since her own messy birth, nearly fourteen years ago. She didn't know who she was or what she was, if she was alive or dead. She didn't even know if she had a body.

But then she smelled her own sweat, felt the cotton folds of her pajamas. Now the salient details of her life came trickling back in bullet points. She was Mia Farisi, fresh out of middle school with a 4.0 GPA and a weight of 150. She was born and raised in La Presa, where she lived in a two-story house with her father, her grandmother, and three burly brothers. A fourth one served in Afghanistan with the U.S. Army. Mia made him e-mail her every day, just to let her know he was okay.

Except . . . Things were not okay. Something bad had happened right here in La Presa. Something that sounded a lot like war.

Her mind flashed back to the thunderous booms that shook the house at 4:42 this morning, when all the clocks stopped and all the planes fell to earth. Within moments, Peter Farisi burst into his daughter's room, shirtless and panicked.

"Take Nana to the basement! Don't come out till I tell you it's safe!"

"Dad, what—"

"Just go!"

It was in the basement that something terrible had happened. A strange vibration on her wrist. An unexpected light. A rumble from above. And then . . .

"Nana?"

The word rolled up Mia's throat like sandpaper. She'd screamed herself raw before fainting, but she didn't know why. The last few moments of her memory were still a muddled blur.

She scrambled to her knees and fumbled through the darkness. The floor around her was concave and covered in dirt. No, it *was* dirt. She stood up and felt the wall. Also dirt, also curved. As Mia crossed to the other side, her bare foot slipped on a pair of smooth wooden planks. Her honor student brain—now working at two bars of power—processed the data and came back with a flustered guess. *Loose steps from the basement. You were standing right on them.*

She continued to feel the walls—perfectly curved all around, like someone had taken an eight-foot ice cream scoop to the earth and carved out a perfect sphere.

Or an egg.

Mia gasped. She remembered the egg of light now. It had encased her on the basement steps. Her grandmother had clawed at its ethereal shell, feebly trying to extricate her. Mia remembered seeing white steam in Nana's cries. Winter breath in the third week of July, in a town ten miles north of the Mexican border.

"Nana?"

At three bars of power, Mia's brain finally introduced her to the problem at hand.

"Oh no. No . . ."

She reached up as far as her five-foot frame would let her, feeling nothing but air. She seized a stair plank and jabbed it at the ceiling. Crumbs of dirt drizzled down on her.

"Oh no. No, no, no, no . . ."

While she continued her frantic stabs at the earth above, words of alarm scrolled along her inner news ticker. *You're buried. You're buried. You're buried alive. You're buried alive and you're gonna die.*

"It's nothing to get upset about," Nana had insisted. "These things happen."

At ten o'clock last night, Vera Farisi entered the dimly lit kitchen and found Mia rummaging through the cabinets in busy fluster. She bounced from shelf to shelf, scanning the calorie counts of every food item and mark-ing them in her notebook. An unfortunate encounter at the mall had left her tense and despondent.

Vera flipped on the light switch. "Sweetheart—"

"Leave it off. I can see."

"Those girls were only teasing you because they're insecure."

"No, Nana, that's . . . You just don't understand."

Vera flicked a spotty hand in exasperation. In her eyes, Mia was a beauti-ful girl with sharp hazel eyes, flawless olive skin, and a lush brown mane that any woman would kill for. Yes, the child was a little chubby, and had an un-fortunate penchant for dark and frumpy clothes, but she was nothing close to the six-chinned horror she saw in the mirror.

Mia read the nutrition label on her favorite dessert snack, then croaked a surly groan. There was nothing even remotely dietetic in the house. The men in her family were all built like tanks. They could eat a plate of lard and burn it off by suppertime.

"That was just a sneak peek of what I'll get in high school," she insisted. "I'll be a walking target every day."

"You don't know that."

"Yes I do. And I deserve it for letting myself get this fat."

For the thousandth time, Vera cursed the girl's mother, a vain and selfish *stronza* who'd abandoned the family years ago. Mia needed female guidance. All she had was this wrinkled old crone who hadn't been a teenager since World War II.

"Tell me what I can do for you, peanut. Can I make you something?"

"No! Are you even listening to me?"

Mia lowered her head and winced at herself.

"I'm sorry, Nana. I'm just . . ."

Her grandmother smiled softly. For all the girl's neurotic self-loathing, she was still the darling treasure of the family, the one who stayed sweet and sensible while her brothers swung through the house like wrecking balls. The Farisi men loved her with such fervent devotion that Vera pitied the first boy who was foolish enough to give her grief.

"Come here, angel."

Mia crossed the kitchen and embraced her, sighing with self-rebuke. It was hard to forget how Vera had grown up in fascist Italy, a barefoot orphan who'd lived from crumb to crumb. And now here was her granddaughter, wailing over a weight gain like it was the end of the world.

God help me, Mia thought, as the kitchen lights flickered. *God help me the day I have real problems.*

Mia blindly thrust the plank at the ceiling, her breath spilling out in high wheezes. Dirt rained down in clumps—falling into her hair, onto her face, down her pajama top. She felt an unpleasant tickle as something crawled across her cheek on tiny legs. Screaming, she dropped the board and furiously slapped her skin until the wriggling stopped.

She fell to her knees and wept. For all she knew, she was miles underground. Even if she stood just three feet under grass, she'd never make it out. She was too short. And digging would only bring the world down on her anyway. All things considered, she'd rather die with stale air in her mouth than fresh dirt. If she was lucky, she'd die sleeping.

A faint light suddenly pierced the blackness of the grave. Mia looked up to see a luminous white disc hanging in the air, two feet in front of her. It started out the size of a coin but then expanded vertically. Two quarters tall. Five quarters. Twenty.

At forty quarters of height, the strange object dropped into the soil.

Dumbfounded, Mia picked it up. It was a cigar tube made of some glow-in-the-dark metal. Unscrewing the lid revealed ten smooth plastic sticks, all wrapped in a long strip of paper with handwriting on the outside. She unfurled it, squinting at the words in the dull radiance of the tube.

PS—Shake the lumicands to light them up.

She shook one of the sticks, then squawked in surprise as a small flame ignited at the end. The fire was fluorescent white and gave off no heat whatsoever. Mia put her free hand above it and then in it. The flame licked her palm harmlessly.

In the new light, she caught more handwriting on the other side of the note.

Mia, there are only 16 inches of dirt between you and sunlight. Use the lumicands. Use the boards. Keep digging. Trust me.

She had to be imagining all this. Maybe she was hallucinating from oxygen deprivation. She noticed her breaths were sharper now. The air felt thicker.

Crazy or sane, she was running out of time.

Mia shook each of the candles and then stuck them into the walls, as if decorating a cake from the inside. By the tenth and final flame, her grave was as well lit as an office cube.

She took a moment to notice her silver bracelet, a strange new adornment that had mysteriously appeared overnight. It terrified her to think that someone had crept into her room and slipped it on her while she slept. She didn't even know how that was possible. The band had no seam and was too tight to slide over her hand. Her mysterious gifter would have had to break her thumb.

She shelved the puzzle and resumed her frantic digging. After two minutes, she managed to carve a small hat of air at the top of the egg, but she had yet to pierce daylight. Her shoulder muscles screamed with strain. She couldn't take a breath without coughing. She couldn't stop crying as dark memories came trickling back.

"Nana . . ."

"I'm sorry," Mia said, as she shivered beneath a blanket.

She huddled with her grandmother in the basement, stashed against the wall between old moving boxes. A dusty kerosene lamp burned at their feet, casting jittery shadows on the stone. The electricity had been out for five hours now. The Farisi men went out to investigate the clamor four hours ago. They had yet to come back.

Mia's eyes glistened in the flame light. "I should have never gotten so worked up about those stupid girls at the mall."

Vera squeezed her arm. Though the woman put on a brave face, Mia could hear the strain in her voice. Every instinct she had was screaming that her son and grandsons were dead.

She stroked Mia's arm. "I know, peanut. I'm just sorry you never had proper advice on these matters. You could have used a mother in your life. Or a sister."

Mia rested her head on her grandmother's shoulder. "You're all the mother and sister I need."

Vera bit her lip and looked away. She hadn't prayed since September of 1943, when Allied tanks rolled into Salerno. Lord only knew what was happening out there now. She held Mia tight and sent her broken thoughts upward. *Please, God. Don't let her die. If I should fall, please bring her to someone who'll care for her.*

A loud creak from upstairs turned Mia's gaze. "Dad?"

She jumped to her feet. Vera clambered after her. "Mia, wait . . ."

"Dad, is that you?"

Halfway up the steps, she felt a strong vibration on her wrist. Mia barely had a chance to notice the glimmering bracelet before a bright yellow haze enveloped her, surrounding her in a near-perfect sphere.

Vera threw off her blanket. "Mia!"

"Nana, what's happening?"

The walls trembled with violent force. The piercing creaks of metal and wood filtered down through the ceiling. The entire house above them seemed to be screaming. The whole world was coming apart.

The candles in the grave began to sputter. Mia clenched her jaw and kept digging, her throat whistling with each desperate gulp of air. She couldn't shut out the image of her grandmother, helplessly clawing at Mia's egg of light as she cried puffs of steam. Winter breath in the third week of July . . .

"No . . ."

. . . in a town ten miles north of the Mexican border.

"No!"

And then something terrible happened. The house, the roof, the heavens themselves, came down on top of them. In a span of a scream, everything Mia knew disappeared in a sea of white. Gone.

"NANA!"

With a final shove, Mia fell back against the earth. The plank pierced the ground and toppled over. Mia caught a soft new glow across the ground. She looked up.

Sunlight glimmered down through a thin slit in the ceiling. Little blades of grass flapped around the edges. Beyond that, a hint of blue sky and clouds.

As she breathed in the air of a whole new world, Mia Farisi curled into a ball and cried.

She had no idea how long she stayed there in the dirt. Minutes. Hours. A lifetime. At some point in her stupor, she caught a quick shadow above her. A fat black nose traveled up and down the slit, sniffing excitedly. Yellow paws tore at the hole. Soon the retriever was yanked away. Now Mia looked up into the wide blue eyes of its owner.

"Sweet Jesus . . ."

After twelve minutes of digging, the hole was wide enough to lower a stepladder. Mia emerged into the side yard of a two-story home in some posh but foreign suburb. She'd been buried so close to the house that a few lateral scrapes would have revealed the foundation.

Her rescuer, a thin and elderly man in a faded maroon sweat suit, stared at Mia like she'd fallen from space. He scratched his cheek in bewilderment.

"This is crazy. I'm thinking I should call someone but . . . Christ, it's my yard. What will they think?"

Mia didn't reply. Her tears had made streaks of clean on an otherwise dirt-caked face, but now her gaze was dry and distant.

"I can't even fathom what you've been through, girl. And I want to help you. But before I call the police, I need to know that you can talk. You have to tell them I didn't do this to you."

The retriever ran barking to the front lawn and returned moments later with a stout young woman in a pea-green uniform. She consulted a small device in her hand, then looked to Mia.

The old man waved his palms. "I found her like this! I didn't do this!"

"Ease it, gramper. You're not in any trouble."

The woman kneeled down by Mia, brushing the dirty brown hair from her face. She studied the bracelet on Mia's wrist.

"You poor thing. You must've been through hell and back. What's your name, kitten?"

She continued to stare ahead, speaking in a tiny doll's voice. "Mia."

"Mia, my name's Erin Salgado. I work for Salgado Security. We've been hired to find you and bring you to safety. You're going to be okay."

The old man furrowed his brow. "You were hired to find her but you didn't know her name?"

Erin shot him a frosty glare. "If you're doubting, call the poes. I fig they'll have more questions for you than for me."

"Look, hey, I was just asking."

Erin squeezed Mia's hand. "Listen, sweetie, I need you to trust me. My clients—"

"Bobby."

"What?"

Mia finally looked at Erin, her lush lips trembling with anguish.

"My brother's name is Robert J. Farisi. He's with the Fourth Brigade Combat Team in Afghanistan. I know his e-mail address. I need to write him."

"Mia . . ."

"He needs to know I'm alive."

As Mia fell into soft new tears, Erin pulled her into her thick arms and held her. This poor thing. This poor lost child.

Hand in hand, Erin led Mia to a long green van that waited at the curb. A burly young man leaned against the passenger door. From his stout face, wide nose, and scattered brown freckles, Mia figured he was more than Erin's associate. They were siblings, possibly twins.

The Salgado brother gawked at Mia's wretched state. "Jesus. Where are these people coming from?"

Erin narrowed her eyes at him. "Start the engine. And get me the soapsheets."

She opened the rear doors and helped Mia inside. A pair of long cushioned rows lined each side of the van. In the center of the left seat, a tall and skinny young woman hunched forward, either unaware or unconcerned about her new company. Erin studied her cautiously.

"You doing all right there?"

The woman offered a meager shrug without budging her gaze from the floor.

"Well, let me know if you change your mind about that epallay," said Erin.

"Who is that?" Mia asked.

"Someone like you. She also had a bad morning. But she'll be all right. You both will."

Mia took a seat on the right side, near the back doors. Eric Salgado opened the gate from the driver's seat and rolled a fat plastic cylinder down the length of the van. Erin popped it open, producing a small wet cloth that smelled like bubble bath. She dabbed it at Mia's face.

"We have to get moving, so I'll let you do the rest. No need to be thorough. There's a hot shower waiting for you in Terra Vista."

"Okay . . ."

"If you need anything else—a blanket, some juice, a baby spot—just yell, all right?"

"Thank you." *Baby spot?*

Erin closed the back doors and rejoined her brother. As the van pulled away, Mia meekly dabbed her skin with the soapsheet and took a moment to examine the stranger in the other seat. She was an enviably lithe woman in a scuffed white blouse and jeans. Her left wrist was wrapped in a makeshift splint and splayed out on a folded pink jacket on her lap.

Mia's large eyes popped at the sight of her other wrist.

"Uh, excuse me . . ."

The stranger looked up. Mia could see that the woman was at least twice her age. She'd certainly be pretty under normal circumstances, but now her face was marred with grief and trauma. Her stare was dull. Lifeless.

"I'm sorry," Mia said. "I just noticed that you have a silver bracelet like mine. I don't . . . I don't know how I got this thing. Do you know how you got yours?"

The woman studied Mia through hanging wisps of red hair. She took a good long time before answering.

"No."

She gazed down at her feet again and was quiet for the rest of the ride. But Amanda felt hot stabs of guilt all throughout her psyche. In the span of an hour, she'd lost her mind and broken her wrist. And now she'd just lied to an orphan.

FIVE

She'd stepped outside the office for a much-needed cigarette. There in the alley, among the puddles and flies, Amanda blew tense puffs of smoke at her sneakers while the near and distant sirens of emergency vehicles shrieked from every corner of the neighborhood. She didn't care about the world's problems at the moment. She had a sister who didn't want her there, a job that didn't fulfill her, and a festering sickness in her marriage that had become all but terminal.

She fumbled with her necklace, pressing the golden crucifix to her collarbone like an intercom button. Her Lord wasted no time responding, though He only confirmed what Amanda already knew. She couldn't run from her issues, no matter how much she wanted to. Dramatic exits were for actresses. Nurses worked to mend what was broken.

By the end of her cigarette, Amanda formulated a shaky plan to heal her life, a lofty to-do list that included everything from counseling to Zoloft to a second stab at medical school. The new resolve did little to soothe her anxiety. Her left hand itched like she had spiders on her skin and she felt an odd sense of spatial unease, as if something huge and heavy dangled high above her.

The echoey clops of wooden heels filled her senses, growing louder with each merry step. Amanda looked up and down the alley but couldn't see anyone. She peeked behind the dumpsters on the slim chance they obscured the approach of a very short woman. Nothing.

The footsteps came to a stop. Amanda turned around and gasped at the pale and smiling creature who leaned against the wall, a mere ten feet away. She wasn't short at all.

"Hello, child."

She had a young girl's voice to go with her young girl's figure, and her curly brown locks were tied in a young girl's ponytail. But the faint lines around her eyes betrayed her as a woman of middle age. Her patterned beige sundress flaunted every contour of her slender frame.

The moment Amanda looked into her coal-black irises, an emergency barrier sprang up in her mind. She refused to find the woman familiar.

The stranger launched from the wall and walked a casual circle around Amanda. "Look at you, my pretty rose. How tall you've grown. How red. Did I foresee this? I believe I did, though now I spy you black in many futures. The color doesn't suit you."

Amanda's heart pounded. She took a clumsy step toward the utility door. "Listen, I need to—"

"You don't remember me, flower? It hasn't been that long. Or perhaps you choose to pretend."

Amanda noticed the woman's strange inflections, her over-pronounced d's and t's. Whether it was an accent or an affectation, Amanda didn't know. She didn't care. The vault was open now. She remembered.

The woman shined a crooked grin at Amanda's gaping revelation. "Ah, now she recalls."

"Who the hell are you?"

"Ask me nicely," the stranger insisted. "Ask my name."

"What's your name?"

"None of you ever ask my name. Thirty-three circlets and not a single . . . Wait, did I not give you your circlet?" She scanned Amanda's bare wrists, then winced at herself. "Forgive me, child. I grow careless at the end."

Like a skilled magician, the woman rolled her wrist and produced a large metal loop in her hand—a thick silver bracelet, shiny and featureless. She deftly balanced it on the tip of her finger.

"It's so exciting. I've seen a terminal fold before but never from the surface. The air crackles with ionization. I should really take samples. Esis."

"What?"

"My name. My first name. I'd tell you my last name, but my wealth insists on guarding it. He overplans, as always."

"Look, uh, Esis—"

The bracelet fell to the concrete. Amanda watched it roll in a circle and settle on its side. By the time she looked up again, Esis's expression had completely changed. The smile was gone. Her dark eyes narrowed. Now she glared with furious umbrage, as if Amanda had just spit on her.

"You stupid, stubborn girl."

Esis grabbed ahold of her hair. Her voice dropped two octaves.

"Why do you have to be so difficult? Why can't you do what you're told?"

Amanda writhed in her grip. "Let go of me!"

"Do not entwine with the funny artist. I grow tired of telling you this. You entwine with your own, you won't be a flower. You'll just be dirt."

"Let GO!"

Amanda broke free and stumbled back to the wall. She pointed a trembling finger at Esis. "You're insane."

"And you're ungrateful. I save you and save you, and yet you never follow the strings."

"Just leave me alone!"

"Not yet."

"Fine. I'll leave."

Amanda hurried back to the building. She felt a sudden hot breeze along her side and heard what sounded like a flat drumroll. Before she could process the new stimuli, Esis stood right in front of her, blocking the door with her limber form.

"Not yet."

Amanda jumped back with a shriek. This woman just moved twenty feet with the speed of a gasp. *That's not the kind of thing crazy people do,* her muddled thoughts insisted. *That's the kind of thing crazy people see.*

"What are you?"

With a coy smile, Esis slung her ponytail over her shoulder and stroked it like a pet. "A wife. A mother. A French Canadian, by ancestry. Oh, and I'm a doctor. Unlike you, I finished my schooling. Curious how you and your sister both dawdled on this world, living far beneath your potential. Perhaps on some level you knew it didn't matter. This is all just prelude."

Amanda's whole body trembled. She took another step back. "Please leave me alone."

"I will," Esis replied with new empathy. "But first you need to don your circlet. It's rather crucial. In three minutes, you'll know why."

A thin white tendril suddenly sprang from Esis's palm. Like a frog's tongue, it seized the silver bangle on the ground, yanking it back into her grip. Amanda's eyes bulged with horror.

The bracelet split apart into four floating corners. Esis gently guided the pieces over Amanda's fingers, tickling her with static. They reunited around her wrist with a loud metallic *clack*. The seams melted away. The bracelet contracted to fit snugly over her skin.

Amanda fought a high scream. "W-what is this?"

"A life preserver," Esis replied. "That's twice I've rescued you now. I don't expect your thanks, being as ungrateful as you are. Just remember my warning about the funny artist. He's not for you. Silvers don't entwine with Silvers."

She swept her hand in a lazy circle. A round white portal bloomed on the concrete wall.

A half moment passed before Esis's upper half abruptly resurfaced. "Sorry, child. Forgot to mention. Don't move. You'll want to stay at ground level. Trust me on this."

Amanda pressed her palms to her wincing eyes, trying to will the universe back into order. By the time she dared to look again, Esis and her portal were gone.

She huddled against the wall and pressed her crucifix to her collarbone like a broken call button. There was no divine wisdom to be found on the other end of the line. Suddenly her Lord had nothing to say.

Against the madwoman's advice, Amanda ran back into the building, up the stairs, and down the long hall. By the time she reached the door of the medical office, her face was flush with strain.

She stopped to gather her wits and form some semblance of a strategy. Should she tell Derek about the crazy thing that just happened? Would he believe her? Would *anyone*?

Hannah.

Yes. Of course. Her sister was just a little girl when the first encounter happened, but she'd remember. She'd believe.

Amanda pulled her cell phone from her jacket, cursing at the little spin-ning radar dish. In all the chaos, she'd forgotten about the signal issues today. *Maybe I should drive to her place. See if she's—*

The screen on her phone suddenly went dark, along with every light in the hallway. The blackout was so thorough that Amanda had to use her cigarette lighter to rule out blindness.

She opened the door to the office and saw a second lighter come to life behind the reception window. Amanda had no trouble recognizing the face above the flame.

"Derek!"

He squinted through the glass. "Amanda! Where the hell were you?"

"Outside. What . . . what's going on?"

"Power outage. And to think of all the money we paid for that backup generator."

"Derek, something happened . . ."

"Help Leni get everyone into windowed rooms. I don't want people trip-ping and suing us."

"I was just in the alley—"

"Wait. First help me find the blankets. It's freezing in here."

"Derek, I'm trying to talk to you!"

"Can it please wait? We're in the middle of a crisis here!"

Her silver bracelet vibrated. Suddenly the waiting room was bathed in a lambent glow. When Derek looked at his wife again, she was encased in a seven-foot egg of shimmering light. They stared at each other through the hazy wall.

"No," Amanda replied, in a low and trembling voice. "It can't wait."

The new plan was to evacuate. Chandra Wilkes, the junior oncologist, orga-nized the cigarette lighter exodus. No one needed their Bics in the waiting room. They had Amanda.

Chandra poked a nervous finger at Amanda's baffling light shell. "What the hell is this?"

"Just go," Amanda urged. "Get everyone out of here."

A thunderous quake rocked the building, knocking half the pictures off the walls. Chandra shepherded the evacuees, shouting them forward while they all stopped to process at Amanda.

For nearly a minute, Derek had tried everything he could to break her free of her enclosure. Then his hands grew numb, his face burned with arctic chills, and it finally occurred to him that Amanda was safer than he was. Now he lounged on a waiting room chair, blowing smoke through shivering lips.

As the last of the patients cleared out, Amanda fixed her wide eyes on Derek. "You should go too."

He took a deep drag of his cigarette. "Nah."

"It's not safe!"

"Honey, it's ten below and dropping. If it's that bad in here, what do you think it's like outside?"

As a man who fought cancer for a living, Derek was no stranger to the fine art of the mercy yield. There were simply times when, despite all efforts, the battle was lost. He'd told Amanda time and again that he hoped to face his death with the same dignity as his best and bravest patients. Amanda found his resolve to be vain in all respects, never more so than now.

A new quake shattered the reception window. The walls began to splinter, along with Derek's calm façade. "Oh God . . ."

"Derek, please go!"

He tried to get up but merely tumbled to the floor. He pressed his palms against Amanda's light.

"This is what I get?"

"Derek—"

"This is what I get for working hard? For saving lives?"

"Just try to get up! You can still—"

"Why aren't you feeling this? Why were you saved?"

A huge new fissure split the ceiling. Tiles fell. Dead wires dangled. As the building screamed in distress, Derek narrowed his eyes at Amanda. His skin cracked with frost.

"Guess G-God thinks you're pretty damn great, huh? At least you two h-have that in common."

Warm tears spilled down her cheeks. "Don't do this . . ."

"I'm actually glad we're going to d-different places. What does that s-say about you?"

The roof finally gave way. The upper floors rained down on them.

"DEREK!"

He disappeared into the crumbling wreckage. Amanda fell to her knees, covering her eyes while the building collapsed all around her.

"Please stop. Please stop. Please. Please . . ."

The metal squeals fell silent. The darkness gave way to bright white nothing. By the time Amanda pried her hands from her eyes, the scenery had changed. She saw small buildings all around her. Blue sky. She was outside again, and everything seemed fine except for her.

She caught her reflection in the nearest window. She floated sixteen feet above the ground, hovering on a cutaway disc of office floor. Before she could even begin to process her surreal state of being, the blue light of her bracelet faded, the protective egg vanished, and Amanda plummeted to earth.

She met the new world, hand extended. It welcomed her by breaking her wrist.

The Salgado van was not a gentle vessel. Every bump on the road jostled her screaming injury. She had no idea where she was or where she was going. From the moment Esis sent her down the rabbit hole, Amanda existed in a raw and tender state of rejection. Only the pain of her fracture kept her tethered to the reality of her situation, such as it was.

She'd woken up forty-two minutes ago in the back of a city ambulance. From inside, Amanda had no idea that the vehicle was flying at second-story altitude or that it was moving at an external clock speed of 312 miles an hour. The only odd thing she'd noticed was the coffin-size device that rested against the opposite wall. An ominous orange sticker brandished a curious warning: THE UNAUTHORIZED USE OF THIS REVIVER IS A FEDERAL FELONY. ALL ILLEGAL REVERSALS ARE INVESTIGATED BY DP-9 AND CAN RESULT IN A MAXIMUM PENALTY OF TEN YEARS IN PRISON AND A FINE OF $200,000.

Upon arriving at the emergency room, a dour young nurse pulled Amanda through a gauntlet of daft and impenetrable questions, asking for her CID, her FIP/N, and eight other alien acronyms. Even stranger were half the conditions on the medical history checklist—Casparitis, Tillman's Malady, Severe Time Lag. After several blinking nonresponses, the nurse put down her tablet and left the scene. Amanda had little doubt she was calling for a psych consult.

She'd languished in bleary solitude until the curtain opened to a freckle-faced brunette in a green security uniform.

"Are you taking me to the psych ward?" Amanda had asked.

"I don't work here," Erin Salgado assured her. "And I don't think you're crazy."

Now after one stop, one girl, and twenty minutes of foreign suburbs, the van weaved its way up a twisty, tree-lined driveway. Erin turned around to her two passengers.

"We're here."

Amanda glanced out the window at the looming gray structure, a three-story complex of glass and brushed metal. Though she'd initially processed the building as a corporate office, she noticed derelict gazebos and leaf-strewn tennis courts on the property.

The van rolled to a halt and the Salgados stepped outside. Amanda took a long look at her fellow passenger—a chubby, sweet-faced adolescent. The poor girl wore enough soil on her pajamas to fill a small planter. She looked like she'd crawled out of her own grave.

"I'm sorry," Amanda offered.

Mia looked up. "What?"

"This whole time I've been sitting here in my own world. I never asked if you were all right. I never even asked your name."

The girl blinked in dazed disorientation. She'd spent the ride in a dull static haze, furrowing her brow at all the alien cars and baffling store signs. Now a loud banshee scream congealed in her throat like an air bubble. She couldn't move it up or down.

"I'm Mia. Mia Farisi. I'm not hurt, but I don't know what's going on. I just want to wake up from all this. I want to see my grandmother again."

Amanda bit her trembling lip and nodded. "I know, Mia. Believe me, I know what you're feeling. I wish I could say something to make it better."

"What's your name?"

To Amanda's surprise, the question stung. In all the pain and turmoil, she'd nearly forgotten the shape of her other wound, the one Derek had planted.

I'm actually glad we're going to different places. What does that say about you?

Now she blew a hot, jagged sigh as old syllables rolled up her throat.

"Given," she told Mia. "My name's Amanda Given."

Erin opened the back doors. "You need help getting out?"

"No," Amanda said. "We'll manage."

As she climbed out of the van, she extended her good arm to Mia.

"Listen, I'm just as scared as you are. I have no idea what's going to happen. But I'm glad to know I'm not alone. If you don't mind, I'd really like to hold your hand. Can I?"

After a moment of addled thought, Mia weakly nodded and obliged her.

Hand in hand, the refugees walked together—the widow and the orphan, the woman who fell from the sky and the girl who climbed out of the ground.

Soon they could spy a small crowd of people watching them through the glass of the lobby. Beyond their shadowy heads, Amanda saw a wall engraving in large gold letters. A word. A name. A last name. *Pelletier.*

SIX

Like uneasy dreamers, Amanda and Mia pushed through the doors and drank in their opulent new surroundings. The lobby was a sweeping chamber of glass and gray marble. Roman columns loomed three stories high while sunshine flooded down through skylights, glinting off every polished surface.

Amanda had to squint through the refractions to study the crowd at the reception desk—eighteen men and one woman, all pasty white and dressed in casual weekend garb. She found them all smart-looking, in a docile sort of way.

Eggheads, she realized. *They're all scientists.*

As Amanda and Mia moved closer into view, nineteen ardent smiles deflated into slack surprise. The crew had expected to find disoriented visitors, but these two looked battered, begrimed, and hopelessly bereaved. They didn't just drift into this world on a freak cosmic updraft. They crashed here like meteors.

While Amanda drew dark comfort from their sympathetic expressions, Mia's stomach twisted with stress. Their wide stares fell on her skin like hornets, making her feel like some wretched little thing they'd found under the porch steps. She meekly hid behind Amanda.

Spying the girl's distress, one of the scientists turned around to his peers. "You know what? This is overwhelming them. Can we, uh . . .?"

He was rotund and diminutive, with spiky brown hair and a scraggly chin beard. He reminded Amanda of a woodchuck, though from his sharp eyes and cultured British accent, she figured he was a phenomenally sharp one.

The scientists slowly departed through multiple exits, leaving only the bearded Englishman and a mousy young blonde with a clipboard.

"I apologize," said the man. "Curiosity got the better of us. We certainly don't wish to cause you any further discomfort. I . . ." He trailed off at the sight of Amanda's wrist. "Good Lord. Is that broken?"

Amanda looked down at her makeshift splint. "I don't know."

"We'll get that looked at right away. We have a fully equipped medical facility here."

Mia suddenly caught movement at the edge of her vision. Past a bubbling fountain and down a hallway, a wet-haired boy peeked out from one of many doors. A teenager. He spotted Mia's gaze and shyly retreated from view.

"I still don't know who any of you are," Amanda said.

The Englishman nodded amenably. "Of course not. Sorry. I'm Dr. Constantin Czerny, Secondary Executive here at the Pelletier Group. This is my associate, Dr. Beatrice Caudell. May I inquire as to your names?"

"I'm Amanda Given. This is Mia Parisi."

"Farisi," Mia corrected.

"Farisi. Sorry."

While Caudell scribbled their names into her clipboard, Czerny studied their tightly clasped hands.

"I can't even begin to imagine what you two have been through. I apologize again. We're all temporal physicists here. As such, we've been overly excited by recent events. For your sake, I implore you to remind us and forgive us should we ever take your state of mind for granted. Your well-being is our absolute priority. I can't stress that enough."

Amanda nearly wept with delirious relief. The bleakest part of her mind had prepared her for more madness, more Esis. But these people seemed mercifully kind. She was willing to forgive God long enough to ask him to please, please, please don't let this be a screw job.

"How did you find us?" she asked Czerny. "How did you even know we were coming?"

"Ms. Given, there'll be time to—"

"What's *happening* to us?"

"I'm afraid we don't have any more than a shard of the overall picture, but I promise we'll share everything we know. That's a task for my superior, Dr. Sterling Quint. He's not here yet, which is just as well, because there are still a few more of you in the vicinity. We're gathering them as we speak."

"Are we the first?" Amanda asked.

"You're the second and third. In fact . . ." Czerny peered down the hallway, then back at Amanda's wrist. "If you can endure without treatment a few more minutes, I'd like to introduce you to young David. I imagine he'll be quite relieved to see he's not alone in his ordeal."

Erin's handphone beeped twice. She read the screen, then tugged her brother's sleeve.

"It's Dad. He wants us downtown." She looked to Mia. "We're hitting the road again, kitten. But we'll be back soon. Sit easy. You're in good hands."

"Good luck," said Czerny.

The Salgados left the way they came. Czerny tapped an anxious finger on Caudell's clipboard. "Get the maid to prepare three more rooms. We'll need six at a minimum."

As Czerny spoke, Mia could see that he was struggling to hold back a grin. He reminded her of a kid at Christmas mass, hearing about the Lord but thinking about the presents.

"This building was originally a hotel," he informed them. "Now it seems it will be again. Funny how the universe works."

The first-floor game parlor was a popular break-time refuge for the Pelletier staff. Aside from hustlers and gamblers, nobody appreciated billiards more than physicists.

The boy named David Dormer stared at the table with wavering concentration. He'd never played pool in his life and had no intention of starting now. Instead he took four boxes of dominoes from the game shelf and arranged the pieces in a winding spiral construct on the felt. When he realized he was building himself a precarious galaxy, he placed a cue ball in the center to serve as the core.

On hearing Czerny's voice, he fluffed his wet blond hair in the mirror. He'd taken a long hot shower earlier, only to discover upon emerging that one of the so-called Pelletiers had snatched away his clothes and wristwatch. They'd left him a plush white robe in compensation, thankfully a long one. David was six feet tall and still growing.

Czerny peeked in the doorway. "How fares my young friend?"

David emitted a less than genuine grin. "Keeping myself busy, I suppose."

"I can see that. Anyway, I have a wonderful surprise—"

"Yes. I'd very much like to meet them. If they're up for meeting me."

Czerny cocked his head in surprise. David shrugged. "I peeked."

"Ah. Of course. Can't say I blame you." He beckoned to people in the hall. "Come. Come."

Amanda and Mia stepped into the doorway, and now David smiled for real.

For a split second, Amanda's primal instincts growled like a Doberman. She'd expected to find someone in the same wretched condition as herself and Mia. Instead she saw this gorgeous blue-eyed boy, one so clean that he practically glistened. And then there was the smile. He's *smiling*! For a tense beat, Amanda drank him in with ice-cold suspicion. *Uh-uh. No way. You are not one of us.*

While Czerny handled the introductions, Amanda took a deeper look. Now she caught the uncertainty in David's eyes, the work of anxious self-distraction on the pool table, the shiny silver bracelet on his wrist. Her judgment was six miles out of whack today. *He is one of us.*

"I don't mean to grin like an idiot," he told Amanda, as if he'd read her concerns. "I've just been wondering for the last hour if anyone else managed to survive whatever it is I survived. I'm only smiling now because the answer's obviously yes. That's the first good news I've gotten all day."

The last of Amanda's doubts melted into a gooey puddle. Now she fought the urge to hug him.

"It's nice to meet you, David. I'm so glad you're okay."

"I'm not sure 'okay' is the operative word. But I'm alive. I suppose I should be thankful for that."

She finally got around to noticing that David, like Czerny, had an unmistakable accent.

"You're Australian."

"Yeah. I grew up there. First Brisbane, then Perth. But I've been traveling with my father these last six years and I haven't been back. Hello."

His greeting was aimed at Mia, who'd once again taken refuge behind Amanda. After all the terrible events of the morning, her mind was in a state of wreckage, a crushed and crackling fuse box. And yet one teenage circuit seemed to work just fine. Like a special news bulletin, it interrupted her grief to announce that there was an insanely beautiful boy in the room, wearing nothing but a robe. It also reminded her that she was still in her pajamas, still covered in dirt, and—lest she forget—still really fat.

"Hi," she said in a barely audible whisper.

Czerny clapped his hands together. "Okay. I apologize for the brevity, but Ms. Given needs medical attention. Mia, would you like to stay here a bit or would you prefer a shower?"

"Shower, please."

He smirked. "I thought as much. Beatrice, would you?"

"Of course." Caudell gestured to Mia. "Come with me."

As they unlinked hands, Mia and Amanda exchanged a brief glance, a wordless agreement to reconnect soon. It scared Amanda to think how very un-Christian she'd become if anyone here mistreated the girl.

Czerny glanced at David. "They'll be back soon. And there are more arriving."

"Wow. That's excellent. I'm very encouraged to hear that."

"How old are you?" Amanda asked him.

The question earned her another smile. This one was softer, hand-rolled with evincible pain.

"I just turned sixteen," David said. "Yesterday, in fact."

She couldn't imagine a worse thing to do right now than wish him a belated happy birthday.

"I'm so sorry."

"Thank you. I'm sorry for your losses as well."

Orphans, she thought. *It's just me and orphans.*

"We'll be back," Czerny repeated to David. "Let us know if there's anything you need."

"At some point, I'd like real clothes. I also wouldn't mind some more information about . . . you know, all of this."

"Soon," Czerny promised. "Soon to both."

He escorted Amanda back to the lobby. David blew a smirking sigh.

"Right. I'll just keep amusing myself then."

He took another look at his careful spiral construct. After a moment's consideration, he flicked the trigger domino, then watched the pieces fall.

"Remarkable, isn't he?"

"I'm sorry?"

Czerny continued to position Amanda's wrist in the scanner. "David. Hard to believe he's just sixteen. I know it's premature to say, but I suspect he's a genius."

The medical lab was once a hotel meeting room. Only the conference tables had been removed, replaced by expensive-looking machines that were utter mysteries to Amanda. The device Czerny currently used on her arm had six Frisbee-size metal rings, all connected by gooseneck rods to a contraption that resembled a photocopier. Czerny had called it a free-induction tomograph. She assumed the imaging was electromagnetic, like MRI scans.

As the machine hummed in busy analysis, Amanda writhed uncomfortably at the odd sensation in her healthy arm. It tingled nonstop with invisible flurry, as if a thousand ants crawled all over it.

"From what he told me, he had a very unique upbringing," Czerny said. "His father was a world-renowned theoretical physicist, much like our own Dr. Quint. The two of them traveled the world. David's lived in Mexico, England, Japan, Holland. Never in one place more than a year."

"Did he mention anything about his mother?"

"No. I was curious but I didn't ask. He looked pained enough talking about his father."

Amanda vented an airy sigh. "He seems to be handling this so much better than me."

"We all react differently to trauma. In your defense, he's not saddled with a broken wrist." He studied the new image on the monitor. "A distal radius fracture, from the looks of it."

Amanda squinted at the scan, unable to make heads or tails of it until she followed Czerny's finger.

"Oh there it is. Good. No compounding. Doesn't look like joint damage. I don't even think this'll need realignment. Do you?"

Czerny stared at her in muted wonder.

"I'm a nurse," she told him.

"I was about to guess you were a doctor. In any case, you're right. This was a nice clean break."

"Good. Thank God."

"Now, let's see what we can do about making you a better splint."

Amanda watched Czerny carefully as he rooted through the supply drawers. "You seem to know a lot about treating people."

"I was a field medic in the British army. I've seen my fair share of broken limbs."

"What part of England are you from?"

His genial smile turned sour. "The part they call Poland."

"Oh. Sorry. I assumed from your accent—"

"Common mistake. Like most of my people, I was taught the King's English and sent to fight in his wars. Anyway, Pole, Jackie—it hardly matters now. I'm a naturalized citizen of these great United States. God bless the peaceful eagle."

Amanda's stomach lurched. The invisible bugs on her arm scurried faster. "You, uh . . . you wouldn't happen to have a cigarette, would you?"

Czerny paused his work, momentarily thrown. "I'm afraid not. If you're looking for a chemical relaxant, we have a few on hand that are far less toxic than nicotine." He eyed her cautiously. "And far more legal."

She blinked at him stupidly. "You're telling me cigarettes are illegal?"

Czerny fought another wild grin. *Marvelous. Absolutely marvelous.*

"They've been contraband for thirty years now. Not that they can't be found. If you're truly in need, I can ask my colleagues. One of them might have a pack of Chinese nicquans hidden away."

Amanda covered her mouth, stifling a black and hopeless chuckle. Czerny gently squeezed her shoulder and reached into his pocket.

"Ms. Given—Amanda—I can only imagine what a trying experience this is for you. But you will adapt. I promise. Until then, here."

He pressed a warm coin into her hand. Though it was the size of a dime and decagon-shaped, it was clearly a copper-colored one-cent piece. It still said "In God We Trust." And it still had a side-profile engraving of Abraham Lincoln.

"One of ours," Czerny told her. "From the pennies we found in David's pocket, it seems your currency is different, but still a little the same. Next

time you're overwhelmed, just remind yourself that this isn't completely foreign. This isn't square one. Things are different, but they're still a little the
same."

His words, though well intentioned, were worth less than the money
he gave her. Amanda looked at the surgical table in the center of the room
and thought about her new predicament. She was an otherworldly being
in a building full of scientists. It seemed all but inevitable that, dead or
alive, she'd end up on that table. And while Dr. Czerny cut Amanda open,
the mousy little blonde would scribble on her clipboard, taking copious
notes on how the subject's vital organs were different, but still a little the
same.

By the time Mia returned to the game parlor, David had switched his interests
from astronomy to engineering. A pair of shaky domino towers rose two feet
from the surface of the pool table. They'd each been built at subtle angles,
meticulously designed to lean toward each other until they ultimately connected. He took a quick moment to process Mia.

"You cleaned up nicely."

"Thank you," she said, blushing.

She took a seat in an overstuffed recliner, carefully holding the flaps of her
robe. The last thing either of them needed right now was an unscheduled
peep show.

"Mia Farisi," said David, as he placed another tile. "I like the cadence of
that. It could work as a single name, like Christo or Madonna. I'm guessing
your last name's Italian. Am I right?"

"It is."

"Yeah. It was a toss-up between Italian and Turkish, and you don't look
Turkish. May I ask what your surname means?"

Mia found herself smiling even as her brow furrowed. This beautiful
Aussie was just a little bit strange. "I don't know."

"Tell me to shut up if I'm being annoying. I have the social skills of a
rock crab. I think that's why they put me in here and told me to amuse
myself."

A misplaced domino caused the left tower to collapse in wreckage.

"Son of a bitch." He gave her a sheepish look. "Sorry."

"It's okay. I've heard worse."

He resumed work on the remaining tower. "They took my wristwatch. I hope I get it back. It's an antique heirloom. Fully mechanical. I have to wind it and everything."

"Wow."

"Yeah. It kept on working, even when all the electronics died. Were you awake for that?"

"I'm sorry?"

"This morning at 4:41, the electricity went out everywhere, even in battery-powered devices. My father woke me up, all excited. He suspected it was some kind of electromagnetic pulse wave. It lasted nine and a half minutes."

Mia thought about her own father, who'd taken a much bleaker view of the power outage.

"My dad's a scientist," David told her. "He lives for this kind of stuff. He was so thrilled by the E-M pulse, he kept me up all morning, bending my ear with wild theories. When I suggested the possibility that this was a man-made occurrence and not entirely benevolent, he dismissed it. He wasn't scared at all. He just . . ."

He noticed Mia wasn't listening anymore. She aimed a grim and distant stare at the floor.

"Anyway," said David, "I think I've hit my limit on these diversions. Godzilla."

He swiped the tower, sending it crumbling to the felt. In search of new entertainment, he began juggling a trio of pool balls.

Soon Mia noticed him again. She lightened up. "You're good at that."

"Yep. I may not have my father's aptitude for science, but I am a prodigy in *commedia dell'arte*." He raised an eyebrow at her. "Tell me you know what that means, Italian girl."

She smiled, despite herself. "Old-school theatrical comedy."

"Very old."

"So what does your name mean?"

"Dormer. French-Latin. It means 'sleeper,' which has never been more appropriate. Despite my awesome showmanship, I feel like I could nap for a month. Heads up."

He gently lobbed a pool ball in her direction. She caught it with a yelp of surprise. David took another ball off the table, then resumed his juggling act.

"Maybe there's some scientist in me after all, Miafarisi, because I find myself tempted to ask you about your experiences today, just to compare them to mine. I don't want to cause you any more grief. It's just that I've seen so much madness in the last two hours that I don't know how to process it. I still haven't ruled out the possibility that I've completely lost my mind. That would certainly explain the voices."

Stuck for a response, all Mia could do was shake her head in empathy.

David had set her up to help him attempt a four-ball juggle, but suddenly thought better of it. He dropped the balls on the table and ran his fingers through his shaggy blond hair. Mia once again noticed how eclectically lovely he was, like an alt-rock angel.

"Just tell me one thing," he pleaded. "Did you see the person who gave you your bracelet?"

"No. Whoever it was, they put it on me while I slept."

He blew a loud puff of air through fluttering lips. "Lovely. Could be anyone then."

"What about you?"

"I'm pretty sure I have an alibi."

"No, I mean did you see who gave you your bracelet?"

"I know. I was just being . . . Yeah, I saw her. I even talked to her. We both did. Me and my dad."

"A woman?"

"A tall one," said David. "Very beautiful. She said her name was Esis."

They both turned to look when Amanda stepped into the doorway. She offered Mia a shaky smile.

"Look at you. I knew there was a pretty girl under all that dirt."

Mia studied the thick new splint on Amanda's left wrist. She found it strange that the fingers of Amanda's good arm were the ones that twitched uncomfortably.

"I thought you were getting a cast."

"In a few days," Amanda explained. "Once the swelling goes down."

Now Amanda looked to David. She started and stopped herself three times before speaking.

"I'm sorry. Did you just say Esis?"

A loud *thud* suddenly filled the parlor. A gruff male voice rumbled through the halls.

"WE NEED HELP HERE!"

The lobby once again teemed with people. Physicists burst out of every door to surround a newly arrived trio. The two standing men wore the same green uniform as Erin Salgado. One was young and square-headed. The other was older and sported a thick walrus mustache. They tended to an unconscious patient on a stretcher—a young Asian man in a faded Stanford sweatshirt. Thin trails of blood trickled from his nostrils.

Czerny emerged from the elevator and made a waddling dash toward the action. He caught Amanda and her young companions at the edge of the hallway.

"Take the kids back to the parlor. It'll be all right."

"Can I help?" Amanda asked.

"Thank you, but we've got this. Return to the parlor, please."

The noisy mob disappeared down the corridor, leaving the guests to themselves. Mia eyed the small splatter of blood by the front door.

"God. What do you think happened to that guy?"

"I dunno," David said. "I was more distracted by the cot beneath him. I can't figure out what was holding it up."

"Do you think he'll be all right, Amanda?"

The widow didn't respond. She was too busy staring in wide-eyed disbelief at the listless young woman who lingered outside. Her face was obscured by tousled black hair. Her T-shirt and jeans were scuffed with dirt. Her left arm was wrapped in a sling.

The woman pushed through the glass doors and hobbled toward the reception desk in a dreamy daze. She took no notice of the three people watching her.

Mia held Amanda's arm. "Are you okay?"

She was not. From the moment the newest guest entered her view, Amanda's brain had fallen into hot conflict. She was convinced she was crazy and convinced that she wasn't. Convinced that the person in front of her was a stranger, and convinced that she was anything but.

Her mouth quivered as she struggled to find a voice.

"Hannah?"

The woman turned to look, brushing the messy strands of hair from her face. There was no denying it now. One world over and thirty feet apart, the Great Sisters Given were reunited again.

SEVEN

No one ever guessed that the two women were siblings. One was a tall and skinny redhead with piercing green eyes. The other was a short and curvy brunette with the wide brown stare of a deer. They had different noses, different jaws, different voices, different walks. The only visible trait they shared was an unwavering intensity. No one ever accused the daughters of Robert and Melanie Given of being too relaxed, though Hannah came close to earning that distinction now. While Amanda froze in white-faced shock, the actress exhaled with breezy relief, as if the sisters had lost and found each other at the mall.

"Oh, hey. There you are."

Amanda made a slow trek toward Hannah, her lips tangled on a hundred burning questions. All she could manage were a few stammering *wuh*s.

"Martin left me in the van," said Hannah. "I wasn't sure if I was supposed to stay there or . . ." She threw her dizzy gaze around the lobby. "What is this place? It looks like a Hilton."

Hannah suddenly noticed David and Mia watching her with puzzled interest. "Kids in robes. Weird. I hope this isn't a cult. Hey, has Zack arrived yet? Skinny guy? Carries a sketchbook? I left him back at the marina. He has my stuff."

Amanda gripped Hannah's chin and turned her face left and right. She thought about the otherwordly penny in her pocket and wondered now if this woman was a similar entity, an ersatz version of the old familiar thing.

Hannah crunched her brow. "Okay, Amanda, you're freaking me out. Can you please say something?"

"I-I'm sorry. I just . . . I can't believe I'm looking at you. I mean I can't believe it's you."

"It's me."

"Do you remember seeing me last night?"

"Yeah. Of course."

"Do you remember where we were? What we talked about?"

Hannah slit her eyes in suspicion. "What exactly are you testing me for?"

"Your pupils are dilated and you're unfocused. You're talking about people named Martin and Zack. I just need to see you're in there. I need to know you're the Hannah I know."

The actress sighed with exasperation. If there was ever any doubt that this was her very own Amanda, she'd just erased it with her singular brand of well-meaning condescension.

"I saw you at the theater," she replied. "At my premiere of *Damn Yankees*. You made it perfectly clear that you weren't a fan of the Hindu version."

Amanda let out a brusque cry and wrapped her in a sobbing embrace. Hannah rubbed her back.

"It's okay. It's really me. And it's really you. And I'm really, really glad I found you."

Amanda wiped her eyes, then shined a trembling grin at the orphans.

"Mia, David, this is Hannah. She's my sister."

David blinked in amazement. "Sister? Wow. That's . . . I mean it was obvious you knew each other but . . . wow. That can't be coincidence."

"That we're sisters?"

He stared at Hannah blankly. "That you both got bracelets."

"Oh. Right. I wonder how many other people got these." She studied Amanda's broken wrist. "Hey, what happened to you?"

Amanda was distracted by Mia's dark and cloudy expression. God only knew how many loved ones the poor girl lost today.

She turned back to Hannah. "I fell. What happened to your arm?"

"I hit a bus."

"What?"

Hannah stopped to read the brass sign on the wall. "Pelleh-*teer*."

"Pell-tee-*ay*," David corrected. "It's French-Canadian. I asked."

Now Hannah zeroed in on David as if he just turned visible. "Holy shit. You're gorgeous."

"He's sixteen," said Amanda.

Hannah glared at her. "I was remarking. I was not angling."

Amanda noticed a little black sticker at the base of Hannah's neck. She peeled it off.

"What is this?" She sniffed the sticky side. It had a faint medicinal scent. "It's a drug. They drugged you. No wonder you're acting so . . . Let me look at your pupils."

"I'm fine! It's just a baby spot. A mood-lifter. It works great. It did wonders for me and Theo."

"Who's Theo?"

Hannah stared with fresh discomfort at the scruffy green baseball cap in her hand. Amanda quickly connected the dots.

"Wait, is he the guy they carried in here? The one who was unconscious and bleeding from every orifice? Are you kidding me, Hannah? Are those the wonders you're talking about?"

"You don't know it was the drug that did that."

"Then what happened to him?"

Sighing, Hannah crunched the cap in her grip. In truth, she had no idea what happened. Even in a lucid state, she'd have a hell of a time explaining the curious case of Theo Maranan.

Thirty-two minutes ago, she'd discovered the ultimate recipe for joy: a baby spot and a comfortable seat in a fast-moving vehicle. The view outside the window was poetry in motion, an ever-changing canvas of color and light. Every time the van stopped at a traffic signal, she'd snap out of her euphoric daze and launch chirpy, childlike questions at her two Salgado escorts. *What makes ambulances fly? Are we getting Zack next? Do you know the white-haired man? Why isn't everyone in the world addicted to baby spots?*

With dwindling patience, Martin fielded her queries (*"Aeris," "Maybe," "Who?" "Because the more you use them, the less they work"*). His son raced through yellow lights just to keep her quiet.

Soon the van pulled into an alley behind a supermarket. Hannah peered through the front grate and studied Martin's handheld computer. The screen contained a grayscale city map, peppered with four blinking red dots.

"What are the dots? Are those the people you're looking for? And how are you finding us anyway? Our bracelets?"

The Salgados opened their doors and hurried outside.

"We'll be back in a couple," said Martin. "Just sit back and stay easy, okay?"

Hannah let out a cynical snort. "You sound like my last date."

She spent the next few minutes in cushy silence, pinching her lip with growing fluster as the awful sounds of apocalypse came trickling back into memory. The booming crackle of the hardening sky. The horrible crunching noise of the frozen corpses . . .

The back doors of the van suddenly sprung open. Hannah saw Gerry Salgado struggling with a thrashing young Asian. He wore a dirty gray hoodie over khaki shorts and sandals. Sun-bleached letters on his chest advertised Stanford University. An Oakland A's baseball cap lay askew on his head.

Martin affixed a small black sticker to the stranger's neck, then joined his son in the tussle. The captive helplessly writhed in their grip.

"Let me go! Please! I'm not ready for this!"

The Salgados forced him into the seat opposite Hannah, then held him in place until he sat still. Hannah noticed a pair of foreign script symbols tattooed on the inside of his left wrist. The silver bracelet on his other arm was all too familiar.

"There we go," said Martin. "You feeling better now?"

The man nodded at Martin. Hannah could see he was in dire need of a shave and a haircut. He couldn't have become this disheveled just from one morning.

"I'm not ready," he repeated.

"Not ready for what?" Hannah asked him, eliciting glares from both Salgados.

The stranger finally noticed her. His twitchy gaze stopped at her bracelet.

"You're kidding, right?" He glanced at the Salgados. "Is she kidding me?"

Martin rubbed his arm impatiently. "Okay, listen, we need to get moving again. I'll trust you two to get along back here. You're both in the same fix and you're both gonna be okay."

Soon they were traveling again. Hannah wasn't pleased that her window view was now obscured by 160 pounds of discombobulated Asian, but she didn't want to offend him by moving away.

Screw it, she thought. *Might as well mingle.*

"Hi. I'm Hannah. What's your name?"

He took off his cap and fluffed his messy hair.

"Theo," he replied hoarsely. "Theo Maranan."

"Hi, Theo. How you feeling now?"

He smeared his bleary eyes. "Fluffy and awkward. Like rabbits are screwing in my head."

Hannah grinned. "Yeah. That's the baby spot. It gets better."

"What's a baby spot?"

"The little patch on your neck. It's a drug. A mood-lifter."

His face crunched with confusion. "They have drugs here?"

"Yeah. Sure. Why wouldn't they?"

"I don't know. I just assumed."

For all his wear and tear, Hannah found Theo to be somewhat easy on the eyes. He wasn't especially burly but he had broad shoulders and finely chiseled features. On a better day, in a better state, she might have even flirted with him.

He raised a loose finger at her arm sling. "You mind if I ask how, uh . . . ?"

"Oh, this? I had some kind of weird mental seizure. Then I hit a bus."

"Wow. Damn. That would do it."

She looked again at the script symbols on his arm. "Maranan. That's Filipino, right?"

He nodded, impressed. "Yeah. Very good. Most folks guess wrong."

"Well, I dated one of your people."

"Fair enough. I dated one of yours."

The two of them plunged into giddy chuckles, prompting Martin to turn around and check on them.

"Okay, I see what you mean about the baby spot," Theo said. "I shouldn't be laughing at all, given what's coming."

Hannah's smile died away. "What's coming?"

"Are you kidding?"

"That's the second time you . . . No, I'm not kidding. I have no idea what's going on."

"You're better off. Trust me."

They both fell quiet for a few blocks. Theo studied her cautiously.

"Can I ask you something personal, Hannah? You don't have to answer."

She shrugged. "Try me."

"What's the worst thing you've ever done?"

The question didn't bother her as much as she expected. She chewed her lip in contemplation.

"I had a big emotional breakdown when I was thirteen. I cut myself pretty badly."

"Your wrists, you mean."

"Yes."

"Across the vein or up and down?"

She eyed him strangely. "What does that matter?"

"Well, to me it's the difference between a cry for help and a serious attempt at suicide."

Her pleasant buzz began to falter. "I guess it was a cry for help then. Still a horrible thing to put my mother and sister through."

"What about your dad?"

She looked away. "He died the year before."

Theo nodded with clinical intrigue. "I see. Suicide?"

"Cancer. Can we please change the subject?"

"Sorry. Didn't mean to upset you."

The van sailed through three green lights before Theo spoke again. "I hope you don't think I was judging you. Believe me, I'm in no position to wag the finger at anyone. I'm a law school dropout, a rehab washout, and an all-around blight on the family tree. If I told you the worst thing I ever did, you'd get the strong and rightful urge to push me out of this van."

Hannah pulled her gaze from the moving scenery and back onto him.

"I also tried suicide," Theo added. "Five years ago. It wasn't a cry for help. It was a full-fledged attempt to end it. The only reason it didn't work is because apparently, among my many faults, I'm also bad with knots."

Hannah let out a churlish giggle. She covered her mouth, mortified.

"Oh my God. I'm sorry. I didn't mean to laugh."

Theo smirked with good humor. "It's okay. You're picturing me falling through a half-ass noose, right onto my full ass. That's pretty much what happened."

They both fell into dizzy laughter again. Theo moaned and wiped his eyes. "You know what's even crazier? For all my attempts to kill myself, both quickly and slowly, I don't even know what did it in the end. I have no idea how I died."

Hannah's humor vanished in an instant. She stared at her new companion in deep bother.

"Theo, do you . . . Jesus, I don't even know how to approach this."

"Just ask."

"Do you really think you're dead right now?"

He stared at her, expressionless, for a full city block. "Okay. This is tricky. I don't want to upset you again."

"What do you mean?"

"Well, let's take this step by step. You told me you got hit by a bus . . ."

"No, I said I hit a bus. It was parked. I only dislocated my shoulder."

Theo sat forward now, his eyes darting back and forth in busy thought. Hannah blinked at him in fresh bewilderment.

"Oh my God. You think this is the afterlife for both of us."

He held up a hand. "Okay, wait now. Before you mock me—"

"I'm not mocking you, Theo. I just—"

"I was enveloped in a ball of hard, glowing . . . something. And then everything went white. When it stopped, I found myself in this place with glimmering walls and flying trucks. I mean, what am I supposed to think?"

"I don't know," Hannah confessed. "I still don't know."

"Then how do you know I'm not right?"

In a more sober state, it might have occurred to Hannah to ask the Salgados to settle the matter. Instead she found herself considering the notion that she was in fact riding the jitney to her own eternal judgment. She imagined the panel would deliberate for ten seconds before sending her to the hazy gray place where mediocre people went.

"I'm sorry, Theo. I don't think you're right. I'm alive. I'm screwed up right now, but I'm alive. It's the only thing I know for sure."

To Hannah's surprise, the idea only seemed to unnerve him more. He furiously tapped his bracelet.

"I talked to someone," he said. "I'm not religious at all, so please don't mistake me for the kind of person who sees angels everywhere."

"Go on."

"He found me at the bus station this morning. He was fierce-looking and—I say this heterosexually—very pretty. He said his name was Azral and that he'd never seen so much wasted potential in a person. He wasn't the first to tell me that, by the way, and he certainly wasn't telling me anything I didn't already know. But then he said I was moving on to a new world. That I'd finally make myself useful there. Then he gave me this bracelet . . ."

Hannah listened and nodded. She already had her next question lined up.

Theo shook his head at himself. "God. You must think I'm an idiot."

"I don't. Really. When I first got here, I thought this was Canada."

After scanning her for ridicule and finding none, Theo leaned his head back and laughed. His face twitched briefly, like he was shaking off a fly.

"I'd been riding all night from San Francisco," he told her. "So I was already at diminished capacity when I met the guy. I'll also admit that I wasn't entirely sober."

"Theo . . ."

"My point is that I wasn't thinking straight."

"Theo, did this guy have white hair?"

He stared ahead serenely. At this point, he'd lost all capacity for surprise.

"Yeah. I guess you met him too."

The van pulled to a stop along the curb. Hannah looked out the window. They were still downtown, in a decidedly less ritzy area than the one she'd arrived in.

"We'll be back," said Martin. "We got two signals, so you'll be in good company soon."

The Salgados disappeared down an alley, between a dilapidated post office and a grungy diner. Hannah and Theo fell into an awkward silence. Suddenly the actress felt an eerie chill on the back of her neck, as if someone was watching her. She turned around and scanned the street. No one.

Soon Theo's head dipped and his eyelids fluttered erratically. Hannah left him to his twitchy nap.

"Azral," she muttered, in a vacant daze. It was strange to learn the name of the white-haired man after all this time. He was no angel. As sure as Hannah knew she was alive, she knew he was no force of goodness.

Four minutes after leaving, the Salgados returned without company.

"What happened?" Hannah asked. "I thought we were getting more people."

Martin hurriedly texted his daughter. "False alarm."

Hannah could practically feel his tension. His son looked downright disturbed. She opted not to inquire further. She'd had enough agitation for one ride.

The vehicle started up again. Soon Hannah drifted off into uneasy thoughts. A floundering actress, a droll cartoonist, and a law school dropout who got plastered at bus stops. *Why us, Azral? What could you possibly want from—*

"He's right," Theo murmured.

Hannah looked at him again. His eyes were still closed. She couldn't tell if he was addressing her or merely talking in his sleep.

"I'm sorry. Who?"

"Zack. He's right. It's not enough money to get to Brooklyn."

She sat forward. "Wait, what?"

A few drops of blood trickled onto his sweatshirt. Then a few more. Then his nose became a faucet. It didn't take a nurse to see that something very wrong was happening inside Theo Maranan.

While the first two floors of the Pelletier building had been converted to office space, the top flight stayed true to its hotel origins. Thirty suites remained fully furnished with beds, chairs, and dressers. Only the locks and lumivisions had been removed, by order of the new owner, Dr. Sterling Quint.

Amanda emerged from her shower to discover that one of the physicists had taken her clothes for study. All she owned now were her gold cross necklace and diamond wedding ring. She was willing to let science have the ring, if science asked.

She fastened her robe and crossed the hall into Hannah's suite, listening to the running shower through the bathroom door. She pushed it open a crack.

"Hannah? You okay?"

Amanda could see her silhouette through the gauzy white curtain, the buxom shape that Derek had ogled fourteen hours ago. Hannah leaned against the tile in somber repose. The mood-lifters were wearing off, turning her thoughts to stucco.

"I'll be out soon," she said in a dismal voice.

"There's no hurry, Hannah. I just wanted to check on you."

"What's her name?"

"Who?"

"The quiet girl in the lobby."

"Mia."

"Yeah. Mia. She didn't look very happy."

"She just lost her whole family."

"That's what I figured," Hannah said. "It's got to hurt a little. I mean to see that we didn't."

Amanda sat on the edge of the sink and closed her eyes. "I don't know."

"You know Mom's dead, right?"

The spider-leg tingles came back to Amanda's right arm. Her fingers twitched uncontrollably. "Hannah . . ."

"This wasn't just San Diego. It was everywhere. A kid with a radio said so. The whole goddamn world."

Amanda could hear her sister's choking sobs over the water. "Hannah, you're coming down off a very strong drug . . ."

"No, I'm coming down off everything! I'm crying about our mother! How come you're not?"

A powerful chill seized Amanda's hand. She pulled back her sleeve and gasped at the mad new blight on her arm. Her skin was covered in tiny white dots from her fingertips to her bracelet. The beads looked as hard and shiny as plastic, but they moved with a life all their own. Amanda watched with frozen horror as three flea-size spots shimmied up her thumb.

Oblivious to the crisis, Hannah rested her head against the wall. "I didn't . . . Look, I don't know what I'm saying right now, okay? Don't listen to me."

Amanda shook her hand with hummingbird zeal until the dots disappeared. She searched every inch of her skin for remnants.

"Amanda?"

She threw her saucer gaze at the shower curtain. "W-what?"

"I didn't mean to say that. I'm sorry."

"It's all right. I'm not . . ." She flashed back to her alley encounter with Esis, the strange white tendril that had burst from her hand. *What did she do? What did she do to me?*

Amanda jumped to her feet. "I should . . . I should check on the kids."

"Let me know if you find out anything about Theo."

"Yeah. I'll ask."

"He said he was a blight."

Amanda stopped at the door. "What?"

"Theo. He made himself out to be some god-awful person, but he didn't seem so bad."

Hannah smeared hot water against her eyes. "I don't want him to die."

Amanda kept staring at her flushed pink arm, lost in dark imaginings. God only knew what the scientists would do if they found out about her white affliction. They'd probably have her vivisected by sundown.

"He'll be okay," the widow said, without remotely meaning it. "We're all going to be okay."

Amanda returned to the game parlor, her arm still tingling from her outbreak. She noticed David and Mia keeping a curious vigil at the window.

"What's going on?"

Mia turned to her. "Erin's back. She found another one of us."

"Looks healthier than the last guy," David added. "Though he doesn't seem pleased."

Before Amanda could peek for herself, the procession moved inside. Loud voices echoed from the lobby.

"—not until you tell me what the hell's going on! I mean, why so cryptic? Are they paying you to generate suspense? Because trust me, I'm all stocked up."

David smirked at his companions. "He's certainly spirited."

Mia noticed Amanda's tense expression. "Are you okay?"

She forced a thin and shaky smile, even as her thoughts churned with hot new worries. She'd held Mia's hand earlier. What if she infected her? What if they both had the alien blight now?

Amanda studied Mia's fingers as casually as she could. "I'm okay. How . . . how are you feeling?"

"Numb," the girl replied. "Tired. I'm happy for you, though."

"What do you mean?"

"Your sister."

"Oh." Amanda blinked in confusion, then reeled with guilt. "Yeah. I still can't believe she's alive."

"Are you two close?"

"Uh, well—"

The argument in the lobby got louder, closer. Now they could hear Beatrice's chipmunk voice.

"Sir, if you would just give me your name . . ."

"My name is Up Yours until I get some answers. What is this place? Who are you working for? What the hell do you want with me?"

"Sterling Quint will answer everything—"

"Sterling Quint? Sounds like a Bond villain. I'm not appeased. But if you can get him here and talking in five minutes, I'll become a lot nicer."

The group appeared in the doorway. Between Beatrice and Erin stood a lanky young man with wavy brown hair. His rumpled black oxford was torn at the left shoulder. He clutched a spiral-bound pad against his chest. A sketchbook.

Zack examined the three refugees in bathrobes, then chucked a hand in hopeless dither.

"Okay. Now I'm at a spa."

Czerny stopped at the end of the second-floor hallway. He squeezed a drop of clear liquid into each eye and shot a blast of eucalyptus spray up his nostrils. After several blinks and sniffs, he was finally ready. He knocked on the door to the Primary Executive's office, and then once again stepped into Rat Heaven.

Scattered among the Persian rugs and sculptures stood ten huge glass aquariums, each filled with scampering mice of the brown and white varieties. Despite the apartheid arrangement, both breeds enjoyed a life of murine opulence, filled with fresh mulch and lettuce, frequent mating opportunities, and the greatest luxury of all: time. As physicists, the Pelletier Group experimented with math, not mammals. None of these creatures would see the business end of a scalpel. Not for a few generations, anyway. Their caretaker was breeding a special strain for his wife, a university neurobiologist. Czerny could tell from the devoted pampering that these creatures were more than a pet project to Sterling Quint. They were pets.

A fat white mouse roamed free on his great mahogany desk. Quint stroked her back as she chomped a piece of radicchio.

"I'm not encouraged by the blood on your shirt."

Czerny breathed through a scented tissue. "I'm afraid the Oriental has fallen into coma, sir."

Quint scowled in pique. "Idiots."

"I'm sorry?"

"The Salgados. They should have smelled the alcohol on him. They had no business drugging him in the first place."

"As it stands, I agree. Shall I dismiss them?"

Quint pondered the matter a moment, then slowly shook his head. "No. The last thing we need are disgruntled ex-contractors spilling our secrets. Raise their wages, but give them less responsibility. Have them guard the property or something."

"Of course, sir. Clever thinking."

It had been remarked by people crueler than Czerny that Sterling Quint kept mice to make himself feel larger. A quirk from his father's genes had left him with achondroplasia, which stopped his growth at four-foot-five. While he struggled with his stature as a child, he'd made peace with it in his adult years. Now, at the distinguished age of fifty-five, he took comfort in the fact that "little" languished at the bottom of his list of pertinent adjectives.

"That doesn't solve the problem of our unfortunate guest," said Czerny. "I fear his condition exceeds my expertise."

"Maranan won't die," Quint assured him. "I have a specialist coming tonight."

Czerny knew better than to press his boss for details, or to inquire how he knew the Filipino's name. He glanced at the three-by-three bank of monitors on the wall. Seven of the screens showed empty rooms. He saw Amanda, Zack, and the teenagers on one. On another, he caught Hannah running a towel over her wet, naked skin.

Blushing, he forced his gaze back onto Quint. "Uh, I suppose you already know that our sixth guest has arrived."

"Sixth and last," Quint responded. "That's all of them."

This was news to Czerny, especially since there had been nine signals from the start. One led to a corpse. He was eager to learn what Quint knew about the other two.

"Okay. I'll inform the team. I take it you'll be introducing yourself soon?"

"Yes. I'll be down in a few minutes."

Czerny sniffed his tissue again. "Excellent. I'll let you prepare."

"Constantin . . ."

He turned around at the door. Quint leaned back in his leather chair, shining flawless white teeth.

"It's okay to smile. This is exciting stuff."

Czerny laughed. "You have a gift for understatement, sir."

Alone again, Quint held the free-roaming mouse and petted her with euphoria. There were six new people in his building today, six people who didn't exist on this world yesterday. As far as science was concerned, this was a game changer. A game *winner*. Now all he had to do was follow the wisdom that Azral had texted him twenty minutes ago.

Keep them safe. Keep them content.

Quint wasn't worried. It was easy to keep them safe when no one else knew they existed. Keeping them content was harder, given their state of mind. It was also less important. When these six people lost their world, they lost their options. In the end, they had nowhere else to go.

PART THREE

TEMPORIS

EIGHT

Zack Trillinger had earned enough screaming condemnation in his life to know that his wisecracks weren't always appreciated. His mother had called it a "cheek problem." He couldn't help himself. Serious people brought out the Bugs Bunny in him, and no amount of blowback could get him to temper his snark. On a day like today, when taxis flew through the air and actresses moved at the speed of missiles, it seemed especially important to embrace the scathing absurdity of the universe, no matter who it bothered.

Unfortunately, he wasn't prepared for the wrath of Amanda Given, a woman who was uptight even on good days, and who was still reeling from the white-specked lunacy on her skin. It took only twenty-nine seconds of mutual acquaintance for her hand problem to meet his cheek problem. She slapped him hard enough to turn his whole body.

"You shut your mouth," she hissed, her voice wavering between fury and tears. "I don't need that from you. You hear me?"

Shell-shocked, Zack held his red and stinging face. "Okay."

"I don't need that."

"I understand."

"Not today."

"I know," he said. "It was a bad joke. It was in poor taste. I'm sorry."

The moment Erin and Beatrice left him alone with his three fellow refugees, Zack had finally revealed his name. He'd introduced himself to them one by one, signing each handshake with an appropriately stupid gag, a half witticism. Upon hearing David's accent, he said. "G'day, mate." To Mia, he proposed that OMGWTF?! should be their new default greeting.

With Amanda, his first impulse was to offer some wordplay bouquet about how she looked pretty intense and intensely pretty, but then bashfully nixed the idea. The moment he spotted her golden cross necklace, his comedy writers jumped to plan B.

"Where's your messiah now?" he'd brayed, in a passable Edward G. Robinson impression.

Before either of them knew what was happening, her right hand sprung like a cobra and struck him. Amanda didn't need to see the gaping horror on Mia's face to know that she'd overreacted. Worse, she realized she might have infected Zack with whatever disease she now carried.

David rose from his chair and raised his palms in nervous diplomacy. "Okay, look, we're all in a state of disarray right now . . ."

"South California," Zack uttered.

"What?"

Zack resumed his stance in the doorway, hugging his sketchbook with vacant anguish. "We're in the state of South California. It split in 1940 when the population got too big for Senate representation. They cut the line right below San Jose. I learned this downtown, in a bookstore called Scribbles."

When Erin Salgado had traced the final signal to Zack, he'd been standing in the reference section, eliciting curious stares from his fellow browsers. It was odd enough to see a grown man gawk in stupor at the pages of a children's atlas, but this man wore a gaping tear on his left shoulder and a woman's handbag on his right. Both the bag and the tear were the personal effects of one Hannah Given.

"Zack!"

The shout came from the hallway. Zack turned around just in time to feel wet hair, soft flesh, and terry cloth pressed against him.

He awkwardly returned Hannah's hug. "Hey, there you are. Speedy McLeave-a-Guy. You know, I'm used to women running away from me, but not at ninety miles an hour."

She pulled away from him. "What are you talking about?"

Amanda blinked at them in bafflement. "Wait. How do you two know each other?"

"This is the guy I was telling you about. We met at the marina." Hannah turned back to Zack. "What do you mean ninety miles an hour?"

"You don't remember what happened?"

"I remember everything going all blue and super-slow."

"No, you went all red and super-fast. You buzzed around the bench like a hornet on crack, talking so quickly I couldn't understand you. You ripped my sleeve, then ran away. And I don't mean Benny Hill speed. I mean you were a freaking blur." He eyed her sling. "What happened? Did you break your arm?"

"No." Hannah shook her head, dumbfounded. "That can't be right. That's not possible."

"Yeah, that was the consensus at the marina."

David matched Hannah's befuddled look. "Forgive me, Zack, but even after everything that's happened today, I have a hard time accepting what you're saying."

Zack shut the parlor door, then addressed the others in a furtive half whisper.

"I don't want to upset anyone more than I already have, but I think there's more than one kind of weirdness going on here. Beyond the flying cars and new state lines, I think something might be . . . different with us. Hannah's not the only one doing strange stuff. Look."

He opened his drawing pad, flipping through a series of crisp white pages. "Last night, I only had three blank sheets left in this thing. Now I have eight. My last five drawings disappeared like I never did them. And then there's this one . . ."

He turned to a rough sketch of a nerdy couple, the two lead characters of his comic strip.

"This used to be finished. Now it's not. I lost about a half hour of pencil work. That's the kind of glitch that happens on computers, not paper."

"What makes you think you caused it?" David asked.

"Because I watched it happen," Zack said, with a delirious chuckle. "The drawing changed right in front of my eyes."

Hannah shook her head in turmoil. Amanda nervously tugged her sleeve over her hand. "Look, I don't think this is the best time to—"

"I'm hearing voices," David blurted. "I'm sorry, Amanda. I didn't mean to cut you off. I just had to get that out. Since this morning, I've been sporadically hearing people that I can't see. People talking to each other, laughing, whatever. I only hope it's related to this phenomenon you're discussing, because otherwise I've lost my mind."

"You're not crazy," Hannah assured him. "At least not more than the rest of us."

Zack studied Mia's dark and busy expression. "Got your own weirdness to share?"

She looked up at him. "Me?"

"Yeah. You're a quiet one, but I noticed you got even quieter when we started talking about this. Is it something you can tell us?"

For a man who'd just been slapped, Zack was awfully perceptive. Mia had been thinking about her own incident—the glowing tube with the candles and the note, a special delivery that somehow managed to find her eight feet underground. She didn't know how to bring it up without sounding insane.

"Not really."

Zack eyed her skeptically. "You sure?"

"Leave her alone," Amanda growled. "She's been through enough."

"We've all been through enough. But we're all old enough and smart enough to speak for ourselves."

Mia nodded at Amanda. "It's all right."

"It's *not* all right. We're still traumatized. Still grieving over the people we lost. The last thing we need right now is to fill our heads with supernatural nonsense."

Zack peered down at Amanda's crucifix and swallowed his next slap-worthy zinger. "Look, I'm just trying to make sense of this."

"And I'm telling you it's too soon to try."

"Too soon for *you*."

"Too soon for all of us!"

Zack chuckled darkly. "Really? How interesting that you already know me better than I know myself. Is this a new psychic power or just an old trick you learned at Judgment Camp?"

As Amanda stood up, Hannah took a reflexive step back. Over the course of her life, she'd seen every dark facet of her older sister. Shoutmanda, Nagmanda, Reprimanda. Hannah knew, as both a summoner and a witness, that few things were less desirable than a visit from Madmanda.

"You unbelievable piece of shit. Are you such a sociopath that you need to mock people just hours after they've lost everything? Is that how you were raised?"

Now it was Zack's turn to step back. His wide eyes froze on Amanda's hand. "Uh . . ."

"I don't judge! I don't preach! I don't condemn the people who don't share my faith!"

Hannah leaned forward, blanching at the bewildering new change in her sister. "Amanda . . ."

"What I *do* condemn are people who disrespect my beliefs, especially when I've done nothing to provoke you but wear a tiny little symbol!"

"Amanda!"

She spun toward Hannah. "What?"

"Your hand!"

The widow peered down at her fingers and got a fresh new look at her weirdness.

The blight had returned in full force, coating her right arm in a sleek and shiny whiteness. Though the substance looked like plastic, it fit her as snugly as nylon.

David and Mia jumped up from their chairs. Hannah covered her gaping mouth.

"What the hell is that?!"

Bug-eyed, gasping, Amanda dropped to the recliner. The glistening sheath felt cool on her skin, like milk fresh out of the fridge. She could feel every bump and fold of the armrest as if she were still bare-handed.

"I don't know. I don't—"

The sisters both screamed as Amanda's long white glove erupted in rocky protrusions. Her silver bracelet creaked in strain, then snapped into pieces.

By the time the jagged fragments fell to the floor, Amanda's arm looked like it was covered in rock candy. The crags rose and fell in erratic rhythms, an ever-shifting terrain.

David looked to the door. "Uh, maybe I should get one of the—"

"No!" Zack and Amanda yelled in synch. "Just watch the hall," Zack said. "If someone comes by, keep them out."

Amanda flinched at Mia's approach. "No, stay back! I don't want to hurt you."

Zack inched toward her, fingers extended. "Look, you just need to calm down."

"*Calm down?*"

Mia nodded tensely. "He's right. This whole thing started when he got you angry." She moved behind Amanda's chair and stroked her shoulders. "You're going to be okay. Just breathe, Amanda. Breathe."

Hannah cringed with guilt as she watched Mia soothe her sister. *I should be doing that. Why didn't I think to do that?*

David peeked through a crack in the door. "Someone's coming."

A four-inch spike erupted from the back of Amanda's hand. Her other arm erupted in a rash of tiny white dots. Zack jumped back.

"Jesus. All right. It's definitely stress related. If you just relax—"

"How do you expect me to relax right now?!"

"It's Dr. Czerny," David announced. "And an extremely well-dressed midget."

Amanda squinted her eyes shut. *Oh God. Please. Please . . .*

"Hannah, maybe you should run distraction," Zack said.

"What should I say?"

"Anything. I don't know. You're the actress. Improvise."

Amanda forced her mind into calming memories—the nature hikes she took with her father, her honeymoon cabin on the French Riviera, all the young patients who cried happy tears when they learned they were in remission.

Soon the milky crags and dots began to melt away. Mia squeezed her shoulder. "It's working. You're doing it."

Amanda opened her eyes and peered down, just as the last of the whiteness retracted into her skin.

"They're almost here . . ." David cautioned.

"It's all right," said Mia. "It's gone."

Zack wasn't relieved. He scooped up the remnants of Amanda's bracelet, then threw a quick glance around the room.

"Look, I don't know who these people are, but I don't trust them. Until we learn more, we need to keep this to ourselves. We'll talk about the big weirdness. We won't talk about the other stuff. Agreed?"

Hannah, David, and Mia accepted his premise with shaky nods. Amanda had the least trouble with Zack's proposal. On this matter, she couldn't have agreed with him more.

Two hazy shapes appeared in the smoky glass. David opened the door to

Czerny and a diminutive companion. They studied their five skittish guests with leery caution.

"Is everything all right in here?" Czerny asked. "We heard noises."

Zack hurried across the room to greet him. "The strangest thing just happened, actually. Amanda bumped her arm against the pool table and her bracelet broke apart."

Czerny furrowed his brow at the warped silver fragments in Zack's hand. "Huh. That is strange." He looked to Amanda. "Are you all right?"

"She'll be fine. I'm Zack, by the way. You Sterling Quint?"

"That would be me," said the other man, in a stately baritone.

The guests all took a moment to study him. He was indeed a little person, as David implied, but he carried himself with the regal airs of a maharaja. He wore a lavish three-piece suit with a red silk ascot, and his feathered gray coif was flawless to a hair. Zack figured his jeweled rings alone could fund a man's food, clothing, and shelter habit for nearly a year.

"So you're the answer man."

Quint nodded. "As it stands."

"Good," Zack replied, with an anxious breath. "Because as it stands, we have questions."

The conference room was a perfect oval of hardwood and gray marble. In lieu of overhead lightbulbs, the entire ceiling glowed with milky iridescence. Mia noticed a pair of multitiered switches on the wall—one to control the ceiling's brightness, the other to change its color.

Quint sat at the head of a long oak table, shining a sunny smile at each guest as Czerny introduced them. For five people who'd made such a remarkable journey, none of them seemed particularly remarkable themselves. *Why them, Azral? Of all the souls to sweep across existence, why these?*

"Thank you for being patient with us," Czerny began. "I know we haven't revealed a lot—"

Hannah waved a shaky palm. "Wait. Hold it. Sorry."

Mia's eyes narrowed to frigid slits. She didn't want to dislike anyone, especially on a day like today, but from the moment Hannah stumbled into the lobby with her tight clothes and ditzy airs, she struck a sour chord. She was every living Barbie doll who'd broken her brothers' hearts, every gum-chewing mallrat who'd mocked Mia mercilessly.

"Before we get to the big stuff, I just want to know how Theo's doing."

Czerny had to wait for Quint's nod of approval before answering Hannah's question.

"Fortunately, he's okay. Still unconscious, but stable. We expect he'll pull through just fine."

Amanda sat rigidly in her seat, her hands hidden deep inside her sleeves. "What happened?"

"I regret to say it's our fault," Czerny admitted. "Our security men gave him apacistene, a dermal sedative more commonly known as a baby spot."

Hannah averted her gaze from the giant neon *TOLD YOU SO* that sat in place of her sister.

"It's not a harmful drug by itself," Czerny explained, "but it can be particularly strong on first-time users. The problem in this case is that Mr. Maranan had a high amount of alcohol in his bloodstream. The combination caused a toxic reaction and . . . well, you saw the results."

"When can we see him?" Hannah asked.

"Not for a while," Quint replied. "Once he's sufficiently detoxified, he'll be sure to join you."

Zack glanced around uneasily. "I'm late to the party. I take it Theo's another one of us."

Hannah nodded. "Yeah. I met him right after you."

"Wow. You do move fast."

No one appreciated the joke, least of all the sisters. As he cooked in the heat of their smoldering glares, his inner Libby shook her head at him. *You never learn.*

David wound his finger impatiently. "I'm glad Theo's okay, but can we please get to the main topic at hand?"

Once again, Czerny deferred to his superior. Quint took an expansive breath.

"I know Dr. Czerny has told some of you about our organization, but for those who came in late, let me explain again. The Pelletier Group is a privately funded collective of physicists, all specialized in the study of temporal

phenomena. We're not beholden to any college or corporation. Our only mission is to follow the science, no matter where it takes us. It was through keen
observation and a little dumb luck that science took us right to you.

"There's a unique subatomic entity called a wavion that's been fascinating
physicists for decades. It moves differently, spins differently, clusters differently than any particle known to man. Though we still have much to learn
about it, we know for a fact that wavions, when positively charged, move
backward in time."

David opened his mouth to speak. Quint cut him off with a curt finger.

"Thanks to their atypical nature, wavion clusters are easy to detect with
the right technology. In fact, one of our first discoveries, four years back, was
a fist-size concentration in a San Diego parking lot. Soon we discovered a
handful of others, all scattered within a ten-mile radius. They were all the
same size, all expanding at the same slow rate. After thirty months, the clusters had each grown into the same specific form."

"An egg," David mused.

Quint grinned at him. "Yes. Each eighty-one inches tall and fifty-five
inches wide, all invisible to the human eye but very perceptible to our scanners. The images became even more interesting, one year ago, when we began
to notice a distinct hollowness inside each formation. To our amazement, every gap took the frozen shape of a human being. Although we're seeing you
today for the first time, we've been familiar with your silhouettes for nearly a
year."

The room fell into addled silence. David shook his head. "That's insane.
You're saying you've been observing us for months when it all just happened
a few hours ago."

"Like I said, charged wavions move backward in—"

"He gets the concept," Zack said. "We all do. We're just having a hard time
stapling it to reality."

David nodded at Zack. "Exactly. Yes. Just the notion of anything traveling
back in time. I mean the logistics, the paradoxes . . ."

The physicists exchanged a brief glance, filled with quizzical interest
and—in Czerny's case—deep astonishment. *They're surprised,* Mia noted.
Surprised at our surprise.

Quint stroked his chin in careful contemplation. "If there's one thing we've learned in the past five decades, it's that time is more . . . flexible than we ever imagined. That's the gentlest explanation I can offer at the moment. You seem like a smart young man, Mr. Dormer, and I'll be happy to discuss it more in the days to come. But for now, in the interests of keeping things manageable—"

Zack cut him off with a bleak chuckle. "Oh, I think that ship has sailed and sunk, Doctor. But here's something you can answer. You say you spent four years watching us from a distance, waiting for our eggs to hatch. I wasn't anywhere near mine when your security goons got me."

"Me neither," Amanda added. "I was at least two miles away. How did you find us?"

"You're still teeming in wavions," Czerny replied. "They're emanating from the silver bracelets you share. It's nothing to fear. The particles are harmless. But they did make you easy to track."

Zack curtly shrugged. "Okay, fine. But none of this explains how we got here."

"Or where 'here' is," Hannah added.

"Or what these things are," said David, brandishing his bracelet.

Quint nodded at them with forced patience. "Yes. These are all pertinent questions. Mr. Trillinger, we don't have an answer for you. Not yet. We can't even offer a working theory until we speak with all of you in detail and get a better sense of the events leading up to your arrival. Mr. Dormer, we don't have an answer for you either. Not yet. Now that we have the broken pieces of Ms. Given's bracelet, we're very eager to study them."

Hannah didn't learn until Czerny's introductions that Amanda had dropped her married name. She'd thrown her sister a baffled look, only to get a vague and heavy expression in reply.

Now Quint turned to Hannah. "In answer to your question, I can only tell you what you already suspected. You're on Earth, but a far different version than the one you knew."

Hearing it out loud, delivered so bluntly, was enough to make several stomachs churn with stress.

"We've made tremendous advances in the field of temporal science," Quint continued. "But for all our progress, our understanding of alternate timelines has never advanced beyond hypotheticals. I've devoted my career to these theories, but it's not until today that I've been graced with proof. Actual living proof. Trust me when I say that your arrival is unprecedented. There's nothing on record that's even remotely similar to what we're seeing now."

Zack threw his hands up in frustration. Quint pursed his lips.

"You still seem to have a problem, Mr. Trillinger."

"As a matter of fact, I do. Look, don't get me wrong. You're excited and I'm happy for you. But at the moment, you have five people—sorry, six—who couldn't give a crap about the advancement of temporal science. We're confused and scared as hell. If you don't have answers to the big questions, then at least tell us what you plan to do with us. And before you say we're not prisoners here, you can drop the whole Mister/Miss thing. It's not helping my tummy ache."

Quint leaned back in his chair and eyed the cartoonist for a long, cool moment. "As you correctly guessed, Zack, we're not holding you here. You can leave anytime you want. But you seem like a clever man, so I probably don't need to tell you that you're not equipped to venture out on your own. You have no contacts, no valid identity, no legal currency, and little to no information about your new environment. You're not just foreigners here. You're aliens. It would be in your best interest to stay with us, at least in the short term."

"As it stands, I agree with you, Sterling. But I'm thinking ahead. And I believe I speak for the others when I say we don't want to spend the rest of our lives as specimens."

"Understandable, but—"

"Good. Now surely a smart man such as yourself realizes that without options, we *are* prisoners here. So I suggest a deal, a *Quint pro quo* if it tickles you. We tell you everything we know about our world, you tell us everything you know about yours. We give you our time, our testimony, our spit samples, whatever. In exchange, you give us money. A thousand dollars a week for each of us. You can keep it all in a safe until we choose to leave. I don't care. The important thing is that when we do leave, we won't be as helpless as you so eloquently described."

All eyes turned back to Quint. He studied Zack through a face of stone.

"That all sounds perfectly reasonable."

"Good. See? We're connecting now. But before we shake on it, I'm adding a

rider. No invasive medical tests without our consent. You tell us what you're doing before you do it, and if we don't like it, you stop. That's a deal breaker."

Quint narrowed his eyes in umbrage. "You seem to have a sinister notion
about our methods."

"I don't know crap about your methods. I'm just covering all bases. As you
said, we're aliens here. Should we happen to do alien things, like sprout a third
eye or levitate, I just want to make sure there are limits to your scientific curiosity. If you were in our shoes, you'd want the same comfort."

Amanda suddenly realized, with dizzying inertia, what a good thing it
was to have Zack around.

"That's easy to agree to," said Quint, "as we're not in the habit of vivisec-
tion. Anything else?"

"Actually, yes. Not a rider. A question." Zack launched a cursory glance
around the room, studying every corner of the ceiling. "Got any hidden cameras in the building?"

In the all-too-telling silence, Mia felt a hot rush of blood behind her face.
Oh God . . .

"It's not a big deal," Zack said. "You've known for a year that those eggs
would hatch people. I assume you prepared for us. You know, cameras, beds,
a medical lab. Makes sense. I just want to know."

David saw Czerny's knuckles curl tightly around his pen. Quint remained
stoic.

"Yes. We have cameras."

The sisters cracked the same frosty scowl.

"I wish someone had told me that before I showered," Hannah griped.

"I wish someone had told us in general," Amanda said. "This isn't the way
to get our trust."

Quint shook his head. "I apologize. It wasn't our intent to deceive you.
Ever since the six of you appeared, we've been scrambling to catch up. Rest
assured you're only being monitored for your own well-being. Furthermore,
in the privacy of your rooms, you're only being watched by someone of your
own gender. This I swear."

"And of course you swear not to release any footage of us without our
consent," Zack said.

"Yes," Quint replied, with all the warmth of a glacier. "Of course."

Sensing the end of his employer's affability, Czerny stood up.

"Look, you've all been through an unprecedented trauma, and you're all coping with remarkable bravery. It won't seem like it now, but you're very fortunate. Fortunate to be alive. Fortunate to be together. And fortunate to be here with us. No one knows more about parallel world theory than Dr. Quint. If anyone can solve this puzzle, he can. In the meantime, have patience and have faith. You're going to be okay."

The guests sat in anxious silence, their muddled thoughts bubbling with a thousand and one concerns. Despite all of Quint's rosy promises, Zack knew there was no way on Earth—*any* Earth—these scientists would let such prize discoveries walk away. To truly leave, they'd have to run. It wasn't a plan right now—it was an option. Zack needed one, as much as the fair and fiery redhead needed a benevolent God.

As his head throbbed and his inner self screamed with childlike hysterics, the cartoonist leaned back in his seat and forced a cheery grin.

"Well, that was a fine presentation, gentlemen. I'm sold. When's lunch?"

They spent the afternoon in an aggregate daze, more like ghosts than guests. They gazed out windows without truly looking, flipped through books without really reading, and wandered the hallways with no clear purpose or direction.

As the sky turned to dusk, a pair of scientists arrived with bags of store-bought clothing—a generic assortment of T-shirts and sweatpants, plus the most basic cotton socks and undies. Soon the refugees stopped looking like day spa clients and now resembled an intramural volleyball team. Mia noticed, with silent distaste, that Hannah had seized the snuggest tank top in the collection. *Yes. We get it. You're blessed.*

An hour later, their evening meal arrived by physicist. Whereas lunch had been a casual buffet set on the pool table, Czerny had opened up the dining room for supper. In its hotel days, it was known as Chancer's, an upscale bar and bistro that hosted gospel brunches on Sundays. The scientists had briefly used it as a cafeteria before shyly settling back to desk dining.

The guests served themselves from steaming tins. Amanda and Zack were the first to sit down, each with a grilled chicken breast and a scoop of pasta salad.

"They're sure leaving us to ourselves a lot," Amanda observed.

"They're probably giving us a day or two to adjust. I figure come Monday . . ."

Zack trailed off as Amanda lowered her head and closed her eyes in prayer. Hannah wasn't sure if the blessing was real or just a showy middle finger to Zack. She didn't know how anyone could thank God after everything that happened today.

The actress sat down with a plate full of greens, the only thing her ailing stomach could handle. "Okay, here's a stupid question. If we're on an alternate Earth, does that mean there are alternate versions of us walking around somewhere?"

"No," said David, from the serving table.

"Doubtful," Zack added.

"Why not?"

Zack lazily motioned to David. The boy sighed and turned around to Hannah. "Okay, obviously our two worlds have a shared timeline. If they didn't, people wouldn't be speaking English here. They might not even be humans as we know them. So clearly our histories split at some point. From what Dr. Czerny told me, they still have Abraham Lincoln on their pennies. But from what Zack discovered, they separated California in 1940. That suggests the point of divergence occurred sometime between the American Civil War and the start of World War Two."

Mia stood behind David, eyeing him with rapt fascination as he expounded.

"Now, even if it's the latter end of that spectrum, the butterfly effect can change a lot in seven or eight decades. Our grandparents may have still existed as children, but the odds of them meeting and breeding as adults, then the odds of their own children meeting and breeding as adults . . . it's just astronomically small. And that's not even factoring the biology. The same sperm, the same gestational factors, the same hereditary toss-ups. At the most, you'd have a genetic relative walking around. But as you and Amanda prove, even genetic siblings can look quite different from each other. So, long answer short, no. Don't expect to find a twin out there."

In the resulting silence, David surveyed his stunned audience. He raised a cautious brow at Zack. "Was that, uh . . . was my answer somewhat in line with yours?"

The cartoonist chuckled grimly. "I was just going to say it's cliché. Jesus. I'm glad you went first."

"How the hell did you put that all together?" Hannah asked David.

"The only thing my dad loved as much as science was science fiction. We read a lot of books together. Guess I picked up a thing or two."

Amanda bit her lip as she thought back to her own reading nights with her father. "I bet he was so proud of you."

David rolled his shoulders in a dismal shrug. "I guess so. He wasn't the type to say."

As Mia sat down, Zack shined a contemplative gaze at Amanda and Hannah. "David has a point. You two don't look a thing alike. You're not half sisters or adopted, right?"

"Full sisters," Hannah replied. "It's a little more obvious without our dye jobs."

"And you both got bracelets," Zack pondered. "That can't be coincidence."

David nodded. "That's what I said."

Amanda kept silent as she sliced into her chicken. Zack could see she was agitated by the subject. He didn't care. He was just a stiff breeze away from a fierce and unseemly breakdown. He needed this distraction.

"Yeah, that's a hint right there. The question is why would, uh . . ."

His attention was seized by David, who sat down at the table with a teeming plate of green peas. The boy sprinkled heaping dashes of salt onto his pile, then looked up at his four confounded friends.

"Quite an interesting diet there," Zack said.

"Just fussy," David replied. "She did mention something about our potential."

"Who?"

"The woman who gave me my bracelet. Esis."

"*Ee*-sis?" asked Hannah.

"Yeah. Tall and lovely woman. She told us—me and my dad—that I was very important. She said that I was part of something larger now, and that I had the potential to help bring about a great and wonderful change to all humanity. That's not verbatim, of course, but—"

"She's insane."

The others looked to Amanda. She aimed her dark gaze down at her plate.

"I'm sorry, David. If we're talking about the same person, then I wouldn't trust a single thing she said. She was completely out of her mind."

From his frigid expression, David clearly didn't enjoy her analysis. "I had a hunch you met her too. What did she say to you?"

"I don't remember the specifics. I just know her behavior was completely erratic. One second she was complimenting me, the next she was grabbing my hair. She . . ."

Thinking about her sister, Amanda decided to censor the part where Esis launched across the alley with blurring speed. That part struck a little too close to home now.

"She was just crazy."

David shrugged. "Well, the Esis I met seemed intelligent and kind. Not even remotely crazy. In either case, you and I would be dead without her intervention."

"Am I supposed to be grateful? For all we know, they're the ones behind all this."

"Oh, come on. You have no evidence to support that."

Zack raised his palms. "Okay, hold it. Wait. David, I agree we're getting ahead of ourselves—"

"I don't even know why we're talking about this at all," Amanda snapped. "Can't we have *one* night to recover?"

"Hey, I was about to throw you a bone. As it stands, I'm deep on your side of the crazy issue. I didn't meet this Esis, but I have nothing nice to say about the guy who gave me my bracelet."

David raised an eyebrow at Zack. "Do tell."

"There's not much to tell. He wore a mask. All I could see were his eyes. But he looked like he was having the time of his life while people were burning to death all around us. That alone makes him someone I'd very much like to unmeet and hopefully never come across again."

"That's how I feel about Azral," Hannah added. "The white-haired man. I mean I know he saved my life twice, but he still scares the living—"

"What do you mean twice?" Zack asked.

Hannah could see her sister tense up across the table. She figured any mention of their childhood incident would send Amanda to tears.

She lowered her head. "It doesn't matter."

Frustrated, Zack glanced over to Mia, the lone holdout in the conversation. She stabbed at her food with a dismal expression.

"She didn't see anyone," David replied on her behalf. "She was asleep when she got her bracelet."

Zack scratched his neck in edgy thought. "So from the looks of it, we're dealing with two, possibly three different people."

Three, the sisters thought in synch.

David scooped another forkful of peas. "We don't have enough information about them to form any theories."

"I think we do," Zack replied. "The fact that Amanda and Hannah are here right now is a big fat clue that these people chose us for genetic reasons. Why else would they give bracelets to two biological—"

With a choked sob, Mia pushed her chair back from the table and fled the room. Amanda rose from her seat, shooting a harsh green glare at Zack before trailing out the door.

The cartoonist sighed at Hannah. "Your sister's not the most relaxed of women."

"She just lost her husband."

"I know. I just . . ." Zack frowned with self-rebuke, then flicked a somber hand. David listlessly poked a fork at his peas.

"We lost people too," he told Hannah. "We're just trying to figure out why they died. And why we didn't."

Hannah could finally see a hint of strain behind the boy's handsome face. She figured she could live to be a hundred and still not understand the way men handled their emotions.

Amanda and Mia returned eight minutes later, their faces raw from crying. Mia brushed her bangs over her puffy eyes and stared down at her half-eaten dinner.

"I have four brothers," she announced, with matter-of-fact aloofness. "I know for a fact that they're my biological siblings and I'm all but sure they didn't get bracelets."

The room fell into bleak silence. Zack placed a hand on Mia's wrist.

"I have an older brother back in New York. Josh. We're about as different as two siblings can be, but we get along." He gestured at Amanda and Hannah. "When I found out these two were sisters, my heart nearly jumped out of my chest because it made me think that maybe he got a bracelet too. Who knows? With all the crazy things that happened today, maybe we both have a brother out there."

Mia raised her head to look at him. "I don't know. I hope you're right."

By the time Czerny came back to check on them, the clock on the wall had reached 8 P.M. The food had grown cold and the conversation had settled back to mundane mutterings, increasingly hindered by gaping yawns.

Czerny suggested, with droll understatement, that perhaps it was time to call it a day.

In a sleepy drove, the group—which Zack took great pleasure in calling the Sterling Quintet—climbed the stairs to the third floor. Zack and David disappeared into their chosen suites without so much as a good-night. Never had a sentiment seemed so pointless.

Amanda urged Mia to share a room with her and Hannah, just for warmth and company. Though tempted, Mia politely declined. She expected to do a lot more crying between now and dawn. She didn't want to muffle herself out of some misguided sense of courtesy.

After three restless hours, she regretted her decision. No matter what she did, she couldn't get comfortable in her room. When the lights were off, the darkness pulled her straight back to her morning grave. She could feel the dirt in her hair again, the creepy-crawly bugs on her skin. When the lamp was on, she couldn't stop thinking about the scientists who watched her every move.

Just as her eyelids finally fluttered on the cusp of sleep, a soft and tiny glow seized her attention. It hovered directly above her, like a distant moon or a penlight. The radiant circle spit a small object onto her nose, then disappeared in a blink.

Baffled, Mia sat up in bed and retrieved the item from her pillow. It was a small scrap of paper, tightly rolled into a stick. She turned on the lamp and unfurled the note.

> *You just survived the worst day of your life. I won't say it's all candy and roses from here, but it does get better. Hang in there. Put your faith in Amanda, Zack, and the others. They're your family now.*

The note was punctuated with a U-shaped arrow, a symbol Mia herself often used to indicate more content. She flipped the note over.

> *Yeah, that includes Hannah. Cut her some slack. She's a really good person. She even saves your life.*

Mia read the words over and over, her heart thumping with agitation. She remembered the curvy feminine letters of her first note, the one that had encouraged her to keep digging for air. Not only did the penmanship on this message match her memory of the original, it triggered a new and disturbing sense of familiarity.

She climbed out of bed and flipped on the desk lamp, transcribing a snippet of her note onto a blank sheet of stationery.

After comparing the two handwriting samples side by side, Mia choked back a gasp. She wasn't sure if she should laugh or cry at the true scope of her weirdness. She wasn't speeding or blanching. She wasn't hearing voices or losing artwork. She was simply getting notes. Notes of prescient knowledge. Notes in her very own pen.

Mia lay awake for hours in furious bother. By the time her eyes finally closed, the darkness had given way to pink morning light. Her second day on Earth had already begun.

NINE

There were nine Silvers at the start.

Though Sterling Quint's physicists had monitored all nine arrivals in progress, only six of the refugees made it to the Pelletier compound in Terra Vista. The remaining three signals led the Salgados to a dead woman, a dead man, and a cracked and empty bracelet.

Quint was upset to learn that he'd lost a third of his future case studies, but his benefactor strangely didn't seem to mind. Azral assured Quint that the three fallen subjects were expendable in the grand scheme.

But what of the missing one? Quint had texted. **I assume the owner of the empty bracelet is still at large.**

An hour later, while Quint sat in the conference room with his new guests, the handphone on his desk lit up with a curt new message.

You're better without him.

Before his cosmic migration and universal upgrade, Evan Rander wasn't a fan of his native Earth. His favorite things in the world, in fact, were the ones that helped him escape it. Sci-fi movies. Video games. Internet smut. He was—by sight, sound, and self-acknowledgment—a geek. Even in his rare bouts of style and swagger, he resembled a meerkat with his narrow frame, sloping shoulders, and hopelessly juvenile features. At twenty-eight, he was continually mistaken for a ginger-haired boy of seventeen. He'd given up correcting people.

With each lonely year, Evan became increasingly convinced that Earth wasn't a fan of him either. Most of his frustrations came from the pretty young women of his world, who continually rejected his awkward attempts to engage them, his creepy leers. It had been theorized in more than one ladies' room that Evan Rander had a stack of restraining orders at home. Or worse, a stack of bodies.

If his lovely detractors could have seen inside his mind, they would have learned that his fantasies, while hardly chaste, were actually quite romantic. But after a lifetime of cold shoulders, Evan feared he didn't have the looks to attract a suitable girlfriend. He certainly didn't have the money. His lean existence as a part-time computer specialist had left him in a sinkhole of debt, enough to force him out of his apartment and into his father's house in City Heights West.

No baron himself, Luke Rander was far from happy to share his meager abode. For years, his best hope for Evan was that the boy's baffling nerd proclivities would one day lead to some profitable nerd venture. Soon his furtive disappointment began leaking out of him like sweat. *No work again today, huh? You should be pounding the pavement instead of playing computer games. At least get some exercise. How do you expect to find a woman if you're all pasty and scrawny? Guess the family name's dying with you. No work again today, huh?*

Round and round the record spun, until the stress caused Evan to wake up with ginger hairs on his pillow. The only ray of sunshine in his dismal life was Shannon Baer, a young account executive at his main worksite. Though she'd failed to make his A-squad of office lusts, she was an indisputable cutie, and she bucked the trend of her peers by treating Evan with smiles and banter. He even detected flirting when she teased him about his LEGO coffee mug.

Eager to learn her feelings without the risk of asking, Evan used his administrative access to log into her e-mail archives. She'd only invoked his name three times. The first two mentions were work related. The last one, in response to her teasing boss, was a knife in the eye.

> Oh shut up. It's not like that at all. I just feel sorry for him. Anyway, Evan's not as creepy as everyone thinks. Of course if I ever go missing, be sure to check his basement first. :)

The next day, he returned to the office in his nicest clothes and warmest grin. After engaging Shannon in friendly chitchat, he told her he needed to install a new antivirus program on her PC. He joked that she was getting the special package, despite her misguided hatred for LEGOs. She laughed and let him do his thing.

Unfortunately for Shannon, his "thing" was a custom malware script that, at the stroke of midnight, erased her project files from her computer and every backup server. Thirteen months of work, irrevocably destroyed. For Evan Rander 1.0, it was the cruelest punishment he was capable of inflicting, though he'd spent the night imagining far worse.

His vengeance quickly backfired on him. Once his handiwork was discovered, the president of Shannon's company had him blackballed from all his freelance agencies. With a simple series of phone calls, Evan had become a toxic commodity, unemployable.

Luke Rander gritted his lantern jaw when he learned of his son's comeuppance. "You know, for all your flaws, I never thought you were stupid until now. But you did it. You screwed up your life, all because you couldn't handle a little rejection."

For the last three weeks of his endemic existence, Evan moved through the house in a grim and listless state, his thoughts frequently dancing around the handgun under his father's bed. Maybe it was time. Maybe it was high past time to put the world out of his misery.

On the third Saturday of July, he woke up in freezing cold, his gadgets blinking in confusion. He barely had a chance to process the new peculiarities before a large, round pool of radiant white liquid bloomed on his wall like an oil slick.

Evan watched in bug-eyed wonder as a towering stranger stepped through the surface, a white-haired being of crystalline perfection. Despite his splashing entrance, there wasn't a hint of wetness on his skin, his hair, his tieless gray business suit.

Expressionless, the man approached the bed and addressed Evan. His voice was honey smooth, peppered with an anomalous accent.

"Listen up, boy. Time is short and I have much to do. In five minutes, everything around you will cease to be. If you wish to continue living, extend your wrist quickly."

Evan raised his arm with meek and dreamy deference. Azral's thin lips curled in a smirk.

"Your cooperation is a welcome change. I won't forget that."

He procured a featureless silver bracelet from his pocket. Evan's thoughts screamed as he watched it break into four floating elbows. They glided over Evan's fingers, reconnecting at the thinnest part of his wrist with a *clack*.

"What is this?" Evan asked in a tiny voice. "Am I dreaming?"

"I don't have the time or mind to explain your situation, child. Just keep your head. Stay where you arrive. Help will come for you shortly."

Azral squinted with revulsion at the unwashed garments on Evan's floor. "You'll wish to find proper clothes, if you have them. Then say good-bye to your father. You won't be seeing him again."

Amidst all the daft and scattered notions in Evan's head, it occurred to him that he'd rather eat his own arm than suffer one more look of disapproval from the bearish old man.

Suddenly Azral's white brow crunched in wrathful scorn. He lurched forward and grabbed Evan by the collar.

"Only a weak man fails to honor his parents. You should be grateful. It was your father's unique genes that saved your life today. Clearly I didn't choose you for strength of character."

As the fearsome stranger walked back to his white liquid portal, Evan suddenly found himself in a small pool of yellow.

"Pathetic," said Azral, before disappearing into the breach.

Over the course of his long and lawless existence on Earth's wild sibling, Evan would find many reasons to hate Azral Pelletier. Near the top of the list was the ridiculously short amount of time he'd given Evan to prepare for his great upheaval. He'd only just zipped his jeans over fresh boxers when the silver bracelet buzzed with life. Shirtless and barefoot in his father's moldy bathroom, he was sealed in light, safely preserved as the house and sky collapsed around him.

It was in that final moment that he forgot his fear. In the space between worlds, the space between lives, he was briefly at peace with himself. The old Earth faded away to an empty white void, and Evan Rander felt nothing at all but gratitude.

As the proprietor of a dreary midtown mini-market, Nico Mundis was used to seeing odd behavior in his store. Aside from the typical assortment of ne'er-do-wells who would rob him at gunpoint or speedlift his wares, he'd suffered his fair share of rants, raves, threats, and propositions. The sexual come-ons always baffled Nico the most, as he was sixty-eight and quite obese.

His favorite strange incident occurred three years ago, when a group of egghead scientists traced an invisible signal to his canned goods aisle. The group leader, a spiky-haired Poler named Constantin Czerny, offered Nico three thousand dollars to let them affix a small device to his wall. Some kind of particle scanner enhancer thingy. Sure, why not? Money was money. At the end of the transaction, Czerny gave Nico his phone number and advised him to call should anything unique happen. Nico had no idea what Czerny meant by that and wasn't sure if Czerny knew either.

Now, just minutes before opening for Saturday business, something unique happened.

As Nico filled the register, the overhead lights died. The table fan came to a stop. Even his electronic watch went blank. Only the white tempic barrier continued to function. It coated the windows from the outside, giving the shop a hazy, snowed-in look.

A flash of light filled the back of his store. Nico grabbed his shotgun and aimed it at the disturbance. He blinked through the dancing brown spots in his eyes and reeled to see a shirtless young man where previously there'd been no one.

Evan blinked twice at the gun, then raised his scrawny arms in terror. "Don't shoot! Don't shoot!"

Nico moved closer to survey the damage. The blast had taken a curved bite out of his store, leaving a concave groove in the wall and slicing half the cans and shelves around the intruder. Tiny wet vegetable morsels dripped onto the floor, covering broken pieces of bathroom tile that had come from God knows where.

"Who are you?" Nico shouted. "What are you doing here?"

"Look, just don't shoot, okay? I have no idea! The last thing I—"

His eyes rolled back into his head and he launched into violent convulsions. Nico took an anxious step back. He couldn't tell if the boy was suffering an epileptic seizure or an otherworldly possession. He wasn't entirely wrong on either count, but what he was truly witnessing at the moment was nothing less than the death of the original Evan Rander.

As Evan stood and stirred, a tidal wave of cerebral data flooded into him. Millions of vivid new facts and memories. They filled his brain node by node, reshaping his psyche. On the outside, he was still a twenty-eight-year-old man with a seventeen-year-old face. In his altered consciousness, he was older now. Many years older and exponentially sharper.

His upgrade had arrived.

Evan breathed a weary moan, as if he'd just given birth. For a moment Nico feared the intruder would fall into tears, but Evan soon let out a delirious laugh.

"Oh man. Man oh man oh man."

He swept his blinking gaze around the store. Nico was amazed at how differently the stranger carried himself. He looked fiercely confident now. Not even a tad confused.

With a hammy grin, Evan spread his arms out wide. "Nico! Nico-Nico Mundis! *Ti kanis?*"

The shopkeeper took another step back. "How do you know my name?"

"Ah, Nico-Nico. You and I go way back. You're my Square One Buddy, buddy. Always here at the beginning to greet me with a friendly smile. And since we're such good buddies, hey, why don't you put down the boom-stick?"

Evan was unsurprised to see the gun remain fixed on him. As he sighed and stretched, his hidden hand seized a can of string beans.

"Well, I figured it was a shot in the dark, no pun intended. Guess I can't blame you for being sore. For years you've been praying for some young and topless beauty to pop into your *Efta-Edeka*, and here I am. You should've been more specific."

He swung his gaze to the cloudy white doorway. "Oh, hello, bishop."

As Nico reflexively turned his head, Evan hurled the can—a perfect throw that connected squarely with the shopkeeper's temple, driving him down. Evan rushed around the counter and grabbed the shotgun off the floor. He jammed the barrel into Nico's stomach, then his nose.

"Why must we do this dance every time, Nico? You know I don't like hurt-ing you."

Evan launched a swift kick into his ribs.

"Well, I like it a little. So do us both a favor. Waddle your ass over to that wall and stay there. I'll be gone soon enough. I just need to do a little convenience shopping."

Snorting through bloody nostrils, Nico crawled to his checkout stand and sat up as best he could.

Evan unwrapped an epallay and stuck it to his chest. "Oof. Mama. These reboots never tickle. My head's all fourped. But who am I to complain? I'm alive, right?"

Nico eyed the silent alarm button at the floor of his station. It was so easy when he could just step on it. Now it was five feet away—a mile in his condition.

Evan sauntered over to Nico's sparse selection of clothing. He threw on a black *Viva San Diego* T-shirt and cheap bresin sandals.

"Since I last saw you, Nico-Nico . . . well, I'll be honest. This last round sucked. Everyone was extra annoying. The Pelletiers. The Gothams. The Deps. And don't even get me started on You-Know-Who. Hannah had her tits in such a wringer, I had to kill her to keep her from killing me. And then her sister came looking for blood. Nearly killed me with her goddamn tempis."

Evan grabbed a handbasket and filled it with items: a quart of rubbing alcohol, a pint of orange juice, a hammer, a hunting knife. He stopped at the soda/vim dispenser and grabbed a large drinking cup.

"Between you, me, and the green beans, Nico, I'm still kinda pissed about it. So now I have two Givens at the top of my shit list."

Evan retrieved a near-empty tube of Crest from the floor. It had traveled with him from his father's bathroom and was now a one-of-a-kind relic. He stashed it in his basket.

"I don't know, Nico. Part of me's tempted to sit this one out. Maybe find an island somewhere and sip margaritas while the idiots do their idiot dance. I haven't written myself out of the story since . . . God, what round was it? Twenty-five? Twenty-six? Oh, hey. That reminds me."

Evan unwrapped a magic marker and drew a large "55" on the back of his right hand. It was a mnemonic device, a way to help organize his multiple sets of memories. He'd eventually hit the laser-brand parlor and get a more lasting reminder. For now, this would do.

"Aw, who am I kidding? I can't stay away from the fun and games. You didn't believe it for a second. You know me too well."

Nico had managed to halve the distance between himself and the alarm trigger. He shuffled another inch to the right, then froze when he spotted Evan's smirking face above the dog food bags.

"Pathetic, man. You're usually within slapping distance of the button by now. Are you even trying?"

"Please. I have children . . ."

"No you don't. Stop it. You're embarrassing yourself."

Evan doubled back to the checkout stand and emptied his goods into a knapsack. He popped open the cash register, then arranged the crisp blue bills into a folded pile. There was no need to count it. It was $212, just like always.

"All righty. The power's coming back and I have a date with a sweet Georgia peach. So this is where we . . . wait! The synchron! May I have your watch, *parakalo*? I need it more than you do."

Nico hurriedly removed his timepiece and held it out to Evan. He snatched it away and wrapped it around his wrist.

"Thanks. Now we're ready."

He checked the ammo in the shotgun, then blew dust off the barrel. Nico crawled backward.

"No! Please!"

Evan aimed the gun at his face. "You know, I remember a time, long ago, when I was the one crying and begging for my life. You didn't kill me but you still weren't nice. I'm just saying."

"Please, sir! Please!"

Evan lowered the weapon. "'Sir'? Did you just call me sir?" He laughed in amazement. "Wow. Fifty-four times and you never called me sir. I'm not sure how to feel. I mean I like it, obviously. I love it. But how much?"

Staring ahead in whimsical thought, he opened the shotgun. Two fat shells dropped to the floor.

"That much, it seems. Good job, Nico, you silver-tongued devil. You just charmed your way to a minor life extension."

Just as he tossed the gun over his shoulder, the overhead lights flickered back to life.

"Hey, look at that. Right on cue."

Evan turned the keylock next to the register, causing the tempic barrier to vanish. Cars and pedestrians became visible on the other side of the glass.

He grabbed his bag and patted Nico's cheek. "Always a pleasure, my friend. Until next time."

Evan ventured outside to a City Heights West that—unlike its shabby, old-world counterpart—actually resembled a city. Split-level houses had become replaced with sprawling office complexes. Trees had given way to animated lumic billboards. He chuckled at how he noted the difference every single time.

Soon his smile disappeared and he stopped cold. Evan didn't let Nico Mundis live very often, and he just remembered why. The fat man's testimony to the local police would enter the national law enforcement database, where certain key phrases would ring bells among the eagle-eyed *federales* in DP-9. Most of the Deps were easy enough to evade, but some, like the exotic Melissa Masaad, were annoyingly sharp. She could make Evan's life that much harder.

He closed his eyes in concentration until his head went light and he felt a full-body tingle, as if swimming in seltzer. Wild colors streaked all around him as the clock of his life reversed ninety-two seconds. Soon Evan found himself back inside the store, back behind the barrier, back with a loaded shotgun aimed at Nico Mundis.

With no memory at all of Evan's prior clemency, the shopkeeper raised a thick hand, crying. "No! Please!"

"Sorry, buddy. I forgot I had my reasons for doing this."

"Please, sir! Please!"

Unfortunately for Nico, Evan was no longer surprised or charmed by the honorific. He fired the shotgun. A cracking boom. A spray of blood. A good portion of Nico spattered onto Evan.

"Oh great. Lovely."

Evan rewound ten seconds, this time killing Nico from a slightly safer distance. He left the store clean.

As a hopeless perfectionist with a very unique talent, Evan Rander was no stranger to repetition. The act of undoing and redoing had become as natural to him as breathing. Sometimes the tedium was enough to drive him crazy. But it sure as hell beat living the one-take life, with all its indelible gaffes and consequences. Regret was something Evan had abandoned a long time ago. It died on his native Earth, with his father, his debt, and his crippling insecurities.

He returned to the street and hailed the first cab he saw. Evan knew the driver's name before the car even stopped, but chose to play dumb.

"Take me downtown, my good man. Childress Park. I'm on a squeeze, so 10× and aer it."

Before the driver could question him, Evan pressed two blue twenties against the glass. Proof that he could afford the speed and flight surcharges.

With a steamy hiss, the vehicle ascended forty feet to the taxi level, then folded its tires inward. The doors and windows locked shut, the classic winged-foot icon lit up on the fare meter, and the cab shot off like a bullet.

It took sixty-three seconds to cross five miles of urban scenery. Inside the taxi, eleven minutes passed. Evan stared out the window at his slowed surroundings. He spotted a puffy plume of chimney smoke that, in the sluggish blue tint of the world, reminded him of Marge Simpson's hair. He sighed with lament. They had nothing like *The Simpsons* here in Altamerica. Satire escaped these fools.

The taxi landed at the edge of an enormous green park, a lush oasis in a field of modern glass office towers. Like the rest of the business district, the place was sparse of life on Saturday.

Evan tossed sixty dollars at the driver. "Don't go away. I'll be back in five."

As he exited the cab, the synchron on his wrist beeped, informing him that it had readjusted to local time. By external clocks, it had only been seven minutes since he and his fellow Silvers crash-landed into this part of existence.

Some crashed harder than others.

In the middle of the park, on a flat patch of grass between picnic tables, a fetching young blonde lay sprawled on her back. Unlike the scattered homeless dozers who malingered here on weekends, the woman was barefoot in a lacy pink nightgown. The silk was marred with dirt and gashes. Only her silver bracelet remained spotless.

She fixed her cracked red eyes on Evan, speaking through wheezes and bloody gurgles.

"I can't move. I can't feel anything. I don't know what's happening. Please help me."

Evan kneeled by her side, clucking his tongue with sarcastic pity. She must have been ten stories up when the whole world changed on her.

"Oh, Peaches," he said, in a mock Savannah drawl. "I do declare this is not your day."

Evan made a habit of visiting Natalie Tipton in her dying moments. By his twentieth encounter, he'd pieced together her life in fragments. She was born Natalie Elder in Buford, Georgia, the only child of a waitress and a rail worker. She'd overcome dyslexia to earn a full scholarship to Emory University, where she studied to become a veterinarian until a well-placed kick from an ailing mare shattered her knee and ambitions.

But life had a way of working out for the terminally pretty. She soon met Donald Tipton, a campus football legend. They fell in love, got married, then moved out west when Donald scored a place with the San Diego Chargers.

If there was any drama during her time as a footballer's wife, Natalie didn't say. In the face of her demise, her only regret was not finishing college and becoming a veterinarian. She'd confessed this to Evan, back when he bothered to feign sympathy.

Having no recollection of their previous encounters, Natalie stared in terror at this creepy, grinning stranger.

"W-what happened to me?"

"You've taken a dreadful fall, sugah. And now you're bone soup, ah say, bone soup from the neck down."

"Please. Call an ambulance. I'm begging you."

"Oh, I've tried that, darling. But it's a big park. The paramedics never find you in time. Shame too, because they have a machine that could fix you right up. Reverse those injuries like they never happened."

"Why are you doing this to me?"

"I'm not the pilot of this plane wreck, sweetie. Just a passenger with a better seat. If you're looking to file a grievance, the people you want are the Pelletiers. Though in their defense, I'm pretty sure they warned you to stay on the ground floor."

He was right. Natalie had woken up in the utility room of her building, twenty floors down from her penthouse suite. A hand-scrawled note on the floor strongly advised her to stay where she was. She didn't listen. When the power died, she was stuck in the elevator between the eighth and ninth floors. Then her bracelet shook, the scenery changed, and Natalie Tipton had nowhere to go but down.

"I don't understand why this happened," she cried.

"Oh, honey bear. You don't even have time for the short answer. Trust me. You're not long for this world either."

Natalie closed her eyes and wept. "Why are you so cruel? What did I ever do to you?"

For once, her dialogue crossed into new territory. Evan's smile dissolved.

"Huh. Weird. I usually get that question from Hannah, not you. For her, I have a long list of grievances. For you?" He gave it some thought. "I don't know. Maybe you remind me of her. You both go wet for dumb muscle. You both seem to confuse lust with love. Now, granted, I never met your husband. But somehow I doubt you would have fallen for him if he was a professional chess player."

Natalie turned her head, wincing. "Oh God. I just want this to stop."

"Well, you're about to get your wish." Evan checked his watch. "It's curtain time."

While her shallow breaths settled and her consciousness slipped away, Evan stroked her arm and stared pensively at the trees.

"You know, I chat with the Pelletiers on occasion. I once asked them why they didn't stop you from falling. I mean they can see the futures better than anyone. They could have tied you down, broken your foot, done a hundred other things to keep you on the ground floor. Hell, they could still go back and save you. I'm not the only one with a rewind button.

"So when I asked, that crazy bitch Esis just gave me a shrug and said, 'Natalie's but one of many.' Can you believe that? They destroy a whole damn world to bring us here and we're still nothing to them. Just rats in their maze."

He checked her pulse, then breathed a wistful sigh. Natalie Tipton was gone.

"Ah, Peaches. You're better off. I've seen the way this story ends, again and again. It never changes."

Evan reached behind her and unhooked her necklace. The chain ended at a dime-size silver disc, engraved with the electric bolt logo of the San Diego

Chargers. Despite his utter disdain for football and the people who watched it, the trinket had become a cherished piece of old-Earth memorabilia. Worth the trip every time.

With a creaky groan, Evan clambered to his feet and clasped the charm around his neck.

"I'd stick around for the wake, darlin', but I've got a meeting with my old platoon commander and he's a real bear about punctuality. Sorry to say your whole life was pointless, and your death even more so. But what can you do? That's just the way the peach crumbles."

He walked away whistling, quietly resolving to be nicer to Natalie next time. In the grand scheme, she never did him wrong. She was the only Silver he could say that about.

While the cab soared to its next destination, Evan dumped the contents of his knapsack onto the seat. He stashed the drinking cup between his thighs, then poured himself a cocktail of rubbing alcohol and orange juice.

The noise of glooping liquids caused the cabbie to peer through the mirror. Evan smirked at him.

"Ease it, flyman. I won't spill a drop."

He stirred the concoction with his new hunting knife, then plunged his fist into the cup. The moment his silver bracelet became submerged, the liquid churned with hissing bubbles.

Soon the taxi landed in a run-down patch of the Gaslamp Quarter. Evan tossed another pair of twenties to the driver, then made his way down a dingy alley. As he crossed into the dark shadow of an elevated highway, he could hear a man's heavy breaths.

Evan bloomed a devilish grin. "Hello, hello, hello? Is there anybody in there?"

He stepped on a circle of concrete that was darker than the rest—a patch of the old San Diego, fused into the new. The upper half of a guitar case, complete with upper half of guitar, lay nearby. It had been sliced in a smooth curve. As always, the Great Cuban Leader hadn't ventured far from his landing spot.

"Just nod if you can hear me," Evan teased. "Is there anyone home?"

In the darkest corner of the alley, between two metal trash cans, a thirty-year-old man huddled against the wall. Black-haired, olive-skinned, and powerfully built, he wore a silk blue button-down over jeans. Even in his rattled state, the man was disgustingly handsome. Evan had lost count of the number of women who'd made complete fools of themselves to get his attention. Unlike Nico and Natalie, people he'd only encountered a few minutes at a time, Evan had years of experience with Ernesto "Jury" Curado. There were few folks on Earth he knew better, and few he hated more.

Evan watched with great amusement as Jury pressed his fingers against his temples, trying to will the universe back into order.

"¿Qué bola, asere? Welcome to beautiful downtown Other San Diego. Don't forget to try our Other Krullers. They're out of this world."

"Shut up," Jury said.

"Hey. Ouch. Hostility. What seems to be the problem, officer? Are we having a bad trip?"

Jury rose to his full six-foot-two height, grumbling at Evan through a sleek Cuban accent.

"Look, I don't know if you're a hallucination or a street nut. All I know is that someone drugged me and I'm freaking out. So go away."

Two years ago, upon receiving a Certificate of Commendation for exceptional performance, Officer Jury Curado had been called a "man of absolute conviction" by the Deputy Commissioner of the California Highway Patrol.

Yesterday morning, his twin sister had a different way of phrasing it.

"You're a stubborn ass!" she screamed, from behind her locked bedroom door.

Ofelia Curado knew better than anyone that when Jury got an idea in his head, there was no force in the heavens that could get it out. When they were fourteen, he was convinced that leaving Cuba was the only way to save Ofelia from their monstrous father. He was right. In Miami, he was convinced it would be better to fight for citizenship than to buy fake papers. He was right. He was right about better opportunities in California. He was right about his sister's hideous boyfriends. He was right about her drug problems and her eating disorder. He was right. He was right. He was right.

"I can't take it anymore!" she yelled. "You make my life a living hell! Just leave me alone!"

Like Jury, his sister was a raven-haired stunner, even on bad days. Sadly, the lingering traumas of childhood had made every day a bad one for Ofelia. She was, as Jury sang, a beautiful mess, and he had frequent cause to rescue her from some not-so-beautiful men. Whether they were lowlifes who exploited her for fun and profit or Lawrence Nightingales who sought to become her savior-with-benefits, they'd all left Ofelia worse for the wear. Some of them had nearly killed her. At Jury's hands, some of them were nearly killed.

Six months ago, his sister had found solace in the arms of a good woman. Martina Amador was a social worker, a squat and ugly matron who was a full twenty years older than Ofelia. Jury could only imagine their coupling was just another form of self-punishment for his sister, another way to lash out at the universe. And yet under Martina's care, she actually improved. First she got clean. Then she got hungry. And finally she found employment as a receptionist. She *worked* now.

Despite all improvements, Jury remained wary of his sister's lover. When Ofelia declared her intention to move out and live with Martina, the twins fell into strife. They screamed Spanish at each other through her bedroom door twenty-six hours ago.

"How long before she moves on to another fixer-upper?" Jury asked. "How long before she leaves you for a woman even younger, prettier, and more screwed up than you?"

"That's what you want, isn't it? You want me to fall back into my old ways so you can be my protector again!"

"You're wrong!"

"No, *you're* the one who's wrong this time! *You're* the one who needs a screwed-up woman to take care of. So just go out and find one already. I can't be that person anymore!"

Friday was a bad day for Jury Curado, which made it an awful day for the moving violators of Interstate 5. Over the course of his final workday, he reduced three different speeders to sobs and nearly broke the arm of a belligerent drunk driver.

Every Friday night, he played guitar at a tiny downtown coffeehouse. Most of his songs were mellow instrumental numbers, though he'd occasionally sing in Spanish when there was a fetching young woman in the audience. On the eve of his final performance, melancholy and desperation pushed him to snare his chords around a middle-aged bottle-blonde with a screeching, high laugh. He followed her home for drinks and debauchery, then woke up in her bed at 7 A.M. with the scent of bad sex in his nostrils and a thundering drum in his skull.

On the long walk back to his apartment, the oddities of the world began to stack up and unnerve him—the white sky, the chilled air, the blinking traffic lights. He turned a blind corner and was shoved against a building by an unseen aggressor. The guitar case fell to the ground.

"What the hell are you doing? Are you crazy?"

With cold hands and shocking strength, the attacker bent Jury's arm behind his back.

"You don't want to do this," Jury said. "I'm a cop."

"Shhhh," a silky smooth voice whispered in his ear. "You hush now, *hermano*."

Jury could feel something cool and metallic clasp around his right wrist. He was sure he was being handcuffed, but the second loop never clicked.

"What are you—"

With a warm blast of air, he was suddenly freed from his armlock. He launched from the wall and scanned the area. The only other soul within eyeshot was a tall man in a black T-shirt and slacks, watching him from two blocks away. He tipped his baseball cap at Jury in mock courtesy, then dashed away at a speed normally reserved for cheetahs.

His thoughts in free fall, Jury grabbed on to the nearest logical explanation. That batty woman he slept with must have laced his drinks with something. PCP. Mescaline. There was no other explanation.

Soon he reached his neighborhood, and the end of all doubt.

The debris of a crashed commercial airliner had turned 13th Street into a hellish horror. A battered nose cone lay in front of his local bodega. A smoldering pile of wreckage stood where his apartment building used to be. Jury covered his gaping mouth, stifling a delirious cackle. No. This was just a psychedelic nightmare. A jet plane never crashed into his home, his sister.

Thus Jury Curado, the man of absolute conviction, rode his fervent denial through the end of the world and into the next one. He kept crouched and still in a quiet corner, waiting for the hallucinations to go away.

Unfortunately, the new stranger—this smirking little imp—made the situation more difficult.

"Who the hell are you?" Jury asked.

Evan stood upright and rigid, his lip curled in sharp ridicule. "Sir! Evan Rander reporting for duty, sir!"

"Why is your hand in that cup?"

"Sir! I'm trying to start a trend, sir!"

"Why are you *talking* like that?"

Evan relaxed his stance. "Can't help myself. You're our great leader. Our stalwart commander. You whipped our sorry maggot asses into shape and turned us into a crack fighting unit. Well, except for Mia. Poor little thing."

Jury clenched his fists, trembling with frustration. Evan exhaled in sympathy. "I know. It's all very confusing. You want to know why my hand's in a cup? The answer's right there on your wrist."

Now Jury examined his new silver bracelet, the most innocuous of all the recent anomalies. "What is this?"

"You know, I asked Azral once. I mean I know what the bracelet does, but I wanted to know how it does it. He gave me a haughty little grin and told me that any answer would be futile, like explaining a handphone to an ancient Egyptian." Evan laughed. "Asshole, right? Well, what Mr. Snooty McFuture doesn't realize is that even an ancient Egyptian can figure out how to break a handphone. Look."

Evan removed his hand from the liquid. The band on his wrist was now cracked and white, as if frozen solid. He pulled the hammer from his knapsack and tapped the surface until a small section shattered. The remainder slid easily over his hand.

"Ta-da! See? If you want to ditch your own, feel free to use my mixture. It's a special cocktail I invented. I call it the Unscrewdriver."

Jury resumed his huddle. Evan shrugged nonchalantly.

"Suit yourself, Sarge. But you should know that there are people tracking us through these things. The Salgados will be here in two minutes to take you to their fancy building in Terra Vista. You don't want to go there. Trust me. In six weeks, that place will be a bloodbath."

Jury sprang to his feet, red-faced. "*Shut up! For God's sake, just shut up.*

I'm freaking out right now and the last thing I need is some creepy little geek who makes no sense!"

Evan's glib smile vanished. Now Jury could see the hatred on his face. Though the policeman had fifty pounds of muscle on his new acquaintance, he raised his palms in contrition.

"Look, I'm not myself this morning. I took a drugged drink and . . . God, you wouldn't believe the stuff I'm seeing."

Evan fished through his knapsack with fresh cheer. "Well, why the hell didn't you say so? Just so happens I have something that can help you."

He carefully approached Jury, his hand still buried in the bag.

"Now, I want you to keep an open mind, okay? The thing about this—"

He plunged the hunting knife deep into Jury's chest.

"—is that it really hurts."

Gasping, Jury fell back against the wall, feebly clutching the hilt of the knife as he sank back to the ground.

Evan furiously stood over him, pinching a thumb and finger. "You know, I came this close, *this* close, to letting you live this time. I was ready to find a whole new way to screw with you, just for variety. If you were living the same five years over and over again, you'd know how crucial it is to mix things up."

In Jury's final moments, Evan no longer existed. The whole world bled away. All he had left were thoughts of Ofelia. He realized she may have been right after all.

"But no," Evan continued, "you had to remind me why the world's a better place without you. So now once again, you've reduced yourself to a bit role. You don't get to play the hero. You don't get to lead the Silvers. You certainly don't get the big-titted love interest. Nope. So sorry. No Hannah for you."

By the time Evan finished ranting, the last spark of life had left Jury Curado. His eyes fell shut and his head dropped back against the brick.

Evan crouched down and hissed a gritty whisper in his ear. "Rot in hell, *pendejo.*"

A long green van rolled to a stop at the mouth of the alley. Evan plucked the wallet from Jury's pocket, then climbed the fire escape ladder. He smiled down from the roof as Martin Salgado and his square-headed son traced their wave signal down the alley. They squawked in fluster at the sight of Jury's corpse.

"A little too late there, fellas," Evan murmured.

He scurried to the front of the roof and looked down at the van. From his high angle, he couldn't get a glimpse of Theo Maranan, the great Asian prophet. But Evan had a perfect view of Hannah.

"Come on, baby. Turn around and show me those big browns."

Hannah twisted in the cushions and aimed a nervous glance out the window. Evan chuckled. For all her twitchy instincts, the actress had no idea what she just lost in that alley, the great and awful edit that Evan just made to her story. When left to their untampered fates, Hannah Given and Jury Curado would meet in Terra Vista and smack together like magnets—the man of absolute conviction and the woman of no conviction at all, locked in a vapid dance of physical worship and wall-piercing orgasms. It was an excruciatingly painful spectacle that Evan had suffered a long time ago, back in the days when he tried to be a good little Silver.

Fighting bitter memories, he plucked the twenty-dollar bill from Jury's wallet and sniffed it deeply. Ah, the green, green cash of home. Funny how he'd hated his Earth so much when he lived there and now he missed it terribly. Sadly, his rewind talent stopped at the canned goods section of Nico's store. He couldn't jump back any further. Home was forever just a few seconds out of reach.

Now here at the start of his fifty-fifth play-through, his fifty-fifth trip through the same half decade, Evan Rander was not a fan of his adopted Earth. He knew there was only one escape from his carousel hell, and yet he couldn't find the nerve to end himself. What else could he do then but keep on spinning? What better way to fill his endless days than by punishing the sisters and Silvers who'd wronged him?

As the Salgado van pulled away from the curb, Evan stood up and straightened his shirt. He whistled a happy tune on the way back to the fire ladder. He didn't know where he'd heard the song before. He wasn't even sure which Earth it came from.

TEN

Sunday was a day of rest for the Silvers. Though the physicists attended to their needs like conscientious butlers, the guests were left to wallow and mingle amongst themselves. Amanda learned that Mia harbored authorly ambitions, and had earned an academic award for the fifty-page biography she wrote about her grandmother. Hannah learned that David was a fellow stage performer, one who'd danced and crooned at high schools all around the world. His bare rendition of "Johanna" from *Sweeney Todd* was gorgeous enough to melt her. She spent the rest of the day uncomfortably aroused.

Zack, meanwhile, discovered that plastic was called *bresin* in this neck of the multiverse. He also learned that he could bend time.

He remained tensely withdrawn in the wake of his revelation, sketching tiny shapes in the corner of his pad and then erasing them with the sheer act of thought. By his thirtieth undoodling, he finally saw the prudence of Amanda's argument. It was too much to deal with, too soon.

On Monday, the work began. The group was ushered through an eight-hour gauntlet of medical tests. To Quint's surprise, Zack remained perfectly docile through all the pokings and proddings. This time it was David who caused the trouble. The boy refused to submit to a single examination until the scientists gave him back his heirloom wristwatch. The moment they complied, his cordial smile returned and he became fully cooperative.

On Tuesday, the guests were ushered to individual rooms and asked to recount the awful events of Saturday morning. They relayed their tales with varying degrees of detail and tears, Hannah winning readily on both counts. She was also the only one brave enough to divulge her weirdness, her strange attack of acceleration at the downtown marina. The news triggered an avalanche of chatter among the physicists, forcing Quint to send a staff bitmail.

People, let's not get ahead of ourselves. We need to understand the basics before we get to the unusuals.

The interviews continued throughout the week, question after question about the Earth that no longer was. The Silvers were asked to name the U.S. presidents in reverse order, a task that four of them botched after Franklin Roosevelt. Only Mia, six weeks fresh from her eighth-grade history final, was able to rattle off names without pause. Her interviewers stopped her at William McKinley.

By Friday, the queries had turned from vague to specific to suspiciously pointed. One in particular had the group talking at dinner.

"'Do you know of any historical event that occurred on October 5, 1912?'"

"Yeah, they asked me that one."

"Me too."

"What did you say?"

"*Titanic.*"

"I said *Titanic.*"

"That happened in April."

"Really? Damn. I was so sure I got that."

"Don't feel bad," David told Hannah. "I think they got the answer they were looking for."

"What do you mean?"

"They're cataloging the differences between their history and ours. Trying to pinpoint the first major event that happened on one world but not the other. Given the fact that none of us know the significance of October 5th, 1912, I'd say they found it."

While the table fell silent in heady dither, Zack scribbled furiously into his sketchbook. "This is bullshit. Quint promised us a two-way exchange of information. He hasn't told us a thing."

He pressed the pad to his cheek and aimed it at the ceiling camera. A large and angry word balloon pointed to his mouth. *WE WANT INFO!*

One floor up, Quint leveled an icy stare at his monitor. He dialed Czerny from his desk phone.

"I think our guests are in need of entertainment."

The next day, physicists installed a sleek device in the lounge: a dark gray console the size of a pizza box. Above it, a five-foot pane of smoky black glass rested on metal stands.

The group watched Czerny with puppy-headed interest as he inserted a small cartridge into the machine. For the next two hours, the Silvers sat wide-eyed, mesmerized by their first taste of lumivision. Crystal-clear sounds filled the room from every corner. The colors popped off the screen like oil paint. Mia couldn't spot the image pixels, even when pressing her eyes to the glass.

They were soon given a teeming box of blockbuster movies, enough to keep them busy for months. It didn't escape anyone's notice that the films were all space operas and fantasy sagas, nothing that would shed light on the world outside their window. Once Mia figured out the console controls, she confirmed Zack's suspicion that the physicists blocked their access to live broadcast channels.

"It's nothing sinister," Quint later assured them. "We're merely trying to limit your culture shock. Have patience. When the time is right, we'll tell you everything we know."

None of them were convinced, but at least now they were distracted. The Silvers gradually settled into their routine like office drones, cooperating with the scientists by day and retreating into escapist entertainments at night. By the end of July, even Zack had grown lazy in limbo. The shock of apocalypse had settled into a more enduring malaise. He wasn't in a hurry to have his mind jostled again.

On August 6, a million angry pathogens invaded the property on the skin of a sniffling physicist, clobbering the foreign immune systems of every guest. Only David got off lightly with a runny nose. The rest were thrown deep into flu.

For Beatrice Caudell, part-time biologist and full-time germaphobe, this was Armageddon. She squeaked a litany of worst-case scenarios to Czerny—tales of viral mutation and global decimation. None of her fears came to pass. But when Hannah sneezed her way into a whole new velocity, when a fever dream caused Amanda to pulverize the ceiling, when Mia received a get-well note from her future self, and when everyone started hearing the voices in David's head, there was no more hiding from the issue. For Sterling Quint, his physicists, and the poor beleaguered Silvers, it was finally time to address the weirdness.

———

Zack was the first to get a handle on his new peculiarity.

From the moment he grasped the temporal nature of his talent, he embarked on a cautious secret mission to study it. He retreated under his blanket with a penlight, squinting at the pencil strokes on his sketch pad until they disappeared at will. Zack found it a basic but slippery trick of concentration, like spelling words backward.

After a mere day's practice, he was able to banish all sorts of paper-related maladies to a state of never-happenedness—crumples and smudges, rips and spittle. Anything doable was suddenly undoable, a prospect that terrified him as much as it thrilled him. He began smuggling fruits into his room to unslice and de-ripen.

On the day the flu virus invaded his body, he tried to send an orange on an accelerated journey back to its infancy. Instead he accidentally aged it rotten. To Zack's astonishment, he could spin the clock in both directions, though it would be weeks before he gained control of his fast-forward feature.

On August 9, he warily revealed his weirdness to his hosts. Quint, Czerny, and a trio of associates eyed him from the far end of the conference table as he blew his nose into a tissue.

"Okay, this cold's knocking the crap out of me, so I'll keep it short. I seem to have acquired the ability to affect time. I can reverse or advance the chronology of small objects, like a sheet of paper or a piece of bread. I don't know how or why this is happening. I just know that I'm too freaked out to keep it to myself anymore. I'll also stab the first one of you who tries to dissect me. Questions?"

They had questions, enough for Quint to assign a dedicated team to study Zack's new talent. The physicists observed him in a laboratory, recording and measuring as he worked his way through an endless gauntlet of test materials. Glass, metal, bresin, stone—there was seemingly nothing he couldn't de-age. He even restored the missing leg on a wooden horse figurine, though the new limb looked bleached by comparison.

When Zack described his feat to David at their next dinner, the boy became vexed.

"That's insane. I assume the original horse leg still exists somewhere. Did it magically teleport from its location when you restored the figurine? Or did you somehow create a duplicate?"

"The eggheads seem to think it's a duplicate."

David shook his head in agitation. "I can't tell you how much that violates the basic laws of science."

Zack had expected to see the same amount of hair-pulling from the scientists themselves, but they remained oddly placid. If anything, they seemed more interested in the biology behind Zack's power than the physics.

Soon Zack felt daring enough to test his magic on his silver bracelet, with surprising results. Just a small bit of reversing caused the band to break apart into four even quarters, all perfectly polished at the edges.

After showing his accomplishment to Hannah, Mia, and David, he indulged their request to undo their own adornments. Mia hugged Zack with gushing relief. The bracelet had been a wasp on her wrist for days now. She thought it would never go away.

When Amanda learned about Zack's stunt, she pulled him aside in the hallway.

"That was reckless. You could have overshot and hurt someone. You don't know what your time stuff does to living creatures."

The next morning, he found out. Quint interrupted Zack's lab session to release a tiny brown mouse on the table. It had glassy white eyes, a chestnut-size lump on his left side, and several battle scratches.

"This poor fellow's at the end of his road," Quint told Zack. "See if you can fix that."

All throughout dinner that night, the cartoonist remained uncharacteristically quiet. While the others conversed, he stared ahead in vacant consternation.

Mia touched his arm. "You okay?"

"Yeah. I . . ." He stammered a moment, then let out an incredulous chuckle. "I reversed a mouse today. The thing was old and dying. And then suddenly it wasn't. Quint says I sent it all the way back to adolescence."

The others eyed him through deadpan faces, waiting for a smirk or some other indicator he was kidding. He stared in wide-eyed wonder at his hands.

"Jesus Christ."

While David and Zack discussed the philosophical implications of his ability, Mia envisioned his next bombshell announcement. Today Zack rejuvenated a live rodent. Tomorrow he could be resurrecting a dead one. Hannah couldn't help but wonder if his skill worked the other way. Could he turn a young mouse into an old one? Could he do it to a human? *Would* he?

It was Amanda's thoughts that concerned Zack the most. She remained silent for the rest of the meal, and stone-faced throughout the evening movie.

At bedtime, she approached her room and noticed Zack watching her from his doorway.

"What?"

"You've been quiet since I mentioned my mouse trick. Did it upset you?"

"A little," she admitted.

"You want to talk about it?"

She crossed her arms, bathing him in the same inscrutable look that had bugged him for hours.

"No. I'll work it out." She opened her door, then eyed him one last time. "Good night."

Amanda skipped her hygiene and prayers and went straight to bed, her jade eyes dancing in restless bother. She'd devoted half her life to God and medicine and now suddenly this mordant atheist could heal with a flick of a finger. And what came out of her hands?

She rolled on her back and cast a contemptuous glare at her creator. Apparently, among His other faults, the Lord had Zack's sense of humor.

The sisters weren't eager to face their paranormal afflictions.

For their first two weeks in Terra Vista, Hannah and Amanda lived in quiet hope that the churning forces inside them would simply go away—a one-time outbreak, like chicken pox.

Fearing that anger was the catalyst of her unholy white weirdness, Amanda kept an iron lid on her temper. She sat calmly through her daily scientist interviews, answering all questions with clenched-jaw amenity. She held her tongue when Hannah voiced her growing attraction to David, and held her scream when David spoke glowingly of Esis. She ignored all the puns, cracks, and antics of Zack Trillinger, a man who irked her even when he was being nice.

Though the restraint nearly burned her an ulcer, Amanda's perseverance paid off in exactly the way she hoped. For fourteen days, her hands remained blessedly pink and normal.

On August 7, illness and sibling disharmony eroded the walls of her composure. The sisters were the first and worst victims of the invading virus. They spent the afternoon laid up in their room. By nightfall, their foul moods turned on each other.

"I'm just saying he's sixteen, Hannah. It's not healthy."

"Would you shut up about that? I told you we're not doing anything. We're just taking walks together. Jesus."

"Well, you need to be careful. You don't always make the best decisions when you're grieving."

Hannah covered her face. "Oh my God."

"What? Am I wrong? Do you not remember—"

"No, Amanda, you're absolutely right. I make cruel and awful decisions. Like, you remember how I dropped my married name an hour after my husband died? Oh wait. That was you."

Amanda raised her head from the pillow. "I can't believe you said that. I honestly can't believe you just said that."

"Yeah, well, here's a cross and some nails. Have fun up there."

After an hour of livid silence, Amanda fell into fevered dreams. She replayed her final moments with Derek in the waiting room—the frost on his nose, the bitter rage in his voice. *I'm actually glad we're going to different places. What does that say about you?*

A thunderous crash jerked her awake. Coughing in dust, Amanda turned on the lamp and found half the room covered in broken plaster. The outer shell of the ceiling had rained down on them, leaving a rug-size patch of dangling wires and cracked wooden beams.

Hannah had gotten the worst of the downfall. Her face and hair were white with dust. Thin trickles of blood oozed from her forehead, her shoulders.

Amanda rushed to her side. "Hannah! Are you okay?"

"No! What happened?"

"I don't know. I think maybe it was an earthquake. I . . ."

Amanda suddenly registered the jarring nakedness on her arms. Her shirtsleeves were shredded. The fiber cast on her wrist had mysteriously vanished. Even her wedding ring was gone.

Oh no . . .

Three hours later, she sat in the medical lab, staring darkly at her lap while Czerny made a replacement cast for her.

"Your sister's fine," he assured Amanda. "She's already sleeping. The damage—"

"I want to see the surveillance footage."

Czerny paused his work. "I'm not sure that's wise, Amanda."

"I have to see it. Please."

Soon she sat in his office, watching a bird's-eye recording of the sisters in slumber. As Amanda writhed in bed, a thick and craggy whiteness expanded from the skin of her arms—snapping her ring, rending her cast. She threw her palms upward in somnolent fury. They exploded like fire hoses, shooting flowing cones of force at the ceiling camera. The video turned to snowy static.

The shock of the incident sent Amanda into self-imposed exile. She retreated to her new single, accepting no visitors, opening her door only for food trays and sedatives.

"I don't care what it takes," she told Quint over the phone. "I'll consent to any test. Any procedure. Just find out what's in me and *get it out.*"

At noon, Hannah shambled out of bed and joined the others for lunch in the bistro. She poked a feeble spoon at her chicken soup, her body wallowing under its many new aches and bandages.

"Has anyone spoken to my sister?"

"I did," Mia replied, through a sickly rasp. "She'd only talk to me through the door. She won't let anyone come near her until she's cured of her thing."

Zack shook his head. "There's no cure. She just has to learn how to control it."

"Tall order," David griped. By all accounts, the boy was having his own weirdness issues—strange, ghostly sounds that plagued him day and night. Just five minutes before Hannah came downstairs, an invisible baby cried right in his ear. Zack and Mia heard it too.

"Maybe you can talk her out," Zack said to Hannah.

She snorted cynically. "I was never able to convince her of anything. And after the awful thing I said to her last night, I'm better off . . . just . . ."

Hannah turned away for a soul-rattling sneeze. The moment it passed, she felt a deep chill on her skin. She saw her own spray fluttering lazily in the air, like tiny bumblebees. Her vision turned a deep shade of blue.

"Okay, this is strange. I . . ."

She noticed others staring at her in motionless silence, their eyes widening at a creakingly slow pace. The steam from David's tea dawdled in fat, languid puffs.

Hannah launched from her chair. "Oh no. It's happening again. Oh God. Someone get Dr. Czerny!"

She realized that none of them could understand her in her accelerated state. Her words were probably coming out as fast as shoe squeaks.

She made a stumbling exit from the bistro, praying to any available god to please, please, please let this madness be temporary. She couldn't think of a worse hell than spending the rest of her life in prestissimo, an incomprehensible blur to the people around her.

Determined not to dislocate another shoulder, Hannah proceeded up the stairwell with tightrope caution. She knocked on the door to Czerny's office, then pulled her hand back in agony. Her knuckles throbbed like she'd just punched a mailbox from the window of a speeding car.

By the time Czerny stepped outside, Hannah's velocity spell had ended. He found her crouched against the wall, crying and holding her injured hand.

"What's happening to me?"

After a baby spot, a hand splint, and a long night of rest, Hannah met with the physicists for her first controlled attempt at triggering her anomaly. She concentrated, meditated, ruminated for hours. Nothing. The next day, a stray thought accidentally brushed the ignition switch in her mind, triggering seventeen seconds of blue acceleration. Czerny patted her back and offered lyrical promises of a better day tomorrow.

He was right. At 8 P.M. the next night, Hannah excitedly knocked on her sister's door.

"Amanda? It's me. Open up."

Amanda stumbled out of bed, her eyes drooped and bleary from opiates. "Hannah?"

"Yeah. I have good news but you have to open up."

Amanda cracked the door three inches, studying her sister through an anxious leer. By now all Hannah's cuts had healed into faint red lines. A new wire splint kept her sprained knuckles flat.

"Did I do that to you?"

"No. I did it. I had another attack but I'm okay. Dr. Czerny helped me find the trigger. I can control it now!"

"I have no idea what you're—"

"My weirdness," Hannah explained. "I can turn it on and off. Once I found the mental switch, it was so easy. Like going from talking to singing. If I can do it, so can you."

Amanda eyed her jadedly. Hannah's smile faded away. "Look, you're going to have to do something. You can't stay in there the rest of your life."

"I almost killed you, Hannah."

"Well, you didn't. I'm fine now. And I'm not the only thing that got fixed up. Look."

Hannah passed her a small item from her pocket, Amanda's diamond and gold wedding ring. Despite its violent expulsion from the widow's finger, the band seemed good as new.

"I found it in the wreckage," Hannah told her. "The thing was so messed up, it looked like a half-melted horseshoe."

"It looks great now. How did you fix it?"

"Zack. He says, 'You're welcome.' And I'm saying come out and join us again. Please? We miss you. *I* miss you."

The next morning, Amanda sat alone in a second-floor lab, surrounded by towers of elaborate monitoring equipment. A team of physicists watched her from the next room, assuring her through the intercom that it was safe to conjure the whiteness. Though Amanda tried for three hours, the creature wouldn't come out. She was mostly relieved.

Hannah, meanwhile, continued to work with the scientists to gauge the limits of her velocity. On Monday, she crossed the lawn at an external clock speed of ninety-two miles an hour. On Tuesday, she topped out at ninety-nine. On Wednesday, she broke the three-digit barrier, then nearly snapped her leg when she tripped on a sprinkler nozzle.

"You need to be careful," Czerny reminded her. "Though it doesn't feel like it, you're moving with ten, twenty times your usual momentum. In that mode, you're all but made of glass."

On Thursday, Hannah reached a running speed of 128 miles per hour. She fought a giddy cackle at the readout. Time had consistently gotten away from her in her old life, leaving her in a perpetual state of scrambling lateness. Now suddenly the clock bent to her will like a love-struck suitor. This world would be rushing to catch up to her.

"It is amazing," David admitted. "You've been given a true gift."

The two of them had made an evening custom of strolling the property together. They walked arm in arm inside the fenced perimeter, trading feather-light chatter and crooning soft duets of pop classics. Normally they refrained from discussing their burgeoning paranormalities, but things had been going uncommonly well for one of them.

"Well, let's not go nuts," Hannah said. "I'm just zipping around."

"It's not the speed I'm marveling at. It's the way you experience more time than the rest of us. You could live a full hour in the span of a minute, or a day in the span of an hour. Now that we're aware of how fragile the universe is, our time seems more precious than ever. And now you have the power to make more of it. That's pretty incredible to me. But what do I know?"

Hannah studied David with uneasy regard. For all her protests, she knew she'd become a little infatuated with the boy. He was a world-class genius, a vegan, a thespian, a sweetheart. All that and gorgeous too. She was almost grateful that he was sixteen, and quite possibly gay. The actress had enough drama to handle.

She squeezed David's arm and breathed a wistful sigh.

"You know plenty. For a kid."

While Hannah continued to conquer her talents, Amanda languished in hopeless stagnation. Frustrated, she tracked Zack to the kitchenette. The cartoonist had grown tired of catered food tins and insisted on making his own meals. His culinary prowess didn't extend far beyond cold cuts.

Amanda watched in bother as he reversed a burnt sandwich roll to a healthy golden brown.

"How do you do it, Zack?"

"If you're asking about the science, you're talking to the wrong nerd."

"I'm asking how you got control," she said. "You seem to have a perfect handle on your condition. I feel like I have a big white beast living inside of me."

"Well, that's your problem right there."

"What is?"

"The way you're looking at it. Whatever's going on with us, it's not a disease. It's not a beast. It's just a new muscle. You're never going to control it if you're too afraid to flex it."

She narrowed her eyes at him. "That's easy for you to say. You heal things with your hands. I hurt things with mine. One wrong move and I could kill someone."

"So?"

Amanda blinked at him. "What do you mean 'so?'"

"I mean 'so what?' You think this is the first time you've been at risk of killing someone? You're a nurse. The wrong injection and *boom*, dead patient. That never stopped you from working. You could run over three people on the way to the office. That never stopped you from driving. You did these things, despite the risks, because you knew they were necessary to living. Well, guess what? Controlling this thing of yours is now a necessity. It's your new day job. So if you're as strong as I think you are—and I think you are—you'll stop worrying about the maybes and do your job."

On August 13, Amanda successfully summoned the beast. The whiteness neatly emerged from her hands and only mildly spiked when a physicist approached her. The next day, she formed solid blocks around her arms, then just as quickly dispatched them. Contrary to Zack's assumption, Amanda found her talent worked less like a muscle and more like a language. Each construct was a sentence, one she could make long or short, crude or elegant. The choice was hers, as long as she kept calm.

Two days later, she indulged Zack's request for a demonstration by forming little shapes around the tips of her fingers. Cubes, spheres, pyramids, cylinders. She coated an arm in a sleek sheet of whiteness, an opera glove that moved perfectly with her wiggling fingers.

Zack leered in bright marvel. "Holy crap. That is . . . wow, you're like Green Lantern without the green. I'm officially jealous."

"I'd trade you if I could," she told him. "I'd rather heal mice."

"Come on. You have to like it a little now."

She didn't, but she hated it less. Though Amanda now wore her wedding ring on a cheap string necklace, she no longer worried about fatal outbursts. She'd acquired enough control to move forward, into the larger issues.

"I still don't know what this stuff is," she told Czerny, at the end of a long practice session.

He promised her the answer was coming. Dr. Quint was preparing a presentation that would soon explain many things.

The following week, Amanda dazzled her fellow Silvers with an eight-inch snowflake, beautifully complex and symmetrical. It balanced on the tip of her finger, slowly rotating like a store display. She took a satirical bow to the applause of her friends.

Though Hannah had joined in on the clapping, her cheer was half performance. She didn't know the name of Amanda's aberrant energy. She just knew that it was the same white death that had rained down on their world, toppling buildings and crushing bodies. Since the eve of her sister's sleeping attack, Hannah had suffered a few nightmares of her own. In her cruel visions, Amanda didn't just bring down the ceiling. She brought down the sky.

While the other Silvers wrestled with their formidable new talents, Mia Farisi became a growing enigma to the Pelletier physicists. Unlike her companions, who brazenly broke the laws of time and nature, the girl had yet to display a single hint of chronokinetic ability.

In truth, Mia had been struggling with her weirdness from the day she arrived. Her temporal quirk was too subtle for the cameras to register, too insane to share with others. She figured even Zack wouldn't believe her when she showed him her precognitive paper scraps. He'd probably assume her mind had cracked into split personalities. She wasn't ready to rule out the possibility herself.

On her third night in Terra Vista, Mia returned to her bed and found a tiny new roll of paper on her pillow. Unfurling it revealed a fresh missive, once again scribbled in her handwriting.

I know you're freaking out right now. So was I. I know you're skeptical about these notes. So was I. But trust me when I say that our power's a blessing, not a curse. I'm loving it now. And I'm only six months older than you.

She continued to manage her problem in secret, receiving at least one new dispatch each night. The messages ranged from the obscure to the inane.

Took my first ride in a flying cab today. Holy @$#%!

Commemoration has to be worst holiday ever. Learn to dread October 5th.

If you see a small and creepy guy with a 55 on his hand, run. That's Evan Rander. He's bad news.

There are no words to describe what they did with New York. So beautiful, it brings me to tears.

On her fifth night, Mia finally saw a portal up close. A shimmering disc, as small as a button and as bright as a penlight, hovered a foot above her pillow. Its tiny surface rippled like a thimble of milk. Before Mia could get a closer look, the portal spit a new note and then shrank out of existence. She unrolled the paper.

Don't trust Peter. He's not who he says he is.

Ten minutes later, she was awoken by another tiny breach just inches above her face. A new piece of paper dropped onto her nose.

Disregard that first note. I was just testing something. Peter's good. He's great, actually.

Daunted by all the baffling new intel, Mia asked Czerny for a journal. "Just to collect my thoughts," she told him, with loaded candor.

The next day, he indulged and insulted her with a ferociously girlish pocket diary—neon-pink, and covered in cartoon hearts. She tepidly thanked him, then transcribed every note she'd received. The original papers were flushed into the sea.

Soon it became routine for the others to find Mia scrutinizing her journal, tapping her pen in deep contemplation.

"What are you writing in there?" David asked her one night. He playfully peeked over her shoulder. "Anything about me?"

She slammed the book shut. "No. Go away."

Despite his blistering intelligence, David often displayed the social tact of an eight-year-old. He openly guessed that the scar on Hannah's wrist was self-inflicted. He idly observed that Amanda and Zack had nearly identical builds. He informed Mia that she would suffer fewer stomachaches if she ate more sensible portions. After each thoughtless gaffe, he turned sheepish in the heat of his victim's stare.

"I was raised by a brilliant scientist with atrocious personal skills," he explained to Mia. "From an early age, I was dragged through a gauntlet of foreign nations, each one with different rules of etiquette. Suffice it to say I'm a little bit strange. I might as well be from a third Earth entirely."

Once Mia caught David canoodling with Hannah, walking arm in arm around the property like old Victorian lovers, she lost her fluttering crush on him. For all his alleged nonconformity, his fondness for large-breasted dingbats made him tragically typical. On the upside, Mia could finally relax around him. Her stomachaches gradually stopped.

On the second night of August, she received a tear-stained message on a scrap of motel stationery.

God, it makes me sick to look at you. The fat, clueless idiot I used to be. You think you're adjusting? You think you're getting a handle on your new life here? Trust me, hon. Your problems haven't even started.

Beatrice Caudell watched on the monitor as Mia crumpled the note into an angry ball. An hour later, while the Silvers dined, Beatrice searched Mia's room and found the paper under the bed. Soon it lay flat and wrinkled on the desk of Sterling Quint.

He suddenly became very interested in his youngest guest.

Brace yourself, an older Mia warned her. *Things are about to get hairy.*

On August 7, twelve hours after Amanda brought the ceiling down on her sister, Mia stood outside her door with Czerny, hoping to coax her out of exile. While the good doctor expounded with flowery optimism, Mia teetered miserably with flu. She would have killed for some of her grandmother's minestrone, or at least a good long nap. But Amanda needed her support.

Don't ever take her for granted, her future self insisted. *She's the best person you'll ever know on this world.*

Suddenly Mia noticed a shimmering disc of light in front of her. She assumed it was another spot in her vision until it spit out a roll of pink paper.

Czerny furrowed his brow at the tiny object. "What is that?"

She scrambled to pick it up. "Nothing. I dropped something."

Unconvinced, the good doctor harangued her until she finally confessed her predicament. The news spread like current through the building. Quint was exuberant to the point of giddiness. The Holy Grail of temporal physics was now resting under his roof, nestled inside a meek little girl.

It wasn't until the hullabaloo of the day finally ended that Mia remembered to read her latest message.

Sorry you're sick. Feel better soon.

She rolled her eyes. "Thanks."

Two days later, Mia lunched in the bistro with Zack and David, chortling with laughter as they tried to one-up each other with tales of past social blunders. A small glow suddenly materialized above the table like a firefly. David and Zack jumped back in alarm.

"It's okay," Mia told them. "It's mine. A note should come out any second."

The men leaned closer to look, but nothing emerged. As she moved toward the portal, Mia was stunned to discover that, for the first time, she could glimpse through the keyhole. She saw her own face, red-nosed and puffy-eyed. Her future self was sick with flu. *Again?*

No. The more she saw through the portal, the more she *felt* through it. She could feel herself standing outside Amanda's door, nodding off to Czerny's blather.

"Oh my God . . ."

"What?"

"I'm looking at the past. That's me two days ago."

David squinted at the portal. "I can't see a thing. How can you tell?"

"I don't know. I just can."

"So what does this mean? That you're the Future Mia this time?"

"I'm not sure. I think so. I mean I got a note. I told myself to feel better."

Zack watched the shimmering breach with antsy trepidation. "I don't want to panic you, but you might want to do exactly that."

Panicked, Mia flipped through her diary, scanning her archives until she found the right message. *"Sorry you're sick. Feel better soon."* [Pink paper, blue ballpoint.]

She'd been so ill and distracted that day, she never realized that the pink paper was from her diary itself. Mia ripped a half sheet from the back, then hurriedly scrawled the six-word message. She rolled it up and popped it through the hole. The portal disappeared in a blink.

The incident left her rattled for days. What if she'd sent different words on different paper? What would that do to her memories? What would that do to *time*?

"Paradox," she uttered to David, as if the word was acid. "Maybe that's what happened back home. Someone forgot to dot the 'i' on a time-traveling note and it ripped the whole world apart."

The two young Silvers had embarked on a morning walk around the property, stopping at the thistle-covered tennis courts. As David jumped back and forth over the sagging net, Mia leaned against the fence, wrapping her fingers around the chain metal links.

"I don't know," David mused. "It seems like a paradox already. I mean you wrote 'feel better' because you thought you had to. And the Mia who sent your note presumably wrote the words because *she* felt she had to. So we have a chicken/egg conundrum. Who first chose the words? Who decided that 'feel better' was just the thing to say?"

Mia could feel her brain trying to jump out of her skull. Just three weeks ago, her biggest concerns were weight gain and the impending start of high school. Now she was trying to wrap her head around the mysteries of time, for health reasons.

Worse, Quint insisted that Mia spend four hours a day in a second-floor laboratory, twiddling her thumbs under a million dollars' worth of monitoring equipment in the hope that a new portal would arrive. The sessions were ex-cruciatingly awkward for Mia, especially with Beatrice on the other side of the table. The mousy young physicist was utterly humorless, and had a ten-dency to treat Mia like the Virgin Mary in her third trimester.

At the start of their sixth session, Beatrice surprised Mia with a large chocolate cupcake. A white-flamed lumicand protruded from the frosting.

"What is this?"

"A small thing," Beatrice replied, in her nervous high voice. "I thought you might like some recognition."

"For what?"

Beatrice cocked her head. "Isn't this . . . ? I'm sorry. Our files say you were born on August 19."

"I was."

"Okay, well, that's today. Today's August 19. Happy birthday."

As the calendar finally caught up with her, Mia covered her mouth and fled the lab. She spent the rest of the day sequestered in her room.

That night, David sauntered into her room without knocking and took a casual perch on her desk. He rolled a tennis ball over the back of his hands. Mia glowered at him.

"I don't want to talk about it, okay?"

"Never said you had to," he replied. "However, if you'd like to see some-thing interesting, put your socks on and come with me."

She grudgingly followed him to the polished stone lobby. He stood at the reception desk and pressed his fingers to his temples.

"David, what are you—"

"Shhh. I need to concentrate for this."

In a sudden instant, more than seventy people materialized across the vast marble floor—rich men in tuxedos, young women in cocktail dresses, bar-tenders, caterers, even a few photographers. A nine-piece orchestra played merry party music. Confetti and streamers flew everywhere.

Mia stared incredulously at the busy new scene. "What . . . what is this?"

"My issue," David informed her, with a coy little grin. "My weirdness."

For four weeks now, the boy had suffered a growing problem with ghosts. What started out as phantom sounds had evolved into strange visual anomalies that rattled everyone in the building. On August 10, the blurry upper half of a waitress interrupted the Silvers at dinner, passing through the bistro like a floating specter. Four days later, David's evening stroll with Hannah was cut short by a week-old slice of sunshine that nearly blinded them both. And just last Thursday, David and Zack turned a hallway corner, only to pass through a day-old apparition of Zack himself.

David desperately worked with the physicists to understand the nature of his temporal manipulations, his ability to reproduce the past as sound and light. As far as his friends knew, he was still struggling to control it.

That situation had clearly changed.

Mia spun a sweeping glance around the lobby. The ghosts were jarringly crisp, nearly indistinguishable from the two living beings in the room. It was only when the partygoers passed through the furnishings of the present that they revealed their ethereal nature.

A young black caterer obliviously walked through Mia. She gasped and jumped out of his way.

"God. This is unreal. Who are these people?"

"This building was once a luxury hotel," David explained. "What you're seeing now is the opening night gala. This all happened about six years ago, give or take."

"And you just plucked it right out of the past."

David jerked a humble shrug. "It takes some effort. But it gets easier each time. Come on."

He moved to the dance floor and held out his hand. Mia eyed him cynically.

"You can't be serious."

"Sure am."

"You want us to dance with ghosts."

His expression turned somber. "You've been dancing with ghosts all day, Mia. It's been clear to everyone."

She crossed her arms and looked down at her feet, speaking in a tiny, broken voice. "It's my birthday."

David nodded in grim understanding. "I'm sorry. I know that must hurt. If I had the power to bring your family back, even for one night, I would. You'll just have to settle for me and these people."

With a sly grin, he raised his beckoning hand. "Come on. If we're going to dwell in the past, let's do it in style."

She slowly joined him on the dance floor, fighting a daft grin. "This is the strangest thing I've ever done."

"These are strange times, Miafarisi. Might as well embrace it."

He took her hands in his and together they danced—the boy with an eye in the past and the girl with a foot in the future. They twirled to the music in their sweatpants and socks, six years late to the party.

The next morning at breakfast, Hannah sniffed her slice of honeydew, then gave it to Zack to freshen up. Amanda dropped her fork and retrieved it with a long white protrusion that sprang from her palm like a frog's tongue. Mia declared that she was tired of movies and wanted to see some live lumivision programs for a change. The others agreed. They'd demand that Quint unblock the channels sometime after the morning's big presentation.

"What's the official topic of this thing, anyway?" Amanda inquired.

David responded through a mouthful of apple. "I asked Quint that very question."

"And?"

"He just said, 'Temporis.'"

Hannah cast a befuddled look around the table. "Does anyone here know what that is?"

She received nothing but shrugs and head shakes in reply.

"Well, this should be interesting."

At 9 A.M., Czerny popped his head into the bistro and asked his guests if they were ready. They were. In quiet harmony, the Silvers cleared their plates from the table, and then moved on.

ELEVEN

Sterling Quint came to work at 7 A.M., looking more dapper than ever in his double-breasted Benaduce suit, Vanya silk tie, and four-hundred-dollar pocket square. His wrists were garnished with eighteen-karat-gold cuff links that were molded in the elaborate pattern of watchworks, the closest thing he had to a lucky charm. He'd first worn them ten years ago at a grand convention hall in Havana, where he stood before two thousand of his fellow temporal physicists and assured them in his most regal baritone that Earth was not an only child.

"We are surrounded by infinite kin," he'd declared. "Siblings and half siblings. Distant cousins. Even twins. These parallel realities share our physical space, lying just outside our perceptions. I believe that one day we'll be able to access them, like so many frequencies on a radio."

Quint was not the first scientist to present that notion, but he did offer a mathematical description of his multiverse in action, a theoretical equation that unified two competing ideas about the nature of time and purported to explain most if not all of the paradoxes involved with temporal manipulation.

Though his Radio Worlds Theory was untestable and could neither be proved nor disproved, it went on to dominate the university chalkboards and make him a global star of the physics field . . . for a time. Eventually his scientific peers, no better than teenage girls with their fickle tastes and fad worship, discarded his theory for a newer and shinier rival.

Now Quint could only grin at the thunderous uproar he'd create at the next temporal physicists' conference. The looks on their pasty white faces when he unveiled the scientific find of the century.

The meeting room was large enough to seat a hundred, but only six folding chairs had been set in front of the dais. Most of Quint's employees stood along the walls. Another few scurried onstage, rushing to prepare the mechanical devices that Quint would soon demonstrate for his guests.

Shortly after nine, Czerny arrived with five Silvers in tow. They approached their seats in a slow single file, their curious gazes fixed on the many strange contraptions up front. Hannah cast a baffled glance at a young and lanky post-grad who was dressed from head to foot in a blue rubber suit.

"What's with the deep-sea diver?"

"It's not a diving suit," Quint told her. "You'll see what it does."

Zack sat down last. He dragged the sixth folding chair in front of him and used it as a footstool.

"Okay, Sterling. We're here. Dazzle us."

Quint glowered at him. "Put that back."

"Oh, I'm sorry. Is this for the prophet Elijah?"

"I think you already guessed who it's for."

"I have," Zack admitted. "You could have just told us, you know."

Amanda eyed him strangely. "What are you talking about?"

The double doors opened again. Now Beatrice escorted a young Asian man in a dark blue sweatsuit. He swept his nervous gaze through the crowd, recognizing only Quint and a handful of physicists. The five people in folding chairs triggered a cloudier air of familiarity, as if he'd seen them all in dreams.

One in particular stood out, just as she stood up.

"Oh my God . . ."

Hannah had only met him once, for a short but eventful eighteen minutes. Still, with nearly seven billion people gone, it was a drop of medicine to see him again. It was just so damn sweet to find another survivor from her world.

She wrapped her arms around him and held him tight.

"Hi, Theo."

The last any Silver had seen of Theo Maranan, he lay unconscious on a stretcher, bleeding from his nose and mouth. The Salgados had given him a baby spot sedative, which reacted violently to the alcohol in his bloodstream, which threw him into a coma.

Though Azral had been surprisingly tepid to the loss of Natalie Tipton, Jury Curado, and the elusive Evan Rander, he was far less pleased about Theo's plight. Four weeks ago, just moments after Theo's bloody arrival in Terra Vista, Quint received an irate text message.

<That was an infuriating error, Sterling. Foolish and avoidable. I trusted you to find competent help.>

Quint blanched as he keyed his reply. <I take full responsibility. Rest assured I have access to one of the nation's best neurologists. I can have him here by sundown.>

<Keep your butcher. I have a specialist of my own. We come tonight.>

The news stunned Quint. For five long years, all of Azral's instructions had come from prerecorded videos, all mysteriously delivered to some corner of Quint's house and accompanied by staggering amounts of cash. On the morning the nine Silvers became flesh in this world, Azral suddenly began communicating through mobile texts. Now suddenly he was coming in person.

At midnight, a round white portal bloomed on the wall of Quint's office. An exquisitely tall couple stepped through the surface. Though Quint had no trouble recognizing Azral from the videos, the brown-haired woman was new to him. She wore a fluffy fur coat over a sheer cocktail dress. The shopping bag in her hand was adorned with Japanese text. Quint reeled to wonder if the pair had just stepped away from a sunny afternoon in Kyoto. (It was actually Osaka.)

Mercifully, Azral appeared to be in a genial mood now. With a soft grin, he introduced his companion as Esis Pelletier. Quint had no idea if she was his spouse, his sibling, or possibly both. (She was neither.) He had a hard time believing she was the medical specialist in question. The woman dressed like a European prostitute and grinned like she was high on four different opiates.

"Precious Sterling," she cooed. "We gave them silver in honor of your name. We found it amusing. It still makes my heart laugh, when no one's looking."

Despite her questionable state of mind, Esis wasted no time getting to work. Quint watched with rapt fascination as she cut a bloodless path through Theo's forehead, using tools and gels Quint had never seen anywhere. After seventeen minutes of tinkering, she closed Theo without a trace of incision. He looked exactly as he had before, except now his eyelids fluttered with restless life.

"He'll awaken tomorrow," Azral informed Quint. "It's fortunate. That one's of particular value to us. Had we lost him, I would have held you responsible."

Quint felt a cold squeeze around his heart. "I apologize again. Are you . . . do you wish to see the others while you're here?"

"Let them sleep," said Azral. "They had a trying day. I would like to meet your staff, however. Please summon them."

By 2 A.M., the physicists and Salgados had assembled in the lobby, sleepy and perplexed. To all subordinates, even Czerny, Azral Pelletier was merely an obscure Canadian philanthropist who'd given Quint carte blanche to run the operation. Azral did little to counter that notion. He shook everyone's hands, congratulated them on their fine work, then wished them a merry evening.

Esis smirked at Quint's befuddlement. "If you saw the strings like we do, you'd know the need for this charade. My wealth labors now to prevent future difficulties."

Once the staff left to return to their homes and beds, Azral summoned a new portal in the wall. He turned around at the rippling surface and looked to Quint.

"Keep Maranan isolated. Until he recovers from his alcohol addiction, he'll be a negative presence among the others."

"And be extra nice to David," Esis added, with a teasing smirk. "He's my favorite."

"I'll do that. I promise. But . . ."

The pair eyed Quint quizzically, waiting for him to finish his thought.

"I've followed your instructions for five years now, Azral. I've done everything you asked. I'm just wondering when I finally get the chance to learn about you. I mean . . . where do you come from? *When* do you come from? What's your ultimate purpose with these people?"

The Pelletiers smiled with enough wry amusement to make Quint regret his outburst.

"How soon you turn from seeking forgiveness to favor," Azral mocked.

"I'm a scientist. Do you expect me to be incurious?"

"We expect you to be patient, Sterling. This is just the beginning of our relationship. For now, your focus should be on the Silvers. Keep them comfortable. Keep them content."

"Our task will be simpler if they remain here willingly," Esis added.

Quint's thoughts turned to Zack, who'd been so stubborn and clever about securing an independent future. "And if they choose to leave?"

Azral's deep blue gaze turned chillingly severe. "Then this won't be the beginning at all."

The couple disappeared into the shimmering circle. It shrank away to nothingness.

As he waited for his thumping heart to settle, Quint cursed himself for his whimpering subservience. For all he knew, Azral was a mediocrity in his native era—a fraud, a mental patient. And yet here was the great Sterling Quint, begging for knowledge like a dog begged for scraps.

Still, indignity was a small price to pay for this scientific windfall, a chance to forever rise above his simpering peers. For the greater prize, Quint resolved to do his job. Most important, he'd do it without any more mistakes. On the short list of things he didn't want to learn from Azral was how he handled the people who disappointed him.

Hannah pulled away from Theo and studied him. When she first met him, he looked like a shipwreck victim. Now his face was clean-shaven and his hair was trimmed to a more civilized shag.

"I had no idea you were awake," she said. "I must have asked about you a hundred times. All they told me was that you were hanging in there."

Theo processed her with awkward, busy eyes. She recognized the look.

"You forgot my name, didn't you? It's all right. I'm Hannah."

Czerny stepped in. "I'm afraid it's worse than that. Due to his unfortunate mishap, he doesn't remember his first day here."

She looked to Theo again. "You don't remember me at all? That talk we had in the van?"

As he raised his palms in shrugging remorse, his sleeves rolled back, revealing the Asian script tattoo on his left wrist and the shiny silver bracelet on his right. It had been nearly two weeks since Zack removed her own bangle. She never thought she'd have to look at one again.

"Okay, well, I can fill you in later. I'm just glad you're all right."

Theo thanked her, even though the state of all-rightness seemed about as distant as Alpha Centauri. He'd spent the last month tucked away in his one-man rehab unit on the second floor, with his own catered meals, his own lu-mivision, his own sweaty struggles. On the upside, he was truly sober for the first time in years. That made him only slightly prepared to be integrated with the other survivors. He was only slightly ready to hear what Quint had to say.

The esteemed physicist motioned Theo to the empty chair. "If you would."

Theo sat down at the end of the row, drumming a nervous beat on his leg. The cartoonist offered him a smile and a handshake. "Zack Trillinger."

"Theo Maranan. Hi. Did we, uh, also meet before?"

"Nope. This is our first time."

"Okay," he said, suppressing the hot urge to laugh. Zack already seemed as familiar as a best friend. He had no idea why.

Quint nodded to Czerny, who dimmed the lights and switched on the lu-miplex. He cleared his throat, then the presentation began.

The first image to appear on the screen was a satellite photo of the world. Though Czerny ran the projector-like device from the other side of the room, Quint was able to move in front of it without casting a shadow or wearing the swirling colors of Earth on his skin.

"To start, I'd like to thank you all for your patience. You've gotten a lot of nonanswers to a lot of pressing questions. I know how frustrating that can be. Believe me, it was never our goal to keep you in the dark. We just want to portion out the information in a way that doesn't overwhelm you. Given all the strife with your physical anomalies, you can understand why we'd hold off on discussing the many quirks and differences of this new world."

Theo scanned his fellow refugees, wondering if he'd failed to notice goat horns or cat eyes. When David caught his gaze, he turned his attention back to Quint.

"But now we feel enough progress has been made to attempt a basic orien-tation. This is only the first of what I hope to be many sessions. For today, we'll start small. Constantin."

Czerny pressed a button on the lumiplex. The wide shot of Earth changed to an illustration of an ancient Egyptian pyramid. As Quint spoke, familiar images advanced in quick order. The crucifixion of Christ. The *Mona Lisa*. The American Civil War. The montage ended with a grainy photo of a walrus-like man in a dark business suit.

"From our many interviews with you, we feel confident that the history of your world and ours are identical up to the early twentieth century. The man on-screen, William Howard Taft, is the last president our two Americas have in common."

Mia and Zack scribbled into their respective books. Zack's notation was a quick doodle of Taft, with "1912?" written underneath.

Quint continued. "So, what changed? What was the first thing to happen on one Earth but not the other? Under current limitations, it'd be impossible to pinpoint the exact moment in which our timelines diverged."

The screen changed to a black slide with a single line of text. *October 5, 1912.*

"However, we've identified the first *major* event to occur on just one Earth. That was simply a matter of asking. We learned that the date on-screen holds no significance to any of you. And yet it's a day that everyone on this world knows by heart. It even has its own holiday."

Now the screen gave way to a movie clip, a pulled-back view of a grand old city at the brink of dawn.

"This scene is from a 1978 historical drama called *The Halo of Gotham*. In addition to being one of the most acclaimed films of all time, it provides an extremely faithful reenactment of the event I'm about to discuss. There's no footage of the actual—"

"What city is that?" Hannah interjected.

"New York," said Zack.

"This is New York," Quint replied with mild annoyance. "Hence the 'Gotham.' Anyway, on the fifth of October, 1912, at 5:52 in the morning, the entire—"

The Silvers gasped as a dome of white light erupted in the center of the city. It grew in all directions, devouring everything in its path. By the time Czerny paused the video, the dome had overtaken the scene, splitting the clouds and stretching deep across the landscape.

"We call it the Cataclysm," Quint said. "A massive discharge of energy centered in northern Brooklyn, in the area once known as Winthrop Park. In five seconds, the burst expanded 4.7 miles in every direction, destroying 24 percent of Queens, 22 percent of Brooklyn, and 68 percent of Manhattan. Everything below the upper reaches of Central Park."

Hannah and Theo covered their mouths. Amanda watched the screen in wincing anguish.

"How many people?"

"A little over two million," Quint replied.

Mia clenched her jaw in tight suppression. She was a hairsbreadth away from bawling at the unbearable fragility of existence, but she didn't want to cry. Not here. Not in front of Sterling Quint, a man who had a very cruel definition of "starting small."

"To call this a transformational event would be an understatement," he continued. "For America and the entire world, everything changed in an instant. Countless books have been written about the rippling effects of the Cataclysm—on culture, on politics, the economy. Those are all topics for another time. For now, I want to discuss how the event forever changed science."

The projection advanced to sepia-toned photos of the altered New York landscape. A quarter skyline of Manhattan. A ten-story building, maimed at the base by a giant curved bite. A bird's-eye view of Central Park, with a diagonal arc of wreckage separating the surviving greenery from acres upon acres of flat gray ash.

"As you can imagine, the mystery of the Cataclysm became a top priority for scientists worldwide. The explosion clearly wasn't man-made, as the damage went far beyond the limits of any human weapon. It left no heat signature, no radioactive fallout. A person standing just five feet outside the blast radius could have gone on to live for decades. In fact, the last known survivor from that famous halo—an infant at the time—only recently passed away."

The next image was an old photo of three pale men in lab coats, posing in front of an elaborate machine. David motioned to the one in the center.

"That's Niels Bohr. He was my father's idol."

Quint smiled. "Mine as well. Though the cause of the Cataclysm has yet to be discovered, the energy itself was successfully reproduced by Bohr and his fellow Danish scientists in 1933. They called it the *femtekraft*, or 'fifth force.' Over the next two decades, it went on to adopt many other monikers. White force, whitewave, nivius, cretatis. In 1955, when its true nature was at long last discovered, it took on its final name. Temporis."

The screen went blank. The overhead lights came on. The Silvers all winced in adjustment.

"Today we know enough about temporic energy to fill a library," Quint declared. "And yet it'll take a dozen more generations to get a true grasp of its nature. Simply put, the Danes had it right. Temporis is yet another governing force of the universe, the quantum building blocks of what we perceive as time. Though the cost was great, the Cataclysm triggered a scientific revolution like none other. We've acquired the means to bend time like a prism bends light. More than bend it, we can stretch it, harden it, even reverse it. Through temporis, we've accessed the watchworks of existence itself."

Quint could see from his guests' fidgety stances that he was flustering them. He swallowed the rest of his spiel and took the shortcut back to their concerns.

"For the last few weeks, you've wondered if you're unique in your abilities. The answer is both yes and no. With the exception of one of you, all the amazing things you can do have been done countless times before by others, myself included. The difference between you and us, what truly makes you special, is your innate ability to wield temporis."

He gestured at the showcase of gadgets behind him. "The rest of us need machines."

Quint moved to the left side of the room and opened the door of a boxy white appliance that looked like a quarter-scale clothes dryer. He retrieved a banana from inside and tossed it at Zack.

"Before I demonstrate the first device, would you do me a favor and age that?"

"Uh, okay."

Though the act of reversing had become as simple as third-grade math, Zack had a trickier time sending objects the other way. He grimaced with effort. Soon the banana turned spotted, then brown, then pungently rotten. Quint directed him to put it back in the machine.

As Zack returned to his seat, Theo drank him in with saucer eyes. "Jesus Christ."

"I know. Trippy, isn't it?"

Quint closed the door, then pressed a few buttons on the contraption's keypad. The box quietly whirred.

"This machine is known as a rejuvenator or, informally, a juve. The technology was invented in 1975 but didn't reach the consumer market until 1980. At first there were certain issues with tooping, which we can talk about another day."

The juve let out a high *ding*. Quint popped the door, then brandished a perfect yellow banana to his audience.

"As you see, the device matches Zack's talents by creating a localized field that reverses the flow of time. It can restore anything that fits inside it, though it does irreparable damage to electronic circuits and batteries. Its primary function is exactly what was demonstrated: the restoration of food. Today you'll rarely find a kitchen without one."

Zack wasn't sure how to react. From the moment he gained control of his weirdness, he'd felt like a borderline superhero. Now he realized he was only as skilled as a common household appliance. He was as impressive as the hero who could turn bread into toast.

"Can it also advance an object's timeline?" David asked.

"Yes. That feature's used for accelerated defrosting and marinating."

Amanda thought about the coffin-size device she'd noticed in the ambulance on her traumatic first day. "What about people? Couldn't that same technology be used to heal?"

"Good question. There is indeed a device that works on the same principles. It's called a reviver. They're expensive and highly regulated. You need a special medical license to operate them."

Zack snapped out of his dolor. "Wait a minute. If you guys have the technology to undo all the bad things that happen to people, wouldn't that eliminate the nagging problem of, you know, death?"

Amanda nodded. "That's what I was wondering."

"Unfortunately, no," Quint replied. "As human beings are far more complex than your average food product, there are risks in using temporis to revert people to a prior state—neurological issues, vascular problems, infertility. The further you bend the clock, the greater the chance of adverse effects. As a result, revivers are mostly limited to life-or-death situations, and usually for traumas that are less than twelve hours old. It's certainly not a tool for fighting something like cancer."

Mia raised her hand until Quint acknowledged her. "What about the recently deceased? I mean if someone died six hours ago and you reverse them seven hours . . ."

"Revivers can indeed restore the spark of life to a dead body, but not a dead brain. The temporis turns a corpse into a living vegetable, and even that typically lasts a couple of hours until death comes again. The technology gets more sophisticated each year, so who knows how long these limits will remain? I can say that revivers are much safer on animals. Veterinarians use them to extend the life of household pets."

Hannah gaped with revelation. "Oh, *that's* what it was."

Upon receiving a roomful of glassy stares, she described the first person she met on this world, a pony-haired teenage activist who sat outside a supermarket, urging a stop to pet extensions. Hannah finally knew what the term meant, but she couldn't understand the controversy.

"There are people out there who see all forms of time manipulation as unnatural," Quint explained. "Even unholy. And then there are other, more rational individuals who simply believe that animals, like people, have a right to die with dignity. When you consider that the oldest dog in America is currently forty-one years old, it's hard to dismiss their argument."

David whistled in wonder. "Forty-one. That's amazing."

"It's awful," said Mia. "You'd think that poor dog would want to die at this point."

Quint shook his head. "Keep in mind that reversal is total. When you undo a year of life, you undo a year of memories. From the dog's perspective, he's merely reliving the same year over and over. He's frozen at a mental age of ten."

"Huh. Just like Zack."

Half the room erupted in chuckles. Zack wagged a wry finger at Hannah. "Well played. Well timed. I hate you, but kudos."

Theo clenched his fists until they throbbed. He was two bombshells away from structural collapse, and yet the others seemed to be handling it just fine. *Why aren't they freaking out? Why am I the only one ready to scream?*

Unamused by Zack and Hannah's silliness, Quint motioned Charlie Merchant to the stage. The slender young physicist looked slightly ridiculous in his blue rubber suit. Insulated wires connected his thick gloves to a small electronic console on his back. The Silvers watched in quiet bemusement as he wrapped a dangling hood over his head and snapped a clear bresin guard-mask over his face.

Hannah winced with concern. "He's not about to get younger, is he?"

"No," Quint replied. "You in particular will appreciate what he's about to do."

Charlie pressed a button on his glove. The device on his back whirred to life. A mesh of glowing blue lines appeared on his suit. Before the Silvers could process the odd display, he dashed back and forth across the stage— fifty feet each way, five times in each direction.

He did this all in a blurry six seconds.

The guests gaped as he came to a panting stop. Wisps of steam rose from his shoulder blades.

"The device Charlie's wearing on his back is called a shifter," Quint explained. "The outfit itself is called a speedsuit. As you've no doubt gathered, the gear doesn't imbue the wearer with any special motor skills. It merely creates a temporic field in which time is accelerated. What was six seconds to us was a full minute to Charlie."

Quint patted the young man's shoulder. "Thank you. You can go change."

Hannah watched Charlie exit. "God. Is that what I look like when I do it?"

"It is," Quint told her.

"And is there one of those in every house also?"

"No. Speedsuits are expensive and difficult to maintain. But the technology isn't limited to clothing. A temporic shift can be generated in any enclosed space. There are special cinemas where you can watch a two-hour movie and yet only lose twenty minutes of your day. Restaurants have special booths where a busy diner can enjoy a leisurely lunch in minutes. The technology's been around for over three decades. Most of us can't remember a time when our personal day was fixed at twenty-four hours."

"How far can it bend time?" Zack asked. "I mean, is it possible to squeeze a year into a day?"

"No. By federal law, no shifter can go beyond twelve times normal speed, or 12x, as they call it. And there are limits, both legal and physical, to the number of consecutive hours one can spend in a shifted state. In most places, the cap is twenty."

Amanda looked to Hannah with fresh concern. "What's the danger of going beyond those limits?"

"That's a source of endless debate," Quint responded. "Aside from the small bouts of resistance one might encounter when tampering with their body's natural clock, some psychologists believe the human mind can only handle so much disruption to its natural cycle without suffering . . . issues. Most of their concerns are either theoretical or anecdotal."

Neither Given took comfort in Quint's assurance. *Great,* thought Hannah. *Now she's going to treat me even more like a time bomb.*

Moving on, Quint retrieved a small object from a display table. It looked like a ten-inch dinner candle without the wick.

"There are other forms of temporis that are specific enough in application to earn their own names. One of them . . ."

Pressing a button at the base of the candle caused a floating white flame to appear.

". . . is lumis."

While the others squinted curiously at the fire, Mia started a new page in her journal. She'd seen lumicands on two occasions now and was eager to learn how they worked.

"Temporic energy moves in waves, as does light. Using one to manipulate the other has opened up some interesting new avenues. This isn't a real flame. It's merely a temporal projection, a visual ghost that's been digitally brightened and desaturated."

Quint stepped inside a structure the size of a phone booth. It had no walls, just four metal posts supporting a thick ceiling. A series of round glass lenses lined the inside of each column.

"Over the last quarter century, lumis has been adopted into hundreds of everyday devices, and has made dozens more obsolete. The television. The lightbulb. Even windows and mirrors are being replaced by more versatile lumic screens. And as you've seen from this little device, lumis is the key to holographic imaging."

Quint flicked the candle four more times, then exited the contraption. From the back of the room, Beatrice entered commands into a handheld console. Suddenly a second Quint appeared inside the booth, indistinguishable from the original except for the faintest of shimmers. Both Quints addressed the Silvers, though no sound came from the duplicate's mouth.

"This machine is called a ghostbox. Like David, it reproduces images from the past with lifelike accuracy. These devices come in all sizes and are used for everything from store displays to forensic imaging."

Just as Quint had done fifty seconds prior, his ghost lit the lumicand four times, then departed the booth. It vanished between posts.

"Does it come with audio?" Mia wondered. "Or are these all silent ghosts?"

"As we have yet to discover a way to restore sound waves through temporis, ghostboxes are forced to rely on standard digital recorders. This machine is currently muted."

"But David's ghosts come with sound."

Quint nodded. "Yes. I was surprised to learn that myself. Obviously his abilities go well beyond the current technology. Perhaps with his help, we'll be able to catch up."

David leaned back in his seat, releasing a grin that was smarmy enough to make his friends chuckle. Theo wasn't as amused. He'd noticed the boy earlier and felt a strange sense of outrage, as if David were mocking everyone in the room. He figured the mistrust was his own personal hang-up. Theo knew a prodigy when he saw one, and he had very strong opinions about prodigies.

Quint moved on to a large steel apparatus that resembled an empty doorframe. As he turned a key at the base, the metal hummed with power. Amanda jumped in her seat.

The machine suddenly turned opaque with a waxy white substance that by now was familiar to everyone but Theo. He cocked his head in puzzlement.

"Tempis," said Quint. "First discovered in 1984. Made commercially available in 1990. Some people refer to it as solid time, but that's a misnomer. It's merely air molecules, temporally manipulated into a uniquely solid state."

David leered suspiciously at the bright white plane. "How can you adjust the speed of air molecules without creating a temperature shift? I mean we should be feeling it from here."

Quint beamed. If he'd had more students like David, he wouldn't have hated teaching.

"I'd love nothing more than to discuss it with you, one-on-one. For now, I'll just say that tempis is one of the most perplexing substances known to man. It has the atomic structure of a hard transition metal but the weight of a noble gas. Somehow it exists in a paradoxical state in which it can be both airy and dense."

"Huh. Just like Hannah."

More people laughed as the actress irreverently narrowed her eyes at Zack. He shined her a preening smirk.

"Don't start a battle you can't finish, honey."

"Oh, I'll finish it."

Determined to ignore them, Quint looked to Amanda. "I noticed you reacted to the energy before the barrier was even activated."

"Yeah. It felt like someone tapping my shoulder from twenty feet away. What does that mean?"

"It suggests you have an innate sensitivity to all tempis. That's fascinating."

"Is it safe to touch?" Mia asked.

Quint thumped his fist against the surface. "Perfectly safe. Many specialized workers wear it as protective gear."

"How?" David asked. "It's a flat pane."

"Tempis can either be projected through lenses, as it is with this barrier, or generated along conductive metal wires. Using a flexible mesh, the substance can be molded into virtually any shape."

Zack noticed a thermos-size generator at the base of the frame. "So this runs on electricity."

"No. Most temporic devices are powered by something called solis. That's for another session."

Amanda studied the barrier with heavy eyes. Now that she knew the name of the force inside her, she rolled it around her thoughts like a boulder. *Tempis, tempis, tempis.* She squeezed her golden cross, praying for the day this beast, this madness, this tempis-tempis-tempis stopped scaring the hell out of her. It didn't help that her sister seemed equally frightened by it.

Quint peered at the clock on the wall. "Does anyone have any questions?"

"Yes," said Zack and Hannah, in synch.

David raised a hand. "Me too."

"Okay. Hannah first."

"I once asked Martin Salgado what makes all the cars and ambulances fly, and he said 'aeris.' Where does that fit in?"

"I was going to save that for next time," Quint said. "But since you asked, aeris is just an altered form of tempis, one that can be molecularly compelled to move in a specific direction, even up. With enough aeris, you can lift entire buildings. Since its introduction twenty years ago, aeris has replaced jet propulsion as the primary means of commercial flight. It can be found in roughly a third of all automobiles. I imagine in another twenty years, ground cars will be an antiquity. Zack?"

"Have there been any other cataclysms since 1912? And has anyone developed a weapon that more or less does the same thing?"

"Mercifully, no to both. The Cataclysm has been a one-time occurrence. And though temporis has certainly been weaponized in various ways, no one's invented the means to re-create an event of that scale. If anyone does develop the technology, it'll be either England or China."

"Why not the U.S.?"

"America hasn't been involved in war since 1898."

Quint wasn't surprised to see six hanging jaws in response. He sighed patiently.

"Again, a broader topic for another day. I'll just say for now that among its many other effects, the Cataclysm drove us inward as a nation. David, you have a question?"

"Yes, I gather from your omission that there isn't a device that does what Mia does. Correct?"

Quint emitted a smile that made Mia want to hide under her chair. "That is indeed the case. For all our advances, the act of time travel itself remains purely hypothetical. At least it did until our lovely young Mia came along. As far as science is concerned, she's the first person in history to transport physical matter from one point in time to another."

While Quint spoke, Zack furtively edged his sketchbook into Theo's view. Among all the notes and doodles was a large query, circled twice.

What's your weirdness?

Zack had left his pencil out for Theo's use, but after five seconds of addled silence, he took it back to add a postscript.

Just being nosy. Forget I asked.

A few moments later, Theo commandeered the pad and wrote his reply. Zack eyed him in blinking turmoil. "Are you kidding?"

"Afraid not."

"Wow. I don't even know how to react to that."

"Guess I don't either."

"Is everything all right?" Quint asked them.

"Yeah," Zack replied. "Just a lot to absorb. I think our heads are about to spin off."

"Well, why don't we stop here then?"

Theo fled the room as fast as politeness would allow. Hannah watched him exit, then cautiously approached Zack.

"Is he okay?"

"I don't know," the cartoonist replied, still vexed. When he asked Theo about his weirdness, he'd steeled his mind for yet another metaphysical brain-bender. But Theo's answer truly threw him. A four-word deposition, delivered straight from right field.

I don't have one.

That night, Theo ate his first dinner with the group. He kept a tense gaze at his food, forcing his eyes away from all the notable distractions—Amanda's cast, Hannah's chest, David's teeming pile of raw sliced carrots. Even worse were Zack's sporadic displays of time-twisting madness. He undid Theo's bracelet with a tap of the finger, then proceeded on two separate requests to freshen up breads and vegetables. No one else seemed bothered by the sheer insanity of his table trick. And these were supposedly the people from Theo's world.

Though he tried to stay quiet through the course of the meal, he was dragged through a gauntlet of idle queries by David. *Maranan. Is that a Thai name?* Filipino. *Did you grow up in the Philippines?* Nope. I was born and raised in San Francisco. *How old are you?* I'm twenty-three. *Do you have any siblings?* No. Just a whole mess of cousins.

"What made you decide on law school?" Zack asked.

Theo massaged his liberated wrist while he danced through the minefield of his past.

"Honestly, I don't know. I'm from a big clan of overachievers. There was a lot of pressure to be someone. I think the plan was to get my JD, then a few years of public crusading, then local politics, then national politics, and then . . . I don't know. My own monument, I guess. Something in a nice onyx."

Zack smiled. He knew he liked Theo for a reason. "What did you do after you left?"

Theo's dark chuckle was enough to make Zack regret the question. "Let's just say I bummed around for a while."

Hannah stroked her lip as she recalled their first conversation. He'd called himself a rehab washout, a blight on the family tree who'd tried to hang himself at least once. She didn't think a lousy time at law school would be enough to send him on such a spiral.

David stirred his carrots with an idle fork. "How long have you been an alcoholic?"

"David!"

He looked to Amanda in surprise. "What? We're all friends here. Must we pretend?"

In the wake of Mia's stern glare, David sighed at Theo with grudging reproach. "If I crossed any lines of decorum, I sincerely apologize."

Theo grinned softly. If anything, the faux pas made him appreciate David now. The kid was a fellow misfit, all brains and no wisdom. He reminded Theo of himself, in better days.

"It's okay, David. You're not the first one to bring it up. And you're right. I've had a problem for . . . shit, it started about two years after law school, so it's been at least five years."

"That's a long time," David said.

"You're telling me."

Zack furrowed his brow. "Wait. You said you're twenty-three."

"I am," Theo responded, with a weary exhale. *Here we go again.*

"And yet you dropped out of law school seven years ago."

"I did."

Hannah shook her head in amazement. "Holy crap. You were *sixteen*?"

Theo shrugged nonchalantly. "I told you I came from a clan of over-achievers."

"That goes beyond overachieving," Amanda remarked. "You're a full-on prodigy."

He shrugged again. "Well, that's what they called me, but I never thought I was particularly brilliant. Just good at tests. In any case, I did a fine job squandering any promise I might have had. I flamed out early, then went on to do very stupid things. I won't bother you with details. I'll just say that when my karma finally comes rolling around, you're not going to want to be anywhere near me. You're going to want to find another planet."

Upon seeing the heavy sets of eyes around the table, Theo felt a pang of guilt for darkening their day. His inner demon wanted to keep on pushing, to list his crimes and grievances in such exquisite detail that none of them would speak to him again. He'd become quite adept at burning bridges, and there was a certain comfort in setting these five flames in advance.

Indeed, just twelve hours later, Mia received a rolled-up warning from future times.

Don't let Theo push you away. He's a good man who's hanging by a thread. He needs you all. The time will come when everyone will need him.

And I mean everyone.

———

Three days after the presentation, Quint finally agreed to remove the clamp from the lumivision. Czerny unlocked the console to the whole broadcast spectrum—thirty-nine channels, no waiting.

"Just thirty-nine?" Zack asked.

Czerny assumed Zack was joking. To Europeans like himself, even thirty-nine channels smacked of American overindulgence.

Despite the simple geographical hierarchy, the Silvers had an impossible time telling the stations apart by content. Whether it was National-1, Southwest-6, or San Diego-13, it was all the same archaic tripe. The sitcoms were filled with pratfalls and slide whistles. The dramas were as bland as meringue. Even the advertisements were blunt, unsophisticated objects—suit-clad spokesmen delivering the joys of soapsheets to fluffy-haired housewives.

Soon only Zack had the stomach to watch live programs. He lingered mostly on newscasts, and ran to Czerny whenever he encountered some impenetrable word or phrase.

"The reporters keep referring to some people as Deps. What are those?"

"Nickname for Domestic Protections agents," Czerny replied. "They're our federal law enforcers. Our FBI, as you call them."

"What are predictives?"

"Predictives are illegal pills that supposedly allow people to channel their 'inner temporis' and see the future. It's all bunk. Most are just cheap hallucinogens."

"Why does the anchorman close out each newscast by telling me to 'keep walking'?"

"It's just an American way of saying 'Be well.' Dates back to a famous Roosevelt speech. I mean Teddy Roosevelt. I keep forgetting your history has two."

One news report shook Zack to the core, a nostalgic look at the reconstruction of Manhattan. In the wake of the Cataclysm, the world's greatest engineers came together to design a second-draft city, one that would carry the island into the next century and beyond. The present-day New York was a marvel to look at, with brilliant glass spires of all shapes and colors, tempic tubes that connected buildings at the highest floors, ethereal ghost billboards, and ten different levels of aer traffic. The images reduced Zack to wet-eyed wonder.

As August turned to September, the others began to notice a change in Zack's behavior. His once relentless wit died down to the occasional lazy quip. He spent more time alone in his room. When asked if he was okay, he merely replied with one-word answers. *Sure. Yup. Spiffy.*

On September 3, David and Mia played an impromptu game of "red hands" in the lobby, giggling as they attempted to thwart each other's palm slaps. Zack watched from his drawing chair, stone-faced, until he suddenly dropped his sketchbook and marched upstairs to Quint's office. For once the cartoonist met him with a serious face.

"You remember our deal, Sterling? About the money?"

"Of course. A thousand dollars for each of you. For each week of your continued cooperation."

"Right. Tomorrow it'll be six weeks."

Quint's stomach lurched. "And your point in bringing this up?"

"You know why," Zack replied. "Get your cash together. I'm leaving."

The Silvers' next meal was a loud one.

"For God's sake, Zack! Why?"

He'd announced his upcoming departure with drab triviality, as if he were merely changing e-mail addresses. The others weren't so blasé.

"I mean, what will you do when the money runs out?" Hannah asked. "Street caricatures? You gonna go door-to-door offering to freshen up vegetables?"

Zack smirked. "I like that. I'll start a whole business. They'll call me the Wandering Juve."

"This isn't funny! This is the rest of your life!"

"Right. My life. My decision. And I decided enough is enough. Every day I stay here, I feel more and more like Quint's house cat. I eat his food. I lounge on his chairs. I beg for information about the world when I should be out there seeing it for myself."

"But where will you go?" Mia asked.

"I'll make my way to New York. If it's anything like my hometown, it's still

Alien Central, which means there'll be people hiring under the table. I'll work for a living. And when I'm not working, I'll look for my brother."

The dining room grew quiet as the others retreated into thought. David came back first.

"Zack, I'm going to be blunt with you in a way you won't like. I say this because I respect you—"

"Just spit it out already."

"You won't find your brother," David said. "Even on the slim chance that a handful of people in New York received bracelets like we did, there's no guarantee Josh is one of them. And even if he was, you're not going to find him in a city of eight million people. It's just unrealistic."

Zack tensely shrugged. "I suppose it is. But if there's a chance, even a small one, I have to try."

"And to hell with us, right?"

From the moment he dropped his news, Zack had simmered in the heat of Amanda's harsh green glare. Her cast had come off an hour ago. She held her mended wrist, wiggling her fingers as if she were playing an invisible trumpet.

"I don't enjoy the thought of leaving you guys," Zack insisted. "In fact, anyone who wants to join me is more than welcome."

"Bullshit. You never asked. You never even tried to convince us."

He looked at Amanda in flummox. "Wait. You're mad because I didn't ask you to come with me?"

"No, I'm mad because you decided to leave us all without a second thought. You're the most adaptable one out of all of us. Maybe we need you. Maybe you need us. Maybe it would hurt you to lose the only people you know from your world. Did any of that occur to you? Or does none of it matter because you're feeling antsy?"

"If you think I came to this decision lightly—"

"That's *exactly* what I think."

Sitting silent and rigid at the far end of the table, Theo awkwardly scanned his companions. He'd been an erratic presence in their lives over the last two weeks. Some days he'd join them for all three meals. Other days he'd never leave his second-floor sanctum. He wished today had been one of those other days. He felt like a guest at a family brawl.

Hannah held Zack's wrist. "Look, we get your decision . . ."

"*She* doesn't," he snarled, in Amanda's direction.

"She wants you to stay. We all do. We just don't understand the rush. Why can't you wait a month or two?"

"You think we'll be any more prepared? It's been two weeks since Quint's presentation. Have there been any follow-ups? Where's the net-accessible computer he promised us ten days ago? Wake up, Hannah. He *wants* us to stay clueless. He wants us to be scared and dependent on him, because we're his meal ticket."

Mia anxiously twisted her napkin. She agreed with everything Zack said and hated the fact that Quint's scheme was working. The thought of facing the outside world still terrified her.

"I'd go if we all went," she meekly offered.

David tapped the face of his wristwatch in absent bother. "That's not going to happen. I'm sorry, Mia, but I see no need to leave this place."

"I do," Amanda declared. "But I'm not ready."

"Me neither," said Hannah, with a tender glance at Zack. "Look, you're right. It's your life and you know what you're doing. It just breaks my heart to lose you. It would kill me to learn that something bad happened to you out there on your own."

Amanda reeled with envy at her sister's warm finesse with men. Even as a child, Hannah's effortless charm had boys falling all over her. She disarmed them as easily as Amanda set them on edge.

Zack's tense brow unfurled. He patted Hannah's wrist. "I'm sorry. I didn't want to start a whole drama. But after everything that's happened, I just can't stay here anymore. I have to get out and do something."

He pushed his chair back and stood up.

"I need a purpose."

As Zack retreated from the table, his companions glumly stared at their half-eaten dinners. Theo blew a hot sigh through his nose.

"I'll go."

Zack turned around at the door, wearing the same look of surprise as the others. Theo himself seemed caught unaware by the announcement. He had no clue where his idea came from, but assumed it wasn't a place of bravery.

"I'll go with you," he said. "If that's all right."

Quint's lantern jaw went slack as he continued to monitor the discussion from his office. Azral had already assured him that Trillinger's departure was an acceptable loss. The cartoonist was expendable and wouldn't be missed. But if Zack turned his exit into an exodus, if he convinced even one of the crucial Silvers to escape with him . . .

The handphone on Quint's desk suddenly lit up with a new text message.

<Maranan must not leave.>

Quint rubbed his eyes in tension. Of course. Of course Azral already knew. He stroked his neck in dark contemplation before keying a reply.

<Maybe we should dispose of Trillinger. Convince the others that he left alone, without word. They'd believe it. And if they hear he died in travel, it would be ages before any of them dared to leave this place.>

Azral responded immediately. <You'd do this?>

Quint scowled at the screen. He was hoping Azral would do the dirty work himself. Of course it wouldn't be that easy.

<You once told me your project was for the greater good,> Quint typed.

<A greater good than you can possibly imagine.>

The esteemed physicist could only sigh.

<Then yes. I reckon I would do it.>

Four minutes later, Azral's final message arrived. Quint could see the smile behind the words.

<I chose you well, Sterling. Do this right and we'll have much to discuss.>

Quint leaned back in his chair and pondered the variables of this new equation. He promised Zack he'd have his parting cash on Monday. That gave him two and a half days to plan his attack. Two and a half days to rid the world of a man who shouldn't exist at all.

The rest of the weekend was tense for all six Silvers. The sisters snapped at each other over silly little trifles. Mia barely left her suite. David followed Zack around like a cloud of doom, raining negative scenarios about his impending journey. Zack was, as David cautioned, a fairly obvious Semite on a solitary trek through a regressed American south. Zack told him it sounded like a great screenplay, then reminded him he wouldn't be traveling alone.

"Yes you will," David attested. "You'll lose Theo at the first liquor store. If you're lucky, he won't steal all your money beforehand."

Though Zack scoffed at the unkind notion, it had already made several laps around his own head. Even Theo found the idea far too credible for his liking. His tricky demon never stopped reminding him that sweet relief could be found just outside the property. It filled him with increasing dread about staying there. By the end of the weekend, the voice in his head had fallen to abject panic. *Get out. Get out. Get out now.*

Of all the Silvers, none seemed more anxious than Future Mia.

On Sunday night, the younger Farisi received four portal dispatches. The messages ranged from the obscure to the alarming:

The steering column is the gearshift. Press the white triggers on the inside of the wheel to switch the van out of Park.

The motorcycles have sped ahead to set up a tempic barrier on the highway. There's no getting around it, but Zack will know how to get through it.

The winter blonde's name is Krista Bloom. Use it. It may buy you a few seconds.

The fourth and most disturbing note had been scrawled across an entire ripped page, filled with a large and shaky version of Mia's handwriting. The author was clearly not in a good state.

Do not let Amanda get out of the van. Listen to me, you stupid girl. Do not let Amanda get out of the van. If she gets out of the van, they will shoot her. They will shoot her and she will die.

Mia's hands trembled as she transcribed the notes into her book. Her sunniest thought was that all these warnings were from a future that, for one reason or another, had become moot. Or perhaps these events wouldn't occur for years to come.

At midnight, a final message dropped to her bedspread. The ivory scrap had been ripped straight from her journal, the words written hastily in bloodred ink.

They hit you all at sunrise. Sleep with your shoes on. Get ready to run.

TWELVE

Erin Salgado was the first to meet the newest guests.

As the pink light of dawn washed over the premises, she carried her gun down the winding driveway. She had no idea what to expect from her last-minute patrol. All she knew was that Mia had scared her something fierce.

Shortly after midnight, Erin had spotted the girl on camera, fretfully pacing the third-floor hallway. Mia paused at David's door in dilemma, then Amanda's, then Zack's, and then repeated the cycle all over again.

Soon Erin went upstairs to find her. "Honey, are you okay?"

Mia hugged her journal, her face a quivering mask. "I don't know what to do. I don't want to start a whole panic over nothing. I mean I once got a note saying 'Don't trust Peter,' and then another note saying to disregard the first note. So I've gotten bad messages before."

Erin stroked Mia's shoulders, hopelessly lost. The physicists didn't go out of their way to explain things to the Salgados. Most of what the family knew was gleaned through surveillance and eavesdropping. Erin had overheard some very odd chatter about Mia.

"Is there any way I can help?"

Mia's eyes lit up. "Can I come with you to the security room? Is that where you see everything?"

Erin knew her clients would frown upon her bringing one of the subjects into the monitoring station, but Mia had a way of tugging her heartstrings. They were both husky gals, both from a large family of men. Erin could only imagine how she'd be if she lost her dad and brothers.

She took Mia downstairs to the cramped little office that, to everyone on night watch, had become synonymous with boredom. As Mia perched at the console and watched the nine color screens, Erin sat behind her and twisted her long hair into braids.

"What exactly are you looking for, kitten?"

"I have no idea. It's probably too early to see them anyway."

Erin eyed her nervously. "People here are saying you can tell the future. Is that true?"

"I don't tell the future," Mia replied, through a gaping yawn. "The future tells me."

At 3 A.M., she finally succumbed to fatigue. Erin led her to the worn green couch at the back of the room and draped a blanket over her.

"Wake me up before sunrise," Mia mumbled. "They're supposed to hit at sunrise."

Unnerved, Erin popped a can of orange vim, then resumed the monitoring. At 6 A.M., her twin brother Eric arrived to relieve her. He eyed Mia quizzically.

"Let her sleep," Erin whispered. "She had a bad night."

"What, like nightmares?"

"I think so." *I hope so,* she thought. Otherwise, trouble was coming right about now.

Instead of driving straight home, as her weary thoughts demanded, Erin drew her pistol and took a cautious sweep around the perimeter of the building. She walked down to the front gates, testing them. The property was sealed within a ten-foot iron fence. Good enough to keep most stragglers out.

By the time Erin returned to the family van, the sun had climbed above the trees. She stashed her gun and texted her brother.

Okay. This is silly. I'm going home. Keep an eye on M

A reflective gleam caught her eye. She turned to spy a wiry man standing on the front lawn, forty feet away. He cut an ominous figure in his dark jeans and black leather jacket. Erin couldn't see his face through the shaded visor of his motorcycle helmet, but he was clearly looking at her.

The gleam had come from the three-foot Japanese sword in his right hand.

Wide-eyed, Erin reached for her gun. Her fingers barely touched the holster before the man sped past her in a dark blur. She felt a hot blast of air, then an odd tug in her midsection. Erin Salgado considered the very strange thing she just witnessed, then fell to the ground in two pieces.

Eric was pouring sugar into his coffee when his sister's death occurred on the upper-right screen. It wasn't until the image looped back to the driveway, fifty-five seconds later, that he glimpsed the long blood spatter on the side of the van. His coffee mug shattered on the floor.

"Erin!"

Mia woke up, startled, as Eric sped past her. He ran down the hall and stopped short at the lobby. Two intruders stood by the reception desk. One was petite and unseasonably dressed in thick winter clothes. A long blond ponytail poured from a hole in the back of her ski mask. The other was tall and wore a simple gray tracksuit. His face was covered in a rubber novelty mask molded in the smiling semblance of Teddy Roosevelt.

Both strangers turned to Eric as he reflexively aimed his pistol.

"Don't—"

With fearful eyes, the woman raised her hand. A quick burst of light enveloped Eric, freezing him solid in an instant. Everything within five feet of him glistened with a fresh coat of frost.

The man in the Roosevelt mask flicked his wrist, causing long tempic whips to emerge from his fingers. They broke off little pieces of Eric, toppling his corpse like a statue.

The woman glared at her companion. "Why'd you do that?"

"I wanted to see if he'd shatter."

"You really are sick."

"Maybe. But you're the one who killed him when you could've just frozen his gun."

The blonde looked at her victim in dismay. Winter mist escaped with each shallow breath.

"I panicked."

"No fooling. You need to mettle up, honey. We haven't even started yet."

She glared at him. "Just go upstairs and help Rebel. I'll take care of the one down here."

Mia swallowed her scream. She'd witnessed Eric's death on the monitor and now frantically scanned the security console for something, anything that could help. One button caught her attention: hot red, with a flame-shaped icon.

She slammed it hard, and the building came to life.

Czerny launched awake in the futon. A chain of loud *woops* filled his office. The entire ceiling flashed with red lumis. He scrambled for his shirt.

Beatrice blinked at him several times, holding the blanket to her naked chest. "What's going on? Is it a fire?"

"Don't know. I'm hoping it's just a glitch."

Czerny donned his glasses and keyed a three-digit number into his desk phone. He was surprised to find a frightened girl on the other end of the line.

"Hello?" she said, in a frantic half whisper. "Who is this?"

"This is Dr. Czerny. Who . . . Sorry, I was expecting someone else. Who am I speaking to?"

"It's me! It's Mia!"

"Mia? What's going on? Why are you in the security room? Where's the guard on duty?"

"He's frozen or petrified. And I think Erin's hurt. I see four different people on the monitors. One of them's really big and he has a gun."

"My God!"

"There's a woman in a ski mask. I think she's coming this way. I don't know what to do!"

Panicked by proxy, Beatrice rushed to get dressed. Czerny cradled the phone and finished buttoning his shirt.

"Okay, Mia. Listen to me. I want you to stay calm. If you haven't already locked the door—"

"I locked it. And I pushed the couch in front of it."

"Good. Smart girl. Now I want you to deactivate the fire alarm. Just press the red button twice."

"Should I? I mean—"

"Mia, please trust me, all right?"

Five seconds later, the clamor came to a stop. The emergency lights disappeared.

"Good. Good, Mia. Now you just stay where you are. Help is coming."

"I think they all have a—"

He hung up before she could finish. For lack of a better term, she was about to say "weirdness."

Beatrice clutched his arm. "Constantin, what's going on?"

He fished a small item from her purse, a gray metal gadget that resembled a baby air horn.

"If our youngest guest hasn't lost her poor mind, then I fear we have armed intruders."

"Oh my God! Should I call the police?"

"No. Call Martin. Get him and his son to come as quickly as possible. Then call the fire service and tell them it was a false alarm."

Beatrice peered anxiously at the little weapon in his hand. "You're not seriously going out there with my chaser, are you?"

"If I had my pistol, love, I'd be wielding that."

"Don't go! You'll get killed!"

Czerny caressed her cheek. The two of them had come together six weeks ago, under the influence of red wine and scientific exuberance. They'd been together almost every night since. It was the worst-kept secret in the building. Even the Silvers knew.

"Stay here," he told her. "Stay hidden. Don't come out until I tell you it's safe."

"But what if they come looking for me?"

With a heavy sigh, Czerny opened the door. He had the strong urge to tell Beatrice he loved her. Instead he remained ever practical.

"I don't think we're the ones they're after."

Thirty seconds after the alarm stopped, the two oldest Silvers emerged from their suites. Zack had taken the time to get decent in a shirt and sweatpants. Amanda was content to let her T-shirt hang down over her underwear. As Zack's higher functions pondered the circumstances behind his rude awakening, his sleepy id admired her long and shapely legs.

"Hellooo, nurse."

Amanda threw him a cool squint. She had yet to forgive him for his impending exit.

"What was that? The fire alarm?"

"Sounded like it," said Zack. "It's probably a glitch."

Or a trick, he mused. Though Zack knew Quint wasn't his biggest admirer, the little man had been far too cavalier about losing one of his alien specimens. He must have had something up his sleeve.

David stepped out of his room, fully dressed in a T-shirt, jeans, and sneakers. He glanced around the hall, his handsome face lined with worry.

"Where are the others?"

Zack shrugged. "Still in bed, I guess."

"Lovely. Why get up for something as trifling as fire?"

"I don't think it's a real fire," Amanda said.

David knocked on Mia's door three times before pushing it open. He scanned the room.

"She's not in there," he said.

"What?"

Amanda rushed across the hall and thumped on Hannah's door. David hurried to the stairwell.

"Where are you going?" Zack asked him.

"First floor. She might be in the kitchenette."

"Amanda's right. It's probably a false alarm."

"It can't hurt to see if she's okay. And it won't hurt you to check on Theo."

As David disappeared down the steps, Amanda opened the door to Hannah's room. She looked inside, then checked the bathroom. Her sister was nowhere to be found.

Three minutes earlier, just as Erin Salgado finished her sweep of the rear property, Hannah stepped out to the patio and stretched her calves. Her inner clock had become muddled from all the time-shifting she was doing. For the fifth day in a row, she woke up at the crack of dawn with no hope of falling back to sleep.

On Thursday, Charlie Merchant suggested that she try something called exertion therapy, a tight regimen of exercise and catnaps, all strategically timed to loosen the body's circadian rhythm. Hannah wondered if it would be easier just to get her exertion from Charlie himself. He was kind of cute for an egghead.

Once her limbs were sufficiently loosened, she straightened her tank top and trotted along the path that looped around the property. She made it only fifty feet before the building alarm sounded. Hannah could only guess that she'd triggered it somehow, since no one else was awake at this ungodly hour.

Wincing at the thought of all the apologies she'd have to offer, she dashed back to the patio. She caught a quick gleam in the reflective glass of the door, then spun around. No one.

Something in the air felt strange, the same smoky aura that Hannah had come to associate with speeding. Once the alarm stopped, Hannah heard a noise that sounded like a flat and heavy drumroll.

The hairs on her arms stood up. A tiny voice in her head offered urgent advice.

Shift.

She flipped the switch in her mind. Once again the world turned blue and sluggish. The drumbeat slowed to the sound of hurried footsteps. She turned around in the shadow of a six-foot man in a motorcycle helmet. Another half second of hidden advantage and his sword would have lopped her head off.

As it was, Hannah had just enough time to scream and duck.

The man overshot, stumbling over a patio chair. White-eyed, Hannah jumped back. Unlike everything else around her, the man existed at a normal speed and color. She could see every glistening red speck on his blade, his clothes. Her throat closed when she considered the notion that she was looking at her sister's blood.

Hannah fled, and the Motorcycle Man followed. He'd been walking at a brisk pace until his quarry decided to shift. Now he was forced to run.

Czerny paused in the stairwell, debating his next move. Should he go up and warn the others or go down and help Mia? The girl was safely barricaded in the security room, but there were also tools in there that could help the situation—weapons, surveillance monitors, a building-wide intercom system.

He went down.

Five steps into his descent, a tall man popped around the corner and stepped onto the landing. He and Czerny jumped at the sight of each other, then reflexively raised their hands in battle. Unfortunately for Czerny, his trigger finger was delayed by two perplexing observations about his opponent: his rubber Teddy Roosevelt mask and the fact that he'd aimed nothing but his bare palm. For a crucial split second, Czerny took it as a stop sign, a call for mercy to the man with the upper hand. It wasn't.

A tempic tendril burst from the stranger's fingers, snaking ten feet up the stairwell and embedding itself in Czerny's gut. The physicist screamed as the Roosevelt Man twisted his thoughts, causing the engorged end of the projectile to expand and bloom thorns.

Half-blind with agony, Czerny raised the electron chaser in his hand and fired.

Temporis and electricity had a complex relationship. While one could be used to generate the other, electric current proved stubborn to most forms of temporal manipulation. It couldn't be advanced, reversed, sped up, or slowed down. It could, however, be steered through the air with laser precision, a development that made power cables a thing of the past. It also allowed for some interesting new weapons.

The moment the invisible bolt struck the Roosevelt Man, his tempic tendril disappeared and he stumbled backward over the railing. He fell nine feet, cracking his skull on the reception desk before crumpling into a motionless heap on the marble.

Czerny dropped the chaser and examined his bleeding stomach. He knew from battlefield experience that abdominal wounds, while painful, were typically slow to kill. With the proper triage, he'd have hours to get himself to a reviver.

His legs grew weak. He teetered backward. In his feeble attempt to gain balance, his heel slipped on a patch of his own blood.

He went down again.

The Motorcycle Man moved faster than Hannah. He gained yards on her every time she looked back.

Their high-speed foot chase took them past the front of the building. As soon as Hannah passed the entrance, she felt the man's cool glove on the strap of her shirt. He'd been running too fast to swing his katana. His goal now was to pull her down.

Frenzied, Hannah broke to the left, toward the green van parked in the driveway. She spied a pair of heavy boots on the far side of the vehicle, toes pointed upward. Beyond them, Erin's freckled arms lay prone on the asphalt.

The last working piston in Hannah's brain registered the sight as two dead Salgados, until she turned the corner around the van and saw just one woman in two places.

Suddenly her mind and limbs all quit in synch. She fell to the lawn.

The actress wriggled away on her stomach, gasping in panic. The Motorcycle Man de-shifted and approached her at a leisurely pace. His sword swayed idly in his grip.

Hannah flipped over and scuttled backward out of his shadow. "Why are you doing this? What did I do to you?"

The Motorcycle Man stood over her, pointing his blade at her stomach. All he had to do was lean in and she'd be impaled through the gut, stabbed on the grass like park litter.

It was at that moment that Hannah discovered something hard beneath her. As the Motorcycle Man leaned into his stab, she screamed into velocity. She rolled over, grabbed the rock from the grass, and then hurled it with all her strength.

It flew from her hand at 205 miles an hour and careened off her aggressor's helmet. The visor cracked. His balance teetered. He toppled back to the grass.

Hannah climbed to her feet and lunged toward him in a furious streak, thumping his chest as he made his slow-motion fall.

"You asshole! You killed her! You cut her to pieces!"

Hannah hit him five times before he collided with the ground. On her final punch, she felt something snap inside his rib cage. She chucked his sword over the gate and then watched him writhe from a safe distance. She knew she should go inside and check on the others, but she couldn't seem to work her muscles. A cruel little voice in her head insisted that the people she cared about were already gone. *Everyone dies, Hannah. You should know that by now. Every friend. Every sister. Everyone under the sky.*

The actress crumpled to her knees at the base of the fence. She wept at high speed.

Mia cursed her future self for not teaching her the security console. In her frantic button-mashing, she'd somehow constrained her surveillance images to the second-floor cameras—six in test labs, two in the hallway, one in Theo's room. The former prodigy was awake and fully dressed. He nervously paced the rug with a wooden post in his hand, a leg he'd unscrewed from his desk chair. He'd been on high alert since 5 A.M. without having any idea why.

Through the monitors, Mia saw a very good reason for him to be scared.

A bald-headed gunman patrolled the hallway at a methodical pace, as if sniffing for prey. Though Mia couldn't tell his height from her bird's-eye vantage, he carried the thick frame of a wrestler. His sleeveless black T-shirt advertised every bulge of his powerful arms. His face was concealed by a bandana mask and sunglasses.

Mia didn't know if he was moving farther or closer to Theo. All she could see was that his revolver looked powerful enough to shoot through walls.

For the third time, she grabbed the public address microphone and furiously hit its buttons.

"Theo? Theo, can you hear me?"

He kept pacing, oblivious. Mia cursed again.

The intruder suddenly ducked into a lab. He placed his back against the wall, aiming a vigilant gaze through the door crack. He was ambushing someone. Who?

On the second hallway monitor, Zack popped into view. Mia blanched.

"Oh my God . . ."

The cartoonist stepped off the landing with a listless yawn. He wasn't fully awake yet, and he was nervous about all the wrong things. His mind was still trying to predict Quint's next move.

He saw the door to Quint's office and fought the temptation to reverse the lock. Maybe his parting cash was already in there. Or maybe he would find some smoking-gun evidence that would convince the others to leave with him. The closer Zack got to his departure with Theo, the worse he felt about splintering the group.

Sighing, he abandoned his burglary scheme. Odds were slim he'd find anything useful in there. And knowing Quint, he probably trained his mice to attack.

He continued down the hall, glancing in perplexity at the many unmarked doors. He cupped his hands around his mouth and projected his voice.

"Uh, hey, Theo? It's Zack. Just thought I'd play fire marshal and see if you're okay. The thing is, I don't know which room is yours. Can you give me a yell? Or better yet, come out?"

After ten more seconds and two more calls, Zack reeled with fresh unease. Three of his friends seemed to be missing in action. *Half my world's population,* he bleakly mused.

"Okay, Theo, I'm at orange alert now. Last chance to speak up before I get twitchy."

Theo kept his back to his door, his face trembling. He couldn't bring himself to move. His higher functions and lower instincts seemed united in the fear that Zack would die if he made a sound.

Frustrated, Zack began testing locked doors. He soon noticed one that was open a crack.

As he touched the knob, a tinny squeal filled the building, loud enough to make him wince. Mia's high voice blared down from the ceiling.

"—*AWAY* FROM THERE! THERE'S A GUY WITH A GUN IN THERE! ZACK!"

The door flung open. A large man shoved Zack across the corridor, pinning him against the elevator doors. Hot air escaped his lungs.

The intruder pressed his gun to Zack's temple. Mia screamed through the speakers.

"NO! I ALREADY CALLED THE POLICE! THEY'LL BE HERE ANY SECOND!"

The man kept his gaze and his muzzle fixed. He spoke in a deep graveled voice, peppered with the unmistakable inflections of a native New Yorker.

"Would you please do something about the girl?"

Zack shook his head. "I don't know what you want me to—"

"I wasn't talking to you."

Zack could see a small microphone clipped to the man's collar.

Mia debated extending her bluff. In truth, she had no luck reaching anyone on the phone. The concepts of 0 and 911 were purely old-America. There were no signs, no stickies, no wisdom again from Future Mia on how to reach the authorities.

She suddenly felt a deep chill on her skin. She saw the steam of her own breath. Mia turned around, just as the door to the security room grew white with frost. It creaked. It splintered.

The moment the gun touched his skin, Zack lost his foothold on time. He existed in a breathless state of suspension, in which every sensation and detail was exponentially magnified. He could feel each bead of sweat on his skin, count every peach-fuzz hair on the scalp of his assailant. He could see through the man's sunglasses, into his dark brown eyes. *Early thirties. Italian. Maybe Jewish. Doesn't look crazy. Doesn't even look angry.*

For all his hyperclarity, Zack couldn't reach the trigger to his own special weapon. His weirdness rested deep on the other side of his mind, behind a cyclone of fearful distraction. He didn't want to die here. Not like this. Not without knowing why.

"Who are you? Why are you doing this?"

Without taking his eyes off Zack, the large man fired his gun at two different parts of the ceiling. Zack grimaced at the booming gunshots, then noticed the new glass fragments on the floor.

He shot the cameras. He shot both cameras without even looking.

The gunman pulled down his bandana. He had a wide and bumpy nose that had clearly been broken more than once, plus several tiny scars along his cheeks and chin. Zack could only guess that he'd been picking fights from the moment he left the crib.

"Folks call me Rebel, but that doesn't matter. All you need to know is that this is my world and you ripped a hole in it."

Zack spotted a hint of movement in the corner of his vision. He fought to keep his gaze on Rebel. "You think it was my choice to come here?"

"Doesn't matter either. The longer you people live, the worse the problem gets. I've seen the future, brother. I'll do whatever it takes to stop it from happening."

He pressed the gun to Zack's chest. What was once a cool muzzle now burned like a stove.

"No!" Zack yelled. "Just go! Go!"

"Sorry. This is how it's gotta be."

Zack wasn't talking to Rebel. Ten feet away, Theo continued his sneaking approach. He'd crept out of his room, chair leg in hand, then deftly skirted the broken glass on the floor.

Sadly, none of his stealth mattered. The moment he got within eight feet of Rebel, the man's muscular arm swung like a hinge.

He shot Theo without even looking.

Five seconds and fifty-one degrees ago, the microphone dropped from Mia's numb fingers. It crashed at her feet, among the shards of Eric Salgado's coffee mug.

She knew exactly how he died now.

A gloved fist struck the door, knocking away a frozen patch of wood. The blonde in the hall was barely an inch taller than Mia. The lines around her sharp blue eyes revealed her as an older woman. Mia could see from her thick white parka that she was also much, much warmer.

She registered Mia through a wide, unblinking stare. "God. You really are just a kid."

Mia desperately scanned her memory, trying to recall the note she'd received about the Winter Blonde. Her future self had given her the woman's full name and advised Mia to use it as a stalling tactic. For the life of her, she couldn't remember it now.

"I didn't do anything to you! Please don't kill me!"

The blonde's voice cracked with anguish. "I'm sorry. I don't want to do this. But I have a daughter your age. She has to live."

"What does that have to do with me?"

"I'm afraid it has everything to do with you. All of you. I'm so sorry. There's no other option."

The blonde took a step back. Thick tears ran under her mask.

"This'll be quick. I promise."

As Mia felt her entire future whittle down to milliseconds, she closed her eyes and thought about her family. If there was truly justice in the multiverse, then she would travel back across the great divide and rest in the afterlife with her dad, her brothers, and Nana. She didn't want to end up in this world's Heaven, where she'd only know one or two Salgados.

Suddenly a pair of radiant orbs materialized in front of the woman's eyes. She covered her face just as a piercing electronic squeal—an echo of the feedback that had blared from all speakers a minute ago—erupted inside her ears. She fell to the ground screaming.

By the time Mia dared to open her eyes, David faced her through the broken door. He pointed to a metal prod hanging on the wall.

"Can I have that, please?"

"What?"

"The baton, Mia. The zapper. I need it. Quickly."

With shaking hands, Mia tossed the weapon to David. He studied every side of it until he found the power switch. Now he jabbed the electric end at the back of the Winter Blonde's head. She shrieked again, then fell silent.

Mia stared at David, dumbfounded. "She was going to kill me."

"I know. I saw. Listen to me—"

"She was going to kill me!"

David grabbed her shoulder. "Mia, I know you're upset but you have to pull it together. Please. We're not safe yet."

Krista Bloom. Her name was Krista Bloom. Mia recalled the note now. Too little, too late. She remembered a few other things as well.

"Oh no! Zack!"

She spun around to the monitors, only to find that her view of the upstairs hallway had gone dark. The cameras had been shot and killed by a very dangerous man.

Theo slid down the blood-flecked wall. He couldn't help but wonder if his latest move had been a first attempt at heroics or merely a second try at suicide.

In either case, he knew he'd failed. A last-second twitch had thrust a less vital piece of himself into the path of the bullet. It cut a nasty gash across his arm, slicing the skin before piercing the wall. As he examined the mess below his T-shirt sleeve, his legs gave out and he slumped to the floor.

While keeping Zack pinned to the elevator, Rebel turned to look at Theo. Something had gone wrong. He'd foreseen the bullet's entire journey before pulling the trigger. In his thoughts, he watched it go right through Theo's heart.

Perplexed, Rebel re-aimed his weapon at Theo. Once again he took a glimpse into the immediate future, checking to see if his shot would connect.

The vision he received, though accurate, was not good news at all.

"No!"

He had just enough time to face Zack, right as the cartoonist rediscovered his weirdness.

Suddenly Rebel's gun flared with cool white light. A thousand needles of pain covered every corner of his hand. Bellowing, he dropped his gun and hostage.

Zack stumbled backward, startled by his results. He'd focused his thoughts on rusting Rebel's weapon. Now the revolver lay on the ground, nine weeks older but still very functional. Rebel's hand, however, had become a gruesome horror. The skin was white and bloodless, with scaly splotches of rot. His fingernails had turned a gangrenous black.

He lashed out with his good arm, striking Zack in the jaw and knocking him down to the carpet. Rebel stooped to reclaim his gun from the floor, testing its weight and feel in his left hand.

"Son of a bitch." He groaned as a new wave of pain overtook him. "I swear to God, if this kills me—"

Rebel's eyes suddenly rolled back in his head. He shuddered violently in place before crumpling to the floor.

Eight feet behind him, Amanda kept an anxious vigil from the stairway landing. Zack dazedly blinked at the peculiar little device she continued to aim at Rebel.

"What . . . what is that?"

She looked down at the electron chaser in her quivering hands.

"I don't know."

_____

She'd gone downstairs in search of Hannah and found Czerny instead.

The physicist lay on the stairwell, holding his bunched shirt to his stomach. His skin was pale, his breathing labored. He was lucid enough to tell Amanda which medical supplies could be found in which cabinets.

"Be careful," he wheezed. "There are still intruders."

The only stranger Amanda encountered in her trip to the medical lab was the man in the Teddy Roosevelt mask. He lay unmoving at the foot of the reception desk, a terrifying sight with his eerie rubber grin. Worse, Amanda could sense a familiar energy coursing inside him. He had the same beast as her. The tempis. From Czerny's grievous wound, it was clear how he enjoyed using it.

The moment she returned to Czerny's side, Mia's frightened voice filled every speaker in the building, warning Zack of an impending ambush.

Amanda covered her mouth. "Oh my God. Zack . . ."

"Where is he?" Czerny asked.

"I don't know. I went back to my room to get dressed. By the time I came out, he was gone."

They heard the sounds of struggle upstairs, followed by two loud gunshots.

Czerny thought of Beatrice, then fumbled for the chaser with a bloody hand. He thrust the weapon in Amanda's grip.

"Go help them," he implored her. "Please."

She did.

Amanda had no idea how long she stood in the hallway, aiming the chaser at the twitching man on the floor. Once her gaze fell to Theo, her nurse's mind took over.

He watched her anxiously as she examined his wound. "How bad is it?"

"You need stitches." She turned around. "Zack . . ."

The cartoonist climbed back to his feet, fixing his shell-shocked gaze on Rebel's rotted hand.

"Zack!"

He snapped out of his trance. Amanda motioned to the stairwell. "Dr. Czerny's badly hurt. We need to get him to a hospital. Can you get Theo downstairs?"

He wiped the blood from his mouth. "Yeah. Go help Czerny."

Amanda hurried back downstairs. Zack lifted Theo to his feet. They both kept a wary eye on Rebel.

"Jesus," Theo uttered. "What did we ever do to that guy?"

Zack wasn't sure he followed the man's vague account of ominous holes and preventable futures. All he knew, from looking at that hand, was that Rebel sure as hell had a reason to hate him now.

By the time Zack and Theo rejoined Amanda on the landing, the orphans had entered the lobby from the east hall. With a high cry of relief, Mia ran up the steps and wrapped her arms around Zack.

"Oh my God! I thought you were dead!"

Zack returned the hug, reeling with guilt. When he'd first decided to leave the others, he didn't think his absence would hurt them any more than the loss of a funny co-worker. In the wake of Mia's hug, her warm correction, he never felt so cruel.

"It's okay. I'm all right."

Amanda passed Zack a roll of sterile gauze and some alcohol wipes.

"Take Theo down to the couches. Clean his wound and wrap it as best you can. Mia, keep his arm raised above heart level. That'll slow down the bleeding." She looked down the steps. "David, where did you go?"

"Right below you."

Zack reached the ground floor and saw David kneeling at the side of the Roosevelt Man. The boy had two fingers pressed against the intruder's neck.

"Are you insane? Get away from him!"

David stood up. "I was just checking his pulse. It's weak but he's alive."

"Yeah, well, be careful. He still could get up."

Theo had the same concern about the large man upstairs. He'd snatched away Rebel's revolver, fiercely determined to keep it away from its owner.

Amanda peered over the railing. "David, go to the medical lab and find a stretcher. We need something to move Dr. Czerny."

David nodded, then left the way he came. Mia stared at Czerny's wound with nauseous dread.

"Will he be okay?"

"I'll be fine," Czerny weakly assured her. "Just have to get to a reviver."

"Can't Zack heal you now?"

"No," said Amanda and Zack, in unison.

"No offense to him," said Czerny, "but his healing experience is currently limited to a four-ounce mouse. Should he fail to capture all of me within his temporic field, the results would be far worse than my current predicament."

Zack turned his white gaze to Czerny. "Wait. What do you mean?"

The physicist grimaced as Amanda placed a bandage on his wound.

"To manipulate the flow of time on a living creature is to manipulate the flow of blood. If you reverse just part of a person, it creates chaos in the vascular system, which can lead to all things from blood clots to a fatal embolism. That's why revivers are full-body devices, and why shifters only work in enclosed spaces."

Zack felt a high scream in his throat. For all he knew, he'd just sent dozens of air bubbles on a murderous path to Rebel's heart. He may have just killed a man.

Throughout all the blood and chatter, Amanda kept glancing at the frozen corpse of Eric Salgado. She fought back tears.

"Can someone *please* go find my sister?"

"I'm here."

Hannah hobbled through the west archway, covered in scrapes and grass stains. She looked ten years older now, and utterly miserable.

Amanda moaned in relief. "Oh thank God! What happened?"

"Some asshole with a sword tried to kill me."

"Are you hurt?"

"I'm all right. I got lucky."

"Where's the sword guy now?" Theo asked Hannah.

"Out on the front lawn. I hit him with a . . . Jesus, Theo! What happened to you?"

"Got stupid. Got shot."

Mia glanced at the unconscious man on the floor. "I think that's all of them. I only saw four people on the monitors."

"I don't care," Zack said. "We're getting out of here. All of us."

"And going where?" Hannah asked.

Amanda finished placing her bandage on Czerny. "We have to get to the hospital as fast as we can."

Czerny debated the notion of mentioning Beatrice, who was still hiding in his office. He figured her best chance for survival was to stay here, away from the targets.

"How exactly are we getting there?" Theo asked.

"Driving," said David. He emerged from the north wing, an aerostretcher in one hand and a jingling key ring in the other. "I grabbed these from the security room. I assume one of them starts the Salgados' van."

Zack grabbed the keys from him. "Good thinking."

"Are you okay driving? I'm not sure how differently the vehicles operate here."

"I'll figure it out. Let's just go."

Mia looked through the windows at their escape vehicle. She recalled the warning she'd received ten hours ago about Amanda. *If she gets out of the van, they will shoot her. They will shoot her and she will die.*

A large round portal bloomed on the wall near Rebel. A tall figure emerged from the whiteness. She was a young woman of Indian descent, as slender and pretty as Amanda. Her hair hung in a braid that extended all the way down the back of her black nylon bodysuit.

Her dark eyes popped at the sight of Rebel. "Oh no! Richard!"

Ilavarasi Sunder was the only one who called him by his real name. As his match, his mate, it was her prerogative. He simply called her Ivy. They all did.

A second figure stepped through the gateway. Gemma Sunder was a slip of a girl, barely five feet tall. She wore a sleeveless silk blouse over a black leather miniskirt, plus a garish amount of makeup. Her appearance was pure defensive strategy, a way to minimize the fact that she was technically ten years old.

Upon seeing Rebel's unconscious frame, Gemma crossed her arms and scowled. "I warned him. I told him the breachers were fast learners."

Ivy glared at her niece. "I don't have time for your attitude. Just give me the picture."

"Working on it."

Once the MacDougals stepped through the portal, Ivy closed it shut. The redheaded brothers were short and stocky, and utterly indistinguishable from each other except for the color of their tracksuits.

The twins helped Ivy roll Rebel onto his back. She screamed when she saw his withered hand.

"Oh God, he's been rifted!"

"He'll be okay," Gemma said. "He won't—"

The girl's head suddenly jerked back as if she just woke up from a nap. She looked to the stairwell in hot alarm.

"They're getting into a van. Right now. They're leaving and they're not coming back."

"Damn it!" Ivy shot to her feet, then pushed the MacDougals to the stairs. "Go!"

The brother in green pointed to his concerned face, then the ceiling.

"Forget the cameras!" Ivy yelled. "Just go! Stop them! Kill as many as you can!"

The weather inside Mia's head was wet and foggy. She could barely hold a thought as she watched her friends in action. While Zack hurried around to the driver's side of the van, David helped Amanda load Czerny's stretcher into the back. Hannah stayed to the side with Theo, propping up his wounded arm as he kept a nervous eye on the lobby. Everyone seemed to have a task. Mia could only clutch her journal and ponder Krista Bloom, a woman who didn't seem particularly crazy or evil. Why did she want them dead? Why did she make it sound so crucial?

She noticed Erin's boots on the other side of the van and mindlessly moved toward them.

"Mia! No!"

With a burst of speed, Hannah blocked her way. "You don't want to see that. She's . . . gone."

"But that's Erin."

"I know. I know it is. But if you see her like that, that's all you're going to see whenever you think of her. Please trust me."

Mia idly reached behind her head, to the fading braids that Erin had tied six hours ago. She bit her lip to keep from crying.

David poked his head out the back doors. "Ladies, we need to go."

"I need someone up front with me," Zack yelled.

Hannah moved to the passenger door and climbed inside. She saw Zack fumble the key ring with shaking hands. For him, there was no avoiding the sight of Erin Salgado. He had to step over her bisected corpse to enter the van.

The actress put a calming hand on his arm. He looked at her. "You saw her."

She grimly nodded. Zack suppressed the mad screaming fit that had been eluding him since day one.

"Goddamn it. Goddamn it."

David tapped on the metal mesh that separated the front seats from the back. "Dr. Czerny says the hospital's not far. Make a left at the front gate, then keep going for two miles."

"Okay."

Hannah spotted rapid movement through the lobby windows. "Oh no . . ."

David pressed against the grate. "Two more are coming this way, Zack! We need to go!"

"I'm trying!"

The Salgado family had three vans, four cars, and two motorcycles between them. All keys were present, and none seemed to fit the ignition.

The front doors of the building swung open. A pair of stout, red-haired twins stepped outside. They fixed their stoic gazes on the Silvers.

Hannah cocked her head at them. "Why are they just standing there?"

The MacDougals each raised their outer arm, aiming an open palm at the van.

Theo went pale. "Shit. I don't like this . . ."

Zack jabbed another key at the ignition. "What? What are they doing?"

A loud metallic squeal filled the van. Suddenly the passenger-side windows turned cloudy and cracked.

Hannah looked up at the creaking roof. "Are they crushing us?"

Amanda rooted through the first aid kit, struggling to stay focused on her task. Czerny's skin had turned cool and clammy. He'd lost too much blood. He was slipping into shock.

Mia kept her tense gaze on her. "Amanda, you have to promise me you won't leave this van."

"What?"

"I got a note—"

"David, keep Theo's arm raised!" Amanda lifted Czerny's legs to push circulation. She glared at Zack through the grate. "Would you start the damn van already?"

"I'm looking for the right key!"

"Amanda, you have to promise me you won't leave this van until I tell you it's safe!"

"Okay, Mia! I won't! I promise!"

Hannah screamed as a door hinge came loose. Patches of rust grew along the edge of the windows.

"They're not crushing the van," David said. "They're aging it."

Cursing, Zack isolated the failed keys, then held the ring out to Hannah. "Take over."

"What are you doing?"

"I'm undoing! Just go!"

Hannah grabbed the ring and bent uncomfortably toward the ignition. Her door let out another rusty groan. She tried not to think what would happen if the twins got an open line of attack on her.

Zack concentrated on the windshield, reversing away the clouds and cracks. He could see the blue-suited brother in front of the van, raising a palm at the hood.

"Shit. He's going for the engine."

David pressed against the metal mesh. "Open the gate!"

"What?"

"I can take him, but you need to open the gate!"

Zack slid the grating. David squeezed his upper body through the opening and aimed a hand at the attacking twin. Suddenly the man's head became enveloped in seven-year-old construction noise, localized and amplified for maximum effect. The twin covered his ears, wincing in agony.

"Good, David. Good!"

"Just get us out of here!"

"I'm trying!" Hannah screamed.

Fortunately, her sixth key was the right one. The electric motor came to life with a loud whirr.

"I got it! I got it! Go!"

Zack reflexively reached for the space where a gearshift would be. There was nothing there but a cup holder. He scanned the wheel and dashboard. "Where the hell . . . ?"

"What's the problem?"

"The gearshift. I can't find it."

Hannah searched with him. "Did you check the other side?"

"I'm looking everywhere. I can't see it."

The second hinge rusted away. Hannah's door fell to the asphalt with a loud crash. The green-suited twin stood fifteen feet away. He aimed his hand at the actress.

"Oh God!"

She shifted into high speed and clumsily hurled a walkie-talkie. It shattered at the man's feet, cutting his ankle with a bouncing piece of shrapnel. He lost his concentration.

The window behind Theo crumbled with age. "Zack, why aren't we going?!"

"The controls are all weird! I can't find the gearshift!"

Mia snapped to attention and opened her journal. She'd been so busy worrying about Amanda that she forgot the other notes she received.

"The steering column is the gearshift!" she yelled. "Press the white triggers on the wheel to—"

The rear doors suddenly flew open. Mia screamed as a bloody glove grabbed her arm.

The Motorcycle Man was out of patience. His cracked helmet had been removed, revealing his gaunt, leathery face. By official records, he was twenty-nine years old. A lifetime of shifting had done a number on his body, not to mention his mind. The six people in the van all looked like Hannah to him. He was fairly sure he was hallucinating again, but what did it matter? Rebel said they all had to die. If he killed them one by one, he'd eventually get to the bitch who broke his ribs and took his sword.

The moment he seized Mia, Amanda's mind went white.

"NO!"

A geyser of tempic force erupted from her palm. It split evenly around Mia, converging on the Motorcycle Man in the form of a twenty-inch hand.

The tempis shoved him with enough force to knock one of the rear doors off its hinges. It crashed to the driveway. The Motorcycle Man crashed harder.

Amanda stammered in shock as she eyed her broken victim. She'd acted without a single thought and yet somehow the tempis knew who to save and who to hurt.

Zack pressed the white triggers on the steering wheel and pushed the column forward. He floored the pedal. The Salgado van peeled away, its one rear door swinging loosely on its hinge.

Nobody spoke a word as Zack navigated the long and winding path to the exit. Hannah looked out her empty door at the moving trees. Mia gazed at the shrinking building behind her. David peered ahead to the front gate. Amanda stared down at her bloody, trembling hands.

Only Theo glanced around at the others in the van, his fellow survivors. He'd lost his memories of the apocalypse they'd endured. Now he had a strong idea of what he'd missed.

"Jesus," he said, in a croaking rasp. "Jesus Christ."

Gemma Sunder screamed.

She'd been in the middle of a calm sentence, a theory as to how the breachers might have been alerted to their attack, when her head snapped back and her face contorted with sudden terror.

"We have to get out of here! We have to go right now!"

Ivy took a step back. Her niece didn't just see the future. She lived it one minute at a time. Her nonlinear lifestyle made her a strange and difficult child, but she was rarely one to panic.

"What are you talking about, Gemma? What's going to happen?"

"I don't have time to explain! Just make a door and get us out!"

With a circular wave, Ivy drew a new portal in the wall. Rebel forced himself up to a standing position. His muscles still throbbed from the chaser attack. His hand screamed with stabbing agony.

"Not leaving without the others . . ." he groaned.

"There's nothing we can do for them!" Gemma yelled.

Ivy shook her head. "No. I have to get Krista."

"Goddamn it! Why don't you two ever listen to me?! If we don't get out of here in the next twenty seconds, we're dead!"

"Gemma, what's coming?"

"Something bad," the girl replied. "Something really bad."

Hidden among the bishop pines at the front of the property, Slim Tim Witten readied his weapon. At sixty-three, he was a clan elder, one of the last of the third generation. If his slight build and advanced age hadn't been enough of a perceived liability, he had a talent that didn't lend itself well to combat. But he'd begged to come along on this crucial mission, and Rebel ultimately gave in. Ivy had stashed him among the trees by the main gate. His task was to shoot any stragglers who tried to escape.

With quick concentration, he refreshed the earthly hues of his skin and beard—his lumiflage, as he called it. He blended among the foliage like a chameleon.

Now he could spot the van's approach in the curving driveway. He saw two people behind the windshield, with hints of more in the back. *Fourping hell, Rebel. Did you get any at all?*

Once the vehicle reached the straight and final homestretch, Tim aimed his rifle at the wavy-haired man up front. The augurs said he was some kind of artist, and that he could be dangerously clever if given half the chance. Whatever he was, he was the driver, and so he was first. Tim lined Zack in his sights and fired.

The bullet traveled fourteen inches before disappearing into a small white portal. Tim cocked his head, flummoxed, until a cold hand grabbed his shoulder from behind. In the span of a heartbeat, he advanced in age—from gray to white to ancient to desiccated. At last Slim Tim Witten crumbled into dust, fertilizer for the shrubbery.

Standing in his place, Azral Pelletier watched his young Silvers approach. He had just arrived. He was not happy.

THIRTEEN

The moment the van crossed the sensors, the iron gate retracted on squeaky wheels. Hannah peered at the street beyond. She'd only experienced the outside world once before, for a quick but crazy eighty-one minutes. She wasn't ready for more trans-American culture shock, but the fears of moving forward were just a gentle breeze compared to the nightmare behind her. Her safe little limbo, her Ellis Island, had been irreparably breached. She never wanted to go back.

As the vehicle idled in front of the sliding gate, the actress nervously tapped her fingers. She glanced out her missing door, then froze in the light of a familiar face.

"Oh my God."

"What?" Zack asked.

"That's him."

"Who?"

"The guy who gave me my bracelet. He's standing right there."

Zack leaned in to Hannah's vantage as the Silvers in the back peered through the shattered window.

Azral returned their gazes, still as stone. He wore a white oxford under a sharp gray business suit that was peppered with London rain. Even at twenty yards' distance, his blue eyes popped with eerie vibrance. To Mia, he was the most terrifying thing of beauty she'd ever seen in her life—part vampire, part archangel, and (God help her) part David. He shared the boy's small nose, bright eyes, and flawless symmetry, but there wasn't a shred of kindness in his expression.

Hannah fumbled a hand in Zack's direction. "I think we should—"

"Yeah."

The passengers kept a fretful watch behind them as Zack lurched the van through the gate.

"Is he doing someth—"

The sound of crashing glass and metal suddenly filled their ears. Zack jumped in his seat.

"What happened? Are we hit?"

"It's the other back door," said Mia. "It fell off."

Zack checked the damage in the rearview mirror. "He's not following us?"

David shook his head, his eyes slitted in busy thought. "He appears to be letting us go."

The van turned left onto a narrow suburban road. Theo peeked through the gateway. "Hannah, what did you say that guy's name was?"

"Azral."

"That's what he told you?"

"That's what you told me," Hannah replied. "Right before your coma."

Czerny mumbled something faint. Amanda leaned in closer.

"What did he say?" Mia asked.

"I don't know. I couldn't make it out. I don't think he's—"

"Pelletier," he repeated. "His name's Azral Pelletier."

The passengers fell quiet for the next sixty yards, until Zack aimed his wide stare at Czerny.

"What?"

Krista Bloom staggered back into the lobby, still reeling from David's assaults. Her head throbbed beneath her ski mask. The sounds of the world filtered in through a teakettle shriek.

Through the dancing spots in her vision, she saw her fallen teammate by the reception desk. She checked his wrist for a pulse. Nothing. It was hard to muster sympathy. The man in the Roosevelt mask had been a pariah among his people, banished long ago for unconscionable acts of cruelty. Rebel had offered him a spot in this mission as a chance to earn his way back into the clan. Krista found it sad that the path to forgiveness was carved through the murder of innocents. These were desperate times. Frightening times.

The glass doors swung open. Krista could make out the MacDougals. She had to squint to identify the unconscious figure they carried between them. The Motorcycle Man was just one violent incident away from becoming another exile. He'd been such a sweet young boy. But as he grew older—faster—his good nature and sanity withered away. Krista noticed from the freakish way his nose bent that it wasn't just his mind that had snapped.

"Will he live?"

The brothers replied with a grim stare. She wasn't sure if that meant yes or no. They weren't his biggest fans either.

"Well, did you at least kill any of the breachers?"

The freckled twin shook his head. There was no point in asking for details. The MacDougals hadn't spoken a word since they were eighteen. Their vow. Their sacrifice.

"Damn it! How could this have gone so wrong?" Krista pressed her collar mic. "Ivy?"

No response. Her blond brow furrowed. "Ivy, are you there? Talk to me."

After attempting to call the other missing teammates—Rebel, Gemma, Slim Tim—Krista read the worry on the brothers' faces.

"No. No way. Ivy wouldn't leave us behind." *She wouldn't leave me*, Krista thought.

"Oh, but she did."

Startled, Krista spun back to the reception desk, where Esis sat atop the polished marble. She dangled her legs off the desk, kicking her feet like a bored child.

"Your friend has departed the premises, along with her niece and the stubborn ape she mates with. Foolish creatures, all of you. I grieve to call you ancestors."

Krista eyed Esis strangely. The woman wore a damp yellow raincoat over a short and leafy vest dress. It was a hip fashion among the progressive youth in London but utterly alien here in the States.

"Who the hell are you?"

Esis jerked a thumb at the brass *Pelletier* sign. "You broke into our house with your fearful schemes and wrongful notions. You've inconvenienced us greatly. We are not amused."

She removed an English hippie sandal from her foot and curiously studied it.

"You should be making love, not war."

Krista and the brothers each raised a hand to attack. Esis dropped her shoe. By the time it hit the floor, the Scottish Twins, the Motorcycle Man, and the Winter Blonde were all brutally slaughtered. Krista didn't even have a chance to think her daughter's name.

Amanda knew that Czerny shouldn't talk in his condition. But like the others, she was anxious to learn why the terrifying being known as Azral also happened to own the name on the lobby wall.

The physicist spoke through pained grunts. "When Hannah provided her initial testimony, she told us she received her bracelet from a white-haired man named Azral. We found that highly peculiar considering that just thirty-six hours before, we'd finally been introduced to our organization's financier, a gentleman who perfectly fit that description."

David opened his mouth to speak, but Amanda touched his wrist. *Wait.*

"Upon broaching the matter with Dr. Quint, I was . . . He didn't take it well. He said I was being an idiot, thinking like a conspiracy theorist instead of a theoretical physicist. He threatened to fire anyone who brought up the subject again, even in jest. So we put it out of our minds. All things considered, coincidence still seemed the likeliest explanation."

He closed his eyes in pained lament. "I'm sorry, friends. I'm afraid we've all been a little misled."

"Not a little," Zack hissed. "And not Quint."

Czerny weakly nodded. "Yes. You're right. I'm certain now that Dr. Quint knew the truth. I'm sorry for that too. I can't even begin to guess the reasons behind the deception."

"What were they planning to do with us?" Mia asked Czerny.

"Not sure. Our only task was to keep you safe and comfortable while we learned as much as we could. Dr. Quint never once said anything to make me believe he wished you harm."

"And if he had?"

Czerny tilted his gaze at the driver's seat. "If he had, Zack, there would have been mutiny in his ranks. We may be scientists, but we're still human beings."

"I know you are," Zack replied. "And Quint knew too, which is probably why he kept you in the dark. God only knows what they were planning for us."

"You think it has anything to do with those killers back there?" Hannah asked.

David shook his head. "I don't think so. I also question Zack's view of Azral's intentions. I mean he had us dead to rights and he let us go."

"I have no idea what he's planning, David. I just know that if he set this place up years ago, just for us, then he's playing a long game. He's not done with us."

Mia fixed her anxious stare out the missing back doors, her journal squeezed tightly in her grip. She held a whole book of prophecies in her arms and yet she didn't even know where she was sleeping tonight. The future had become a fierce, wild creature. And she still had two warnings left about the events of the day.

Azral grimaced as he opened the lobby doors. The carnage was unpleasant to look at and even worse to smell. He hailed from a more civilized age, and wasn't accustomed to the raw scent of blood.

Esis remained barefoot in the center of the lobby, standing among the bits and pieces of her four latest victims. Unlike Azral, she'd adjusted quite well to the savagery of this era. Her hands had become long white scythes. Streaks of gore ran at crossed angles across her coat, her face, her tempic blades.

She reverted her hands to humble pink flesh, then reversed the blood from her clothes and skin. Her dark eyes narrowed to a petulant squint. She wasn't pleased with Azral right now, for reasons he couldn't refute. She'd warned him about the possibility of this attack and he didn't listen.

Despite the setback, Azral assured Esis through soft, foreign words that the situation was far from tragic. It wasn't the end of all their hard work. It was merely the end of Quint's.

A curved screen of light appeared an inch above his wrist. Countless words of a strange alphabet scrolled past his vision at dizzying speed. He paused on one, a verb that was four syllables long. The definition fell somewhere in the space between *cleanse* and *amputate*.

With a wistful sigh, Azral activated the command.

At 6:32 and 58 seconds, an invisible swarm spread across the globe, a breed of subatomic particle that modern science had yet to name or even notice. The energy was undetectable to all but one species of beetle and harmless to all but twenty-one unfortunate souls in the state of South California.

Charlie Merchant was showering at home, thinking how nice it would be to rub soapy lather on Hannah's naked body. While his imagination flourished, a thin trickle of blood escaped his nose. His eyelids fluttered. His muscles clenched. And then Quint's youngest employee fell to the drain. Dead.

Martin and Gerry Salgado were speeding toward the office in their Royal Condor. Beatrice had phoned them nine minutes ago with shrill cries of deadly intruders. Now while Martin floored the aerovan's accelerator, Gerry desperately tried to hail his siblings on the radio. Martin didn't care about Czerny or Beatrice or any of the freakish guests. All he wanted were his two youngest children. He prayed that Erin and Eric were okay, even as dark instincts told him otherwise.

Suddenly both father and son slumped forward in their seats. The aerovan lulled into a drifting spin, languishing twenty feet in the air like a half-filled balloon. For the next hundred yards, the Condor twirled a lazy path over Terra Vista. Dead.

In a fraction of a moment, twenty-one people came to an end. Everyone who worked for Sterling Quint. Everyone who'd met Azral Pelletier on the night of the Silvers' arrival.

Of the staff, only Beatrice Caudell had noticed the strangely gritty texture of Azral's handshake. She'd considered pouring rubbing alcohol on her palm, a move that would have saved her life. But red wine and romantic thoughts had overtaken her that night. She resolved to stop being a germaphobe for once.

Now she wrapped her arms around her knees, crying tears of relief from the underside of Czerny's desk. The intruders were gone. The crisis was over. *Oh thank God. Thank God. Thank God.*

She then felt a warm trail under her nostril. She touched the blood on her lip. Her eyes rolled back and she collapsed to the floor. Dead.

Five miles away, Sterling Quint continued to sleep in good health, blissfully unaware that his staff had been let go. Safe and snug beneath his Asian silk blanket, he dreamed of time travel and Nobel Prize medallions.

The van was still a mile from the hospital when Constantin Czerny reached the end of his string. He turned his head to the window, thought of Beatrice, and then moved on.

Amanda rushed to the head of the stretcher and checked his pulse.

"No, no, no, no. Don't do this."

Hannah turned around and watched with dread as her sister began resuscitation measures. With each chest compression, little rivers of blood oozed from the edges of Czerny's stomach bandage.

David watched with dark discomfort. "You seem to be aggravating his injury."

"I don't have a choice," said Amanda. "If I don't do this, he has no chance at all."

"At the risk of upsetting you . . ."

Theo cut him off with a sharp, grim look. *Don't.*

Amanda pinched Czerny's nose and forced two breaths down his throat. She resumed compressions.

"Cardiac arrest is not the same as death," she said. "If we can get him to a defibrillator in the next five minutes . . . Goddamn it, Zack! Why are you slowing down?"

Hannah followed Zack's nervous line of sight. Two vehicles approached in single file from the opposite lane. They were both dark blue and sneaker shaped, as if some mad mechanic had slapped a minivan rump onto a sports car. Bright white letters on the hood and roof advertised the cruisers' affiliation with the Terra Vista Police Department.

The actress looked to Zack. "What's the problem? We didn't do anything."

He eyed her cynically. "We're riding in a van that's not even remotely ours, with a dying man in the back and a two-foot spatter of Erin's blood on the driver's side. We do not want their attention."

The cruisers met the van. Zack fixed his gaze ahead with as much aloofness as he could muster. Once the police cars disappeared over the hill, Zack stomped the gas pedal. Hannah ran a shaky hand through her hair.

"God. I can't take this."

Amanda was on her fifth round of chest compressions when she noticed that the Silvers in the back were looking at her, not Czerny. Even Mia's young face teemed with fatalism. Amanda wanted to scream at them. Did they think she was deluded? That she didn't know death when she saw it? She was a cancer nurse. She knew.

"This doesn't . . ." She shook her head at Czerny. "It doesn't make sense. A person with his injuries usually goes through four stages of shock. They progress to tachycardia. Tachypnea. They don't jump straight to . . ."

She looked at the blood on her hands. Her lips quivered. "He's already cold. He shouldn't be cold already."

Suddenly Zack let out a chain of profanities, a machine-gun blast of foul exclamations that only a native New Yorker could properly achieve. For a moment, Amanda thought she was the target of his wrath. Then she noticed everyone aiming their hot attention past her, through the missing back doors.

The police cars had come back. They rapidly approached the van from behind, then lit their flashing colors.

FOURTEEN

As his limbs turned to stone and his fingers clenched like hooks around the steering wheel, Zack took an anxious trip down the many branching futures. He knew there were no good outcomes left. Just a tightrope path to the least catastrophic.

His heartbeat doubled as he stomped the gas pedal.

Hannah grabbed his sleeve. "Zack, what are you doing? They want us to stop!"

In lieu of spinning roof lights, the twin cruisers were covered with lumic panels. Every inch of the chassis now flashed red and blue. Once Zack accelerated, the sirens blared. A gruff voice boomed through the speakers.

"PULL OVER! NOW!"

Theo veered his wide gaze between the police cars and Zack. "I'm seriously questioning your plan right now."

"Me too!" Mia yelled.

Zack spotted a sign for Highway V. He'd learned from his preparative map studies that all the interstates here had roman numerals. V stretched all the way north to Sacramento.

"Okay," he said. "I'd like everyone to listen to me while I explain the shitty situation we're in. We have no identity here. Whether we're suspects or perps or just people of interest, those cops will ask us our names. They'll look for us in their databases and they will not find us. Working under the correct assumption that we're hiding something, they'll hold us. Once they find out what happened to the original owners of this van, I imagine they'll hold us a good long time."

"But if we explain—"

"Explain what, Hannah? That we're from a parallel Earth? That we popped into the world six weeks ago and have been staying at a hotel run by physicists until we were attacked by people with swords and guns?"

Zack rushed through a red light. A garbage truck and a commuter bus both screeched to a halt as the van cut between them.

"PULL OVER BEFORE SOMEONE GETS HURT!"

Mia shook her head. "But there are still people who can vouch for us . . ."

"Who, Quint's people? Do you really think we're safe with them after everything that happened?"

"Zack's right," said David. "We have to keep going."

Theo gestured at the cracks and broken hinges. "I'm not arguing your reasons. I'm just saying we'll never be able to outrun them in this thing. It's falling apart."

That was indeed a problem. In addition to the wisps of white smoke that snaked from the engine, a dashboard gauge casually informed Zack that the vehicle had enough power left for 25.2 miles. The last time Zack breathed, it was at 28.

Hannah turned in her seat, her hair blowing wildly from the wind of her missing door. "Look, they're going to stop us one way or another. Let's just tell them the truth. They'll think we're nuts, but we have proof. I mean the things we can do—"

"No."

The objection came from behind her. Amanda had taken her own bleak trip through the future. She envisioned them all in a government lab, some antiseptic Guantánamo staffed by scientists even crueler than Quint. They'd probably hold them for six months in barren cells before making full use of their scalpels.

"No more authorities," she said. "We keep going on our own."

Hannah gaped at her. "What are you going to do? Blast them away with your tempis?"

"THIS IS YOUR LAST CHANCE!"

Zack steered the van up the entry ramp and onto northbound Highway V. He was relieved to find traffic sparse on both the ground and aer level.

David threw a pensive glance at the police cruisers as they split into a side-by-side formation.

"I have a way," he offered. "It's not pretty, but I think it'll work."

"Will it hurt them?" Mia asked.

"Most likely. Yes."

She swallowed her objections, even as her thoughts fell back on Krista Bloom. Mia wondered how many slippery-slope incidents it would take before she and her friends were apologizing to their own murder victims. *I'm so sorry. There's no other option. This'll be quick. I promise.*

Zack glanced at David in the rearview mirror. "Look, I trust you. Do whatever you can to stop them without hurting them."

"Do *everything* you can to avoid hurting them," Amanda stressed.

"You guys are insane!" Hannah shouted. "This is insane!"

David flashed a palm at her. "Your objections are noted. Now please be quiet, all of you. I need to concentrate."

He leaned forward in his seat, squinting as he rummaged through a whirlwind montage of local history images. Seven seconds later, he returned to the present, with company in tow.

An eighteen-wheel truck materialized behind the police cars. The cab was deep black. Its liquid tank trailer was garnished with hazard signs. The cargo had been heptanoic acid, an organic compound used primarily for fruit soda flavoring. It also had a vital role in the production of black market cigarettes. On Christmas Eve, an aspiring bootlegger hijacked the vehicle and absconded down the freeway at 120 miles an hour.

This had all happened eight years ago. To local eyes, it was happening again.

The Silvers watched in stupor as the ghost truck overtook the cruisers, forcing both drivers to swerve in opposite directions. One slid into the guardrail. The other veered across the median, into southbound lanes.

"No!"

Hannah covered her mouth as a delivery van smashed into its trunk. The cruiser spun a full 360 degrees before hitting the opposite guardrail. The motor died in a shower of smoke and sparks.

As quickly as it arrived, the phantom tanker disappeared. David scanned the view out the rear doors, then emitted a weak chuckle.

"Wow. That was . . . I'd never done anything like that before. That was intense."

The Silvers all regarded David with varying shades of disquiet. He quickly turned somber.

"I'm sorry. I didn't expect him to cross into opposing traffic. That wasn't my intent."

Amanda knew she wasn't in a position to judge after what she did to the Motorcycle Man. And yet a wary voice in her head reminded her that she hadn't chuckled afterward.

Theo peered out at the other police car, which had already recuperated from its guardrail scrape. "We still have one on our tail."

Hannah jumped in her seat as a highway patrolman appeared outside her door. His motorcycle was a powerful-looking machine, as thick as a horse. The driver was covered from neck to foot in a blue rubber suit.

"Shit. We have two again."

"Three," Zack corrected. He had a motorcycle cop outside his window too. "I think these guys are wearing speedsuits."

The floating wires of Mia's memory connected. She rushed to the grate. "The motorcycles are going to speed ahead!"

"What?"

The suits of both patrolmen suddenly lit up with a mesh of glowing blue lines. The cycles shot forward in a hot blur. They disappeared over the horizon.

"How'd you know they'd do that?" Theo asked.

"I got a note." Mia flipped to the last active page of her journal. "It said the motorcycles will speed ahead to set up a tempic barrier on the highway. We won't be able to get around it, but Zack will know how to get through it."

"What?"

"That's what it said."

"I don't know how to get through a tempic barrier!"

"I'm just telling you what it said!"

The highway once again descended to ground level, splitting the north and south arteries around a thick strand of trees. A sign on the right announced the next exit a mile away. Zack was sure the motorcycle cops would raise the barrier before that. And now he couldn't turn around.

Amanda gasped as if someone touched her back with cold fingers. Mia held her arm. "What's the matter?"

"Tempis."

The Silvers looked behind them as a long white panel extended from each door of the cruiser. The vehicle slowed down, leaving yards of empty space behind the van.

"What are they doing?"

"Isolating us," David said. "We're about to be boxed in."

Hannah saw the motorcycles up ahead. The patrolmen had disembarked to set up a pair of thick metal posts on opposite sides of the road. With a flip of a switch, the space between them filled with solid white energy. It stretched across the highway like a tennis net.

Caught between the tempis and the trees, Zack had no choice but to step on the brake. Hannah eyed him nervously. "What now?"

"I don't know."

"This was your idea! Think of something!"

Zack watched the police car come to a halt. Two tall men in uniform stepped out, guns drawn.

"David, ghost the doors."

"What?"

"The doors. The windows. We need them back now."

"Okay."

The policemen stopped, perplexed, as the missing doors to the van reappeared like magic. Hannah ran a hand through the clouded window next to her. Nothing but painted air.

"Does this mean you have a new plan, Zack?"

Yes. "No. I'm just buying time."

The motorcycle cops approached from the front. They pointed their pistols at Zack and Hannah.

"Turn off the engine and get out of the van! Now!"

Taking a cue from the Scottish Twins, Zack aged the windows until the glass turned clouded and cracked. He closed his eyes and took a deep breath. If his friends hated his last idea, they'd truly despise this one.

"Theo, do you still have Rebel's gun?"

"You've got to be kidding me."

"You can't do that!" Hannah yelled.

Zack raised his palms. "Calm down. I'm not going to fire it. I'm not even going to point it. I just need it for . . . veracity."

"What are you talking about?"

He let out a feeble sigh. "Look, we're obviously going back to the police station. There's not much we can do about that. But if we coordinate our story, only one of us will be put in a holding cell. All you have to do is tell them I kidnapped you—"

"No!"

"No way!"

"It's the only chance we have of escaping!" Zack insisted.

"For us," Amanda shot back. "Not for you."

"There has to be a way through the barrier!" Mia exclaimed. "Why would I write it to myself if it wasn't true?"

Amanda winced in frustration. She could feel the tempic wall in her mind. She could even touch it, in ways she couldn't explain. But as sure as she knew anything, she knew she couldn't do more than make a few ripples in the surface.

Twenty feet from the passenger side, a policeman shouted through the ghosted window. "Turn off the engine and step outside with your hands up. It's the only way you're getting out of this in one piece."

Theo lifted Rebel's gun by the edge of the handle, then carefully placed it under his seat. "I hate to say it, but I think we're out of options."

"Let's just do what they tell us," Hannah said, her eyes welling with tears. "I don't want to die. I don't want to see any of you die."

"But what'll they do to us?" Mia asked.

"I don't know, sweetie, but is it any worse than getting shot to death?"

David shook his head in bother. "I can't believe what I'm hearing. We just survived six murderous people who had talents like ours. They attacked us without warning and we still beat them. Now after all that, you're looking to surrender to four mere coppers?"

"It's not that simple," Amanda said.

"Of course it is. They have weapons. So do we. We know theirs. They don't know ours. If we work intelligently, we could disarm them before they even know what hit them."

Once again, everyone leered at David in dark wonder. He was getting used to the look.

"That's crazy," Hannah griped. "You're going to get us all killed."

Theo nodded. "She's right. We only got out of that building through dumb luck. We push it again and someone's going to die."

Mia bit her thumb in tense deliberation. She fell well on the side of the cautious majority, and yet she knew that without David's reckless gallantry, she'd be a frozen corpse in the security room.

Zack kept his tense gaze fixed on the windshield. He could see hints of the tempic barrier through the clouds and cracks, an urgent puzzle that taunted him. If only Quint hadn't been so damn stingy with his information.

His brow suddenly rose. His mouth fell open. "Oh. Wait a second."

While David continued to argue with Theo and the sisters, Zack turned around in his seat.

"Wait a second! Guys!"

He got their attention. Between his wide eyes and hanging jaw, his friends saw a glimmer of hope.

"I know how to get through it."

Zack's good news wasn't good at all to the Great Sisters Given.

"No!" Amanda yelled. "Absolutely not!"

It took him just nineteen seconds to explain his idea. While he filled in the others, he removed the Salgados' nightstick from the door holster and passed it to an incredulous Hannah.

"One of those two posts has the generator. It could be on the outside. It could be on the inside. In any case, you break it and the wall goes away."

Two weeks ago, when Quint demonstrated a tempic barrier in action, Zack had noticed a thermos-size power pack on the frame. According to Quint, tempis didn't run on electricity. It was fueled by something called so-lis. But power was power. Lack of power, in this case, was freedom.

There was, however, one significant drawback to the plan.

"You're risking my sister's life!" Amanda snapped.

"It is a risk," Zack acknowledged. "I'd do it myself if I could. But Hannah's the only one who can smash it. She's the only one fast enough to get away."

"It could work," David said. "If she attacks from the woods, as Zack suggested, they won't even notice her until the barrier's down."

Mia peeked out the ghosted window as stealthily as she could. "But the motorcycle cops are wearing speedsuits . . ."

"Yes, but they're not wearing shifters," Zack replied. "The shifters are in the bikes. They can't speed on foot."

"How the hell do you know that?"

He looked back to Amanda, suddenly sheepish. "I saw it on lumivision."

"Oh my God . . ."

"I'm right about this. I'm telling you."

"No. I'm not letting you do this. You're not throwing my sister's life away on some stupid—"

"I'll do it."

"—half-assed plan that doesn't even make sense."

"I'll do it," Hannah repeated, in a tiny voice. She held the nightstick with white-knuckled fear. Rubber and wood, against two metal posts and four men with guns.

"Hannah, you can't!"

"If there's a choice besides dying and getting arrested, I'll take it," she said. "I don't want us getting separated. I don't want to end up in some government facility or wherever they put people like us. I just want to live in a nice apartment and do musical theater. I'm sick of all the weirdness."

Theo looked to the semblant rear doors. Gloved fingers briefly popped through the surface, testing the nonmaterial before hastily retreating. His mind fell into a jackhammer refrain. *Tear gas tear gas tear gas tear gas . . .*

"Tear gas," he said. "They know the back door's fake and they're going to throw in tear gas."

"What?"

"How do you know?"

"I think I just overheard it."

He didn't, but he was right all the same.

"We have about a minute before—"

The van was suddenly filled with a blast of heat, accelerated air molecules spreading in all directions. The Silvers winced. By the time they opened their eyes, Hannah was gone.

———

She ran into the woods at 155 miles an hour. Pebbles flew like buckshot from beneath her sneakers. The air around her was icy cold and her vision had turned almost uniformly blue. There was a fresh new ringing in her ears that, when she focused on it, sounded a little bit like music.

The actress slipped between the trees, then surveyed the road from a hidden distance. In her accelerated vision, the tempic barrier swirled with smoky gray wisps. She studied the thick metal posts of the blockade. She wasn't sure she could break them, even at top speed.

"God, Zack. What were you think—"

"Quit squirming!"

Hannah scanned the area in a startled twirl. The words had come through a woman's harsh whisper, but there was no one else around. She shouldn't have been able to hear anyone in her shifted state.

She figured her nerves were playing tricks on her, with good reason. The motorcycle cops had caught her blurry dash to the trees and were now beginning a slow turn in her direction. Hannah watched their speedsuits in breathless anticipation. They didn't light up. *Oh thank God. At least Zack got that part ri—*

"I mean it, Jury! Quit moving! I don't want to rift you!"

Hannah glanced to her left and now saw a young, dark-haired couple hiding behind a nearby tree. The man was olive skinned, muscular, and exquisitely handsome. He wore a black T-shirt over jeans and grasped his companion tightly from behind. Though the woman's face was obscured, she was built and dressed like Hannah. Her shoulder-length hair was even beginning to show its brown roots, just like Hannah's.

The pair kept an anxious vigil on an empty patch of highway, twenty yards north of the tempic barrier. Despite their edgy posture, Hannah saw the tender way the man and woman touched each other. They were clearly intimate.

Before Hannah could speak, the brunette brushed her hair behind her ear. Now Hannah had a clear view of her face. *Her* face. Her own side profile, as seen in countless photos.

With a high scream, Hannah fell out of velocity and toppled to the dirt.

The illusive couple disappeared in a blink. Hannah reeled in mad perplexity. She couldn't shift. She couldn't move. She couldn't stop looking at the empty space where her ghostly self and lover once stood.

Four seconds after her sister left the van, Amanda heard her fragmented shriek from the woods. Her mind stammered in panic. *Something, something, something went—*

"Wrong. Something went wrong. She's in trouble."

Zack launched a nervous stare through the clouded glass. "She just left. Give her time."

"No. This was a bad idea, Zack. You're going to get her killed."

Theo flinched in worry as Amanda moved in front of a clear window. "You shouldn't stand there."

David nodded. "He's right. Please sit down."

Amanda ignored them. Her green eyes bulged as the highway patrolmen proceeded, guns drawn, to the edge of the woods.

"No. No. No no no no . . ."

Mia kept her wary gaze on Amanda. She had one warning left from her future self, the worst one by far. Now all the alarms in her head were ringing.

"Amanda . . ."

With frantic eyes, Amanda looked to the intangible rear doors. Mia slid down the seat, speaking in a low and maternal tone. "Amanda, you can't go out there . . ."

"She's my sister."

"You promised me you'd stay in the van."

"They're going to shoot her."

"They'll shoot *you*! If you leave this van right now, they will shoot you and you will die! It already happened! I got the note!"

The men eyed Mia with fresh apprehension. This was news to them.

"I really think you should listen to her," Zack implored Amanda.

"Please! Please listen to me!"

Amanda's shallow breaths slowed down to gulps. "Okay. Okay."

Mia closed her eyes and exhaled. *Thank God.*

"I'm sorry, Mia . . ."

"It's all right. You listened. It's not—"

"I'm sorry."

Amanda turned to the window. "I'M COMING OUT! DON'T SHOOT!"

"No!"

With a final look of remorse, Amanda brushed past Mia. She hurried through the ghosted doors, out into the open air.

"Amanda!"

In another string of time, another elsewhile, Amanda might have burst through the illusory hatch without a hint of announcement. Her sudden emergence might have startled a policeman into firing a fatal shot. But Mia's warning prompted Amanda to issue one of her own. With five shouted words, she eased the pressure on the policemen's triggers just enough to exit the van unharmed.

The cruiser cops raised their guns at her. Amanda kept her bloody fingers pointed at the ground.

"Show me your hands!" a cop shouted.

Amanda eyed them with savage defiance. "Call your other men back here."

"*Show me your goddamn hands!*"

"You call your other men back here *right now!*"

Blood rushed to Mia's face. She scrambled to the exit, only to be caught by her shirtsleeve.

"Let me go!"

"No," said Theo, grimacing in pain. "No more bad ideas."

It was Theo's bad idea to grab her with his wounded arm. She broke free and sprinted toward the doors. David rushed after her.

"Mia, don't!"

It never occurred to Mia that she already saved Amanda's life, or that she was making the very same mistake she helped Amanda avoid. The moment she burst through the ghosted doors without warning, the policemen aimed their pistols at her head.

One of them fired.

Mia Farisi never considered herself a lucky girl, any more than she considered herself tall or svelte. And yet there were a few scattered nights on this

world when she marveled at the miraculous circumstances behind her continued existence. She'd been spared from apocalypse by mysterious forces,
saved from asphyxiation with the help of a future self. And then just twelve
minutes ago, she was rescued from death by a brave and beautiful boy who,
for reasons she'd love to hear one day, preferred a world with her in it.

She was lucky, never more so than now.

The bullet flew past Mia's face, brushing her cheek with warm air before
passing through the van and piercing a hole in the windshield.

The moment the shot rang out, Amanda stopped thinking about her sister. Her skin turned hot. Her mind went blank.

She showed the policemen her hands.

The tempis exploded from both palms, launching up the highway in two
jagged cones. In the half-second journey between Amanda and her targets, a
giant white hand had bloomed at the end of each projectile. They grabbed the
policemen like rag dolls, pinning them down to the concrete. Amanda could
feel every button on their shirts, each newly broken rib in their chests. She
idly began counting the fractures as if she were merely having a strange
dream.

"Amanda, stop!"

The tempic arms vanished at the sound of David's voice. Amanda cast a
stunned gaze at the cops, then David, then her own twitching palms.

"What . . . what did I . . . ?"

"Come on!"

David seized Mia and Amanda by the wrists, pulling them back inside.
Zack hit the gas pedal. The van traveled a hundred feet before the fog of Mia's
shock cleared away.

"Wait. What happened to the barrier?"

"It's down," said Zack. "Hannah did it."

Amanda looked through the grate, at the empty passenger seat.

"Where is she?"

Hannah heard the loud standoff between the cruiser cops and Amanda.
Even in her muddled state, she could tell her sister had once again become
Madmanda—unyielding, unforgiving, impervious to fear or reason.

When the gunshot was fired, Hannah finally broke her paralysis. She jumped to her feet and scanned the area. Amanda was still standing, thank God, but the cruiser cops weren't. The sight of her sister's giant tempic arms was enough to rattle the two motorcycle patrolmen. They retreated from the edge of the woods and raised their pistols at Amanda.

"NO!"

Hannah shifted back into high speed and rushed toward them, thumping the barrel of each gun with her nightstick. As the weapons fell to the earth in a slow-motion twirl, Hannah noticed the twisted bouquet of broken fingers she'd left behind on each patrolman. Their faces were already beginning to contort in pain.

"Oh my God! I'm so sorry!" she yelled, hopelessly incoherent.

She ran to the tempic barrier, smacking the metal post with her baton. The reverberation shot all the way up her arm, rattling her bones. The barrier seemed no worse for the wear.

"Damn it! Come on!"

Hannah ran to the other post and noticed a metal protrusion on the outer edge. It was the size of a salt shaker, and sported three tiny green lights. Maybe Zack was right after all.

"Come on. Please."

She struck the protrusion. The barrier flickered for a moment, then recovered.

"COME ON!"

A final desperate swing, and the generator exploded in a ball of sparks. The nightstick broke in half. Hannah de-shifted and clutched her throbbing hand, then scanned the results of her last strike.

The tempis was gone.

Zack didn't waste a breath hitting the gas pedal. Hannah watched the clouds disappear from the driver's-side window as the van screeched past her. Zack caught her gaze and pointed straight ahead. Hannah threw her arms out, flummoxed.

"Wait. What does that mean? Where are you going?"

The vehicle moved on without her, a fact that hadn't gone unnoticed by the others.

"What the hell are you doing?!"

Zack threw a quick glance back at Amanda. "We need to get off the high-way before those other cops get back on their motorcycles. It's the only chance we have."

"You left her back there!"

"She'll catch up."

"Not if she's hurt!"

"She's not hurt. I saw her."

"Zack, turn around and get her! Now!"

"Listen to me. Your sister can run at over a hundred miles an hour. This van can't even crack fifty. She'll catch up. Trust me."

"After all your stupid decisions, I don't trust you at all!"

"You're criticizing *me* for stupid decisions? What you just did—"

"Zack, I'm telling you for the last time . . ."

A small hand grabbed Amanda's shoulder, turning her around. She barely had time to process Mia before the girl slapped her across the cheek. Heavy tears ran down her face.

"You didn't listen! You didn't listen to me and you almost got killed!"

Stunned and hurt, Amanda took a step back. "Mia . . ."

"Don't you *ever* do that again! You *listen* to me!"

"I'm sorry."

"I can't lose anyone else!"

"Mia . . ."

"I can't lose anyone else!"

Amanda pulled her into her arms, holding her tight with aching grief. The two of them had met right here, in the back of this very van. Six weeks had never felt like such an eternity to Amanda. Time never felt so broken.

Theo scanned the empty road behind them, then turned grim. "Zack . . ."

For the twentieth time in the last ten seconds, Zack checked the rearview mirror. The exit was approaching fast, and Hannah wasn't. His stomach seared with acid.

"She'll catch up," he uttered. "She knows what she's doing."

Amanda took a deep wet sniff over Mia's head. "Zack, I'm begging you . . ."

She didn't have to. He slowed to a stop at the off-ramp. He hated making mistakes, even on small things. This was not a small thing.

"All right. I'm turning around."

A dark blur crossed the windshield. Another blast of heat filled the front of the van. By the time Zack turned to look, Hannah glared at him from the passenger seat.

"Go!"

With a hot breath, Zack stomped the pedal. The van hugged the winding exit from Highway V, then disappeared into the tree-lined suburbs of South California.

FIFTEEN

Quint didn't like what he saw in the mirror. At every stop on his morning commute, he examined the dark new bags under his eyes, the jaundiced hue of his skin. He'd spent a long and sleepless weekend devising a scheme to kill Zack Trillinger, for reasons he convinced himself were absolutely vital to science.

By the time he reached the garage, at 7:25, he'd smothered the last of his doubts. This could work. This *would* work. The plan would go off without a hitch and everything would be okay again.

At 7:26, the universe sharply corrected him.

Quint's knees buckled with strain as he eyed the bloodbath in the lobby—four dead strangers in multiple pieces, plus a frozen body that Quint could only guess was once a Salgado. He sidestepped the blood on the landing, only to find another spatter on the wall of the second floor hallway.

Having spotted Czerny's car in the garage, Quint unlocked the door to his office and found Beatrice Caudell splayed dead on the rug. Her small blue eyes were bloodshot and frozen open in shock.

Quint held the wall for support and staggered down the hall. His office was the last room in the building to contain life—ninety-eight rodents, plus two surprise visitors he only loosely deemed to be human.

"Hello, Sterling."

Azral sat on the edge of Quint's desk, his face a calm and genial mask. Esis stood among the mouse cages, petting the fur of a small white youngling. Quint noticed that all the other rodents were engaged in rampant copulation. The madwoman had redistributed his creatures, mixing browns with whites, males with females. Five years of meticulous breeding, ruined.

"What in God's name happened here?"

"The facility was attacked," Azral informed him.

"Attacked? By who? Who are those people downstairs?"

"Brown mice," said Esis, with a look of wry mischief.

Though Azral smirked with humor, the joke flew several feet over Quint's head. He wanted to wring both their necks.

"They're natives like yourself," Azral told him. "Though a more unique strain."

"I don't understand. How could this have happened?"

"How indeed?" Esis asked, with a pointed glare at Azral. He sighed with soft contrition.

"The error is mine. I underestimated these people, despite the warnings of my ever-wise mother."

Esis crossed her arms in a showy pout. Quint studied her in daft surprise. The woman looked ten years younger than the man who called her Mother.

"Where's everyone else? What happened to the subjects?"

"The Silvers are alive," said Azral. "But they won't be returning. The plan has changed."

"Changed how?"

"That's no longer your concern. Though I hold you blameless in this latest trouble, I'm afraid this is the end of your involvement in our project."

Dumbfounded, Quint studied Azral in the vain hope that this was just another peculiar gag.

"No. You can't cut me loose after all this time, without any explanation."

"You'll find I can indeed do such a thing."

"You owe me answers, goddamn it! One of my employees is dead!"

"All of your employees are dead," Esis casually informed him.

The nausea came back full force. Quint leaned against a bookshelf. "What? Why?"

"A necessary evil," Azral sighed. "I seek to prevent future complications. If it's any comfort, none of your people suffered much. Most of them died in their sleep."

Quint took no comfort in that at all. "Then why . . . why am I . . . ?"

"I wanted to thank you for all your hard work, Sterling. You did everything I asked of you. And aside from that early issue with Maranan, you handled your tasks superbly. Know that we'll always value your contribution."

Quint's eyes darted back and forth in busy thought. "Look . . . look, why don't we compromise, okay? Just give me the girl. Give me Farisi and we'll go our separate ways."

"Sterling . . ."

"You said she was expendable!"

"To us," Azral said. "Not to them. The Silvers will be traveling now. They'll need her unique insight."

"But—"

"Furthermore, you misunderstand your situation. I said I wanted to thank you. I never said you were spared."

The walls of Quint's mind suddenly constricted into a narrow tunnel, as a million floating concerns melted away to just one. White-faced, he fumbled the knot of his tie until it came loose. He knew that pleading for his life would be futile, like begging the mercy of a great white shark or a snowy avalanche.

Suddenly the esteemed physicist erupted in a low and untimely chuckle. The Pelletiers watched him with furrowed bother.

"Did you not understand what—"

"Oh, I got it," Quint said, still chortling. "I may be many things, Azral, but I'm not stupid."

Esis eyed him warily. "And yet you laugh in the face of your own demise."

No one was more surprised than Quint, a man whose whole life had been an upward climb, filled with endless battle. Now after fifty-five years, there was nothing left to do. No one left to fight. The revelation was . . . liberating.

"I'd explain it," he said, through dwindling snickers. "But I doubt you'd understand. If the two of you represent the future of mankind, then this is an excellent time to stop progressing."

Azral and Esis exchanged a stony glance, then bloomed a matching set of grins.

"Oh, the pride of the ancients," said the son.

"Truly a sight to behold," said the mother.

Their condescension cracked the walls of Quint's serenity. He shot a wrathful glare at Azral.

"Just get it over with already, you stretched stain. You chalk-faced bowel.

If I have one regret, it's that I won't get to see all your plans crumble right on top of you. Don't think it won't happen. You're clearly not as smart as you think you are."

Expressionless, Azral rose from the desk and approached Quint. The physicist smiled.

"It'll be even more amusing if your grand design gets foiled by the very people you brought here. The great Azral Pelletier, brought low by an actress, a cartoonist, and all their little friends. It's a shame I'll miss that. Talk about a sight to behold."

With a soft and solemn expression, Azral rested a gentle hand on Quint's scalp.

"I thank you again for your help, Sterling. Your work here is done."

Quint closed his eyes in anticipation of pain, but he felt nothing more than a faint and bubbly tickle under his skin. He peeked an eye open.

"What—"

He dropped through the rug as if it were nothing more than mist. Down he fell, through the floorboards and wires, the lobby chandelier. He passed through all objects like an apparition but he plummeted like a stone.

When he reached the underground parking lot, Quint finally screamed. He disappeared through the concrete and then continued in darkness. By the time he succumbed to suffocation, he'd already descended an eighth of the way into the Earth's crust. His body kept on falling, all the way to magma.

Grim-faced and silent, the Pelletiers exited the complex. The moment they reached the front yard, Azral turned around and closed his eyes in concentration.

A dome of piercing white light suddenly enveloped the building—a bubble of backward time moving at accelerated speed. Inside the field, corpses vanished, plants shrank, mice perished as zygotes. The hint of past life appeared in split-second intervals, like aberrations in a flip-book.

By the time the dome disappeared, the entire structure had been reversed fifty-two months, reverted to the failed hotel that Quint had yet to purchase. Every file, every photo, every mention of the Silvers was now erased from existence.

Esis peevishly crossed her arms and addressed Azral in a foreign tongue, a byzantine blend of European and Asian languages that was still over two millennia away from being invented.

"I warned you not to overlook our ancestors, *sehgee*. You should have listened to me."

"I know."

"You and your father both."

Azral held her hands, his sharp eyes tender with affection. "Just forgive us, *sehmeer*, and embrace the new course."

Esis heaved a wistful breath and fixed her dark stare at the blooming sun.

"I can't help but worry for those children. There are so many futures open to them now. So many strings."

"There's only one outcome that matters," Azral insisted. "They go east. To Pendergen."

"Assuming they don't fall on the way."

Azral wrapped his arms around Esis and cast a soulful gaze down the driveway.

"They will not fall," he assured her. "Not the important ones, at least."

Nobody knew where they were going, least of all Zack. His only goal now was to avoid looping back into police search paths. Every chance he got, he drove east into the rising sun.

Twelve miles from the site of their standoff, the engine fell to sickly whirrs. Zack veered onto a narrow forest road and pulled over to the dirt. He felt relatively good about ditching the van here in a desolate area, under the thick canopy of trees. He could only assume that the police hunt had extended to helicopters or whatever they used here to make pigs fly.

He gave everyone five minutes to gather their wits and scant belongings, but Amanda insisted on ten. She'd discovered a sterilized pack of sutures at the bottom of Czerny's med kit and was determined to close Theo's wound before they all proceeded on foot.

While the others exited, she remained with Theo in the back of the van. She saw him wincing with every stroke of the needle.

"Sorry," she said. "I'm an oncology nurse. I don't do this very often."

"You're doing fine."

Theo studied her as she made her final stitches. Her expression was tight and unsettled, like crumbling stone.

"They have those healing machines," he reminded her. "Anything you did to those cops will be undone."

"Not if I killed them."

"I don't think you did."

Amanda didn't think so either, but she couldn't escape the grim possibilities. She'd pinned those men down with the hands of a giant. Another ounce of thought and she could have crushed them like eggs. It had taken her years to accept cancer as part of God's great plan. She didn't even know where to start with tempis.

Twenty feet away, Mia paced the side of the road, kicking tiny stones with vacant bother. She couldn't shake the tickle from her cheek, the strip of skin that the policeman's bullet had kissed with hot air. Someone just fired a gun at her face. And yet somehow she was still standing.

David chucked acorns at the treetops, startling numerous birds.

"What's going on in that head of yours, Miafarisi?"

"I was just thinking how you saved my life back in that building. I never even thanked you."

David shrugged as if he'd merely lent her a nickel. "No worries. Just glad we're all still breathing."

He caught his oversight and turned to Mia in hot remorse. She threw her dismal gaze inside the van, at the blanket-draped corpse of Constantin Czerny.

"Shoot. Mia, I didn't mean—"

"I know what you meant," she told him. "I just feel bad leaving him like this."

"We can't bury him," David said. "There's no time. No reason. The police will only dig him up."

Mia didn't think she had any tears left in her, and yet her eyes welled up again.

"He was nice."

David pulled her into a soft embrace, resting his chin on her scalp. Such a sweet thing, this Miafarisi. Such a sweet child.

Zack leaned against the driver's door, nervously tapping his foot. Between all the traumas of the recent past and all his worries about the near future, he found the energy to mourn the sketchbook he'd left behind in Terra Vista. It was the last surviving relic of his old life. Now he had nothing left but memories.

Hannah emerged from the woods, red-faced and puffy-eyed. She'd gone into the trees to vomit, but it turned out all she needed was a few good minutes of unabashed weeping. She wiped her eyes and rested against the van.

"You okay?" Zack asked.

"Yes. Thank you. You're still an asshole."

He'd already apologized twice for making her run after the van. She didn't care. She was suffering the second-worst morning of her life and she needed to be irrational about something.

He took her hand and pushed a small silver disc into her palm. "There."

"What's this?"

"Restitution. I found it in the cup holder."

Hannah studied the coin. It was twice the size and value of a standard quarter, and bore the side-profile portrait of Theodore Roosevelt. She found the inscription under his head—*We Persevere*—to be ominously cryptic. She could only guess it had something to do with the Cataclysm.

"That's all the money you found?" she asked.

"That's all the money we own."

She pocketed the coin. "Fifty cents. Lovely."

A red sedan turned a sharp corner onto their road. Hannah tensed up and squeezed Zack's arm. He squinted at the approaching vehicle.

"It's okay. It's not a cop car."

Loud country-rock music blared from within as the vehicle rolled to a slow stop beside Zack and Hannah. The young driver turned off his radio and leaned over to the passenger side, whistling in wonder at the dilapidated van.

"Hoo-EE! I've seen some threeped-up rides in my time, amigos, but that is one unhappy son-of-a! You folks doing all right here?"

The man was slight in stature, but he dressed and acted to compensate. Beneath his wide gray cowboy hat were a pair of sunglasses large enough to qualify as novelty shades. His red denim shirt was garnished with rhinestones. The man practically drowned his new acquaintances in his proud Southern drawl.

"We're fine," Zack assured him. "Bought a clunker. Clipped a deer. You know how it goes."

"I hear that. Sure as hell do. Sometimes life just grabs you by the jangles and gives it a good ol' squeeze!" He tipped his hat at Hannah. "If you'll pardon the expression, ma'am."

Even with his absurd shades, Hannah could tell he was aggressively unconcerned about her delicate ears and quite interested in the goods beneath her tank top. She crossed her arms uncomfortably.

"Sure I can't help?" asked the cowboy. "I'm mighty handy with a wrench." Zack shook his head. "No thanks. We're fine. We appreciate it though."

The man kept smiling, his high cheer peppered with a hint of wry amusement.

"All righty. I'll just mosey on along then. But if you're ever feeling blue, just remember: it's a brand-new day and the sun is shining bright. Yes, sir!"

He lowered his shades and offered Hannah a quick wink that was creepy enough to distract her from all her recent woes. Zack was intrigued by the "55" tattoo on the back of his right hand. He wondered if the significance of the number was cultural or personal.

For Evan Rander, it was very personal.

He revved his engine, then offered his two fellow Silvers a final preening smile.

"Y'all take care now. Keep walking."

"Keep walking," Zack repeated.

He and Hannah continued to watch the car as it disappeared to the east. Zack could have sworn he heard laughter over the loud, noxious music.

Hannah kept her gaze on the car's dust trail. "Why'd you say 'Keep walking'?"

"American expression. Means 'Be well.' 'Stay strong.' That sort of thing."

"Oh." She vaguely recalled the pony-haired girl at the supermarket saying the same thing. At the time, Hannah had taken it as a rude brush-off. Guess the kid was being nice.

Once Amanda finished Theo's bandage and the last of the van's useful items were collected into bags, there was little else to do but move on. The Silvers gathered at the side of the road.

Amanda watched Hannah caress her aching hand, then grabbed it for inspection.

"What are you doing, Amanda? I'm fine."

"You're not fine. You keep rubbing it and wincing."

"Well, you're not making it better by squeezing it."

"Just let me check, okay?"

"Ow! Goddamn it!"

Amanda dropped Hannah's arm. "We'll have to wait and see, but I don't think it's fractured."

"It is now!"

"Yes, thank you for yelling at me. That's just what I need right now."

Mia watched their exchange with dark fascination, then looked away when Amanda noticed her.

Zack pointed to the elevated highway in the distance, stretching deep into the sunrise. "I don't know the name of that road, but it runs east. I say we travel underneath it until we hit the next town. Along the way, we can figure out what to do about money and food and all that. Is everyone okay with that idea?"

In slow succession, they all nodded. Zack studied their grim and weary faces.

"All right then."

The group took a final mournful look at Czerny, then slowly proceeded down the road. Two by two, they traveled east—rarely talking, frequently yawning.

Soon a commuter aerotrain crossed high above them on invisible tracks. The bottom of each car sported glowing white struts that varied in formation from trailer to trailer. From below, the whole thing looked like a giant string of dominoes.

The group stopped in place, craning their necks until the final car passed from view.

"They have flying trains," Hannah uttered. "Did anyone else know they had flying trains?"

From the blank expressions of the others, it was clear that they didn't. "Jesus."

Amanda rubbed her back. "Come on."

With a deep breath, the actress picked a pebble from her sneaker and then joined the others. The Silvers followed the road to the elevated highway, and then kept walking.

PART FOUR

ALTAMERICA

SIXTEEN

September 6 was a bad day to be a morning commuter on Highway V. A tempic police cordon blocked all northbound lanes at Terra Vista while bright lumic arrows diverted vehicles to the nearest clogged exit. The ghosted image of a U.S. flag slowly rippled above the barrier. A glimmering overlay asked drivers to be patient and kind to their fellow Americans.

Beyond the cordon, twenty state and local policemen gathered to investigate the odd standoff that had occurred here ninety minutes ago. The Terra Vista police chief scratched his jowls in confusion as he processed the testimony. He was a fat and hairy man of churlish disposition. No one had cause to find humor in the fact that his name was James Bond.

The chief was in a particularly foul mood this morning. Two of his men had been banged up in a high-speed road chase that went bizarrely awry. Another two were laid up with cracked ribs and punctured lungs. They rested on stretchers, waiting for the court recorder to arrive. Before their wounds and memories could be undone by revivers, they had to give their sworn statement about the woman who hurt them—a tall and skinny redhead who'd discovered a bold new way to resist arrest.

Everyone glanced up as a pair of ash-gray aerovans appeared above the treetops. The doors of each vehicle were garnished with the familiar golden logo of a spread-winged eagle, perched behind a large number 9. With a pair of steamy hisses, the vans unfolded their rubber tires and descended to the pavement.

Just as the chief expected, the Deps had come out to play.

The Bureau of Domestic Protections was formed in 1961, at the peak of the New Simplicity. The government's goal was basic: to consolidate their national law enforcement agencies under one umbrella, with clear delineations of purpose between each of the eight new divisions.

In 1988, the Bureau created a ninth department to tackle the growing crimes of high technology. In addition to chasing down the new and savvy breeds of cracker (hacker), jacker (pirate), ripper (scammer), and creeper (pervert), DP-9 was tasked with curbing the felonious misuse of temporis. Each new method of bending time created at least a dozen new ways to break the law. The most common infractions involved swifting (causing mayhem in a speedsuit), rifting (accelerating only part of a victim's body), clouding (vandalizing the sky with lumic projections), and tooping (using rejuvenators to create illegal copies of objects).

When the preliminary report of the morning's altercation reached the federal wire, two words—*weaponized tempis*—raised eyebrows at DP-9 headquarters in Washington. A team was quickly dispatched from the Los Angeles office.

The policemen watched with cynical interest as eight agents emerged from the vans. Six of them were merely boys in suits, technicians with badges. Their leader was a gray-haired shellback with an Old West mustache and enough leathery experience on his face to ease the chief's mind.

The final Dep was something else entirely.

While her companions were pasty, her skin was a smooth cocoa brown. She wore a short red skirt over stockings and a sleeveless white blouse that flaunted every curve of her sculpted arms. Intricate brass earrings dangled from her lobes like chandeliers. Most intriguing of all were her twelve-inch dreadlocks, finger-thick and scattered like fern leaves. It was an alien hairstyle in this country, even among the odd folk.

A dozen stares followed the woman as she surveyed the scene. She was certainly easy to look at, but between her strange hair and features—her overpronounced cheekbones and near-Asian eyes—she seemed far too exotic to be an agent of the Eagle.

The seasoned Dep-in-charge noticed the chief and approached him. They traded a firm handshake.

"Andy Cahill. Supervising Special Agent, DP-9."

"James Bond. Poe-Chief, Terra Vista."

"We hear six of your men came across some interesting sinners."

"Four of my men," the chief corrected. "The cycle jocks are State Patrol."

"They get hurt too?"

"A few broken fingers each. Apparently some queer-looking swifter knocked the guns right out of their hands."

"Queer-looking how?"

"She moved too fast to get a full eyeball, but the men say her speedsuit was torked to look like normal clothes."

Cahill stoked his jaw. "Huh. That is strange. What prompted the chase in the first place?"

"My men noticed a bloodstain on the driver's side of the vehicle. They attempted—"

"Sir, I apologize for cutting you off," said the female Dep, "but it takes time to set up our drills. If you could point us to the location of the tempic attack, that would facilitate our work here."

The chief blinked at her, befuddled. The woman spoke with a scholarly foreign accent, a quasi-British twang he'd never heard before. *Hell and wonders. She's not even American.*

Cahill smirked. "This is Melissa Masaad. Don't let the skirt fool you. She's smarter than us."

Offering the friendliest smile she could muster, Melissa gave the chief a handshake that rivaled Cahill's in pure ferocity. It was one of the first customs she learned here.

"Masaad," said the chief, as if her name were all asterisks and ampersands. "That's quite unique. What part of the world—"

"I'm sorry, sir. Where did you say this attack occurred?"

Melissa was born in British North Sudan. At seventeen, she moved to the motherland to attend Oxford, where she earned advanced degrees in mechanical science and criminology. She spent the next six years in London as an analyst for Military Intelligence, specializing in the study of temporal weaponry. Ten months into her tenure, she received a Royal Commendation for tracking the perpetrators of a deadly rift attack at a Cambridge aerport.

Two years ago, at age thirty, she was offered one of the four hundred immigration slots that the United States extended annually to exceptional applicants. She didn't hesitate to renounce her British and Sudanese citizenship, one of the chief requirements of naturalization. America demanded sole allegiance from its adopted children. Melissa was prepared to give it.

"You're making a terrible mistake," Sir Edgar Ballott had warned her. He was an old British manatee, an Assistant Director-General of the Security Service. More than her mentor, he considered himself her father figure, albeit one who often imagined her naked.

"The United States may be a peaceful nation, my dear, but it's teeming with racists, isolationists, and every other breed of regressive bigot. If you believe they'll embrace a foreigner and a negress as their equal, then I fear you're in for an abrupt education."

Melissa had kept silent at the time. She saw no purpose in drawing out a futile conversation.

"I don't care what the documents say," Sir Edgar insisted. "England will always be your home."

England had stopped being her home a long time ago, since the military began using her research to improve their temporic arsenal. She feared it'd be a matter of years, not decades, before His Majesty's Armed Forces managed to squeeze an entire Cataclysm into the nose of a long-range missile. God help their enemies then. God damn her if she ever played a part in that.

The policemen watched the Deps assemble their devices on the highway—four black obelisks, each eight feet tall and covered in glass lenses. They were placed forty feet apart in a perfect square. Thick cables connected them to a portable computer.

As Melissa helped prep the towers, two state patrolmen eyed her through slitted eyes.

"Huh. I didn't even know they had duskers in England."

"Yeah. The limers set their flag in a bunch of savage countries. Guess they brought a few back."

Melissa ignored them. In her thoughts, Sir Edgar Ballott raised a smug eyebrow.

A half hour later, the ghost drills were ready. Each system cost two million dollars and required five technicians to operate, at a taxpayer cost of seventeen thousand dollars per hour. All that expense and effort to achieve what David Dormer could do with a wave of his hand.

Inside the perimeter of the towers, the recent past came to light. The dilapidated Salgado van reappeared in front of a disembodied strip of white tempic barrier. The projections were as brown and grainy as a Civil War photograph until the technicians made their adjustments. Soon the van could almost pass as the real thing.

Cahill pointed at the ethereal vehicle. "Why are the back doors transparent?"

Melissa squinted at them. "I've only seen that effect during a double-echo, when you view the ghost of a ghosted image."

"Ghosted van doors? We don't even have that technology. What's it doing on a ten-year-old junker?"

While setting up the drills, Melissa had kept an ear on the discussion between Cahill and Bond. She listened with great interest about the phantom truck that appeared on the highway, sending one police cruiser into opposite lanes. The ability to create a three-dimensional image of that size—on a fast-moving freeway, no less—was far beyond the capability of any lumic projector.

Suddenly a colorful streak emerged from the passenger side of the van, disappearing beyond the confines of the ghost field.

"Whoa! Did you see that?"

"Rewind and replay," Melissa told her teammate. "Tenth speed."

Even at slow playback, it took three attempts for the technicians to catch Hannah in motion, and then another twelve adjustments to achieve an unblurred freeze-frame. Now every law enforcer fixed their stare on the frightened young thing with the nightstick in her hand, a woman who moved at triple-digit velocity.

The Deps crossed into the image field, studying Hannah up close. Like breathing underwater or walking through fire, speeding was a perfectly mundane accomplishment with the proper gear. But in her flimsy cotton tank top and grass-stained running shorts, this woman did not have the equipment to do what she was currently doing.

Cahill tossed a muddled glance at Melissa. "I fig you never saw anything like this in Europe."

"No, sir. Nothing even close."

While Hannah's speedy feat was enough to rattle all investigators, her sister's angry hands truly shook their world.

Thirty-two more seconds of playback passed before Amanda emerged from the van. Though the ghosts were soundless, the lip-reader on the team relayed the tense words exchanged between the redhead and the two local policemen. A short teenage girl suddenly burst through the ghosted rear doors. One of the officers fired his gun in surprise. Then things got weird.

Now all the cops and Deps on scene stared in muted wonder at the frozen image of Amanda's tempic outburst. The technician paused playback just as the policemen were slammed down to the pavement by her shimmering white hands, each one the size of a coffee table.

Melissa walked a slow, shambling circle around Amanda, straining her mind to find a sensible explanation. To accept this sight at face value involved pushing her skeptical boundaries five yards away from reason, toward the land of aliens and vampires.

She made several notes in her handtop before rejoining Cahill at the edge of the ghost field.

"So what are you thinking?" he asked.

"I'm thinking the Bureau may owe Wingo an apology, sir."

Cahill chuckled. Alexander Wingo was a dark legend among the Deps. He'd been a rising star at DP-1, known all throughout the Bureau for his deductive brilliance and flamboyant eccentricities. Thirty-six years ago, a perplexing homicide investigation took him into strange territory, and he became obsessed with a secret society of time-bending superpeople he dubbed the Gothams.

Wingo soon quit the Bureau to become a full-time crusader. His bestselling book, *Children of the Halo*, inspired a generation of rumors, myths, and hoaxes. To this day, the Gothams remained a favored topic among the crackpot fringe.

"Let's table the crazy stuff for a moment," said Cahill. "What do you make of the people?"

"They're all young and frightened. Given the state of the van, as well as their injuries, it's clear they engaged in battle before the police discovered them. I wouldn't be surprised if we find more casualties in their wake."

"Motley assortment here. Four adults and two teens. I'd guess they were all kin if it wasn't for the chinny. Where do you think he fits in all this?"

Melissa studied Theo's ghost. "They wouldn't have left him near the revolver if they didn't trust him. Whoever he is, he's one of them. He's not Chinese, by the way."

"How do you know?"

"The tattoo on his left wrist is Baybayin. It's an old writing script of the Philippines, pre–Spanish colonialization."

Melissa had been on Cahill's staff for twenty-two months now. In her early days, he feared she was hopelessly out of her element, a fish in the desert. Now he wished he could clone a whole team of her.

"If you want to embarrass me further, you can tell me what the ink says."

"It's been years since I studied the language," Melissa confessed. "Best I can figure, it says *rama*. Or possibly *kama*."

"Kama?"

It wasn't until she said it out loud that Melissa fit the pieces together. "Karma, sir."

For the hundredth time, Cahill locked his gaze on Amanda and her great tempic arms.

"I get the sense that none of these people are out hunting for victims. They only attack when cornered. I suppose I should find some comfort in that. At the moment, I just want to break out the wet card and drink myself silly."

"Understandable, sir. I imagine you'll be postponing your sunset now."

"Why in worlds would you think that?"

Melissa laughed. "Are you joking? A case like this?"

Andy Cahill was set to retire in three weeks. He'd been a Dep for over forty years, since the days before tempis and aeris, juving and shifting. Like the Silvers, he'd been born into a world where time only moved in one speed and direction. Cahill had adjusted to the new reality better than most of his generation.

But now it seemed the game had changed again, and this time he wasn't ready to follow. He was old, he was tired, and he had Melissa now. She was sharper than anyone he'd ever worked with. She had decades left to her.

"Darling, the minute I get back to the office, I'm making you the lead on this case."

"Sir, I'm not at a level to—"

"You will be. I'm putting in those papers too. You're ready for this. Trust me."

"All respect, sir, it's not my readiness that concerns me. The directors—"

"I'll handle the idiots above me. You'll have to handle the idiots below. A lot of them won't like the fact that you're cutting in line. And others . . . well, I don't have to tell you why they'll have problems. You'll just have to earn their trust or push them out of the way."

Cahill held her arm, then jerked his head at Amanda's ghost.

"Just promise me you'll find these people. Whoever they are, they're scared, they're reckless, and they're powerful. You track them down. You haul them in. And for the ones who hurt those troopers, you make damn sure to give them their due karma."

The chief interrupted them with updates. His men had just discovered the original van in question, abandoned twelve miles away at the edge of a national forest. Additionally, the registered owner of the vehicle—one Martin Salgado—had been located in Terra Vista. He and his son were found hunched forward in the front seat of a drifting aerocruiser. Cause of death was currently unknown.

Having two fresh new avenues to explore, two dotted lines to the dangerous oddities, Melissa Masaad took a heavy breath, then plotted her next several moves.

SEVENTEEN

For those traveling east, Ramona was the last pocket of suburbia in San Diego County. The town was home to fifty thousand people, twice the population of the Ramona that had existed on the Silvers' world. In the wake of the Cataclysm, millions of East Coast emigrants made a cold rush on California, crowding every city, burg, and hamlet until the state cracked in half. By 1940—when Ramona, CA, became Ramona, CS—the local headcount had tripled and the town had bulged a half mile in every direction.

Theo groaned like an old man as he hunkered down on a wooden park bench. He'd spent the last four hours trekking through the margins of civilization, all the ranches and branches and gulches of South California. He wanted nothing more than to take a deep nap, but he knew from experience that cops didn't take kindly to rumpled dozers. The last thing the group needed was more police attention.

At 11:30 on a Monday morning, the playground park was only minimally occupied by human life—two mothers, three toddlers, and four weary Silvers. A string of single-level storefronts lined the street across from Theo, brandishing offers both familiar and strange. An auto supply shop professed to be the number one place for custom liftplates and swore that none of their parts were tooped. A spa clinic advertised a special on Circadian Adjustment Therapy, inviting all to *Extend Your Day the Natural Way*. A business called Farsight Professional Augury peddled fortune-telling services with the elegant veneer of a bank. A fancy sign boasted that their staff had a prediction accuracy rating of 68%.* Theo was too far away to read the asterisk's fine print.

He rested his face in his palms, dreading all the new headaches ahead of him. He was used to wandering cashless through California, but never sober, and always alone. He wondered if he'd be better off without the group, and vice versa. He didn't know them very well (and vice versa). Besides, what did he bring to the table? He wasn't all that resourceful, and he didn't sport an eerie talent like each of them did. Of course, after witnessing Amanda's tempic blowup, Theo didn't feel too bad about being left off the weirdness wagon.

A three-year-old girl in a little pink romper wandered away from the playground and studied Theo from a curious distance. It took a few moments for him to notice her.

"Uh . . ."

Theo scanned the park behind him. The two mothers on scene remained rooted at the swing set, hopelessly distracted by the sight of a shirtless David.

He shined the girl an awkward smile. "Hi."

She shyly bit her fingers. On seeing Theo's bloody arm bandage, her half grin melted away.

"It's just a scratch," he assured her. "A little owie. Listen, you should probably—"

One of the mothers, a chubby woman not much older than Theo himself, hurriedly scooped the girl into her arms. She shot Theo a glare of nervous judgment, as if he were holding a fishing rod with candy on the hook.

With a jaded sigh, Theo turned his gaze back to the augury service. He wondered if people were all that friendly here in Altamerica.

Hannah rested in the comforting shade of a sugar pine tree, her mind even more exhausted than her legs. All throughout her trek, her thoughts had run circles around her. *I wish I knew what Azral was wow I bet every cop in the state is looking for Christ I really broke their fingers when damn we're all gonna starve if Amanda can't Jesus what did she do to those policemen?*

By the time she'd reached Ramona, she couldn't conjure anything more than a few impure notions. David stood bare-chested against a nearby elm tree, staring off into the distance like a high-fashion model. For a teenage genius who didn't eat a lot of protein, he sported a surprising amount of muscle tone. The skin on his chest was hairless and glistening. To the women of the park, he was the thing to look at. He wasn't just the group's David anymore. He was Michelangelo's.

"What are you thinking about?" Hannah asked him.

He continued to gaze at an empty patch of grass as he absently tapped his wristwatch.

"David?"

He shook his head and blinked at Hannah. "I'm sorry?"

"Just checking up on you. You look so lost."

"Actually, I was scanning the local past in my head. I can't help myself. Everywhere I go now, I nose through history like a curious dog."

"Yeah? See anything interesting?"

"Oh yes. Every year, around October, they host a candlelight vigil in this park. Everyone wears white robes and masks, and no one says a word. It's quite eerie. There was also a gruesome murder here about five years ago. Some poor woman got stabbed in the neck."

"Ewww. God. Why would you even look at that?"

"Guess I'm just in a grim mood." He grew a sheepish smile. "Though I admit I keep coming back to a sunbather who was here last weekend. She's . . . quite nice to look at."

Hannah was sure the girl would feel the same about him.

"You probably think that's creepy," he said. "It is creepy. I should stop."

"Sweetie, you do whatever makes you feel good."

Mia sat alone at a nearby picnic table, forcing her anxious gaze at her journal. For the fifth time in four minutes, she lost the fight against her teenage id and drank David in. In the corner of her vision, she caught Hannah smirking at her. Mia suddenly grew hot with humiliation and anger until she took a second glance and saw that the actress wasn't mocking her at all. Merely empathizing.

Mia reeled with guilt. She kept misjudging Hannah, even after everything that happened today. While Mia had to be rescued from her attacker in Terra Vista, Hannah saved herself. While Mia couldn't handle her one simple job of keeping Amanda in the van, Hannah did everything that was asked of her. She took on armed policemen with just a nightstick and set her friends free.

Too tired to find the right words, Mia shined Hannah a look of warm regard, and then quietly resolved to think nicer of her in the future.

The future . . .

She focused on her journal again, scanning all the hints and warnings of her elder selves. If the notes were right, then Mia was due to visit the rebuilt New York ("*So beautiful, it brings me to tears*") and ride a flying taxi ("*Holy @$#%!*"). She was supposed to meet a man named Peter, who was either great or untrustworthy, depending on which of the two contrasting notes she chose to believe. And of course the prophecy remained that Hannah would one day save her life. Mia no longer had trouble envisioning that scenario.

On the second page of her notations, an old message jumped out at her.

If you see a small and creepy guy with a 55 on his hand, run. That's Evan Rander. He's bad news.

Mia had originally filed the warning away as a distant concern, as none of the physicists matched the description. Now it merited some thought. She decided to wait a bit longer before burdening the others with this information. They were all running on shattered nerves right now. She feared one in particular was dangerously close to snapping.

Amanda bit her thumbnail, tapping a nervous beat on the counter as the sweaty man conducted his tests. She could see from the pawnbroker's license on the wall that his name was John Curry and he was twenty-nine years old. Genetics had unfortunately screwed him in two directions, giving him the acne of a teenager and the hairline of a middle-aged man. To make matters worse, he carried both the shape and smell of an overstuffed trash bag. Amanda was too unglued to think charitably, and could only assume that one of the torments that awaited her in the infernal beyond involved handcuffs, a bed, and John Curry.

He'd already examined her wedding ring through a grading loupe, inspecting every curve and facet for impurities. Now he put it inside a device that resembled an Easy-Bake oven. As the machine whirred, the pawnbroker fixed his appraising eyes on Amanda. He studied her in a way that made her empty stomach churn.

She turned around to check on Zack. He'd accompanied her to the store to help negotiate a good sale price. Now he strangely hung back near the entrance, browsing the hocked watches.

Amanda threw him a tense, baffled shrug. *What are you doing?*

He replied with a nod and an assuring palm. *It's okay. You're fine.*

Though Amanda had been through hell and a four-hour hike, and was forced to wear David's T-shirt to cover the bloodstains on her own, she was still a fetching sight. Zack saw the pawnbroker's eyes pop with interest the moment she stepped through the door. He figured Amanda would have a better shot handling the business on her own.

The pawnbroker scratched his pitted cheek as he pondered the machine's analysis. "I'll give you five hundred."

Amanda balked at him. "Five hundred? The ring cost eight thousand dollars."

"I doubt that."

Zack wasn't able to remind her that she was working from another world's economy. All the same, the offer was disappointing. *Come on, man. You know she puts the "dish" in disheveled. Cut her a deal.*

"How about six hundred?" Amanda asked.

"No way. I'd be taking a loss."

"How? This is eighteen-karat gold with five diamonds."

"Right. And it's also been juved."

Zack was surprised to learn that his work left traces, and that reversal affected the resale value.

"Five fifty," Amanda offered.

The pawnbroker removed the ring from the scanner, holding it out to Amanda as if he were proposing the most cynical marriage ever.

"You only have two choices here: five hundred or keep walking."

She slapped her palm on the counter. "Look, I wouldn't be selling this if I didn't need the money! I guarantee the extra fifty dollars will mean a lot more to me than it will to you."

The pawnbroker stared in turmoil at the cash safe under his desk. The moment Amanda struck the counter, the tempic shell rippled like jostled milk. It took five seconds for the walls to settle back to normal.

"Look at me, John. My name's Amanda Given. I'm not a gambler or a drug addict. I'm not . . ." Once again she suffered a tactile flashback, and could feel the broken ribs in the chests of those policemen. "I'm not a criminal. I'm just someone who's hit bad times. A bunch of us need this money for food. Now, you're going to make a profit on this ring regardless. I'm asking you out of the goodness of your heart to raise your offer. Please."

Between the freakish incident with his safe and Amanda's unbearable intensity, the pawnbroker's sexual interest became replaced by a burning desire to get her out of his store.

"Five ten. That's my absolute last deal. Take it or go. Just decide fast."

Frustrated, Amanda glanced at Zack. All he could offer was a hopeless shrug.

She turned back to the pawnbroker. "Fine, John. Fine."

He counted out a thin blue wad of bills. Amanda snatched it from his hands.

"Fine deal. Fine profit. Fine person you are."

While the pawnbroker glared, Amanda took a final look at the ring that had traveled with her across the multiverse. Her thoughts teemed with images of Derek, a flip-book chronicle of decline that began with his marriage proposal and ended with his last spiteful words.

She joined Zack at the exit and passed him her money with trembling hands. "It's not enough."

He led her outside. "It's enough for now."

"No. It's not enough money. I should . . ."

She fumbled for her golden cross necklace, tucked away under two T-shirts. "I should see . . . I should see how much . . ."

"No."

"It's just a symbol."

"Amanda . . ."

"I don't need a symbol to be a good Christian."

The walls of her composure crumbled away. She fled down a narrow alley between the pawnshop and a bakery. There among the boxes of old discarded bread, she crouched to the ground and wept into her hands.

Zack followed her down the alley and took a seat on the milk crate next to her.

"I should have listened to Mia," Amanda confessed. "I should have never gotten out of the van."

Zack knew this wasn't the best time to agree with her. "They're being fixed. Whether it's through temporis or good old-fashioned medicine, those cops—"

"Doesn't change the fact that I did it."

"No. Can't say it does."

Zack fixed a dreary stare on the abandoned loaves and rolls. He assumed it was only professional pride that kept the bakers from selling rejuvenated bread.

"I hurt that guy back in the building. Rebel. I panicked and I aged his hand. If Dr. Czerny—rest his soul—was right about what that does to a body, then I probably shot a bunch of fatal air bubbles into his heart."

"You were defending yourself," Amanda said. "That man was trying to kill you."

"Yeah, and you didn't attack those cops until one of them fired a bullet at Mia. It's also worth noting that Rebel would have killed me and Theo if you hadn't stopped him. I'm sorry I never thought to thank you until now. I just hope the next time you think about the two men you hurt today, you also remember the two you saved."

Amanda looked up at him with red eyes. Though she was loath to praise him in their tense early days together, she'd noticed from the start that Zack was humble to the point of self-deprecation. There wasn't a vain bone in his body.

She took a deep wet sniff and gazed across at the bread boxes.

"They'd have to be big bubbles."

"What?"

"Rebel. You'd have to make big bubbles in his bloodstream in order to kill him. A few centimeters at least. Even then, he could still survive if he got treated in time. You don't need a reviver. Just a hyperbaric chamber. Most hospitals have one, at least where we come from."

Zack almost laughed at his conflicting reactions to her information. He was relieved to be that much less a murderer, and worried that Rebel would be that much more alive to murder Zack someday.

"Thank you. It's been bugging me all morning. I needed that perspective."

"No problem," she replied, with black humor. "I'm here to help."

What began as a snicker soon escalated into a series of near-maniacal giggles. She caught Zack's puzzled grin.

"I was just thinking about that pawnbroker. The expression on his face when I got all pissy on him. I can't tell you how many times I've gotten that look from people, Zack. Complete strangers. My husband always said I made a strong first impression on people. It wasn't a compliment."

The cartoonist smirked sardonically. "That's all right. I once had a woman slap me just thirty seconds after meeting me."

Amanda laughed. "Yeah. I remember. Guess I made a strong first impression on you too."

"Well, part of me."

She wiped her eyes and brushed back her hair. She realized now that she'd have to dye it a different color. *God. I'm already thinking like a fugitive.*

"Zack, why does that trash bread look so good to me?"

"Because we haven't eaten all day. Come on."

He rose to his feet and extended a hand. As he helped her up, she wrapped herself around him.

"Oh. Hey. Huggage."

"Thankful huggage," said Amanda. "I'm glad you were still with us when all this stuff happened. I'm glad you're still with us now. You're a good man, Zack. Sometimes, on rare occasions, you're even funny."

He grinned along to her surprisingly droll humor, his hands falling awkwardly on her back. As a jaded New Yorker from an aloof and broken family, he was severely unskilled in the art of physical contact. But there was something jarringly beautiful about this embrace. They were both the same height, with the same limber frame. Her warmth and symmetry were a little too nice to handle right now.

At the end of their hug, Amanda suffered a sudden flashback to Esis Pelletier. The madwoman had approached her in an alley much like this one, uttering words so bizarre and cryptic that Amanda quickly forgot them in the chaos that followed. Except now a tiny fragment came back to her, an angry warning to not entwine with something. Or someone.

She crumpled the thought into an angry little ball and buried it in the back of her mind, along with the policemen, the pawnbroker, and Derek's harsh words. No more of that business. It was time to be strong again.

They returned to the park with nourishing goodies, their first meal on Earth that wasn't provided by physicists. For a gratifying twenty minutes, the Silvers sat around the picnic table, devouring their bounty like a pack of wild predators.

Amanda returned David's T-shirt after the meal. She watched with puzzlement as he sniffed the fabric. She wasn't sure if he was checking for sweat stink, cooties, or something worse.

While the others waged a run on the nearby department store, Amanda stayed in the park with Theo. Their clothes were too bloody for close public mingling. Theo was in no condition to go shopping anyway. Once Amanda finished changing his bandage, she led him to the shade of the pine tree and ordered him to take a nap. Though he insisted he was fine, he quickly drifted away on a bed of grass.

Amanda rested against the tree, mindless in the wake of her meltdown. She occasionally heard Theo mumble in his sleep. He called out to a woman named Melissa, then mumbled something about a girl with two watches. Amanda hoped he was at least having a good dream.

An hour and a half later, the others came back with fresh supplies. New clothes for all. Better shoes for some. A map. A compass. Two flashlights. Six knapsacks to carry it all.

Amanda wasn't encouraged by Zack's crabby expression. "How much do we have left?"

"Don't ask."

"Tell me."

He sighed defeatedly. "About a hundred and fifty."

"What?"

"We bought the cheapest stuff they had. But even bargain basement clothes add up when there are six of us."

"So what are we going to do about money?"

"I don't know," he said. "You think you can write the Harry Potter books from memory?"

Amanda fought a grin. "No."

"*Twilight*?"

"Zack . . ."

"I have some ideas. We can talk about it later. In the meantime, you may want to have a chat with your sister. Or Mia. Or both."

"Why? What—"

Hannah dropped her bags on the picnic table, then brusquely walked away. Her face was grim. Her eyes were red from crying. Mia soon slapped her own purchases on the table and shuffled off in the other direction. She looked even worse.

When Amanda turned to Zack, he chucked his hands in hopeless quandary. He had no idea what happened between Hannah and Mia. Neither one of them was talking.

They'd split up four ways inside the Harvey Mark, with a plan to reassemble in an hour. Mia wandered the aisles in a moony daze, marveling at the daft embellishments to this otherwise familiar environment. A stock boy pushed giant boxes on a hovering aeric platform. A two-dimensional ghost woman hawked the benefits of a Harvey Mark purchase account. A young boy hobbled after his mother on legs of pure tempis.

More alarming were the fashions, a mix of 1950s and 1980s clothing styles, flavored with a twist of madness. Mia saw two teenage girls dressed in sleeveless turtlenecks with cleavage holes cut in the fabric. One wore a bob of orange-red hair that was teased to looked like flames. The other sported blond bangs that were long enough to obscure her eyes. Mia couldn't tell if the girls were cookie-cutter trend slaves or bold fashion rebels. All she knew was that she'd never be anything more than an alien here.

Soon Mia and Hannah spotted each other in the women's clothing section. Their overwhelmed expressions were identical, enough to evoke a mutually nervous giggle.

"This place is like Wal-Mart on acid," Hannah said. "It's freaking me out."

Despite Mia's resolve to think nicer of Hannah, she found herself squinting with reproach at the box of black hair dye in her handcart. *Your sister sold her wedding ring so we could eat and live, not touch up our roots.*

It was actually Amanda who'd requested the product for herself. Though Mia had misjudged again, Hannah wasn't entirely innocent this time. She'd convinced her sister to go black over blond just so she could use the leftover dye on her roots.

Peering into Mia's cart, Hannah winced at the pair of dark, long-sleeved shirts she'd chosen for purchase. *Oh sweetie. You're going to bake like a muffin in those things. Is it worth getting heatstroke just to look slimmer for David?*

Loath as she was to jeopardize Mia's fresh goodwill, Hannah plotted a course of delicate pestering. "Uh, hey, listen—"

"Oh, you've got to be kidding me."

Mia spun a quick circle, urgently scanning all shoppers within eyeshot. From her panicked expression, Hannah feared the girl was on the verge of a gastric catastrophe.

"Are you okay?"

"No. She couldn't have picked a worse time. What the hell is she thinking?"

"What? Who are you—"

A bead of light suddenly appeared ten inches in front of Mia's chest. Hannah took a step back.

"Whoa. Jesus. Is that . . . is that the thing your notes come from?"

"Yeah."

Mia raised her handcart until it obscured the glowing breach. Hannah skittishly peeked inside.

"Wow. I've never seen one of these before. It's like a tiny sun. How long before a note pops out?"

"It varies," said Mia, increasingly tense. Something wasn't right about this delivery.

"And does it usually—"

"Hannah, I can't talk right now. I need to focus on this."

"Okay," she said, dejectedly. "I didn't know. I'm sorry."

Wincing with guilt, Mia bent her knees until she was eye level with the portal. She could see another Mia through the tiny circle, anxiously pacing the carpet of her Terra Vista suite. She was dressed in the same clothes Mia wore now, and radiated a sense of worry that was painfully easy to recognize. It was her just fourteen hours ago.

Mia's skin blanched as she grasped the scope of her new problem. "Oh God. Oh my God."

"What? What's the matter?"

"This is a past portal. I'm not receiving, I'm sending. I know exactly what I need to write but I don't have the right pen. You need to find me a red pen, Hannah. It has to be ballpoint and it has to be red."

"Uh, okay. Why—"

"I'll explain the rest when you get back! I promise! Just please go! Hurry!"

Hannah rushed toward the school supplies, wondering just how scared she should be. She vaguely recalled David mentioning something about Mia's newfound fear of paradoxes, the devastating consequences of changing the past. He didn't seem to share her concern.

"I don't believe it works the way she thinks it does," he'd told Hannah. "I certainly can't imagine that some minor inconsistency in her notes will somehow bring the universe to collapse. Then again, what do I know?"

David knew plenty, enough to alleviate Hannah's fears. Still, after everything that happened to their world, she could understand why Mia would be deathly afraid to screw with time.

Hannah quickly returned with an assortment of red pens. Thin trails of sweat rolled down Mia's temples.

"Oh thank God. I don't know how much longer it'll stay open."

"I'm here. I have it."

Hannah shielded the portal from all prying eyes while Mia tore a pen from its packaging. She ripped a careful swatch from the back of her journal and then double-checked the archive of her original message. She didn't know why she bothered. The words had been laser-burned onto her psyche.

They hit you all at sunrise. Sleep with your shoes on. Get ready to run.

During the eighty-two long seconds of Hannah's absence, Mia had considered all the things she wished she could write in place of that vague warning. With the right words, she could have ensured that the building was evacuated hours in advance. Nobody would have died.

Conversely, she pictured what would happen if the portal closed without any warning sent at all—a revised chain of events in which Rebel and his people killed everyone in their sleep. It was too terrible to think about. It was worse to think that it could still occur retroactively, just because Mia didn't have the right pen.

Mia rolled up the note and deposited it into the breach. As the portal vanished silently into the ether, she wrapped Hannah in a delirious hug of relief.

"Oh God. Thank you so much. I'm sorry I made you go running like that. And I'm sorry if I was ever cold or mean to you. It's just stupid jealousy. You're so pretty and you have this amazing body. But I know you're a good person too. And I promise from now on . . ."

She suddenly realized that Hannah wasn't returning the embrace. Mia pulled back to find her white-faced with horror, stammering as if Mia had stabbed her.

"You knew."

"What?"

"Your note. I saw it. You knew we were going to be attacked today and you didn't say anything."

Mia tensely shook her head. "No. Hannah. I didn't know. I mean not for sure."

"'They hit you all at sunrise'? 'Get ready to run'? What did you think it meant?"

"You don't understand. I've gotten bad notes before. Conflicting notes. I wasn't sure what was happening and I didn't want to worry people without—"

"You didn't want to *worry people*?"

In hindsight, it sounded pretty bad to Mia too. "Hannah, I'm so sorry."

The actress didn't care about Mia's remorse. She didn't care how this whole scene looked to the bystanders who were watching. Her mind was trapped six hours in the past, lost in battle with the Motorcycle Man.

"I went out jogging at sunrise," she cried to Mia. "Do you think I would have done that if . . . do you know how close I came to dying?"

"I'm sorry!"

"Sorry doesn't fix it, Mia! People died! Czerny died! Erin got cut in half, all because *you* didn't want to worry people!"

The tears flowed wildly on both of them now. Hannah held up a trembling hand.

"I can't even look at you."

She retreated down the aisle, crashing into a fellow shopper as she brusquely turned the corner. Both their handcarts fell to the floor.

"Oh God. I'm so sorry."

"My fault," the man assured her.

He wasn't wrong. It took five rewinds for Evan Rander to stand in just the right place for a spilling collision. Now he shined a cordial grin as he stooped to gather Hannah's belongings.

"Oh, you don't have to—"

"No, no, no. I insist. What kind of gentleman would I be?"

Even in a better state of mind, Hannah wouldn't have recognized him from their first encounter. Evan had swapped his ostentatious cowboy getup for a simple gray business suit. His hair had been respectfully parted to one side, and he wore soulful blue contact lenses behind rimless glasses. He was the humble good Samaritan now. He was Clark Kent.

Soon he presented Hannah with a refilled handcart. She sniffed and wiped her nose. "Thank you."

"No worries. I sense you're not having the best of days."

"Yeah. That's putting it mildly."

"I saw you arguing with your sister back there. Listen, I have siblings myself. These things always blow over."

Hannah rubbed her eyes. "She's not my sister."

"Oh."

"Look, I'm sorry. I really need to go."

"Of course. Of course. I understand. You take it easy now, all right?"

There was very little for Hannah to find creepy or suspicious about this incarnation of Evan. And yet as she made her brisk journey to the restroom, a dark voice in her head urged her to not look back. She couldn't shake the feeling that the man was still standing at the scene of their accident. Still watching her. Still smiling.

David studied the map on the picnic table. The nearest cradle of civilization was ten miles to the north. Their abandoned van lay a scant eight miles to the southwest. It wouldn't be long before the police search made its way to Ramona, if it hadn't happened already.

"We can't do ten more miles today," Amanda insisted. "We can't even do two miles. Look at us, David."

Over the boy's grumbling objections, the Silvers bought two rooms in a cheap motel off the main drag. The accommodations were pitiful compared to their suites in Terra Vista, but each room had two beds and each bed was soft. By three o'clock, they were all out cold.

Mia woke up four hours later, groggy and alone. Purple clouds peeked in through the curtain gaps. She could hear the shower running.

As she sat up, her hand brushed a small object on the blanket, an eight-inch cigar tube. Future Mia must have sent another delivery in her sleep.

She unscrewed the lid and shook out a roll of blue currency. Her jaw went slack as she counted fifteen hundred-dollar bills.

Mia used her finger to fish out the other two pieces of the parcel: a small white scrap containing a Brooklyn address and an eight-by-ten sheet of note-book paper densely crammed with text. The lettering was blocky and angular. A man's handwriting.

> *Hello, Mia,*
>
> *You don't know me yet, but I'm a friend of your future. In fact, you're sitting next to me as I write this. The Mia I know is fourteen, just like you. But this one traveled across the country to get to me. She made it here with flying colors, along with all her friends.*

Mia spotted her own scribble in the margin. Hey girl! See you on the other side!

The author continued:

> *It's of great importance that I earn your trust, which makes this next part all the more difficult. I'm sorry to say that the people who attacked you in Terra Vista are my people. My clan. There's a group of us who live in the outskirts of New York: forty-four families, all natives of this world, all gifted like you and your friends. We even have a few folks who can fly on wings of aeris, though they can't do it as often as they'd like. Through discipline and the occasional use of misdirection, we've managed to keep our talents hidden from the public at large. We don't want to be lab rats any more than you do. For us, the price of living free is living quietly.*
>
> *Recent developments, however, have put us all in a bad state. In the*

weeks since your arrival, several of our own have gone missing. Worse, the augurs of our clan—the ones who can see the future, live the future, and hear from their future selves—have all gotten wind of a terrible event coming. A second Cataclysm, of sorts.

Shortly after our troubles began, a man named Richard Rosen (you know him as Rebel) determined that the disaster ahead can be averted by destroying all the new people who arrived in this world. He believes you're all living ruptures in the fabric of time, breaches that need to be plugged. Though his theory isn't entirely based in fiction, it's deeply flawed. Unfortunately, fear won out over reason and Rebel got the clan to see things his way. For your sakes, I wish I'd fought better. All I managed to do was get myself banished from the councils.

But I'm not out of the game yet. I've got my own plan to stop what's coming, one that doesn't involve murder. Unlike Rebel, I don't think you and your friends are part of the problem. In fact, I believe you're part of the solution. One of you in particular.

So I'm writing you now, Mia. I'm asking you to come find me at the enclosed address. I can provide you all with shelter, safety, and crucial information. For those of you looking for a purpose on this world, I can sure as hell give you that too.

Come to Brooklyn. You won't have to worry about Rebel for a while, but there are other people on your trail. I'll let your older half tell you about those folks, on the other side of this note.

I'd say I look forward to meeting you, but I already have and I'm already glad. I'll just say I look forward to you meeting me.

All the best,
Peter Pendergen

Beleaguered by all the new information, Mia turned the letter over. The other side was written in Mia's hand, an assortment of quick thoughts scrawled at various angles. A passage at the top caught her attention. It was circled twice and garnished with a smiley face.

Apology from Hannah in 3 . . . 2 . . . 1 . . .

Mia jumped when the door opened. Hannah stepped out of the steamy bathroom. She adjusted her towel wrap and aimed a soft expression at Mia.

"Hi."

"Hey. Where's, uh . . . ?"

"She's checking on Theo. How are you doing?"

Still reeling from the letter, Mia could only shrug. Hannah fixed a somber gaze at her feet.

"Listen, I talked to Amanda. She told me you spent all night in the security room with Erin, looking out for intruders. She also said you're the one who pulled the fire alarm and warned Zack about Rebel. I'm . . . I don't know what came over me. When I learned about your note, I just flipped out and assumed you didn't do anything with the information. But it turns out you did a lot. So, I'm sorry. And I'm so sorry for saying you were responsible for Erin and Dr. Czerny. Can you forgive me?"

Mia bit her lip, nodding in warm accord. Hannah leaned against the doorframe and crossed her arms.

"Okay. Now that I got that out, I have a favor to ask. In the future, should you get another—"

"Evan Rander."

Hannah blinked at her. "What?"

"A note I got. A warning. If you see a small and creepy guy with a '55' on his hand, run. That's Evan Rander. He's bad news."

Though Hannah had failed to notice any numbers on anyone's hands, she could think of two different men who'd set off her creep alarms today.

"Okay. Wow. I don't know what to make of that yet. But I'm glad you told me. Thank you."

Hannah glanced at Mia's journal on the end table, then nervously scratched her neck.

"Is there, uh . . . is there anything else from the future I should know?"

With a flustered sigh, Mia looked down at the fresh new dispatch in her hand. Yeah. There was something else.

EIGHTEEN

Nobody knew what to make of Peter Pendergen. The Silvers convened in one motel room, debating all the revelations and implications of his letter. When they didn't talk over each other, they fell into a pensive silence, one so deep they could hear the slow drip from the showerhead.

Hannah dumped the empty plates and wrappers of their takeout dinner into the trash, then reclaimed her spot on Zack's bed. She peeked over his shoulder as he sketched a man's face on motel stationery.

"I don't trust him," she uttered.

"Me neither," Amanda said from the desk chair. She kept an eye on the muted lumivision. The nine o'clock news would begin in five minutes. She fully expected to be the top story.

"I don't think any of us are ready to marry the guy," Zack replied, "but are you both suggesting we avoid him completely?"

Zack had made it clear that he was very much in favor of meeting Peter. He admitted that his vote was influenced by his desire to go to New York and search for his brother. It also didn't hurt that Brooklyn was 2,500 miles away from the site of their police standoff.

Amanda flicked her hand. "I don't know. It just feels like a trap to me."

"What are you basing that on?" David asked.

"Azral let us go. Maybe this is the reason why. After everything we learned about Dr. Quint today, is it really such a stretch to believe that Peter's also working for the Pelletiers?"

David shook his head. "I think you're being overly paranoid."

"I think she makes a damn good point," Hannah said. "I also find it weird that he didn't include a way for us to contact him. No phone number. No e-mail."

"Well, keep in mind this letter's from Future Peter," Zack said, aware of how silly he sounded. "Maybe the current Peter isn't in a position to hear from us. It might put him at risk somehow. Or put us at risk."

The sisters crossed their arms in synch, wearing the same dubious frown.

"I don't buy it," said Hannah.

"Me neither," said Amanda.

"And what about the fact that Mia got a warning flat-out telling her not to trust him?"

Mia sighed from the foot of David's bed. She'd spent an uncomfortable amount of time in the hot seat tonight, answering numerous questions on behalf of her future selves. She knew she couldn't talk about Peter without mentioning the two conflicting messages she'd received about him five weeks ago:

Don't trust Peter. He's not who he says he is.

Disregard that first note. I was just testing something. Peter's good. He's great, actually.

After reading the messages aloud, Mia had glanced up to five dim and bewildered faces. "Yeah. Now you know what I've been dealing with."

Sadly, there was nothing in this latest parcel to clarify the confusion. On the flip side of Peter's letter, Future Mia addressed the matter with a virtual shrug.

I wish I could explain those notes, but I still don't know why we got them. All I can tell you is that I've known Peter for six months now and I trust him with my life. He's a good man. He's not half as funny as he thinks he is, but he's a good man.

Below her passage, Peter scribbled a brief retort. *I am very funny.*

"I'm honestly not sure what to think about him," Mia said. "But if he is who he says he is, if he really does have shelter and safety to offer us, then I'd hate for us to blow our chance because I got a bad message."

David nodded vigorously. "Exactly. This is an opportunity. I can't speak for the rest of you, but I still want the answers that Quint and Czerny promised us. Maybe Peter can provide them. On top of that, there's also the matter of that second Cataclysm. If Peter's right—"

"—then we'll be walking right into it," Hannah griped.

"He didn't say it was happening in New York," David replied. "He just said it was happening. He also said we're potentially part of the solution. Don't you think that's worth investigating? Isn't that a better way to spend our days than aimless wandering?"

Once again, the discussion hit a weary lull. Theo sat cross-legged on the desk, staring out the window at a municipal impound lot.

"Theo?"

He glanced up at Zack. "Huh?"

"You've been Johnny Tightlips over there. What are you thinking?"

There was no safe way to answer truthfully. From the moment Mia revealed her surprise cash endowment, Theo's dark inner demon had snapped awake in its cage. It eyed the money hungrily, calculating the sheer amount of liquid solace that $1,500 could purchase. It would carry Theo for miles, all the way to the next world.

"I don't know. I mean I understand what David's saying. I respect it."

"But?"

"But this is our first day out in the world. We're still flailing around like newborns. And now you're talking about crossing the country to help some stranger stop a Cataclysm? That's not just ambitious. It's nuts."

Theo saw David's eyes narrow to a cool squint. The dark demon smiled. *The boy doesn't like you. He sees you for the burden you are. You think he's the only one?*

"Looks like we're split down the middle on this," Amanda said.

David chucked a hand in frustration. "You guys can do what you want. If I have to go to New York alone, I will."

"Hey, come on . . ."

"David!"

Zack raised his palms. "Okay. Stop. We've had enough drama for one day. Can we just agree in the short term that we need to get the hell away from California?" His posit was greeted with soft nods. "Good. Then we can all keep going northeast. Maybe Mia will get more info along the way. Maybe we'll dig up our own. The point is that we have days to decide."

Everyone tensed up as the sound of police sirens filtered in from the street. The Silvers sat motionless, fingers extended, until the noise faded away.

Zack sighed exhaustedly. "We also have more pressing concerns."

Mia's older self had succinctly explained the scope of their legal problems.

It's not the cops you need to worry about. It's the Deps. DP-9 is the federal agency that handles temporic crimes, and they're very good. They already know what we look like and what some of us can do. They're extremely eager to meet us, especially Amanda.

The news had caused five stomachs to drop, and sent Amanda to the bathroom with dry heaves. But the warning came bundled with advice, three simple rules for avoiding detection:

1. Stay away from civic cameras. That means no hospitals, no bank machines, and no public transportation of any kind. They're all heavily monitored. You will get spotted.

2. Don't get friendly with the locals. The more you talk, the more you expose yourself as foreigners. They do not like foreigners here.

3. No public displays of weirdness, ever. Keep your talents hidden. Even if you think no one's looking, assume they are. It's the only way you'll make it to New York.

David lurched forward in bed, matching Mia's prone position. He playfully brushed her shoulder.

"Thanks to our invaluable messenger here, we have nearly everything we need to keep ahead of the federal agents. The one thing we're missing is transport. If we can't take buses or trains, then we'll have to acquire a car."

Amanda eyed him sharply. "I hope you're not talking about stealing one."

"I am, actually. Is your objection moral or practical?"

"Both," she said.

"For the moral objection, I assume they have auto insurance on this world. Anyone we steal from will be reimbursed."

"Yes, and I assume they have LoJack on this world, or some other high-tech system that makes it easy to track stolen cars. Are you really that eager for another police chase?"

"Well, that's the practical objection, but—"

David stopped at the sound of Theo's dark chuckle. For a moment, the boy's expression turned so cold that Mia felt the unprecedented urge to move away from him.

"I was about to say that we could target an older vehicle, one less likely to have a tracking device. But by all means, Theo, go ahead and mock me. At least I'm offering options."

"I'm not mocking you, David."

"Then why were you laughing?"

Theo couldn't safely answer that question either. He remembered what it was like to be sixteen and fearless. He remembered the false security his own brilliance afforded him. Now, at twenty-three, it was far too soon to play the role of the hardened old crank. And yet here he was, chuckling at David's impertinence, fighting the urge to say, "Boy, it ain't that easy."

"I was mocking myself. But for what it's worth, you're right that we need wheels. We're going to hit desert soon. That won't be fun to walk."

Zack continued his memory sketch of Evan Rander. "As long as we bring enough water and don't pray to any golden calves, we'll make it through the desert. I'm more concerned about the financials. Fifteen hundred isn't enough to get us across the country."

"You don't think so?" Amanda asked. "I mean we're stocked up on supplies now. If we're careful—"

"If there's one thing I learned today, it's that 'cheap' times six equals 'expensive.' Unless Future Mia fronts us another loan, we'll have to come up with more."

"I'm not so sure."

Theo shook his head. "No, Zack's right. It's not enough money to get to Brooklyn."

Hannah leered at him with sudden puzzlement. He caught her hot stare. "What?"

"You said that before."

"Excuse me?"

"That thing you just said. You used those exact words back in the van."

Now it was Theo's turn to become baffled. "I don't recall saying that."

"I don't recall him saying that either," David attested. "I was there the whole time."

"No. I don't mean the van today. I mean six weeks ago. When I first met you."

In the wake of everyone's dumbfounded looks, Hannah bared her palms. "I'm not making this up! We were on our way to Terra Vista. You'd fallen asleep. And then suddenly you mumbled, 'He's right.' I said, 'Who's right?' and you said, 'Zack. He's right. It's not enough money to get to Brooklyn.' Then your nose got all bloody and you fell into your coma."

The showerhead dripped ten more times before Zack broke the muddled silence.

"Uh, normally I'd write that off as a strange coincidence. But after everything we've seen, Theo, I'm going to go out on a limb and suggest you might not be entirely weirdness-free."

Theo felt a hot rush of blood in his face. He stammered for a response.

"I really don't see how—"

"Oh my God!"

The others followed Mia's gaze to the lumivision, where the nine o'clock news had just begun.

Contrary to Amanda's expectations, the broadcast didn't open with her police sketch. In fact, the standoff on Highway V would merit just forty seconds of airtime. In the absence of any fatalities, and the coordinated silence of all law enforcers on scene, the incident was treated as just another police chase. Another irksome traffic jam.

The top story of the day was much juicier. The star of the tale was Sterling Quint.

———

At 6:34 this morning, operators at Triple-5 Emergency received eleven distress calls of the exact same nature—eleven spouses, lovers, and siblings who'd all succumbed to the same fatal stroke. When record checks revealed that the deceased were all employees at the same organization, authorities suddenly became quite interested in the goings-on at the Pelletier Group.

By sunset, the last of the bodies had been discovered. Four names on the payroll had yet to be accounted for: Erin and Eric Salgado, Beatrice Caudell, and the head honcho himself, Sterling Quint. The world-renowned theorist had left for work at 7 A.M. and was never heard from again.

The story quickly caught fire at newsrooms across the nation. Some broadcasts filled their screens with juxtaposed photos of a dour Quint and a nervous Beatrice—a saucy suggestion that the pair had perpetrated the massacre and were now lovers on the run.

The Silvers watched the lumivision with wide eyes and white faces, processing the deaths of everyone they knew outside the motel room. Hannah thought of poor Charlie Merchant, barely a year older than her. Her eyes welled up with tears.

"I don't get it. Why would he kill them?"

"I assume you're not referring to Quint."

"You know I'm not, David. Come on. I'm talking about Azral."

"It had to be him," Amanda said. "Him and Esis."

The widow couldn't get her mind off Czerny. His death had seemed so inconsistent with his type of injury. Now she knew why. She bit her trembling lip.

"They threw them away. They didn't need them anymore, so they just tossed them like garbage."

David shook his head. "For all we know, this was the work of Rebel's people."

"Doubtful," said Theo. "If Rebel's people had the ability to kill remotely, they wouldn't have come at us with guns and swords."

Mia couldn't bear the thought of anyone having that power. She pictured Azral standing before some necromantic circuit breaker, shutting off lives from miles away. She could only imagine he had six more buttons, all labeled with the names of people in this room.

"Do you think maybe Beatrice got away?" she asked.

The lack of response was enough to confirm her grim suspicion. She took a moment to mourn the poor woman who'd baked her a cupcake for her birthday.

Zack remained silent from his perch on the bed, stewing over the large new problem this tragedy created for them. The Salgado van and the body of Dr. Czerny were two thick chains that tied the Silvers to the Pelletier slaughter. While the media continued to chase ghosts, the federal agents would have a stronger notion of who to blame.

By ten o'clock, Melissa Masaad was angry enough to break the law. It took twenty minutes of research to uncover the location of the nearest tobacco den, hidden away beneath a Terra Vista bowling alley. Six more minutes of digging earned her the passphrase.

"Are your bathrooms clean?" she asked the cashier, just as she was told.

For once, Melissa's foreign attributes worked in her favor. The greasy old man at the counter would have never suspected she was a Dep. Even if she had been with DP-4, the illicit substances division, she wouldn't have wasted time on such a piddling sting. The Bureau didn't care about smoke-easies.

"We have a clean bathroom downstairs," the cashier replied. "They're pay toilets."

"How much?"

"Twenty dollars."

"Goodness. Do these exceptionally clean toilets come with Eaglenet access?"

For an extra ten dollars, they did. Melissa carried a handtop under her arm. She was determined to keep working, all through the night if she had to.

Two stairwells and one purchase later, she sat in an overstuffed recliner in the corner of a dim and smoky lounge. She closed her eyes as she savored the taste of the cigarette, her first in twenty-two months. She'd been hoping to enjoy her life in America without the crutch of nicotine, but today was a day of extraordinary frustrations.

"It's out of my hands," Cahill told her, five hours ago. "We hunt where they tell us to hunt."

Melissa had crafted a no-nonsense approach to tracking the fugitives—a strategic sweep of every pawnshop and panhandle park in the ten-mile radius of the abandoned van. From all appearances, these runners were low on resources. Finding them was simply a matter of anticipating their chosen method of fund-raising.

Unfortunately, the mystery of the dead physicists crashed her plans like a wayward truck, dominating the team for the rest of the day. Nine hours ago, Melissa walked through the empty corridors of the Pelletier building, marveling at the results of her wave scans. From all gauges, the entire building had been temporically reversed, a feat that was as bizarre and unlikely as broiling a high school. Soon policemen stumbled across a bloody Japanese sword, just one foot outside the property perimeter, a discovery that made even less sense. The only encouraging find was a missing door from the stolen van, direct evidence that the fugitives had been there.

Seven hours ago, Melissa sat at the bedside of Janice Salgado, the widow of Martin and mother of the three security guards who were either missing or dead. She was a heavyset woman with a cherry-red bouffant that matched her freshly cracked eyes. A constellation of baby spot sedatives was peppered across her neck, twisting her mouth into an unholy union of a smile and a scream.

"There were six people living in that building," Janice told Melissa. "Marty didn't know where they came from. He said they just showed up one day with bracelets on their wrists and . . . weird stuff. They could do weird stuff. Erin took a real shine to one of them. Young girl named Mia. Poor child. Erin said . . . she said the poor thing lost her whole . . . she lost her whole . . ."

Janice sobbed and clutched at Melissa's blouse. "Please. Please find my youngest. I know in my heart they're gone, but they need to be buried with the family. Please."

Five hours ago, Melissa stood at the city coroner's office, watching through a window as men in masks examined Constanin Czerny. As they finished their work, her handphone rang. Cahill didn't sound pleased.

"Just heard from the directors. Our scope has changed. For the short term, they want us to devote all our resources to finding Sterling Quint."

"What? But sir, the runners—"

"I know. I know. It's all image control. The story's gone national. They reckon we'll look like humps if we can't track one of the country's most famous dwarves."

Melissa clenched her jaw. She had a grim hunch that Quint, Caudell, and the two Salgados had all been inside the Pelletier building when it was mysteriously reversed. Dead or alive, their bodies would have been erased out of existence. The British referred to the process as "nulling." The Americans called it "zilching." In both countries, it had become the cornerstone of waste management, as well as a favored tool for criminal evidence disposal. They'd never find Quint.

"Sir, this is the most perplexing case I've ever seen. There's so much I don't understand. But one thing I know is that every trail leads back to those six people. We need to find them."

"I agree with you, hon. But look at the bigger picture. I'm still five signatures away from making you the new me. This isn't the time to kick sand."

Twenty minutes later, she received a preliminary autopsy report on Constantin Czerny. He had died of the same subarachnoid hemorrhage as the other victims. But from the unique attributes of his abdominal wound, he'd been stabbed by a projectile made of pure tempis.

Melissa was downright smarmy when she updated Cahill.

"Shame we don't know anyone who can cause such an injury, sir. Perhaps Dr. Quint will know."

That was when Cahill told her, with a hopeless sigh, that it was out of his hands. If Melissa wanted to do more digging on the tempic redhead, he wouldn't stop her. But she had to put in face time on the Quint search. Such was the price of career advancement.

After three hours of pointless legwork, Melissa escaped to the tobacco den, puffing cigarette after cigarette as she scanned through digital mug shots. The red-haired woman was, as Melissa feared, a virgin to the justice system. Odder still, there was nothing in the news archives about a girl named Mia who lost her entire family. Were these people in *any* systems?

In a desperate last effort, she accessed the Eaglenet bitboards and launched a keyword search through today's online discussions. There was much talk of tempis and even more talk of redheads, but not a lot of chatter about both. After wading through a number of false double-positives, Melissa found an interesting post in a customer support forum for a popular brand of armored safe:

> This incredibly intense redhead came into my store today and slapped her hand on my counter. Suddenly the tempis on my Shellbox started rippling. Has anyone else seen anything like that?

A profile search on the author revealed him as John Curry, a pawnbroker here in South California. His shop was just eight miles from the site of the fugitives' abandoned vehicle.

Melissa took a final drag of her cigarette, closed her handbook, and hurried outside to the company van. She steered it thirty feet into the air and then shifted to 10×. She could still taste the tobacco on her lips as she shot through the night like a missile, straight toward Ramona.

NINETEEN

Amanda didn't know how to feel about her latest transformation. She watched her reflection from the desk chair while Hannah brushed inky dye into her tresses. Stroke by stroke, lock by lock, red to black, red to black.

At midnight, the job was finished. Now Amanda stared in wonder at the dark-haired stranger in the mirror. To her surprise, she didn't hate the new color. And yet she couldn't help but lament the latest upheaval to her personal status quo. She was a widow now, an alien, a fugitive, a brunette. Mad events were slowly turning her into a parallel-universe version of herself. Bit by bit, piece by piece, she was becoming Altamanda.

Hannah removed the drip-stained towel from Amanda's shoulders, then studied her reaction. "I did the best I could."

"What? No, you did great, Hannah. It's perfect. I'm just upset about the reasons behind it."

"Well, it'll work. I doubt anyone who's looking for you will recognize you now."

"That's really all that matters. Everything else is . . . I just need to get used to it."

Amanda bounced a mirrored gaze at Mia. "So what do you think?"

Mia had peeked up from her journal many times to watch the recoloring in progress, this strikingly cozy endeavor between women. Having grown up in a house full of brothers, it was strange for her to witness the feminine rituals of siblings.

"Looks good," she listlessly replied. "You two finally look related."

Hannah tossed her rubber gloves in the sink. She was too tired to color her own hair. Too upset. She plopped herself onto her bed, sending Zack's drawing fluttering down to the floor. She was sick of thinking about the bothersome man in the picture.

On the flip side of Peter's letter, Future Mia had reserved some words for a new orbiting threat.

I'm not even sure how to explain Evan Rander. He's from our world, but he acts like he's been here forever. He knows us all disturbingly well, and yet none of us know him. We still have no idea why he hates us so much. He always seems to find us when we're alone and at our most vulnerable. He likes to twist the knife, especially on Hannah.

Once Evan's identity was uncovered in retrospect, Zack worked with Hannah to provide a composite sketch of the smiling cowboy who'd greeted them at the side of the van.

"It makes no sense," said Hannah. "What could we have done to make him so angry? What could *I* have done?"

Mia shrugged. "I don't know. Maybe he's just crazy. If I had spent the last six weeks wandering alone out here, I might have lost my mind too. I probably would have slit my wrists."

The sisters traded a dark look in the mirror. Amanda tensely wrung her fingers.

"I don't know who this guy is. Right now, I don't care. We have bigger problems."

"Easy for you to say," Hannah growled. "He hasn't singled you out."

Amanda turned her sharp gaze on her. "Do you want to trade places? Because I'd rather have a stalker chasing me than a team of federal agents."

"Hey, fun fact: the feds are after me too."

"And this Evan guy is following all of us! Why do you . . ." Amanda closed her eyes and waved a tense palm. "I can't handle a fight with you right now."

"Then don't start one."

Amanda tightened her towel wrap and shot to her feet. Mia watched with puzzlement as she closed the bathroom door behind her.

"Okay, what just happened?"

Hannah threw herself back onto the mattress, throwing a dismal gaze at her scarred wrists. "It's nothing. Old wounds."

"Will she be okay?"

"She'll be fine," the actress replied, with dripping venom. "She's a rock, that one."

Mia returned to her journal, her thoughts twisting with unease. She wondered if she dodged a bullet by not having sisters. All things considered, she preferred the way men fought.

Zack and David crossed midnight like frigid old spouses, puttering away in parallel beds. While David browsed a local paper, Zack drew an elaborate pen sketch of Bugs Bunny. There were only a handful of people who'd recognize the poor rabbit now. Zack wasn't even sure David was one of them.

The boy glanced with concern at the stack of glossy blue cash on Zack's nightstand. He checked the door to the bathroom, where Theo had been showering for forty long minutes.

"Maybe we should put that money in a safer place," David suggested.

"What, you mean a hedge fund?"

"No. I mean perhaps I should give it to Mia or one of the sisters."

"Oh, you're just hoping to catch them in their undies, you scamp."

"Zack, I think you know what my issue is."

Zack did know, and he was trying not to get angry about it. "What do you have against Theo anyway?"

David lowered his voice. "Nothing. I'm sure he's a fine person. But at this stage of his alcoholic recovery, he's a liability to all of us."

"That liability got shot trying to save me."

"I'm not asking you to expel him from the group. Just hide the cash."

"Fine. You asked. And I'm saying no. Now drop it."

They languished in icy silence for several minutes. Zack finished his sketch and let out a loud exhale.

"Look, I'm as cynical as the next guy. Normally you wouldn't have to tell me to be nervous about someone. The problem is that we have too many problems already. Rebel and his people are looking to kill us. The Deps want to lock us away. God only knows what the Pelletiers are after. And now we have some twisted little creep following us around like our own personal Gollum.

Given all that, I'm in a rather desperate need to trust the people in my tent. Do you get that?"

"I do," said David. "Just as long as you understand my concern."

"Yeah. You don't want to lose the money."

"I don't care about the money, Zack. I'm sure Mia could send herself more if she had to. But after reading Peter's letter, it seems absolutely crucial that we get to New York. Not just some of us. All of us. For all we know, Theo's the 'one in particular' who stops the second Cataclysm."

Zack lowered his pad and studied David carefully. The boy was usually logical to a fault, but now he treated Peter Pendergen's words like they'd come down from Mount Sinai. It was an odd shift for one such as David, but who knew? Maybe the kid needed to believe in Peter as much as Zack needed to believe in his friends.

"Look, I'll make you a deal. We'll leave the cash out for one night. If it's still here in the morning, we'll know we can trust him and that's one less thing to worry about."

"And if it's not?" David asked.

"Then I'll dance on the street for money till I can buy you an apology bouquet."

David eyed him with furrowed bother until he emitted a dry chuckle.

"I like you, Zack, but you can be awfully strange sometimes."

"Says the kid who eats like a six-foot rabbit."

"I just hope you're right about him."

Zack looked to the bathroom door and heaved an airy sigh. "Guess we'll find out."

Once his long shower ended, Theo wiped the steam from the mirror and stared at his chest. An angry red scar ran across his left pectoral—six inches long, five years old, and as jagged as the mouth of a demon. Theo was well acquainted with its voice by now. It had pestered him all throughout the evening, dousing him in noble reasons to break away from the group. *They'd get so much farther without your mouth to feed. They'd be so much less conspicuous without an injured Asian among them. They'd have a chance, Theo. Why must you rob them of their chance?*

By the time the steam cleared, the matter had been settled. He'd leave them tonight, after Zack and David fell asleep.

Ecstatic in victory, the demon took no time to rest. As Theo dried himself off, it broached the delicate subject of severance pay.

The squad room was a slice of Old London, a dank basement of dripping steam pipes and moldy gray brick. Melissa found it a refreshing contrast to the unrelenting modernism of South California. The whole damn state seemed obsessed with hiding its history.

Fourteen law enforcers eyed her cynically from their chairs as she paced in front of the screenboard. Half the men were uniformed officers here at the precinct. The other half were her fellow Deps, all summoned to Ramona in the middle of the night for reasons they had yet to process. Even Cahill seemed skeptical as she activated the display. The flat ghost images of all six Silvers loomed behind her. She pointed to one with her coffee-cup hand.

"Her name's Amanda Given. At least that's what she told the local pawn-broker at 11:36 this morning, when she sold him a wedding ring." Melissa motioned to Zack's picture. "She was accompanied by this man, the driver of the stolen van and quite possibly the leader of the group. Now there are several factors—"

"That was fifteen hours ago," an agent griped. "What makes you think they're still in town?"

"There are several factors that lead me to believe the fugitives are still here in Ramona. We can assume they didn't steal a vehicle. Only two cars were reported missing today. One was recovered. The other was a two-seater, far too small for this crew. We know they didn't leave by bus, train, or aership. Their facial maps were entered into the Blackguard database. Had they approached any ticket counter, the civic cameras would have recognized them. Excuse me."

Wincing, she reached up the back of her blouse. Several sleepy eyes lurched awake as she pulled a lacy black bra from her sleeve.

"Sorry. I've been wearing that thing for twenty hours."

Cahill shook his head at her in dark wonder. With a small grin, she continued.

"It seems unlikely that a group this size could hitchhike out of town. I also believe they were too fatigued to walk. Given their state and their fresh influx of money, the likeliest scenario is that they're resting in one of the twenty-one budget motels that are currently open for business in Ramona."

She distributed a series of clipped packets, each one containing a list of motels, plus a color printout image of every Silver.

"Check the numbers on your handouts. I've split you into seven pairs, with the task of covering the three circled motels on your list. If the night clerk doesn't recognize the photos, find out if any double or triple room purchases have been made with cash today. If you get a lead, call me. If you should see any of these fugitives, do not engage them. They don't look it but they're dangerous. They already hurt six policemen today and may be responsible for at least two dozen deaths."

Melissa took another sip of coffee, then checked the wall clock: 2:45 A.M.

"I can only imagine they'll be making an early start out of town. That means we have a limited window to take them by surprise. Does anyone have any questions?"

No one did. "Good. Let's move out. And please be cautious."

Despite her call to action, nobody moved. The Deps looked to Cahill, who eyed them sternly. "Did anyone have trouble hearing her?"

The men grudgingly proceeded upstairs. Cahill smirked at the bra in her hand. "You sure like to poke the hive, don't you?"

"It was mostly a comfort decision."

"I wasn't talking about the skimpies, hon. You have any idea what you're risking here?"

"A pay raise, I imagine."

"That and more. It wouldn't have killed you to wait until these people surfaced again."

"No, sir, but it might have killed someone else."

On seeing his weary face, Melissa took his arm. "Come on. You can lecture me in the car."

Cahill didn't lecture her. He finally saw the futility in trying to instill political sense in this woman. Melissa Masaad was ultimately her own creature—gifted and reckless and hopelessly strange. Cahill could see why she had an easy time getting into the heads of these six runners. Perhaps on some level they were odd birds of a feather.

Theo rose from his blanket on the floor and gauged the sleeping breaths of his roommates. After five years of drunken hookups and trespasses, he'd become quite skilled at the art of the stealthy escape. He could move through the dark like a cat, even while his head pounded, his body throbbed, and his sense of worth dangled low enough to trip him.

He tied his shoes by the light of the moon, then slung his knapsack over his shoulder. Between all his frantic inner debates over staying and leaving and robbing his friends blind, a lone voice gibbered in unrelated panic. *Run run run. People are coming. Run run run from the people who come.*

As he spied the glistening currency on the end table, Theo's demon assured him that the group would be fine without it. Mia Farisi was a temporal cash machine. Hell, her next delivery would probably include tomorrow's winning lottery numbers.

He snatched the money, moving two shaky steps toward the door before halting with a guilty wince. He counted eight hundred dollars from the top of the stack and returned it to the table. Maybe now he could slink away as a half bastard, a half wreck of a human being.

While passing the desk, he noticed Zack's skillful rendition of Bugs Bunny on a stationery pad. Theo seized it and scribbled on the lower corner of the sheet.

I'm sorry, guys. I'm just not

He struggled on the next words until he realized he didn't need any. It was perfect just like that. As he closed the door behind him, he caught a reflected gleam in David's eyes, as if the boy were looking right at him. Theo's heart lurched. He shut the door and fled.

Soon he returned to his bench at the playground park, his heavy gaze fixed on the one store that remained open. The Genie Mart was embellished with faux-Arabian minarets and sported a cartoon mascot that looked like a sneering devil in a turban. A beer poster in the window hinted at great treasures within.

Theo pulled the money from his pocket and studied it. Nestled between two twenties was a scrap of paper he'd been carrying since Sunday, the phone number of Bill Pollock. He was one of Quint's older physicists—a husky, white-haired genius who could have passed for Santa Claus were it not for his eternally dour expression.

As the only recovered alcoholic on staff, Bill had been put in charge of Theo's rehabilitation. He'd wasted no time professing his unsuitability for the task.

"I honestly don't know how to help you," he'd told Theo, as the young man thrashed and screamed in withdrawal pain. "If I were any good with people, I wouldn't have become a scientist. The only argument I can make is a mathematical one. It seems you're one-sixth of your world's remaining population. You're the living marker for a billion people. Given the numbers, I suppose it'd be especially tragic if you threw your life away now. It wouldn't just be suicide. It'd be genocide."

As the weeks passed, the two men grew into their roles as counselor and patient, improving in synch until Theo finally became clean. When Bill learned that Theo was leaving with Zack, he came to work on a Sunday just to hand off his phone number.

"Look, I think your departure's premature, but you're strong enough to make your own decisions. Just call me if you ever feel weak or tempted. I won't tell Quint a thing."

Now, forty-two hours later, Theo felt weak and Theo felt tempted, but he couldn't call Bill Pollock because Bill Pollock was dead. Good people kept dying and yet Theo kept on living. The karmic balance of the universe was fatally broken.

He squeezed the money in his hand and took a teary-eyed glance at the Genie Mart. Whether it was suicide or genocide or something else entirely, the living marker for a billion people was ready to drink enough for all of them. He rose from the bench.

"Finally."

Theo spun around in surprise. Twenty feet away, a ginger-haired man leaned against the swing set, casually examining his cuticles. He was dressed like Theo from head to toe—same jeans, same sneakers, same gray sweatshirt. It was a surreal and discomfiting vision, like staring at a true dark genie.

"Who the hell are you?"

Evan grinned. "You'll figure it out in a minute."

"How long have you been standing there?"

"As long as you've been sitting there. I saw you wrestling with your conscience and I wanted to see which way you'd go. Now, while I respect your decision to party like there's no tomorrow, I'm afraid it was all for nothing. You can't buy liquor. Not without one of these."

Theo squinted as Evan flaunted a small blue photo ID. He held it up as he approached.

"They call it a wet card. You can apply for one when you turn eighteen. Just take a one-day class, a one-hour test, and then ta-da! License to drink. You have to be careful though. You get caught in a drunken misdemeanor, the card's suspended. Get caught in a felony, the card's revoked. And if you serve alcohol to someone without a wet card, even in your home, you're in for some hefty fines, fella. The civil liquortarians shit a blue pickle when they heard about this plan. But when they saw what happened to cigarettes, they suddenly became a lot more flexible."

Now he stood close enough for Theo to read the card, which featured Evan's cheery photo next to a cryptic pseudonym.

"Gordon Freeman?"

"The card's a fake," Evan explained. "So's the name. Zack would get the reference. He's awesome that way."

The pieces finally came together in Theo's head. "You're Evan Rander."

"Ding ding ding! Told you you'd get it." Evan laughed. "Oh, that Farisi and her spoilers."

Theo tightened his grip on his book bag and took a hasty step back. "Listen—"

"Oh relax, guy. I'm not so bad. In fact, I come bearing gifts and valuable info. Just hang a bit. You won't regret it."

He hopped over the bench, then motioned for Theo to join him. After a few silent moments, Theo took a wary perch on the far end.

Evan shined a soft grin at the Farsight Professional Augury. "You know, folks here are nutty about the future. Obsessed with it. Corporations have their own augurs on staff. Politicians rely on them like pollsters. It's still a bunch of crap. All cold readers and educated guessers, spouting flowery babble that could be twisted to mean anything. None of these people are gifted like our sweet little Mia. And she's not gifted like you."

He grabbed a bottle cap from the concrete and flicked it from his fingertips. Theo watched it sail toward a light post, knocking a fat moth out of the air.

"Once Mia makes it to New York, *if* she makes it to New York, she'll get out of the note-passing business and find a better use for her portals. You'll inherit the keys to the spoiler shop. You'll be a lot better at it."

"You talk like you can see the future yourself."

Evan chuckled. "Me? Nah. I'm no augur. I'm just a guy who's been around the block a few times."

He flicked another bottle cap. Theo watched with grim fascination as it killed another moth.

"How do you know so much about us?"

"Well, T'eo me lad, it's a wee bit complicated. I'm certainly familiar with *your* storied past. My goodness. Graduated high school at twelve. Got your undergrad degree at fifteen. The youngest person to ever enroll at Stanford Law and, subsequently, the youngest to drop out. When people ask why you quit, you insist that it wasn't the course work. It wasn't the pressure. 'No,' you say, with a wistful sigh, 'I just got tired of being special.'"

Theo felt a cold lurch in his heart. He used to say that often, exactly the way Evan described.

"I also know what happened five years ago," Evan added. "How you got that scar on your chest."

He pantomimed a driver flailing at the wheel. His cartoonish screeching sounds ended with a spittle-flecked crash.

Theo brusquely stood up. "Go to hell."

"Come on, man. How long you gonna keep punishing yourself for one little car accident? Folks have done worse. Hell, I know three people who destroyed a whole planet on purpose. They sleep just fine."

"Thanks for the perspective," Theo replied, while walking away. "Enjoy your night."

A bottle cap sailed by his head, just a half inch from his cheek. Theo stopped.

"Is that some kind of stupid threat?"

"Nope. Just a stupid trick to get you to turn around and look at your gift."

Theo turned around and watched Evan procure a sixty-ounce bottle of vodka from his knapsack.

"What do you want with me?"

Evan hunched his shoulders in a shrug. "Just passing the time, brother."

"Maybe you should find a hobby."

"Maybe I already have. Oh, hey, that reminds me. Has Hannah started flirting with you yet?"

Evan laughed at Theo's dim expression. "Guess not. Well, she will, but don't get a big head over it. You're just her default choice. She knows by now that David isn't biting and Zack's got eyes for Sister Cherry Pious. She used to have a fourth option, but I removed it. Poor Hannah. Simply can't exist without a man to wrap around her little finger. Are you going to take your present or not? I went to a lot of trouble here."

Theo returned to the bench, examining the bottle from every angle. A frightening new voice in his thoughts suggested a darker use for it. *Hit him. Kill him. Kill him now. Trust me.*

"Well, I hope you enjoy it," Evan said. "You and I don't cross paths very often. You're usually busy with other stuff. So while I wouldn't hang your photo in my locker, I can't say I hate you. Mostly I just pity you."

"Why? Because I'm a drunk?"

"No, because you're special," Evan replied. "You *are* special, Theo, even among us freaks. You're only scratching the surface of your weirdness now. When you find out what you can truly do, man oh man, your life will change. Everyone will want a piece of you. Your friends. The Pelletiers. The U.S. government, eventually. And Peter Pendergen. He'll be the worst of all."

Evan laughed. "I love the way he says your name. He's got an Irish brogue, so to him you're not Theo Maranan, you're *T'eo Maernin*. And he'll say your name a lot. Oh yes. He's got plans for you, my friend. To him, you're Jesus, Neo, and Frodo rolled up in one tortilla. The minute you get to Brooklyn, he'll set you on a great and impossible task. You'll spend the rest of your life trying, and you'll die knowing you failed. There's your future, Mr. Self-Punishment."

He leaned over and tapped the tattoo on Theo's wrist.

"There's your karma."

While Theo reeled over all the new information, Evan stood up and let out a stretching groan.

"Well, it's been fun chatting, T'eo, but it's way past my bedtime. So I bid . . ." He suddenly slapped his forehead. "Oh crap! I totally forgot the whole reason I came here. Jesus."

"What are you talking about?"

"The Deps," Evan said, while checking his watch. "They're hitting your motel in fifty-two minutes. Your friends are going bye-bye unless you get them out now."

Theo shook his head. "Bullshit . . ."

"Come on. You already sort of knew they were coming, just like you sort of knew that Rebel's people were coming. You gotta start listening to that inner voice, man."

He wasn't wrong. Theo could hear the panicked chatter in his head right now. *Run run run from the people with guns. People with guns. People with guns and badges.*

"Why would you warn me? What do you get out of helping us?"

Evan walked backward down the street, flashing a droll smile.

"What can I say? I get no kick from champagne. Mere alcohol doesn't thrill me at all. But I do have a hobby. And if you guys got arrested then, gosh, I'd have to learn macrame. Who wants that?"

He turned around and kept ambling. "Oh, and tell Booberella to check her damn pockets already. I can't do everything for her."

As he watched Evan leave, Theo suddenly felt the weight of Rebel's handgun in his knapsack. A cool voice in his head, neither devil nor angel, calmly demanded that he use the weapon to end Evan right now. It insisted that it would be an act of mercy, a one-time chance to prevent future tears, future misery, the future deaths of some very good people.

You'll look back on this night, the voice told him. *You'll wish you had done it. And so will Hannah.*

The night clerk at the Aurora Motel nearly dropped her soup when two young police officers entered the lobby. She was a forty-year-old bachelorette, and was highly unused to encountering quality men at her wretched job. When they asked her if any multiple room purchases had been made with cash to-day, she didn't hesitate to look through the registry. *Yes, indeed. Rooms 115 and 116 were purchased with cash at 2:56 p.m., about six hours before my shift began. This isn't my career. I'm actually a . . . Oh, what's this?* She looked at the photos of six young people, only one of whom looked familiar. *Yes, sir. I did see a fellow of Oriental persuasion pass by my window earlier. I'm pretty sure it was him. He seemed to be in an awful hurry, both times.*

At 3:41 A.M., a cadre of policemen and Deps assembled outside the motel. On Cahill's signal, they made a simultaneous seige of the two rooms.

Both of them were empty.

Five minutes later, Cahill found Melissa sitting at the desk in Room 116. He dropped an empty box of hair dye in front of her.

"Found it in the bin. Guess the redhead's not a redhead anymore. Nice of her to let us know."

Melissa shook her head in bother. "Amateurs. They're all amateurs at this."

"You seem disappointed."

"It makes no sense. If they're such amateurs, how did they know we were coming?"

"They didn't. They just got a lucky head start."

Melissa slid the stationery pad across the desk. The top page was graced with Theo's sloppy handwriting.

We didn't kill the physicists.

Slack-jawed, Cahill sat down on the bed. "Well, screw me."

Melissa launched her dark gaze out the window. Cahill was retiring soon. If these outlaws had an honest-to-God augur among them, then she was the one who was screwed.

Winded and sweaty, the Silvers perched atop a dark hill and looked back. Beyond the tempic gates of the impound lot, they could see the reflected glow of emergency lights from the motel.

Hannah looked to Theo in flushed confusion. "You going to tell us how you knew?"

He'd come pounding on their doors twelve minutes ago, their own Paul Revere. He was both relieved and disturbed to see that the British had actually come.

"It's complicated. I'll explain once we start moving again."

Zack narrowed his eyes at the distant lights. He took no comfort at all from their close getaway. The Deps shouldn't have found them this quickly.

He shined a flashlight on his compass, and then at the trees. "We need to go north, which means we'll have to cut through the woods. I hope nobody has dark-forest issues. We have two flashlights. It shouldn't be bad."

"I can make more light if we need it," David offered.

"Third rule," Mia sternly reminded him. "No public weirdness."

He raised his palms. "When you're right, Miafarisi, you're right."

Amanda slung her knapsack over her shoulder. "We should get going."

As they moved toward the woods, Theo furtively pushed the stolen cash into Zack's palm.

"Sorry."

Zack patted his back with tense distraction. "Don't worry about it."

Theo checked on David, anticipating a far less charitable response. To his surprise, the boy merely eyed him through a quizzical leer.

"You're just not what?" he asked Theo.

"What?"

David removed Zack's pen sketch from his pocket and pointed to the incomplete scribble that Theo left in the corner. *I'm sorry, guys. I'm just not*

"Oh." Theo scratched his neck in contemplation. "I don't know how I was going to finish that."

"Well, I suppose you have time to figure out what you are and aren't."

Though David had said the words amicably, they still didn't sit well with Theo. He'd spent the last five years in a liquid state, living without a single care for the future. Now suddenly he found himself insanely concerned with events to come. He was concerned about Evan, concerned about New York, and now very concerned about Peter Pendergen.

He straightened his book bag and followed the others into the woods. By the time they emerged, the sun had come up and the Silvers were five miles closer to Brooklyn.

TWENTY

They marched north, through a seemingly endless terrain of dirt roads and grassy hills. Yesterday's clouds had all but vanished. Now the late-summer sun raged away at their skin, repeatedly forcing them to take shade under sprawling oaks.

When they traveled, they plodded forth in a drowsy trance. It was only while resting that thin reeds of chatter sprang up between them. Virtually all the conversation came from Amanda and the men. Mia had fallen into a bleak silence. Amanda didn't like her flushed color or the way she occasionally staggered on the grass. Mia had to assure her twice that she was fine. Just quiet.

Everyone knew why Hannah wasn't talking.

It was at their first oak tree respite, four hours ago, that Theo relayed a message from Evan Rander.

"He said check your pockets. I have no idea why. Just . . . be careful."

At first Hannah couldn't find anything in her shorts but the silver half-dollar Zack had given her. She opened her knapsack and fished through the jeans she'd purchased yesterday. Tucked away in the back pocket was the driver's license of a handsome thirty-year-old man. After a few seconds of tense perusal, she passed it to the others. Zack was the first to speak his name.

"Ernesto Curado. Huh."

"You don't know the guy?" David asked Hannah.

She didn't, but she was sure she recognized Ernesto from her hallucinatory vision yesterday, the muscular man who'd held another Hannah so closely from behind. Her ghostly double had called him Jury.

Amanda studied the license with fidgety unease. "It doesn't make sense. How did Evan get this in your pocket?"

"He did it yesterday when I bumped into him at the department store. He put all my stuff back in the handcart. Guess this was why."

"But what was he hoping to accomplish? I mean if he was trying to upset you, why use the driver's license of a man you never met?"

"I don't know," said Hannah, with distant bother.

Zack returned the license to her. "Well, whoever he is, he's from the unified state of California. He's one of us."

"Was one of us," David corrected, with enough detachment to make Hannah want to scream.

Theo frowned at him. "You don't know he's dead."

"I think the message is a pretty clear indicator."

Evan had placed a small and ominous sticky note on the back of the card. *You would have liked him.*

Hannah obsessively studied the license for the next two miles, until all his information was chisel-etched into memory—his height (six-foot-two), his weight (205 pounds), his hair (black), his eyes (brown). She knew his address on 13th Street, not far from where the 747 had crashed. She knew he was an organ donor and that he shared a birthday with her mother.

She also knew that Jury Curado was dead. There was no maybe about it. He survived the end of the world, but he didn't survive Evan Rander.

At noon, the Silvers rose from their fifth shady rest stop. Hannah watched jadedly as Amanda once again enlisted Zack to help her to her feet, a surprisingly dainty move for a woman who was normally self-reliant to a fault. The actress had caught enough lingering stares from Zack to know, even if he didn't, that he harbored some attraction for Amanda. It wasn't until her sister's second outreached hand that Hannah realized the door swung both ways.

Great, the actress seethed. *She gets a funny love interest. I get a deranged stalker.*

Theo walked alongside her on the unpaved road. She glowered at his tender concern. "My sister send you to check on me?"

"I'm checking on my own," he insisted. "I feel bad. I should have waited until we were settled before—"

"Settled? When are we ever getting settled? We can't go a day without someone jumping us."

"Things will get better."

"Is that a premonition or just a platitude?"

Theo wasn't sure. Ever since he stepped out of the woods, he'd carried an odd surplus of optimism, more than he knew how to handle. His body beamed with giddy anticipation, as if there was a recliner and an ice-cold lemonade waiting for him on the other side of the plains.

"Hannah, I'm really sorry I threw that Evan stuff on you. I should have waited."

"I'm mad at you for the opposite reason."

"What do you mean?"

"You're holding out on me. I know he talked about me, but you're not telling me what he said."

In relaying his tale of last night's discussion, Theo had censored Evan's uncharitable mentions of Hannah. He was stunned she'd sensed the omissions. The woman could be jarringly perceptive.

"I didn't think it was worth sharing," he said.

"Well, it's about me, so why don't you let me decide?"

"It's about both of us, actually."

"What do you mean?"

As Theo formulated his reply, Amanda and David both shouted in alarm. Now the others followed their gaze to the middle of the road, at the still and crumpled form of Mia Farisi.

She'd blacked out once before. Last year, at the end of a school assembly, Mia felt the auditorium spin into a vortex of bright lights. Before she knew what was happening, her eyelids fluttered and she toppled back into her classmates.

It was her own damn fault. Her latest weight tantrum had thrown her into a six-day regimen of cabbage soup and rice cakes. She never expected her crash diet to become literal.

Her oldest brother picked her up from school. Though Bobby Farisi was six-foot-four and built like a fortress, his baby sister had a way of turning him to porcelain. After a half mile of stony silence, he fell into blubbering tears.

"You pull any stupid shit like that again, I swear to God I'll kill you. Don't *ever* scare me like that!"

"I'm sorry . . ."

"Don't apologize," said Amanda. "Just drink."

She woke up in the shade, with her head in Amanda's lap and a bottle pressed against her lips. Her head pounded. Her skin throbbed as if she were one continuous bruise. Mia took a sip of warm water and then scanned her surroundings. She could only see Amanda and Zack.

"What happened?"

"You fainted," said Amanda. "You're overheated. A body can only take so much."

"Where are the others?"

"They went to get water. They'll be back soon."

"Water from where?"

David had spotted the green bolt logo of a vehicle charging station behind a line of distant trees. None of the others could see it, even after following his pointed finger. The boy had thrown Zack a lordly grin. "And you mock my love for carrots."

Zack wasn't feeling very humorous at the moment. He paced the grass with furious distraction.

"You should have told us you weren't feeling well. We would have rested more."

"I didn't want to slow us down," Mia said.

"You think there's a speed trophy waiting for us in Brooklyn? Our only reward is getting there alive. So you tell us next time. You pull this martyr crap again, I'll tape you in a box and mail you to Peter."

Amanda squinted at him. "Ease up. She doesn't need a lecture now."

On the contrary, Zack's wrath was like water for Mia's soul. Though the cartoonist could probably fit inside one of her brother's arms, he carried the same masculine vulnerability, the same caring passion. It was scary how much she loved him right now.

Zack let out a self-defusing sigh, then sat down with the others. "I don't like splitting up like this. Not without cell phones."

"They'll be fine," Amanda assured him. "They know the way back."

At least the men do, she thought. Her sister had the directional skills of a leaking balloon.

Once Amanda caught Zack's gaze, she motioned to Mia's free hand. He took it in his grip. Though he offered her a weak smile, he had to suppress his other new concern. If things were this tough in the grasslands, they didn't have a prayer of making it through the desert.

Hannah's calves burned with fury as she climbed the steep ridge. Her only comfort was the malevolent twinge of glee she drew from Theo's matching strain. She'd forcibly volunteered him for the water-gathering mission, the Jack to her Jill. Though the task hardly required three people, David insisted on coming along. The boy barely broke a sweat.

"You could have left your backpack with the others," he told Hannah.

"It's okay. It balances the weight up front. Not that you ever noticed these."

David eyed her with perplexed indignity. "I noticed. I just never said anything. Was I supposed to?"

"No, but you're a teenage boy. I should have caught you looking by now."

He jerked a tired shrug. "I don't get the fascination with large breasts. I won't say it's a purely American fetish, but it does seem to be rampant in this culture and era. I admit I'm intrigued by the unique disparity between you and your sister. From what I can see, she barely has a chest at all."

Hannah slapped Theo's shoulder. "See? David knows how to get on my good side."

"If I acknowledge your superior endowments, will you stop being mad at me?"

"Just tell me what Evan said!"

"He said you'd flirt with me soon!"

Hannah stopped at the top of the hill and stared at Theo in puzzlement. "That's it?"

"That's the bulk of it. Yes."

"Jesus, that's nothing. I flirt with people all the time. I flirt with David."

The boy nodded. "It's true. She does."

"Theo, why did you think that would bother me?"

He flicked a tense hand. "I don't know. He said you'd flirt with me by default, that you can't exist without a man to wrap around your finger, which I thought was pretty unkind."

"It's also kind of true," Hannah admitted. Throughout her adult life, the actress had rarely gone a week without some fling, tryst, or other quasi-romantic dalliance. She gravitated toward partners who were meek enough to put her on a pedestal, a handy way to control the terms of the relationship. She wasn't proud of it, but she was aware enough to recognize the pattern. The real mystery was how Evan knew it.

"There was one other thing," Theo cautioned. "He told me you used to have a fourth option, but he removed it."

Now Hannah was bothered. For the twentieth time, she procured Jury's license from her pocket. Evan's teasing note still burned fresh in her mind. *You would have liked him.*

"I don't understand. How could he say I had the option if I never got a chance to meet him?"

"He must have his own temporal talents," David mused, as if merely discussing the weather. "We know from Mia that it's perfectly possible to tamper with the past. Maybe Evan can do the same. Maybe we exist in a branching chronology that he created, an alternate-alternate timeline where Ernesto Curado never became part of the group."

Hannah trembled as she tried to wrap her mind around the implications—a human being removed not just from life but from the memories of everyone who knew him. She couldn't think of a crueler thing to do to a person, and yet Evan clearly took joy in his feat. Worse, he was determined to fill in the blanks for Hannah, to make sure she knew exactly what she lost.

David continued to ponder the idea. "Actually, given how much Evan knows about us, I'm starting to think he used to be part of our group as well. Maybe he'd been with us from the beginning, until he decided to change that. What I can't figure out though—"

"David . . ."

"—is how his own memories would be preserved."

"David, stop."

At Theo's words, the boy glanced up at Hannah's pained face. He flinched with remorse. "Sorry. I was channeling my father again. I could be wrong about all of this. I probably am."

She rubbed her eyes. "It's all right. Let's just keep going."

Eight minutes later, they reached the MerryBolt chargery, a facility that looked less like a gas station and more like a drive-in theater. The lot contained over two dozen generator spaces for cars. A large screen kept motorists distracted with commercials and cartoons.

Thankfully, the place included a mini-market that was stocked to the roof in ice-cold refreshments. After downing a full cherry vim, Hannah felt her inner gauges swing back into the green. She blithely locked arms with her companions, like Dorothy in Oz, as they proceeded down the road with their new bags of bounty. She considered talking about her breasts again, just for positive attention, then cursed herself for being so damn insecure.

A hundred yards from the chargery, David came to a sudden halt. He aimed a curious gaze up a long dirt hill.

"Huh."

"What's the matter?"

He broke from Hannah's grasp. "Wait here. I want to check something."

Theo shook his head. "Uh-uh. We've split up enough already."

"Fine. Then come with me."

"David, are you sure this is a good idea?" Hannah asked. "Mia really needs water."

"I know what Mia needs. If this is what I think it is, she'll benefit most of all."

Hannah and Theo traded a dim expression as they followed David up the slope. Whatever the boy was looking at was invisible to them. All he would tell them, as he led the charge, was that something interesting came up this hill two days ago and never came down.

By the time they joined David at the crest, they could see exactly what he was talking about. The recent past had met up with the present. And quite a present it was.

The luxury van glistened in the sunlight, resting serenely near the edge of a cliff. Aside from the dirt and grass on the tires, the vehicle looked as pristine as a showroom special. Through the tinted windows lay six plush bucket seats. A metal emblem on the rear door heralded the van as a Royal Seeker. It was painted in shiny silver.

Hannah held her mystified gaze on the abandoned vehicle.

"Huh."

———

Zack ambled back and forth in the leafy shade, clucking his tongue to a forcibly cheery tune. If pressed to name the song in his head, he could only peg it as a number from *The Little Mermaid*. The one the crab sings.

Soon he spotted the dry chagrin of Amanda and Mia and became smirkingly contrite.

"Sorry. That used to drive my girlfriend nuts too."

"Sit down. You're making us nervous."

He rejoined them at the tree, rapidly drumming his thighs as he scanned the grassy distance.

"You never mentioned a girlfriend before," Mia said.

"She was an ex," Zack clarified. "We broke up two years ago but we still lived together."

"That's a strange arrangement," Amanda mused.

Zack rolled his shoulders in a sullen shrug. "It was a good apartment."

Sensing the end of his effusiveness, Amanda dropped the topic and ate another peppermint. Zack had noticed her popping them like crazy over the past fifteen minutes, ever since Hannah and the others crossed into worrisome tardiness.

As she reached for the last candy, an odd new thought occurred to him.

"Wait. Don't eat that."

She paused. "Huh?"

"Hold that mint. And hand me the box, please."

Confused, she passed him the little square tin of Breezers she'd purchased from the motel vending machine. Zack brandished the container like a stage magician.

"Now, what do you think would happen if I reversed this?"

"What do you mean?"

"I mean, do you think I could refill this box with mints of the past?"

Amanda stared at him blankly as she pondered his premise. "I don't like the idea of half-digested candies suddenly disappearing from my insides."

"I'm pretty sure that won't happen."

Zack placed the tin on the ground and concentrated until it gleamed with light. He opened the lid to a fresh new heap of white candies.

Mia's mouth went slack. "Wow."

"Wow," Amanda said.

"Wow indeed." Zack looked to Amanda. "Do you feel any less minty?"

"No. I feel exactly the same. I can still taste the last one I ate."

"Yeah. These are doubles. Holy crap. I made copies." He laughed. "David's going to blow a synapse."

For all his awe, Zack suspected his feat was pitifully mundane to the civilized natives of Earth. He was right. The process of tooping had been a part of modern culture for decades. Using any rejuvenator, a container could be reversed to create temporal duplicates of its former contents, whether they were mints or apples or shiny gold nuggets.

Unfortunately for wealth seekers, tooping was an inherently flawed process, one that always resulted in inferior copies. Precious metals became rusted and worthless. Gems turned cloudy and cracked. Most tooped foods were inedible, though certain grains and vegetables were able to survive the process with a tolerable loss of quality. There were over a thousand toop-friendly recipes that had been discovered through years of experimentation—pastas, breads, and rice dishes that were easily saved by fresh seasonings.

Though tooping was prohibited by federal law, the authorities could only do so much to stop it in the kitchen. In the end, nobody craved shoddy cloned sustenance. It was just the fiscal reality. The middle class had leftovers. The lower class had do-overs.

In the grassy wilds, Zack received a quick education on the limits of tooping. The moment he sampled a re-created mint, his face contorted in comical disgust. Mia and Amanda covered their laughs.

"What's wrong?"

He spat his candy into the dirt. "It's awful. Like eating a dust bunny."

"That's disgusting."

"I'm serious. Try one."

Amanda pushed his arm away. "I believe you!"

"God, that sucked. Let me have the original." He took the mint from her hand, tested its structural integrity, and then ate it. "Yeah. Okay. I think Breezers were meant for one-time use."

"Maybe they added a special chemical," Mia said. "Like copy protection."

Zack stared ahead in thought. "You know, I bet that's one of the things that pawnbroker was testing for. To see if your wedding ring was a clone."

"And I bet that's why the cash here is all blue and glossy," Amanda added. "It's probably some fancy ink that can't be duplicated."

"Great," Zack sighed. "Guess I can't make a figurative mint either."

Mia shook her head, frustrated. "We still have so much to learn about this place. I mean everything we figured out just now is stuff a third-grader already knows."

"We'll catch up," Amanda assured her. "Someday."

Once again, Zack looked out to the hills, rapidly drumming his thigh until Amanda pressed his hand still. As their fingers touched, he realized that she rarely mentioned her husband. He made a note to ask about him someday, carefully, when he had a few less items on his plate of worries.

"Where the hell are they?"

Hannah wasn't sure which of her two friends would explain the Royal Seeker first. David and Theo circled the van at polar ends, one scanning the past, the other peering into the future.

After two revolutions, David seized the winning edge.

"Look, I adore Mia. I respect her rules for avoiding federal detection. But we're well out of sight. It would be far easier to show you what I've learned than to tell you. May I?"

Before Theo or Hannah could answer, David closed his eyes in concentration. A ghostly copy of the Seeker appeared at the edge of the hill, rolling up the grass until it merged with its present counterpart. Soon a spectral door opened and a handsome young man in hiking clothes stepped into the sunlight. From his long blond ponytail and sideburns, Hannah figured he represented the haute couture of the Altamerican progressive.

The driver took a panoramic sweep of his surroundings, then shut his door. Hannah's heart lurched as he moved to the edge of the fifty-foot drop.

"David, if he jumps, you tell me now. I don't want to see that."

"He doesn't jump. Watch."

For the next several seconds, he kept his expressionless gaze on the canopy of trees below him. Then, with triumphant fury, he threw the ignition key over the cliff.

"Oh no!"

"It's all right," David assured Hannah. "We'll find it."

The man procured a handphone from his pocket and pressed a single button. "Yeah, it's me. It's over. I'm out. Thanks for everything. Go fourp yourself."

Satisfied, he chucked the phone into the trees, then turned around and left the way he came. The ghost disappeared in a ripple.

David beamed at his companions. "He walks back down the hill, still smiling. Whatever decision he made, it was a good one. For him and for us."

"But who was he?" Hannah asked.

"Who cares? We have a vehicle now. An unstolen luxury van."

"I'm not so sure about that," Theo said. "For all we know, this guy just quit his job as a car thief."

David sighed impatiently. "It's been sitting here for two days. If it was stolen, then it wasn't reported. If it was reported, then it wasn't tracked. This is our van now. We just need to find that key."

They descended the hill and scoured the woods in a three-pronged sweep. The search felt like a needle-in-a-haystack conundrum to Hannah, but then she knew it was never wise to bet against David Dormer.

Theo took a break from his halfhearted hunt, wiping his brow with the lip of his T-shirt. Hannah was momentarily stunned by the sight of his finely muscled stomach, the hint of a scar on his left pectoral. She was wise enough not to ask about old wounds.

"You okay?"

"Headache," he said. "Probably just lack of sleep. It'll pass."

"Did you see anything futurish when you looked at that van?"

"It's hard to say. I got a bunch of vague flashes, but I can't tell if they're predictions or just my usual thoughts. Mia's lucky. At least her future's written out for her."

"Well, were they good flashes or bad flashes?"

"Both," he replied, with jittery uncertainty. "I feel like that van will take us all the way to New York, but that could just be wishful thinking. I also feel like that scene we witnessed up there wasn't entirely genuine, but that might just be paranoia."

Hannah grew tense all over again. There was something about the driver's expression, right after he threw the phone, that slightly reeked of acting. She'd also filed the suspicion as paranoia. Certain parties had given her plenty of reason to be skittish.

"Found it!"

David bounded through the trees, grinning with triumph. He jingled a key chain in his hand.

"So who feels like driving?"

Hannah mentally cursed Theo and David as she climbed behind the wheel. She had two certified geniuses in her company and yet she was the one who had to pilot the crazy Royal Seeker. There were buttons and switches every-where. This was no Salgado clunker. This was the goddamn *Enterprise*.

After ten minutes of wary experimentation, in which Hannah nearly sent the Seeker over the cliff, she finally got a handle on the controls. Soon the splinter group returned with their four-wheeled surprise. Zack's fear turned to bafflement when he spotted Hannah behind the wheel.

He stood up and chucked his arms at full wingspan. "What . . . ? How?"

The passenger window opened to David's chipper face. "Shall we discuss it inside?"

Soon the Silvers filled the six plush seats, basking in cool comforts. Be-tween the air-conditioning, the fresh water, and her ridiculously cozy perch, Mia felt a full-body relief that was almost religious in intensity.

She glanced around in muddled awe. "I can't believe you guys just found this lying around."

David smiled at her. "After the last few days, I think we're due for some random good fortune."

"It just seems a little too random," Zack fretted.

"And a little too good," Amanda added.

Hannah narrowed her eyes. They weren't even a couple yet and they were already making her ill with their cuteness.

David scowled at them. "This wasn't delivered to our doorstep. It was abandoned in a distant patch of wilderness two days ago. Don't you think that's a little dodgy as far as traps go?"

"By the old rules, yes," Zack replied.

"So, what are you saying?"

"I'm saying that in a world where time can go wibbly-wobbly and pretzel-bendy, it's entirely possible that we were meant to find this Mystery Machine."

"Meant by who?"

"Do you really have to ask, David? Do you think this is the first silver gift we've gotten?"

Amanda nodded darkly. "Exactly."

Theo and Hannah remained outwardly neutral, though images of Azral had been circling their thoughts from the moment the van came to life. Theo fumbled with a thin metal attaché case he'd discovered under his seat. The lid was held shut by a convoluted system of clasps. He couldn't tell if it was locked or just strange.

David flicked a curt hand. "I don't know what to tell you. If you want to give yourself an ulcer over paranoid conspiracy theories, feel free. Just leave me out of it."

"Hey come on, David . . ."

"Why are you getting so angry?" Amanda asked. "We're just talking."

"Except none of us have thanked him yet."

The others looked to Mia as she straightened her seat back. Her expression was both remorseful and stern.

"Thanks to David, we don't have to walk across the country now. We don't have to worry about deserts or dehydration. We could be in Brooklyn in four or five days instead of two or three months, thanks to David. And he did it all without robbing or hurting anyone."

She looked to him now. "Thank you, David. You probably saved my life again."

The van fell quiet. Hannah scanned the bright new smile on David's face, then confronted the disturbing new possibility that she'd be traveling with two couples soon.

Zack let out an attritional sigh. "Look—"

The attaché case loudly sprang open, startling everyone. Theo exhaled with relief. A few more minutes and he would have started smashing it.

The others stared at him, dumbfounded, as he procured a neatly wrapped stack of shiny blue cash. Hannah leaned forward and read the paper band.

"Holy shit. Five thousand dollars?"

Zack blinked in stupor. "Are you serious?"

"That'll last us all the way to New York," said Amanda. "Easily."

"Guys, you're not getting the full scope of this."

Theo turned the case on his lap, revealing a tray of identical bricks. Lifting one revealed another, then another, then two others. Fifty stacks in total. A quarter of a million in cash.

The group fell into bewildered silence. Soon Zack found his way to the only sane response.

"Thank you, David."

Nervous giggles spread through the van as the others followed Zack's dizzy lead. The grin on David's handsome young face slowly flatlined. He looked to Zack contritely.

"I'll admit that your suspicion seems a little more plausible now."

"Look, trust me, I'd rather be wrong. If Azral's the one who gave us this stuff—"

"No," said Hannah, frantically waving her palms. "I'm sorry. Between all the bad stuff of yesterday and the good stuff of today, I'm about to get the bends. Can we put away the big issues for a couple of hours? Can we just enjoy this? Please?"

No one had trouble agreeing to her request. After a cozy respite, Hannah oriented Zack on the van's controls. David plotted a course on the computer navigation system. Soon the Silvers joined the speedy bustle on Highway X, snaking east through the South California grasslands and into the desert.

By the time the Seeker crossed into Arizona, the sun had set and David fell fast asleep in his seat. The five waking Silvers tumbled back into the larger issues. Some thought about Azral. Others thought about Peter. All of them wondered why one was so eager to help them get to the other.

TWENTY-ONE

The Power Boy chargery crackled with life, a pocket of activity in a bare patch of Kansas. Two hundred travelers ambled the station, stretching limbs and killing time while their vehicles drank from electric wells. The plaza offered two diners, four stores, an arcade, and a mini-theater. It also sported a tea lift, a diversion so unique that Zack nearly drove off the freeway gawking at it.

While the van replenished at a generator, the Silvers split up and wandered in pairs. Only Zack and Theo chose to brave the antigravity madness of the tea lift. They were loaded into a two-seat metal cup, which rose ten stories into the sky on a remote-controlled saucer of aeris. Despite the panorama of sun-drenched plains, Zack and Theo couldn't take their eyes off the other riders—twenty cups of people, all floating through the air in a slow and synchronous halo.

Theo saw Zack's stupefied expression and raised him a jagged chuckle. "This is some Willy Wonka shit right here."

"I know. My inner physicist is sobbing right now. He demands we plummet."

"Why did we do this again, Zack?"

"Oh, you know. When in Rome . . ."

". . . fall as the Romans fell?"

The cartoonist shrugged. "We can't be country rubes forever. If this is what they do at gas stations, just imagine their theme parks."

An electronic chirping sound emanated from Zack's pocket. He retrieved his handphone and checked the screen. *Amanda Calling.*

He answered her with a grin. "Hey. You'll never guess where we are."

"I know where you are. I saw you in line. You're both crazy."

"You should try it. It's amazing."

"Yeah, no thanks. I'm just making sure you're not holding each other and screaming."

"Well, we're not screaming."

Amanda laughed. "Just try not to die, okay? I don't like driving the van."

"Where are you now?"

"At the base of the statue."

He peered down at the thirty-foot sculpture of Power Boy—a chubby blond tyke with button eyes and an electric-blue superhero outfit. Two black-haired women stood at the feet of the eyesore. Even from a hundred feet up, Zack could see Hannah's fidgety agitation. He was starting to share Amanda's concerns about her.

"Yeah. I see you. Stay there. We'll be down in a few minutes."

Two days ago, Zack had purchased six handphones from an Arizona vendor, all bare-bones models that were prepaid for a generous amount of usage.

On Wednesday afternoon, shortly after the van crossed into New Mexico, Hannah's screen lit up with a chain of malevolent texts. The sender was only identified as *A. Sonnet*.

> Hey Hannah Banana, Always-Needs-a-Man-a. I guess you found Jury in your pants.
>
> He would have entered your knickers a hell of a lot quicker if I hadn't messed with events.
>
> In previous times, he was the pearl in your clam. You were the honey on his plantain.
>
> Wherever we stayed, it was always the same. We'd all hear your screwings. Your melodious oohings.
>
> It was not meant to be, unfortunately. He adored you, I assure you, but he always died before you. :(
>
> You'd cry at the dirt in your little black skirt and you'd swear to us you loved him.
>
> And yet within a week, we'd hear the mattress squeak.
>
> The bump-bump-bump of a brand-new chump.
>
> If only these men knew the real and awful you.
>
> Rest assured I do, oh Hannah Banana.
>
> :)

Now the actress paced the feet of the Power Boy, anxiously scanning every man in the crowd. She barely knew a thing about Evan Rander and already she hated him more than anyone she'd ever known. She hated him for singling her out, for chipping away at an already broken psyche.

While Amanda talked on the phone with Zack, laughing her radiant laugh, Hannah swallowed a high scream. As if her stalker problems weren't bad enough, this voyage was quickly becoming a couples cruise, a romantic slow dance across the floor of the nation. The disparity of fortune killed her. It tortured her for reasons that were vain and petty enough to make her ashamed.

Soon Zack and Theo returned to the ground and rejoined the sisters. On the way back to the generator lot, Hannah clasped fingers with Theo. Despite her smile, her grip was tight and desperate. She hated herself for the plan she was hatching. She hated Evan for knowing her.

To Mia and David, the only thing better than having the Royal Seeker was having it to themselves. The moment they finished lunch, they dashed back to the van like secret lovers. Classical music played from the radio as they propped their legs on empty seats and buried themselves in nonfiction. David read *Temporis in a Nutshell*, an ironic title for an 594-page tome. Mia pored through *The Annotated History of America, Volume IX (1912–1940)*. The cover was graced with a haunting old photo of a broken doll in rubble, a shot of post-Cataclysm New York.

Mia sneaked a quick glance at David over the top of her book. She could only imagine that the teenagers of the world would roll their eyes at what these two did in the back of vans, and yet recent events had forced her to wonder. Ever since she spoke up for him on Tuesday, David's smiles for her grew a few shades brighter and he touched her arm every time he brushed past her. She didn't think it meant anything until Hannah slipped her a furtive whisper in the hotel garage. *You might have just started something.*

Over the next three days, his affections simmered down to old levels, enough to stop her stomach pains. She had no idea what was going on behind that beautiful face of his. Maddeningly, Future Mia was no help at all on the matter. She could have ended the conundrum with a single spoiler, but chose to let her younger self twist in the wind. Mia had received time-traveling intel about Hannah and Amanda and Theo and Zack, but nothing about David. For baffling reasons, her future had yet to mention him once.

An advertisement on the outdoor movie screen suddenly caught her eye. She watched through the windshield as a trio of cartoon handphones danced atop a forty-foot tagline. TRIPLE-8 IS ALL YOU NEED TO FIND ANY-ONE IN AMERICA, ANY TIME!

Mia's mouth fell slack with revelation. It had been an irksome catch-22 that she didn't know the phone number for Information. Now that she had it, she had a chance to shed some light on the other mystery man in her life.

David glanced up as she dialed her phone. "What are you doing?"

She shushed him with a finger. "Hi. Brooklyn, New York, please. Peter Pendergen."

Mia spelled out his last name, then listened to the operator with faint surprise. "Oh. Okay. Is that near Brooklyn?"

David crinkled his brow at her. He didn't know how any of these people could tolerate holding phones to their ears. The electronic squeals and crinkles were infuriating to him, like a whistling teakettle covered in firecrackers.

She scrawled a phone number into her journal. "Okay. I'll try that. Thank you."

"Success?" David asked.

"No listing in Brooklyn, but there's a Peter Pendergen in Quarter Hill, just north of the city."

"Could be an old number," David speculated. "Or it could be where his handphone's registered."

Mia bit her thumb in dilemma. "Can you think of any reason why I shouldn't try calling?"

"I can think of several, but you have me all curious now. I say do it."

She stepped outside, restlessly pacing beside the van as she dialed the number. Her heart skipped when someone answered on the fifth ring.

"Hello?"

Mia was surprised to hear a high young voice, a boy caught in the wavering chords of puberty. She wasn't sure if she'd laugh or scream if she learned that Peter was her age.

"Hi. Is this . . . this isn't Peter Pendergen, is it?"

The boy fell into a suspicious pause. "Who is this?"

"I'm a friend."

Another pause. The boy took a bite of something crunchy, then spoke through chews. "My dad's not known for his maturity, but I'm pretty sure he doesn't have any ten-year-old friends."

Relieved, intrigued, and a little indignant, Mia stopped pacing. "I'm fourteen."

"Okay. Fine. You're fourteen. And you apparently have no idea what your friends sound like."

"Well, I never actually talked to Peter. I'm sort of his pen pal."

The boy choked on his snack. "Excuse me?"

"What?"

"If I heard you right, and if you're not rubbing me, then I don't think you meant to say 'pen pal.'"

"What do you mean?"

"You're implying you had homosexual relations with my father in prison. I don't even know where to begin with that."

Mia flushed hot red. "What? No! I didn't . . . that's not what it means where I come from!"

"Who *are* you?"

"I'm Mia Farisi, and I promise you that Peter really wants to talk to me! Is he there or not?"

The line fell silent again. Mia could almost feel the air in the boy's hanging mouth.

"Holy Christ. You're one of them. You're a breacher."

Mia scoffed. "I'm pretty sure I don't like that term."

"Are you insane calling here? Do you have any idea what you're doing?"

"Look—"

"If you value your life, hang up! Hang up right now and get rid of your phone!"

With a panicked yell, Mia hurled her phone. It sailed over a chain-link fence and disappeared into bramble.

Soon the other Silvers returned to find David and Mia embracing at the side of the van. Hannah was convinced the needle had finally swung all the way into romance until she saw the girl's shattered expression. Mia fixed her frantic eyes on Zack.

"I think I told Rebel where we are."

They fled the Power Boy with an 88 percent battery charge, and didn't stop until they were halfway into Missouri. Mia was the last to unclench her fingers from the seat rests. The theoretical danger had theoretically passed. They were as safe from Rebel as they always weren't.

The group ate dinner at a highway truck stop, their first experience in a bona fide speedery. Each booth and table was encased within a large glass cube. The place looked more like a human aquarium than a greasy spoon diner.

Theo was the first to spot the peculiar dial on the table, right above a sticker advising pregnant women and epileptics to avoid using it. After confirming that nobody in the booth suffered either condition, he turned the knob to 10. Suddenly the door to their enclosure locked, the glass lit up with a crosshatch of bright lines, and the outside world became ten times slower. Waitresses creaked their way between tables. Coffee poured like syrup from tilted pots.

As she casually perused her salad options, Hannah welcomed the others to her world.

Theo watched through the kitchen window in awe as a flipped burger rose and fell in slow motion.

"I just bent the fabric of time at a roadside grill. With a knob that sits next to the napkin holder."

Amanda suffered a tense flashback to the fuel truck that dawdled over the Massachusetts Turnpike, seventeen years ago. She hid her bother behind a glib smirk.

"Great. A way to make the service even slower."

"I'm pretty sure it's not meant to be used until after you get your food," David said.

"Yes, thank you. I'd worked that out already."

"So this is what you see every time you shift?" Mia asked Hannah. "It goes all blue like this?"

"Yeah. The faster I go, the bluer it gets. And colder. Sometimes I see my own breath."

And sometimes she saw more. Hannah thought back to the hallucination she'd suffered on Monday—the handsome Jury Curado, embracing a second Hannah from behind. *He adored you, I assure you, but he always died before you.* :(

Mia pressed a finger to the glass. "You think this would work if the walls weren't here?"

"The enclosure's just for safety," David explained. "If you put your hand beyond the field, it would exist at a different speed than the rest of your body. According to the book I'm reading, that's called rifting, and it's not a pleasant experience."

Amanda checked Zack's stony expression, still fixed on his menu. He'd been morbidly quiet since they'd fled the chargery. This wasn't the best time to learn the term for what he did to Rebel.

Hannah looked to David with sudden concern. "Wait. I don't have glass around me when I shift. I don't have a suit. Am I in danger of rifting myself every time I speed up?"

"I imagine if you were, it would have happened already," he mused. "I'd guess you're more a danger to others. I certainly wouldn't suggest touching anyone in your accelerated state."

Czerny had told Hannah the exact same thing, some weeks ago. She'd assumed he was just worried about high-speed bruising and breakage. Apparently there were worse dangers.

David turned to Zack. "Come to think of it, you also create an open temporic field. I imagine you'd be just as much of a risk as—"

"I know."

"He knows," said Amanda, at the same time.

Zack closed his menu and twisted the knob back to 1. Life outside the glass returned to normal.

"Let's just pick what we want and order."

That night, they rented three rooms at a quaint little inn on the outskirts of Jefferson City. Though the Silvers had forsaken fleabag motels in the wake of their new riches, Zack urged sensible restraint. "This isn't just travel money," he'd told them. "It's build-a-life-in-Brooklyn money."

All the same, Zack readily caved when David asked for his own room. The boy made a prickly bedfellow, and became downright surly when he didn't get his personal space.

Amanda stepped out of the shower at ten o'clock to find she had the women's suite to herself. She saw Hannah outside the window, lounging poolside with Theo. She could only guess that Mia was reading in David's room, her new evening ritual.

Edgy in solitude, she texted Zack on her phone.

<What's going on with you? You've been grim all evening.>

<Can't draw and type at the same time,> he replied. <Come ask in person.>

Two minutes later, he opened the door to Amanda. With her wet hair and white robe, her appearance was a throwback to his first recollection of her. She was a much more formidable presence than the high-strung redhead who'd slapped him seven weeks ago. Without a proper frame of reference, he couldn't tell if she was changing into a whole new person or settling back into the person she was. Most of his thoughts were stuck on how good she looked with wet hair.

"I think I know what we need," she said as she swept past him.

"So you're skipping over the whole 'What's going on with you?' part."

"Shut up and listen."

Zack fought a grin and returned to his sketchbook. He'd been on a cultural preservation kick since buying his new art supplies, dedicating his pencil to faithful re-creations of old-world icons. His current subjects were Calvin and Hobbes.

"We should take the weekend off," Amanda declared. "Find a nice hotel with a sundeck and just relax. We're all at wit's end and we need to unwind. What do you think?"

Zack kept drawing, expressionless. "I think the others will love your idea."

"What do *you* think?"

"I think what I think is moot, considering I'll get outvoted."

"Zack, you more than anyone else deserve a rest. You've done almost all the driving."

"I'd drive all night if you guys would let me. I just want to get there already."

"You think our problems will stop the minute we get to Brooklyn?"

On the contrary, Zack was terrified of what was waiting for them there. Ever since acquiring the van, he'd been plagued by nightmares that weren't even his own. For three nights in a row, Theo had lurched awake from sleep with an anguished cry. Each time he apologized to Zack but never explained the specifics. He insisted he was only having bad dreams, not previews.

Earlier that day, as the two men floated high in the Kansas tea lift, Theo finally spoke of the future.

"I have this bad feeling about Peter. Not like he's an enemy. More like a doctor with bad news. I have no idea what he's going to tell us, Zack. I just know we need to hear it. I know it's going to hurt."

Zack chose to withhold that tidbit from Amanda. She didn't need more reasons to fret.

"I don't think our problems will stop in Brooklyn," he told her. "But I do think we'll get answers. And about goddamn time too. I'm sick of having this 'in over my head' feeling, like I'm trying to read *Lord of the Rings* in Farsi. I'm so desperate for information right now that I don't even care if it's bad news. I just want to know."

Amanda crossed her arms. "You're right. That is a minority opinion."

"I'm not saying it's right or wrong. I'm just telling you what's going on with me."

"Well, I'm really worried about Hannah. You've never seen her break-downs. I have."

Zack jerked a limp shrug. "Okay, then sell your idea to the others. I won't fight it."

"I was hoping to get more than martyred resignation from you."

"And I was hoping to be in New York already. I guess we'll both have to settle."

Zack continued to sketch in full awareness of her harsh green glare, an-other throwback to their early days. Amanda wished him good night with all the warmth of a cadaver, then left him to his doodles.

Four hours later, bad dreams once again hit Zack by proxy. Theo shot up in bed with a yell, then stared at his trembling hands.

Zack rolled over to face him. "This isn't good, man."

"I'm sorry."

"I'm not complaining. I'm just worried about you."

"It's all right. I'll manage."

"Is this one of those recurring dreams where you're falling?"

"No."

"Is it a recurring dream where *I'm* falling?"

Theo fought a smirk. "No. I swear to you, Zack, I'm not seeing the future in my sleep."

"How do you know?"

"Because in my dream, I'm floating in front of a glowing white wall that stretches out to infinity. Does that sound realistic to you?"

Zack admitted that it didn't, though he would have once said the same thing about floating teacups over Kansas.

"And what exactly are you doing in front of this wall?" he inquired.

"I'm looking for something. That's the part that keeps getting me. In my dream, I'm desperately trying to find this tiny little object that means everything to everyone. And I just can't find it. I don't even know if it's there."

"What is it?"

Theo dropped his head to the pillow and blew a heavy breath at the ceiling.

"A string," he replied. "That's all I know. Just some stupid little string."

Zack woke up at 6 A.M., stirred by the sound of gentle knocking. He rubbed his eyes and made a sleepy lurch to the door. Amanda and Mia greeted him from the hallway, both crisp and suspiciously sunny. Mia brandished a rolled-up note in her hand.

"It's for you."

"What?"

"I got a note last night. It's from me but addressed to you."

Zack wasn't lucid enough to handle Mia's temporal juju, or the furtive grins of both women. "What are you two up to?"

"Just read it!"

He blinked several times until his vision came into focus, then took the sheet from Mia.

Dearest Zachary, brother of my heart,

A clever man once told me that there's no speed trophy waiting for us in Brooklyn. He was right. Now follow your own damn wisdom and slow down. This second Cataclysm isn't happening for another four to five years. For your own sakes, it's much more important to get here in a strong state of mind than it is to get here fast.

My advice is to take Amanda's advice, and then some. Find a ridiculously expensive hotel and hole up there for a week. Treat yourselves on comforts until you're all ready to pop. Don't worry about blowing the cash you have. Peter's filthy rich, just like all his people. Money's one of the few things you'll never have to worry about again.

Zack, if you trust me, then listen to me now. This is the note we wish we'd gotten. This is your chance to avoid one of our biggest regrets. Slow it down. Live it up. Heal your weary minds. Enjoy the simple pleasures of life, before life becomes less simple.

With love, always,
Mia

A cynical voice in Zack's head suggested that Mia was pulling a clever ruse, forging a note from her future self in order to keep him from souring Amanda's plans. His theory dissolved when he saw his own handwriting at the bottom of the page.

I'm Zack Trillinger and I approve this message.

He couldn't help but laugh in the wake of his self-correction. He could just picture the canny smirk on Future Zack's face as he scribbled his authentication. *He'll need this. Trust me. I know the guy.*

Amanda leaned against the doorframe and sneered with vindication. "Get the message?"

He reskimmed Mia's words. Her last line struck an ominous chord, a dark complement to Theo's grim portent. Fortunately for Amanda, the note instilled Zack with just the right amount of fear. The future could wait a little while longer.

TWENTY-TWO

The Piranda Five Towers was a sparkling jewel of the Midwest, a gleam in the "I" of Indiana. Amanda found a brochure at a chargery kiosk and fell in love with the photos. A quintet of tall glass spires loomed like fingers around a great palm grotto. At night, each building glowed with heavenly lumis while a great floating ghostbox provided a kaleidoscopic light show for anyone willing to crane their neck. The rooms were gorgeous and the resort had enough amenities to keep guests busy around the clock.

As the sun set on Saturday, the Silvers entered their new accommodations on the tenth floor of Tower Five. The Baronessa Suite was a 3,800-square-foot palace with two levels, three bathrooms, a full-size kitchen, and a hot tub veranda.

Hannah dropped her knapsack and forged a gawking path into the living room. She was the only one who'd taken issue with Amanda's choice of hotel, only because it was located in the ominously named city of Evansville. She was glad no one listened to her.

"Oh my God. This is . . ."

"Incredible," Mia finished. "How much did this cost for the week?"

"A fraction of what we have," Zack told her. "No worries."

Giddy with pleasure, Amanda threw her arms around Zack's neck. "Say it."

"Smugness doesn't become you, Given."

"Say it!"

"Fine. Yes. This was a brilliant idea. You're the goddess of gratification. I bow to you."

David returned from his walk-around inspection. "There are six beds, but only three bedrooms. If no one has a problem with a coed arrangement—"

"Theo and I can share," said Hannah, with an arch grin. "Easy breezy. Problem solved."

Mia wasn't sure whether to thank or slap Hannah for cutting off David's thought. Theo nodded in shaky accord.

"That's fine. Whatever works."

Zack flipped through the elaborate room service menu and stopped at the page of lobster options.

"Oh, this works. This really, really works."

Their stay in the Baronessa Suite was one of the nicest weeks of their lives, with an asterisk. The events of checkout morning would forever mar their recollection, though the healing distance of time would eventually allow them to catalog the week as "mostly lovely," or "perfect until. . . ."

When stored in their own bottle, the first six and a half days shined from every angle. The Silvers enjoyed a level of carefree comfort that had eluded them on two worlds. They lived without worrying about finances or federal agents, sword-wielding killers or citywide Cataclysms. For 156 hours, they existed in the sweet haze of the moment. They coddled themselves in manners both shallow and deep, conventional and strange.

It was on their first morning that Amanda Given, the goddess of gratification herself, stretched the definition of leisure to the snapping point.

"I'm going to church," she announced at breakfast. "Anyone care to join me?"

She'd aimed the question at Zack in droll jest, and was stunned when David leapt at her offer. He'd always wanted to experience a Christian worship service, just to see how the pious majority lived.

Following the directions of the concierge, they attended mass at a Roman Catholic church in downtown Evansville. Amanda dreaded all the daft adjustments to her old and familiar liturgy, but she was soon amazed by the wonderful sameness of it all. There were no tempic altars, no speed knobs on the pews, no peculiar rites or parallel-Earth prayers. For a brief time, two worlds converged and Amanda was back in the Chula Vista parish. She could almost feel Derek sitting next to her, a sensation bittersweet enough to draw quiet tears.

David sat through the ceremony like an overcaffeinated tourist, launching his fascinated smile in all directions. It was only during the penitential rite that Amanda noticed him staring at the floor with a grim and heavy expression. Like her, he'd injured two policemen on Monday, when his ghosted truck sent their cruiser into a rough collision. By outward appearances, the boy had written off his actions as a necessary evil. Now Amanda wasn't so sure.

At noon, she parked the van in the hotel garage, then aimed a pensive stare at David.

"I think I want to find the names of those cops we hurt and send them some of our money."

"That's a horrible idea," he said.

"Why?"

"Because the Deps will know who sent the cash and why. They'll determine our general location from postmarks. And they'll seize your gift as evidence. Those policemen will likely never see a dime of it."

She stared ahead in busy contemplation. "Crap."

"If you're looking for absolution, why didn't you stay to make a confession?"

Amanda debated it, but then realized that she'd either have to suppress the details of her tempic transgression or tell the priest the whole truth. She didn't want to think how he'd react to her ungodly white monstrosity.

"I just want to do it to feel good," she said. "I mean, that's what this week is for, right?"

David bit his lip in churning thought. "I suppose we could give a portion of our money to local charities. People in need. I mean if we're careful—"

"We?"

He gave her a shrug and a soft grin, then admitted he was never one for hot tubs.

To the bewilderment of their four companions, Amanda and David spent their week as wild roaming philanthropists, a bizarro Bonnie and Clyde. They rode the streets of Evansville with fifty thousand dollars of goodwill and a marked-up city map. They weren't choosy in their targets—churches, temples, children's centers, animal shelters. They even donated eight hundred dollas to the Natural Life Foundation, a group that was starkly opposed to all uses of temporis.

For discretion's sake, they never contributed more than a thousand dollars to a single charity, never gave their names, and never stayed too long to receive gratitude. David even swapped his native Australian accent for a flawless American dialect. "Your sister's not the only actor in the group," he told Amanda, with an impish grin.

It wasn't until their weeklong venture together that Amanda dropped her last thread of unease about David. Unlike Hannah and Mia, who'd both been smitten from the start, Amanda had always sensed something slightly off about the boy. She routinely detected a spark of effort behind his deep blue eyes, as if he were perpetually flexing a muscle or censoring a thought. By their second cozy lunch, she realized she'd been overjudging him, punishing him for the fleeting way he reminded her of Derek. When unfettered by those chains, David was a delight to be around. He dazzled her with knowledge on virtually every subject, amused her with anecdotes from his time among the Dutch and Japanese. He broke her heart with descriptions of his mother, a geneticist who fell to ovarian cancer when he was nine.

"She's the one who gave me this wristwatch," he told her, brandishing his vintage silver timepiece. "Her dying wish was that every time I wind it, I find one reason to be thankful. I honor her request each time. Like clockwork, as they say."

On Friday afternoon, they donated the last of their cash to a fledgling theater company that was performing *Titus Andronicus*. Amanda was depressed to reach the end of her charity run. If she didn't think Zack would blow a gasket, she'd ask for another week and fifty grand.

As their elevator climbed the side of Tower Five, David clutched Amanda's arm and shined a tender smile.

"Thank you. This was a wonderful way to spend a week."

"Thank *you*. It was your idea."

"Yes, well, even I didn't know how therapeutic it would be," he admitted. "I come from a 'big picture' family. Big thinkers, with our heads always high in the clouds. Sometimes I forget the pleasures of small endeavors."

Amanda squeezed his hand. She couldn't have loved him more.

"So do you think you have it now?" David asked her.

"Have what?"

"Absolution."

The elevator opened. Amanda didn't find her answer until they reached the door of their suite.

"I can't speak for God, but I think I can say I've forgiven myself."

"Well, that's something."

"What about you?"

David pulled back from the door, shooting her a look that was harsh enough to unnerve her.

"I never said I was seeking forgiveness."

"I saw you at church, during the penitential rite. You looked upset. I assumed—"

"Amanda, I would hurt a dozen more policemen to keep us from being incarcerated. I would kill a hundred to keep us alive. We can argue the ethics until we're both old and gray. This is the new reality. I'm sleeping just fine."

As she cast her silent prayers that night, Amanda forced herself to stay positive. She thanked God for David Dormer—his strength, his insight, his kindness to his friends. All the same, she found herself grateful that he could only throw sound and light at his enemies. She shuddered to think what a boy like that could do with tempis.

Zack never thought he'd get tired of lounging in luxury. And yet by Monday morning his liquid daze congealed into a hard and restless boredom.

While Hannah and Theo canoodled in their room and Amanda and David embarked on their mad giving spree, the cartoonist dropped his sketch pad and idly flipped through a dictionary of modern American slang. Ten minutes of baffling word study was all he could take before he jumped to his feet and plucked the history book from Mia's hands.

"Come on. We're out of here."

They hailed a cab to Evansville and caught a big-budget suspense film, a tale of a killer shark that was uncreatively called *The Killer Shark*. The theater was shifted at 12×, allowing Zack and Mia to suffer two hours of atrocious cinema while ten minutes passed in the outside world. Sadly, there was no escaping once the movie began. The best they could do was dawdle at the concession stand until the building de-shifted and the front doors unlocked.

They recuperated at a quiet seafood restaurant. Zack brought Mia to teary-eyed laughter with his tirade about the film, which he called a "cranial

crucifixion" and a "developmentally disabled children's production of *Jaws*."
She nearly choked on her soda when he went on to explain the new-world
jargon he'd learned from Mia's slang book.

"Okay, so the act of cloning objects through temporis is called 'tooping.'
We already knew that. But when you take tooped food and toop it again, it
makes a noxious, smelly goo that people call 'threep.' You with me?"

Mia bit her lip in quivering suppression and nodded.

"Now, in addition to being a prime element of pranks and hazings, 'threep'
is the all-purpose word for anything awful. It could be used as a noun, as in,
'Hey, who cooked this threep?' Or an adjective, such as, 'Man, this job is truly
threeped.' If you're looking for something stronger, 'fourp' is . . ."

Mia burst into another fit of giggles. With a droll smirk, Zack proceeded.

"'Fourp' is mostly used for emphasis, as in, 'Wow, that movie was a fourping torture fest,' or—"

"There's not a 'fivep,' is there?"

"See, now you're just being silly."

Mia realized now that Zack was the crucial ingredient in her feel-good
week. On the cab ride home, she rested her head on his shoulder and told him
that, like it or not, she'd be glued to his side for the next five days. He breathed
a furtive whisper through her hair, a sneaky proposition that they break the
leisure accord and research the fourp out of Peter.

She squeezed his arm and told him she loved him.

Their work began on Tuesday, in the hotel business center. Sitting side by
side at a rented computer, they spent half the morning teaching themselves
the gruesomely hostile operating system, which Zack likened to an eight-bit
horror from Soviet Minsk. They tabbed their way through an endless maze of
text menus until they found the door to Eaglenet, a web that was anything but
worldwide. A digital wall had been erected around the borders of the nation,
ensuring purely American data for purely American eyes. Despite its rigid
structure, the network allowed free public access to fifty years of news
archives.

A keyword search for "Peter Pendergen" generated 1,206 articles. When
he wasn't a sound bite in someone else's story, he was the author in the byline.
Mia was surprised to learn that her pen pal (of sorts) was a freelance journal-
ist who'd written for forty different publications. The subject of his stories

was always the same: people who professed to have amazing temporal abilities. In some pieces, he called them "temporics." In others, they were "chronokinetics." Mostly he referred to them as Gothams, a term that deeply intrigued Zack and Mia.

A keyword search for Gothams generated 1,014,353 articles.

Zack tossed his partner a bleary stare. "We're gonna need a bigger boat."

The topic consumed them for the rest of the week. For twelve hours a day, they sat at adjacent workstations, catching up on decades of Altamerican legend. In the 1950s, at the dawn of temporis, new rumors swirled of people who could innately bend time in one manner or another. The explanations ranged from the scientific to the mystical to the purely divine.

Thirty-six years ago, a former Dep named Alexander Wingo breathed new life into the myth. He dubbed these people Gothams after the Halo of Gotham, the miraculous ring of land where more than sixty thousand souls survived the Cataclysm of 1912. Though they'd stood mere feet from the edge of the blast, the damage they suffered was purely emotional. The only exceptions were the pregnant women, many of whom birthed children with crippling defects. If Wingo was to be believed, a fraction of the infants had mutated in more interesting ways. Some developed strange talents. Some grew up to find one another and bear talented offspring of their own.

In his book, *Children of the Halo*, Wingo claimed to have discovered a clandestine community of third- and fourth-generation Gothams. Though normal citizens in public, they secretly operated under their own arcane laws and rituals. Their strict mating customs made each generation stronger than the last. Wingo feared it was just a matter of time before they began birthing gods.

The book created a huge stir among starry-eyed believers, spawning novels and movies and one long-running lumivision series. It also sparked an endless chain of incredible claims and sightings. At least once a month, some bold attention-seeker would come forward with nebulous proof of Gotham activity, only to get exposed as a fraud or dupe. Usually the one exposing them was Peter Pendergen. The man clearly had a taste for irony.

On Friday evening, while the Silvers digested their dinner on the balcony, Zack and Mia shared the fruits of their labor.

"He's thirty-seven and widowed with one son," Zack told them. "When he's not out disproving the existence of his own people, he likes to write fiction. He has two published novels, both set in medieval Ireland. He claims he can trace his ancestry all the way back to King Arthur's father."

"Yes, and I'm related to Beowulf," David mocked.

Zack laughed. "We didn't buy it either. From his age, I assume he's a fourth-generation Gotham, which is pretty mind-blowing when you think about it. I mean we're nouveau weird. These people have been carrying it in their genes since 1912."

"They sound like interesting people," Theo offered. "Shame they want us dead."

Amanda forked a piece of Zack's cheesecake. "I don't understand what Peter's trying to accomplish with his articles. Why write about fake Gothams?"

"Misdirection," Mia explained. "The more he highlights the phonies and crazies, the less people believe in the real thing."

"Oh. Well, I guess we didn't help his cause when we fought those policemen."

Zack vented a heavy sigh. "No. We made a bunch of new believers on Monday. I'm sure that's another reason Rebel wants us dead."

Hannah stewed in the bubbling hot tub, scowling with ill temper. This was supposed to be a week of luxurious self-indulgence, and yet two of her people blew it all on research while another two went wild with charity. Stranger still, they all seemed happier for their efforts. Obviously she and Theo screwed up somehow. They had devoted their week to more intimate pleasures. Now they both felt perfectly wretched.

They'd spent their first night in separate beds. Once the lights went out, the actress and the augur blew airy topics of chatter back and forth—favorite songs, pet peeves, complaints about their mutual companions. They moved on to discuss past loves, though Theo confessed to having just one. Hannah noticed he wasn't particularly eager to talk about her.

At 2 A.M., she bid Theo good night, and then offered him the prospect of a great night.

"Let me know when you want me to come over there," she said.

Five seconds passed before Theo turned on the lamp. He stared at her with tense, bulging eyes.

"Uh, what exactly are you proposing?"

She opened the drawer on the nightstand, revealing a box of Admiral John condoms. Beneath the stylized logo, a bearded man in eighteenth-century naval garb smirked at Theo.

"Wow. Jesus, Hannah. I . . . don't even know what to say."

"Did you honestly not see this coming? I've been hanging all over you. I practically insisted we share a room."

"I don't know. I thought it was just flirting. I certainly never expected . . . What's this supposed to be, anyway? A one-night stand? A weeklong fling?"

"It can be whatever we want it to be. And I'm sorry if my directness bothered you. I know we're attracted to each other. I'm just trying to save time."

Theo couldn't get over her sudden transformation. Hannah was normally a rickety construct, perpetually unsure and unsettled. Now she propositioned him without a speck of doubt or worry.

"I really don't think it's a good idea, Hannah. I mean if things go bad—"

"Okay. Suit yourself."

She turned off the lamp. Theo continued to stare at her in the dark. "Look, I'm really sorry. It has nothing to do—"

"Theo, it's fine. Seriously. I've been at both ends of this process. I get it."

"So you're not mad."

Hannah aimed a sly grin at the ceiling. She didn't get mad in these situations. She got ruthless.

On Sunday, the actress began her formal assault on Theo's better judgment. She hit the boutiques for a sleek haircut and a bag full of seduction supplies. That afternoon, she entered the hot tub in her new swimsuit: a shiny silver one-piece with a neckline plunge that derailed even David's train of thought. At dinner, she reached past Theo for the salt shaker, filling his nose with a strawberry scent that pushed him another step closer to madness. At midnight, she showered with the door slightly open, singing a rendition of Leonard Cohen's "Hallelujah" that was beautiful enough to make Theo wince. She emerged from the bathroom in a chest-hugging half shirt and boy shorts, then asked him if there was anything he felt like doing.

Theo now understood why she'd been so cavalier last night. She saw the inevitability of his surrender long before he did. She wasn't just the confident one in this duo, she was the augur.

"You sure know how to make a guy feel stupid for turning you down."

"I haven't said a word about it," she coyly replied.

"You think I wasn't already tempted?"

"I have no idea what's going on in your head, Theo."

Frustrated, he dropped his book on the nightstand. "Convince me that a fling won't end with us hating each other."

"Convince me that it will."

"I could spend an hour listing all the dark possibilities."

"I could spend a week listing all the better things we can do with that hour."

After a few silent moments, their tight faces cracked away in laughter. Theo shook his head at himself. "I'm trying to talk a beautiful woman out of sleeping with me. It's come to this."

Hannah turned off the overhead light and sat at Theo's side. In the soft haze of the night lamp, she held her palm against his cheek.

"Look, I'm sorry for the way I offered myself to you last night. I shouldn't have been so cold about it. If I wanted a meaningless encounter, I'd go to the bar and pick up a stranger. I'm coming to you because I want intimacy with a man I know and trust. We're both adults, Theo. We can be affectionate without falling in love or hating each other later. We can make each other feel good on every level. But in order to do that, you need to stop worrying about the future, just for a little while. Can you do that? Can you put it all aside and just be with me?"

Caught between his doubts and desires, the inevitable regrets of his yes and no answers, Theo ran a cautious hand down her arm.

"When you are in your element, Hannah Given, you're a force to behold."

Smiling in victory, she reached for the lamp. "Sweetie, I haven't even started."

Sunday was a great night for both of them. At 5:23 and four Admiral Johns, they finally agreed to rest their elated bodies. Hannah pressed against Theo's side as he drifted off to sleep, enjoying the rhythmic sound of his heartbeat. The thump thump thump—

(of a brand-new chump)

—was hypnotic, almost enough to clear the turmoil in her thoughts. She wanted to burrow a hole in Theo and hide inside him until everything was right with the universe again.

They spent the next four days like newlyweds, devouring each other at every turn. In daylight hours, when the others embarked on their missions, they frolicked through the suite—kissing in the kitchen, spooning on the sofas, basking in the balcony hot tub. It was only during their evenings of mixed company that they kept their hands off each other. They agreed to keep their arrangement hidden, if only to spare themselves from Zack's jokes, Amanda's concerns, and David's awkwardly intrusive questions.

With each secret act of pleasure, their emotional cords became tangled in ways that were both subtle and obvious. By Wednesday, their conversations had become as intimate as their lovemaking.

"I don't miss my parents," Theo confessed. "I was only their son when they could brag about me. The moment I stopped being the glowing prodigy, I simply stopped existing. They never even visited me in the hospital after I tried to kill myself."

Hannah held him in bed, somberly staring at the wall as she traced a finger across his chest. "That might be a blessing. Amanda visited me and it only made things worse."

"How so?"

"She sat next to my mother and looked at me like I was some kind of criminal, like I'd tried to kill some other girl. It made me want to die all over again. I mean I still love her but . . . I don't know. If she hadn't gotten a silver bracelet, I'd probably be telling you now in all honesty that I don't miss her."

In the predawn hours of Friday, they reached the peak of their union. Their fifth encounter of the night had turned so passionate that all they could do was stare at each other in astonishment as they fought to catch their breath.

"Hannah . . ."

"Don't."

"Don't what?"

"Don't say anything that's going to change things."

He eyed her with hot resentment. "I wasn't going to tell you I love you."

"I didn't say you were."

"I was just going to say things may have changed."

"Well . . . don't."

Theo rolled off her, then shot a dark gaze at the ceiling.

"I haven't had any bad dreams since Saturday. They stopped when we started."

He checked her expression. "Is that okay for me to say? Or does that freak you out too?"

"That doesn't freak me out, Theo."

"So, any response to that?"

Hannah turned away from him, grim-faced.

"I guess our friendship comes with all sorts of benefits."

That morning, Theo's handphone beeped. The display announced nine new texts from a person only listed as *A. Fact*. Each message was fifteen characters or shorter. Theo couldn't delete them without being forced to read Evan's whole nasty dispatch.

> She will never
> Love you, Theo.
> She simply
> Isn't capable.
> Save yourself.
> Get out now.
> If you won't
> End it,
> Azral will. :(

After lunch, they soaked in the hot tub. Theo rolled drops of water down Hannah's shoulders. He didn't need Evan to cast a cloud of doom over their relationship. With each passing hour, he felt a cold wall of grief drawing toward them like a tidal wave. He wasn't sure if he was suffering premonitions or merely jitters.

"What was your longest relationship?" he asked her, out of the blue.

"Nine weeks, more or less. Why?"

"How did it end?"

"I mostly dated actors," Hannah replied. "Typically I'd lose them to another woman, another man, or Los Angeles. As it stood, I lost Nine Week Boy to a woman in Los Angeles. Why are you asking?"

"Just being nosy."

"Okay. Fine. My turn. How did you and your girlfriend—what was her name?"

"Rachel."

"How did you and Rachel break up?"

After a brief silence, Hannah slid off his lap and faced him from the other side of the tub. "You're not going to tell me?"

"We didn't break up," he replied.

"So she died."

"Yes."

"When everyone else did?"

"No."

Hannah chucked her wet hands. "This is turning into Twenty Questions."

"I'd rather it turn into No Questions."

"So you get to delve into my past, but I can't delve into yours."

"I'm choosing not to answer. You could have done the same. It's not like we need to know everything about each other. We're not a couple."

Hannah could have frozen the whole tub with her stare.

"Are you just venting right now? Or are you trying to sink the whole ship?"

"We've been sinking from the start, Hannah. I'm just putting on a life vest."

She climbed out of the water and wrapped a towel around her waist. "I'll let you stew for a while. If you have any interest in preserving what we have—"

"We can't preserve it. That's what I'm trying to tell you."

"We have *weeks*, Theo! We could enjoy each other for weeks!"

"Until what? I become discouraged enough to leave you for another woman? Another man? Los Angeles? Aren't you getting sick of this pattern?"

She glared at him in hot exasperation. "Are you trying to make me hate you?"

"No."

"Then look to the future and see where this gets you."

She slammed the patio door behind her. Theo looked out to the other four towers. He could only imagine that Evan was sitting on one of those balconies, grinning as he watched their bubbling troubles through binoculars.

They kept their distance from each other for the rest of the afternoon, and avoided eye contact during dinner. While the Silvers ate their desserts on the balcony table, Hannah crawled back into the hot tub. Her companions spent most of the evening talking about Gothams and Peter Pendergen, as sure a sign as any that the vacation was over.

Once the others retired for the night, Theo finally dared to face Hannah alone. He saw her through the crack in the bedroom door, staring somberly at a small item in her hand, the driver's license of Ernesto Curado. She spotted Theo and quickly hid the card behind her.

"So. Is this going to be a reconciliation or another fight?"

He took a weary perch on the cedar desk. "In the spirit of you and me, I think it's going to be something in between."

"I never lied to you, Theo. I told you from the start what I wanted."

"Yes. You did. It's my fault for not being able to handle it. But in retrospect, it was silly for us to think we could have something casual in the middle of uncasual circumstances."

"That's exactly why I wanted it casual! I thought it'd be easier to enjoy each other without all the emotional baggage that comes with relationships. Why do I keep finding the few men on Earth who can't grasp that concept?"

"I don't know. Why do you keep resenting the fact that we want more than sex from you?"

She shook a brusque finger at him. "Don't turn this into a head-shrink session. It won't end well."

"Then tell me what I can say right now."

"To do what?"

"To end this well."

She looked at him with pained surprise, then flicked a hand in surrender. "You want out? Fine. Abracadabra. We're friends again. Frankly, I think this was a problem that needed a wrench, not a chainsaw. But I guess you have your own way of doing things."

"I'm trying to avoid a bad situation for everyone," he insisted. "The six of us are going to have to rely on each other, probably for the rest of our—"

She threw her book to the floor. "Look, you wanted an exit, you got one. But don't pretend you're leaving for noble reasons. You got scared. You bolted at the first sign of trouble. You don't get to wear that as a feather in your cap!"

Her eyes began to moisten. Her entire face quivered. She was no longer

Hannah in Her Element. She wasn't even the rickety Hannah that Theo had known before. She was falling apart.

"We could have had weeks, you asshole. We could have healed each other."

"That wouldn't have happened."

"Oh, just get the hell out of here already. You're such a coward, I can't even look at you."

"Hannah . . ."

The tears flowed freely down her face. "Theo, I swear to God you have three seconds to get out of this room before you see the real and awful me."

He took her at her word and left. He sat motionless on the living room sofa for over an hour before stretching out for sleep.

At 1 A.M., Hannah emerged with a folded blanket and pillow, then dropped them on his stomach. Theo saw his phone in her hand. A tiny bulb flashed green in announcement of new text messages.

"Don't read that. It's—"

"I know who it is."

She stepped outside to the balcony, hurled the phone over the railing, and then raised her middle fingers high in the night. It was her own message to Evan Rander, in whatever patio he'd chosen as his spying perch.

Theo watched her cautiously as she marched back through the living room.

"Give me one night to hate you," she said.

"Okay."

He wrapped himself in the blanket, steeling himself for the return of bad dreams. On the plus side, he knew he had only one night to spend on the sofa. Their feel-good week would finally end in the morning. At long last, the Silvers were checking out.

As the sun rose on Saturday, September 18, a tiny breach of time opened above Mia and spat an urgent message. The note rose and fell with her sleeping breaths for ninety-five minutes, until a waking turn rolled it into a blanket crevasse. She yawned her way to the bathroom, unaware.

Hannah woke up five minutes later, dark eyed and unrested. She shook

Theo awake in the living room and pulled him back to bed. She didn't want the others to see him sleeping on the couch like a punished husband. The less they knew about the whole debacle, the better.

While Hannah showered, Theo lay awake on the mattress, lamenting the loss of access to her ravishing body and suffering a vague new sense of dread. There was a bad wind blowing from the future, and it was centered around the sisters. Theo relaxed when he spotted Amanda in the living room, as cheery as he'd ever seen her. A week of rest and charity had done wonders for the widow's state of mind.

By ten o'clock, everyone was dressed, packed, and waiting at the balcony table. In light of the beautiful morning weather, Amanda insisted on having a final patio brunch. Zack led a sardonic round of applause when she wheeled in the food cart. Room service had taken over an hour to deliver their order.

"They're having some kind of bellhop crisis," Amanda explained. "A hotel manager had to bring this. He gave us free mimosas as an apology."

David leered at the six flute glasses. "That's strange. He didn't ask to see your wet card?"

Zack scowled in mock outrage. "Can we go one morning without your crude euphemisms?"

The boy ignored him. "They have laws against serving alcohol to people without proper ID. The manager's putting the hotel at serious risk."

Amanda shrugged. "Well, it was a young guy. He's probably new. And who cares? Is anyone here planning on reporting them?"

"I am."

"Shut up," she said to Zack. "You're having a drink with me. Who else wants?"

Amanda turned sheepish when she saw Theo's heavy expression. "There's probably an ounce of champagne in these things. Not even enough for a buzz."

"It's okay. I'll pass."

Amanda wasn't surprised when the teenagers abstained, but Hannah's refusal threw her. "Are you sure? You used to love these."

"I said I don't want any."

Raising her palms in surrender, Amanda backed away. Soon everyone took turns at the kitchen juve, reversing their food to a piping-hot state. Amanda passed Zack a glass and a whisper.

"There are at least three of us here in bad moods. Please save me before I become the fourth."

"I can do that."

The two of them quickly dominated the meal with their boisterous celebration, trading silly quips and toasts between each sip of mimosa.

"To happy fugitives," said Amanda.

"To well-rested fugitives," said Zack.

"To tall and skinny atheist fugitives who can be somewhat cute when they're not obnoxious."

Zack retracted his glass. "Sorry. Can't drink to that without correcting you."

"You're not cute?"

"I'm not an atheist. I have no idea if God exists or not."

"Then why do you make fun of the people who do?"

"Because I'm obnoxious," Zack replied. "That part of the toast was accurate."

"I see. You're an obnoxious agnostic. You're agnoxious."

"I'm antaganostic."

Amanda roared with laughter. "How could you think you're not cute?"

"I never said I wasn't!"

Though Mia giggled at their goofy banter, the other three Silvers remained grim and humorless. Halfway through Amanda's second drink, her fingers turned shiny and white. When Mia awkwardly told her that her weirdness was showing, Amanda laughed, shook her hands pink, and then raised a toast to tempis fugitives. The pun launched Zack into bellowing guffaws.

"I'm thinking those drinks are stronger than you realized," David mused.

Zack waved him off. "We're not hammered."

"We're just having fun," Amanda insisted, with a pointed glare at Hannah.

It had taken only five minutes of her sister's excruciating revelry to make Hannah swallow down the three spare mimosas. But instead of joining Zack and Amanda in tipsy exuberance, the actress felt worse than ever. Her skin burned. Her legs bounced uncontrollably. Angry notions exploded in her mind like popcorn.

Once Amanda propped her feet on Zack's thighs, Hannah stood up fast enough to wobble.

Theo grabbed her. "Whoa. You okay?"

Hannah yanked her arm away. "I'm fine."

She washed her face in the bathroom, gritting her teeth as a sneering inner voice taunted her. *Hey, Hannah Banana, Always Needs-a-Man-a. Funny how you can't keep them while your sister can't keep them away. Shame Jury's not here to balance things out. Oh well. That's just the way it goes here in Evansville.*

She returned to the balcony with forced poise, determined to ignore Theo's patronizing look of concern and the escalating flirtations between her sister and Zack.

"It's true!" Amanda insisted. "You have physical contact issues. You don't like hugging."

"That is bull-pucky of the highest order. I hug everyone. Even my enemies."

"Remember that time we hugged in Ramona? You were awkward about it."

"That's because we were in an alley. I could feel the hobos judging us."

"There were no hobos, Zachary. You have issues that need fixing. Stand up."

"No."

"Fine. We'll do it sitting down."

Amanda planted herself on Zack's lap, fastening his arms around her slender waist.

"And what is this supposed to accomplish?" he asked.

"Immersion therapy. You need to get over your resistance."

"Boy, the charity never stops with you."

She leaned back against him and blew him a frisky whisper. "This isn't charity, you clueless man. I want more hugs."

Hannah jumped to her feet, rocking the table. As drinks spilled onto plates and laps, the actress threw an empty glass to the floor. It exploded all around her shoes.

"What the hell is wrong with you?!"

Shocked into sobriety, Amanda climbed off Zack's lap. She raised her taut fingers.

"Okay, take it easy . . ."

"Do you even see how pathetic you're being right now? You've been a widow for eight weeks! Eight weeks, and this is how you act!"

David held Mia's arm. "Let's get the bags ready."

Mia gave him a shaky nod. They disappeared inside. Amanda fought to stay calm.

"Look, I don't know what's really bothering you . . ."

"You think it isn't upsetting enough to watch you disrespect Derek?"

"You barely even knew him!"

"I know he'd hate to see you give a lap dance to some other guy!"

Zack shook his head in seething pique. "Hannah, you're way off base and way out of line."

"Well then let me be the second one to call you clueless. I swear to God, there isn't a single man in this group who knows a single thing about women."

"Look, you're angry at me," Amanda said. "Don't take it out on him."

Hannah laughed bitterly. "Oh, you just love being noble. The great and noble Amanda Given. Oops. Sorry. I meant Amanda Ambridge. Hey, Zack, I hope you're not intent on having her take your name. She'll just drop it the minute you die. That's how noble she is."

Amanda gritted her teeth. Her eyes filled with tears. "You sad little child . . ."

"Yeah, the child. Your other favorite meme. You just love being better than me."

"Well, you make it so easy!"

"Oh, go to hell!"

"*You* go to hell! We did this for you! We took this whole week so you could feel better! Of course you'd do everything in your power to stay miserable! That's all you know how to do!"

"Shut up!"

Theo reached for her. "Hannah, don't—"

She turned to him, red-faced. "You do not say a word to me. You do not say a word!"

Amanda eyed the two of them with dark revelation. She burst into a caustic chuckle.

"Oh, I get it now. I see why you're so pissed."

"Shut up! You don't know a thing!"

"And you call me the pathetic one? Amazing. You never learn."

Theo and Zack both yelled as Hannah hurled a second glass. This one hit Amanda in the face.

Mia gathered her bags from her room, her stomach churning with bitter acids. For all she knew, this latest fight would plague them for months. Worse, it could split them up forever. What would happen then? Who'd go with who?

As she adjusted her bedspread, she noticed a rolled-up note. She read it with growing fear, then fled back to the living room.

The flute glass cracked in two against Amanda's forehead, leaving a pair of gashes along her brow. She touched her new wounds, then stared in trembling rage at the blood on her fingers.

Hannah covered her mouth in white-eyed horror. "Oh my God . . ."

Zack made a furious beeline for Hannah. "What the hell's wrong with you?!"

The cartoonist could suddenly feel every molecule in Hannah's body. It scared him to think that he could rift her dead with a single thought. Scarier still, a part of him wanted to.

Mia ran to the door. "Zack, stop! The drinks were drugged! You're all drugged!"

Though her future self hadn't elaborated, the chemical that affected them was called pergnesticin. It was initially developed as a mood enhancer, as it did a fine job turning good feelings into great ones. Unfortunately, it also had a tendency to turn bad moods into violence. The drug was illegal in the United States but remained wildly popular as contraband. In dermal patch form, it was appropriately known as a leopard spot.

Theo could suddenly see the shape of the problem ahead. He knew now that Evan wasn't content to return a middle-finger gesture at Hannah. He was going to give her the whole hand.

"Hannah, you need to get out of here . . ."

"I'm sorry, Amanda! I didn't mean to do that!"

The widow's world fell hot and silent as chemical rage overtook her. There was no sister, nurse, or Christian inside her anymore. There was only the tempis.

The whiteness exploded from her left palm, a spray of solid force that toppled everything in its path. A wooden chair fell while another snapped to pieces. The dining table flipped over, spilling drinks and dishes everywhere. By the time the tempis reached the other end of the balcony, it took form as a six-foot hand. It shoved away the two men who had the unfortunate luck of standing near Hannah. Theo toppled to the right, colliding painfully with the hot tub. Zack flew to the left, flipping over the side of the balcony railing. He caught a loose hold of the edge.

The tempic palm barreled into Hannah, shoving her six feet through the air. Amanda retracted her hand in time to see Hannah crack her head against the far brick wall. She spilled to the floor in a lifeless heap.

David lunged toward the railing, rushing to grab Zack before he lost his grip. Between the blood in her eyes and the many alarms in her head, Amanda processed the simple but devastating notion that the boy wouldn't make it in time.

Indeed, just inches before David could reach him, Zack's fingers lost their hold. He dropped from the side of Tower Five.

Ten days ago, as he floated over Kansas in a giant teacup, Zack wondered what it would be like to plummet to his death. He debated how much time his mind would give him to process the sad and messy end of his tale.

The answer, he now knew, was "quite a bit."

For the second time in his life, the cartoonist fell into a state of breathless suspension, an almost supernatural acuity that allowed him to register dozens of details in the span of a blink. He could count the number of balcony railings between him and the ground (*eight*). He could scan the unforgiving elements of his future impact zone (*wood and concrete*). He could envision the reactions of his surviving friends and enemies (*Oh God, Amanda . . .*).

As he passed the fifth-floor balcony, something odd happened. The shift in his momentum was so abrupt and painful that he feared he'd already hit the pavement. A cold, hard pressure immobilized Zack's body, as if he'd been packed in dense snow. When he opened his eyes, he could see the ground fifty feet below him. It wasn't getting any closer.

He turned his head and caught his reflection in a patio door. A giant tempic fist had seized him, snatching him from above like the hand of God itself.

She caught me, he thought. *Jesus Christ, she caught me.*

Zack once again gazed down at the grotto, where dozens of bystanders began to gather in a messy clump. They pointed up at him, gawking and shouting, snapping photos.

His last thought before blacking out was of Peter Pendergen, a man who'd worked so tirelessly to keep the public cynical about chronokinetics. Zack cast him a weary apology for the unwitting countereffort. All the minds they changed today. All the new believers.

TWENTY-THREE

Evan woke up in a sour mood on Saturday, haunted by the memories of his multiple pasts. They leapt at him from his cutting room floor—scenes deleted but not forgotten, words unsaid but not unheard, all the hurtful actions of a woman he'd cherished but now despised. They always hit him worst in the morning.

With a drowsy yawn, he crossed the floor of his hotel suite. He showered and shaved, dressed himself in a sleek charcoal business suit, then tucked his hair beneath a wavy brown wig. Once he applied his putty nose and chin, Evan chuckled at his reflection. He could have passed for Zack's dapper young brother.

After a hearty breakfast in the grotto café, Evan rented a room on the tenth floor of Tower Five, just a few doors down from his fellow Silvers. He ordered six mimosas from room service and then called the front desk to launch an incoherent complaint about his new accommodations.

Soon a manager knocked on his door. He was bald and barrel-chested, with a strong lantern jaw that unpleasantly reminded Evan of his father. The manager did a double take at Evan's suit, a nearly exact replica of his own.

"Good morning, Mr. Freeman. I'm Lloyd Lundrum. What seems to be the problem?"

Evan tapped the square brass pin on the man's blazer. "Lloyd Lundrum. Good name. I like it. Listen, the room's fine. I'm just hoping to play a gag on some friends down the hall. I'll give you a thousand dollars to lend me your name tag for an hour."

The manager's eyes narrowed to frosty slits. Evan laughed.

"Okay. Wow. You even glare like my dad. I guess there's no point in raising my offer."

"No, sir. There's not. And I don't appreciate you calling me here under—"

Evan's skin tingled with tiny bubbles as he reversed his life fifty-eight seconds. He straightened his sleeves, then answered the knock at the door.

"Good morning, Mr. Freeman. I'm Lloyd Lundrum. What seems to be the problem?"

"Well, Lloyd, there's an ugly red stain on the carpet and frankly, I'm not happy about it."

Sixty seconds later, the manager lay crumpled at the foot of the bed, a trickling bullet hole between his frozen white eyes.

Evan stashed his silenced .22, then stooped to remove Lloyd's ID pin. He could only imagine that Luke Rander was shaking his head from the great beyond. His father never understood him in the old world and sure as hell wouldn't get it now. In Evan's Etch A Sketch life, nothing mattered. All that was done was inevitably undone. The screen would wipe clean for Round 56, and Lloyd Lundrum would live again to scoff at wealthy pranksters.

Evan whistled a chipper tune as he stirred a vial of crushed pergnesticin into the mimosas. Soon he heard Amanda in his earpiece, placing the room service order. He waited in the hallway until a freckly young porter emerged from the elevator. Fortunately the kid was more flexible than Lloyd, and was happy to relinquish the food cart for a thousand dollars. Evan dawdled in his room for another half hour before wheeling the cart down the hall.

He stashed his hatred behind a genial grin when Amanda greeted him at the door. Evan couldn't look at her without recalling the trauma from his last life, the cold and rainy night she jammed a tempic sword through his chest. That Amanda had died before Evan could get his revenge. But this one was standing right here, just ripe for the plucking.

"Good morning, ma'am. I'm Lloyd Lundrum. I sincerely apologize for the delay."

"What happened?"

"We're short on bellhops today. It's a madhouse. I've been delivering food all morning."

Amanda looked over the cart. "Are you sure this is our order? Those drinks—"

"I threw in the complimentary mimosas as our way of saying sorry. If you don't want them—"

"No, that's fine. My sister loves those."

Evan smiled. "Well then I hope you and your sister have a wonderful brunch."

As Amanda processed him with her sharp green gaze, he fought the urge to rewind and start over. But soon she passed him a twenty-dollar tip and then pulled the cart inside. Evan grinned all the way to the elevator until he realized the bitch never once looked at his name tag.

Twelve minutes later, he sat on the balcony of his Tower Five rental, listening to Zack and Amanda's giddy banter in his earpiece. When Evan first discovered they were staying in the Baronessa Suite, he rewound two days and became its previous occupant. Tiny listening devices were concealed in various parts of the living room, the balcony, and of course Hannah's bedroom.

The hardest part of Evan's week was having to once again hear her dulcet moans of pleasure, each one a pinch of salt in a very old wound. But he knew her fling with Theo never lasted long or ended well. Evan had only seen two men pierce the formidable shell around Hannah's heart. He'd already killed one of them. The other would crash her life next year, with deliciously tragic consequences.

Evan had been wiping the makeup off the back of his hand, scrubbing his "55" tattoo back into visibility, when Hannah smashed her first flute glass. He launched forward with the binoculars, hoo-hooing and oohing as the sisters traded angry barbs. When the second glass cracked across Amanda's forehead, Evan squealed with delight. This was a thing of beauty, a moment so perfect that he had to watch it six times.

His smile vanished when Amanda's tempic hand knocked Zack off the balcony. Evan shot to his feet now, staring in alarm as Zack lost his grip and fell. Screaming, Amanda threw herself against the railing and launched a tempic arm at Zack. She caught him at the fifth floor.

Evan closed his eyes and moaned with hot relief. He didn't want to reverse such a beautiful chain of events, but he would have done it to save Zack. The cartoonist was the focus of Evan's next mission. More than that, he was a friend.

Amanda's mind howled with chaos, a fire in a crowded theater. Panicked thoughts trampled each other on the way to her mouth as her body twisted painfully over the railing. Her hands were submerged in an enormous white arm, fifty feet long and as thick as a manhole cover. She could feel Zack's body in her thoughts, resting limp and unconscious in her titan grip.

"I got him. I got him. Oh my God."

David pressed up against her backside, holding her in place. "Okay. Good. Good, Amanda. Now you have to bring him back."

"It's not working! I can't control it!"

"Yes you can," said David. "Concentrate."

Six weeks ago, Sterling Quint's physicists had attempted to gauge the limits of Amanda's tempic talent. Her creations took an increasing amount of willpower to maintain. At sixty seconds, it felt like squeezing a tight fist. At two minutes, it felt like squeezing a tight fist around thumbtacks. Czerny had stopped the endurance test at 148 seconds, when Amanda began to cry and bleed from her nose.

David laid his hands on Amanda's wrists. She could feel the giant arm contract.

"What are you doing? David, how are you doing that?"

"I'm not doing anything," he said. "It's all you. Just keep focusing."

Theo fumbled his way up the side of the hot tub, throbbing with pain. He yanked a small shard of glass from his thigh, then looked to Hannah. The actress lay motionless on the floor.

Amanda turned her head as much as she could. "Theo! Are you okay? Is Hannah okay?"

"Concentrate on Zack!" David yelled.

Theo took an anxious reading of Hannah's pulse and future, then exhaled at the presence of both.

"She's all right. She's okay."

"Don't move her. She could have a broken—"

Amanda screamed when Zack slipped in her grasp. David seethed at her.

"Goddamn it, Amanda! If you care about him . . ."

"I do! I'm sorry!"

Theo looked to the patio doorway, where Mia stood frozen in dread. Her inner voice chanted Zack's name over and over.

"Mia . . ."

The urgent note from the future still dangled from her fingertips, warning her of Evan's drugged cocktails. If only she'd seen it sooner . . .

"Mia!"

She snapped out of her daze. Theo jerked his head at the living room.

"Security's coming. We need to go fast. Gather as many bags as you can carry. Leave the stuff we don't need. Can you do that?"

She gave him a trembling nod, then disappeared inside.

Theo scooped Hannah in his arms, praying she didn't have a spinal injury. He saw a thick stream of blood trickle down her hair. *Goddamn you, Evan.*

By the time Zack reached the ninth floor, Amanda's brain felt like it was wrapped in barbed wire. David wiped sweat and blood from her forehead.

"Hold on. Just a few more seconds."

"I can't hold it . . ."

"You can, Amanda. You have to. You'll never forgive yourself if you let him drop."

With a final scream, she raised Zack to eye level. David grabbed his arms just as the tempis vanished. He pulled Zack over the railing, then checked his vitals.

"He's okay, Amanda. You did it."

Amanda fell back onto the one chair that was left standing, her face drenched and white.

Theo turned around in the doorway and looked to David. "You think you can carry him?"

"Yeah. I can get him to the van."

With a loud grunt, David hoisted Zack into his arms. Amanda cast a shaky palm.

"Be careful! He could have a broken neck! They could both . . ."

Now the images in Amanda's head turned melodramatic, a theater in a crowded fire. She pictured Zack and Hannah as paraplegics. Her fault. Her hands. Her tempis.

"Oh my God. I did this . . ."

David gritted his teeth. "Amanda, we don't have time."

"He's right," said Theo. "I know you're drugged and I know you're hurting, but you need to pull yourself together. We have to go right now."

Wincing, she struggled to her feet. "Okay. Okay."

They turned their gazes to the airy distance, at the sound of approaching sirens. Now Theo's future howled. There was no way they'd make it to the van without being spotted. There was no hope of making it out of Evansville without another chase.

Zack came to life on the way to the elevator. Hot knives of pain stabbed his chest while his body bobbled and dangled in David's arms. He raised a weak gaze.

"David . . . ?"

Amanda rushed to his side. "Zack! Are you all right? Can you feel my hand?"

He fought a cracked and addled laugh. *I think we all felt your hand, honey.* "I'm okay. Anyone else hurt?"

"Hannah. She's unconscious. I don't know how bad it is yet."

As Mia jabbed the elevator call button, Theo checked the progress displays above all four doors. Two of the cars were on their way up, one from the first floor, the other from the fourth. His thoughts flashed with images of six security guards in the lower elevator.

He pointed to the north-side doors. "This is going to be close. We need to jump in that thing the second it opens."

"Put me down," Zack said. "I can walk."

The moment he touched the ground, he winced at another painful chest stab. Amanda held his arm. "What is it? What's wrong?"

"Nothing. I'm all right."

The elevator was two floors away. Theo shifted Hannah in his arms. "We're never going to make it through the lobby. Not like this . . ."

"We have no choice," David said. "We'll have to fight our way through."

Amanda eyed him with dark concern. "There has to be a better way."

"Here it comes . . ."

As she lifted her knapsacks, Mia felt a familiar twinge in the back of her mind. *Oh no . . .*

The doors opened to an empty elevator. "Come on!" Theo yelled. "Hurry!"

They rushed into the lift. Mia dropped her bags and propped a door.

"What the hell are you doing?" Theo asked.

"I'm getting a note!"

A small bead of light floated a foot above the carpet, an arm's length outside the elevator. Theo looked to the display across the hall. The other elevator was at Floor 7.

"Forget it! We don't have time!"

"It could be important!"

"Mia, I'm almost positive there are six security guards in that other elevator . . ."

"We wouldn't be in this mess if I'd seen my other note! I'm not making that mistake again!"

David pressed the hold button. "I got this. Move your hand."

Mia pulled her arm inside. David ghosted a pair of closed elevator doors just as a chime issued from across the hall. The Silvers stood frozen behind their illusive cover, listening to the gruff voices and heavy footsteps just ten feet away.

The clamor quickly moved down the hall. David breathed a whisper at Mia. "Be careful."

She dropped to the ground and crawled through the ghost doors. Once she plucked the note from the carpet, she glanced down the hall. Theo was right. Six armed guards now stood outside the Baronessa Suite. They didn't bother to knock before keying into the room.

With a deep exhale, she backed into the lift. The real doors closed over the ghosted ones. Mia read the note with bulging eyes, then pressed the emergency stop.

"What are you doing, Mia?"

"We can't go down. We have to go up."

David blinked at her. "Are you insane?"

"What's the message?" Theo asked.

"'You won't make it to the garage without hitting cops. Go up to Suite 1255. It's being repainted but nobody will touch it until Monday. Hide in there until things quiet down.'"

She pushed the cancel button until the lobby light went dark, then reset their course for the top floor.

David shook his head. "I don't like this. In a matter of hours, this place will be crawling with Deps. They have ghost drills. They'll track us."

Amanda felt ill at the thought of federal agents watching a spectral re-enactment of her balcony attack. If that didn't put her on their Ten Most Wanted list, nothing would.

"They need warrants to use ghost drills on private property," Mia told him. "We have at least forty-eight hours before they start."

"Yes, I read the same book you did. The law could have changed since that was written."

"David, why would I send that note from the future if the plan didn't work?"

"Because there's more than one future! Why haven't you figured that out yet?"

Mia looked to David with wide-eyed hurt. He lowered his head.

"Let's just go there," Zack said, through a pained wince. "At least until Hannah wakes up."

They scanned the hall for witnesses, then made a run for Suite 1255. In Zack's impaired condition, it took him four tries to reverse the door lock.

Their new hideout was just a quarter size of the Baronessa Suite, with only two beds and one bathroom. Half the furniture had been stowed in a bedroom while the other half was covered in spattered sheets.

The smell of new paint made Amanda light-headed. She wobbled toward Theo.

"Put her down on the couch. I need to check her head. Mia, get me some hand towels from the bathroom. Soak one in cold water."

David held her arm. "I think you need to rest."

"Someone has to sneak out to a pharmacy. I'll make a list. We need bandages . . . We need . . ."

Amanda's eyelids fluttered. Her legs turned to jelly. David caught her in mid-faint.

She woke up in bed, grimacing. An awful taste filled her mouth, like cardboard dipped in sour milk. She touched her forehead, surprised to feel adhesive bandages over her cuts.

Hannah lay unconscious on the other side of the bed. Someone had wrapped a long gauze strip around her skull, securing a folded towel to the back of her head.

Mia watched her from the doorway. "You all right?"

Amanda dazedly blinked at her. "How long was I out?"

"A while. It's almost four o'clock now."

"Did you do the bandages?"

"Yeah. I hope they're okay."

"They're fine. Who got the supplies?"

"David. He was careful. He brought back a little food too, if you feel like eating."

The thought made Amanda queasy. She tested Hannah's vitals. "If she doesn't wake up soon, I'm taking her to a hospital."

"You know you can't do that."

"I'm not going to lose her."

"You'll lose her to the Deps if you take her to a hospital. You'll never see her again."

Amanda pressed her palms to her bleary face. Mia hesitated before throwing the next issue at her.

"Listen, I only gave Zack an epallay. I wasn't sure how to do the rest."

"What do you mean? I thought he was okay."

Mia sighed, focusing hard on the Amanda who saved Zack and not the one who hurt him.

"I think you should go see him."

The second bedroom was a miniature labyrinth of stacked wooden furniture. In the center of the maze was a full-size bed, in the center of the bed was a stretched-out man, and in the center of the man was a cruel and jagged problem.

Zack bit his lower lip, swallowing his cries while Amanda tested each rib for damage.

"This one?"

"Yeah."

"Okay. Hold still."

Mia sat on a dresser, feeling more and more like a voyeur as she watched Amanda place adhesive tape on Zack's chest. There was something uncomfortably sensual about the way Amanda touched Zack's shoulder whenever she reached for a new strand, the way he stared at her neck as she worked on him. Once Mia felt sufficiently educated about the treatment process, she left the bedroom and closed the door behind her.

Amanda ran a taut finger along another rib. "This one?"

"No."

"You sure it doesn't hurt?"

"I have no reason to lie about it."

"You also have no reason to act macho around me."

"I think the last thing either of us needs today—"

He sucked a sharp breath when she found the next cracked rib. Amanda peeled a new strip of tape. Her mouth quivered in tight suppression.

"Can you please just yell at me a little bit so I feel less awful?"

"I told you—"

"I know. I was drugged. I wasn't responsible. Everyone keeps saying that. But be honest. Would you accept that excuse if you had rifted me today?"

"Probably not," Zack admitted. "But if I had unrifted you immediately afterward, I'd go a lot easier on myself."

She shot a sardonic grunt at his bandages. "Right. No harm done."

"I still can't believe you caught me."

"Me neither. It was insane. I didn't have a single thought in my head. It's like the tempis just took over."

"Well, I'm glad the tempis likes me."

"It likes you," she sighed. "There's no question of that."

In the center of Zack's cruel and jagged problem was a hot new urge. He wanted to run his hands all over Amanda, explore her with his fingers like a blind man would. He assumed whatever drug Evan had slipped him was still floating around in his veins, eating away at his formidable inhibitions.

Amanda finished mending him, then helped him slide his shirt back on. She told him that he'd have to take it easy for the next few weeks. Zack humored her as if such a thing were possible.

After clearing away the bandage debris, she finally met his stare with deep green sadness.

"She'll wake up," Zack assured her. "I know it."

"How? How can you be sure about anything? It seems like no matter what we do—"

"Amanda . . ."

"It's just going to get worse."

"Hey." He reached for her golden cross necklace and squeezed it between his fingers. "Whatever happened to the woman of faith?"

"Today happened. Now where's the agnostic with no answers?"

"He was saved," Zack replied, with a dark and feeble smirk.

Amanda placed a soft hand on his cheek. Her sister's angry words still stuck in her thoughts like a bee's broken stinger. *You've been a widow for eight weeks! Eight weeks, and this is how you act!*

She pulled away. "Don't sleep on your side. And force a few coughs to break up the fluid in your lungs."

"Amanda . . ."

"I'll check on you later."

She fled the room without looking back. Zack watched her depart, then groaned his way back to the mattress. Though he folded his hands over his chest like a serene cadaver, his eyes danced with life and uncertainty.

While Hannah and Zack convalesced, the others passed the time in the small living area. Amanda and Theo sat on the couch like waiting room strangers— staring at walls, avoiding each other's gaze. They both had Hannah on their minds, a hanging mobile of worries that would only spin faster if they acknowledged each other.

At seven o'clock, David made everything worse by turning on the lumivision.

"Sorry, Amanda. We need to know."

As they feared, their awful brunch had become a top story nationwide. More than a hundred photographs had been snapped during the eighty-eight seconds Zack dangled in a great tempic arm. Most of the pictures were worm's-eye shots from the grotto, distant enough to obscure his features. Mia balked at the most damning photo—a crystal-clear image of Zack that had been shot through a telephoto lens. One reporter remarked that he looked like a mouse being crushed by a python, an observation that sent the python to tears.

Mia rubbed Amanda's back. "This isn't your fault. It's Evan's."

"It doesn't matter. Everyone's going to recognize Zack now."

David tilted his head at the image. "No they won't. Unless he finds another way to float horizontally with a contorted expression of pain, no one will make the connection."

Soon the news report transitioned to a live Q&A with the lead Dep on scene, shot downstairs in the lobby. Andy Cahill was a leathery codger who delivered curt words through a bushy mustache and a sandy baritone. His whiskers curled in a patient smile as he indulged the reporter's questions. *Are the people involved still at large?* Yes. *Do you believe they're foreign terrorists?* Doesn't seem likely. *Do you think the shooting death of the hotel manager is somehow connected?* That does seem likely. *Anything you can tell us about the tempic device that was used today?* Nope.

When teasingly asked if he considered the possibility of Gothams, Cahill chuckled softly and told the reporter she watched too many movies.

All throughout the interview, Theo sat forward in rapt attention, fixing his gaze on a female agent in the background. Though she moved too fast to provide a decent look, her dark skin and flowing dreadlocks were enough to ring every bell in Theo's head. His thoughts screamed with recognition, as if she'd been a crucial part of his life from the moment he first drew breath.

Once the scene changed, he snapped out of his trance and flipped his mirrored senses. It wasn't the past he knew her from. She was a towering presence to come. That dark and faceless woman loomed over every corner of his future.

Propriety went out the window at bedtime, when Mia crawled under the covers with Zack, and David asked Amanda for permission to sleep with her sister.

"I'm not a beagle," the boy declared. "I can't just doze on some couch or rug. I need a bed. I promise I'll be a perfect gentleman. And I'll wake you right away if Hannah's condition changes."

Amanda traded a dim look with Theo, then gave David an acquiescent shrug. She raised a worried eyebrow when he closed the door behind him.

"Did I just make an awful mistake?"

Theo smirked. "Even if she was conscious, Hannah wouldn't mind."

"You mean if he shares a bed with her or if he tries something?"

"Yes."

She covered her laugh with a hand, feeling guilty to be glib under the circumstances. She slipped out of her sweaty T-shirt and into a tank top, stunning Theo with her sudden lack of inhibition. What a strange unit the six of them had become. He already felt more at home with the Silvers than he ever did with the Maranans.

Amanda turned off the light and stretched out on the long sofa. Theo had curled up in the love seat, his bandaged thigh dangling awkwardly over the edge. She asked him if he'd be okay like that. He assured her he was quite the beagle.

At dawn, a shrill electronic chirp blared throughout the suite. Zack's eyelids fluttered in jarring disruption. He dazedly processed the teenage girl in his bed, then plucked his ringing handphone from the dresser.

Mia rolled over and opened a groggy eye. "What time is it?"

"Early."

"Who's calling?"

"Well, that's the weird thing."

He held the phone in front of her. She squinted at the screen. *Mia Calling.*

For a brief disturbing moment, Mia wondered if her future self had discovered a new venue. Once the ringing stopped, she stumbled onto the saner theory.

"Someone found my phone. The one I threw away."

Zack had a strong idea who it was. When the phone rang a second time, he painfully scuttled out of bed. Mia sat up in worry.

"Wait. You're not going to answer that, are you?"

"I'll be all right."

"But it could be—"

Before she could finish, Zack pressed the phone to his ear and heaved a sigh into the speaker.

"Hello and up yours, Evan."

From the airy balcony of his newest suite, Evan laughed. This was his fifth trip through their conversation. Zack always started the same way.

"Good morning," he said, with sunny cheer. "How are the new digs?"

"Spiffy," he'll say, and then inquire my purpose in calling.

"Spiffy," Zack said. "Are you calling to gloat or is there another reason?"

"For you, my friend, I'm all rainbows and kittens. Come outside. Let's talk privately."

Beyond the sliding glass door, two naked corpses bled out on the bed. This suite's balcony was the only place Evan could get a decent view of the Silvers' new hideout. Tragically, the room had been occupied by a pair of young newlyweds who were light sleepers and loud screamers. Evan had to rewind twelve times before he was able to murder them quietly. It didn't help that he'd invaded their room in a smiling gray goblin mask.

Evan pressed binoculars to his eyeholes, waiting for Zack to emerge onto the patio.

"By the way, I'm sorry about the mimosa prank. I only wanted the sisters to shriek and pull some hair. I didn't expect a full tempic smackdown. Jesus."

Zack stepped outside and slid the door shut. He scanned Tower Two, the only spire within view.

"Over here," said Evan. "Top floor."

Zack squinted across the distance at the tiny waving goblin. "You're wearing a mask."

"No. This is just how I look in the morning."

"Why the mask? I've already seen your face."

"It's for the Deps and their damn ghost drills," Evan explained. "They can be a real hassle when they've got your mug in their system, as you'll soon discover. The woman on your tail is particularly smart. In fact, I'd say she's your next big problem."

"I'm still stuck on the current one."

Evan sighed. "I know. I'm a handful. Look, you took this call because you're hoping to reason with me, to convince me to leave you guys alone. The good news is that there's a way. Let's just . . . Whoops. Here comes the concern brigade."

Mia, Amanda, and Theo stood at the glass door, all watching Zack with leery caution. Theo and Amanda backed off at the sight of Zack's assuring palm. Mia kept her nervous vigil.

Evan chuckled. "Ah, that Farisi. Such a little sweetheart. Enjoy it now before she changes."

"I don't want to hear it."

"I mean all teenagers are wet clay, but Mia really takes a different shape. Sometimes she becomes a thin and pretty slut-tease, the Third Little Given. Other times she hardens into a fat and angry ass-kicker. That's when she's really fun."

"Evan . . ."

"Most of the time, she just dies. It's weird. She's like the team's cannon fodder. She rarely makes it to Year Two."

Zack's empty stomach churned. "You're obviously trying to upset me."

"No. If I wanted to upset you, I'd tell you how David turns out."

He'd called Zack at the crack of dawn in the hope of dulling his sharp edge. And yet in the first four run-throughs of the conversation, Zack kept finding new and clever ways to gain the upper hand. Evan was determined to keep him off balance in Round 5.

"Why do you hate us so much?" Zack asked. "What did we ever do to you?"

Evan exhaled impatiently. It was like living in a world full of senile people. They never remembered.

"It's not worth getting into. Just know that I only really have it in for the Givens. Theo and the kids? Meh. Take them or leave them. But you, *mein Freund*, I can never stay mad at. Truth be told, I really miss our chats."

He grinned at Zack's furrowed perplexity. "Strains the brain, doesn't it? Once upon a time warp, I was part of the gang. We started out as an eight-piece band. You guys, me, and Jury Curado."

"You mean the guy on the driver's license."

Evan laughed. "You're lucky that's all you know him from. You should be thanking me. He was a real asshole. Always yelling. Always convinced he was right. He was decent enough to the womenfolk, especially Hannah. He wasn't so nice to us beta males, especially me."

"So why don't I remember any of this?"

"Because the story changed. I changed it."

"How?"

Evan waved a curt hand. "Ah, I'm sick of talking about it. Let's talk about culture."

"Why don't you just get to the—"

"I know you weren't crazy about your old life. I hated mine. But man, do I miss the culture. You must have noticed how bad it is here. The shit that passes for entertainment."

Zack sighed with forced amenity. "The movies are pretty bad."

"It's all bad. You know why? No foreign geniuses to shake things up. No Charlie Chaplins or Alfred Hitchcocks or Sergio Leones. Foreign films are illegal here. You think George Lucas would have come up with *Star Wars* if he hadn't been able to see *The Seven Samurai*? Of course not. But they sealed the doors and nailed the curtains shut. So now all we have are five hundred brands of American vanilla."

"I do miss *Star Wars*," Zack admitted.

"God, I'd kill to see the original trilogy again. I'd only maim for the prequels."

Zack was amazed to find himself smiling. "If I had known what was coming, I would have packed a portable movie player and a suitcase full of discs."

"You and me both, brother. It kills me that I only had a few minutes to prepare. I think about all the things I could have grabbed from my room. Even the cheapest piece of crap would have been a treasure to me now. But oh no. Azral, King of Time, was running late and had to rush me."

Zack tapped the railing, debating whether or not to press Evan for intel. Could his information be trusted?

"I'm guessing you know a lot more about him than I do."

"Oh, you wouldn't believe the things I know, Zacky. I've seen this tale from start to finish. You really want to know about the Pelletiers?"

"Tell me."

Evan took a deep breath. He knew he was sailing into dangerous waters now.

"They're Gothams," he explained. "But from way the hell in the future. Distant descendants of Peter Pendergen's people. Fiftieth generation, hundredth—I have no idea. I just know they're insanely powerful. They're one family you don't want to mess with. And yet you always do."

"How many are there?"

"There are three. Papa Bear's on special assignment. He'll rear his ugly head next year. That won't be a fun day for any of you."

Zack thought back to the scary man in the tempic mask, the one who gave him his silver bracelet.

"What do they want with us?"

Evan cracked a dark laugh. "If I told you that, they'd come down on me like the Monty Python foot. They don't want you knowing yet. All I can say is that we share a rare quirk in our DNA. Nothing that ever made us stand out from the crowd, though we do tend to fall on the brainy side. Even Hannah's got some wattage in the noggin, though it sure did take a thumping, didn't it?"

Zack slitted his eyes at Evan, swallowing his wrath. "How many of us did they bring over?"

"They gave out ninety-nine bracelets in ten different cities. Not sure how many of us are still breathing. Our group lost two. The Violets are down five."

"The Violets?"

"Pelletier lingo. They like to call us by the color of our bracelets. Isn't that cute? The Violets are the London folk. The ones in Osaka are the Rubies. The Pearls of Guadalajara are my favorites. All-girl group. Eight Mexicans and one hot Cuban."

Zack remembered what the masked Pelletier had whispered, shortly after sealing the bracelet around his wrist. *Any other weekend, you'd be one of the Golds.*

His heart lurched. "There's a New York group . . ."

"Yep. Motley bunch. Their Sterling Quint's a Chinese woman. Some big-name biology professor. Easy on the eyes, but not the nicest gal. I know what you're about to ask, by the way."

"My brother's from New York. If the Pelletiers are picking siblings—"

"Now, Zack—"

"Is my brother alive?!"

Evan scratched the skin beneath his mask. "We have reached the end of the 'free information' portion of our discussion—"

"Goddamn it! Just tell me!"

"—and have now commenced the part in which you need to be careful. There are things you want. You won't be able to shout them out of me."

As Zack struggled to compose himself, Evan grinned behind his mask. He knew this would be the final take of their discussion. Round 5 was a keeper.

"You realize you're getting worked up over a guy you weren't that close with. I mean when it comes to being different, the Trillingers make the Givens look like Siamese twins."

"Who told you that?" Zack asked.

"You did. I'm stealing your own joke."

"He's still my brother."

"Is it him you really need right now? Or are you just looking for a quest?"

The cartoonist turned away in clenched fury. Evan softened up.

"Listen, Zack, I know what you're going through. You survived an apocalypse. You learned just how nasty the universe can be and now you're scrambling to give your life meaning. And since you're too smart to cram Jesus into the equation, you've fit everything into a neat Hollywood structure. In your mind, you're on a hero's journey, with allies and riddles and big epic quests. You even have a love interest, an uptight hottie who's slowly warming up to your wisecracking ways. Better than being a speck of dust in a senseless world, am I right?"

Zack gritted his teeth. "You don't know me at all."

"Oh, I do. And please don't think I'm judging you. I used to be the exact same way. I thought I had all the same things you did. I went to Brooklyn and listened to Peter Pendergen. That man . . . God, what a prick. He dominated our lives with big ideas and Holy Grail quests, and we ate it up with a spoon because we needed to believe it. You want to know how it all turned out?"

"No."

"Good," Evan said. "That's why I called. I want to spare you from all that. There's no need to throw your life away on a wild-goose chase. Screw it. Ditch the Silvers. Come join me."

Zack looked up from the railing. "Are you kidding me?"

"Not at all. You and I, we're nerds of a feather. I'm more of a brother than your brother ever was. We could have fun together. Reminisce about pop culture. Buy the attentions of hot and shallow women."

"Buy them with what?"

"Oh, don't you worry about money, Zacky. I've got bundles. While you were all futzing around in Terra Vista, I hit the casinos. With power like mine, you can't even call it gambling. It's more like synchronized winning."

"What is your power, exactly?"

"Come with me and I'll tell you. I'll answer any question you have. You'll get every spoiler about Rebel, Azral, Peter, *Amanda*. Trust me. It'll be better to hear it all secondhand than to live it."

"And you'll leave the others alone?"

"Zack, if you come with me, none of them will ever hear from me again. I swear it."

Evan was mostly sincere in his promise, though he knew there was an opportunity coming up soon, a rare and golden chance to shatter both sisters at once. If Zack joined him, Evan would have to sneak out for an evening.

"I need some time to think about this."

"Okay," Evan replied, with a cautious leer.

"But there are two things you could do to help convince me—"

Evan pounded his fist on the railing. "Oh, goddamn it!"

"What?"

"You keep forgetting that I know you, Zack! If you were really considering my offer, you would have drowned me in a dozen more questions. But no, you jump right to the demands."

"That's not necessarily—"

"Let me guess. You want me to promise to leave you guys alone for a week. Or two weeks. Or until you get to New York. Just as a good faith token. Am I right?"

Zack hissed an inner curse. That was exactly the angle he'd planned.

"And then you were going to press me about your brother again. So you could get something out of me before turning me down. Clever, Trillinger. Always the clever one."

Zack hunched over his railing, his face an angry mask. "Did you really think I'd come with you? You've harassed us. You've *poisoned* us—"

"Oh, now you drop the ruse."

"Hannah could still die because of you!"

"She won't die. Azral won't let her."

"What are you talking about?"

"No, no, no. You don't get any more info. You blew it. I mean, shit, Zack. I really thought I could convince you this time."

"Evan, listen to me—"

"Well, you'll find out the hard way that the universe doesn't care about your three-act structure. There's no epic saga. No Holy Grail to find. You don't even get your love interest. That's another thing Peter takes from you. See, he's a spiritual man, unlike you. With a better face and body. In a perfect world, the looks wouldn't matter. But Amanda's a woman. She's a Given. It matters."

Evan chuckled at Zack's frozen expression, caught between despair and distrust.

"That's okay. Don't believe me. You'll see for yourself soon enough. It's just one of the many pains that await you, my friend. When you see tomorrow's paper, you should clip that photo of you getting squeezed by the big tempic fist. Because that is you for the rest of your pathetic life."

Evan leaned forward, hissing a whisper. "Oh, and by the way? Your brother's dead. He was here. He was a Gold. But Rebel got him three days ago. Oops. So much for that quest."

All the blood fled Zack's face. The world outside faded away to a swirling haze. He dropped his phone over the railing, then returned inside without so much as a look at the goblin in the tower.

Screaming, Evan overturned the patio table. He raised a chair to throw through the glass, then froze at the sight of a tall couple in the bedroom. He had no trouble recognizing them.

"Shit . . ."

Azral curled a long white finger, sternly beckoning him. Esis stood at his side and shook her head in reproach. Evan knew there was nothing he could do to allay their displeasure. No matter where he rewound, the Pelletiers would be there, still aware of all events. Still angry.

He dropped his chair and removed the mask. There was no point in wearing it now. The Deps wouldn't see a thing with their ghost drills.

His heart jackhammered as he joined the Pelletiers in the bedroom. When he'd first witnessed Azral's wrath, centuries ago, he wet himself in terror. Never again. He'd never again show his fear to these people.

He plopped himself down in the overstuffed easy chair and forced a chirpy smirk.

"So. Is this a lecture or a spanking?"

Amanda stared at her tense reflection in the lumivision glass, pondering her next steps. Zack had traipsed back to his room with barely a word. She'd never seen him so distraught.

After five anxious minutes, she cautiously followed him into his room.

Zack leaned against a dresser, keeping a crossed-arm vigil at the window. She knew it was a painful position for a man with cracked ribs. He didn't budge an inch at her approach.

"I asked you all to give me some space."

"I know, Zack. I just—"

"Did you think you were an exception?"

"I was kind of hoping I was."

Now he turned to face her. His eyes were gray and cold, the color of knives. "You're not."

Amanda took a pained step back, then retreated from the room. The cartoonist resumed his window stance. He stood for two hours like a stone figurine, lost in the pain of his many new fractures.

TWENTY-FOUR

Hannah dreamed in high speed, a whirlwind barrage of fleeting scenes and images. She danced high in the sky on a floor of aeris, her long white gown twirling in the wind as Azral spun her under his finger. He dipped her halfway to the floor, ravishing her with a smile so flawless that she didn't mind the freezing cold.

She ran crying through the streets of an old and foreign city on the brink of dawn, leaving footprints in the snow as she carried a bundled infant. She knew the Cataclysm was coming but she didn't have time to warn anyone. She had to get her son to safety. He was all that mattered.

She stood onstage in a majestic old theater, a sprightly little child in a pretty white dress. As she sang her angelic rendition of "I'll Fly Away," her parents and sister smiled at her from the front row. Amanda's hands were sleek and white, as if her skin wasn't skin at all but—

No . . .

She lay in a void of pure whiteness. The air chilled her to the bone. A brown-haired woman eclipsed Hannah's view. She was a fearsome beauty with coal-black eyes and a fiendishly crooked grin. The actress struggled to move but she was held in place by something cold. Not ice but—

"No. No tempis. Get it off me. Please!"

Esis raised an alabaster hand. "Hush, child. You're mended now. Sleep."

Her palm flashed white, and Hannah disappeared into a dreamless oblivion. Once her brain rebooted, she found herself awake in strange quarters. Someplace beige. Someplace warm.

Bleary thoughts floated through her head like dandelion puffs as she registered her new surroundings. The room smelled like paint and was devoid of all furniture except her bed. A familiar mop of shaggy blond hair poked out from the covers next to her.

Hannah traced a fumbling path through her memory. All she could see were the hazy images of a very bad brunch. Now she was in bed with a sixteen-year-old boy who—God help her—she wasn't above seducing.

"David?"

He rolled onto his back and blinked in sleepy half awareness. His eyes popped open and he launched to a sitting position.

"Hannah! You're awake! Wow, that's . . . Hi."

"Hi."

"How are you feeling?"

She held the blanket in front of her chest as if she were topless. "Confused. What's going on?"

"I'll explain, but let me get Amanda first."

"Wait!"

He paused at the edge of the bed. As she studied the wrinkles in his T-shirt, she waded through a tangled patch of queries and stopped at the thorniest one.

"How mad is she?"

"Who? Amanda?"

"Yeah. You were there this morning. You saw the way I acted."

David eyed her in dim, blinking stupor. "Okay. Huh. Well, the good news is that she isn't mad at all."

"What's the bad news?"

"Not bad news. Just . . ." He checked his wristwatch. "You've been unconscious for twenty-two and a half hours. That whole thing happened yesterday."

"What?"

"Let me get Amanda."

Baffled, she traced a finger along her forehead bandage and removed the blood-soaked hand towel that rested against the back of her skull. Despite all evidence of injury, she felt perfectly fine.

David soon returned with Mia and Amanda. Hannah was stunned by her sister's dismal appearance. She looked like she'd gained ten years and lost two more husbands.

Amanda wrapped Hannah in a tight embrace. "Oh thank God. I was so worried."

"I'm okay. I'm so sorry."

"It's all right. It's not your fault. How are you feeling? Are you in pain?"

"Not even a little." Hannah glanced at her bloody towel. "What happened to me? Did I fall?"

Amanda's expression grew cloudy and dark. Hannah saw David and Mia trade an anxious glance.

"Okay, someone needs to tell me what's going on."

"What's the last thing you remember?" Amanda asked her.

"You sat on Zack's lap. Then I got all bitchy at you. I said horrible things. I think I threw a glass at the floor."

Hannah blanched at the sight of Amanda's brow bandages. "Oh my God. Did I do that to you?"

"It's not your fault. You were drugged."

"Drugged? How?"

David filled her in on everything she missed—the spiked mimosas, the tempic hand, the rushed escape to Suite 1255.

Hannah listened quietly, staring down at the bedspread with increasing agitation. By the time he finished, her eyes were filled with wet, seething rage.

"He needs to die."

"We'll worry about Evan later," Amanda insisted. She hugged Hannah again. "I'm just so glad you're okay."

She suddenly caught the scent of shampoo in Hannah's hair, an odd smell for a woman who hadn't showered since yesterday. She ran her fingers along the back of Hannah's scalp.

"You checking my wound?"

"Yeah."

"Must not be too bad if I can't feel it."

It bothered Amanda that she couldn't feel it either. No broken skin. No scabs. Not even dried blood in her hair.

Hannah peeked into the empty living room. "Where's Zack?"

"He's in the other bedroom," Mia replied. "He just had a long phone call with Evan."

The news surprised David as much as Hannah. "He did? What did he say?"

"I don't know. He just went straight to his room. I'm worried about him."

"He'll be all right," Amanda said, unconvincingly. Still mystified by Hannah's condition, she looked to David. "Did anything strange happen here last night?"

"Strange how?"

"I don't know. Anything."

He shrugged in drowsy detachment. "I slept like a stone. If anything happened, I missed it. Why?"

Amanda shook her head, dismissing the issue. For all she knew, accelerated healing was a new aspect of her sister's weirdness. There were certainly worse problems to have.

As the fog slowly cleared from Hannah's thoughts, she suddenly remembered her other recent drama. She looked into the living room again.

"Where's Theo?"

Twenty-four hours after Amanda flexed her great tempic arm, the incident continued to plague the Piranda Five Towers. The property bustled with law enforcers and news reporters, plus an ever-increasing influx of fanatical Gotham-seekers.

Theo felt like a rock star in disguise as he crossed the crowded lobby. He lowered his baseball cap, adjusted his sunglasses, and cast his eyes down at his shopping bag.

Sometime during his food run, management had called in the cavalry. Security guards blocked the path to all stairs and elevators now, refusing entry to civilian nonresidents.

Unfortunately, the only key Theo possessed belonged to the hotel's most infamous suite. He counted the cash in his pocket. He had $653, enough to rent a basic room.

He approached the reception desk. The small blond clerk studied Theo skeptically.

"No luggage, sir?"

"It's in the car."

She slitted her eyes at him. "If you're only here to investigate the disturbance—"

"I'm not," Theo insisted. "I swear it."

The glass doors swung open to heavy-footed bustle. Theo anxiously studied the large cadre of men who'd just arrived. They wore the same navy blue windbreaker with a golden eagle logo on the breast. Giant yellow letters were stitched on the back.

DP-9.

Theo froze in place as the Deps moved his way. Four of them lugged tall metal towers on dollies—ominous black obelisks that could have come straight from the Death Star.

Ghost drills, Theo realized. *Shit.*

He took his new room key and joined the line at the security checkpoint, lowering his gaze as the agents brushed past him. His heart jumped when he noticed the lone female in the group—dark skinned, with finger-thick dreadlocks that sprouted from her head like fireworks. Though Theo could only glimpse her from a rear angle, he knew she was the woman he'd seen on lumivision last night, the one who'd filled him with a prophetic sense of familiarity, a *préjà vu.*

Now she passed close enough for him to hear her strong voice and exotic accent. His recognition was so powerful that he could practically taste her name. It rolled around his thoughts like childspeak. *Missah Massah. Missah Massah.*

Theo swallowed his panic as it became his turn to pass them. He pulled down the lip of his baseball cap and made a sharp left at the elevators, all the while battling his urge to peek at this woman, this *Missah Massah.* For all his strange new intimacy, he had yet to see her face.

It was extreme luck on Theo's part that Melissa had yet to see his.

She sighed patiently into her handphone. "Sir, I understand your concerns, but if you limit our ghosting area, we'll have a much more difficult . . . Yes, sir. I'll hold."

Howard Hairston watched her scowl. He was a young and freckly redhead, one of the few agents on the team who didn't resent Melissa for her recently announced promotion. If anything, she'd make a better boss than Andy Cahill, who treated everyone under thirty like a high school intern.

"No luck with the judge?" he asked her.

She covered the phone. "No. He doesn't want us scanning outside the crime scene."

"Lovely. Why not make us wear blindfolds too?"

Melissa did a double take at the fast-moving Asian who slipped into the stairwell. She'd lived and breathed the fugitives for two weeks now, studying their ghosts from every angle. She knew their bodies, their postures, their gaits. That man moved a hell of a lot like Theo Maranan.

Can't be, she thought. The fugitives should have been three states away by now. They certainly weren't crazy enough to linger here at the crime scene. Were they?

She shelved the debate when the judge returned to the line. While Melissa continued her plea for a more expansive ghost warrant, she bandied Theo's name in her thoughts. She never guessed for a moment that he was doing the same with her.

David barely had time to answer the coded knock at the door before Theo swept past him in a flushed and winded huff.

"We have to go."

"Why? What did you see?"

"Exactly what you were afraid of."

David closed the door. "Ghost drills. Marvelous. I knew it wouldn't take forty-eight hours."

"We can't wait for Hannah to wake up. We'll have to move her somehow."

"Move me where?"

Theo nearly dropped his bag at the unexpected sight of Hannah. She looked so spry and healthy that for a moment he thought he was hallucinating.

"Hannah. Wow. You're up. When did . . . ?"

She eyed him through a cool squint. For all her miraculous recovery, Theo could see that she had yet to forgive him.

"Yeah. I'm fine. Why are you freaking out? What did you see?"

"The Deps. They're going to start ghosting any minute now. We can't—"

A bedroom door creaked open. Zack stepped outside. His skin was pallid. His face was racked with grief. Now Hannah knew exactly why Mia was worried about him.

He offered her a feeble hint of his old smirk. "Hey. Welcome back."

Hannah rushed toward him in gushing empathy. Amanda raised a palm. "Don't hug him. He has broken ribs."

She took his hands instead. "Oh God, Zack . . ."

"I appreciate the pity, but I'm all right."

"It's not pity, you schmuck. I know what you did. I know you tried to reason with that psycho."

"Yeah, well, it didn't work."

"I didn't think it would. But I love you for trying."

Unnerved by Theo's urgency, Mia looked to the door. "I really think we should go."

They gathered their bags and masked themselves as best they could. While the men hid under hats and shades, the women fixed their hair in ways that were previously anathema to them. Hannah sported a ponytail for the first time since she played Sandy Olsson in a high school production of *Grease*.

The group split up into innocuous pairs and took three different routes to the parking structure. Hannah rode the service elevator with Zack. Even with painkillers, the cartoonist was in no condition to take the stairs.

He gazed at the doors through dark sunglasses, his face a dismal mask. Hannah caressed his wrist.

"He really did a number on you, didn't he?"

Zack jerked a listless shrug. He wasn't even remotely ready to talk about it.

Hannah rested her head on his shoulder. "We're going to make it through this, Zack. All of them. The assholes in our lives will fall away one by one, and the six of us will find a nice quiet place to settle down."

"You really believe that?"

Strangely enough, she did. Her new optimism surprised them both. Yesterday, she was a muddled wreck. Now her thoughts were clear and bright. If she'd known a concussion would do her so much good, she would have cracked her skull a long time ago.

Soon the Silvers reunited at the Royal Seeker. While Amanda drove a slow and careful path down the driveway, the others kept their wide eyes peeled for flashing lights. No one followed them.

The moment they crossed the front gate, they let out a collective exhale. Amanda peered back at the shrinking glass towers. This was the second time her tempis had brought the law down on them, the second time they'd been saved by luck and Theo Maranan. Though she wasn't an augur like him, she couldn't shake the inevitability of handcuffs in their future. Sooner or later, the Deps would find them. Their wrists seemed all but destined to carry the weight of silver bracelets.

TWENTY-FIVE

On a wet Thursday morning in a tiny lakeside village, Mia Farisi's weirdness got a little bit weirder.

The sisters had gone to Main Street on a grocery errand, with the two youngest Silvers in tow. Once Hannah and Amanda disappeared inside a barn-size market, David and Mia explored the quaint surroundings. Nemeth was a rustic hamlet in the southeast corner of Ohio, home to 188 people. It graced the lip of a thousand-acre lake that teemed with striped bass and wall-eyes. Half the wooden shop-signs included some reference to bait or tackle.

Mia loved everything about Nemeth. In saner times, she'd dreamed of becoming a big-name author who retreated to the quiet country whenever she needed to finish her latest magnum opus. The fantasy included a posh lake cabin, two dogs, and a miraculously compliant husband who only appeared when she needed him.

She felt the edge of a high girlish cackle when David put his arm around her, even though she knew it was merely a gesture of purpose. Holding her under their shared umbrella, he led her to a two-story building that served as both post office and town hall. A sprawling twelve-month calendar graced the front window.

David counted the squares from Armageddon to now. "Wow. It's been sixty-one days."

"Which way are you surprised?"

"Feels like longer. Hell, it feels like a month since we came to Nemeth."

Mia cringed at the scorn in his voice. The lake-house layover had been her idea. David wasn't shy in voicing his opposition. In the four days since settling into their secluded retreat, he took numerous opportunities to remind everyone that Brooklyn was just 488 miles away. A one-day drive. A single battery charge.

"Look, when Zack gets better—"

"I know," he replied. "I'm not angry."

"You're impatient."

"I'm concerned. Let's just leave it at that."

He leaned in to study the dozens of handwritten notations on the calendar. "Huh. Look at all those birthdays. I bet this thing lists the birthday of every person in town."

"That's so sweet. See, this is why I love the country."

"Yes, it's all sweetness and light until they spot a minority in their midst." Mia batted his hand. "That's not always true."

"It is. I've seen it all over. Small towns create small mind-sets."

"Yeah, isn't it terrible the way they generalize?"

Her jibe evoked a laugh and an affectionate squeeze from David. Amidst the flurry in her thoughts, she felt a twinge of an impending portal.

She nervously glanced around. "Crap. Here we go again."

A bright white bead materialized in front of her chest like a penlight. Fortunately, the rain obscured the floating breach from the few townsfolk straggling about.

David hunched forward and leered at the anomaly. "Wow. My father would have given an arm to study one of these."

"I'd give an arm to stop getting them in public."

"Are you receiving or sending?"

"It's a delivery."

After the incident in Ramona, in which she was caught off guard by a past portal, Mia kept a shoulder bag with her at all times. It contained her journal and an assortment of colored pads and pens. Hannah called it the Emergency Paradox Prevention Kit.

A rolled-up note slowly emerged from the breach. Mia cupped her hands to catch it, then experienced an unpleasant new twitch, as if a shady stranger had violated her personal space. Suddenly the note combusted in angry flames.

Mia blinked in bewilderment as smoldering black flakes snowed down on her palms.

"What . . . ? David, what just happened?"

"Not a clue. You ever see that before?"

"No."

She wiped the ash from her hands, trying hard to shake the feeling of sabotage. "God. I hope the message wasn't important."

"Oh, I'm sure it was just a warning about me and my sweeping generalizations."

Mia fought a grin. "I already knew about that."

"Right. No big loss then."

Amanda and Hannah emerged from the grocery store. They made a clumsy dash through the rain and loaded their shopping bags into the Seeker. David lost his humor and sighed with resignation.

"Guess we're going home."

Mia had found the lake house in a booklet of vacation rentals. The photos could have been ripped straight from her fantasies, from the cedar walls to the stone hearth fireplace to the windows and skylights and patios galore. Better yet, it was buffered by nature in every direction. The nearest human neighbor was half a mile away.

With uncharacteristic fervor, she convinced the others that it was a perfect place to hide and heal, a welcome change from their usual digs. She was right. From the moment the landlord left the Silvers to themselves, the ones who weren't David felt a gushing love for the place. They'd spent the last two months in a state of flux—as guests of the world, guests of the physicists, guests of the hotels and motels of Altamerica. Now they had a house all their own. Those who craved a slice of domestic tranquility suddenly found one on a platter.

For the Great Sisters Given, serenity lay at the bottom of a cooking pot. Though neither one considered herself a culinary goddess, Amanda and Hannah took fervent glee in playing house chef. They spent hours each day twirling around the kitchen, passing spoons and spices between each other as multiple mixtures bubbled on burners.

While they worked, they smiled and giggled. When they disagreed, they disagreed kindly. Their knockdown brawl on the hotel balcony filled them with a desperate need to be perfect to each other. Soon their forced rapport snapped into place and they found themselves speaking intimately for the first time in years. Amanda finally shared the details of her broken marriage with Derek, his vicious last words. Hannah revealed the mystery of Jury Curado, from her strange ghostly vision to Evan's cruel hints of love undone.

The only topics they dodged were their current thorny entanglements. Hannah swore that everything was fine with Theo, though the tension between the ex-lovers was clear for everyone to see. Amanda claimed she wasn't worried by Zack's grim new state of being, a ceaseless black mood that filled the house like smog and only intensified in her presence.

"It's just pain," she insisted. "Once his ribs heal, he'll become his old self again."

Hannah wasn't so sure. For the first four days in Nemeth, Zack carried all the textbook signs of depression. He stopped shaving. He rarely spoke. He spent most of his time alone, either sketching in his tiny bedroom or staring out at the lake from a patio lounger.

On their third night in Nemeth, Zack finally opened up about his fateful phone call. He shared everything he learned about Evan's alternate history with the Silvers, plus the stunning but questionable revelations about the Pelletiers.

Though everyone sensed Zack was withholding something, only David succeeded in drawing it out of him. Late Wednesday night, the boy invaded Zack's room and pestered him until he divulged the fate of his brother. Zack relayed the news with matter-of-fact aloofness, never once looking up from his sketchbook.

David leaned against the dresser and gazed out at the rain. "As with all of Evan's information—"

"I know."

"I'm just saying you should take it with a grain of salt."

"You're the one who told me I shouldn't get my hopes up about Josh."

"I did. I still believe you shouldn't. The odds suggest he died on our world like everyone else."

Zack took dark pleasure in David's tactless candor. It made a nice contrast to the delicate tiptoe everyone else walked around him.

"I don't know how you always manage to stay so rational. Doesn't this stuff ever get to you?"

"Of course it does," David attested. "Why do you think I'm so eager to get to New York? I'm convinced that Peter Pendergen can provide us with all the shelter, safety, and crucial information he promised us. You used to feel the same way."

Zack put down his pencil and looked at him. Evan's harsh words about Peter were never far from his thoughts.

"Well then maybe it's my turn to tell you not to get your hopes up."

"Zack . . ."

"Think about it. If Peter's information's so crucial, why didn't he include it in his letter? If getting to him is so important, why didn't he offer to meet us somewhere halfway? And then there's the big question. Why do the Pelletiers want us to go to Peter? Why did they give us the van?"

David chucked a loose hand. "I can't answer any of that. I just know in my heart that he's our only hope. Unfortunately, I see the way the others react whenever I mention Brooklyn. Now I'm scared that we're about to add Peter to the list of people we're avoiding."

"They just need time," Zack said. "*I* need time."

David opened the door and turned around, his face a somber veil.

"Sooner or later, Zack, our problems will come find us again. It'd be nice for once if we met them on our terms."

The next day, while the group ate lunch in the dining room, David told the others about Mia's strange incident in town, the self-combusting note from the future. No one seemed willing to explore the issue with him.

"It's nothing to worry about," he assured Mia. "For all you know, your future self used a new type of paper, one that doesn't handle time travel very well."

She rolled her shoulders in a feeble shrug. "Maybe. I don't know."

Zack watched from the end of the table as the others stared down at their food. That seemed to be the default reaction now whenever David soiled their haven with real-world matters.

The cartoonist dropped his napkin over his plate and vented a loud, wistful sigh.

"We need to get better."

Everyone turned to look at him. It had become a rare occurrence for Zack to join a discussion, much less start one. He tapped the table pensively.

"The way I see it, we have four different threats out there and Evan's the least of them. And yet he kicked our asses worse than the Gothams, the Deps, and the Pelletiers ever did. Hell, we kicked our own asses for him, all because some of us still can't control their weirdness."

Hannah took umbrage at his stern implication. "It's not Amanda's fault. She was drugged."

"So were you. So was I. And yet we didn't go crazy with the shifting and juving."

Flushed with guilt, Amanda looked down at her fingers. "He's right."

"No, he's not," said Hannah. "This was nobody's fault but Evan's. And by getting pissy at you, Zack's playing right into his hands."

"I'm not saying this to be pissy."

"Bullshit. You've been cold to my sister for days. Everyone sees it. And I don't think it's fair."

Now it was Zack's turn to blush. He couldn't look at Amanda now without recalling Evan's teasing hint of the future, her predestined romance with Peter Pendergen. He was ashamed to let it bother him so much, and doubly ashamed that it was noticeable.

"Look, all I'm saying is that we need to get a better handle on these things we do. They're our biggest advantage when they work right and our biggest liability when they don't."

David nodded his head. "I agree. I mean if we're staying here awhile, we might as well put the time to good use. We're hidden away now. No one will see us if we practice."

"You sure about that?" Mia asked. "If you're wrong, the Deps will be all over us again."

"Maybe. And maybe someday soon you'll get a portal in public that can't be concealed. Wouldn't you like to learn how to avoid that?"

She narrowed her eyes at David. "That's not up to me."

"You sure about that?"

Zack gestured to Theo and Mia. "To be brutally honest, I think you two need the most work. You're our early warning system. If you were both a little more attuned to the future, maybe we could have avoided Evan's prank before it blew up in our faces."

The two resident oracles stared at Zack with pained astonishment.

"Now you're really being unfair," Theo griped.

"Now Zack's right," Hannah shot back. "Did you get a flash of warning at all when we were drinking our spiked mimosas?"

Theo glared at her. "I would have told you if I did."

"Well then you just proved Zack's point, didn't you?"

"Hey, you know what else I can't foresee? An end to your grudge against me."

"This isn't about that. Get over yourself."

"It is about that, so why don't we both get over me?"

Amanda raised her hands. "Okay, stop. This isn't helping. Now Zack needs at least two more weeks to properly heal. If some of you want to spend that time practicing, then do it. If not, then don't. But we can't fight each other like this. We have enough problems."

In the cool silence, Zack uncovered his plate and stared at it until it glowed. The others watched now as his razed corn cob repeatedly vanished and reappeared, each time with more kernels. The ash-gray clone of a chicken breast re-formed itself piece by piece.

Soon the dish regressed to an empty state. Zack squeaked a finger across the pristine surface.

"Mia, what's the term for the thing I just did?"

"I think that's called zilching."

The others studied Zack in wonder. More surprising than his table trick was the bright look on his face, his first smile in days.

"Zilching," he said. "I like that."

The rain went away that night and didn't come back until the first of October. In the nine-day space between storms, the Silvers spent a lot of time thinking about temporis. They endeavored in their own unique ways to become better acquainted with their peculiar talents. Their results, like the weather, were a mix of scattered clouds and sunshine.

No one was surprised to see David blaze his way to the head of the class. Rarely a day went by without him demonstrating a mind-blowing new aspect of his weirdness. On Thursday, he created miniaturized ghosts of the group at dinner, displaying them on the table like a shoe-box diorama. On Sunday, he filled the backyard with constructs made of last night's darkness. On Tuesday, he summoned five real-time projections of himself. They surrounded him like bodyguards, matching his every move and sound.

The next night, he premiered his greatest special effect yet.

"Bear with me," he said, as the others watched from chairs and sofas. David stood by the fireplace, pressing his temples with squinting concentration. His friends chuckled at his comical intensity until the air around him rippled like pond water. Suddenly the boy was gone.

Five grins melted away to hanging gapes. Theo shook his head in bafflement. "What . . . ? How did you . . . ?"

A disembodied laugh rang from the front of the room. "Guess it worked then."

"Yeah, you're completely invisible! Can't you tell?"

"No. I see myself just fine over here. I can't see any of you though."

Once Theo stood up and saw the oddly skewed perspective of the fireplace, he understood the trick. David had created a flat ghost image of an empty living room and cast it in front of him like a movie screen. Hannah poked her head through the illusive wall and now glimpsed David clear as day.

"Obviously the deception falls apart under scrutiny," he admitted. "But in a pinch, it could get us out of a tight situation."

The actress didn't share his success in breaking new ground. After two hours of running in high-speed circles and one afternoon skimming *Temporis in a Nutshell*, she lost her urge for higher knowledge. She soon fell back into the joys of cooking and sibling harmony.

"I'm fine with what I already know," she told her sister as they diced vegetables together. "I'm not in the mood to discover any new complications. I sure as hell don't need another case of time lag."

Amanda shared her reluctance. She spent one hour moving paint cans around the basement before she realized the futility of practicing her tempis. She had perfect control of it when she was calm. It was stress that made her dangerous. She enlisted Hannah to teach her some relaxation techniques. They spent an hour each day on theatrical breathing exercises.

Annoyed by the Givens' denial-and-yoga approach to handling their powers, Zack found Hannah in the kitchen and placed an open book on her cutting board, a mid-chapter spread from *Temporis in a Nutshell*. Hannah balked at the gruesome photos of people with rotted limbs. One poor casualty was mummified from the neck up.

"Eww. God. That's disgusting. Why are you showing me that?"

"They're all victims of rifting," Zack explained. "You and I work with loose temporal energy. We're like microwave ovens without the door. If we're not careful, we'll make more victims like this. It might even happen to some-one we like."

"What do you want me to do, Zack? I tried practicing. All I have is an on/off switch and a gas pedal."

"If you're stuck, go talk to the sensei."

Hannah grudgingly took his advice and told David about her impasse. He scrutinized her from the porch swing, stroking his chin in scholarly contemplation.

"It's an interesting issue. I have a theory about this temporic field you cre-ate. I'd like to test it, with your permission."

"That depends," said Hannah. "What does it involve?"

"A swimsuit, if you're modest."

An hour later, she soaked in the claw-foot bathtub, feeling self-conscious and skeptical as David watched her from the edge of the sink.

"Okay. Shift."

She turned the key in her mind. Time slowed down all around her. The water in the tub took on the sluggish consistency of a milkshake. When Han-nah dragged her arm across the surface, the liquid near her skin still rippled normally.

"Wow. You were right. I can see the field. It's barely . . ."

David was still lost in a hazy blue languor, unable to comprehend her. She de-shifted.

"You were right. I saw it. All the water within a half inch of me was mov-ing normally."

"Huh. That's a thinner field than I expected. The temporis seems to cling to you like spandex."

"So does that mean I'm not the nasty threat Zack thinks I am?"

"Well, I wouldn't suggest hugging anyone in your accelerated state, but I don't think you're in danger of accidental rifting."

"Wow. That's great. Thank you, David. This was really clever."

"We're not done yet. I'm curious to see if you can expand the size of your field."

Hannah crunched her brow at him. "Even if I could, why would I?"

"Because in case you haven't noticed, we make a lot of hurried exits. With enough practice, who knows? Maybe you could shift us all."

After five more baths, Hannah found the switch in her thoughts. Soon she was able to double the thickness of her temporic sheath, then quadruple it. By the end of September, she was able to shift all the water in the tub. Though the act of expanding her field was as easy as puffing her cheeks, she couldn't maintain it for more than forty seconds without getting a blinding headache.

There was of course another downside to her new skill.

"I keep thinking about those photos you showed me," she told Zack, as they rocked on the porch swing. "As much as I love the thought of us all zipping away like Road Runner, my new biggest fear is rifting one of you. Or all of you."

Zack could relate. The image of Rebel's withered hand still haunted him at night. Rather than explore new aspects of his talent, he worked to improve his aim. He spent hours each day attacking a family of bananas, ripening and unripening them from various distances.

On September 29, he staged a backyard demonstration of his new prowess. The sisters and David sat in folding chairs, eyeing the three banana bunches that dangled from the porch awning.

"Nice decorations," Hannah teased. "Is it Monkey Day or something?"

"It's Shut Up and Watch Day. Shall I tell you how to observe it?"

"No. I think I get it."

Zack aimed his finger like a pistol and rotted the X-marked banana in each bunch. As a crowd-pleasing finisher, he repeated the trick while the targets spun and swung on their strings.

Hannah led the others in applause. "Wow! Very impressive, Zack!"

"Thanks. Maybe the next time someone points a gun at me, I can rust it without rifting them."

David cynically pursed his lips. "And while you're taking the extra time to preserve the gunman's precious fingers, he could end your life."

"Even rifting a finger can be fatal," Zack countered. "If an air bubble—"

"I'm just saying you shouldn't put your enemy's well-being ahead of your own."

"Well, I consider 'not being a murderer' to be a part of my overall well-being."

Amanda held his arm. "I think what you're doing is admirable, Zack. You're a good man."

He gave her a lazy shrug and told her the bananas would disagree.

The quiet time in Nemeth had done wonders for the cartoonist. As the pain in his chest diminished to a sporadic moan, he slowly began to resemble the man the Silvers knew and missed. And yet despite all progress, Amanda could still feel a maddening wall of space between them, as if Zack had demoted her to the status of neighbor or colleague. She stewed about it so deeply one night that she unwittingly shredded her socks with short spikes of tempis. She had no idea it could sprout from her feet.

On the last day of September, she joined Zack in the kitchen, drying the lunch plates he washed.

"I think Theo's coming down with something," she said, for lack of a better topic. "He's looking a little peaked."

"I noticed."

"I wish he and Hannah would work out their issues already. It's been frustrating to watch."

"Yup."

Scowling, Amanda rubbed a plate into a state of squealing dryness.

"Not like us," she said, through seething black humor. "You and I are doing great."

"Amanda—"

The back door flew open. Hannah rushed into the kitchen and seized Zack's wrist.

"We need you! Come with me!"

She'd been exploring the woods with David, a brisk morning hike to fight their growing cabin fever. Soon they heard a soft animal whimper and traced it to a clearing. A spotted fawn had splayed itself out on the leaves, taking pained and shallow breaths. One of her legs was bent at an unnatural angle. Blood trickled from her nose and a deep gash in her chest.

Hannah returned to the scene with Zack and Amanda. David lay a calming hand on the deer's neck.

"Poor thing staggered here from the road," he told them. "Must have been clipped by a car."

Hannah tugged Zack's wrist. "You have to heal her!"

"I don't know if I can."

"You might as well try," David said. "She's not getting up from this."

Zack looked to Amanda, who remained dryly pragmatic. She'd seen children die of leukemia. Her threshold for weepiness hovered high above Bambi.

"Don't push yourself if you're hurting."

Zack sighed. "No. I can do it. Everyone step back."

He closed his eyes and concentrated, enveloping the creature with his thoughts until he could feel every hair on her pelt. The others watched with fascination as her body took on a luminescent sheen. The pool of blood at her chest began to shrink and drip upward. The deer's leg straightened and the gash closed like a zipper.

Zack fought a delirious cackle as he felt his magic at work. Suddenly, he was more than just a helpless speck in the cosmos. He was a minor deity, the Jesus of Nemeth.

Just as the deer's last trace of injury vanished, Zack felt a painful lurch in his mind. The fawn convulsed, squealing in agony while her chest ballooned. Before Zack could curtail his temporis, the creature exploded in a torrent of blood and organs.

The sisters gasped through their covered mouths. David balked at the carnage.

"God! What happened?"

Zack stared at the corpse in stammering shock. "I don't know. I-I just lost control. Jesus. Hannah—"

The actress sped out of the clearing in a windy streak. Amanda held Zack's shoulder.

"She's not mad at you. She's just upset."

"I don't get it. It was working."

"Living creatures are complex," David offered. "Could be one of a thousand different things. It also could be worse."

"How could it be worse?"

"You could have done it to one of us."

The thought of Mia lying in place of the disemboweled deer made Zack queasy. He leaned on Amanda.

"I need to get out of here."

The mood in the house was still somber at dusk, when Theo and Mia returned from the public library. As David filled them in on the incident in the woods, they listened with dark distraction, nodding along as if he were merely talking about the coming rain.

"That's awful," said Mia.

"Hope Zack's okay," said Theo.

David studied them with new concern. "Are you all right?"

The two of them had become inseparable lately, a miniature guild of augurs. They'd embroiled themselves in research in the hope of learning more about the nature of precognition. Their quest bore little fruit until three hours ago, when the future came and found them at their study table. They didn't like what it had to say.

TWENTY-SIX

The Marietta Public Library was a daily slice of Heaven for Theo and Mia, a perfect place to hide from friends and enemies alike. The building was located fourteen miles south of Nemeth, a sleek glass ziggurat nestled between a leafy green park and the great Ohio River. Every floor had dozens of plush window seats. Portable music players were available to anyone who asked.

The pair spent their first couple of days dawdling on novels and videos, as well as the pleasure of each other's company. Theo was amazed at how much Mia bloomed when removed from the group. She brought him to tears of laughter with her spot-on imitations of the others—Zack's mordant sneer, David's quizzical leer, Hannah's flailing arms of fluster, Amanda's furrowed brow of concern.

Mia, in turn, finally got a glimpse of Theo's inner prodigy. The man ripped through books like he was wearing a speedsuit, displaying freakish recall of every word ingested. When she asked him his IQ, he merely shrugged and told her it fell somewhere in the space between chickens and David. She loved Theo's humility, even if it was peppered with hints of self-loathing.

On their third day, they finally agreed to take a stab at their research mission. They were surprised to learn that Altamerica had quite a bit to say about people like them.

The temporic revolution of the late twentieth century had forever changed society's expectations of what was and wasn't possible. Once Father Time proved to be a more lenient parent, the concept of precognition moved away from the flaky fringe and into the collective "maybe."

In 1981, a shrewd investor named Theodore Norment capitalized on the shift by launching Farsight Professional Augury, a chain of upscale boutiques in which customers could hear their future from courteous and attractive specialists while sipping complimentary coffee from a chaise longue.

Norment's venture was a huge success, and soon others joined in on the propheteering. By the turn of the millennium, the concept of fortune-telling had been stripped of all mysticism and repackaged as a store-bought amenity. Anyone could claim to see the future through an innate connection to temporis. Today, there were nearly a million registered augurs in the United States. They even had their own union.

Naturally, skeptics remained. An escalating war of books had brewed between the doubters and devotees, enough to fill a wall of the library. The more Theo and Mia read into the debate, the more isolated they felt. They were living proof that the naysayers were wrong, and yet it seemed increasingly obvious that their fellow seers were just posers.

On September 30, just as the other Silvers in Nemeth witnessing the grisly demise of a poor young fawn, a portal found Mia in the library restroom. She glared at the tiny floating disc from the toilet seat, wondering if her future self was deliberately choosing awkward moments to contact her.

She caught the note as it fell, then unrolled it.

The Future of Time. Page 255. Third paragraph. Wow.

The book in question was located on the second floor. Mia's older self neglected to mention that the author was someone she knew and detested. *The Future of Time* was Sterling Quint's second best-seller, a collection of speculative musings that had been rushed to print at the peak of his fame. Though his cold and haughty prose was enough to trigger bad memories, his passage on page 255 shined a strange new light on Mia's talent.

At the risk of lending credence to the fools and frauds of the augur trade, I'll admit that precognition by itself is not conceptually impossible. Still, in a multiverse of infinitely branching timelines, the act of seeing one true future is about as likely as breathing just one molecule of air. A real augur, if he existed, would foresee many different outcomes for any situation, possibly even millions. If the power didn't drive him mad, it would certainly render him useless. Every time he tossed a coin, he'd become bombarded with multiple premonitions of heads and tails, unable to discern the true outcome until it stared at him from his wrist.

Mia rejoined Theo at the study table, watching him read the passage with vacant consternation. She noticed that he'd become sluggish and distant over the past few days. She often found him skimming the same page over and over, or staring out the window with a glazed expression. Though he insisted he was fine, Mia feared he was coming down with an illness.

He closed Quint's book and passed it back to her. "I'm not sure what to make of that."

"Me neither. But I keep thinking back to Ramona, when I got the fifteen hundred dollars from the future. You remember that?"

Theo could hardly forget. He'd stolen off into the night with half of it. "What about it?"

"The next day we found a quarter of a million dollars in the van. That always confused me. I mean why would that Mia bother sending me cash if she knew we were about to be swimming in it?"

"So now you're thinking she didn't know."

Mia nodded. "Right. Maybe she was from a different future, one where we never found the van and money."

Theo pressed his knuckles to his lips as he fell back into his own conundrum. His foresight had gone into overdrive these past couple of days, barraging him with split-second glimpses of moments that had yet to occur. Though most of the visions were vague and benign—moving snapshots of strangers in strange places—he was particularly struck by the ones that involved Melissa Masaad. In one flash, the stalwart Dep bound Theo's wrists in handcuffs on a crisp and cool evening. In another, she shot him in the rain. In a third, she handed him a DP-9 identification card with his name and photo. And in yet another, he rested his cheek on her taut and naked belly, feeling the flutters under her skin as she stroked his hair. Even if these were premonitions and not just figments, he couldn't believe they were all from the same timeline.

"That's . . ." He pressed a taut thumb to his chin. "Huh."

"Yeah. I can barely wrap my head around it."

"If there are an infinite number of futures and we're just seeing one or two at a time, then what's the point? We're no better than guessers. We're not even educated guessers."

Mia puffed in bother. "I don't know. I just know this is exactly the way David said it was. How does he always know these things?"

"He reads a lot of sci-fi. I'm still not convinced it works that way."

"I'm thinking it does," said a third voice.

They turned to the woman who sat two tables away, a honey-skinned blonde in a flimsy white sundress. Though she carried herself with the self-assuredness of an adult, she could have passed for a teenager with her large hazel eyes, cute waifish body, and cropped pixie haircut. Theo was intrigued by her nebulous ethnicity, an incongruous blend of European and Asian features.

The girl closed her book and approached them, standing at their table like an auditioning actress. Mia noticed the pair of watches on her right wrist. One was analog with an ornate silver band. The other was digital and cheap-looking.

She flashed the pair a pleasant smile. "Sorry. I hate to be a snooping Susie, but you two are having a *very* interesting discussion."

Mia turned skittish. "We're just messing around. You shouldn't take us seriously."

"Don't worry. I'm not a psychologist. I'm probably nuttier than both of you. But I do know a thing or two about futures." She motioned to a chair. "May I?"

Theo and Mia exchanged a wary glance before indulging her with nods.

"Cool." She took a seat, then studied their research pile. "Well, no wonder you're confused. These books are crap. If I really wanted to stick my nose in your business, I'd put you in touch with an experienced augur. I mean a real one."

"Frankly, we're not sure there are any real ones," Theo said.

The girl grinned at him with enough mischief to make Mia suspect a flirty hidden motive.

"Oh ye of little faith. Are you familiar with the Gunther Gaia Test?"

Theo nodded. It had come up several times in research. In 1988, a wealthy skeptic named George Gunther publicly offered twenty million dollars to anyone who could correctly predict five natural disasters in the course of a calendar year. The test had become an annual lottery to the would-be augurs of America, with thousands entering each January. So far only a handful had managed to get even one forecast right, an endless source of swagger for the nonbelievers.

"Well, I have it on good authority that this year's challenge isn't going quite the way Gunther likes," the girl told them. "There's a man who entered a whopping seventeen predictions, and so far he's been right on the money. He has four guesses left, all for the last three months of the year. I have no doubt they'll happen too. You might want to steer clear of Tunisia this Christmas."

Mia sat forward in rapt attention. "Who is this guy?"

"He says his name's Merlin McGee, though I know for a fact it isn't. Young fella. Very shy. Very cute. I've met him twice now. He's the real deal. When I congratulated him on his impending wealth, he merely shrugged. He said he's not sure if Gunther will honor the arrangement."

"If he can truly see the future, wouldn't he know?"

The girl tapped Mia's hand. "I asked him the same question. You know what he told me? He said he only wished that people were as easy to predict as God."

Theo winced as a hot knife of pain cut through his mind. The first one had hit him three days ago. Now they seemed to come every hour.

Mia held his arm. "You okay?"

"Yeah. I'm all right. It's nothing."

From her sympathetic expression, the girl clearly disagreed. "You know, there's a health fair going on at the other side of the park. You don't need insurance. They'll take anyone."

"I appreciate it, but I'm okay."

Despite the kindness of their new acquaintance, Theo grew suspicious of her. It seemed odd that a person so friendly hadn't offered her name by now, or asked for theirs.

Mia brandished Quint's book to the girl. "This guy says a real augur wouldn't know anything because he'd see every possibility at once."

"Oh, please. There's an expression people like to give me whenever they notice my wrist. They say, 'A girl with two watches never knows what time it is.' That's bullshit." She checked her dual timepieces. "It's 3:30."

"How do you know for sure?" Theo challenged.

"Because they're synchronized. That makes me twice as sure. What Sterling Quint, God rest his missing soul, doesn't take into account are the redundancies. You look at a million possible outcomes, you start to see repeats. From repeats come patterns. From patterns come probabilities. A true augur can look at the big quilt and see which futures have the best chances of happening."

She tilted her head at Mia as if she suddenly just noticed her. "You have *amazing* hair."

Mia fought a bashful grin. Theo remained skeptical. "It's still guesswork though."

"So?"

"It wouldn't matter for coin tosses, but for life-or-death situations . . ."

The girl waved him off. "Oh, suck it up, man. You're never going to be a good augur if you live in fear of regret."

"Who said I wanted to become an augur?"

"You're already an augur, Theo. You're just not a good one."

Now both Silvers stared at her in hot alarm. She sighed at herself.

"Shit. I didn't want to make a whole thing of this. I don't even know why I came here. This isn't my battle."

"Who are you?" Mia asked.

"I'm nobody. Just a stupid girl who can't mind her own business. You both seem like nice people and you looked so lost. I just wanted to give you a push in the right direction and then flutter away."

"You won't even give us your name," Theo griped. "Why should we believe anything you say?"

The girl shrugged. "You don't have to believe a word, hon. Doesn't affect me one bit. It also doesn't change the reality of your situation. Big things are coming, whether you like it or not."

"Yeah? Like what?"

"Like you," she told Theo. "You have no idea how much power you're carrying in that stubborn brain of yours. There's a great prophet buried in there. Now he's clawing his way up through all that trauma and liquor damage. I wish I could tell you the process will tickle, but those headaches you're getting are just previews. Come tomorrow, you're really not going to like being you."

"What are you talking about?"

"What does it matter? You don't believe me anyway." The girl looked to Mia. "I'm hoping you'll be a little more receptive to what I have to say. You're a sweet and pretty girl with a sharp mind and killer hair. But one thing you're not and never will be is an augur."

Mia's heart lurched. "What . . . what do you mean?"

"You don't have the sight like me and Theo. You just have your portals, and they aren't meant to be used the way you're using them. It's not your fault. Nobody told you. It's just that there are a lot of Mias out there in the future. The stronger you get, the more of them you'll hear from. If you're not careful, every minute of your life will be a ticker-tape parade. I don't think you want that."

The thought turned Mia white. "I don't! What do I do?"

"Talk to Peter. He'll set you straight. The man can be a pigheaded fool sometimes, but he sure knows his portals."

Theo eyed her cynically. "Is that what you are? A Gotham?"

"No, but I've met a few. They hate being called that, by the way."

The girl rose to her feet and slung her purse over her shoulder.

"You know why Merlin McGee only predicts natural disasters? Because he's lazy and they're easy. They're constants across the many branching futures, well outside our influence. It doesn't matter which way we zig or zag. It's still going to rain in Nemeth tomorrow."

She fixed a heavy gaze on Theo. "Bad times are coming. First for you, then your friends. If there was a way around it, I'd tell you. You're all just going to have to stay strong and weather the storm."

The girl walked ten steps to the bookshelves, then took a final look at Mia.

"I really do love that hair."

She disappeared in the aisles, leaving her new friends in quiet turmoil. Theo aimed his dull stare out the window. Mia's gaze danced around the letters of Quint's book jacket.

"Are you okay to drive?" she asked him, a half hour later.

"I think so."

"Okay. I think I'd like to go home."

"Yeah."

They left the library in grim silence, without looking back. They didn't need foresight to know that they wouldn't return here. They'd already learned more than they wanted to know.

The grandfather clock ticked away as the Silvers sat behind the remnants of their supper. Ten elbows rested on the dining room table, ten fists propping five chins. Only Theo sat slouched in his chair. He wished Mia hadn't told the others about the girl with two watches.

"She's either a skilled augur herself or a time traveler," David surmised. "I can't see how else she'd profess to know about Theo's potential."

Amanda peered at David's plate, still half-filled with boiled peas. The sisters had initially tried to prepare more elaborate vegan dishes for him. He never took more than a few polite bites before returning to his vegetable piles.

"And we're absolutely sure this woman wasn't Esis?" Zack asked.

David squinted at Mia. "Describe her in detail."

"I don't know. She was thin. Pretty. Short."

"No," said David.

"No," said Amanda. "Esis is not short."

The cartoonist shrugged in grim surrender. After exploding a deer today, he wasn't confident in his opinion about anything.

Hannah sat back in her chair and seethed. In the four hours since the death of the fawn, her melancholy had turned into something hard and prickly. She found herself despising everyone at the table for reasons of little merit. She hated David for his stupid vegan diet. She hated Mia for her inexhaustible sweetness. She hated Zack and Amanda for not screwing like rabbits already. She hated Theo for all the usual reasons.

At the moment, she hated the fact that her companions were all brilliant in one way or another, and yet none of them considered the obvious.

"She's an actress."

The others glanced up at her with blank expressions. She met their gazes one by one.

"Evan's messing with us again, only this time by proxy. He hired that woman. Coached her through and through. And now once again we're all dancing to his tune, wondering if up is down, left is right. It'd be funny if it wasn't so tragic."

The clock ticked five more times before David broke the silence.

"That's a very solid theory."

Zack nodded. "I've been wondering why we haven't heard from him in a while."

"I don't know," said Mia, her nervous eyes fixed on Theo. "I'm hoping it's all a lie."

Hannah peered across the table and was surprised by the tender smile Theo shined at her. He didn't think she was right at all, but she killed the discussion and he loved her for it.

At five minutes to midnight, Hannah made a drowsy trip to the kitchen and poured herself a glass of water. She crossed into the darkened living room and jumped at the shadowy figure in the easy chair.

"Just me," Theo croaked.

She pressed her chest. "Jesus. You scared the hell out of me."

"Sorry."

She turned on the lamp and faced Theo from the sofa. His eyes were dark. He slumped against the cushions as if he were boneless.

"Are you okay? You don't look good."

Theo couldn't help but grin. Hannah never looked better in her snug white tank top and panties, her bed-tousled hair. While the angel on his shoulder plotted a course of emotional reconciliation, the devil in his sweatpants insisted he was a few deft moves away from couch sex.

"I'm okay," he assured her. "For now."

"So you think that girl was telling the truth."

"I know she was. I see it now, clear as day. Right after breakfast, I'm going to get a nosebleed. Then a splitting headache. By noon, I'll barely know where I am."

Hannah sat forward. "God, Theo. Are you sure this isn't some self-fulfilling, psychosomatic thing?"

"Yup."

"That's crazy. You were talking about infinite futures at dinner. How can this be so certain?"

"Well, there's some wiggle room on the nosebleed."

"This isn't funny. I'm worried about you."

"I know. I can see that. I have to say it's kind of nice, all things considered."

Hannah shot a hot breath at the floor, then matched his lazy stance.

"I've been pretty pathetic, haven't I? Taking two weeks to get over a one-week fling."

"Well, I certainly haven't helped."

"I don't know," she said. "I think I've been angry just for the sake of being angry. Hell, I got mad at you all over again today when that poor fawn died."

"How was that my fault? I wasn't even there."

"Exactly. I was upset and I needed someone to screw me numb. I'm not like my sister. I can't just draw on inner strength. I don't have any."

"That's not true."

"I don't know. Feels like it. So while I understand your reasons for the breakup, and even agree with them in retrospect, I'm still mad that you took away my crutch."

Theo struggled to stay noble, even as he ripped the clothes off her mental image.

"I'm sorry I can't handle the kind of relationship you want, Hannah. Sorry for both of us. I'm looking at you now and I'm thinking about what's coming. I wish I could screw us both numb."

The grandfather clock chimed in the midnight hour, heralding the official start of October. By the twelfth echoing ring, Hannah clenched her jaw in tense resolve.

"First thing tomorrow, I'll go to the pharmacy with Amanda. Get you a ton of painkillers."

"They won't help."

"Well, we'll try, goddamn it. Just because it's destined to happen doesn't mean we can't fight it."

Once again, she was surprised by Theo's thin and tender smile, out of place given the situation.

"Yesterday I had a snapshot premonition of you and me," he told her. "We were sitting just like this, chatting away at midnight in our sweatpants and underwear."

"Is that why you came down here?"

"No. This was somewhere else. Some house on an army base. You looked a bit older. My guess is that it's still a good four years away."

"Wow."

"Yeah. It's nice to know there's at least one future out there where you and I are still alive in four years. Still friends."

Hannah glumly stared out the window, listening to the owls.

"Friends. Strange word to use for any of us. I can barely separate you guys from Amanda anymore. It's like you're all my siblings now. Even you, as screwed up as that sounds."

The two of them sat in silence for another long moment. Hannah rubbed her eyes.

"You're a good man, Theo. You're a good man and I love you and I really hope you're wrong about tomorrow. You don't deserve it."

The augur breathed a long sigh of surrender. It seemed a cruel joke of the universe that the easiest things to predict were the ones that couldn't be prevented. The pain. The rain. The natural disasters. And yet he couldn't help but disagree with Hannah's last sentiment. The girl with two watches had attributed alcohol damage as a primary cause of his neurological crisis. That made it his fault, which strangely made it easier to accept. For once there was justice, there was balance, there was karma in the situation. Theo planned to wield it like an umbrella. Like Hannah's screwed-up love, he'd carry the blame with him, all the way through the storm.

Everything happened as foretold. At 5:02 in the morning, the sky over Nemeth offered ten seconds of warning drizzle before coming down in sheets. Dawn arrived in the form of a hundred lightning flashes.

At 9:20, Theo glanced down at his eggs and noticed a fresh drop of blood, another warning drizzle. He pressed a napkin to his nose, then looked to his troubled friends.

"Shit."

The pain hit him like a cyclone. His muscles turned to liquid and he fell out of his chair. By the time David carried him to the couch, he'd lost all sense of time and place.

Theo lay on his back, writhing on the cushions like an uneasy dreamer. He was only marginally aware of the conversations that occurred around him, the feminine hands that comforted him in turns. While Mia stroked his fingers with sisterly affection and Amanda tended to him with clinical diligence, it was Hannah's intimate caress that brought him back to the present. He lifted the damp cloth from his brow and tossed her a bleary stare.

"What time is it . . . ?"

She checked the grandfather clock. "Quarter after one. How you holding up?"

"Worse than anything I ever felt. I wanna . . . I wanna die."

Hannah squeezed his hand. "Oh, sweetie. Just hang in there. The pain won't last."

"It's not the pain . . ."

"What do you mean?"

Amanda rushed into the room and pulled at Hannah's shoulder. "Let me look at him."

"Just a second. We're talking." She looked to Theo. "What do you mean? Are you having visions?"

"I'm not just seeing," he moaned. "I'm feeling. I keep feeling you guys . . . dying. Over and over. I feel Zack's blood all over me. God. I can smell it."

He seized Amanda's arm, his eyes red and cracked. "I can't take it. You have to knock me out. I don't care how you do it. Just knock me out. Please."

Amanda rooted through their pile of store-bought painkillers, then fed him the one with the drowsiest side effects. He gradually drifted off to sleep. Judging by his somnolent moans and cries, it seemed the future followed him there.

The next forty-eight hours passed like weeks for the sympathetic Silvers. By the morning of Sunday, October 3, they were all as pale and unrested as Theo.

They sat around the living room in a dreary daze, watching David jab the fireplace with a metal poker. Hannah cradled Theo's head in her lap as he twitched in restless half slumber. Nobody thought he was getting better.

Hannah spoke in a hoarse and weary rasp. "We need to do something. He can't take another day of this."

"I'll go to the drugstore," Zack offered. "See if there's something else."

Amanda curled up with Mia on the love seat, absently stroking her hair. "We've been there twice. It's all the same weak stuff. He needs a prescription-strength remedy."

"We're back on this," David complained.

"Yes, we're back on this. I've made up my mind. I'm taking him to Marietta."

Yesterday, during their umpteenth discussion of Theo's plight, Mia shared the information that the girl with two watches had given her about the local health fair. Amanda confirmed by phone that it was still going on and that anyone was welcome to bring their untreated ailments.

Even as she'd broached the idea, Mia wasn't sure it was a good one. David had a stronger opinion on the matter.

"Perhaps you didn't hear me last time . . ."

Amanda sighed at him. "I heard you, David. I understand your concern. But a health fair isn't the same as a hospital. There's no reason to assume it's being monitored."

"It's a place where fugitives are likely to seek treatment. Of course it's being monitored. You might as well phone the Deps now and tell them you're coming."

"David, I've worked at these things—"

"On another world."

"They're understaffed, overcrowded, and wildly disorganized. Even you wouldn't be able to find us in that chaos."

"You're willing to bet your freedom on this?"

"I am," said Hannah.

"I am," said Amanda. She looked at her sister. "You're not going."

"Bullshit. You think you can lift him by yourself? Your arms are like pipe cleaners."

Amanda shook her head. "We can't carry him in. He'll have to walk. I can get him there."

"I'll go with you," Mia said. "I know the way."

"No."

"Hell, no," Zack uttered.

David chuckled with bleak derision. "Like lemmings off a cliff."

"What do you suggest we do instead?" Hannah asked.

"You know what I suggest. We could be there by nightfall."

She flicked a brusque hand. "Of course. I should've guessed. Peter, Peter, Peter. Your magic-bean solution for everything."

"He may know the nature of Theo's illness. He may have a cure."

"Or he could be a trap," Amanda countered. "Or a Pelletier. Or he might not be there at all. We're not ready to face the next step, David. Not with Theo like this."

David threw a pleading look at Zack. "Are you going to help me here? Or are you relishing the thought of a smaller group?"

The cartoonist exhaled from his easy chair, splitting his pity between Theo and David. The boy's rational insights were consistently drowned out by the emotional concerns of the majority. Clearly he was about to be outvoted again.

Zack looked to Amanda. "For what it's worth, I agree with him. You're taking an insane risk for a bunch of pills you might not even get. I mean without ID—"

"I'm bringing a sick man and a fat wad of cash. That'll be enough."

"And if they give you a written prescription?"

"They should have samples. I'll ask for extra. I'll pay through the nose if I have to."

Zack shrugged with hopeless uncertainty. "Well, you know that scene better than I do. I'm just telling you where I stand. That said, if I were the one in Theo's shoes, I wouldn't want this put to a group vote. It's his pain and your risk. It should be his decision and yours."

Amanda leaned back on the couch and looked to Hannah's lap. In all the hubbub, nobody had noticed until now that Theo was awake. He fixed a dull gaze at the ceiling.

"Did you hear all that?" Amanda asked.

"I heard enough."

"What do you think?"

He barely had the space for thoughts. Over the last two days, the future had been thrown in a blender and funneled into him. He'd progressed beyond fretting over individual images and now worried about the patterns. Hannah kept suffering at the cruel hands of Evan. Zack kept dying at the tempic hands of Esis. The skyline of San Francisco kept crumbling in a distant cloud of dust.

Between all the flashes and glimpses, Theo detected a hint of a much larger problem, a lingering shade of despair in the minds of his elder selves. It always stayed the same from future to future. The only merciful aspect of his ordeal was that he never stayed in one place long enough to see the true shape of it. Theo didn't consider himself a particularly strong or brave man. He was willing to take any risk, any detour to avoid the awful thing ahead of him.

"I can walk," he said, in a weak and jagged voice. "I can go."

Amanda's preconception of the health fair was generous in hindsight. The admission line was a hundred-yard backlog of impoverished treatment-seekers, all as surly and grim as the weather itself. Volunteer organizers in white rain slickers floated around them like angry ghosts, shouting incomprehensible orders. A line cutter provoked a fistfight, causing a human domino topple that ended ten feet shy of Amanda and Theo.

After snaking through the rain for sixty-eight minutes, they finally reached the admission tent. Amanda filled the reception clerk's ear with an elaborate tale of muggings and lost wallets before learning that ID was required only for those who wished to waive the hundred-dollar entry fee. She paid the money so cheerfully that the clerk wondered why she even bothered with the sob story.

Amanda led Theo to the waiting room tent and sat him down in a folding chair, rubbing his back as he rested his face in his palms. She nervously glanced around for cameras, then jumped in her seat when she spotted an elderly man reading a magazine with her own tempic fist on the cover. In the center of the shot, Zack winced in purple-faced agony while Amanda's giant fingers dangled him from a hotel balcony, cracking ribs.

And you wonder why he's been so cold to you, she thought.

They waited in silence for thirty more minutes, until a young and anxious nurse led them to a small private tent. An hour passed without anyone checking on them, then another. Every time Amanda flagged a staffer, she received a shrug and a jittery assurance that a doctor was coming.

"I don't like this," Theo moaned from the cot. "Something's wrong."

"I told you these places were disorganized."

"No. I don't like this. We need to get out of here."

She parted the curtain and peered at the waiting room tent across the way. Just five minutes ago, it had been packed with patients. Now all the chairs were empty.

Her fingers curled in tension. "God. I think you're right."

Theo struggled to a sitting position. "Shit! Shit! I didn't see it in time!"

"What are you talking about?"

"It's too late. They're here."

"Theo, what—"

"Hold your breath!"

A glass ball the size of an orange rolled through the doorway and exploded in white smoke. While Theo covered his mouth and nose, Amanda breathed a pungent gas that tasted like nail polish remover. Her senses went topsy-turvy. The tempic walls of every tent rippled like liquid for four eerie seconds, until the widow fell unconscious to the grass.

Half-blind, mindless, Theo fled the tent. He only made it a few feet before he was tackled to the ground by three men in black fiber armor. They subdued him like spiders, rolling him around and binding his limbs in sticky white string. Six arms hoisted him above the ground and strapped him to a floating gurney.

Theo looked at his captors—over a dozen armed agents, all wearing the same protective gear. Their faces were obscured by long white gas masks with dark eyeholes. They looked frighteningly surreal, hulking black panthers with possum heads.

Soon the slimmest figure approached and removed her mask. Even with rain in his eyes, Theo had no trouble recognizing the dreadlocked woman in front of him. His lips curled in a feeble smile.

"Melissa Masaad."

Though the Deps within earshot all traded baffled looks, Melissa wasn't entirely shocked to hear her quarry say her name. She'd seen the man's work in two different states. It was because of him that she now believed in augurs.

"Hello, Theo."

He muttered something under his breath before falling unconscious. Melissa looked to her team in confusion.

"Did you hear that?"

"No, ma'am. I couldn't make it out."

Neither could she. The part she heard was nonsensical. She could have sworn she heard him say "private school."

Disturbed, Melissa wiped the rain from her face. "Take him to the hospital. Call me the minute you learn what's wrong with him."

A trio of agents emerged from the tent with Amanda strapped to a stretcher. Even in her unconscious state, the other Deps kept their rifles fixed on her. No one wanted to take any chances.

Melissa approached the gurney and checked her prisoner's pulse. After four weeks of chasing ghosts, it was a marvelous thing to finally touch the real Amanda Given.

She rooted through Amanda's pockets, procuring a handphone. The tiny light flashed green in announcement of a new text message from David's phone.

We haven't heard from you in a while. Is everything all right?

Melissa smiled. She'd just captured two dangerous criminals without spilling a drop of blood. Now she had the tool that would lead her to the rest of the group. Everything was more than all right. It was a beautiful day.

TWENTY-SEVEN

She'd grown used to her conspicuous nature. Everywhere she went in her great adopted nation, she could feel the heat of inquisitive stares. She was a dark-skinned beauty with overpronounced cheekbones, exquisite almond eyes, and a flowing hairstyle that was far too exotic for uncultured minds to process. She spoke with an accent that few Americans had ever heard before. To top it all off, she carried a badge.

Her fellow Deps were no closer to cracking the enigma that was Melissa Masaad. Even those who saw beyond her standing as a dusker, a limer, and an occasional erection-inducer couldn't get around the fact that she was a little bit off. She talked to herself in hallways, chewed on her hair in meetings, and derailed conversations with peculiar non sequiturs. Though she scored her fair share of acrimony for her early rank advancement, it seemed rather fitting that Melissa would seize the reins on the Bureau's strangest case to date.

Now fifteen agents watched Melissa with muted puzzlement as she lay atop her guest desk in the bullpen. She'd spread herself out like a bearskin rug, her chin propped on a thick phone directory. Her handtop rested on the edge of the neighboring desk.

"Advance."

The screen displayed a new page of transcribed dialogue. Through ghost drills, the Deps had reproduced more than seventy hours of fugitive chatter, every word the Silvers had uttered in the Ramona motel and the Evansville resort. Melissa had read all twelve hundred pages. She had enough questions to keep her captives busy for weeks.

Howard Hairston stood at the hallway junction, glaring at the two local agents who peered up Melissa's skirt. She raised her head to look at him.

"Is everything ready?"

"We're all set."

The skinny young Dep had become Melissa's right-hand man in the wake of her promotion. *You can't do it all yourself,* Andy Cahill had warned her, on his last day of work. *The minute you become the new me, you need to find a new you.*

"How is she?"

"Surprisingly calm," said Howard.

"Did you find a—"

He held up a tempic screwdriver. Melissa smiled.

"Wonderful. Thank you, Howard."

She climbed off the desk and arched her back with a wince. After the day's double raids, her spine was a sore and angry beast. Now she was about to interrogate a woman who, under the worst circumstances, could snap it like a breadstick.

The Charleston outpost was a small operation—seventeen employees in an old brick building that stood alone on a tree-lined hill. The hallways were lit by antiquated filament bulbs and stacked with dusty radio equipment. The local Deps specialized in solving broadcast crimes, everything from the illegal transmission of foreign film and video ("mudding") to the hijacking of lumivision signals for the purposes of mischief ("surping").

The most wanted felon in the office was a legendary figure known only as Surpdog. At least twice a month, the mysterious assailant would preempt a random broadcast with fifty-four seconds of guerrilla video, an ever-changing montage of beautiful images from other nations. After eighteen years and 452 surpings, all the agents knew about their target was that he hated American isolationism and was extremely good at covering his tracks. Melissa liked Surpdog's message. She hoped the Deps never caught him, if he even was a he.

She stopped at the door to the makeshift interrogation room and blew a heavy breath. Howard eyed her cautiously.

"Be careful in there. We don't know those machines will work."

"I appreciate the concern, Howard. I'll be fine. Say, when's your birthday?"

"Uh, February 10th. Why?"

When she was a field agent, Melissa didn't do much hobnobbing with her peers. Now that she was a supervisor, she figured she'd have to start asking people how their weekends were. She'd have to give them cards on their birthdays.

"No matter."

She cleared her throat, adjusted her skirt, then opened the door to her eminent guest.

Amanda sat on a worn brown sofa, the only conventional piece of furniture in the large room. Her wrists and ankles were fastened to the floor by thick metal chains, giving her just enough slack to sit upright. She wore a dark blue jumpsuit with the DP-9 logo emblazoned across the right breast, plus a grated metal collar that wasn't tethered to anything. A quartet of slim mechanical towers surrounded her in a perfect square formation. Each one was six feet tall and filled with humming blue bulbs. They reminded Amanda of bug zappers.

Melissa pulled a folding chair to the center of the room. The two women studied each other.

"Well, here we are," said Melissa.

"Here we are," Amanda echoed.

"You like the new color?"

"What?"

"Your hair. That was quite a change, going from red to black."

Amanda blinked distractedly. "Oh. Yeah. I don't know."

"You don't know if you like it better black?"

"I don't know why you're asking me about my hair."

"It's just an icebreaker."

"Well, congrats. You made me more nervous."

Amanda still reeled from the knockout gas. She had no idea of time or place. For all she knew, she was in some government black site in central Asia. Or maybe she'd died and gone to a strange little corner of Hell, where all the demons were beautiful and droll.

Melissa flipped through a stack of color printouts. "And your physical state?"

"Queasy. My ears are ringing like murder."

"Normal side effects of the gas. You'll recover in an hour or two."

"I feel like none of this is happening. Like this is all a dream."

"That could also be a side effect," Melissa said. "Or possibly just denial. In either case, I assure you you're not dreaming. Unless I'm the one in denial."

Amanda eyed her in leery wonder. She'd spent many nights imagining her interrogation at the hands of federal agents. This woman couldn't have been further from her expectations.

"Where are we?"

"West Virginia," Melissa replied. "Roughly eighty miles from your place of capture. Do you know my name?"

"No. How the hell would I?"

"I thought maybe Theo told you. He seemed to know it."

"Is he here? How is he?"

Melissa chewed her lip in contemplation. It was too soon to start bartering for information. Amanda could use a good faith token.

"He's on his way here. He was taken to a hospital for tests. From what I'm told, he's been given painkillers and is now sleeping like an infant."

Amanda let out a dismal chuckle. Melissa cocked her head at her. "What?"

"Nothing. That's all I wanted. I just wanted him to get some relief."

"Well, that you accomplished. I'm Melissa Masaad, the DP-9 agent in charge of this investigation. I've been eager to meet you for quite some time."

"No doubt," said Amanda. "Where are you from? I can't place the accent."

"I'm North Sudanese, formally educated in British schools."

"How long have you been here?"

"About two years," she replied, with a provocative glance. "You?"

Amanda narrowed her eyes defiantly. "Born and raised in the USA."

A storm of mad cackles brewed in Melissa's throat. Seemingly every page of the ghost drill transcripts featured one of the fugitives remarking on how much they missed their world, how different things were on this one. Chronokinesis by itself was difficult enough to process. No one in the Bureau was ready to embrace the idea of chronokinetic aliens.

Heavy chains rattled as Amanda scratched her neck. "You're lucky I'm so stupid, Melissa."

"How are you stupid?"

"I was warned there'd be civic cameras at the health fair. I didn't listen."

Melissa shook her head. "Whoever told you that was misinformed. We have no cameras there."

"You don't?"

"No. Installing a civic camera is a monstrous bureaucratic procedure.

Worse than traffic lights. No one would go through all that paperwork just to monitor a five-day event."

"So how did you find us then?"

Melissa clicked her pen against her chin in busy thought.

"We can discuss that later. I imagine you're curious about some of the devices in this room."

Amanda touched her new metal collar, then examined the four humming consoles around her. "I assume it's some kind of shock fence thing. Like they use for dogs."

"No. The collar's a separate fail-safe. Should you get belligerent, my associate watching through the camera will press a button and the embedded capsules will release more pacifying gas."

"So what's the purpose of these big machines?"

Melissa eyed her suspiciously. "You haven't tried your tempis yet?"

"No."

"Go ahead."

"No."

"It's not a trap, Amanda. I'm genuinely curious."

"I don't care."

"Fine. I'll show you myself."

Melissa procured the tempic screwdriver from her pocket and jutted it toward Amanda. The moment it crossed into the quadrant of blue light towers, the tempic point rippled wildly and then vanished.

Amanda cast a baffled stare at the towers. "What are these things?"

"They're solic generators. Have you heard of them?"

"No."

"If temporis were a family, solis would be the mother. It's the power source behind every tempic device, every lumicand, every shifter, every juve. It's also the catalyst that turns a little bit of sunlight into a lot of electricity. Nearly everything in the civilized world runs on solic generators. These four only look different because I removed the protective casings."

Amanda recalled seeing a tall metal cylinder in the basement of the lake house. She'd figured it was a water heater.

"Will I get sick from all this exposure?"

"Solis isn't harmful to living creatures. The casings are only used to protect the equipment."

"Why is it harmful to tempis?" Amanda asked. "You said it's a power source."

"Yes, in the same way that helium powers a child's balloon. Add too much and it pops."

"Meaning I'll pop if I try."

"I doubt that."

"I'm not a screwdriver. You have no idea how this will work on me."

"I have no idea *if* it'll work on you. We're both taking a risk. But what choice is there? You have a history of violence, especially when threatened."

The room fell into tense new silence, broken only by the hum of the generators. Melissa noticed a rectangular discoloration on the wall behind Amanda—twenty feet wide, five feet tall, and two shades lighter than the faded beige around it. She didn't know why it bothered her.

By the time she focused on her captive again, she saw glistening tears. Melissa pushed a pack of tissues into the solic field.

"Guess it doesn't feel like a dream anymore."

Amanda took a tissue. "No."

"Would you like some time alone?"

"Just ask your stupid questions. I know you have a million of them."

"I do, in fact. Does that mean you'll cooperate?"

"Not at all. I just want to get this part over with."

"I understand why you don't want to talk about your friends—"

"I'm not saying a word about them."

"—but are you willing to discuss your enemies?"

Melissa pulled a printout from her stack, a grainy ghost image of Amanda in the hallway of the Piranda Five Towers. In the photo, she conversed with a slight-statured man dressed like a hotel manager.

Amanda scowled in bristling contempt. "Evan Rander. He's a psychopath. I'd give him to you on a platter if I could."

"He shot a manager to death, five doors down from your suite. The same pistol was used to kill a young couple in another tower. We presume he did it to get a view of your twelfth-floor hideout."

Amanda stayed silent. She'd learned about their deaths on the news. It tortured her to think they'd all be alive now if she'd picked a different hotel.

"We also know he drugged you," Melissa said. "We found traces of pergnesticin on the glass fragments. It's an extremely powerful narcotic. For what it's worth, I don't hold you responsible for your actions that day."

Amanda dabbed her eyes. "Thank you."

"He went to a lot of trouble to poison you. Why does he hate you all so much?"

"I have no idea."

"I think you have some. Zack and Evan had a lengthy phone discussion on September 19. We were only able to reproduce Zack's half of the conversation. What did Evan say to him?"

"I don't know."

"Zack never told you?"

"Zack barely speaks to me now."

"That's surprising. From all the scenes we ghosted, you two seemed quite close."

Amanda closed her eyes in anguish. "I'm not talking about Zack. And I have nothing left to tell you about Evan."

"Fine. Let's jump back two weeks. On September 6, you and your companions were attacked in Terra Vista, in the office of a scientific organization called the Pelletier Group. You've mentioned a man named Rebel as the leader of the assault."

"I have?"

"You all have, in private discussions. Who's Rebel?"

"No idea."

"You're lying. Why are you protecting the man who tried to kill you?"

Amanda kept quiet. She feared any talk of Rebel and Gothams would ultimately lead the Deps to Peter Pendergen.

"Eighteen physicists died that day," Melissa reminded her. "Two went missing."

"That wasn't us."

"An entire family of security guards, dead or missing."

"We didn't kill anyone!"

"Tell me what happened that day."

"Why do you even need to ask? Just use your damn ghost drills."

"We tried," said Melissa. "The entire property had been temporally reversed several years. If it wasn't for city records, we'd never know the Pelletier Group had ever set foot in the building. A feat like that is utterly unprecedented. Who do you think is capable of doing such a thing?"

"Not a clue."

"You're lying again. See, the drills were good for something. I've followed every conversation you had in the Five Towers resort. You believe your generous influx of money came from Azral and Esis Pelletier, a couple who don't exist anywhere on record. You also believe they're responsible for the deaths of the physicists. Tell me about them."

"No."

"Now you're protecting the Pelletiers?"

"Now I'm protecting you."

Melissa lowered her head. "I'm not sure you realize the gravity of your situation."

"Is this the part where you threaten me with jail time?"

"Do I even need to? You know what you did to those policemen. To Constantin Czerny."

"Wait, what?"

"Which part are you confused about?"

"I didn't do anything to Dr. Czerny."

Melissa retrieved a photograph of the ill-fated physicist, lying dead on a coroner's table. A ghastly red wound ran across his bulging stomach.

"Autopsy shows that he was impaled with a tempic projectile. It expanded inside his abdomen, like a blowfish. I know every tempic weapon out there. None are able to change shape like that."

"That wasn't me! I tried to save him!"

"I assume you stabbed him by accident. You were all under attack. Tensions were high. He may have startled you."

"Someone else did that to him!"

"Someone else with your singular talents?"

Amanda fell into hopeless black laughter. There seemed no point in telling her about the tempis-wielding Gotham in the Teddy Roosevelt mask, especially if all trace of him had been erased.

"Fine, Melissa. Pin it on me. Pin every murder on me. It doesn't matter."

"You don't care what happens to you?"

"I care very much what happens to me. I'm saying it doesn't matter what I say or do here. I know how this ends. I'm going into a government lab and I'm never coming out."

Melissa slit her eyes in cool umbrage. "For someone who claims to be born in this country, you don't seem to know how we operate."

"I think the rules go out the window when it comes to me."

"The rules of nature, perhaps. Not the rules of law. You still have rights."

"So what's the plan then? I go to trial? I spend the rest of my days walking around some prison yard with my four solic generators?"

"As we speak, a special cell is being prepared in our Washington headquarters. We plan to hold you under Title 22, Part IV, Chapter 409 of the U.S. Criminal Code, the provision that allows us to detain an undocumented suspect for up to ninety days unless they produce valid U.S. credentials or have their foreign identity confirmed by a representative of their home nation. Should that fail to occur, we'll charge you as a Jane Doe in the assault of two policemen and the murder of Dr. Czerny. Given ninety days, I can all but guarantee I'll find a pharmaceutical remedy to your tempis problem, which will be administered forcibly under Title 23, Part II, Chapter 217—the Prisoners with Special Afflictions clause. You're not too unique for our legal system to handle."

Amanda stared at Melissa through wide, unblinking eyes. The agent relaxed her stance.

"I know you're not a malicious person, Amanda. I don't want to see you incarcerated any more than I want to see you dissected. If you cooperate with us, if you help us solve all these deaths and riddles, we can work out a special arrangement. You can be our ally instead of our prisoner."

"You expect me to believe I'll walk free someday?"

"I can't imagine we'll ever be out of your life. But with time and trust, the chains will come off. This I promise."

Amanda peered down at her lap. "I want to believe you."

"But?"

"It won't work."

"Why not?"

"Because at some point you'll ask me where my friends are and I still won't tell you."

With a soft and frustrated sigh, Melissa pulled a new photo from her pile. It was an extreme close-up of a small silver panel. A sixteen-letter code was etched across the surface.

"What is that?" Amanda asked.

"It's a Serial Registry Pin. Every communication device has one. On Friday, September 17, you left your handphone facedown on the coffee table of your hotel suite. Our drills captured the image. Through the SRP, we got a trace warrant. After that, we just had to wait for you to use your phone before we could pinpoint its location. Ten hours ago, upon your arrival at the health fair, you sent a text message to David. This is how we got you."

Amanda's heart thundered. "What are you saying?"

"Through your phone, I got an emergency trace warrant on David's number. Turns out Nemeth was just a stone's throw away."

"No . . ."

"At 3 P.M. this afternoon, my team raided your four-bedroom house on the lake. I don't need to ask about your friends."

Amanda gritted her teeth. "You're lying. You would have told me if you had them."

"You think I'd tell a woman who can smash walls that her sister's in the next room?"

"Is she?"

"Of course not."

"Stop playing games with me!"

"You first."

"Show me they're here. Show me they're okay. Then I'll talk."

"If I trusted you, Amanda, I might agree to that. Since I currently don't . . ." She chucked a blank notepad on the couch. "You tell me everything you know about Azral and Esis, Evan and Rebel, and then we'll address the matter of your companions. If you'd like some extra-credit goodwill, you can tell us all about Peter Pendergen too."

Melissa smirked at Amanda's slack surprise. "Of course we knew about him. We've been watching him for two weeks now. We've had another team staked out at your rendezvous address in Brooklyn. You never had a chance."

She tossed Amanda a pen. "I'll leave you alone. If you need anything, speak to the camera."

Melissa closed the door and shambled down the hall to the tiny office where Howard sat. He furrowed his brow as she crawled across the surface of his desk, spreading herself out in front of him like a buffet. Andy Cahill never did that.

"Uh, you okay, boss?"

"No. My back hurts."

"Sorry to hear that. You need anything?"

"Just ten minutes on a hard surface." She covered her eyes with her forearm. "I don't think she's from around here, Howard."

"Yeah. I'm getting that sense."

"I would laugh like a jackal if this turned out to be the world's most elaborate prank. I would not be bitter at all."

Howard checked Amanda on the monitor. "She's just staring at her fingers now."

"Huh. I guess they do work."

"Her fingers?"

"The generators. She's finally testing them."

"Jesus. You really poked the lion, didn't you?"

"She'll cooperate," Melissa said. "She knows she doesn't have a choice."

"You going to tell her the truth?"

Melissa exhaled wearily. It was a mean trick she'd played on Amanda, though technically she didn't lie. Her team did raid the lake house in Nemeth today, but Melissa failed to mention that it had been abandoned in a hurry, with David's handphone found smashed to bits on the floor. The other four fugitives were still at large, somewhere out there in the rain.

At 9 P.M., Theo arrived at the office, secured to a wheelchair by gray iron cuffs. His appearance was a throwback to his alcoholic days—ashen skin, sunken eyes, disheveled hair. He wore the same dark blue jumpsuit as Amanda, though his buttons had been misfastened by one.

Despite his haggard appearance, the augur never felt better in his life. An arsenal of powerful relaxants had cleared the maelstrom in his head. For the first time in days, he was free of all pain, free of visions. His relief gleamed like sunshine over every dark facet of his current predicament.

By the time Melissa returned from her clandestine cigarette break, Theo had been sequestered in a small room with two of her burliest and surliest Deps. They circled his wheelchair like predators, attempting to chisel away at his good cheer with overwrought descriptions of the prison ordeals that awaited him.

Theo smiled through all their bluster. He knew more about his future than they did.

Melissa sat in the bullpen, periodically checking the interrogation on the monitor while she browsed Theo's medical report.

"No wonder he's so happy. It looks like they gave him every drug in the lockbox. Ephermanine? That's for schizophrenics."

Ross Daley yawned from a nearby chair. "Who's to say he's not? You should've heard the threep he was spewing at the hospital. He tried to tell me that San Francisco will fall to an earthquake in two years. Said it was a fixed event."

The agent was a young and broad-shouldered man, the only other person of color on Melissa's team. Though she never expected racial solidarity, she was dismayed that Ross was her worst backbiter, covertly casting doubt on her decisions, her qualifications, even her sexuality. Melissa didn't have the time or energy to work on his attitude.

"Did he mention anything about a private school?"

Ross eyed her strangely. "No. Why would he?"

Theo had mumbled something odd in Marietta, just before passing out on the gurney. Melissa wasn't sure she heard it right, but it seemed like more than babble.

"It's nothing," she said. "I'm grasping at straws."

She studied Theo's cerebral tomogram in furrowed bother. The scan revealed a foreign object in his thalamus, a metal ring the size of a mouse's eye. The chief examiner was at a loss as to how it got there. Even with the most advanced surgical equipment, it was impossible to plant an item that deep in a patient's brain without killing him.

A flurry of new activity on the monitor caught her attention. The agents shoved Theo's chair, poking him. Melissa pursed her lips and hurried down the hall to intervene.

"All right. Enough. Take a break. Both of you."

The agents looked at her with childlike innocence. "We weren't hurting him."

"I didn't say you were. But as you can see from his imbecilic grin, he's not responding to your threats. Give it a rest."

The two men shot Theo a menacing glare before exiting the room. The augur adjusted his rumpled collar with his free hand, then reclaimed his smile.

"I really look like an imbecile?"

"You look like a homeless imbecile," Melissa replied. "If you'd been this conspicuous two weeks ago, you would have never made it past us in that hotel lobby."

Theo chuckled cynically. "Okay. Guess you're not here to play Good Dep."

"No. I didn't come to interrogate you. Though now that I'm here, I'm darkly intrigued by a question you're not asking."

"And what's that?"

"'How's Amanda?'"

Theo's smile vanished. Melissa crossed her arms and leaned against the wall.

"You do remember her, right? She's the one who risked and ultimately sacrificed her freedom to get you medical treatment. She asked about you right away."

He fixed his dark eyes at his lap. "You really know how to sling the guilt."

"I'm glad you feel bad about it."

"And I'm glad you're looking out for her. I was afraid you guys wouldn't see beyond the tempis."

"We're federal agents, Theo. We're trained to profile."

"Well, you sure missed the boat on me. If you think I don't care about my friends—"

"You still haven't asked about her."

"How's Amanda?"

"She's managing."

"I knew that," he said, through gritted teeth. "I already knew."

He fixed his sharp gaze at the edge of his wooden desk, then let out another snicker.

"Something funny?" Melissa asked.

"Just admiring your effectiveness. You killed my buzz in record time."

"I'm your arresting agent. Did you expect me to be your friend?"

Theo had certainly expected someone nicer. The Melissa of his visions seemed honest and noble and thoroughly kind, even as an adversary. Unless his prophecies were prone to embellishment, the woman in front of him was just a shade of her future self.

"Guess not," he replied. "So when does the interrogation begin?"

"In a day or so, when the drugs wear off and you're a little more lucid."

"In a day or so, I might not be around for questioning."

"Are you predicting your death at our hands or merely threatening escape?"

"I'm just saying anything can happen."

Melissa eyed him coolly. "You're trying to use your augur's mystique to rattle me. It won't work. If you were as good as you think you are, you wouldn't be wearing our handcuffs."

"And if you were as good as you think you are, we'd all be wearing them."

"You're assuming we haven't been to Nemeth to pick up your friends."

"I know you don't have them," he said. "I overheard your man talking in the car. He's not a big fan of you, by the way. Said you were frigid and arrogant. Frankly, I don't see it."

Torn between her urge to throttle Theo or Ross Daley, Melissa stashed her rage behind a smirk. "We'll have plenty of time to correct our misconceptions about each other."

She closed the door behind her, then marched to Ross in the bullpen. He slouched in his desk chair, reading baseball scores on his handtop. Melissa slapped the screen shut.

"I need a list of all the private schools within a hundred miles of Nemeth, current and defunct."

"Why?"

"Because Theo said something about it earlier. It's a possible lead to the location of the others."

"The guy's out of his skull. If we investigate every crazy thing he mutters—"

Melissa leaned in close, cutting Ross off with a harsh whisper.

"Agent Daley, in forty-five seconds I'm going to employ a supervisory tactic that's not endorsed in the handbook. In fact, it'll earn me quite a nasty reprimand from my superiors. I expect to recover. You, however, will look back on this night for a very long time. You'll wish you'd done things differently. This is your last exit. Nod your head, say, 'Yes, Melissa,' and then do what I ask."

Ross looked around the bullpen at his colleagues, then forced a breezy shrug.

"Fine. Whatever. No need to get menstrual."

"Eight seconds . . ."

"I said fine."

"Seven . . ."

"Yes, Melissa. Yes. I will get you your list of private schools."

She rose to her feet. "Thank you."

Howard swooped in from the stairwell. He looked to Melissa with urgent worry.

"Uh, we have a guest."

The gray-haired man in the lobby was, like Melissa, a conspicuous presence. He stood as tall and thin as a beanstalk, with spindly fingers that were as long as most hands. He wore a fedora, longcoat, and gloves, all woolly black relics from a more conservative decade. Deep wrinkles ran like circuitry across his gaunt, handsome face.

The moment Melissa spied his shrewd blue eyes, she knew and feared his true nature.

"Good evening, sir. I'm Melissa Masaad. Supervising Special Agent, DP-9."

The man removed his hat and procured his government ID. He spoke in a soothing lilt, as if reading a bedtime story.

"Cedric Cain. Associate, NIC."

Melissa scanned his badge. "That's quite a vague rank, sir. Can't say I've heard of it."

"I never need to make my own coffee, if that's what you're asking."

"I suppose I'm dancing around the larger question."

Cain smiled slyly. "You are. But you look good doing it."

The National Integrity Commission was formed in 1913, during the great American panic that followed the Cataclysm. Though their original mission statement involved the "neutralization of foreign threats and influences," their first two decades were little more than a systematic purge of immigrants, illegal and otherwise.

In 1932, the NIC was re-formed into a global network of strategic intelligence operatives. They worked mostly in secret, virtually always outside the nation's borders. Though crackpot rumors of their activities remained, Integrity held a mostly positive reputation among U.S. citizens. To the lay public, they were the stalwart souls who kept the world's problems from becoming America's problem. How they did that was their own business.

Melissa knew the shades would come sniffing around her case sooner or later. The question was whether or not they deemed her fugitives to be a foreign threat.

"Melissa," Cain cooed. "Pretty name. Does anyone ever call you Missy?"

"No, sir."

"Well, I'm going to start calling you Missy if you don't stop calling me sir."

"Apologies, Mr. Cain. My strict British conditioning."

"It's Dr. Cain, actually. You can start there and work your way to Cedric. You smoke?"

"Are you asking me if I break the law, Dr. Cain?"

"I'm inviting you to break the law with me, agent."

Two minutes later, they sat in the parking lot, in the front seat of Cain's black Cameron Bullet. Melissa found it a surprisingly compact car for such a stretched man. The driver's seat had been altered to retract another ten inches, all the way to the back cushions.

"So how's Andy handling his sunset?" Cain asked.

Her mind danced with pleasure as she took a drag of Cain's Cuban cigarillo. "You know Andy Cahill?"

"Oh, we go way back. You were probably in diapers when he and I had our first turf war."

"Really? Who won?"

Cain let out a coughing chuckle. The question was rhetorical sarcasm.

Integrity was the rock to the Bureau's scissors, trumping them on all jurisdictional matters. Only an act of paper from the White House could stop them from taking Melissa's case away from her.

"Andy's fine," she responded. "He says he hates retirement, which I assume to mean he loves it."

"Last of the cowboys, that one. You know, I tried to poach him a couple of times. The man was too damn smart to be a Dep."

"We are a simple folk," she jested.

"Please. I already know you're smarter than Andy. If I thought you wouldn't laugh me out of the car, I'd make you a job offer right now."

Melissa couldn't help but smile at Cain's perceptiveness. After seven hard years in British Intelligence, she'd sooner club baby seals than step back into the world of national defense.

She followed Cain's gaze across the lot, at the silver Royal Seeker that had been seized with Amanda and Theo. Her men had already pored over every inch for prints and fibers.

"How much do you know about this case?" Melissa asked.

"I'll put it to you this way: I only recently started smoking again."

"You'll have to give me more than that."

"I read all your summaries and transcripts," he said. "Stole a gander at the Filipino's hospital report. I sat in this car an hour ago, watching you interview Amanda Given on my handtop. There's not a drop of evil in that woman, is there?"

"That feed was closed-circuit."

"Nothing's closed-circuit. You did a stellar job, by the way. The generators were a brilliant idea."

Melissa blew smoke through a scowl. "So while we've been following these people, you've been following us."

"More or less. But before you beat the war drums, know that I'm not here to plunder. I've only been asked to assess and report. You're lucky they sent me and not someone else."

"Why is that?"

"Because I don't think we're ready to handle this problem," Cain confessed. "Integrity's in a state of flux right now. Bunch of young hard-liners are taking us over, pulling us back to our dark early days. If they got their mitts on these outlaws of yours, it wouldn't be pretty. At the very least, that Maranan fellow would be a goner. The lab boys would fish the ring out of his brain like the prize in a cereal box."

Melissa's stomach twisted in tension. "You can't do that."

"There's no 'me' in that equation, hon. I don't run the Sci-Tech division. Not anymore."

"Obviously you still have some influence if the agency sent you here."

"If I sing the right tune, I can quell their interest for a while. But I can't do it alone. You need to keep me posted on everything you learn, especially about this Azral and Esis Pelletier."

"You seem fine at gathering this information on your own."

"It's harder than it looks. If I get my news straight from you, I'll have better luck spinning my new bosses. Are you willing to work with me?"

"That depends. Why are you really doing this? What do you get out of it?"

Cain sighed a long spout of smoke, then tapped his ashes out the window.

"'Associate' is just a title they slap on the folks they don't know what to do with. There are those who hope I go the way of Andy Cahill. I have other plans. Fortunately for you, they involve keeping these fugitives away from Sci-Tech. At least until I get it back. Now I know you're cynical about us God-and-country folk, but I swear to you I want these people alive. I think we can learn a lot more from their mouths than their corpses. I know you feel the same way. So let's help each other."

Melissa couldn't shake the feeling that she was being positioned like a chess piece, though she saw little choice at the moment. "I'll keep you posted on everything I learn."

"Good. Your big task now is to find those other four runners, fast."

"Believe me, that's my top priority."

"It better be. Because if they make any more headlines, it'll be out of my hands. Integrity will cloud up and rain all over them."

They stared at the Royal Seeker again. Neither the license plate nor the Vehicle Registry Pin existed on record. Either the tags were unparalleled forgeries or the van had somehow been pilfered from the future. A month ago, Melissa would have laughed at the latter theory.

"Guess everything's about to go topsy-turvy again," Cain reckoned. "Everything we know, right out the damn window."

"I only recently resumed smoking myself," Melissa admitted.

"Have you said it out loud yet?"

"Said what?"

"That they're from another world."

Melissa felt a familiar lurch in her gut, the one she suffered whenever mad reality confronted her.

"Not yet."

Cain took a last drag of his cigarrillo, then chucked it away. "Well, maybe it's time to start."

As soon as she returned to her desk, her handphone buzzed with a new text message. Owen Nettles was a blond and bespectacled little man who never made eye contact and rarely spoke above a mumble. But for all his awkwardness, he was one of the Bureau's best ghost drill operators. Melissa had left him at the Nemeth lake house to learn more about the missing fugitives.

His update wasn't encouraging.

<Weird weird weird results. Non-results, actually. Can't be a glitch.>

Melissa frowned as she keyed her reply. <Elaborate.>

<Everywhere I drill, I get nothing but Davids. Dozens of him. Walking, standing, hopping. It's all I see. Unless I'm suffering a schizoid manifestation of my personal fantasies, I'd say the Golden One's learned some new tricks.>

Melissa winced with discomfort. Owen's deep love for ghosting had mutated into an unhealthy fascination with David Dormer. She'd have to talk to him about guarding his tongue around the others. The Bureau didn't look kindly on boyers. She typed:

<Okay,> she typed. <Keep looking.>

She sat at her desk in a state of fidgety distraction, chewing a dreadlock as she twirled Cedric Cain's contact card in her fingers.

"Something, something, private school. Something, something, private school."

Her agents traded dark and baffled glances. Howard waved to her from the edge of her desk.

"Melissa?"

She snapped back to awareness. "Hello, Howard."

"Are you okay?"

"I'm all right. Thank you. How are you?"

"Well, truth be told—"

"Has Amanda written anything yet?"

"No. Not that I saw."

Melissa muttered an expletive and hurried down the hall.

Amanda curled into an uncomfortable fetal position on the sofa, the best she could manage with her chain restraints. Her eyes were dark with fatigue and anguish.

Melissa retrieved the notepad from the floor. A few lines of scribble graced the top page.

I don't think you have the others. If you knew they were okay, you would have told me like you did with Theo. I'm sorry to use your kindness against you, but information's the only leverage I have. I plan to use it sparingly.

For what it's worth, I do believe everything you said about honoring my rights. I pray to God the rest of your people are as decent as you.

With a weary sigh, Melissa sat down on the folding chair and rubbed her throbbing temples.

"When I was thirteen and living in Khartoum, a drunk driver struck me down in a crosswalk. I lost my left arm and my right eye, and my spine was shattered in three different places. It was extreme good fortune that the hospital had installed its first reviver the week before. I woke up inside the machine, fully intact and with no memory at all of the incident. I didn't believe the story until the doctor showed me photos of my mangled body."

Amanda sat up on the couch again. Melissa absently twirled the tempic screwdriver in her fingers.

"That was when I first realized the great and wonderful change that was happening all over the world. To this day, I remain endlessly fascinated by temporis. I built my first tempic barrier when I was sixteen, and then my first ghostbox a year later. I understand these devices better than I understand most people. I love them all. Except for the weapons."

She fixed a heavy stare on Amanda's long fingers.

"When I think about what you and your people can do, I feel like an amateur all over again. I barely know how to process it. And now on top of all the lunacy . . ."

Melissa shook her head at Amanda in bleary awe.

"You didn't have temporis at all, did you?"

"What do you mean?"

"On the world you come from."

Amanda met Melissa's gaze with brief and pensive silence. "No."

"I can't even imagine what you people have been through. The shock and upheaval. It staggers the mind."

The generators hummed without interruption for ten long seconds before Melissa stood up.

"I don't have the others," she confessed. "The lake house was abandoned by the time we got there. My guess is that they're proceeding to Brooklyn in the hopes that Peter can help them locate and rescue you. I assume that's where we'll apprehend them."

"I hope not," said Amanda.

"I understand. But the fact remains that your companions are out there right now, hunted by forces far worse than us. And now they have to function without their seeing eye and their tempic arm. At this point, we're their best option. You'll just have to trust me on that."

She opened the door, then turned around to Amanda.

"I'll do everything in my power to protect you. That's an unconditional . . ."

Melissa took another look at the rectangular discoloration on the wall. Her jaw went slack with revelation. She knew why it bothered her now.

". . . chalkboard."

Amanda looked at her askew. "What?"

"There was a chalkboard there. This used to be a classroom."

"Uh, okay. Why are you—"

Melissa closed the door and ran back to the bullpen, urgently scanning each agent.

"What happened to the local men? Did they all go home?"

"One of them's still here," said Howard. "He's in the bathroom. Why?"

Melissa rushed to the men's room. The heavyset blond at the urinal jumped at her abrupt entrance.

"What the hell are you doing?"

"How long has DP-9 occupied this building?" Melissa asked.

He shook his head at her in exasperation. "You stormed in here just to—"

"How long has DP-9 occupied this building?"

"I don't know! Ten years or so. Why?"

"What was it before you moved in?"

"It was a school! Some fancy little academy. Why the hell are you—"

Melissa bolted down the hall and burst into Theo's room. He tossed her a genial smile.

"What's up?"

She squinted at his free hand, clutched around the edge of his desk table. His grip tightened defensively as she approached. She pried his fingers, revealing a small brown sticker.

PROPERTY OF ARCHER LANSING PRIVATE SCHOOL

Melissa laughed with dark disbelief. "You knew you were coming here. You foresaw this."

"I think you're overestimating my—"

She fled the room and made a beeline back to the bullpen, stopping at Ross Daley's desk.

"Did you leave Theo alone at any point during his hospital stay? Did you leave him within reach of any handphones?"

Ross scowled at her in insult. "No. Of course not. What do you take me for?"

"You don't want me to answer that."

She spun around to Howard. "Call Owen and Carter and anyone else who's not here. Tell them to get back now. The rest of you, grab your guns."

Howard flashed his palms. "Whoa, whoa, boss. Slow down. What's going on?"

Melissa cracked another jagged laugh.

"I don't know how he did it, but Theo got a message to the others. They're right here in Charleston. And they're coming for their friends."

On the dark and chilly patio of a fourteenth-story hotel suite, between the empty lounge chairs and the potted cherry trees, four weary travelers stood side by side at the guardrail. The DP-9 building rested a thousand yards to the east. The Silvers could see lit windows between the trees, and the occasional glimpse of moving figures within.

Hannah stowed away her cheap binoculars and looked to Mia, Zack, and David. Like her, they were dressed in black from neck to toe, and wore their worries openly.

"Okay," said the actress. "Now what?"

TWENTY-EIGHT

Their last hour in Nemeth had passed with creeping dread. Between the *plink-plink-plink* of the rain on the windows and the *tick-tick-tick* of the grandfather clock, David drummed a one-finger beat on the face of his wristwatch. Mia tapped a pen against a page of her journal. Zack paced the hardwood floor in clomping worry, the handphone clutched tightly in his grip. He'd left two texts and a voice mail for Amanda. She had yet to respond.

At the stroke of one, a ringing chime sliced through the house, startling everyone. Zack raised an angry palm at the wooden clock. Suddenly the hands spun like fan blades and the glass turned gray with dust. The oil on the gears dried away to nothingness until the inner workings creaked to a halt. A four-year demise condensed to five seconds. A timepiece choked to death on time.

The cartoonist looked to David and Mia with grumpy contrition. "I'll fix it later."

Suddenly the handphone chirped in announcement of a new text message. Hannah sped down the stairs in a windy blur, de-shifting at Zack's side.

"Is that her? Is she all right?"

Zack furrowed his brow at the screen. "I'm not sure . . ."

"What do you mean?"

"Just read it!" Mia yelled.

"'Sorry, Zack. They made me power off my phone in the exam tent. No news yet. I'll call when I know more.'"

Now the others landed on Zack's uncomfortable perch, caught between their doubts and their wishful thinking. Before anyone could speak, Zack aged the handphone to a husk, then chucked it to the floor. It shattered into rusty fragments.

Hannah grabbed his arm. "What are you doing?"

"When have you ever heard her say she 'powered off' something?"

"Okay, that sounded strange, but that doesn't mean—"

"I'm sorry, Hannah. We're out of rosy scenarios. That wasn't Amanda. That was a Dep."

Hannah glared at Zack. "But why destroy our last phone? If that was her—"

"They wouldn't have tried that trick if they didn't want us to stay here. They're tracking us. We need to go."

"Go where?"

"Go *how*?" Mia asked. "Amanda took the van."

"Our only choice—"

"Stop."

David hadn't said a word in two hours, fearful of the furious invective he'd unleash. He'd warned them all what would happen if Amanda took Theo to the health fair. No one listened. Now Zack was about to leave an oral trail of bread crumbs for the Deps to follow.

"Everyone stay quiet until I finish."

The others watched blankly as he paced back and forth across the living room, adjusting his gait each time. After three treks, he shuffled his way back to the sofa.

"All right. Now gather around me. Sit closely."

They clustered around the coffee table. David closed his eyes. Suddenly the first floor teemed with the recent ghosts of himself, a busy crowd of self-projections that walked, skipped, and hopped in every direction.

David formed a small bubble of space around the four solid Silvers. "This is the only way we can safely talk. If they see us in their ghost drills, they'll read our lips."

Mia wished she was in a state of mind to enjoy the new scenery. Her voice creaked with strain. "Are you sure that wasn't her, Zack? I mean if you're wrong—"

"I'm not."

"—we'll be leaving them. They'll come back to an empty house with no way to find us."

"He's not wrong," David said. "They're in federal custody. There's no time to debate this."

"So what do we do?"

Zack bounced his busy gaze between Hannah and Mia. "You two pack our stuff. As much as you can. David and I will be back to pick you up."

"Pick us up in what?"

Seeing Zack's grim expression, the boy nodded with understanding. "Something borrowed."

They cut through the rain in long-legged strides. Their closest neighbor lived a half mile down the road, in a humble wooden A-frame that was overdecorated with American flags and crucifixes. The owner's Dixon Tumbril rested in the driveway, a boxy white minivan filled with clutter.

While David kept a wary eye on the lit windows of the house, Zack reversed the car doors to an unlocked state. They slid into the Tumbril in quiet synch and pulled down their rain hoods.

"Smells like dog in here," Zack muttered.

"Beggars can't be choosers."

"I wouldn't call this begging. I'm wondering if we should just offer them cash."

"We don't have time to broker a sale, Zack, or soothe your criminal guilt."

"It's not guilt. I'm just afraid this won't work."

"It'll work."

During his nine days of power practice, Zack had conducted a few casual forays into temporal duplication, otherwise known as tooping. He learned thirty years after the rest of the world that metal objects cloned better than most, acquiring unseemly patches of rust but keeping most of their structural integrity.

He concentrated on the keyhole until it shimmered with a faint white glow. Soon a splotchy metal construct grew from within, forming the tip of a key, as well as a broken piece of key ring.

Zack marveled at his new creation. "Holy shit. That's surreal."

"Closest thing to magic I've seen yet."

"Yeah, I'm the Merlin of car thieves. My mom would be proud." His face crinkled with disgust as he touched the key's surface. "It's slimy."

"You probably cloned some of the driver's hand."

Zack didn't want to picture the mass of insentient goo that would result from a fully tooped human. He cleaned the key with his sleeve.

"All right. I'm ready. Do your thing."

David looked to the house. "On my signal. Three . . . two . . . one . . ."

With a flick of his hand, the property was consumed in a booming rumble, a perfect echo of the thunder that had blanketed Nemeth ten minutes ago. Zack started the engine under the loud noise cover, then checked the front window of the house.

"Good job."

Now it was David's turn to marvel. "Wow. I've never thrown thunder before. That was like something out of Norse mythology."

On a better day, Zack would share in his godly thrill. All he wanted to do now was scream. The federal posse on their trail kept pushing them into becoming bigger and better criminals, larger and meaner threats. Zack could only imagine the cycle would spin faster and faster, until he and his friends were killing just for the privilege of living.

Mia and Hannah waited quietly on the porch swing, their collective belongings stuffed into duffels with little semblance of order. They'd packed their bags in grim silence, refusing to speak for fear of ghost drills, refusing to cry for fear of never stopping.

"The Deps wouldn't hurt them," Mia insisted. "I mean they still have rules."

The actress nodded her head, scrambling for the sunniest scenario. "They're probably sedated. I bet they're just sleeping right now."

Mia cast a dismal glance at the lightning. "She called it a storm."

"Who?"

"The girl Theo and I met in the library. She said everything that was happening right now was a storm and we just had to weather it. Maybe that means we'll get them back."

Hannah hoped to God she was right. She'd just made peace with Theo. She'd finally started getting along with Amanda after ten years of thorny distance. Now the two of them were probably in a government plane, speeding away to some top-secret lab in the middle of nowhere.

Soon the stolen Tumbril pulled into the driveway. The Silvers threw the bags into the back, then sped away in a splashing screech.

The moment he crossed the intersection, Zack glimpsed headlights in the rearview mirror. A trio of ash-gray vans hung a sharp left behind him, speeding toward the lake house. His heart hammered.

Seconds, he thought. *We missed them by seconds.*

Three hours after the dramatic capture of two federal fugitives, the Marietta health fair returned to its normal chaos. A lone Dep remained at the scene, patrolling the grounds as a volunteer organizer. Melissa didn't think Zack and the others would be foolish enough to come here looking for their friends, but then she'd underestimated their recklessness before.

For all the same reasons, Hannah was not a fan of the current plan. While their stolen Tumbril idled in the library lot, she studied the temple structures at the far end of the park.

"It's all right," David assured her. "I'll be in and out before anyone can spot me."

"That's just what my sister said to you."

"Yes, well, I plan to be more careful."

"Just watch out for cameras," said Zack.

"Watch out for everything!" Mia added. "Please."

David exited the car, tightened his rain hood, then shined a breezy smile through the window.

"Don't you fret, Miafarisi. You won't lose me today."

Hannah shook her head at him as he hustled toward the fair. "That kid is unreal. Nothing scares him."

"He's amazing," Mia said, with sheepish self-consciousness.

Zack tapped a nervous beat on the steering wheel. "He was right. Amanda should have never come here. I should have helped him convince her."

"You wouldn't have stopped her," Hannah said. "You know how she gets when someone's hurting. She was always like that, even as a kid."

"Why didn't she become a doctor then?"

Hannah hesitated to reply. It seemed crass, especially now, to talk about her sister's stillbirth, a devastating trauma that had knocked Amanda's whole life off trajectory.

"It's complicated," she sighed.

Zack shut off the windshield wipers. Soon the outside world drowned away. Nine minutes passed before a wet and winded David hurried back into the car.

"They're okay. The agents used some kind of sleeping gas on them."

Hannah covered her mouth. "Oh my God."

"Did anyone say where they were going?" Mia asked.

"The Deps? No. But I think Theo might have."

"What?"

"Start from the beginning," Zack said. "What did you see?"

Through hindsight, David had seen everything. As he walked the crowd with his hooded face lowered, he scanned the past in his thoughts. He watched the entire federal ambush from setup to takedown, then stood at Theo's gurney as the augur mumbled something odd. David had placed his ear near Theo's retrospective lips, parsing every syllable of the message.

"Archer Lansing Private School?" Hannah asked.

"That's what he said. I replayed it three times."

"But why? Who was he talking to?"

David smirked in bright amazement. "Strange as it sounds, I think he was talking to me."

Soon Mia returned to the library and sat at a terminal. She learned through Eaglenet archives that Archer Lansing was once a small but prestigious boys' academy in Charleston, West Virginia. A cross-reference search of the address revealed that the building was now a regional office for the Broadcast Crimes Division of DP-9.

When Mia brought her results back to the car, Zack brimmed with guarded optimism.

"That can't be coincidence. That has to be where they're holding them."

David nodded excitedly. "Theo knew I'd come to ghost him. He gave me the future through the past. It's kind of brilliant, actually."

"It's just one future," Mia cautioned. "We don't know if it's the right one."

Zack scoured the road atlas he found under the passenger seat. Charleston was eighty miles south of here, a straight shot down Highway XLI.

"It's the only lead we have. If they're not there, we're screwed."

"And if they are there?" Hannah inquired. "What then?"

The cartoonist matched her uncertain expression, then told her to ask again later.

Two hours after sunset, on the chilly balcony of a West Virginia high-rise, she did.

The Kanewha was the oldest and most prestigious hotel in the state, a blond brick high-rise in the center of the capitol district. History buffs knew it as the place where President Irving Dudley died of a heart attack just days after his 1960 reelection. Had David sprung for the $4,200-a-night penthouse suite, and had he felt the urge to push his ghosting talents, he would have learned the death wasn't entirely natural.

He sat on the patio of his decorous new room on the fourteenth floor, keeping a binocular vigil on the DP-9 building in the hilly distance. He could spy the familiar frame of their Royal Seeker in the parking lot. He'd caught Melissa Masaad, the exotic-looking leader of the Marietta raid, sneaking a cigarette behind the generator towers. Now he watched Ross Daley push Theo up the wheelchair ramp of the building. David smiled at the augur's serene expression.

"I'll never doubt that man again. He's a true prophet."

The Silvers in the living room didn't share David's cheer. They still had no confirmation that Amanda was inside, nor did they have a rescue plan. Shortly after check-in, Mia visited the business center and printed every online photo she could find of the old private school. Hannah and Zack raided the department store, purchasing black clothes and radio transmitters for everyone.

Now the cartoonist rooted through their bag of dark keepsakes from Terra Vista, finding Czerny's small electron chaser (dead), the Salgados' stun baton (dead), and the imposing revolver that Rebel had painfully introduced into their lives. It looked quite functional, with five .44 caliber bullets remaining in the chamber.

Hannah paced the carpet, nervously eyeing the gun. "Am I the only one who thinks this is crazy?"

"No," said Mia.

Zack chucked a hopeless palm. "I'm open to alternatives."

"This is our best chance," David insisted. He returned through the sliding screen and closed it shut behind him. "It's a small building, isolated from its surroundings. From what I can see through the windows, there are only nine or ten agents in there."

Hannah scoffed. "Oh, is that all?"

"You seem to forget we have talents they don't. We also have the element of surprise."

"How do you know they're not expecting us?"

"They can't possibly know we've divined their location," David insisted. "We have the advantage. It's just a matter of using it. I can create a distraction that lures most of them outside. While I keep them blind, you and Zack can look for the others."

"What about me?" Mia asked. "What should I do?"

David regarded her with tender concern, mixed with an insulting amount of doubt. "I think you should stay here and watch from the balcony. You can let us know through the transmitters if reinforcements arrive."

Mia shook her head. "Are you insane? You guys are outnumbered enough already!"

"He's right," Zack said. "I mean none of us are commandos, but at least our weirdness gives us a fighting chance. It's not like you can throw notes at them."

"But what if you get captured?"

"We won't," said David.

"We might," Zack countered. "If that happens, use the money to get to Peter. He'll take care of you. He may even be able to get us out."

"You can't . . ." Mia choked on her words. The thought of being alone on this world made her knees buckle. She failed to notice the tiny new glow in front of her chest.

"You can't ask me to do that."

"Mia . . ."

"You can't ask me to sit here while you guys risk your lives!"

"Mia, you're getting a portal."

"What?"

She looked down at the glowing circle, yet another breach at the worst possible moment. She only seemed to get them when she was sleeping or stressed.

"Oh shit. Not now."

"No, this is good," said David. "It could be useful intel."

She fished her journal from her bag. "It's not. It's a past portal. I'm sending, not receiving."

Hannah's brow rose with cautious hope. "Wait. Where does it go? How far back?"

Mia blushed, thoroughly grateful that none of them could see through the keyhole. Her younger self sat on a toilet in the Marietta library, her pants bunched around her ankles.

"Three days ago," she replied. "Right before Theo and I met the girl with two watches. I need to tell myself about a passage in one of Quint's books."

"Oh my God. That's perfect!"

Zack eyed Hannah cynically. "You can't be serious."

"Why not? You said you were open to alternatives."

"Yeah. Realistic ones."

"How is it any less realistic than storming a building full of Deps?"

Mia was relieved to see David share her confusion. "What are you two going on about?"

"Changing the message," Hannah said. "We can tell Amanda not to go to the health fair!"

David blinked at her like she was selling rainbows in a jar.

"I don't think that'll work."

"How do you know? We never tried it before."

"If it were truly possible to alter past events—"

"It is possible, David. Look." She pulled the license of Jury Curado from her pocket. "We used to know this guy. Now we don't. Evan changed the past. Why can't we?"

Zack eyed the license with a raised brow. "That's a good point, actually."

"Thank you. See?"

Mia blinked in addled stupor, her mind filled with images of apocalyptic carnage. "You're talking about deliberately causing a paradox!"

"Your notes are already paradoxes," Hannah attested. "Just because you write the same words with the same pen color doesn't mean you've created a perfect duplicate of the message you got. There'd be dozens of tiny inconsistencies. Apparently the universe doesn't mind."

"That's what *you* say! For all we know, that's what killed our world!"

David shook his head. "It wasn't. Don't get me wrong, Mia, I don't believe this trick will work. But you're not going to tear the fabric of time just by changing a message."

Hannah gripped Mia's shoulder. "Sweetie, if there's a chance to save Amanda and Theo without throwing us in the path of a thousand bullets, don't you think it's worth a try?"

Mia scratched her cheek in hot dilemma. She could feel the portal slipping away.

"Shit. Shit."

She tore a scrap from her pad and scrawled a frantic message.

Tell Amanda not to take Theo to the health fair! The Deps will get them! Please trust me!

"God. I can't believe I'm doing this . . ."

Hannah squeezed Zack's arm. "If this changes the timeline, you think we'll remember?"

"I don't know," he replied. "If it works, I don't care."

Mia spun to face him. "And if this kills us all?"

"It'll be fine," David assured her. "Do it."

Mia winced and looked away as she placed the note in the breach. The portal swallowed the paper, then vanished.

The Silvers stood rooted in place for thirty taut seconds. Zack and Hannah threw their wide gazes around the living room, nervously scanning for signs of change.

Soon Mia opened an eye and peeked at David. He crossed his arms and leaned against the wall, his expression dancing a fine line between annoyance and amusement.

"And here we still are."

Hannah tossed up her hands. "Goddamn it. How does Evan do it then?"

"Obviously not through notes."

"How did you know it wouldn't work?" Zack asked him.

"Because multiple chronologies exist. This whole world is proof of that. The best I can figure is that Mia created a fork in time, a branching chain of events that runs parallel to ours. If that timeline's Amanda chose to heed the warning, then I imagine these alternate versions of us are having a much better day than we are. They're the ones who benefited from Hannah's idea. Not us."

The actress scowled at her feet. "Great. So they get a happy ending and we still get shot to death."

Mia remained firmly unsettled. Between all her thoughts and apprehensions, she experienced a strange new sensation, as if someone tapped an undiscovered third shoulder.

Zack held her wrist. "You okay?"

"No. Something's not right."

"What, like some kind of—"

"Zack, move!"

She pulled him aside as a new portal arrived where he was standing. The shimmering gateway was the size of a dinner plate. It had a windy pull that was strong enough to ripple all drapes and garments.

The Silvers shielded their eyes at the blinding glow. For a maddening moment, Hannah feared Mia was right after all. This was the paradox apocalypse. It was the Rupture.

"Mia, what's happening?!"

"I don't know! It's a portal but I don't think it's mine!"

"Past or future?"

"I don't know! It's not mine!"

A brown cloth bag suddenly popped through the surface, hitting the rug with the faint sound of clanking metal. A flat manila envelope fluttered out after it. Before anyone could process the new items, the portal shrank away.

Half-blind and teetering on lunacy, Zack reached for the envelope. A line of angular scribble stretched across the front.

To the damn fool Trillinger and his mad boy accomplice.

"Can someone please tell me what's going on?"

Mia scanned the cover. "I don't know. That looks like Peter's handwriting."

Zack opened the envelope and emptied the contents. Among an assortment of maps and sketches was a hand-scrawled message on notebook paper.

You know, for two allegedly clever men, you don't have enough common sense to fill a bee's rubber. You cannot waltz into a building full of armed federal agents and expect to come out again. Hannah knows this. You should listen to her more often.

There's a better way to save Theo and Amanda. At 4 A.M., a group of five agents will leave the building in a Tug-a-Lug truck, heading east toward Washington, D.C. Three Deps will be riding in the trailer, along with your friends. If you position yourselves at the stretch of highway I've marked, you'll be able to intercept the truck at 4:45.

Use everything at your disposal, including the handcuffs I sent you. Be careful around Melissa Masaad, the black woman with the funny hair. She's their leader and she's smarter than you.

I'd come out and help, but my people are still watching me closely. I can't join you without bringing Rebel back down on your heads. All I can say is good luck and godspeed. Don't let Theo die.

—Peter

PS—Don't go to the Brooklyn address I gave you. It's been compromised. When you get to the city, have Mia—and only Mia—call 11-53-34855. We'll arrange a meet from there.

The room fell to silence as Peter's message passed from hand to hand. David dropped the note to the coffee table with a frustrated sigh.

"I have no idea how to react to this. I mean I don't know if this is Future Peter using hindsight or Present Peter using foresight. If it's Future Peter—"

"David . . ."

He threw a nervous look at Hannah. "I'm just trying to make sense of it."

"I understand that. But have you ever hijacked a truck before?"

"Of course not."

"Well, that makes four of us. Maybe we should focus on that."

Freshly stung by Peter's rebuke, the boy nodded. "You're right. You're right."

Zack emptied the bag of handcuffs and spread out Peter's materials. Among the maps was a sketch of a rental truck, and another of the rocky outcropping that would serve as the ambush point.

As the beleaguered Silvers began to formulate their plans, Mia found her gaze drifting back to the little patch of air where she'd just split time. She'd only just gotten used to the idea of multiple futures. Now she had to process multiple pasts. She'd been so worried about destroying the Earth. Now she had to wrap her mind around the possibility that she'd just created one.

TWENTY-NINE

The 3 A.M. chime broke the silence in the interrogation room. Melissa yawned and checked her watch. The building had been on high alert for five hours now, with no sign of intruders.

She sat cross-legged on the desk, her crumpled red bra resting in her lap. As caffeine and exhaustion pummeled her from both sides, a high and giddy chuckle escaped her throat.

"My agents think I'm crazy. Even more so than usual. I'd blame you, Mr. Augur, but really the fault is mine. I've let the surrealism infect me to the point where I actually believe that an actress, an artist, and two minors would dare attack this place."

Theo lay on the folding cot, his arm draped over his eyes. He was coming down off a bevy of neuroleptic drugs, a dilating effect that made the ceiling bulbs burn like desert suns.

In the sober light of reason, he regretted leaving his mumbled clue for David in Marietta. If he'd been wrong, he would have sent his friends on a wild-goose chase. Being right was even worse. He might have lured them into a trap, thanks to Melissa's adaptive reasoning.

"I still can't shake the feeling that they're coming to rescue you," she said. "Perhaps they're waiting for some kind of signal."

"For the hundredth time, I don't know where they are. I don't know what they know. If you'd just let me sleep—"

"No, no. If I have to stay up, so do you. I blame you enough for that."

Theo clenched his jaw. "God, you're ridiculous. Do you even have a life outside this job?"

"Not much of one. No."

"Well then maybe you should live it up while you're still young and hot."

"Thank you for the compliment, but I don't do well with flings. We at least have that in common."

Theo raised his arm to glare at her. "Did you ghost my entire relationship with Hannah?"

"Not the naughty parts," she assured him. "We have rules about that."

"Oh good. So you didn't chuck the entire Fourth Amendment."

She dangled her shapely legs off the table and swayed them like a bored child. "I know you don't have ghost drills on your world, but do you even have Domestic Protections?"

Theo rubbed his eyes. There was no point in pretending.

"We call it the FBI. The Federal Bureau of Investigation."

"Interesting. I like that. And what about the NIC?"

"The what?"

"The National Integrity Commission. I guess you don't have that either, as such."

"I guess not, considering I have no idea what that is."

Melissa sighed a heavy breath. For his sake, she hoped he'd never find out.

Howard poked his head into the room, his eyes dark and bleary with fatigue. Melissa could sense that even he resented her for the overzealous lockdown.

"The tugs are here," he announced.

"Excellent. If I can have four men help me with the generators, I'll escort Amanda myself."

"Okay. I'll round some up."

"What's happening now?" Theo asked.

Melissa hopped off the table and grabbed her gun. "We're leaving."

In their long freeway travels, the Silvers had become quite familiar with the sight of the blue-striped Tug-a-Lug truck. The company had grown so dominant in the do-it-yourself moving business that "tug" was now the casual term for any rented hauler.

At 4 A.M., a trio of sixteen-foot trucks left the field office and split up at the first intersection. The maneuver was a skittish ploy on Melissa's part, a vehicular shell game to thwart any would-be rescuers. Two of the tugs returned to the building within the hour. The third kept moving east on Highway LXX.

The atmosphere inside the trailer was downright eerie. The battery lamps on the floor created a sinister underlighting for everyone but Amanda. She continued to shine like an angel in the blue-tinted radiance of her solic generators.

She and Theo faced each other from opposite walls, their arms handcuffed behind their folding chairs. Beneath the powerful joy of seeing each other alive and well was the pain of greater separation. Theo wished he could talk to Amanda telepathically, to pick her brain about the status of the others without alerting their captors.

Melissa's loud yawn bounced off the metal walls. She and Howard sat perpendicular to the captives, like bridge opponents.

"We'll be in Washington in two hours," she told them. "Your accommodations there will be far more comfortable."

Theo couldn't get over all the chains and safeguards the Deps were using on Amanda, as if this skinny nurse and Christian had become their personal King Kong.

"You going to keep those machines on her for the rest of her life?" he asked Melissa.

"We're completing construction on a special cell that achieves the same effect. She'll have more mobility. If we're fortunate, we'll find a drug that safely suppresses her access to the tempis." Melissa looked to Amanda. "I imagine you wouldn't be too upset about that."

The widow shook her head. Though she retained a wary fondness for Melissa, she didn't like the other two agents in the trailer. Howard never took his nervous eyes off her, as if she'd disembowel him the moment the generators flickered. The other one, a strange and bookish little blond named Owen Nettles, seemed to have a creepy fascination with David. He spent the first few miles pestering the prisoners with questions about the boy. After his sixth failed attempt to gain answers, he sulked in a dark corner, resting on a blanket like the family dog.

"How you feeling?" Amanda asked Theo.

"Better. No pain. No visions. Whatever they gave me did the trick."

Amanda looked to Melissa. "You must have gotten the results of his hospital tests by now."

"I have them," Melissa confirmed.

"Don't you think he has a right to know what you found?"

Melissa fought the urge to withhold the information as leverage, but they had a long struggle ahead of them. She had to start building trust.

"The scanners discovered a foreign object in your thalamus," she told Theo. "A perfect ring, no larger than a crumb. Any idea how it got there?"

Theo had every idea. His only surprise was that he shared it.

"The Pelletiers. Has to be."

"Why?" Melissa asked. "What's the purpose of the object?"

"I have no idea. I can't imagine it's there to kill me. There are easier ways."

"Is there anything you're willing to tell me about this Azral and Esis?"

"I know you'll never find them unless they want to be found," Theo responded. "You'll never get them in an interrogation room. I just hope for your sake that you never become a problem to them. They slaughtered two dozen of their own employees by remote control. They wouldn't hesitate to do the same to you."

Howard's leg bounced in anxiety, sending soft tapping echoes through the trailer. Melissa stroked her jaw in rumination.

"So what do they want from you? Why did they bring you here?"

Theo shrugged as best he could. "I don't know. None of us know."

"I hope we never find out," Amanda said.

The truck veered to the left, then rolled to a quick halt. Melissa raised her radio.

"Carter, what's going on? Why are we stopping?"

The receiver hissed loud static. "We got an accident up ahead. Overturned truck across both lanes."

"Is anyone on scene yet?"

"Yeah. An ambulance and two local poes."

Melissa muttered a curse. Something didn't feel right. "Okay. Talk to them and see if you can get an estimate."

She scrutinized Theo's face for hints of canny awareness, finding none. Frustrated, she turned to Howard. "Call Michael with our coordinates. I want the rest of the team on standby."

Amanda and Theo watched her closely as her thoughts once again bounced with mad leaps of logic. When it came to the fugitives, no assumption was too far-fetched. Nothing was out of the question. Melissa was living in their world now. She didn't like it at all.

———

Carter Rutledge stepped out the driver's door with a tired grunt. At five-foot-four, he rivaled Owen Nettles as the shortest man in the unit. He battled his stature with a ferociously overpumped build. Even his loose wool blazer flaunted the pneumatic bulges of his biceps.

Like Ross Daley—his colleague, gym partner, and current copilot—Carter did not like having an eccentric female foreigner as his supervisor. They certainly didn't enjoy driving a tug through the sticks in the wee hours, all because their batty new boss was jumping at shadows.

They closed their doors and examined the fracas on the highway, a gaggle of emergency lights in the dark middle of nowhere. A fourteen-wheel bread truck had flipped onto its side, spilling across both lanes at a forty-five-degree angle. A young paramedic pushed the injured driver on a squeaky-wheeled stretcher while three doughy state troopers chatted beside their cruisers.

Ross smirked at his teammate. "I love flashing my badge at these country duffs."

"Careful," Carter teased, "I hear they shoot duskers on sight here."

"In that case, maybe we should bring the boss out."

They laughed and approached the policemen. Ross held up his ID. "Excuse me, gentlemen . . ."

The cops kept conversing, oblivious. Ross cleared his throat and raised his badge higher.

"*Excuse me*, gentlemen . . ."

Still no response. Ross looked to Carter in outrage. "Can you believe this?"

"I can understand why they wouldn't *see* you in the dark . . ."

"This isn't funny anymore."

Ross moved to the nearest officer and reached for his shoulder. His hand passed right through it.

"Oh shit."

The entire accident scene disappeared in a blink, leaving nothing on the road but a lone female figure. In the light of the moon and the tug's distant high beams, they had no trouble recognizing Hannah Given and the deadly .44 she aimed at them.

Zack's open sketchbook dangled in her left hand, a large message scribbled in thick marker ink.

ON YOUR KNEES.
HANDS ON YOUR HEADS.
NOW.

Though she had no way to measure it, Hannah was shifted a speed just shy of 22×. She had over a dozen prefabricated messages written out in Zack's pad, one for nearly every anticipated occasion. She would not slow down for purposes of comprehension. She would not take her eyes off their hands. Though her weapon experience didn't go beyond stage pistols, she was ready to fire a warning shot before they even touched their guns.

The Deps processed her ferocious expression, fueled as much by acting as it was by adrenaline. She impatiently shook the pad at them.

Carter raised his palms. "Okay, look, you don't want to do this . . ."

"She's shifted, you idiot. She can't understand you. Now do as she says. This is your last warning."

Ross and Carter looked around, unable to see the young Australian who just spoke in their ears. David's command was a ghosted echo of words he'd uttered fifty-five minutes ago. He'd created some prefabricated messages of his own.

Stymied, the agents grudgingly kneeled on the pavement, their palms on their scalps.

"Now if you value your lives," said David, "you won't move a muscle."

He emerged from behind the rocky embankment and seized their guns and radios. Ross clenched his jaw as he watched his pistol fall into a knapsack.

"I don't care how young you are, boy. I'll tear you open for this."

"Yes, we're all impressed by your manliness. Put your hands behind your back. Hurry."

Melissa's tinny voice crackled through the fabric of David's bag. "Carter, what's going on? Report."

David motioned to Mia, who'd been watching from behind the rocks. The moment she reached him on the asphalt, he passed her two pairs of handcuffs.

"I need to help Zack. Will you be all right taking over?"

She glanced at the men, then gave David a shaky nod. "Yeah. I think so."

"Don't worry. Hannah will keep you covered."

He stood behind the two agents and hissed a whisper into their ears. "Stay still and do exactly what the girl says. You touch one hair on her head, I'll kill you with your own guns."

Mia could only watch in slack-jawed stupor as David dashed toward the truck. Between the shock and concern over his murderous threat was a savage thrill that would haunt her for the rest of her life. She existed in a dreamlike state, only half-present. Only half-scared.

She studied the handcuffs in her grip, then squinted at the Deps. Her voice fell two octaves.

"All right. You heard the man. Hold still. Don't fuck with me."

Melissa scanned the road through the three-inch crack in the trailer gate. She raised it four more feet and climbed down to the dirt. Howard followed her out.

"Keep them quiet," she told Owen. "Watch Amanda closely."

The agent croaked a querulous mutter, then closed the gate. Melissa raised her gun and motioned Howard around the other side of the truck. She advanced up the driver's side, cursing herself for letting Theo spook her about the Pelletiers.

Soon she spied Carter and Ross up the road, both handcuffed and seething as Hannah and Mia led them behind the rocks. A soft sigh of relief escaped Melissa's lips. The only thing better than a foolish enemy was a nonviolent one. This situation could be turned. If Melissa was lucky, she might even reach Washington with a complete set of fugitives.

She heard soft footsteps behind her, then spun around with her pistol. Zack stood at the rear of the truck, his palms raised high.

"Whoa. Easy. I'm unarmed."

"No you're not."

"Well, I'm as unarmed as I can get. In any case, you don't want to shoot."

"You're right. I don't. But if I see one flash of temporis—"

"It already happened," Zack informed her. "Look at your gun."

Melissa studied her weapon. While she was staring up the road, the barrel had aged several decades. She studied the muzzle, now thoroughly clogged with oxidation.

"Goodness. That's quite a trick, Zack."

"I've been practicing."

"You realize you could have rifted my hand."

"Exactly why I've been practicing."

"I appreciate the extra care, but this was foolish. You won't succeed here."

"We just want our friends back. We're hoping to do it without hurting anyone."

Melissa spun at the sound of Howard's brief yelp at the other side of the truck.

"Seriously hurting anyone," Zack qualified.

"What just happened?"

"A flash of light in the eyes. He'll be fine."

With a futile sigh, she holstered her gun. "Zack, listen to me. My name's—"

"Melissa Masaad. Yes. I'm aware."

Melissa blinked in bafflement. She could never tell which of the fugitives knew her name already.

"You can't keep running," she insisted. "You're smart enough to see that. Sooner or later, your luck will run out and someone you care about will die."

"As opposed to the long and fruitful life we'll enjoy in your Area 51."

"I don't know what that is. If you're talking about scientific dissection, that's not the plan for you. That's not what we want. You have to believe me."

"I don't."

David weaved around the front of the tug with a captured Howard in tow. The handcuffed agent squawked in pain as David pushed him to his knees. Melissa held his shoulder.

"Howard! Are you all right?"

"No! That son of a bitch blinded me!"

"Quit whining," said David. "It's temporary."

Melissa watched him with muted concern. She'd observed the boy through countless ghosts and transcripts. There was always something about him that bothered her, a hint of polished reasoning well beyond his age. Now as Zack flinched with moral unease, David stood eerily calm. He aimed Howard's pistol at Melissa's head.

"On your knees, please. Hands behind your back."

She did as he said, keeping her cool gaze fixed on David while Zack hand-cuffed her wrists.

"You seem to be a natural at this," Melissa told David.

"Thank you."

"It wasn't a compliment. I've chased enough killers to recognize one in the making."

"If that's the extent of your psychological insight, it's no wonder we keep outsmarting you."

Zack plucked the radio from her belt. "As much as I'm enjoying this BBC growlfest, we're on a clock. We know you have one last agent in the back of the truck. If you care about him, you'll tell him to come out with his hands up. We won't hurt him. I promise."

Melissa clenched her jaw, formulating her strategy. Howard had called for backup four minutes ago. They had at least twelve minutes before the rest of her team arrived in shifted aerovans.

"Okay, you both need to listen to me very carefully—"

"No we don't," David snapped. "Stop trying to stall us."

"I'm trying to save your life, boy. You have problems you don't even know about."

"Yes, and I'm sure you'll tell us all about them while your reinforcements arrive."

"I can tell you in twenty seconds," she insisted. "There's a government agency called the National Integrity Commission. They operate outside the law, with virtually no oversight. Like us, they don't enjoy the fact that you're running around the country, causing damage and making headlines. If I don't apprehend you soon, they'll come after you with everything they've got. That's when you end up in the Area 51, as you call it. That's when your worst fears about the government are realized. If you come with us—"

"Time's up."

"If you come with us, Zack, we can avoid that. We'll work with you, not against you. We know about Rebel and Evan and the Pelletiers. We want to stop them just as much—"

A booming gunshot cut her off, making everyone but David jump. He lowered the smoking pistol. A tiny new crater graced the asphalt, ten inches from Melissa's leg.

David grabbed the radio and held it to Melissa's face.

"Now you're out of time and warnings."

Hannah de-shifted, grateful to be out of the blue. Thirty-two minutes of her life had passed on the highway. Her right arm throbbed from all the vigilant gun-pointing.

Ross and Carter remained bound on their knees behind the tall rocks. They bathed Hannah in murderous glares as she reactivated her transmitter. She could hear David in her earpiece, trading curt words with a smartly accented woman.

"What did I miss?" she asked Mia.

"There's one agent left in the back of the truck. They're trying to get him out."

"What do you mean 'get him out'?"

"He could be aiming a gun at the door. We don't know."

"He is," said Carter. "It's standard procedure. But I hope your blondie boyfriend tries to get in anyway. He'll look nicer without a head."

Mia spun around, red-faced. "Shut up!"

"Please, honey. You're about as scary as a teddy bear. Now your friend here, the one with the bouncers, she's got crazy written all over her."

Hannah shot him a dark and defiant grin, then turned her back on him.

"Yeah, that's right, girl. Pretend you're not scared. Just wait till I get out of here. I'll show you a time."

Ross bumped Carter's shoulder, shaking his head with caution. *Be quiet.*

Mia followed Hannah to the road and watched the standoff at the truck. They both flinched when David fired a bullet at the ground.

"Jesus. I really hope he's acting."

"Maybe you should go over there," Mia said. "See if you can help."

"I don't want to leave you alone with these guys."

"They're handcuffed. I'll be fine."

Hannah was never more enamored of Mia. She placed Rebel's gun in her hand, then breathed a quick whisper through her hair. "Don't let that asshole get to you. He's just feeling emasculated. The best way to piss him off is to treat him like he doesn't matter."

Still high from David's ferocious act of devotion, Mia fought a wild grin. It was the strangest time to realize what an invaluable asset she had in Hannah. The actress could serve as her sisterly guide to the opposite gender. She might even help her navigate the tricky maze of David.

"Go. Be careful."

"Thanks. You too. Call me if they give you trouble."

Hannah sped toward the truck. Mia looked down at the heavy weapon in her grip. Her father had taken her to the shooting range dozens of times, but she'd never fired anything this large before. Her finger was barely long enough to reach the trigger.

Behind her, Ross carefully wriggled his hands. The girl was inexperienced in shackles and had left too much room in the right loop. He'd worked it over the base of his thumb. He was nearly free.

Owen's nervous footsteps echoed through the trailer. He'd only joined DP-9 for the ghost drills, and had little interest in handling criminals in their solid form. His pistol dangled in his hand so loosely that Amanda feared he'd kill someone just by dropping it.

"You have nothing to worry about," Theo promised him. "If these are my friends, they won't hurt you."

The agent continued to pace and mumble. "That may be a factual statement, but the momentary scream we heard a minute ago would suggest that at the very least, they're willing to hurt Howard. Had it been Carter or Ross, I would consider the mitigating circumstances, as many people wish to hurt them. But the fact remains that Howard's a nice person. I'm a nice person. And your friends seem comfortable inflicting pain on nice people."

Melissa's voice crackled on the radio. "Owen, do you read? Can you hear me?"

He raised the device. "Yes. I hear you. I also hear strain."

"We've been subdued by Theo and Amanda's companions, but no one's been harmed. Zack and David are here right now and . . . Oh. Hannah just arrived rather suddenly."

Amanda closed her eyes, wincing tears. She never thought she'd see her sister again. Now Hannah was just a few yards away, risking her life, sealing her fate as a national public enemy.

"They're demanding you come out peacefully," Melissa told Owen. "I'm ordering you to disregard. Keep your gun at the door. Fire at anyone who—"

David chucked the radio and pressed the gun to Melissa's forehead.

Hannah grabbed his shoulder. "David, no!"

"Put it away," Zack growled at him. "Enough already."

"She's stalling us until backup arrives! Why can't you see that?"

"I see it. Just like she sees you won't really kill her. You're the one wasting time."

On the contrary, Melissa felt quite convinced that David's threat was genuine. She watched the boy carefully as he turned to Zack.

"The man in the truck has a positional advantage. We're out of 'nice' options. We're out of *reasons* to be nice."

"That's not true," said Melissa. "You haven't harmed us yet. It's not too late to—"

"You shut up! You've done enough already!"

Mia watched the drama from her distant rock cover. She'd never seen David so furious. She considered saying something in her microphone to calm him down.

A strong arm suddenly seized her from behind, covering her mouth. Ross switched off her transmitter and snatched her gun. She could hear the jingling of his loose handcuff as he pressed the heavy barrel to her temple.

"You're lucky I'm a good guy or your brains would be splattered all over those rocks. Now I'll burn in hell before I shoot a little girl, but if you make any noise or trouble, God help me, I'll crack you one. You hear me?"

Her heart thumping madly, Mia quickly nodded.

"Now tell the truth, girl, because I'll know if you're lying. Do you have the handcuff key?"

She shook her head. Ross threw a sigh at Carter. "Sorry, man."

"It's okay. I don't need my hands to do a rounder."

"All right. Good plan. Give me two minutes to get in position."

Ross held Mia closer. She could smell his sweat.

"You and I are going to take a walk now. You better hope your friends behave. I got no qualms about putting a bullet in any of them."

Mia's thoughts screamed as Ross pulled her back into the darkness.

The future continued to evade Theo, lost in a dwindling fog of chemicals. He knew from Howard's call that at least eight more Deps would be here in minutes. He wanted to yell the news through the trailer wall, but he didn't know if Zack would hear him. He also wasn't sure how Owen would react. The strange little agent was becoming increasingly unglued.

"This is . . . this is . . . no. I don't like it. I don't like it at all. She was supposed to bring wisdom to the department, like Athena. Instead she calls for violence, like Ares. Or Andy. She has grown the metaphorical mustache and become her predecessor. And now she asks me to shoot."

"Then don't," said Theo. "Just drop the gun and go outside. They won't hurt you."

"The door's locked from the other side. You're trapped in my dilemma. I think—"

A banging noise from outside made Owen flinch. He aimed his gun at the door.

"Okay, Owen, listen to me—"

"Theo, let the man work out his problem! You're not helping!"

Owen tossed Amanda an obliging nod. "Thank you. My inner chorus is loud enough."

Theo looked at her confusedly. Her expression was more pleading than stern. She mouthed a single word. *Wait.*

Soon Owen retreated into his tizzy, mumbling in the rear corner of the trailer. The moment he turned his back, Amanda slumped in her chair, struggling to thrust her right foot as far as it could go beyond the boundary of her solic generators.

Now Theo understood, though he was no less surprised. He had no idea Amanda could generate tempis from her feet. She'd only just learned it herself last week, when she unwittingly shredded her socks in a fit of Zack-related anguish. She wasn't sure if her trick would work now. The white beast inside her felt heavy and languid, as if riddled with tranquilizers. Amanda gritted her teeth in concentration, willing it awake.

Theo kept a nervous eye on Owen. The agent still didn't notice Amanda's new pose, or the fact that her sneaker was beginning to swell.

Hannah paced the road in furious bother while Zack and David studied the back of the tug. It seemed insane that they'd come this far only to be hindered by a single door and Dep.

"I'll open it," said Hannah. "If I'm fast enough . . ."

Zack shook his head. "It's a sliding gate. The moment you lift it, you're a stationary target."

Melissa fought a laugh over their inflated impression of Owen Nettles. The man was more in danger of hurting himself.

"It'll leave your midsection exposed," she told Hannah. "Which is exactly where my man will shoot. He knows abdominal injuries are slow to kill. We'll have plenty of time to get you to a reviver."

"You need to stop talking," David urged.

"You know he has a crush on you, my agent in there. I'm not one to judge—"

"I said be quiet!"

"Or what? You'll shoot me in the head?"

"If that's what it takes!"

"David . . ."

Melissa smiled wisely. "No, Zack. Let him work it out. The boy's gotten a taste for power now. I do believe he likes it."

David lurched toward her. "You don't know the first thing about me!"

"I know you would've killed me if Hannah and Zack hadn't stopped you. I know it wasn't morality that stayed your trigger finger. You care what your friends think. You want them to keep trusting you."

Hannah yelled as David grabbed Melissa by the collar. Her grin turned fierce.

"Go on, boy. Show them. Show them the real you."

"David, stop! You're doing exactly what she wants! You're helping her stall for time!"

He looked to Hannah with wide-eyed revelation. "You're right. You're absolutely right." He tossed a cynical laugh at Melissa. "Wow. I was told you were smart, but you're downright brilliant. You played me like an amateur."

Melissa silently cursed Hannah. She'd hoped the stunt would buy a few more minutes.

"Well, I'm impressed," David said. "Feel free to keep talking. I'm no longer . . ."

His smirk disappeared when he noticed Carter standing ninety feet up the road. Though the agent's hands were still cuffed behind his back, he grinned like all was right with the world.

David raised his collar mic. "Mia?"

Now Zack and Hannah joined him in worry. Hannah tested her own mic. "Mia, are you there?"

Zack turned pale. "Uh, Hannah, can you please—"

She shot up the road in a dusty blur. Zack traded a wary glance with David. "I don't like this."

Neither did Melissa. She had a dark feeling that Carter and Ross were pulling a two-man rounder, a risky tactic used to turn the table on armed aggressors. Unfortunately, its success relied on the enemy's ability to drop their weapons. These people were their own weapons.

She bent a knee in nervous readiness. "Zack, David, I need you both to stay perfectly still . . ."

Thirty feet behind them, Ross emerged from the shadows, his hostage still muffled in his grip. He raised the gun. Mia forced a scream through his fingers, loud enough to turn David around.

Melissa jumped to her feet. "Wait!"

Ross Daley had been fully prepared to shout a warning. The words had moved from his mind to his throat. *Don't move! Don't move!*

Unfortunately, David was quicker. He raised his palm and hurled the first loud noise he could find, the warning shot he'd fired two minutes ago. The ghosted echo struck Ross like a cherry bomb, rupturing both eardrums.

It also prompted him to fire.

David watched helplessly as the bullet cut through his right hand, severing two fingers at the base before continuing into the night. The shock of his wound kept him mindless and frozen for three and a half seconds, through the many events that happened next.

The moment he spied David's bloody hand, Zack lost hold on all reason. For the second time in his life, he focused his weirdness on Rebel's gun without any concern for the hand that wielded it. Melissa shoulder-barreled him before he could launch his attack. They tumbled together to the dirt.

Mia worked her teeth around Ross's index finger, biting him deep enough to draw blood. The agent yelled and threw her to the ground. He aimed the gun at her head.

"Goddamn it! Goddamn! You little bi—"

A sudden windy force slammed him from behind. He flew eight feet through the air, then skidded six feet across the road.

Hannah de-shifted at the place of impact, her stunned gaze fixed on her victim. She'd shoved him in the back at 120 miles an hour, hearing and feeling the snap in his spine. Now he writhed on his back, wide-eyed, broken. The actress covered her mouth with both hands. *God, what did I do to him? What did I do?*

David remained in shell shock at the two gushing stumps on his hand. Once the agony of his wound caught up to him, he fell to his knees and screamed.

Mia pulled off her sweatshirt and ran to him. She tried to wrap the garment around his hand. He savagely struggled away from her.

"David, stop it! Stop! You're bleeding!"

Melissa clambered back to her feet. She glanced down the road at her fallen agent.

"Oh goddamn it. Goddamn it. Zack, you need to let me out of these cuffs."

The cartoonist kept his tense stare on David. "Go to hell."

"Zack, I have a seriously injured man—"

"—who shoots at unarmed kids!"

"Not unarmed! And not a kid! I don't know if you're deliberately blind to your friend's nature, but it's moot now. Look around you. It's over. Your only choice now—"

A loud and echoey *thump* seized everyone's attention. They all turned to look at the truck. A second *thud* bulged the gate as if an angry rhino pounded at it.

Melissa closed her eyes. "Shit."

Now a huge tempic fist knocked the door from its track. It dropped to the road in a resounding boom.

Theo and Amanda stepped out into the night, their broken shackles dangling on their wrists. The relief of escape lasted three short steps before Mia cried from the side of the truck.

"Amanda! Help us!"

She rushed to David's side. "Oh God. Mia, we need alcohol. We have to disinfect this."

"W-we brought a first aid kit. It's in the car. I can get it."

"No. Help me get him there. Backup's coming. We need to go fast."

Hannah kept a wide and unblinking gaze on her victim until Theo gripped her shoulders and gently turned her around. She took a trembling moment to process him, then wrapped him in a tight embrace.

"I didn't mean to . . ."

"It's okay."

"I didn't know how fast I was going."

"It's all right. They'll fix him."

Even as he said it, Theo knew nothing would erase the consequences of her actions. The Deps would remember what Hannah did. They'd probably shoot her on sight next time.

Zack moved behind Melissa and rusted the chain of her handcuffs. She broke them apart.

"Thank you. Now I know you can simulate a juve. What about a reviver?"

His mind flashed back to the dead deer in Nemeth. "No."

"If you could heal him, Zack, it would go a long way—"

"If I could heal people, I'd be healing David."

Melissa ran to Ross and checked his vitals. "It's all right. There's still time to get him help. We can still fix this, Zack. Everything I said still applies."

The cartoonist took Hannah's free arm and helped Theo escort her away. As the Silvers moved up the hill in two hobbling trios, Melissa shouted after them.

"We can protect you! With enough time and cooperation, we'll even free you! We'll give you a life on this world! Citizenship! Identity! What do I have to do to convince you?"

Theo turned around to face her. "We believe it's what you want, Melissa. We don't believe it's what we'll get."

"If you think you're better this way, then you don't know a damn thing about the future. You're walking to your own deaths! Please listen to me!"

They disappeared over the dark crest. Melissa closed her eyes and pressed a fist to her forehead. "Goddamn it."

Soon she heard an electric engine start. She watched a boxy white minivan swerve onto the road, kicking a cloudy trail of dust as it sped to the east. She couldn't read the license plate from her vantage. It didn't matter anyway. The fugitives would ditch the vehicle before Melissa could get a trace warrant. She wasn't dealing with amateurs anymore.

THIRTY

The old man wasn't happy to have guests. The moment the minivan rolled into his garage, he threw an antsy scan around the neighborhood, then closed the power gate. Zack had barely stepped out of the driver's door when a gnarled and stubby finger poked his chest.

"You the leader?"

The cartoonist stammered. He'd never considered the title before and he didn't enjoy wearing it now. "I'm Zack."

"I don't want to know your name. I just want to know if you're the man to talk to."

In his recent portal delivery, among all the notes and handcuffs, Peter included directions to a house in Quinwood, West Virginia, seventeen miles east of the highway ambush site.

His name's Xander. He'll be expecting you. He won't be pleasant but he'll hide you. He has no love for Deps.

He stood just a thumb taller than Mia, with a scrubbed pink face and the flawless gray bouffant of a news anchor. Despite the early hour, he wore a sharp blue blazer ensemble with a red silk ascot and matching pocket square. Zack figured the man stood out like neon in this rustic little town, a Truman Capote in a sea of John Waynes. Not that the Silvers were any less conspicuous. Four of them were dressed like burglars while two sported the blue prisoner jumpsuits of DP-9.

Xander covered his mouth at the sight of David's gory hand, which had already bled through its dressing and now dripped a crimson puddle.

"Oh, Lord no. He didn't tell me you'd have injured people bleeding all over my rugs."

Amanda narrowed her eyes at him. "Peter didn't know. If you have towels—"

"Take what you want," he said, his palms raised in high dither. "I was never here. You're merely robbers who broke in while I was visiting my sister."

The hair-dryer whirr of an aerocar motor turned all heads to the door. Theo peered through the glass.

"Get away from the window!" Xander yelled.

"A taxi just pulled into your driveway."

"It's mine. I was hoping to be gone before you showed up."

He thrust a set of keys in Zack's hand, then gestured at his small red sedan.

"You have three days before I report it missing. If you're still driving it by then, it's your problem."

"I understand. Look, we have money. We'll pay for whatever we—"

Xander cut him off with a scoffing hiss. "You people never change. You think you can buy your way out of any fix."

Zack blinked at him in dark wonder. *He thinks we're Gothams.*

"Listen, if you talk to Peter—"

"I won't," Xander insisted.

"—tell him the Deps are watching him."

He snorted a chuckle. "The Deps are all fools to a man. If they're watching Peter, it's only because he's letting them."

The cab honked. Xander lugged his suitcase to the door, then turned around one last time.

"Don't bleed on my rugs. Don't abuse my cat. Don't be here when I get back. And when *you* talk to Peter, you tell him, 'No more favors.' My debt's officially paid."

He sneered at Amanda's thick metal collar, a remote-triggered gas dispenser that the Deps typically used on lunatics twice her size.

"They finally admit you exist now. At long last, the Bureau believes."

He left them in the garage, all grim and exhausted in the wake of their messy battle. Mia didn't care that she was standing around in her flimsy undershirt, or that she still tasted the blood of the Dep she bit. All her dark thoughts revolved around David. The poor boy had screamed all throughout the van ride as Amanda disinfected his wounds. Now he'd become dark-eyed and listless, a living corpse.

It killed Hannah to see him like this. David had been their strongest wall, their toughest spine. Now the universe had broken him as thoroughly as Hannah broke the back of that federal agent.

She wrapped her arms around Theo, burying her face in his chest. He rubbed her shoulder and looked to the minivan.

"Zack, if that thing has an antitheft tracker—"

"It does. I'll rust it." He scanned the group, his nervous eyes lingering on David. "You guys should get some rest."

Mia held Amanda's arm. "You want me to find a towel?"

Through the garage-door glass, Amanda watched Xander depart. The Deps may have been fools to a man, but she knew they had one smart woman. A second encounter with Melissa seemed all but inevitable. Next time she wouldn't bother with sleeping gas.

Amanda rubbed her brow with a bloody hand, too tired to even cry.

"No. Screw the rugs."

The house was as posh and immaculate as its owner. The living room teemed with modernist sculptures, abstract paintings, and bizarrely shaped furniture that seemed more ornamental than functional.

Mia reclined in a lounger, stroking the neck of a fat black cat while she replayed the events of the morning. She could only imagine how her dad and brothers would have reacted to seeing their sweet little treasure on the highway, growling threats at federal agents as she cuffed their wrists. She might have seized the mantle of Meanest Farisi if she hadn't screwed up so badly.

She chewed her pen in somber thought, then scribbled into her journal.

The time may come when you need to put handcuffs on people. When you do, make them tight. I didn't, and David got shot because of it.

Now that she was freed from the fear of paradox, she could send any messages she wanted through her past portals. It brought her a modicum of comfort to think she could create a branching timeline where that agent never broke free and seized Rebel's gun. The note would make all the difference in the world to a parallel David. She only hoped this one could forgive her.

He slouched at the kitchen table, processing his wound with bleary misery. The bullet had reduced his ring and middle fingers to stubs, turning his right hand into a crude, misshapen trident. The sight of his infirmity, his obscenity, forced his rage into a single vengeful beam. It didn't point at Mia.

"I warned you," he told Amanda, through a hoarse and jagged rasp. "I warned you what would happen if you took Theo to that health fair. Do you believe me now?"

The widow sat at his side, bandaging his hand in grim intensity. "I'm sorry."

"You're sorry. Just like you were sorry when you ignored Mia's warning and confronted those policemen. Just like you were sorry when you nearly killed Hannah and Zack with your tempis."

Amanda hid her torment behind a face of stone. She knew from experience that not all patients were brave in the face of their pain. Some were downright cruel.

"If you would just take an epallay—"

He slapped the patch from her hand. "I do *not* want that chemical filth in my body. I'd sooner wear leeches."

Mia shut her eyes in a tortured wince. She could hear David's every word from the living room and anxiously waited for her due share of the rancor.

"You're a stupid woman, Amanda. As stupid as you are sanctimonious. The fact that you even lecture other—"

The violent slam of a car hood cut him off. Zack treaded in from the garage and threw David a baleful glare on the way to the sink. The boy's deep blue eyes narrowed to slits.

"You have something to say to me?"

The cartoonist scrubbed his greasy hands under the faucet. "He was bald and black."

"Excuse me?"

"The agent who shot you. He was a bald, black man. I'm only telling you this because you seem to have him confused with Amanda."

She raised a palm at Zack. "It's all right."

"No, it's not all right. I know he's hurt right now—"

"Hurt *right now*?" David stood up and brandished his hand. "Do you think this is a temporary condition, Zack? Do you expect to heal me like you so brilliantly healed that animal? At least Amanda's fearsome in her incompetence. You were just a joke out there. The way you took Melissa's side against me—"

"You were acting like a psychopath!"

"I did what had to be done!"

"All you did was prove their worst fears about us! Even I was scared of you!"

"Even you," David mocked. "You're scared of everything. You're the most cowardly man I've ever known."

Amanda shot to her feet. "Okay, stop it! Stop. This isn't the time for this." She looked to David. "Please sit down and let me finish."

"No! I've had it with both of you!"

"David . . ."

"You don't ever *listen* to me! None of you listen! I'm fighting to keep you all alive but you just . . . you . . ."

David sucked a sharp breath as hot knives of fire shot up his arm. All his life, he'd been a stranger to pain. He'd never broken a bone, never pulled a muscle, never suffered a burn or laceration . . . at least not that he could remember. And now here he was, suffering an agony that was medieval in its cruelty. It was powerful enough to shatter every mask and pretense, every chiseled image of the person he fought to be.

As David fell to his knees and cried, Zack winced in self-reproach. He blew a heavy breath. "Listen—"

"No," David sniffed. "I'm done listening to you. I'm done protecting you. You can both go die for all I care."

Mia's heart skipped a beat as David hurried through the living room. He was halfway up the stairs when he heard her high voice, barely a whisper.

"I'm sorry."

He stopped mid-flight to look at her. From the new lines of grief on his beautiful face, Mia guessed he was done being vicious. She expected her rebuke now to be one of gloomy disappointment. *I gave you one task, Mia. One. You couldn't even do that.*

Instead, he continued upstairs without a word.

Mia vented a heavy breath and continued to pet the purring feline in her lap. Her grandmother always told her that black cats were good luck for good people. Mia didn't even think she needed it. While her friends all suffered fractures and gunshots, concussions and amputations, she had yet to get a single scratch. The one bullet that was fired at her had missed her head by millimeters.

She peered down at the cat, her tortured mind bargaining with the forces of fate. *Give me the next one,* she implored them. *Whatever bad thing happens, you leave them alone. You give it to me.*

Hannah spooned Theo on the futon, listening to his gentle snores while she stared at the wall in restless discomfort. The musty little office reeked of old age and iodine, and her wrists still throbbed from shoving that agent. Every time she closed her eyes, she could see his body skid across the highway in slow motion, scraping bloody patches with each impact.

She gave up on sleep and sauntered out to the hallway. Through the crack of a bedroom door, she saw Mia snoozing away on Xander's queen-size bed. The fat black cat sat dejectedly at her side, mewling for his new best friend to give him more love.

The sound of whistling laughter drew Hannah to the stairwell. She crouched down and peered into the living room, where Amanda and Zack stretched side by side on a wide chaise longue. They looked like a cozy married couple in their long T-shirts and underwear. Morning light cracked through the wood blinds, striping their bare legs.

Amanda rolled onto her side and fought an indignant grin as Zack giggled deliriously.

"You just find that hilarious, don't you?"

She'd just finished explaining how she subdued Owen Nettles in the back of the truck. While the peculiar little agent paced and mumbled, Amanda summoned a burst of tempis from her toes. Owen turned around just in time to see the man-size foot coming at him. Before the whiteness could even touch him, his eyes rolled back and he fainted to the floor.

Amanda had been too stressed at the time to find it funny. Even now her humor was tempered by the fact that she owned only one shoe.

Zack wiped his eyes and moaned. "You should've seen us outside the truck. We were so scared of what that guy might do. Melissa made him sound like Joe Kickass."

"He was not Joe Kickass," Amanda said. "I'm just glad I didn't hurt him."

Disenchanted with Mia, the cat sauntered down the hall and rubbed against Hannah. She caressed his back, praying she wasn't her sister's next topic of discussion.

Amanda pursed her lips in a droll pout. "I'm so glad David called me stupid. That's just what my self-esteem needed today."

"At least he didn't call you a coward."

"Right. I lack a brain. You lack courage. All we need now is a tin man."

Zack plunged into another fit of punch-drunk giggles, until his humor gradually melted away. He smeared his bleary eyes.

"I shouldn't have gotten on his case like that. He was probably just blustering out there. It's not like he hurt any of them."

No, Hannah thought. *I'm the one who left a victim.*

"He's just in pain," Amanda told him. "He has a long recovery ahead of him. The best thing we can do is be there for him, without judgment. He needs siblings now, not parents."

Hannah suppressed a jaded laugh. It took an extraordinary lack of self-awareness for Amanda to equate siblings with nonjudgment.

Zack closed his eyes and cracked a boyish grin. Amanda eyed him flippantly. "Still tickled about the tempis?"

"No."

"Then what, pray tell, are you smiling about, Zachary?"

He folded his hands over his chest, his expression serene and contented. "Just nice to have you back."

Hannah scowled cynically in the tender silence that followed. *Shit. Here we go.*

Amanda nestled up against him, resting her hand on his. As their fingers laced together, she suffered an unwelcome flashback to her alley encounter with Esis, the madwoman's stern and cryptic warning. *Do not entwine with the* [something something]. Amanda couldn't salvage the rest from her trauma-scarred memories. She had larger concerns now anyway.

She heaved a jaded sigh across Zack's chest. "You're a schmuck."

He chuckled at her *shiksa* Yiddish. "Why am I a schmuck?"

"Because you're being all sweet and I know it won't last. You always run hot and cold with me."

"Says the woman who sat on my lap, then threw me off a balcony."

"You still blame me for that."

"No. I always blamed Evan."

"Then why did you get so distant after that?"

Zack considered pinning that on Evan too, but then he'd have to explain the teasing hint about Amanda and Peter, a romantic prophecy that still bothered him to no end.

"I'm too tired to open that box," he replied. "Let's just agree I'm a schmuck and move on."

Hannah watched the cat roll around on the carpet, purring in mindless bliss. For a moment, she thought Amanda and Zack would do the same. Now she wasn't sure if they'd kiss, fight, or fall asleep on each other. In any case, it was time to leave them alone.

Just as she rose to her feet, Amanda took Zack's advice and changed the subject.

"I'm worried about Hannah."

A sharp new panic gripped the actress, freezing her in place. Her inner self waved her on with flapping arms. *Go! Leave! You don't want to hear this!*

"She'll be all right," Zack assured Amanda.

"You've only known her ten weeks. I've known her her whole life. I know what trauma does to her."

"You're looking down from the big sister perch."

"I'm not looking down, just back. She has a history, Zack. It's right there on her wrists."

A storm of screams brewed in Hannah's throat. She clenched her fists and vanished into the bathroom. The startled cat bolted down the stairs, past the chaise longue.

Amanda raised her head at the scurrying footsteps. "What was that?"

"Bad luck," said Zack.

"Great. Like we need more."

Amanda fixed a tense gaze at the sleeping-gas collar on the coffee table, a grim souvenir of her incarceration. Forty minutes ago, she asked Zack to reverse the lock, a task he'd initially refused out of fear of rifting her. She had to remind him that he was a man of minor miracles, able to rot a swinging banana from twenty feet away, grow keys out of keyholes, and turn old mice into young ones. He'd led an actress and two teenagers into battle with armed federal agents, and won.

Ultimately he'd indulged her, concentrating on her collar with the sweaty apprehension of a bomb defuser. The moment he popped the lock on her very last shackle, Amanda's regard turned a hot new color and she fought the urge to kiss him. Now as she pressed against him, his heartbeat thumping against her breast, she wished she had her sister's skill with men. She wished she could find just the right words to express her feelings, her qualms.

Then she considered that Zack was an artist. Maybe he didn't need words.

Thin white strands of tempis slowly sprouted from her forearm, twisting around their locked hands like ivy. Zack leered with grinning marvel as small white leaves sprouted from the vines.

"Wow. Amanda, that's beautiful. You ever do that before?"

"No."

Her ropes wrapped tighter around them, driving the point home. The cartoonist aired a loud, somber breath.

"Guess we have a bit of a problem."

"Guess we do," she said.

"I don't know what to do about it," said Zack. "I spent four years in a bad entanglement."

Amanda fixed a heavy stare at her naked ring finger. "Five and a half."

"With everything going on, I'm not sure I can handle another one. I'm not saying it's inevitable. Just possible. And after all the drama with Theo and Hannah . . ."

The tempic leaves withered. The vines retracted into Amanda's skin. Zack checked her grim expression.

"I just pissed you off again, didn't I?"

She shook her head. "No. I understand your hesitation. It's smart."

"Then why do I feel so stupid right now?"

"Because you know."

"Know what?"

"That we don't have much longer to live."

Amanda struggled to her feet. Zack watched her as she moved to the shuttered window.

"You know they're going to get us sooner or later, Zack. Whether it's the Deps or Rebel or Esis, it's just a matter of time. And yet here I am, worrying about being a proper widow. Here you are, worrying about the fights we might have a month from now. There is no month from now, Zack. Not for us. Maybe we should just . . . I don't know . . ."

Zack joined her at the window and gently turned her around. When she realized he was simply drawing her into a hug, she fell into his arms with maniacal relief. Yes, yes, yes. Hugs were good. Hugs were safe.

"I'm sorry, Zack. I'm all over the place. I don't know what I'm saying right now."

He caressed her back. "It's all right. You had a crappy day by anyone's standards."

"Make it better. Say something sweet to me."

"Can it be about your looks?"

"No."

"Because you're very, very pretty."

"I don't care," she said, though she held him tighter anyway. She cared a little.

"All right. Give me a moment to think it over." He rested his chin on her shoulder, amazed that her hair could smell so good after twenty hours of captivity.

"You remember when we were on the balcony—"

"Oh God, Zack."

"No, no. I'm not talking about that. I'm talking about the moments before, when you and I were cracking each other up with silly wordplay. I said I was antaganostic. You called yourself a tempis fugitive."

She bloomed a wobbly smile. "I remember."

"Yeah, well, that's when I started to get nervous, because there aren't a lot of people who can crack bad puns in Latin, or go joke for joke with me like you did. I knew from the start that you were strong and smart and very, very pretty, but nobody told me you were funny."

The widow's lips curled in a wavering smile. Zack pulled back to look at her.

"I have no idea what's going to happen with us, Amanda. I just know that women like you are jackpots to guys like me. You don't think short term with jackpots. You don't screw them on the couch when they're feeling vulnerable. I'll wait as long as it takes for us to get our shit together. I don't want to go the way of Hannah and Theo. We do this right or we don't do it at all."

Amanda held him so fiercely, she feared she'd break his ribs all over again. When she first met Zack, she had no idea that he was a rigid perfectionist, an uptight moralist, a minder, a mender. No wonder it felt so good to hug him. They were practically twins.

She ran a gentle hand down his cheek. "I really want to kiss you right now, but I won't."

"I wasn't saying it to—"

"I know. I'm just thinking ahead. Wherever we end up running, whether it's Brooklyn or Canada or God knows where, the six of us are going to rest and heal. And then once we get our act together, you and I are going to slip away for an evening. I don't care if it has to be the second room of our criminal hideout, we're going on a date. Some things have to be done the normal way. Even for people like us."

His responding smile was warm enough to melt her. Amanda embraced him again, speaking stern but trembling words over his shoulder.

"Just don't die on me, Zack. Don't you dare die on me."

He pressed her back and let out a glum sigh. "I can only promise to try."

"Well, if you ever need more incentive, you think about our third date. I'm not Catholic about everything."

Amanda covered his loud laugh, and then tensely bid him good night. She would have loved to rest with him down here on the couch, but the temptation to do something—

(do not entwine)

—would mess up their wonderful new plan.

She scrambled upstairs in dizzy haste, then conducted a stealthy check on the others. Theo and Mia were visible in their rooms. David and Hannah were tucked away behind closed doors. Amanda stowed her concerns, then climbed into bed with Mia.

As her eyelids fluttered with teeming fatigue, the widow's mind shot like fireworks into the many branching futures. She pondered all the obstacles between her and a happy life, counting her issues like sheep.

Just as she began to drift off, the dangling wires of her memory connected and Esis breached her thoughts once again.

Do not entwine with the funny artist.

Amanda's eyes sprang open in hot alarm. She stayed awake and disturbed for hours.

At the jagged tail end of his twenty-hour slumber, Theo fell into a dream that by now had become painfully familiar. He existed as a disembodied spirit, a formless being drifting slowly through a silent gray void. A bright white wall stretched endlessly in front of him like a vertical tundra, radiating a bitter coldness that chilled him to the core.

Theo dreaded coming here, but this was his job now. There was something he needed to find on this wall. He was the only one who could do it.

He kept moving without any idea of direction. Up, down, left, right. It all looked the same. It was only when he moved toward the wall that he could make out the infinite beads of light that comprised its surface. Each one was burning agony on his thoughts, like a magnified sunbeam. He kept his distance and never stopped moving. He had so much area to cover. Too much. Whenever he thought about it, an arch panic overtook him, *I can't do it, Peter. The wall's too big. The string's too thin. I'll never find it. I don't even think it exists.*

And yet he kept traveling, searching the wall for the one little strand that meant everything to everyone. The only thing worse than being in this cold and dreary hell was leaving it, since he knew he'd have to face his companions and tell them once again that he failed.

Though they always thanked him for trying and assured him that tomorrow would be a better day, Theo could see the heartbreak behind their expressions. They knew as well as he did that there were only so many tomorrows left. While he flittered and flailed on the other side of the wall, his friends were merely waiting. Waiting for the sky to fall again.

He jerked awake on the futon, his chest moist with sweat. He did a double take at the clock when it told him that it was 2:12 in the morning. Theo had slept nearly a full day in this dingy little office. Even his coma didn't last that long.

He relieved himself in the bathroom, gargled a shot of mouthwash, then lumbered down the stairs. The smell of sizzling bacon made his mouth water. He'd barely had a bite to eat since Nemeth.

The moment Hannah saw him, she dropped her spatula in the frying pan and hugged him.

"Thank God. I was starting to get worried. How you feeling?"

"Like Rip van Winkle." He saw Zack and Mia at the table. "You're having breakfast at two A.M.?"

"We did some heavy sleeping ourselves," Zack said.

The cartoonist seemed awfully chipper for a man on vampire time. Mia, by contrast, looked thoroughly morose. She aimed a dull gaze at her lap through her tangle of bangs.

Hannah pushed him to the table. "Sit. I'm making waffles too."

Theo studied her carefully as she returned to the stove. He knew her well enough to recognize the "everything's fine" voice she used when she was bottling her anger at someone. He could practically hear the creak of the crossbow string. Mercifully, the quarrel didn't seem to be aimed at him.

He took a drowsy gander at the map book in Zack's hands. "We leaving today?"

"I don't know. Depends on David."

"Well, you know what he'll say."

"I'm talking about his health, not his preferences. If Amanda says he's not ready, we're staying."

Theo gazed out the window at the lumic lamppost. "She'll be waiting for us in New York."

"Who, Melissa?"

"Yeah. She knows exactly who we're going to see."

"Peter's a dozen steps ahead of the Deps," Zack replied. "He knew just where your truck would be, how many agents were guarding you. I don't think those people are a problem for him."

"You think Peter's an augur too?" Hannah asked.

Zack shook his head. "No. I'm guessing he's more like Mia. The two of them have some kind of portal juju going on."

Mia's expression grew darker. She'd received two new messages from her future self earlier, neither of which offered any practical value. One of them was cruel enough to make her cry. If Peter shared her affliction, she pitied him.

Theo jerked a lazy shrug. "I'm still not sure what to think of the guy, to be perfectly honest. I just hope—"

A sudden stabbing jolt caused him to wince and press his temple. Hannah rushed to his side.

"Theo!"

"I'm all right," he assured her. "It's okay."

"It's not okay. If your problem's coming back—"

"It's just a headache. I'm fine."

Zack eyed him warily. "Have you had any premonitions since they drugged you?"

"Not a one," Theo said, hoping that was true. The great white wall still loomed large in his thoughts.

Mia's stomach gurgled with stress as she recalled the first vague note she'd received from her elder self today.

Don't get too comfortable. You're not out of the storm.

Amanda sat quietly on the guest bed, tending David's wound with edgy distraction. Though the widow had steeled herself with five deep breaths before knocking on David's door, she was pleasantly surprised to find him genial. His pain was just a fraction of yesterday's. The stumps of his fingers showed no signs of infection. Amanda thanked God for the double mercy. She couldn't have handled a second attack of scorn. Not in her state.

David studied Amanda warily as she unwrapped a new roll of bandages. "How's Mia?"

"She's all right. Worried about you."

He sighed with lament. "The way I acted, I don't blame her. I've never experienced pain like that before. It was . . . enlightening."

Amanda eyed him strangely. "Enlightening?"

"Ever since it happened, I've been thinking about the people of the past, the way they accepted agony as just another part of their lives. With all our advancements in technology and medicine, I'm wondering if perhaps we lost something as a species. A certain fortitude."

"No one can accuse you of weakness, David. You're one of the strongest people I've ever known."

"Well, I appreciate you saying that." He cracked a dour smirk. "If Nietzsche's right about the things that don't kill us, then Zack's really going to be afraid of me soon."

Amanda felt a hot stab of anguish at the mention of Zack. She clenched her jaw and kept working.

"He's not afraid of you," she uttered.

"Then why did he call me a psychopath?"

"For the same reason you called me stupid, okay? He was upset. If you had stayed in the kitchen ten more seconds, he would have apologized."

David eyed her with sharp surprise. He'd noticed her tension from the moment she entered the room. Now the woman who'd handled him so calmly yesterday seemed to be coming unglued.

"Amanda, I'm sorry for the way I behaved yesterday. I really am."

"That's not why I'm . . ." Her eyes darted back and forth in quandary. "Can I pick your brain about something? In absolute confidence."

"Of course. What about?"

"Esis."

His sandy eyebrows rose in intrigue. "Wow. Okay. I mean I'm not sure how much insight I can give you. I only met her once."

"Well, you're the only other person I know who's spoken to her. She . . ."

Amanda fought to explain her conundrum. All throughout her sleepless day, she'd replayed her back-alley encounter with Esis, reconstructing it word by word. By sundown, she'd pieced together the woman's full warning. *Do not entwine with the funny artist. I grow tired of telling you this. You entwine with your own, you won't be a flower. You'll just be dirt.*

David listened to the story with abject fascination, stroking his chin with the arched brow of a sleuth.

"Wow. That's . . . huh. At the risk of embarrassing you, it seems fairly obvious who she was referring to, and what she meant by 'entwine.'"

Amanda nodded brusquely. "Yes. I know that. But how did she even . . . I mean . . ."

"How did she know that you and Zack would become intimate?"

She flinched in discomfort. "We haven't. Not yet. But she gave me that warning before I even met him."

"Well, clearly Esis is an augur of some sort. It's not like we don't know any."

"But why would she care who I . . . entwine with?"

The boy gazed ahead in deep rumination. He started and stopped himself twice before speaking.

"She did say something odd to us, me and my father. He was with me when she gave me my bracelet. She just popped into our living room through a glowing white portal in the wall. Now that I think about it, I wonder if it's the same temporal mechanism that Mia uses for her notes."

Amanda wound her finger impatiently. "What did she say?"

"She told us the world was ending in minutes, that I was moving on and my father wasn't. Had the portal not lent her a certain latitude for wild assertions, we might have dismissed her as a lunatic. But my father certainly listened. The whole thing made him rather . . . Well, if you knew him, you'd know how rarely he shows emotion. But at that moment, he was overcome."

David pressed his knuckles to his lips, his face marred with twitchy grief.

"I half expected him to plead for his life, so he could continue the work that was so important to him. But to my surprise, his one pressing question to Esis was 'Will my son be all right?'"

Amanda held his arm. She could understand now how David had become so resilient. The poor boy had practically been raising himself since he was ten.

"Anyway, Esis was sympathetic," he said. "She assured my father that I'd be in good health and excellent company. I remember her exact words on this. She said, 'He'll only be alone for a short while. Then he'll be joined with his brothers and sisters.'"

The floor of Amanda's stomach dropped. The room suddenly felt three times smaller.

David shrugged pensively. "I'd always assumed Esis was being figurative. But now—"

"That's not it," Amanda stammered. "That's crazy. I know who I come from."

"And I know who I come from. I've seen the video of my birth. Doesn't rule out the possibility that our mothers were surrogates."

"How can you even say that?"

"I'm just exploring the options, Amanda. We know the Pelletiers existed on our world. We know they chose us. We just don't know when. Maybe they had an active role in our creation, forging us all from the same genetic template. If that doesn't describe siblings, what does?"

Amanda stood up on watery legs. She leaned against the dresser.

"That's insane. We can't all be related. I mean Theo's . . ."

"Asian. Yes. He might be an exception. Or perhaps their genetic engineering capabilities are more advanced than we realize."

"But no one warned Hannah about entwining with Theo." *Did they?* she suddenly wondered.

David chucked his good hand in a listless shrug. "I don't know. In any case, if the Pelletiers are indeed augurs, then perhaps they knew that Hannah and Theo were destined to fail as a couple. Maybe they foresaw a more lasting union between you and Zack."

Her throat closed tighter. "That's not . . . You're just guessing all this. None of this is proof."

"Proof? No. But Esis did warn you about entwining with your own. And there's one other thing I neglected to mention, something I've pondered every day. Maybe it's why he didn't ask more questions . . ."

"What are you talking about?"

David sighed. "When Esis appeared in our house, my father already knew her name."

Amanda closed her eyes, fighting to hold herself together. She thought back to the incident on the Massachusetts Turnpike, seventeen years ago. Her father never uttered the Pelletiers' names. But then he never asked for them either. Did he already know? Did both her parents know them?

She rushed to David's side, squeezing his biceps with rigid fingers. "Listen to me. Whether you're right or wrong about this, we have to keep it to ourselves. You hear me? Until we get absolute proof, we don't breathe a word of this to the others."

"If you wish."

"You especially don't tell Hannah and Theo. They don't need this."

"I said okay, Amanda."

David watched her cautiously as she cleaned up the bandage debris. "Guess you have strong feelings for him."

"I don't want to talk about it."

"Fair enough. But Amanda, there's something you need to consider . . ."

"No."

"Yes. This needs to be said. Whether you believe we're all siblings or not, you know for a fact that Esis doesn't want you entwining with Zack. You know she gets angry about it."

"What are you saying?"

David studied his bandaged hand with dark and heavy eyes.

"I'm saying that for your sake and his, you might want to start thinking of him as a brother."

At a quarter to three, David joined the others in the kitchen for breakfast. Mia was thrilled to see him swap warm apologies with Zack, and beamed with gushing relief when he squeezed her hand under the table. It scared her how easily David could move her to good and bad places. She wondered if that was a sign of being in love.

The bacon and waffles were nearly all gone by the time Amanda came downstairs. She met Zack's bright cheer with a nervous half grin, then avoided his gaze for the rest of the meal.

Soon Theo sucked a sharp breath in pain, grinding all conversation to a halt. He glanced around at his worried friends, then sighed with futility.

"Yeah. I think it's coming back."

Zack tapped the table in tense resolve. "All right then. That settles that."

"What settles what?"

"As soon as we're ready, we're saying good-bye to the cat and hello to Peter."

He scanned the faces of the others, lingering an extra second on Amanda. "Anyone have a problem with that?"

Hannah, Theo, and Mia slowly shook their heads, censoring their many leery doubts about Peter. Amanda merely stared at her empty plate, deeply lost in other concerns.

David was the only one who smiled. No one needed to ask him how he felt on the matter.

The bathroom mirror was nothing more than a floating lumic projection. It was impervious to fogging, and could reflect at six different viewing angles.

As Mia finished drying herself, her elbow brushed a button on the wall. Suddenly the picture changed to a rear view. Unhappy to be mooning herself, she reverted to the traditional reflection, then squinted curiously at her body. There seemed less of her now than usual. She must have shed at least ten pounds since fleeing Terra Vista.

She slipped on her clothes and ran a drying wand over her hair, examining herself with sunny awe. Between the weight loss and David's forgiveness, her mood was nearly healed from the battering it took earlier, when she received the cruelest message yet from future times.

I hate you. I despise you with every fiber of my being. You're so hopeless, so clueless, so utterly blind to the things happening right under your nose. The Pelletiers are laughing at you, Mia. Semerjean is laughing.

I'd spoil the joke for you if I could, but it really doesn't matter. Just take my advice and kill yourself. We should have never come to this world. We should have died in the basement with Nana.

Even now, hours later, Mia reeled from her own venom. She couldn't spend the rest of her life as the whipping girl for every Future Mia in a black mood. If the girl with two watches was right, then the problem would only get worse.

Mia suddenly heard sharp, angry voices outside the door.

"Okay! All right! I was just asking, Hannah!"

"You're not asking! You're blaming!"

Mia put down the heat wand and groaned. *God. Not this. Not now.*

The sisters stomped through the bedroom, both half-dressed and flailing in jittery rage. While Hannah stuffed unfolded garments into duffel bags, Amanda rummaged through Xander's closet.

"There's a difference between being upset and being upset at *you*," the widow snapped. "I'm upset because I only own one shoe now!"

"And you're upset at *me* because I left your other pair at the lake house!"

"Did I say that? Did you actually hear me use those words?"

"You didn't have to. It was all in your tone. Do you think we just met?"

Amanda shook her head in trembling pique, throwing shoe after shoe over her shoulder. Of course the old man had the narrow feet of a ballerina. She was destined to go barefoot to Brooklyn.

"You always do this, Hannah. Always."

"Always do what?"

"Take your bad moods out on me. I know what you're really upset about."

"Oh do you now?"

"You hurt that agent. I get it. I hurt two cops so I know exactly what you're going through. But do you come to me for help? Of course not. You decide to yell and scream at me, *just like you always do!*"

"Excuse me. Who's screaming now?"

Amanda jumped up from the floor. "I am! I'm screaming at you now because I can't take it anymore! You wear me out!"

Hannah clenched her jaw and looked away, her foot tapping maniacally.

"You think I'm weak. You think I'm so goddamn weak. Have you considered the fact that maybe I'm only weak around you? Maybe *you're* the one who—"

The bathroom door flew open. Mia barged into the room, her wet hair throwing droplets in arcs. She snatched a pair of sandals from under the bed and chucked one at the feet of each sister. She waved a quivering finger back and forth between them.

"No more. I'm not sharing a room with either of you ever again. I don't care if I have to sleep outside in a dumpster. I can't do this anymore."

Amanda and Hannah watched her in matching stupor as she stormed back to the bathroom. She spun around at the door, fighting tears.

"You think I wouldn't kill to have my brothers here? You think Zack wouldn't kill to have his brother here? You have no idea how lucky you are, and yet all you do is fight. There's something seriously wrong with both of you."

"Mia—"

She slammed the door behind her, jostling a picture from the wall.

Dead-faced, silent, Hannah made a slow trek out of the room. Amanda sat down on the bed and calmly gathered the sandals. As she slipped them over her feet, she thought once again about David's theory and realized that the DNA didn't matter. The six of them lived and screamed and hurt each other like family. They were all siblings down to the bone.

The Silvers rode the final leg of their journey in dismal silence. Xander's red Cameron Arrow was a skinny little car with two platform rows that were better suited for couples. Zack's arm brushed Mia every time he turned the steering wheel. She could feel Theo's body tense up whenever he suffered a new flash of pain. She held his hand, caressing it with worry. Her future self once told her that it was more important to get to New York in a strong state of mind than it was to get there fast. She had no illusions about anyone's current condition.

David slept soundly in the back, his head flopping in turns between each sister's shoulder. As Hannah fixed her surly gaze out the window, her dark emotions flew back and forth across the car. She faulted Amanda, then faulted herself. She hated Amanda, then hated herself.

By the time she snapped out of her doleful trance, the Arrow had shot out of a tunnel and into a great urban thoroughfare.

Hannah blinked at the sight of yellow taxis and Jewish delis. "Wait. Are we . . . ? Is this . . . ?"

Zack shined his searchlight gaze around at all the lumic signs and tempic storefronts, these alien embellishments to the city he once knew. Though he was finally back in his native Manhattan, the cartoonist never felt farther from home.

"This is it," he said, with a nervous exhale. "We're here."

PART FIVE

STRINGS

THIRTY-ONE

The traffic light was nothing but a floating disc of lumis, two feet wide and red as a sunset. Fat gray pigeons fluttered through it while a hunched old woman crossed the street between tempic guardrails. A ghosted billboard stretched the length of the intersection, hawking heart-healthy breakfast cereal to idled drivers.

Zack leaned forward and craned his view at the near and distant streams of flying cars. He'd counted seven different levels of traffic when the light turned green, the billboard vanished, and the tempic rails gave way to open road.

Mia tapped his wrist. "Zack."

He snapped out of his trance and pressed the gas pedal, marveling at the taxi in the rearview mirror. A true New York cabbie would have honked him into oblivion for dawdling at a green light. This wasn't Zack's city on any level. Calling this place New York was like calling a dog a zebra, or swapping the concepts of blue and yellow.

"This should be Soho," he uttered. "I mean we came out of the Holland Tunnel, so . . . I don't know. I don't know what they call it now."

Mia stroked his wrist with sympathy. Though she'd never set foot in the old New York, a future self had sold this world's version as a paradise beyond description, beautiful enough to evoke tears. Now she glanced through dry eyes at the windblown scraps of litter, the garish assault of animated ads. *Wrong again,* she seethed. *You just keep giving me bad information.*

Amanda writhed uncomfortably in the backseat. She could feel every tempic construct within a half-block radius, a hundred cold fingers pressing her thoughts. Barricaded storefronts stretched along both sides of the street, each one ready to ripple and dance for their visiting queen.

"What time is it?"

David checked his watch. "Half past ten."

She eyed the stores suspiciously. "Middle of a Tuesday morning. Why is everything closed?"

Hannah stroked her lip in bother. The whole city seemed eerily quiet at the moment. There were only a handful of pedestrians on each block, most of them dressed from head to toe in lily-white garments. A husky street vendor sold a wide assortment of white Venetian masks.

"Something weird is going on here."

"It's not just here," said Zack. "Everything was closed in Jersey too."

Mia's eyes bulged at a masked young couple in white bathrobes and sneakers. The man brandished a hand-painted placard that said *New York Thrives on 10-5.*

"Commemoration," she said.

"What?"

"Ten-five. Today's the anniversary of the Cataclysm."

The Silvers glanced out their windows with fresh unease. They recalled Sterling Quint's discussion of the great temporic blast that destroyed half of New York City on October 5, 1912. The day had become a major holiday in the United States and a near-religious event here in the rebuilt metropolis.

The Arrow turned north onto 6th Avenue. Mia read the scrolling lumic banner that stretched above all lanes. *This is our day, New York. The whole world is watching. Show them why this is the greatest city on Earth, now and forever.*

Zack shook his head in exasperation. "I don't know if our timing's really good or really bad."

Mia plucked Peter's day-old message from her shoulder bag and reread it. "We need to find a pay phone."

"I'm looking."

"Maybe we should look on foot," Amanda suggested. "Get out and stretch our legs. If we can."

One by one, the others checked on Theo in the front passenger seat. He'd spent the whole ride with his head against the window, twitching in restless slumber. Now his eyes were wide open and marked with deep red veins. His headaches had once again become bundled with visions, prophetic flashes too quick and obscure to make any sense. The only clear image he saw was Azral Pelletier. His harsh and handsome face popped up over and over, enough to erase all doubt. The white-haired man was coming back as sure as the moon, and probably sooner.

Theo glanced out at a distant flurry to the east. "I think I see where everyone went."

The Ghostwalk was a ritual that dated back to the first Commemoration in 1913. It began as a silent procession down 3rd Avenue—fifty thousand mourners in white robes and masks, all marching for the souls of the lost. As the years progressed and cracked hearts slowly healed, the Ghostwalk grew a fluffy tail of musicians, dancers, and other sunny revelers who sought to honor the dead by celebrating life. The cavalcade expanded each year until it became known as the March of the Spirits.

Today the twin parades were joined in bipolar harmony, the yin and the yang, the grief and the joy. The event moved to Broadway in 1942, starting at 96th Street and ending at City Hall Park.

The Silvers caught the tail end of the Ghostwalk at 14th Street, at the corner of New Union Square. They hovered at the edge of the crowd, watching the parade through their newly purchased masks. They indulged the vendor when they saw aerocycle cops scanning the crowd from twenty feet above.

Mia felt ridiculous in her butterfly eye-mask, even though half the locals around her wore sillier disguises. She stood on her tiptoes in a vain attempt to peer over the wall of spectators.

David offered her a smirk and a hand. He looked like a superhero in his white domino mask.

"Let me give you a lift."

Mia's brow curled in worry. "You're hurt."

"My spine's just fine. Come on."

She climbed onto his back with wincing dread. To her amazement, he didn't even grunt. Maybe she'd lost more weight than she realized.

"You sure this isn't hurting you?"

"You'd know," David sighed. "As you saw yesterday, I don't handle pain very well."

The procession continued past them. The majority of ghostwalkers wore plain white bathrobes. Some women sported snowy gowns. A few men were decked out in formal ivory vestments that had been passed down for three generations. The one item that never varied was the mask, an expressionless white face with black fabric eyeholes. The uniformity created an eerily powerful effect. For a moment Mia imagined she was watching the departed souls of her world, all the teachers and classmates and neighbors and cousins who didn't get silver bracelets. And to think she'd snapped at the sisters for not realizing how lucky they were. She was alive. She was alive on the back of a beautiful boy with the heart of a lion and an unflinchingly deep regard for her. Mia never stopped replaying the scene on the highway, when David threatened to kill two Deps if they harmed a hair on her head. She wasn't just lucky, she was blessed.

Mia locked her arms around David and heaved a warm sigh over his shoulder. "Don't feel bad."

"About what?"

"The way you acted yesterday. We don't care about that. You've been there for us since day one and we love you. We'll love you no matter what you do."

She breathed a soft whisper into his ear. "I'll love you no matter who you kill."

Though the mask lay still on his impassive face, David's voice carried a thin new tremor.

"You're a rare and precious jewel, Miafarisi. I dread the day our paths diverge."

Everyone turned to look as booming cheers erupted to the north. Exuberant music blared up the street. The last of the Ghostwalk was exiting the square. Now came the March of the Spirits.

Amanda crunched her brow behind her white burglar mask as confetti guns popped and the locals turned jubilant. The crowd had gone from funeral to Mardi Gras at the turn of a dime.

She sneaked an anxious peek at Zack, a parallel study in conflicting extremes. His rabbit-eared mask radiated levity while the eyes behind it screamed with bewilderment. He stood right next to her, but he might as well have been a thousand miles away.

She took his dangling hand in hers. "It has to be hard for you. Coming back to your hometown and finding it so different."

Zack threw an antsy glance at the drugstore behind him, where a public phone lay encased inside an opaque metal cylinder. A red light on the door indicated that the tube was currently occupied.

"I don't know," he said. "It seems like every big difference in this world can be traced back to the Cataclysm in one way or another. Guess I shouldn't be surprised New York changed the most."

The first of the parade platforms approached, ferrying a gorgeous young blonde in a star-spangled minidress. She crooned a bouncy tribute to New York into her microphone while a thirty-foot ghostbox displayed a giant live projection of her buxom upper half. Zack noticed the empty space beneath the platform's hanging drapes. It seemed aeris had turned all the floats literal.

Amanda stroked his hand with her thumb, then grimaced in affliction when he pulled it away.

"Zack . . ."

"It's all right. I understand."

"Understand what? We haven't had a chance to talk."

He pursed his lips in a crusty scowl. "If it's a 'let's just be friends after all' speech, I don't need to hear it. You've been wearing it on your face for the last seven hours."

Amanda threw a quick nervous glance at David, five feet away.

"It's not what you think," she said to Zack. "I've been waiting for the right time to explain it."

"You don't have to explain anything. It happens. It's not like we signed a contract."

Amanda clenched her jaw. She knew Zack well enough to see the mask behind the mask. He was determined to play the breezy teflon shrugger until one of them screamed.

"Would you listen to me? I'm not backing out. There's just . . . a new complication."

Exuberant children in brightly colored jumpsuits lined every edge of the second float. They reached into buckets and flung foil-wrapped candies at the crowd. Zack gave Amanda his full attention, even as a chocolate coin sailed between them.

"I'm all ears."

She shook her head. "Not now. When we're alone again, and when you're less angry—"

"I'm not angry."

"No. Of course not. You're just convinced I dropped my feelings for you on a fickle whim. Why would that anger you?"

"Well, what did you expect me to think? Yesterday we had a nice plan worked out. Today you can barely look at me. I've had seven hours to scratch my head over it. All I have now are a bloody scalp and a few second thoughts of my own. Maybe it wasn't such a good idea after all. Maybe it'll be easier for everyone if we just forget it."

Tiny spikes of stress tempis hatched from Amanda's feet, piercing the straps of her borrowed sandals. She banished away the whiteness, then cast a thorny glower at the parade.

"I swear to God, Zack, sometimes I think you're played by twins. I never know which one of you I'm going to get."

"Great. Maybe the four of us can go out for burgers sometime."

"Go to hell."

Amanda cut through the crowd, her jaw held rigid with forced composure. Zack tossed another glance at the pay phone before trading a desolate look with Hannah. She wished the two of them would get over their issues, whatever they were, and just screw already. She feared she and Theo were partly to blame for their hesitation. They didn't provide the best sales brochure for the carpe diem hookup.

They sat side by side on an unattended shoeshine stand, their faces both covered in weeping theater masks. Theo's head dipped and jerked erratically. Hannah couldn't tell if he was asleep or lost in premonitions. She ran gentle fingertips up and down his forearm. The caress always seemed to soothe him, no matter how far gone he was.

"Where's the happy face?"

Hannah jumped at the high voice next to her. A cute young brunette leaned against the wall. She wore a sleeveless white gown that hugged every contour of her elfin body. Her long brown tresses matched Mia's hairstyle to the strand. If it wasn't for the girl's honey skin and vaguely Eurasian features, Hannah might have wondered if a Future Mia had sent herself back in time.

"I'm sorry. What?"

"You and your fella are wearing the same theater mask," the stranger noted. "It's supposed to be one happy face and one sad face. You know, Thalia and Melpomene. The Muses of comedy and tragedy."

Hannah felt silly to be conversing through a disguise. She pulled it away. The girl studied her.

"Nope. Still sad, but prettier now. Damn, hon, you're a scorcher. I bet you drive all the boys wild."

The actress bloomed a bleak little grin. "Not enough to keep them."

"You seem to be doing all right with that one."

Hannah peered at Theo, oblivious in his torpor. "It's not like that."

"I wasn't slapping a label on it. I just see the way you're comforting him without a second thought or a 'what's in it for me?' Whatever you are to him, he's lucky to have you."

It was the sweetest notion Hannah heard in days. But for all the girl's rosiness, she wielded a sad face herself. She held a glossy mask in her hand, the plain white façade that Hannah had spotted ad nauseam five minutes ago.

"You were in that first parade."

"The Ghostwalk. Yeah. I do it every year, though I never make it the whole way without losing it. I'm probably the only one who still cries about the Cataclysm. Everyone else is thinking about their aunt Jody or that dog who ran out in the road."

"Well, you can hardly blame them. It happened a century ago."

The girl shrugged tensely. "What can I say? I'm a slow griever."

The next float ferried four lithe young women in black rubber speedsuits, prancing around the platform in slow ballet motions. Suddenly their gear glowed with patchwork strips of color and they swayed around each other in a hazy blur. Hannah watched in gaping astonishment as their streaking hues combined to form ethereal images—an ocean sunset, a city skyline, a crude American flag. The crowd cheered wildly with each new tableau.

Soon the quartet de-shifted and resumed their gentle mincing. The girl smiled at Hannah's slack-faced awe.

"Guess you've never seen lumis dancers before."

"No. That was incredible. Jesus. I don't know how they do that without breaking a bone."

"Years of practice," said the girl. "Takes months to rehearse one routine. You should see what the Chinese do with it. Their stage shows are mind-blowing."

"Do they have one here?"

"Here? God, no. You'd have to go to China."

Hannah snorted cynically. "Yeah. That'll happen."

"Hey now. You never know. Someday someone might jaunt you around the world just to put a smile on that sexy face."

"I don't have until someday."

The girl narrowed her eyes. "Sweetie, you know you're in trouble when a chick who just marched in a five-mile death parade is telling you to lighten up."

Hannah smiled despite her mood. She realized how nice it would be to have a friend outside the group, a fun and witty galpal who could bring some sanity back to her existence. If only it were possible.

"I'm Hannah. What's your name?"

The girl kept a busy stare on the parade. "Ioni."

"Wow. That's very pretty. It really suits you."

"Oh stop it. I'm already a little gay for you. You're just poking the fire."

Hannah laughed. "If you can hide me from my life, Ioni, I'm all yours. You can have me any way you want."

"Wow. That's quite an offer. What exactly are you running from, Hannah?"

"Everything," she sighed. "Everyone."

"Even the people who need you?"

Hannah looked to her sister, staring down at the pavement in a somber daze. The thought that Amanda might need her was a strange new concept, as alien as anything in the parade.

"I don't know. Part of me wants to run away on my own. Change everything about myself until no one can find me. The other part of me's sick of travel. Sick of change."

Ioni fixed a sudden nervous eye on Theo. She took a step from the wall.

"We've been running for so long," Hannah continued. "It's taking its toll on all of us. I don't think we can last like this another—"

"Hannah, listen. I need you to stay calm, all right? Don't make a scene."

"What?"

Theo suddenly fell into violent seizures, shaking hard enough to knock his mask off. His eyes rolled back. His skin glowed with a faint and sickly sheen, as if he'd become his own ghost.

Ioni rushed to his side and pressed her fingers to his temples, bowing her head in concentration. Soon Theo's luminescence faded and the convulsions stopped. He fell into restful sleep.

Hannah jumped out of her seat, bouncing her saucer gaze between Theo and Ioni. "What . . . what did you . . . ?"

"He peaked a little too early. I'm buying him some time." Ioni threw a tense glare at the busy pay phone. "You guys really need to get to Peter."

Hannah noticed the dual watches on Ioni's right wrist, and suddenly scrambled to recall her secondhand knowledge of the mysterious stranger who'd approached Theo and Mia in the Marietta library. Odd that Mia had described her as a short-haired blonde. Odder still that Hannah didn't notice her watches sooner. She must have deliberately hidden them behind the ghostmask in her hand. Ioni had been wearing her disguise all along.

Hannah scanned the backs of her other four companions, still occupied with the parade.

"Don't call them," Ioni urged. "I only came here to talk to you."

"Who the hell are you?"

"Calm down. I'm not your enemy."

"Why should I believe you? You lied to me. Pretended you were a stranger."

"I *am* a stranger, Hannah. If I had an ounce of sense, I'd stay that way. This isn't my struggle."

"Then why are you following us?"

"There's no 'us.' Just Theo."

"Why him?"

Ioni looked to Theo and sighed. "It's complicated. Suffice it to say that I have a special empathy for augurs, this one in particular. It gives me a modicum of comfort to help him through this rough patch."

"Help him? You already hurt him!"

"What do you mean?"

"You're the one who told Mia to bring him to the health fair. We took your advice. If you knew what would happen—"

"I knew he'd get treated."

"He got arrested!"

"And then he got treated," Ioni replied. "In the augur game, it's never a direct line from A to B. If you want things done, you have to make bank shots. Theo will learn that soon enough."

Hannah shot her a baleful glare. "People got hurt."

"People always get hurt. There's no such thing as a perfect future. Someone always gets the pointy end."

"Who *are* you?"

Ioni rubbed her weary face. "You can't handle the answer. Not today. Just take comfort that I'll be out of your hair in a minute. Once I'm done here, none of you will see me again for at least two years."

Hannah looked to Theo. "At least tell me what you're doing to him. Are you healing him?"

"There's nothing to heal. These are just birth pains and they're almost done. In thirty-eight minutes, he'll be stronger than he's ever been in his life."

Hannah's brow arched. "I want to believe that."

"You'll see soon enough. But listen, hon, it's not all roses. By the end of the day, he'll have a whole new burden. He'll need you more than ever."

"What are you talking about?"

"He's been doing penny ante stuff up until now. Parlor tricks. Very soon he'll know the true nature of his talent. Power like that can ruin a person, Hannah. You have to keep him anchored. You and Mia and Zack and Amanda, you're his family now. Comfort him. Love him. Yell at him, if need be. Just don't let him fade away into the futures. That's where people like Theo become people like Azral. You do not want that."

Ioni's pretty young face twisted with hatred. She raised a stern finger.

"The time may come when you'll be tempted to trust the Pelletiers. Don't. They destroy worlds, Hannah. They destroyed yours twice."

The actress felt a sharp flutter in her stomach as she tried to process all the new information.

"You're right. I can't handle this."

"I said you couldn't handle my story. I have every faith you can handle yours. I've seen you in times to come, Hannah. You're magnificent."

The actress flicked a hand in hopeless bother. "If you know so much about the future, then help us."

"I just did."

"Tell me something I can use to save someone I love."

"Sweetie, I just did."

Hannah clenched her jaw, exasperated. Ioni lay a gentle hand on her wrist.

"If I could fill your life with smiles and happy faces, I would. But the future doesn't work that way. It's a map that's always changing. I can't even guide you through the minefield of today without steering you wrong. All I can tell you is to be brave, be strong, be there for the people who need you. You do that and you'll be okay."

"If the future's always changing, how can you be sure?"

Ioni bloomed a sage little grin. "There are some events in life that are so reliable, we don't bother predicting them. The sunrise. The full moon. The rainbow after a storm. These are all things that can't be stopped by mere mortals. You know what the augurs call them?"

"What?"

She took Hannah's hand and breathed a soft whisper through her hair.

"Givens."

Ioni kissed her cheek, then backed away. Hannah looked into her palm and found a small folded square of purple paper. A crude pencil drawing of a theater mask graced the front. A happy face.

Once Hannah glanced up again, the girl with two watches was gone.

She took a heavy gulp of air, then reclaimed her seat on the shoeshine stand. She fumbled with the seams of her paper construct until she gave up and stuffed it in her jeans pocket. Her hard drive was already overflowing with wild new data. She couldn't take another byte.

Theo continued to twitch in somnolent anguish. Hannah stroked his arm with her fingertips, rolling Ioni's words around her thoughts like boulders. *You have to keep him anchored. You and Mia and Zack and Amanda, you're his family now.*

A cold flutter gripped Hannah's heart when she caught Ioni's glaring omission. Why didn't she mention David?

The light on the pay phone turned green. The door swung open and a gaunt old woman exited the tube. Zack tapped Mia's shoulder.

"You're up."

She fed enough coins into the slot to buy twenty-six minutes. A recorded voice asked her to close the tube door and kindly spare others from her business. Mia ignored it.

While she listened to the dulcet chirps of Peter's ringing phone, she cleared her throat and peeled off her silly mask. *As if he'd see you,* she chided herself. *As if he'd judge.*

Zack paced her side like an expecting father, doubling her anxiety. She forced her gaze past him, onto the bulky gray bank machine that stood against the neighboring wall. It reminded her of a video poker console with its seven large buttons and crude pastel graphics. A dark glass beacon rested on top like a novelty fez. She assumed it only flared in the event of criminal tampering.

After two minutes and thirty rings, Amanda and David joined Zack in his fretful hovering. Mia shrugged in tense surrender, then hung up. Loose coins drizzled into the return tray.

"You sure you got the number right?" David asked her.

"Yeah. I double-checked."

"Try again in a few minutes," Amanda said. "He could just be—"

The pay phone rang. Mia leapt at the handset, plugging her free ear with a finger. "Hello?"

A taut male voice filled the receiver. "What's your name?"

"What?"

"Your name. Say it."

"Mia. Mia Farisi."

The voice loosened up. "All right. Just had to make sure. You guys in the city?"

"Yeah. We're here. Can you—"

"And you're together. All six of you."

"Yes. We're all together. Can you just ease my mind and confirm that you're—"

"Peter Pendergen," he replied. "You called my house a few weeks back and spoke to my son Liam. The two of you had a misunderstanding about the definition of 'pen pal.' Better?"

Mia sighed contentedly. "Yes. Thank you. And I'm sorry about that call. If I put him in danger—"

"No. He's fine. My people would never hurt him. Listen, I'm being watched. I don't have much time. You got a pen and paper?"

"Yeah. Always."

He dictated an address in the Battery Park district of Manhattan and then, with a brusque impatience that bothered her, made her read it back.

"I'll be there in five minutes," he said. "Come as quick as you can."

"Okay, but can you bring whatever painkillers you have? Theo's—"

He hung up before she could finish. Mia kept a dubious stare on the receiver.

"Everything all right?" Zack asked.

"Yeah. I guess."

"What's the problem?"

"Nothing. He just seemed nicer in his letters."

Amanda moved to the shoeshine stand, flanking Theo's side while Hannah gently shook him awake. He blinked at the sisters in drowsy puzzlement, then surveyed the parade.

"What . . . what are we doing back here?"

"We never left," Amanda said.

Hannah rubbed his shoulder. "Are you okay?"

"No. I'm confused. Last thing I remember, we were picking you both up from the roof."

"What roof?"

He rubbed his eyes. "I don't know. I feel weird."

Hannah fumed at Ioni. *What the hell did you do to him?*

"We're going to see Peter now," Amanda told him. "Are you okay to walk?"

Theo nodded unsteadily. "Yeah. I can walk."

As the group regathered, Mia took a final glance at the bank machine. She knew they were called "cashers" here and that they were maintained by the state government. They could be used to pay taxes and traffic tickets, even renew a drinking license.

Behind the dark round glass on top of the console, the civic camera continued to fix on Mia. It knew a few things about her as well.

Melissa snapped awake in her swivel chair, dazed and half-blind. She brushed the dreads from her face and glanced around the narrow van. A chubby young blond in a sweatsuit yawned at his surveillance console. He was yet another unfamiliar face from the Manhattan DP-9 office. Melissa had dozed right through a shift change.

She arched her sore back. "Did I miss anything?"

"No ma'am," the agent replied.

Quarter Hill was located fourteen miles north of the city, a wealthy little hamlet nestled snugly inside a ten-foot tempic wall. The gates were guarded by a security firm that had been cited several times by police for overzealous force.

Melissa peeked over the agent's shoulder at the thermal imaging display, where two orange silhouettes casually moved around the dark blue backdrop of a living room. From all indications, Peter Pendergen led a perfectly mundane life. When he wasn't typing away at his latest novel or debating Irish history on Eaglenet forums, he lounged around the house with his thirteen-year-old son. If anything, it was the hint of anguish in Liam Pendergen's voice that suggested something wasn't right.

The conversation in the living room came to a halt. The father took his son by the shoulders and drew him into an embrace. The directional microphones picked up a gentle whisper.

"Call your team," Melissa said. "Tell them to get ready. Pendergen's about to move."

"What did he say? I couldn't hear it."

"Neither could I. But that's a good-bye hug if I ever saw one."

Her handphone beeped with a new text message. She pulled it from her pocket.

Case Lead Alert. Oct-5. 11:07am. Civic Camera #NYS-55-1948C (New Union Square). Sighted: Farisi, Mia. Kidguard Facial Recog: 98%.

Melissa opened her computer and logged into the camera alert network. It had been four weeks since she added the ghosted images of the fugitives to the facial map database. As minors couldn't be entered into the Blackguard registry of criminals at large, she threw David and Mia into Kidguard, the archive of missing children. The effort finally paid off.

Her screen displayed a grainy still photo of the group's youngest member. Mia cradled a pay phone handset and scribbled something into her ever-present journal. Three tall people stood behind her. Though their masks prevented the camera from making positive IDs, Melissa had no trouble recognizing David, Zack, and Amanda.

As she phoned the local office, she kept her somber gaze on Mia's frozen image. *Should have kept your mask on.*

Rosie Herrera was Melissa's equivalent at the New York DP-9 branch, a stout and square-jawed matron who endlessly groused about the Bureau's glass ceiling. Fortunately, she wasn't too jaded to help.

"They can't have gotten far," she told Melissa. "Let me call my guy at the precinct."

"No. The police aren't prepared to handle these people. All I need is your fastest ghost team at Union Square. The girl wrote something in her book. I'm guessing it's a new meeting address."

Melissa's phone beeped with an interrupting call from a person marked simply as *Nameless*. She narrowed her eyes at the screen.

"Rosie, hold on." She switched lines. "Cedric?"

Cain chuckled. "Professional pointer: when a shade hides his name, you don't say it out loud."

"Look, this isn't the best time . . ."

"I know. I got the same alert you did. Don't bother with the ghost drills. In five minutes, I'll know exactly where your runners are headed."

Melissa's stomach churned as she tried to guess his methods. Integrity's resources were as frightening as their freedoms.

"I see," she replied. "So this is an anonymous tip then."

"No. That's coming. This is just a heads-up warning to gather your forces and gather them big, because you've got one last chance to bring these people in. They get away this time, it's out of my hands. They'll become Integrity's problem, and vice versa."

Melissa rubbed her aching back. "I understand."

"Good. Make your calls. Get ready for mine. And next time, don't say my name."

He hung up. Melissa heaved a loud breath, then switched lines again. "Rosie?"

"Yeah. I'm here. You still need that drill team?"

"No. Now I need everyone."

The young agent leaned forward in his chair, baffled by the thermal scanner. A moment ago, there were two orange figures on the monitor. Now there was just one. In the blink of an eye, Peter Pendergen had vanished.

Battery Park was one of the few areas of Manhattan that had to be rebuilt twice. In August of 1931, a clash between police and pro-immigrant protesters erupted into a citywide riot known as the Deadsetter's Brawl. It culminated with a massive blaze that killed 112 people and destroyed half the new buildings on Battery Place.

Today the street was a posh and pristine beauty, flanked by acres of lush greenery to the south and sleek glass office towers to the north. Commemoration had turned the business side into a tranquil void. Pigeons merrily strutted about the concrete, free to forage without the usual human bustle.

Zack found a parking spot mere yards from their destination, a twelve-story structure of sloped steel and mirrors. The entire ground floor was enclosed in a thick sheath of tempis.

Amanda swept a nervous scan of the area. "So where is he?"

"Inside," Mia guessed. She motioned to the four-foot metal post that stood near the barrier. "There's the buzzer."

"Seems like a strange place to meet. I mean, why here?"

"I'm sure it's all just part of the zigzag," Zack speculated. "He's dodging his own people as well as the Deps."

Hannah tapped a tense beat into her thigh. She didn't have the strength to tell her companions about her encounter at the parade. Now she reeled in the dark subtext of Ioni's comments. She'd called today a minefield. What if this was the first bad step?

They chose to travel light for their rendezvous, limiting themselves to one knapsack each. Zack nestled the last of their cash in a front flap. The sisters combined their essentials into one bag, saving their strength for an ailing Theo. They propped him up like crutches and walked him to the building.

Mia hunched over the intercom and pressed the call button.

"Uh, hello? Peter?"

After five seconds of silence, a ten-foot square of tempis melted away to reveal a pair of swinging glass doors. They unlocked with a hollow click.

The Silvers moved dazedly through a brushed stone foyer, past the unmanned security desk. The directory listed fifty-four different companies in the building, everything from law firms to placement agencies for corporate augurs. Zack swallowed a daffy chuckle when he noticed a nonprofit advocacy group called the Justice League of America.

Suddenly the tempis sealed up behind them, blocking the doors like a snowdrift. Hannah fixed her round white eyes at the barrier.

"I don't like this."

"If Peter wanted to hurt us, he would have done it already," Zack insisted. "He could've killed us all in our sleep at that old man's house."

Amanda eyed him cynically. "The Pelletiers don't want us dead either. Doesn't mean they have good intentions."

Zack looked to David. "This is the part where you say something smart and assuring."

The boy had little to offer at the moment. A bad bump of the arm had set his wounds on fire. Between the agony in his hand and the area's screaming history, David could barely hold a thought. He cast a blank stare down the hallway.

"We came a very long way to meet this man. Might as well finish what we started."

The hallway soon opened up to a gargantuan lobby of polished green marble. Four towering ghostboxes swirled with abstract holograms while a bubbling stone fountain filled the area with serene white noise. Above the four balcony levels, a giant lumic projection of clear blue sky turned the chamber into a synthetic courtyard.

Mia looked around with discomfort. This stony paradise reminded her too much of the Pelletier lobby in Terra Vista. What if Peter was merely an-other Sterling Quint in waiting? What if they'd traveled 2,500 miles just to come full circle?

"Hello at last."

The Silvers threw their busy stares around the lobby, and soon discovered a brown-haired man sitting alone among the many sofa clusters. He propped his feet on a coffee table and shined them a guarded smile.

"You've been through stitch and strain, my friends, but you did it. You're here. Now the hard part's over and you get some well-deserved rest."

He motioned them over. "Come. Sit."

He was dressed in a simple blue button-down over jeans, with white run-ning shoes that were faded at the soles. His feathered hair was peppered with hints of gray and his steel-blue eyes were marked with gentle crow's-feet. Even while lounging, the man radiated a coarse virility. He was a Hollywood gum-shoe in color, an Indiana Jones between sequels. Hannah figured he was the type of man she'd go wobbly for in ten to fifteen years, when she was finally done with moody creatives.

Amanda looked at his handsome face and saw a hint of something that bothered her, the same artificial cheer that Derek had always carried around terminal patients.

"You're Peter Pendergen."

"That I am," he replied, in the same curt voice that had ruffled Mia over the phone. "Which pretty sister are you?"

"Amanda."

"Ah yes. The formerly incarcerated. Glad to see you guys got out of that fix in one piece." His gaze wandered to Theo, still lost in a harrowed daze. "Mostly."

Mia took the farthest easy chair in the cluster. "So . . . what happens now?"

"Now we talk of a great many things. If you like what I have to say, then we move on together. If not . . ." He forced a nonchalant shrug. "We go our sepa-rate ways with no hard feelings."

Zack perched on the arm of Mia's chair. "You sure it's safe to talk here?"

"Normally it wouldn't be, but you did a good thing by coming on Com-memoration. I paid off the few security guards on duty. We have the whole building to ourselves."

He looked to David, shuffling restlessly behind a love seat. "Have a seat, lad. I don't bite."

"It's okay. I'd rather stand."

Theo moaned with pain and bedlam as the sisters walked him to the sofas. His consciousness had become a rapid-fire montage of premonitions, all as vivid and real as the present. He dodged falling debris in San Francisco and lay dying on a street in Washington, D.C. He danced at Zack's wedding and cried at Mia's funeral. He shouted with joy as he watched Amanda soar above him on butterfly wings of aeris. He saw Hannah in more iterations than he could count. She stood tall and proud over every corner of his future.

This man in front of him stood nowhere.

As Theo cast his bleary eyes on the brown-haired stranger, his foresight screamed at him. He fell to his knees and screamed back.

Hannah and Amanda dropped to his side. "Theo!"

"What happened?"

He gritted his teeth, curling his fists. "Not him . . ."

The man rose to his feet, peering at Theo over the cushions. "What's the matter with him?"

"We were hoping you knew," Zack said.

"That's why I asked you for painkillers," Mia complained.

He threw a quick and helpless glance at the upper railings, then turned back to Theo. "Look, why don't we get him to the sofa, all right?"

Amanda felt his sweaty forehead. "He's burning up."

"Just get him to the sofa and stay here. I'll find a first aid kit."

"Not him," Theo wheezed. "That's not Peter."

Now the other five Silvers eyed their host in wide alarm. He stopped and turned around, his hands raised defensively.

"Look, I don't know what your friend is suffering, but I assure you I'm Peter Pendergen. I can prove it. Just let me . . ."

David caught a reflective glint on the balcony. His eyes popped wide.

"GET DOWN!"

"Hannah!"

Theo pulled her down just as a hissing bullet struck the floor beyond her. A second shot shattered the lamp next to Zack. He fell off the chair.

Mia barely had a chance to process the gunfire when she saw the false Peter run away in a speedy blur. Her mind stammered with shock. *He shifted. He shifted. He's a—*

Zack grabbed her and yanked her down, just as a bullet cracked the arm of her chair. He pulled her under the coffee table.

Amanda's thoughts turned white, and a geyser of tempis erupted from her hands. It quickly bloomed into a crude but massive shield that covered the sisters and Theo. She had no idea if tempis could stop bullets until she heard two gunshots and felt a pair of agonizing stings in her thoughts, like hot knitting needles. She shrieked and toppled to the ground, her barrier vanishing in a blink. A pair of crushed bullets dropped to the marble.

David was the last to stand his ground, caught like a pinball between reason, panic, and rage. For the boy who could dredge up the past, it was easy to look back thirty-one hours and relive his recent errors. He'd hurled a gunshot noise at an armed and twitchy Dep, a foolish move that cost him two fingers. Now he waltzed right into an ambush, ignoring his instincts as this false Peter Pendergen tried to get him to stand still for the rifle scopes.

No more mistakes, he thought, and then dredged up the past again.

The lobby suddenly filled with screaming people and flames, a spectral re-creation of the great blaze that engulfed Battery Place in August 1931. Firemen in tin helmets ran back and forth with axes while smoldering wooden furniture lay juxtaposed among the sleek sofas of the present. The images were so realistic that Hannah shrieked with pain when her arm fell into fire. It took three full seconds to realize she wasn't burning.

"What's happening?!"

Amanda seized her arm, shouting above the ghosted din. "It's David! He's giving us cover!"

"Where is he?"

The pair frantically looked around, but they couldn't see anything through the eighty-year-old smoke. Amanda flinched when a burning woman ran through her.

"I don't know! We'll get Theo out and come back!"

The sisters struggled to ferry Theo through forty yards of ghosted chaos, retreating all the way to the entry hall. Amanda jostled the knob of a utility door, then broke it open with a tempic shove.

They scrambled down a narrow white hallway, its concrete walls echoing with loud clamor. Hannah kicked open the first door on the left, a locker room for security guards. Wooden batons hung from wall hooks while a leaky faucet dripped into a moldy sink.

Amanda swatted the towels from a bench and sat Theo down. He panted with strain, still lost in branching futures. He glimpsed David four minutes from now. Through a half-bloody face, the boy calmly asked Theo not to tell the others about the awful thing he just did.

"I won't . . ."

Hannah kneeled by his side. "What?"

"I don't know. I'm all . . . I'm all messed up."

Amanda doused a towel and dabbed it against his forehead. Hannah looked at her nose.

"You're bleeding."

"Huh?"

The widow ran a finger under her nostrils, then shook the blood off.

"It's okay. It's from the tempis. We need to find the others."

The thundering ruckus from the lobby came to a stop. Hannah and Amanda hurried back to the hallway to see a lone figure stagger through the archway. Blood poured from a thin gash in his forehead, striping the left side of his face.

The sisters ran to him. "David!"

"Are you hit?"

He closed his eyes and leaned on Amanda as she walked him into the maintenance hall.

"I tripped over a coffee table. Smacked my head on the edge."

"Where are Zack and Mia?"

He glanced behind him, throwing flecks of blood. "I thought they came this way. You didn't see them?"

"No."

Hannah covered her mouth. "Oh my God . . ."

"Shit. Shit!" David broke away from Amanda and unslung his knapsack. Between his T-shirts and spare jeans lay the two compact service pistols he'd seized from his Dep hostages. Each one was loaded with a dozen .40 caliber rounds.

Amanda bounced her hot green stare between the gun and David. "Wait, what are you doing?"

"Going back for them."

"The hell you are. You cracked your head open. You probably have a concussion."

"I'll be all right."

"No you won't!" Hannah yelled. A half hour ago, Ioni painted a quick glimpse of the future that had suspiciously omitted David. Now the actress had a dark hunch why.

"Amanda and I will find them. You go in there and watch over Theo. Keep him safe."

"Look, I'm telling you—"

"And I'm telling *you*, David, if you don't listen to me right now, I'll never speak to you again!"

David eyed her with wide surprise, then plucked the baton from Hannah's hand. He thrust a pistol in its place. "Okay, but you're not going out there with that stick. These people are shooting on sight. You can't give them the chance."

While Hannah tested the frightening weight of Ross Daley's weapon, Amanda took a cautious peek into the lobby.

"Those can't be Deps. I mean they wouldn't just fire at us. Would they?"

Like Mia, David had seen the false Peter Pendergen flee the scene in a streaking blur. These weren't Melissa's people at all.

Rebel dropped his rifle against the wall and scratched his stubbly head. He'd dressed for battle like he was going to the gym—black T-shirt and sweatpants, white high-top sneakers. He didn't bother with the bandana mask this time. His wife had commandeered all the security cameras an hour ago while Mercy Lee flooded the lobby with enough solic static to ensure that the Deps wouldn't see a thing in their ghost drills. They'd taken a day and a half to set this trap. Everything had gone flawlessly until forty-one seconds ago.

He pressed his collar mic and summoned his team back to his perch on the mezzanine. One by one, they returned—four men and one woman, each from a different family. They were all inexperienced in long-range weapons, but desperate times had motivated them to learn.

Freddy Ballad, a tall and stringy blond of twenty, threw his hands up in fluster. "What happened?"

Rebel shrugged his broad shoulders. "Maranan got wise."

"Gemma said the augur wouldn't be a problem."

The shrill voice of a ten-year-old girl hissed through their earpieces. "I said he *probably* wouldn't be a problem."

Freddy snarled into his mic. "It's your job to be sure."

"And it was *your* job to shoot the Aussie before he pulled any ghost tricks. How did that work out?"

"Enough," Rebel snapped. "Freddy, settle down. Gemma, I don't want to hear another word out of you unless it's intel."

"I'm working on it."

With a hot blast of air, Bruce Byer de-shifted at the edge of their gathering, flushed with exertion and rage.

"You idiots could have shot me!"

Rebel frowned. He knew Bruce was a self-serving coward, like all Byers. But he was a skilled actor who strongly resembled Peter. No one was better suited to bait the hook.

"Calm down. We knew you'd clear the lobby."

"Really? Like you knew the sick yellow chinny would catch on?"

Mercy Lee gripped her rifle with ire. The willowy young woman was a daughter of the clan's last pure Asian family, though one could hardly tell from the excessive amount of mascara she wore.

"Stow it, penis. No one's in the mood for your mouth dump."

"I said *enough*." Rebel rubbed his eyes, then checked his watch. "In eight minutes, this place'll be crawling with Deps. We gotta work fast." He pressed his earpiece. "That means *you*, Gemma."

"I got it. I got it. Trillinger and Farisi went east. They're hiding in the office cubes. Looks like one of them's bleeding."

"What about the others?"

"Dormer and Maranan are in the maintenance hall. Not sure which part but . . . God."

"What?" Rebel asked. "Are they going to be a problem?"

"No. It's the Givens you need to worry about. In ninety-one seconds, they'll come back through the southern arch. They are . . . Jesus, you guys have to be careful. They've gotten stronger. A lot stronger."

Rebel took an anxious breath. He'd learned to listen to Gemma Sunder's warnings. The girl saw things no one else could.

"All right. Freddy, you go after the boy and the augur. Forget the rifle. Just do what you do."

Freddy smiled. His fists encrusted with spiky tempis. "Now we're talking."

"I want the rest of you on the sisters. Take them out. Do it fast. Mercy . . ."

The young woman nodded nervously. She knew she was Rebel's ace in the hole. "I'll be ready for them."

Bruce narrowed his eyes at Rebel. "Where are you going?"

No one else had to ask. The cartoonist who'd rotted Rebel's hand was in this building right now, hiding in the office cubes.

"Just help the others," he told Bruce. "You all know what's at stake here. Go."

They dispersed. As Rebel hurried to the eastern door, Ivy's dulcet voice rang through his earpiece.

"You be careful, Richard. You hear me? You kill them all and come back alive."

Rebel pulled out his new revolver and checked the chambers. He'd been woefully unprepared in Terra Vista. It cost him six people and a hand. He knew better now. He was ready.

The sisters stopped at the lobby entrance, their heartbeats pounding in synch. Amanda choked back a scream and squeezed her golden crucifix. *Please, God. Please let Zack and Mia be all right.*

Hannah watched her sister's teary prayer and suddenly rued her own agnosticism. She always saw higher meaning as something outside her reach, like fractal math or long-term monogamy. As the gun dangled in her quivering hand, all the actress could conjure was Ioni's bright assurance. *The sunrise. The full moon. The rainbow after a storm. These are all things that can't be stopped by mere mortals. You know what the augurs call them?*

"Givens," she muttered.

"What?"

Hannah looked at her sister through moist eyes. For the life of her, she couldn't remember what they fought about this morning. She couldn't fathom why they wasted any of their precious time on battles.

"I love you."

Warm tears rolled down Amanda's cheeks. "I love you too, Hannah. I love you more than anyone. As soon as you get in there, you go as fast as you can. You don't slow down for a second."

Hannah wiped her eyes. "I won't."

"I will not lose you today."

"You won't," Hannah said. It occurred to her that she wasn't entirely faithless after all.

"Are you ready?"

They clasped fingers in the dainty little way of children, and then anxiously pulled apart. Amanda coated her hands with shiny white tempis. Hannah shifted into the blue.

The Great Sisters Given stepped forward into the fray.

THIRTY-TWO

The matron healer watched the wall of monitors, her sausage fingers curled with tension. In her prime, Olga Varnov had been a knockout blonde of stunning proportions. Now her hair was gray as ash and her body stood a balloon-sculpture parody of its former self. Not that she cared. Her need for beauty had perished at age twenty, when a bad reversal rendered her infertile, unsuitable for marriage. She'd grown content in her role as the clan's beloved nurse and nanny. There wasn't a Gotham under forty who hadn't had their diapers changed or their wounds undone by Mother Olga.

She followed Amanda's progress from screen to screen as the lovely young woman brushed the wall of the lobby, clutching her crucifix necklace in fright. On another monitor, three hazy figures crept down the stairwell, all lumiflaged against the backdrop like chameleons. Olga knew Ben Herrick could sear poor Amanda to a crisp while Colin Chisholm could cut her to shreds with flying knives of tempis. They advanced slowly on their prey, approaching a range close enough to guarantee an instant kill.

Olga clutched her giant bosom and turned away. "I can't watch. This is slaughter."

"You don't have to look," said Ivy. "Just be ready if things go bad."

Ilavarasi Sunder was an Indian beauty of thirty-three, as tall and slender as the woman Olga pitied. She sported the same black bodysuit she wore at the Terra Vista siege, only now the nylon was stretched by a ten-week baby bump. Ivy only had to think of her child to erase all doubt about her mission. She only had to recall the gruesome death of Krista Bloom to shed her empathy for these Pelletier pets.

She stood behind her diminutive niece, who feverishly worked the camera console. As always, Gemma dressed well beyond her ten years of age, sporting the blouzer/skirt combo of a power executive. It was an improvement over the sleek-a-boo tinytops she usually wore.

"See anything yet?" Ivy asked her.

"No."

"I don't mean the cameras."

"I know what you meant. If Azral and Esis were coming, I'd be screaming right now."

Ivy sighed with guarded optimism. It seemed these breachers were on their own. Of course she'd thought the same thing in Terra Vista, just before her best friend was brutally butchered by Esis. *Oh Krista. I left you to die. I failed you so horribly. Please forgive me.*

Their command center was located four blocks north of the ambush site, in a tenth-floor office that was currently closed for renovation. Three of the walls were raw wooden beams. The fourth stood bare in plaster.

Ivy only needed one solid surface for her portals. She was ready to extract wounded teammates at a moment's notice. There would be no more casualties, she swore. Not on her side.

Hannah sped like a missile through the sofa clusters, launching her frantic gaze in every direction. After two dashing circuits around the lobby, a hot cry of relief escaped her throat. There were no corpses to be found here. Zack and Mia must have fled through a different exit.

Beyond the slow-motion dribble of the tiered stone fountain, she caught her sister's laggard form. Amanda kept to the walls beneath the overhang, out of view of any high snipers. Hannah couldn't see any movement on the upper levels.

Her heart lurched when she heard soft footsteps behind her. She spun around and raised her pistol.

Bruce Byer jumped back and threw his hands up. Unlike everything else in the sluggish blue haze, the man who'd impersonated Peter Pendergen moved quickly and carried a faint red tint to his countenance. He squawked fearful words that were too rushed for Hannah to understand. She realized, with mad consternation, that he was shifted at an even higher speed than hers.

She concentrated until his crimson hue vanished and she matched his velocity.

"—not my idea!" he yelled. "I was against this from the start!"

Hannah kept the gun fixed on him. The man had set them up to die like clay ducks in a shooting gallery. Now she'd caught him sneaking up on her. She didn't think it was to apologize.

"Give me one reason why I shouldn't shoot you in your stupid lying face!"

"None of this was my choice! The elders forced me into it! Rebel's got them all—"

"Rebel?! He's here?"

"Yeah. This was his trap. My only job was to take the call and meet you guys here. I wasn't supposed to fight you. I'm not a fighter at all."

Hannah could see that. Any hint of masculinity he'd displayed as Peter Pendergen was now utterly gone. She squinted at him skeptically. "What are you then? An actor?"

"Yes, actually. A very accomplished one. I've been on Broadway."

She knew there were a hundred better questions she could be asking right now, but her mouth got ahead of her. "In what?"

"God. Lots of things. *Angeline, Dog Days, One Summer in Paris.* I was with the touring company of *Babes in Toyland.*"

Hannah's eyes lit up. "I know that one."

"*Babes in Toyland*?"

"Yeah. I did it in college."

"You're an actress?"

"Uh-huh. I played Jane."

"I was Alan."

The two speedsters blinked at each other in addled stupor.

"Why are you people trying to kill us?"

Bruce chucked his hands. "Honestly, I don't even know. A few months ago, all our prophets started madding out, screaming gloom and doom. Then some of our young ones started disappearing and everyone panicked. Rebel's the only one who seemed to have a plan. He says killing you breachers will make everything right again."

"That's crazy! Why does he think that?"

"Who can say with these augurs? They're all nutballs. Of course they think the same thing about us swifters. It's strange to meet a new one after all this time. Do you ever hallucinate when you go real fast?"

A wary voice in Hannah's head cut her off before she could answer. *He's still playing you. He's stalling for time.*

She turned around to check on her sister and now caught the outlines of three shrouded men. They crouched fifty feet behind her, moving in with the blended stealth of crocodiles.

"AMANDA!"

A shadow grew at Hannah's feet. Once again, she spun around to see Bruce raise his fingers in anxious surrender. He'd halved the distance between them while her back was turned. Now Hannah could see the tip of a wooden nightstick protruding from his sleeve. At this speed, he could crack her skull like an eggshell.

"You asshole!"

"It's not what you think. I was just—"

"Fuck you!"

She aimed the gun at his thigh and pulled the trigger. His leg erupted in a bloody torrent.

Olga gasped as she watched Bruce's plight on the monitor. Gemma yelled into her headset.

"Don't all go for the swifter! Someone get the tempic!"

Her warning went ignored. The moment they heard the gunshot, the three Gothams swung their palms at Hannah and launched their attacks in reflex.

A pair of twelve-inch tempic shards shot from the hands of Colin Chisholm, a stocky young blond with a pocked and piggish face. Even in Hannah's shifted state, the projectiles flew at her like fastball pitches. She dove out of their way, her shoulder colliding painfully with the edge of the fountain as she dropped to the tile. Her pistol fell in the water.

Ben Herrick, the gangly beanpole of the trio, fired an invisible blast of heat from his charred right palm, a blurry cone of air that cooked everything in its path. Tables smoldered. Upholstery bubbled. Ceramic lamps burst apart. Hannah ducked behind the concrete fountain. She shrieked as hot steam hissed above her, scalding the hand that remained clasped on the fountain's lip.

There was no escaping the third assault. Nick McNoel was a portly redhead of seventeen, a skilled lumic who'd been bending light since he was a toddler. The cloaking colors vanished from the trio's skin and garments as he channeled his thoughts. Suddenly Hannah became engulfed in a dome of searing white radiance. The light blinded her through the membrane of her eyelids.

Gemma's high voice howled in their earpieces. "Goddamn it! The tempic!"

Amanda clenched her teeth and thrust her hand at the attackers. A spray of white force erupted from her palm, quickly splitting into three long arms that shoved each man back against the steps. She felt something snap in Nick McNoel's back.

The tempis vanished. Amanda rushed to her sister's side. "Hannah! You okay?"

"No! My hand hurts and I can't see anything! I can't see!"

Amanda studied her red, blistered fingers. They looked like second-degree burns.

"You'll be okay. Just hold on to me. We have to go."

"I shot someone," Hannah uttered, in a stammering daze. "I aimed for the leg. Is he . . . is he alive?"

Bruce lay unconscious on the nearby tile. From the way blood spurted from his thigh, Amanda was sure the bullet hit an artery. Her inner nurse and Christian clamored for her to make a tourniquet. She dismissed them both as lunatics.

"He'll be fine. Come on."

A half mile away, Olga grabbed Ivy's arm. "He's bleeding to death! You have to extract him!"

Ivy kept her hot gaze on the sisters. "What are you waiting for, Mercy? Hit them! Now!"

Amanda caught new movement above her. By the time she looked to the second floor and saw the slender young Asian at the railing, it was already too late.

Mercurial Lee was the daughter of augurs. Her birth name itself was a prophecy, a forecast of her future temperament. Though she'd spent much of her life trying to disprove the prediction, there was no denying it. The twenty-three-year-old artist was a turbulent woman, as quick to humor as she was to huff. She heckled the elders at public assemblies and littered the walls with subversive graffiti. She arrived at a wedding wearing nothing but handcuffs, a protest against the clan's forced unions. Her parents would have done just as well to name her Rebel.

Five weeks ago, her teenage brother Sage became the latest young Gotham to mysteriously vanish, a shock that put an end to her incendiary antics. At long last, Mercy stood aligned with her people. Her unique temporic talent, one she'd long considered useless, had single-handedly turned the tide in the battle against the Golds. To Rebel, she was more than a cherished ally. She was the key to destroying the Pelletiers.

With a heavy thought and an unblinking stare, Mercy enveloped the sisters in a field of concentrated solis, the equivalent output of a thousand home generators. The bombardment scrambled the sisters' access to temporis, turning them back to the normal people they once were.

Hannah furrowed her brow at the faint new tickle under her skin. "Something happened. I feel weird."

The moment Amanda wiggled her indelibly pink fingers, she recalled the four humming towers the Deps had used to suppress her tempis. Now the great white beast wasn't just sleeping inside her. It felt all but dead.

She looked to the steps, where Colin Chisholm and Ben Herrick rose to their feet. Then she peered up at Mercy again. The two women traded a look of grim understanding.

"Hannah, take my hand. We have to run."

"Why? What's happening? I still can't—"

"Run!"

She pulled Hannah away. The two angry Gothams watched them stumble helplessly across the lobby. They raised their palms for a second attack.

Gemma turned from the monitors and shined Olga an ugly grin.

"Now it's slaughter."

Rebel followed the blood drops through the elegant reception area, a razzle-dazzle array of neon sculptures and lustrous white furniture. The ground-floor office belonged to Nicomedia Magazines, publisher of such upscale monthlies as *Push*, *Preen*, *American Woman*, and *Taste*. On the dimmer end of the spectrum, they put out *Wonders*, a biweekly pupu platter of weird news items that always managed to include one crackpot Gotham sighting. Seventeen days after the incident, the tabloid continued to swoon over the great tempic arm that dangled a man from a hotel balcony in Evansville, Indiana. Rebel wanted to kill the Silvers just for that headache.

Beyond the white glass wall lay a sprawling grid of office cubes. The blood trail ended at the edge of the first cluster. The targets had wisely plugged the leak before moving on.

Rebel checked his watch. Six minutes until Deps stormed the building. There was no time to search every cubicle. No reason. He pitched his gravelly voice across the room.

"Zack Trillinger. I know you're in here. You know my voice. You know I'm not leaving till you and the girl are dead."

Forty feet away, Zack and Mia crouched beneath a copywriter's desk, both sheet-white and drenched in sweat. As they'd escaped the lobby, ninety seconds ago, Rebel's bullet struck the wall and cut Zack's neck with a flying shard of marble. Mia pressed a folded T-shirt to his laceration. The fragment had missed his jugular by an inch.

Now that she knew who was in the room with them, Mia fought her panic. If Rebel's new gun was anything like his old one, he could probably kill them through six of these flimsy partitions. Worse, Zack had seen him shoot two ceiling cameras and a friend without even looking. He didn't need a line of sight on his targets.

The hulking Gotham prowled the edge of the office, brushing his revolver against the cubicle barriers. With each tap of the barrel, he scanned the speculative future to see the end result of a gunshot. *This little bullet kills a desk lamp. This little bullet cracks glass. This little bullet goes "wee wee wee," all the way into no one.*

"You won't believe me, Trillinger, but I got good reasons for doing this. You people were never meant to come here. If you knew the damage you were causing just by living and breathing, you'd kill yourselves. I'm prepared to do it nicely. I got a bag of sedatives here with me. Just say the word and I'll send you both home with a smile instead of a bullet hole."

Zack fought a pitch-black laugh as his stomach seared with stress. Rebel looked down at his prosthetic hand, a clunky thing of chrome, rubber, and circuitry. He saw the folly of his offer.

"Guess you don't believe that either," he said. "I don't blame you. Last time we tangled, you got me good. Stuck me with this million-dollar meat hook. Can't say I'm happy about it, but I'm not angry anymore. If anything, you're the one who owes me pain."

He raised his revolver in readiness. "I killed your brother."

All the blood rushed to Zack's face as Rebel turned a corner. The gun barrel continued to make loud friction sounds against the cloth-board walls.

"Josh Trillinger. Tall guy. Curly hair. Little scar on his not-so-little nose. He was one of Azral's New York group, tucked away in some fancy building in White Plains. We hit them last month in the middle of the night. Two of the Golds got away from us. Six didn't. Your brother was one of the ones who didn't."

Mia squeezed Zack's trembling hand. Hot tears spilled down both their faces.

"I took no pleasure in it," Rebel insisted. "He seemed like a good guy. When his friends started dying, he came right at me. Faced me like a man. Now here you are, hiding under a desk with the other little girl. I fig your brother would be ashamed to see you right now. He's probably been ashamed of you your whole life."

Rebel could hear the faint sounds of shuffling as Mia struggled to keep Zack still. Though his skin burned red with rage, he only reached for the notepad above him. He plucked a pen from the floor and scribbled hastily.

He's coming this way. I'll hold him off. The second I move, you RUN and don't look back.

Mia shook her head. The girl was only half Zack's age, but she was no stranger to losing brothers. Now she was convinced that she had four more loved ones to mourn. In her dismal thoughts, David and Amanda and Theo and Hannah were all dying or dead. All she had left was the man in front of her. Her entire world was small enough to fit under a desk.

She seized the pad and pen, then scrawled what she could only assume was her final note.

I love you and I'm not leaving you. Don't you dare think I would.

Zack closed his eyes and pressed his forehead to Mia's. From the moment he realized he could end people with a thought, a dark new tunnel opened up inside him. He'd barricaded the entry with warning signs and cattle skulls and enough moral rhetoric to fill a synagogue. Even now he'd rather follow his brother into the afterlife than join Rebel in the dark fraternity of self-excusing murderers.

Ultimately it was the thought of Mia that shattered his obstructions and turned every red light green. He planted a soft kiss on her forehead, then steeled himself to take a path he knew was one-way only. Whether he succeeded or failed, there was no coming back from this.

Suddenly Rebel caught a fresh new glimpse of the minute to come. In his mind's eye, he saw Zack spring out of an office cube, launching his temporis in a thirty-foot arc that would easily rift the Gotham a second time.

Unfortunately for Zack, there was a reason Rebel kept making noise, alerting his targets to his position. Now that he'd flushed out the Zack of next minute, Rebel knew exactly where the current one was hiding.

He ducked behind the corner and aimed his revolver through three cubicle walls. The future had a better story to tell now. *This little bullet cracks the heart of an enemy. This little bullet hits home.*

Hand in hand, the sisters fled across the marble, toward the emergency exit in the north elevator bank. In Amanda's frantic thoughts, she reckoned they *(maybe maybe please)* had a chance if they reached the stairwell. They might even get their defenses back if they escaped the cruel Asian woman with the heavy eyeliner and the Kryptonite stare.

Twelve yards into their dash, a flying white sphere demolished the flower pot near Amanda. Colin Chisholm had ditched the knives in favor of firing tempic cannonballs. His cracked ribs screamed with blunt force trauma. He was determined to pay Amanda back in kind.

At twenty yards, the air around the sisters abruptly doubled in temperature. Ben Herrick might have roasted his targets alive if he hadn't been hobbled by a fresh concussion. All he could summon now was a dry sauna blast, one strong enough to send Hannah stumbling to the floor.

Amanda rained sweat as she struggled to lift her. "Come on, Hannah! Please!"

A loud crack rang out from the balcony. A bullet pierced the coffee table behind them. Amanda threw a savage yell at the distant railing.

"LEAVE US ALONE!"

Mercy pulled the bolt lever of her rifle, her face streaked with mascara tears. It was only just this morning that her parents finally told her they were proud of her. Proud of her for doing this.

The gunshot scared Hannah back to her feet. The sisters ran again.

Once they reached the elevator bank, a tempic cannonball slammed Amanda's left ankle. Her fingers flew from Hannah's grip and she crashed onto her back.

"Amanda! What happened? Where are you?"

The widow cried with pain as she sat up to check the damage. The skin of her ankle was red and distended. Her foot pointed in a horrible new direction. *Broken. It's broken. It's—*

"Over. It's broken. Hannah, you have to go."

"No . . ."

"You have to go," she cried. The temperature around them continued to rise. They could barely draw a breath. "The stairs are right behind you. Please!"

Through the murky brown spots in her vision, Hannah could see two approaching figures. It was already too late.

You were wrong, she thought to Ioni. *You got it all wrong.*

The actress sat at her sister's side, their faces wet with perspiration.

"I'm sorry," Hannah said. "For every awful thing I ever said and did to you. I'm so sorry."

Amanda closed her eyes, squeezing her golden cross with one hand and her sister's wrist with the other.

"Nothing to forgive," she creaked. "You were never that bad."

The two Gothams reached the elevator bank. Hannah shot them a hot wet glare.

"Assholes. You don't even know why you're killing us."

"We know," said Ben Herrick, with a shaky look that betrayed his confidence.

"You know nothing," Amanda hissed. "Just do it already."

The young men raised their palms for a final strike, and then arched their backs in screaming pain. With a sickening bone crunch, a curved white spike burst from the chests of both men, like elephant tusks. The tempis lifted the bodies three feet into the air and then hurled them to the ground like rag dolls.

Standing tall and fierce behind her two crumpled victims, Esis Pelletier shined a crooked grin.

"Hello, Givens."

The high alarm scream of Gemma Sunder filled every earpiece, making Nick McNoel wince and Mercy Lee drop her rifle. Rebel flinched in surprise as he fired his revolver. The bullet cut through two cubicles, shattering the computer screen above Zack and Mia.

He shouted a curse, then pressed his collar mic. "Gemma, what—"

"Get out! Get out! Everyone get out!"

"What do you see?"

"Esis! She's in the lobby! Ivy, get out of there!"

Rebel turned white at the mention of his wife. He made a furious dash for the exit.

Gemma was alone in the command center, her fearful gaze leaping between the monitors and the shimmering portal on the wall. Soon Ivy and Olga returned through the white liquid surface, lugging the ailing Bruce Byer between them.

Gemma frantically motioned them in. "Close it! Close it! Hurry!"

Ivy dropped Bruce's legs and waved the portal shut. "Jesus, Gemma! Are you sure it's—"

"Yes, I'm sure! She's right there! She—"

Suddenly every screen went dark. The static hum of their headsets fell quiet. Ivy tried to hail Rebel three times, then covered her mouth.

"Oh no. No! I have to go back!"

Gemma's head jerked back as if she just woke up from a nap. Like Mia, the girl shared a rapport with her future selves. But Gemma's weren't content to pass her notes. They possessed her body like demons.

Now four minutes older in mind and spirit, she closed her eyes and wept. "You can't go back," she said. "You can't help any of them."

Freddy Ballad floated down the maintenance hall on a disc of radiant white aeris. Though the young blond Gotham stood among the elite minority of tempics who could slip the bonds of gravity, he never got the hang of wing flight. He settled for simple acts of levitation, a handy trick now that he needed stealth. In this narrow concrete passage, his feet would clop like Clydesdales.

Once the clamor in his earpiece died down, he steered his disc around a corner and whispered into his mic. "Rebel? Ivy? What's happening? Are we aborting?"

No response. Even Gemma, that shrieking little bat, had gone quiet. His eyes darted back and forth in busy debate. He didn't want to play the coward here. The Ballads had a history of weakness, both genetic and moral. Freddy had a rare chance to elevate his family's status.

He pressed on with his task, continuing to test every door with long white arms before cautiously peeking inside. He didn't know why he was so scared. His targets were a half-dead augur and a boy who could throw fake fire. What chance did they have against his tempis?

The last door on the right opened to an empty locker room. Freddy moved on, then backed up for a puzzled second glance. Something wasn't right. The angle of the lockers changed oddly when he moved his head, as if he were looking at a forced-perspective painting.

Sharp white spikes grew from his arms. He hopped off his disc and stepped through the door.

Suddenly the illusive screen vanished and two figures turned visible. Freddy barely had a chance to register Theo in the background before his stunned gaze fixed on David and his government-issue pistol. It pointed right at Freddy's face.

A hot stream of urine trickled down the tempic's leg. "Wait—"

The gunshot rattled every surface in the room. Theo watched in wide alarm as the stranger fell backward in a bloody heap.

"God. Jesus. You killed him."

"I saved us," David replied. "Come on."

After a quick scan of the hallway, he escorted Theo to the drab and tiny office of the building security manager. David stashed him behind the metal desk and crouched at his side. Theo saw new flecks of blood on the boy's face. They mingled with the thin wet stripes that dribbled from his forehead gash.

"Stay here while I look for the others," he told Theo. "Keep hidden. You'll be all right."

"I won't."

"Why do you say that? What do you see?"

Theo blinked confusedly. He was responding to something David said thirty seconds from now.

"I . . . never mind. Just be careful. I think Melissa might be coming. I think she's bringing a whole lot of people."

David cursed under his breath. That damn woman was the last thing they needed now.

"All right. I'll be back as soon as I can."

He glanced down at the gun in his hand as if he just remembered it was there. He looked to Theo with pale discomfort.

"I would, uh . . . I'd consider it a kindness if you didn't tell the others what I did. I'd rather they hear it from me."

Theo nodded shakily as time looped again. "I won't."

Once David left the room, Theo's hold on the present slipped away like a thousand balloons. He huddled in the corner, his mind scattering across futures near and—

"No."

—very near. He felt a wave of panic so powerful that his whole body fell to quivers. Something was coming for him. Something terrible.

You have no cause for fear, a cold voice in his thoughts assured him. *In moments, you'll experience a great and wonderful change. Nothing will be the same again.*

"No . . ."

Now a thousand busy screens in his head all united to display the smiling image of a white-haired man.

You are ready, Azral told him. *Come to me.*

Hannah's thoughts screamed with discord as she helped Amanda into the elevator. She didn't need her eyesight to identify their brutal savior. The woman spoke with the same alien accent as Azral, and carried a mincing mischief in her voice that no sane person could muster at a time like this.

Esis propped the door from the lobby and pressed the button for the twelfth floor. She dressed like she was headed for Aspen in her sleek gray ski jacket and black thermal leggings. Her winter boots left glistening blood prints on the carpet. She hadn't bothered to walk around her victims.

"Stay high and out of sight," she told the sisters. "This is no longer your battle."

Hannah hadn't encountered Esis since she was five years old, and was grateful she could barely see her now. Ioni's harsh warning about the Pelletiers still rang heavily in her thoughts. *They destroy worlds, Hannah. They destroyed yours twice.*

"Is . . . Azral here too?" she asked Esis.

"My wealth addresses another concern. He entrusts his mother to end this mayhem."

"W-what about the others?" Hannah asked. "What are you going to do?"

"To which others do you refer, child? Your enemies or your kin?"

"I mean my friends. Will they be okay?"

Esis threw Amanda a canny smirk, as if they were in on a chummy secret joke.

"Your *friends*, as you call them, are alive and in much better condition than the friend you currently hold. Now if you'll excuse me, I have matters to discuss with the unfriendly others."

Unlike Hannah, Amanda had a full view of Esis's first "discussion," one that left two young Gothams disemboweled on the floor. Now as agony and heat exhaustion pushed her to the edge of collapse, the widow scrambled to process this shark-eyed horror in front of her, a woman who slaughtered her enemies and employees without distinction.

"What do you want with us?" she asked Esis, in a parched rasp.

"A little gratitude, to start. I did save your life, and not for the first time."

"What do you *want* with us?"

Esis slitted her eyes in a peevish squint before releasing the door.

"I want you to grow, my stubborn flower. I want you to live. If you wish the same, you'll heed my advice."

Her expression turned frigid. "And my warning."

The elevator closed on her pointed last words, which struck Amanda like arrows. She envisioned a large tempic spike bursting through Zack's chest, throwing him to the floor in a bloody heap.

Hannah held Amanda close as she continued to keep the weight off her broken ankle.

"It'll be okay," she insisted. "The others are all right. You heard her."

The words did little to comfort Amanda. She stared ahead in a morbid daze, too distracted to notice the fifth-floor button lighting up on its own.

"What did she mean by 'kin'?" Hannah asked her.

Amanda fixed her dark green stare on the doors.

"Nothing. She's insane."

The Gothams knew of Esis Pelletier. A week after Rebel's ill-fated mission in Terra Vista, the clan's best ghosters had traveled to Sterling Quint's lobby and watched her slaughter four kinsmen in retrospect. Her tempic savagery was described in harrowing detail at the next elder council, enough to give nightmares to half the tribe.

Mercy Lee had missed that meeting. She'd been off sharing opiates and oral favors with a long-haired delinquent from Nyack.

Now she was all caught up on the matter of Esis.

Mercy hid behind a planter, struggling to hold back her screams as she listened to Nick McNoel's gurgling last breaths. Esis had found the broken boy on the stairwell and wasted no time finishing him with a tempic sword through the neck. Three of Mercy's teammates were dead now. Her commlink was dead. Her solic charge was still drained from her attack on the Givens. *I'm next. I'm dead. Oh God.*

She parted the hydrangeas with trembling fingers, peeking down at the lobby through leaves and iron rods. No one was there. *Maybe . . . maybe she . . . maybe she just . . .*

A cold hand grabbed her ankle from behind. Mercy shrieked as she dangled upside down from a long white arm. The lip of her T-shirt tumbled down to her chin. Esis curiously studied her small breasts and flat olive stomach. A flowery vine tattoo spiraled around Mercy's navel.

"Look at you. As lovely and filthy as an outdoor cat. Tell me, cat, why do you stain yourself with so many inks and oils?"

Thick black tears dribbled down Mercy's temples. "Please! Please don't kill me!"

"You slaughter my Golds and threaten my Silvers, and now you ask for mercy, Mercy?"

"Please! I'm sorry! I never wanted to hurt anyone! I just got scared! My brother—"

"Your brother lives," Esis informed her. "He resides in our care, as healthy and pampered as an indoor cat. Does this news quell your bloodlust? Or must I find a stronger remedy?"

"No! No! Please!"

Esis threw a baffled gaze at the highest railing, beneath the artificial sky. Through the metal bars, she saw Hannah and Amanda hobble out of the elevator. She'd sent them to the twelfth floor, not the fifth. Her dark eyes narrowed in suspicion. *No. Not him. The fool wouldn't dare.*

"Please!" Mercy shrieked. "I'll do whatever you want!"

Esis turned back to her captive. She had no intention of killing Mercy Lee. The child came from an optimal gene line, and her future intersected heavily with Zack Trillinger's. The two funny artists were practically born to entwine.

"You seem sincere, child. Perhaps I will spare you. But know that if you raise your claws against my little ones again, there will be no mercy, Mercy. Do you understand?"

Through her upside-down perspective, Mercy saw a large figure creep up the stairwell. She looked away for fear of alerting Esis. "Yes! I won't! I promise!"

Rebel aimed his revolver through two metal posts. He reeled with doubt as he watched his speculative gunshot pierce the back of Esis's skull. *That can't be right. It can't be that easy.*

Indeed, the moment he pulled the trigger, a small white portal appeared ten feet in front of him and swallowed the bullet whole.

Esis dropped Mercy and moved toward Rebel in a windy blur. He barely had a chance to react before she tackled him down the stairs. He crashed to the floor, his gun sliding thirty feet across the marble.

The mother Pelletier straddled his stomach, pinning him to the floor in a tempic web.

"Imbecilic ape. Did you think you were the only augur here? You see nothing compared to me. You're a blind and stubborn fool and we are out of patience with you."

Five stories above, Amanda took a wincing perch on a cushioned bench by the railing. She'd sent Hannah to the restroom to soak her scalded hand. Now she had a lone view of the conflict below, clear enough to recognize the man beneath Esis.

Rebel bucked and thrashed in her web. "I'll kill you, bitch."

"Your foresight fails you again, Richard. Shall I tell you the future? That crude piece of lead you fired at me will return one day when you least desire it. It'll travel through the skull of your pretty wife. Or perhaps the tiny eye of your child."

He bucked madly. "NO!"

"You've inconvenienced us greatly, Richard. Did you think we would tolerate it? You should have listened to Pendergen. You accomplish nothing by killing these children of ours."

"The breaches—"

"The damage to this world is already done. It cannot be undone, any more than your hand can be unrifted. Cease your foolish crusade and perhaps we'll let you and your family live to see its natural end."

"I swear to God I'll—"

"Kill me. Yes." Esis sighed. "A stubborn fool to the last. So be it. Soon you'll know—"

She threw her head back and gasped in cold shock. Even the most powerful augur couldn't foresee every circumstance. When Esis dropped Mercy Lee to the carpet, she never anticipated for a moment that the terrified girl would rediscover her nerve. And her solis.

With a feral scream, Mercy drowned both Esis and Rebel in an invisible field of energy, dissolving the tempic web between them and flipping the cruel advantage. Esis was a 130-pound woman with slender arms and a delicate beauty. Rebel was not.

Amanda gaped, thunderstruck, as Rebel's first punch drew blood from Esis's nose and sent her flying onto her back. He leapt on top of her, pummeling her with fists both flesh and synthetic.

"You threaten my wife? You threaten my *child*?"

Four blocks away, the screens of the command center flickered back to life. Gemma did a double take at the action on the center monitor. This was not the future she'd seen. Not at all.

"Oh my God. He's alive."

Ivy raised her teary face from her hands. "What?"

"He's alive! Rebel! He . . . Holy shit, he's beating her!"

Olga looked up from her table. She'd just finished tying a tourniquet around Bruce's leg and was now lowering his body temperature in preparation for reversal. Her ice pack dropped to the floor when she saw the two slaughtered kinsmen in the elevator bank. *Dear Lord. No.*

Ivy kept her rapt attention on the middle screen. "Oh God. Richard. Get the gun. Kill her."

"Kill her!" Gemma screamed.

Kill her, Amanda cried in her broken thoughts. *Kill each other.*

Rebel continued his furious assault, reducing Esis to a raw and battered wreck. The woman had been raised in a more civilized era, where only the poorest suffered the indignity of pain. Even a surgeon like her could live her whole life without seeing a drop of blood.

Now as this ancestor ape thrashed her with his brutal fists, a shrill cry escaped her bloody lips.

"SEMERJEAN!"

A nine-foot portal opened on the second floor balcony. A speeding figure burst through the surface and knocked Mercy unconscious. It continued down the stairs in a blurry streak, yanking Rebel off Esis and slamming him against a wall. Two heavy-framed paintings crashed to the ground.

Now Amanda could see this new man clearly. He stood as large and bald as Rebel, with powerful arms and a broadly muscled back. His entire body was glossy white, like a marble statue of a naked Greek god. It took two squinting glances for Amanda to see that he was covered in tempis.

Ivy stared at the screen in slack horror. "Oh Jesus, Richard. Come on. Break free."

Rebel may as well have been crucified for all the force that pinned him. When he tried to kick his aggressor, the man grew a second pair of arms from his hips. They held Rebel's thighs to the wall.

Gemma shook her trembling head. "God. What is that? Is it even human?"

Only Rebel was in a position to glimpse the man behind the tempis. Through the small round eyeholes, he could see pale skin and sandy brown eyebrows. His fierce blue eyes brimmed with savage fury, like a panther in mid-roar.

Rebel hocked a spiteful gob at his attacker. "Fuck you, coward. A real man shows his face when he kills someone."

Semerjean's eyes laughed with a shrewd and vicious mockery that Rebel found even more frightening than his rage. Clearly this creature wasn't just a thug on the family payroll. He was a Pelletier through and through.

Ivy cried out when the tempic man grew a third pair of arms from his rib cage. They struck at Rebel with relentless fury, cracking his jaw, breaking his teeth. Once Rebel's face matched the bloody wretchedness of Esis, Semerjean melted away his extra limbs. He leaned in toward Rebel and hissed a gritty whisper.

"You'll know when I'm killing you, boy. You'll see my true face then."

Rebel moaned in pain as Semerjean traced a finger along each cheek, rifting the skin just enough to scar him. He let his victim collapse to the floor, then gently scooped his wife into his arms.

Amanda watched in bleary-eyed anguish as Semerjean carried Esis through a new portal. The gateway shrank to a close behind them.

All was once again quiet in the lobby as the living fell as still as the dead. In the remote command room, three Gotham women stared numbly at the monitors. Gemma shuddered in her seat while she received new intel from the future.

"It's safe to get Rebel and Mercy," she told Ivy. "But you have to do it fast."

"Why? Are those monsters coming back?"

"No."

Gemma adjusted the camera displays to show a view of the street. A trio of ash-gray vans came to a halt in front of the building, with several more approaching.

The Deps had arrived in full force.

Howard Hairston parked his rental coupe at Bowling Green Park, a block away from the action. The freckly young redhead was the only member of Melissa's team to follow her here. Everyone else had been called back to Los Angeles by the regional director, who sought to sever his office from this quagmire of a case. Until Integrity seized the reins, as everyone assumed they would, the six otherworldly fugitives were officially New York's problem.

The moment Howard reached the siege site, he saw that New York was ready for them.

Seventeen government vehicles flanked the building—armored trucks, reviver vans, mobile thermal scanners. A trio of NYPD aerocruisers circled the roof like buzzards.

Howard scanned the crowd for Melissa, to no avail. He moved in on Rosie Herrera, a small and sturdy woman whose masculine features were only slightly countered by her salmon-pink ensemble. She paced the barricaded entry, commanding her men like Napoleon at Austerlitz.

"I want all exits covered before that tempis comes down. Every door. Every window. Every vent."

"Excuse me . . ."

She held up a finger to Howard, then fumed at the young agent working the gate controls. "Why am I still looking at this barrier, Jules?"

"None of the overrides are working. Someone jammed it good."

"Well, fix it already. We got thirty guys standing here with their twigs out." She turned to Howard. "Who the hell are you?"

He raised his badge. She leaned in to study it. "Huh. Another one from Sunland. You must be Melissa's boy."

"Yes, ma'am. Has she arrived yet?"

"She's here. She's changing."

"Changing?"

"You faced these perps before. How bad are they?"

"Bad." Howard sighed. "One of them broke my teammate's back. Another punched the gate off a Tug-a-Lug truck. They've got an Australian kid who's an ice-cold gangster and a Filipino who probably already knows your middle name. If they slip out this time—"

"They won't."

"—it'll be because of Maranan. That guy just knows things."

Rosie snorted. "Unless he knows how to turn into sunbeams, he's not getting out of there."

The back doors of a truck swung open with a heavy *thud*. Eight imposing agents marched down the ramp. They wore the same padded black armor, with thick-soled boots and gray metal cables that ran between their gloves and their backpack shifters.

The lone female of the group broke away from the procession and approached Howard. He smiled at the dreadlock tips that dangled from the base of her mirrored black helmet.

Melissa raised her visor and flashed him a humble grin. "Hello, Howard."

"Hi, boss. Damn. I guess I don't need to ask if you're ready."

Melissa now had the power to move at twenty times her normal speed. Her armor carried four gas bombs, three flash grenades, two sonic screamers, and a stun chaser. She kept a snub-nosed pistol in her side pouch in case Zack rusted her primary weapon. Most crucial of all were the two reviver vans parked right outside the building. In lieu of winning over her quarry's hearts and minds, she now had the freedom to shoot them everywhere else. This was Melissa's final chance to capture the fugitives alive. She wouldn't waste it on words.

She blew a hot breath, then looked to the barrier. "Let's get this thing down, shall we?"

Hannah eyed her dreary reflection in the restroom mirror. Her vision was coming back in dribs and drabs, enough to let her see the magnitude of her sister's injury. Amanda was in mortal agony and yet somehow she found the strength to fuss over Hannah's trifling burn. *You need to soak that hand,* she'd told her. *Put it in cool water, not cold.*

After forty seconds, Hannah yanked her fingers from the sink in restless anguish. There had to be something she could do for Amanda. Maybe she could make her a splint out of something, or find some painkillers. For once it was time for the dizzy actress to take care of the nurse.

She returned to the hallway and scanned the many glass doors. Though her weirdness was still smothered under a lingering sheen of solis, she figured she could smash her way into any one of these offices if she found something heavy enough.

Her search was interrupted by the sudden presence of music, a faint and tinny riff of jazz lounge trumpets. Hannah looked around and saw that the door to a nearby office—some personal injury law firm—had been opened a crack. Stranger still, she could swear she recognized the song that blared from within.

Soon her suspicions were confirmed by the unmistakable voice of the divine Sarah Vaughan.

Whatever Lola wants, Lola gets.
And little man, little Lola wants you . . .
Make up your mind to have no regrets.
Recline yourself, resign yourself, you're through.

Hannah reeled with fresh perplexity. This wasn't some Altamerican retread of her old favorite showtune. This was a haunting echo from her old dead Earth.

She pushed the door open in a dark and dreamy daze. The law firm's lobby was no larger than her old living room. Drab wood paneling covered every wall, while bubbly white chairs stood out like blisters on the red shag rug. There wasn't another soul in sight.

Through the glass wall of a conference room, she spied a clunky homemade contraption at the edge of a long table. Two large speakers were bridged at the top by a thick square battery. Clipped, split wires curled wildly in all directions.

Resting in the center of the construct, like a beating heart, was a tiny pink device that triggered another sharp flash of recognition in Hannah.

She was looking at her own iPod, the one she'd carried in her handbag on the day the world ended. Last she knew, the thing was dead and gathering dust in Terra Vista. What the hell was it doing here?

Suddenly the ground beneath her vibrated. Eight-foot poles of tempis sprang up all around her in a perfect square formation. Panicked, she shook the bars, then looked down at the metal platform below. A large engraving by her foot reminded owners to check their local laws for restrictions on using this Ellerbee-brand live animal trap.

She covered her eyes. "Oh no. No no no no no . . ."

Soft footsteps approached. A high and merry whistle kept rhythm with the song. Once her captor moved close enough to pause the iPod, Hannah opened her eyes and looked at him.

Evan Rander tossed her an impish grin through the bars of her cage. He tilted his head in mock concern.

"I'm sorry. Is this a bad time?"

Rebel lay flat on the marble, a grim and battered husk. The skin of his face had become as numb as a mask while the bones beneath throbbed with jagged pain. Through the sliver of his unsealed eye, he saw a narrow figure kneel at his side.

Ivy pressed his shoulders. "Don't move, hon. Don't try to talk. Your jaw's fractured. You have four shattered teeth and that creature rifted some skin on your cheeks. But you'll live."

He could tell from her level of knowledge that Gemma had been to the future to get the doctor's prognosis. The girl had probably already spent an evening at his bedside.

"Merzee," he mumbled.

"Olga's getting her now. She's out cold, but she'll make it. So will Bruce."

Rebel couldn't give a crap about Bruce Byer. He sensed from Ivy's grim omission that all the others were dead. Ben. Colin. Nick. Freddy. *We lost four. They lost none.*

"Firdy . . ."

"Richard, don't talk."

"How?"

Ivy closed her eyes. "Gemma says he was shot in the face. She thinks the boy did it."

A guttural groan escaped his lips. Ivy held his arm. "I know. I'm angry too. But right now I'm just so glad you're okay. I can't believe you survived that creature. I just can't believe it."

Rebel knew it wasn't luck. The Pelletiers had chosen to spare him, either out of strategy or sadism. Now that he'd been rifted again, he knew he couldn't be healed through reversal. The temporal discord in his body would kill him instantly, gruesomely. He'd have to recover the slow and painful way, as Semerjean no doubt intended.

While Olga carried Mercy over her shoulder, Ivy helped Rebel back to his feet. She slung his thick arm around her and walked him to her portal on the eastern wall.

Amanda followed their progress from her hidden perch. *Just go already. Leave.*

As Olga carried Mercy through the glimmering gateway, Rebel stopped and noticed his revolver. It had spun all the way through the eastern arch, resting halfway between the lobby and the entry for Nicomedia Magazines. One more second and he would have gotten Trillinger. One more second.

Ivy tugged him along. "Come on. We have to go."

His fresh failures bubbled inside him like boiling water. All the evidence they were leaving behind. All the dead kinsmen. All the living Silvers.

Rebel broke away from Ivy and charged through the archway.

"Richard!"

He seized the gun and fired seven shots through the open door. The first round hit the leg of the reception desk. The next two shattered the white glass wall behind it. The remaining four traveled into the sea of cubicles where Zack and Mia hid. Rebel's foresight was still hobbled by solis. He shot blindly and was now blind to the results.

By the time Ivy caught up to him, he fired empty clicks at the office. She grabbed his arm.

"Richard, stop! Stop! It's over!"

"No!"

"If we're lucky, the Deps will finish them. If not, we'll have other chances. But we have to go!"

Amanda turned white at the distant sound of gunshots. She looked to the southern archway and saw David make a stealthy reentrance. He ducked behind a support column just as Rebel and Ivy returned to the lobby. Amanda's fingers dug into her thighs.

Oh God, David, don't. Just let them leave.

A half mile to the north, Gemma accessed the Nicomedia office cameras and shook her head at the image.

"Christ, Rebel. You lucky son of a bitch."

Olga looked to Gemma. "What are you talking about?"

"He did it." She chuckled in wonder at the screen. "He got one."

Zack sprawled facedown on the carpet, his fingers pressed over his head. From the moment the glass wall exploded in front of him, his body went into system crash. He couldn't move. He couldn't think. He couldn't feel anything but the thundering beat of his heart.

Two minutes after Rebel's hasty exit, Zack and Mia worked their way back toward the front of the office, darting in and out of cubicles like skittish rabbits. Once they'd reached the first row, Zack made Mia wait behind him while he scanned the reception area. He'd only made it as far as the white glass partition when the shots rang out and the world seemed to end all over again.

Now the wall lay in shards all around him. For all he knew, his body was just as broken.

"Zack?"

The sound of Mia's voice prompted him to move. He clambered to a wobbly kneel, then checked himself with trembling hands. He still couldn't feel anything. He couldn't get his mouth to work.

"I . . . I . . . God . . ."

After four more seconds of self-scrutiny, he rose to his feet and blurted a nervous laugh.

"I think . . . I think I'm all right. I'm okay. Jesus, Mia. I . . ."

He turned around and saw her now. Her skin had turned chalk-white. She pressed a weak and trembling hand to her chest. For a hopeful moment, Zack figured she was simply struggling to collect herself. Then he saw the thick blood seeping through her fingers. His delirious grin faded.

"Oh God. No. No . . ."

Mia removed her hand and stared down at the oozing hole in the center of her chest. She thought about the policeman's bullet that had narrowly missed her face a month ago, the ridiculous luck that kept her in perfect health while her friends suffered wound after wound.

She finally understood how the universe worked now. Suddenly it all made sense.

"Zack . . ."

Her legs gave out from under her. She crumpled to the floor.

Four hundred and thirty feet away, in the tiny windowless office of the building security manager, Theo screamed in synch with Zack. His scattered thoughts came together in a unified roar, a thousand voices all wailing in grief, insisting that there were no futures left with Mia Farisi in them.

He clutched his hair, throwing his elbows left and right.

"No! No! No! No!"

It was at that cruelest of moments that a final gear snapped into place inside him. His eyes rolled back, his skin glowed white, and his consciousness took him to a strange new place.

At long last, Theo Maranan was formally introduced to his weirdness.

THIRTY-THREE

Everything stopped.

The ambient hum of the building generators fell silent. The light on the desk phone froze in mid-blink. A fat bead of water halted its drop from a sweaty ceiling pipe. It hung in the air like a miniature planet.

All over the office, all across creation, time held its breath and waited for Theo.

The bewildered augur kept as still as his surroundings as he fought to absorb this latest insanity. What little color the room had was gone. A thin gray mist blanketed the floor and walls. He saw twinkling specks of light through the fog, like distant cities.

Vague time passed—a second, a minute, an hour—before he dared to move. He writhed in his thoughts and suddenly found himself sling-shot to the other side of the office. Dumbstruck, he turned around and reeled at the haggard young Asian in his former place. The man sat huddled behind the desk in a frozen cry of grief, wearing Theo's face and clothes, his karma tattoo. It took five rounds of furious debate for him to accept that he was somehow looking at himself. *What? How is this . . . ?*

The mist on the eastern wall suddenly darkened and swirled like thunderclouds. A tall, reedy figure emerged from the depths, trailing smoky black wisps as he moved.

Azral Pelletier shined a cordial grin at the empty space where Theo's consciousness lingered.

"Welcome, child."

He looked majestically dapper in his stone-colored business suit and tieless white oxford. His flawless skin was now as colorless as his surroundings but his eyes remained a vibrant blue. The good cheer on his face did little to quell Theo's panic.

"Ease yourself," said Azral. "Your mind is still adjusting to the transition. Soon your senses will compensate and give you form."

Though his lips moved when he talked, Azral's cold honey voice hit Theo like a second set of thoughts. He struggled to reply, unsure if his words were spoken or merely imagined.

What happened to me? Am I dead?

Azral smirked. "On the contrary. You're more alive and awake than ever before."

Awake was one of the last words Theo would use to describe himself at the moment.

You're in my head.

"Yes."

His mind flashed back to the results of the cerebral scan that Melissa had shared with him.

You put something in my brain. Some tiny metal ring.

"A harmless device," Azral assured him. "It merely allows us to communicate in this state, little more."

His "little more" struck Theo like a salesman's asterisk. He felt a nervous lurch where his stomach used to be. "And where exactly . . ."

Theo balked at the new echo in his voice. Now he looked down to see a hazy facsimile of his body.

Azral nodded approvingly. "Already you adapt."

Theo was surprised to find himself in his faded Stanford hoodie, his old khaki shorts and sandals. It was his favorite outfit, one that had comforted him through many drunken travels.

"What's happening to me?"

"You're an augur, Theo. Did you think you'd spend the rest of your life suffering random glimpses? No. You're generations ahead of your peers, the so-called prophets of this age. Their talent is a crude cudgel. Yours is a violin. This is where the futures sing at your bow, my friend. This is your true gift."

A thunderous shudder filled Theo. By the time it passed, he appeared as whole as Azral. He could feel the ground beneath his feet again, a simulation of life and breath inside him. The sensation was even more pleasurable than waking life. He felt wonderful now. Except . . .

"Mia. I saw her. She was shot in the chest. Did that really happen? Has it happened already?"

"It has occurred," Azral calmly replied. "She fades from life at this moment."

"No . . ."

"We can address the matter later. For now—"

"I have to find her!"

"Boy, look around you. What do you see?"

Theo took another wide-eyed glance around the office. The fat water droplet still dangled in the air. The clock on the wall remained rooted at 11:56 and 48 seconds, with no signs of letting go.

"So it's not just here," Theo said. "Time stopped everywhere."

Azral emitted a soft chuckle, snugly perched between fondness and ridicule.

"You can't stop time any more than you can stop a desert or a forest. Time is a landscape that stretches across all things. We're the ones who move across it."

Theo shook his head in hopeless perplexity. "I don't—"

"If it helps, think of all the people of the world as passengers on a train. You travel through time at the same speed and direction, perceiving events through your own narrow windows. The concepts of past and future are entirely human constructs. We formulated them as navigational markers, like east and west. Only now—"

"I got off the train."

Azral smiled again. "You're not the first of your kind to achieve this state, though my ancestors only seem to come here by accident. They romantically refer to this realm as the God's Eye. You'd do just as well to call it the Gray."

Theo didn't care what it was called. If he was forever stuck here at the cusp of noon, it was Hell.

"Is there . . . a way back on the train?"

"Of course. You can resume your journey at any time. I'll show you how, but not yet. Come with me. If you wish to aid your companions, there are things you should see."

Theo felt a gentle hand on his back. He'd only taken three steps out of the room when a cold force pushed him forward like a leaf in a gale. By the time his dizzy senses returned to him, he found himself outside the building.

"What . . . what just . . . ?"

"A quicker mode of transit," Azral explained. "Foot travel is a needless formality here."

Theo's next question fizzled in the urgency of his surroundings. More than twenty federal agents now flanked the building—all paused in tense and busy actions. A ghost team fixed their imaging towers around the Silvers' dusty red car while a second group wheeled a large metal device that reminded Theo of a supervillain's death ray. He shuddered to think what it would do once the clock started ticking again.

"Shit. It's worse than I thought."

"Indeed," said Azral. "In one hundred thirty-two seconds, their crude solic toy will breach the barrier."

Theo looked to the eight gun-toting Deps in armored black speedsuits. He could only assume they were all assigned to take down Hannah. "We'll never make it out of here."

"You'll escape. It's the continuing presence of these government agents that troubles me. There may yet be a remedy."

"What remedy?"

"It's my task," Azral curtly replied. "Not yours."

Theo churned with stress as he recalled Azral's remote-button slaughter of twenty-one physicists, another so called remedy. *They worked for you and you killed them. Bill Pollock got me sober and you killed him.*

"I never wished to slay those scientists," Azral replied, to Theo's unease. "I saw the consequences of their continued existence, an elaborate chain of events that would have destroyed you and a great many others. It's the burden of foresight. Our choices often seem questionable to those around us, even cruel. You'll know this soon enough."

Theo saw the dreadlocks dangling from an armored agent's helmet and struggled to avoid all thoughts of Melissa. If the Pelletiers identified her as the face of their federal problem, she was dead.

Azral put his hand on Theo's back. "Come."

In a windy swirl, the scenery changed once more. Now they stood in the vast marble lobby, a place that had seen much violence since Theo left it.

Furniture all around the room had been smashed and singed and spattered with blood. Two wet and gory strangers lay facedown in the elevator bank while a third corpse languished on the stairwell.

Theo looked to the inanimate couple at the eastern wall, poised inches from a glowing white portal. Though the alluring Indian woman was a stranger to him, he had no trouble recognizing the bald and brawny thug who'd shot him in Terra Vista. A stagnant curl of smoke extended like coral from the barrel of Rebel's revolver.

"Goddamn it. It was him, wasn't it? He shot Mia."

Azral glared at Rebel. He'd only just now caught up on the battle in the lobby—the savage beating of his mother, the timely intervention from his father. His voice dropped a cold octave.

"You won't have to worry about him much longer."

"Why is he trying to kill us? What did we do to him?"

Azral shook his head in scorn. "Beneath all that bulk, Richard Rosen is nothing more than a frightened child. He sees a dark event coming and he can't bear the thought of it. So his weak mind conjures a theory, an enemy, a brutal solution. He's hardly the first man in history to blame his troubles on immigrants."

Theo scanned the room and caught David hiding behind a support pillar, his pistol raised high in frozen readiness.

"Oh no . . ."

Azral bloomed a small grin. "He'll be fine. The boy's remarkably capable for his age."

Theo was all too aware of that. Azral gleaned his flip-side worry.

"You believe he'll kill this pair."

"I don't know." Theo eyed the pregnant bulge in Ivy's bodysuit. "I hope not."

"Why would you show concern for those who would slaughter you without hesitation?"

"I'm mostly concerned for David. I don't want to see him go down a dark path."

"Have you?"

Theo had to think about it. He'd suffered countless premonitions over the last several days, but only just now realized how very few of them involved David. His future seemed to fall in a blind spot.

"No."

"Have faith in him then," Azral said. "Let us continue."

The next jaunt took them up to the fifth-floor walkway that overlooked the lobby. The mist was ten times thicker here. Theo had to stand next to Amanda to see her on the cushioned bench.

"God, her leg . . ."

Azral studied her broken ankle. "Yes. Strange that my mother didn't heal her. She favors this one. The child must have angered her."

"You're talking about Esis."

"Yes."

"She doesn't look old enough to be your mother."

"She would adore you for saying that."

"I've only seen her in visions." Theo scowled in hot contempt. "She keeps killing Zack."

Azral frowned. "Trillinger is a buffoon and a nuisance. I see now why Quint found him so vexing."

"He's my friend!"

"If you seek to keep him, his fate is easily prevented."

"How?"

Azral raised a long finger at Amanda. "She knows."

The white-haired man floated deeper into the fog. Theo scrambled to keep up with him, even as his screaming thoughts urged him to flee.

"Why is it so hazy here?"

"Even in this realm, none of us are omniscient. As we move farther from our own sphere of influence, our view grows weaker. Should we venture but one floor higher, I wager we'd glimpse nothing but mist."

That's why you're teaching me, Theo surmised. *You need me to see the things you can't.*

If Azral heard his thoughts, he didn't acknowledge them. He led Theo into a small office that looked like a low-grade law firm. Through the swirling mist, he spotted Hannah inside a small tempic cage. She gripped the bars, her face contorted in a silent scream.

He had to move closer to spot the source of her anguish.

"Jesus Christ! You've got to be kidding me!"

Evan Rander was dressed in the stately beige uniform of a security guard, an ensemble that looked silly on his scrawny frame. Theo could only guess the outfit was part of his personal escape plan. He'd probably put on his best Barney Fife impression for the Deps, give a few shaky statements, and then slip away while no one was looking.

The rogue Silver wore a nasty grin as he fired a bullhorn-shaped device at Hannah.

"What's he doing to her?"

"He inflicts her with a low electric charge," Azral replied. "He seeks to torment, not kill."

"Son of a bitch. Why does he hate her so much?"

"He hates both sisters. The reasons hardly matter. Rander is nothing. A pathetic fool. I only show him to you as a cautionary example."

"What, you're afraid I'll become like him?"

"In mind-set, not temperament. The boy has lived hundreds of years and yet he still fails to grasp the structure of time. He sees the past as his chalkboard, a single line to be erased and redrawn at whim. In truth, he undoes nothing. He merely jumps from train to train, forever dodging the consequences of his actions. I'm hoping you won't be so linear in your thinking."

Theo covered his face in hot distress. His friends were all suffering and Azral was giving him a primer in fiftieth-century metaphysics.

"What will it take?"

"For what?"

"For this guy to see consequences!"

Azral jerked a testy shrug. "His talents give him a unique perspective on events, which in turn provides us with helpful information. But perhaps I should reevaluate his usefulness."

"I don't want him dead. I just want him to leave us alone."

"Yes. I thought I'd dissuaded him when last we spoke. Perhaps I need to make myself clearer."

Azral studied Theo carefully as he reached for Hannah with an intangible hand. "You feel strongly for this one."

"Yeah, but not the way you think."

"You don't know what I think," Azral snapped. "If I deemed your love to be physical, we'd be having a different conversation."

Theo looked to him in wide-eyed bother. "What . . . what do you mean?"

"Just take comfort that you won't lose her. Not anytime soon."

"I know." He turned to Hannah again. "I see her all over my future. She's everywhere I look."

"You say it like it troubles you."

"It troubles me that I don't see the others as clearly. Can you *please* take me to Mia now?"

Azral nodded obligingly, though his handsome face turned grim.

"Come, then."

He'd prepared himself for the worst, but what Theo saw in the magazine office sent his proxy form to chaos. He screamed and cried with two blurry heads, punched at the air with four hazy hands. He paced the floor in all directions while five ghostly duplicates fell to their knees. He was everywhere at once—an army of Theos, all thrashing and grieving over the youngest of the Silvers.

Mia lay cradled in Zack's arms, her eyes wide with vacant horror as he pressed a bloody T-shirt to her chest wound. The cartoonist served a silent contrast to Theo's raging sorrow, a snapshot image of a man in blanket shock. His tears had paused in mid-journey, lining his cheeks like scars.

Azral stood expressionless among the broken glass, calmly waiting for his protégé to collect himself.

"Theo . . ."

One by one, the doppelgängers vanished. A lone Theo crouched by Mia's side. "How long does she have?"

"Moments," Azral informed him. "She dies before the agents breach the barrier."

"Oh God. There has to be something we can do."

"I don't know, Theo. Is there?"

"Don't play games with me! I'm not in the mood!"

"It's your mood that clouds you. Your emotions prevent you from seeing."

"Seeing what?"

"The futures," Azral said, with a sweeping hand gesture. "They reveal themselves in this place. They sing to us from every corner. Have you not wondered about the lights in the mist?"

Theo looked to the northern wall, at the tiny beads that twinkled within the fog. He'd glimpsed them everywhere he turned in this dreary gray world. He didn't know why they scared him.

"What are they?"

"I said your talent was a violin, Theo. These . . ."

Azral moved behind him, plunging his fingers deep into the augur's skull. "These are the strings."

Hot white strands of light converged on Theo from every direction. His consciousness erupted in a screaming torrent of images—a million parallel futures, all as different as siblings but knotted at the ends with the same painful traumas. Every string ended with his own cold death. Every string started with Mia's.

"NO!"

Azral leaned in close, his imperious voice cutting through the chaos. "You see them now. All the branching possibilities. All the endless permutations and patterns. We've been so blind, Theo. Our species has lived for so long like moles in a tunnel. You're among the first to step into the light and see time as it was meant to be seen. This is humanity's greatest evolution. A whole new dimension of perception. It's beautiful, is it not?"

"It hurts!"

"You hinder yourself."

"She keeps dying!"

"You adopt the grief of your elder incarnations. For them, it's too late to save her. Not for you. Detach yourself and perhaps you'll find a brighter outcome hidden among the multitudes."

With a raspy shout, Theo thrust his palms and cleared a six-foot ball of space around him. The strings now ended in a curved wall of pinlights. The bedlam in his thoughts dissipated.

Azral retracted his hands. "Good. Very good."

The augur dropped to his ethereal knees, panting through imaginary lungs. "Go to hell . . ."

"I only seek to aid you. The girl can be saved."

"You're lying!"

"Look again. Search the strings more carefully. You've no reason to hurry. We don't age here. Our bodies don't clamor for food or sleep. In this realm, time is our servant. Use it."

Theo raised his head and squinted at the array of tiny lights. Glancing at it was like staring into an endless crowd of suffering children, searching for the one who smiled. And Azral expected him to do this for days, weeks, years on end. *Is this how you learned the strings, you murderous shit? Is this what turned you cold and white?*

He squinted his eyes shut. "I can't do this! I can't keep watching her die!"

"Then she is indeed lost."

"You know how to save her. Just tell me!"

"Am I indebted to you, boy? Are you the one who rescued me from a dying world, or was it perhaps the other way around?"

"I never asked you to give me a goddamn bracelet! And you wouldn't have saved us if you didn't need us for something. So just tell me! Tell me how to keep her alive!"

Azral sighed defeatedly, a reaction that nearly made Theo burst with jaded laughter. Though he was new to the Gray or the God's Eye or whatever this place was called, he was a decorated veteran in disappointing people. The familiarity soothed him like a warm shot of whiskey.

"It seems I overestimated you, Theo."

"You found me drunk at a bus stop. What did you expect?"

"I found you long before that, but no matter." Azral touched Theo's back. "Come."

Their final journey was different from the others. Instead of twirling around like a leaf, Theo shot forward at blurring speed, his vision a tableau of bright, streaking colors. Occasionally he felt a shift in direction, as if Azral steered them down a branching path. *Forks in the road,* Theo mused, though he imagined it was hardly so binary. There were likely millions of options at every juncture, millions of variations and subvariations, even a few minor miracles.

After an indeterminate period—nestled somewhere in the space between "soon" and "soon enough"—the pair emerged into a sparse but cozy living room. Venetian blinds filtered afternoon sunlight. Taped moving boxes lined the bare walls. A group of mismatched chairs and couches stood in sloppy formation around a circular glass coffee table. The cushions were occupied by five people Theo readily recognized, including himself.

His twin stretched out on a plush recliner, locking his arms around Hannah's waist as she wearily leaned against him. Zack, David, and Amanda all slouched alone in their sofas. Amanda wore a makeshift splint of broken broomsticks and duct tape. The others sported numerous bandages.

The spectral Theo peeked over David's shoulder and examined his wristwatch.

"It's a quarter after one. A little over an hour from now."

Azral cracked a patronizing grin at Theo's muddled notion of "now."

"Where is this?" Theo asked.

"Approximately five miles east of the office tower."

Theo peeked out the window at a red-leafed sycamore tree. "Brooklyn. Jesus, we really did get out."

"In this string, yes."

"But what about—"

Hannah cut him off with a melodious yawn, startling him. He thought the scene was a still frame like all the others. His friends were merely languishing in dull stupor.

Now he heard the clinking of ceramics through the kitchen door. His eyes bulged when Mia entered with a tray of steaming mugs. Though her face drooped with fatigue like all the others', she looked healthy enough to live for decades.

She placed a cup on the end table next to Amanda. "He doesn't have milk. Sorry."

The widow stared ahead in dead torpor, her voice a flimsy wisp. "Okay."

The spectral Theo continued to study Mia in slack awe. "God. It's like she was never shot. How did that happen? Was there a reviver in the building?"

"There was a reviver in that very room," Azral replied. "You simply failed to see it."

"Well, how do I find it then?"

"What do you mean?"

"When I go back. How do I make this the future that happens?"

Azral eyed him with dark disbelief, as if Theo were lost in a broom closet.

"This *is* happening, child. Every path of time exists on the landscape, one as real as the next. Did you think I merely brought you here for instruction?"

Now Theo was truly lost. "What are you telling me?"

"I said you could resume your journey at any time. You have only to concentrate to take your place in that chair. Your life will continue seamlessly from this moment. Is that not preferable?"

Theo blinked distractedly, his mind twisting in furious dilemma. As tempting as it was to be done with all the day's traumas, he couldn't shake the subtle air of incongruity that kept him detached from this scene. These friends didn't feel exactly like the people he knew. This was Zack with an asterisk, Hannah with a caveat.

Azral studied him warily. "What troubles you now?"

"I don't know. I'm just trying to wrap my head around it. I mean if I do this, what happens to the other timeline?"

"It continues."

"Without me?"

"Very much with you."

"How does that work?"

"Far beyond your understanding," Azral replied, with crusty impatience. "To explain it now would be like explaining a sphere to a circle. You're not ready. Perhaps you never will be. You're more like Rander than I feared."

Theo crossed his arms and stared at his other self sandwiched comfortably between a soft chair and a warm actress. There had to be a catch to this bow wrapped present. This string had to have its own strings attached.

"Is this what you do, Azral? You pick and choose the futures you want?"

"As I said—"

"Right. It's beyond me. There's no denying that. But I'm not like Evan. The thought of jumping trains right now makes me queasy. It feels like I'm leaving my friends behind."

Azral shook his head in brusque bemusement. "You beg me for hints and now reject the full answer. You're a fool."

"I am a fool," Theo admitted. "I've been one as long as I can remember. But you know what? You came at me on the second-worst day of my life. You showed me everyone I care about in horrible danger and then somehow expected me to grasp the intricacies of the universe. For a master of time, you have shitty timing. You also killed Bill Pollock. So no, I don't trust this answer of yours. And I don't believe for one second that you just happened to save us from a dying Earth. I'm pretty sure it was healthy until you came along."

In the sharp and frosty silence, Theo grew convinced that Azral's next move would be lethal. Instead the white-haired man merely summoned a single strand of light from the wall. The moment it hit Theo, he felt a vague sense of familiarity, like a numb hand on his arm.

"What . . . what is this?"

"The path of return," said Azral. "This string will lead you back seventy-six minutes to the place you and your companions still suffer. If you proceed slowly enough, you'll witness events in reverse and note all the timely decisions that enabled your escape. Perhaps you'll succeed in duplicating this outcome. Perhaps you'll fail and lose more than one friend in the process. It seems a needless risk to take when you're already here, but I suppose fools will do as they do."

Long seconds passed as Theo pondered the heavy new task ahead. Azral shined his cool blue eyes on Hannah.

"Seh tu'a mortia rehu eira kahne'e nada ehru heira."

Theo eyed him strangely. "What was that?"

"An old expression of my people, a rallying mantra for the soldiers and scientists who kill for the greater good. 'I shall feed Death before I starve her.'"

"Why are you telling me this?"

"You think me a monster when I'm merely a crusader. My parents and I fight for the greatest purpose of all. If we succeed in our endeavor here, we'll save countless trillions of lives. We will starve Death like none other before us."

Theo narrowed his eyes. For a cynical moment, Azral looked as silly as a biologist explaining the benefits of cancer research to his lab mice.

"Small comfort to the ones you serve to her," Theo groused. "When's it our turn?"

"We didn't bring you here to kill you. On the contrary, we've labored to keep you all alive. Do you think it was fate that rescued you from your coma? Was it the hand of God that pulled Hannah from the brink of a fatal concussion? We've provided you with comfort and aid at every turn, Theo. And yet even now as I offer a means to save the child Farisi, you see me as an enemy."

"How am I supposed to know what you are to us when you won't tell us what we are to you?"

"Crucial," said Azral. "There are those among you who are crucial to our plans. I would think that'd be obvious by now."

"But what do you *want* with us?"

Azral regarded him with a jaded leer. "I see the futures better than you, child. Telling you now serves no benefit. You'll know when it suits us."

Theo chucked his ethereal hands. "So we just go about our lives in the meantime, hoping we don't do anything to piss you off."

"If you hinder us by accident, you'll be duly warned as the elder Given was."

And if we hinder you on purpose? Theo wondered, before he could stop the thought.

The mist on the wall grew dark and stormy. Azral floated toward the swirling exit, then turned around to bathe Theo in an icy stare.

"Look to the strings, boy. See what becomes of our enemies."

He disappeared into the fog, leaving Theo alone in this quiet scene, this teasing preenactment of better times. It seemed utterly daft to throw himself back into the fray and risk Mia's life in retrospect. And yet the more he thought of Azral, the more he feared the numbing effects of this talent. If he had access to a billion Mias, how long before he stopped mourning the loss of one or two of them? How long before he shrugged off the death of one measly Earth?

He worked his hands around the lone strand of light and found it as solid as a rope. With a hearty tug, he pulled himself toward the past, determined to reverse engineer their escape from the office building. Theo didn't care how long it took him. He had all the time in the world to get it right.

THIRTY-FOUR

The seconds moved with slow-ticking fury as David watched the last two Gothams stagger toward the exit. While his maimed right hand felt light enough to float away, his other wrist was burdened with a .40 caliber pistol and a vintage silver watch. It had been forty-four ticks since Rebel's last gunshot echoed through the eastern arch, ample time for David to envision all the worst scenarios. The thought of Mia with a bullet in her eye—just one shade darker than the current reality—made his gun arm twitch with a vicious life of its own. *Tick, tick, tick.*

The hands on his watch hit 11:57 when he leapt out from behind his pillar and summoned a line of ghostly duplicates. Eight Davids aimed their pistols in synch, speaking with one firm voice.

"Stop."

Rebel and Ivy turned around at the portal, freezing at the sight of the one-man posse just forty feet away. Ivy jumped in front of her husband.

"Don't shoot us! We're leaving! We're going!"

"Try it," David hissed. "See how well that works for you."

Sixty feet above, Amanda wrung her fingers in screaming tension. *Just let them go, David. You'll get yourself killed!*

Rebel dropped his empty gun and heel-kicked it through the portal. He tried to speak but could only groan a pained garble.

The eight Davids cocked their heads. "I'm sorry. Was that English?"

"He can't talk," Ivy explained. "Look at him."

"Yes. I can see someone already had their fun with him. What's he trying to say?"

"He's asking you to let me go."

"Does he expect me to believe you're innocent in all this?"

"No. But our child is. Look at me."

David narrowed his cool blue eyes at her bulging stomach. "What's your name?"

"Krista."

He raised his gun. "Try again."

"Ivy! My name's Ivy!"

"Well, Ivy, tell me something. Why should I care about the innocent lives in your family when you clearly don't care about the innocent lives in mine?"

Rebel leaned forward in growling defense. Ivy held him back.

"You think we like doing this? We're not assassins. I'm a network engineer. My husband's a security consultant. Freddy was a college student."

"Who's Freddy?"

"The boy you shot in the face."

David balked at her knowledge before hardening again. "You sent him to kill us. I was only defending myself."

"That's just what we're doing! We're defending ourselves and everyone we know! You have no idea what's at stake here!"

"Nor do you," he said, as he peered through the arch. "See, your man just fired seven gunshots and I'm anxious to know where they went. So we're going to walk in that direction and find out together. I swear to you, if any of my people—"

A distant shriek echoed through the chamber, filtering down from the fifth floor. While the trio in the lobby looked up, Amanda turned her white gaze down the hall.

"Hannah?"

Seeing his chance, Rebel wrapped his arms around Ivy and threw them back through the portal. David aimed his pistol at the white liquid pool as it shrank closed. He muttered a curse, then waved away his mirror selves.

The door to the maintenance hall flew open with a kick. David watched Theo with blank-faced puzzlement as the augur bolted through the lobby like a champion sprinter. His urgent expression filled David with dread.

"Theo, what happened? What did you see?"

A second scream rang out from the fifth floor. David launched his troubled gaze back and forth, up and east, before forcing a hot decision.

"Goddamn it."

He ran after Theo. His wristwatch ticked to 11:58.

Theo had no idea how long he'd been in the God's Eye. For all he knew, he spent days on his backtracking path through time, analyzing every twist and turn of their impending escape. He knew how precarious these next few minutes would be. He didn't have an inch of room for error.

He rushed past the reception desk of Nicomedia Magazines, over the broken glass, and into the cubicle where Zack cradled Mia in his arms. The two of them breathed the same shallow breaths in synch, wore the same bombshelled expression. Only Zack looked up and noticed Theo.

"Where's Amanda?"

"Zack . . ."

"Where's Amanda?!"

"She's all right. Listen—"

Zack shook his head, venting all the notions that had stacked up in his mind like greasy dishes.

"I think the bullet missed her heart. If we can keep her from slipping into shock, she'll have a chance. Amanda will know what to do."

"I know what to do, Zack. You have to listen to me . . ."

They both turned at the sound of hurried footsteps. The moment David reached the cubicle, his jaw went slack and his gun fell from his hand.

"Mia . . ." He dropped to his knees and clutched her arm, his bloody face twisting with grief. "No. *No!*"

Mia kept her glazed stare on the ceiling, her consciousness swirling at the bottom of a deep, dark well. She could hear David's voice far above her. She could feel Zack holding her dying body in his arms. Strange how she came into this world buried six feet underground and was now fixing to leave it like a nestled newborn.

From grave to cradle, she thought. *I did it all backwards.*

David brushed the bangs from her forehead. "You stay with me, Mia. You hear me?" He turned to Theo. "You said the Deps were coming."

"They're already here." He glanced at the wall clock. "They'll hit the lobby in eighty-two seconds."

"If they're storming the building, they'll have revivers outside."

"No, David—"

"I'll bring her to them! They'll fix her!"

"And then take you both," Zack said.

"You'll get us back, just like we got Amanda and Theo back."

"You think Melissa won't expect that next time? You think she'll make it easy?"

"Zack, you have to trust me—"

Theo kicked a file cabinet. "NO! She's going to die in *seconds*! That's what I'm trying to tell you! You're the only hope she has, Zack! *You're* the reviver!"

The cartoonist drank him in through saucer eyes. It had been five days since his last healing attempt, one that had gruesome consequences for a poor young fawn. The thought of trying again on Mia, a much larger creature, seemed as safe as closing her wound with dynamite.

"It won't work," he insisted. "It'll just kill her quicker."

David nodded darkly at Theo. "He's right. You didn't see what happened last time."

Theo was all too familiar with the risks. He'd stopped at this very place in the God's Eye to view the alternate outcomes. Zack only managed to save Mia ten percent of the time at best. In nearly all other instances, she ended up a pristine corpse or a desiccated husk. Most horrific of all were the riftings, the times Mia woke up screaming in agony as her distended stomach exploded in a torrent of blood and gases.

Theo had spent long, painful hours analyzing the details, looking for some identifiable factor that separated the wins from the losses. In the end, it all came down to timing. There was a three-second window where Zack succeeded more often than not. It was almost here.

"Zack, I've seen it. I've watched you bring her back to life. But you got to get ready. You have to do it exactly when I tell you. Please."

David gripped Zack's arm. "Let me take her to the agents. It's her only chance."

"David, shut up! You're killing her!"

"*You're* killing her! You have no idea what you're doing!"

Zack tuned out his friends, his addled gaze drifting around the cubicle. He was stunned to find a recent issue of *Wonders* with his own image on the cover, the famous photo of his plummet from a hotel balcony. Once again he saw his face contorted in purple agony as Amanda's great tempic hand squeezed him from above. In cropped context, it looked like God Himself had reached down to smite him. Now the bastard's cruel hand was coming for Mia.

No, thought the cartoonist. *You will not.*

"David, get back."

"Wait. Listen to me—"

"Get back!"

Theo pulled David to his feet. Zack lay Mia flat on the carpet, then joined the others at the cubicle entry. The augur fixed his stare on the wall clock, his finger raised tensely.

"Wait."

Suddenly Mia wheezed a loud and broken gasp. Her eyes fluttered to a close.

"What was that?" Zack asked.

"Her last breath," Theo replied. "Go."

Zack clenched his fists and squinted in nervous concentration. Mia's limp body shuddered. Her skin lit up with a gauzy incandescence. Zack gritted his teeth, struggling to hold the temporis that bucked and swerved like a rickety spotlight. He knew that if any part of Mia fell outside the glow, even for a moment, she'd be lost forever.

Four seconds into his battle, the magazine cover penetrated his thoughts, shaking his focus and plaguing him with an overwhelming sense of futility. He shot his rage upward at the malignant forces of the universe—the ones who took his world, then yanked his brother away on a short rubber string. Now they teased him with a flicker of hope for Mia. He could already see the punch line coming.

Suddenly, Amanda's lovely face bloomed in his thoughts like a sunrise. Her lips curled in a wry and canny smirk.

Oh Zachary, you schmuck. You cynic. You think I wasted time cursing the heavens when you fell from that balcony? Uh-uh. I ran right to the edge and caught you. That's not God's hand smiting you in that photo. That's Him and me saving you.

Warm tears spilled down Zack's cheeks as his inner Amanda stroked his face.

It's so easy to believe, after everything we've seen, that we live in a cold and senseless universe. But as long as we have a world to live in, as long as we have people to love, we are the lucky ones, Zack. We are the blessed.

Now go catch our little sister. Bring her back to us.

With a last cry of strain, Zack engulfed Mia in a cool blinding flash. David and Theo unshielded their eyes to find Mia motionless on the floor. Her feet were bare and her hair was damp from the shower. Her clean silk blouse was unbuttoned all the way to her navel, revealing a perfectly unblemished sternum.

The men stood as frozen as statues while they waited for her body's response. They knew this was the crucial moment, the point where Mia would scream or explode or merely die quietly. Or . . .

She sat up with a lurch, gasping with urgent breath. David and Theo flanked her sides.

"Mia!"

She looked around the cubicle with frantic eyes, and then screamed in bewilderment. This Mia was nine hours younger than the one Rebel shot. She'd only just slammed the bathroom door on the sisters in Quinwood. Then suddenly her whole existence screeched like a yanked vinyl record and she felt the vague sense of drowning. Now here she was in some strange corporate office that looked like it had been through World War II. Zack and David were both marred with bloody gashes. Theo never looked healthier.

Mia glanced down at her open shirt, then anxiously covered herself. "What's happening? Where are we?"

David wrapped his arms around her, hugging her with a gushing relief that scared her as much as it thrilled her. She feebly returned the embrace. "You're bleeding."

He croaked a soft chuckle. "I'm all right. I'll be fine."

"David, what's going on?"

"We'll explain it," Theo promised. "But right now we have to go. David, can you carry her?"

He nodded at Theo, his young brow curled in gentle contrition. "What's the plan?"

"There's a hatch in the generator room. It'll take us underground. We have to move fast."

"I heard someone screaming upstairs. I think it was—"

"We'll deal with that." Theo looked to Zack. The reversal had left him even more shell-shocked than Mia.

"Zack . . ." Theo shook his shoulder. "Zack!"

"Huh?"

"I know that took a lot out of you, but we're not done yet. This is the hard part."

Zack's absent stare turned sharp with worry. "Amanda. Hannah . . ."

"I know."

"We have to get them."

"We will. I promise. Come on."

While Zack regained his footing, Theo avoided David's suspicious leer. It seemed like weeks ago that Azral warned the augur about the burden of foresight. *Our choices often seem questionable to those around us, even cruel. You'll know this soon enough.*

"Soon enough" had come far too soon for Theo. There was no way to prepare his friends, no time to explain why they had to leave Hannah and Amanda behind. Even the best strings turned in bad directions. The sisters had to suffer just a little bit more.

The law office shook with loud orchestral drama. Evan had cued Hannah's iPod to the original Broadway cast recording of *Les Misérables*, thirty-ninth track. Now he danced around the reception area in his security guard uniform, a puckish smile on his face and a cone-shaped gun in his swinging hand.

He minced his way to the dismal corner where Hannah wept, strutting with operatic pomp as he marched to the final battle song.

"Ohh, would you listen to that drama? I'm all tingly. Aren't you tingly?"

The actress lay fetal on the floor of her cage, her hands pressed over her eyes. Evan had drawn three screams from her with his handheld jolter, a weapon legally restricted to riot police. Though its static electric charge could clear a small crowd without causing injury, the blast was far less gentle to those who couldn't flee. Every inch of Hannah's skin throbbed with hot needle stings.

Evan paused the iPod, then heaved a bleak sigh.

"Tragic. The only surviving music from our world and it's all showtunes and crap pop. Typical Hannah. Bouncy, flouncy, mispronouncy. It kills me to think of all the great minds who died while you just keep on jiggling."

She pulled her hands away, only to flinch at his sickening leer. It bore through her clothes and skin, making her feel worse than naked, worse than the dumb animal he'd trapped so easily.

"Bet you're itching to know how I got my hands on your little pink jukebox."

"Go to hell," she croaked.

"Yeah, that's right. Azral gave it to me. He knows I'm a sucker for old-world gewgaws."

"Why?"

"Hey, I have a sentimental side."

"Why would he give you a gift?"

"Oh." Evan's grin deflated. "I guess *he* has a sentimental side."

His last encounter with Azral and Esis had been a tense, mystifying affair. He knew they were mad about his hotel prank, the spiked mimosa cocktails that triggered a near-fatal brawl between Amanda and Hannah. And yet instead of venting their ire, the pair took Evan on a portal jaunt to Amsterdam, treating him to a sumptuous lunch at a five-star floating restaurant.

At dessert, Azral presented Evan with a book bag full of treasures rescued from Terra Vista—Zack's original sketchbook, Theo's Oakland A's cap, Hannah's iPod and *Entertainment Weekly*. The unprecedented bounty had left Evan speechless. After fifty-four lifetimes, he still couldn't figure out the Pelletiers. They operated with the convoluted madness of a Rube Goldberg machine, shaping all their actions on complex calculations and byzantine prophecies.

Once they returned to Indiana, Azral acted more in line with expectations. He'd gripped Evan's arm, chilling him to the bone with his harsh blue stare.

"You will not jeopardize Hannah again. Not until she serves or fails her function."

Esis made it clear, in her own loopy way, that the same applied for Amanda.

As the days passed and his purpose on this world grew muddier, Evan convinced himself that there were still plenty of ways to strike at the sisters without risking their precious bodies. If anything, the challenge made Round 55 a hell of a lot more interesting.

He plucked his handtop from the reception desk. An empty view of the hallway filled the tiny screen. *Christ, sister. Hop to it. We're on a clock here.*

"You know, it wasn't easy bringing your iPod back to life," he boasted to Hannah. "They have none of the right cables or batteries here. I had to jury-rig a solution. And hey, speaking of Jury . . ."

"Fuck you."

"Whoa ho ho! The man's a sore spot already. And just from a driver's license photo. Good thing you never saw his biceps. You'd be inconsolable."

Hannah shot him a murderous glare. From the moment Evan showed his cruel and juvenile face, she sensed an odd frustration behind his loathing. He wanted to do so much more to her than he was currently doing. Clearly it wasn't his conscience holding him back.

"My iPod wasn't a gift," she speculated. "It was a bribe. Azral doesn't want you hurting us."

Evan narrowed his eyes in pique. The woman could be jarringly sharp when she wanted to be. He scrambled for cover behind a sneering grin.

"Nice thought, Giggles, but Azral didn't care when I killed Jury. He won't shed a tear over you. By the way, I have to know. Are you still carrying his license? You can tell me."

"No."

"Liar. Come on. I know you're keeping Jury near your naughty bits. Show me."

"Would anyone shed a tear if you died, Evan?"

"You would."

"I'd cry with joy."

"That counts." He raised his jolter. "Now are you going to empty your pockets or do I need to make you fork over your pants?"

"You'd like that, wouldn't you? That's what this is all about."

"Getting in your pants?" Evan cackled with scorn. "Oh sweet Jesus. The ego on you. If I wanted that, hon, there are easier ways. Spreading your legs is the fastest thing you do."

"For men like Jury," she seethed. "Not like you."

"Amazing how you're proud of your shallow standards."

"Is that why you killed him?"

"Don't play detective, Boopsie. You're out of your element."

"You told Zack you used to be part of our group. You and Jury both."

Evan sighed with ennui. It was always so tedious to watch the Silvers play catch-up.

"In times undone," he told her. "Days gone bye-bye. Don't mistake my wistful look for nostalgia. The memories aren't fond."

"What did I do to make you so angry?"

He checked the screen of his handtop. *All right. Finally.*

"The question you should be asking right now . . ."

He pressed a button on his console.

". . . is what did *she* do?"

Hannah spun around in her cage, just as her sister collapsed in front of the open door.

"Amanda!"

Forty minutes ago, Evan had stashed a video camera and an electron chaser in the planter outside the law office. The moment Amanda hobbled into range, he remotely activated the weapon's charge. In an instant, the widow's world went red with pain and her muscles turned to jelly.

Evan dragged her inside and closed the door behind them. Hannah shook the bars of her cage. "Stop it! Leave her alone!"

"Hush now, darling. Screaming time is over." He snickered derisively. "I swear, you two are so easy to trap. Just a shame it took Peter's Cotton Tail so long to hop her way over here. We're a little behind schedule."

His synchron watch beeped its noon chime. Evan adjusted the handtop to access his lobby cameras.

"Yup. There it goes."

Hannah eyed him confusedly. "What are you talking about?"

"The barricade," he replied, with a savage grin. "The Deps are storming the castle."

At the stroke of noon, the tempic sheath around the building fell to the government's solic drill. The glass doors shattered at the edge of a metal battering ram.

Rosie Herrera shouted a staccato barrage of orders as she led the charge to the lobby. Her motormouth zeal was fueled half by adrenaline and half by fear that Melissa would try to seize control of the operation. To Rosie's surprise, the eccentric agent from L.A. followed the crowd in demure silence. Once she reached the first bloodstain, Melissa uttered a single word.

"Shift."

Eight armored speedsuits lit up with a crosshatch of bright red lines as their wielders jumped to maximum velocity. A temporal voice converter in each helmet allowed the team to communicate with their unshifted brethren, though Melissa had quietly disabled those devices nine minutes ago. The speeding elites were now isolated in their own headset network, Melissa's to command by default rank protocol. *Sorry, Rosie. It's easier this way.*

"Fan out," she ordered them. "Search every corner. You see a fugitive, shoot them in the gut, even if they raise their hands in surrender. These people are never unarmed. And I assure you they have no intention of coming quietly."

The men dispersed in streaking blurs. Melissa moved to the elevator bank and studied the two young corpses on the floor. They looked like they'd been gored by rhinos. No sword or lance could have killed them this brutally.

Tempis, she thought, with sinking dread. *God help you if you did this, Amanda. God—*

—help me.

Amanda lay chest-down on the carpet, her slender frame convulsing with shudders. Her wall-hugging hop down the hallway had been the single most agonizing experience of her life, until Evan's chaser set every nerve ablaze. Now she was a prisoner of her own fractured body, a tiny creature in a cage of screaming flesh.

She had a moment to register Hannah through a sideways glance before Evan crouched to eclipse her view. He chuckled at her bug-eyed recognition, the long pink fingers that wriggled helplessly like earthworms.

"The tempis you're trying to call is currently unavailable," he teased. "Please try again later."

"P-please . . ."

"Hey, don't look at me. I didn't cork your weirdhole. That was the cute Asian solic you met downstairs. Her name's Mercy Lee, but you can call her the Future Mrs.—"

"Leave her alone!"

"—Trillinger." He spun around to glare at Hannah. "*Don't* step on my lines."

"She never did anything to you!"

"*BAAAP!* Incorrect." Evan squinted venomously at Amanda. "She's done plenty."

Though Amanda didn't know it, she and Evan carried centuries of animosity between them, dating back to his first days on this world. Even when he'd tried to be a good little Silver, the sharp-faced bitch never trusted him for a moment, never liked the way he looked at her sister. He, in turn, hated the gooey hold she took on his one true friend. She ruined Zack every single time.

As a full-fledged adversary, Amanda was even worse. Just months ago in his recollection, on a cold and rainy night near the end of his fifty-fourth lifetime, the widow came looking for blood in the wake of Hannah's murder. She took Evan by surprise on a Boston rooftop, swooping down from the sky on her mighty wings of aeris. Before he knew what was happening, Amanda's cold tempic sword burst through his chest. One inch to the left and he would have died instantly.

Instead, Evan spent sixty-two of the longest seconds of his life on the wet concrete, sobbing and pissing and begging for mercy while Amanda looked down at the wretched creature she'd made of him. Though her disgusted pity allowed him enough time to concentrate on a rewind escape, the phantom pain followed him for weeks. The memory still tortured him at night.

Now he walked a slow preening circle around his nemesis, basking in their reversal of fortune. Amanda didn't piss herself, as Evan had hoped, but she was just a few pokes away from full emotional collapse.

"You know, I learned a long time ago why Tits McGee over there is such a train wreck. I know why all your husbands grow to hate you. You just have that effect on people. You beat them down with your high-and-mighty know-it-all-ism until they just want to stab a hobo. Godmanda, Judgmanda, Reprimanda. Hell, even now if I asked you to beg for your life, you'd beg for

Hannah's instead. And it's not because you love her. You don't. You just have to be the noble one."

"She *is* the noble one," Hannah snarled. "Compared to you, she's Jesus in drag."

"What part of 'don't step on my lines—'"

"—do I not understand? I get all of it, you weasel-faced shit geyser, just like I know your threats are worthless. You'll either kill us or you won't. Nothing we say will change that. So why don't you shut your mouth and—"

"'—do what you came here to do,'" Evan said, in perfect synch. He shook his head at her, chortling. "One of these days, you'll come up with new dialogue. As for your 'tough girl' bit . . ."

Evan pulled a snub-nosed .38 from his holster and aimed it at Amanda's head. In a sharp instant, all the bravada left Hannah's face. She lurched forward in her cage.

"Wait! Stop!"

He balked in mock bother. "But . . . I thought my threats were worthless."

"Please! I'm sorry! I'm sorry! Don't!"

Evan chuckled scornfully. "You always were a shitty actress."

He checked the countdown timer on his synchron. Two minutes and twenty-eight seconds until Melissa's speeding bloodhounds reached the fifth floor. He rooted through his duffel bag and placed two gas grenades on the reception desk. Evan had all the right lies and credentials to walk out of this building a free man, but he'd have to send the sisters to sleep so they wouldn't rat him out. That came last, after the fun.

Hannah watched with furious perplexity as Evan donned a mortarboard and glasses from his bag. Now the young security guard was a professor from the neck up.

"What the hell are you doing?" she asked him.

"What I came here to do." He stooped down to poke Amanda. "Hey, honey? Snookums? I know you're on the verge of passing out, but if you don't want me to shoot your sister through her all-access fun tunnel, you'll need to pay attention to what I say now. It's very important. Will you listen?"

Amanda dug her taut fingers into the rug, nodding tensely.

Evan smiled. "Smart girl. Keep it up, A-Cup, and you just might hobble out of here."

He cleared his throat, his brow crunched with scholarly gravitas. Behind his satirical expression, Evan glowed with rapture. This was his favorite part of the show, the absolute high point of his looping existence.

"There's a crucial bit of information you gals have been missing, a piece of the puzzle that ties everything together. Now the Deps won't tell you because they don't know about it. The Pelletiers? Eh. They don't care if you know or not. But the Gothams? Ah, this is where it gets interesting. You might have noticed they're a little . . . edgy about something, some future event that has them all soiling their short pants. They might have even said something about it during their many attempts to kill you. Any idea what I'm talking about, class? Anyone? Bueller?"

Hannah looked to Amanda and noticed a quarter-size spot of tempis on the back of her hand. At long last, the solis was wearing off. Her heart leapt with anxious hope. *Don't let him see it. Keep his eyes on you.*

"A second Cataclysm," Hannah replied. "Peter mentioned it in a letter."

Evan snapped his fingers. "Aha! Yes! Except . . . no. That doesn't add up. The Gothams don't give a crap about anyone outside the clan. If they thought their Habitrail hamlet was going tempo-nuclear, they'd simply pack up and move. So then what's the real issue? Why are they freaking out?"

Hannah kept her tense stare on Evan. *Look at me. Look at me, you worm.*

"What? You're saying Peter lied to us?"

"Through his big Irish chompers. Excuse me a moment."

He aimed the cone-shaped jolter at Amanda and pulled the trigger. Hannah screamed as her sister convulsed in fresh pain. The tempis vanished from her hand.

"You'll have to try better than that, girls. This isn't my first day teaching."

Hannah cried through the bars. "Stop it! Stop! Turn it off!"

"You know if you just paid more attention, you wouldn't be here in remedial class. The answer's been out there. You're just not connecting the dots."

"Then just tell us! Tell us! Stop hurting her and tell us!"

"You tell me, Hannah."

"I don't know!"

"Get it right and I'll stop hurting your sister."

"I don't know!"

"Think harder! This is the lightning round! Take a Hail Mary, shot-in-the-dark, wild-guess stab at the answer! What horrible event do you think is coming?"

"IT'S THE END OF THE FUCKING WORLD!"

"YES!"

He turned off the jolter. The three of them breathed in heavy gasps. Evan took on a new and somber sincerity that Hannah found utterly frightening.

"This world ends," he announced with a heavy breath. "In four years and seven months, it all goes to hell in exactly the way ours did. The sky comes down. The air turns cold. The buildings go *crinkle* and the people go *crunch*. This time no one gets a bracelet. No one gets out alive except the Pelletiers and me. They go forward to their own adjacent future. I go back. Back to the beginning. Back to Nico Mundis and his crappy little store. This is now my"—he brandished the numerical tattoo on the back of his right hand—"fifty-fifth trip through the same time period. I've danced this dance over and over again. Sure, I mix things up, just for shits and giggles, but it always ends the same."

The Givens fell to abject silence, staring ahead in bleak dismay. Evan crossed his arms and studied Amanda. A hard smile returned to his face.

"I know what you're thinking. 'Oh that Evan. Such a meanie. He'll say anything to upset us.' Well, an hour from now, Peter will confirm everything I just told you. And while you're all sobbing into your teacups, he'll falsely assure you that all is not lost. See, just like Rebel, Peter's got a plan to save the world. You'll believe it, of course, because you want to. You *have* to. But the spoiler twist? It doesn't work. I've seen the non-result for myself, again and again and again. You try to stop what's coming every single time. You fail, every single . . ."

He stopped in the wake of Hannah's low chuckle. It began as a mirthful rumble, then rose in volume until her giggles overtook the office.

Evan cocked his head at her quizzically. This was new. "You don't believe me."

"Oh, I believe what you're saying, Evan. It makes perfect sense in its own sick way. What I don't believe is you. You went through all this trouble, you risked life and limb just to give us the bad news before Peter did. You had to see the looks on our faces."

He slit his eyes as she rolled with pitch-black laughter. Hannah wasn't sure if it was a Method act or a sign that her mind had finally snapped for good, but it seemed only right to rob this sick little demon of the one thing he came for.

She wiped her eyes. "God, Amanda. You missed it earlier, when he told me why he hated me so much. You won't believe this."

"I didn't tell you anything."

"You told me *everything*." She laughed. "You drew all the dots. I just had to connect them. You see, Amanda, he used to be one of us. In times undone, days gone bye-bye, Evan lived with us in Terra Vista. Then one day I made the awful mistake of being nice to him. I rubbed his arm. Maybe gave him a hug. Though he creeped me out with his constant eyefucks, he'd lost his world just like the rest of us. I felt sorry for him."

Evan scoffed with forced amusement. "Nice try, but that's not even—"

"And yet instead of realizing that I'm touchy-feely with everyone, Sad Sack over here convinced himself that something hot and heavy was brewing between us. In his twisted little mind, I was one tender moment away from becoming his devoted love cushion."

"Your ego's truly—"

"Shush, now. I'm talking to my sister. Anyway, one night he's walking the grounds, looking for me as usual. Maybe he went by the pool house, or the garden shed, someplace without a camera. And then he heard it. The sounds of my screwing, my melodious oohing. He looked through the door and learned that while he was picking out china patterns, I was spreading my legs for Jury Curado."

Evan's fists clenched with trembling rage. Though the details were off, the gist of her tale was painfully accurate. Her lips curled in a vengeful smirk.

"Oh, how that must have stung him, Amanda, to learn that this brand-new world was just like the old one, where the boys with the biceps got the girls with the tits. Nothing changed. Except—"

"Shut up."

Hannah's smile flattened. Her eyes cracked with grief. "Except it got worse. As time went on, this little shit came to realize that what Jury and I had wasn't all that shallow. He saw the way we looked at each other and he knew we'd developed something strong, something that had eluded me my whole life."

"You don't know that! You don't know anything! You've never even seen the guy!"

"I saw him, Evan. You didn't erase all of him. I glimpsed him with my own two eyes and I know why you killed him. It's because deep down you knew that Jury wasn't just the better-looking man. He was the better man."

Hot blood rushed up Evan's neck. He took off his glasses and rubbed his eyes. Hannah grew a teasing sneer.

"I bet you even tried a round without him, just to see if you could get me on your own. I'm sure that worked out really well for Theo."

"That's because you're a goddamn whore!"

"Right. Hannah Banana, Always-Needs-a-Man-a. Except that man was never you. You stopped trying a long time ago, but you never got over it. So this is how you spend your days. This is what you do between Armageddons. Jesus Christ, Evan. You have got to be the single most pathetic—"

The gunshot shook every wall and window, rattling teeth. While his thoughts and ears rang with clamor, Evan studied the large new spatter of blood on the wall behind Hannah, the trickling hole in her forehead. The two of them traded a wide look of horror before the actress fell dead to the floor of her cage.

For a short hot moment, Evan wondered if perhaps someone else in the room had shot her. He didn't remember aiming his .38 at her head or pulling the trigger. And yet there was the smoking gun in his hand, still raised. Strange. He'd killed Hannah so many times before but something, something, something about this didn't feel right. Something—

He shrieked when a cold white blade cut into his calf. Before he could register Amanda on the ground, she jammed her tempic knife through the back of his knee.

Screeching, Evan swung the pistol down and fired a bullet through the top of her skull. Her face splashed down into her own exit blood and she fell still. He only just now realized that Amanda had been howling along with him. She'd been screaming the whole time between gunshots.

Wide-eyed, bleeding, Evan stumbled against the wall and pondered the consequences of his actions. The Deps surely heard the blasts. They'd be here in seconds now, but they were the least of his problems.

"Oh no . . ."

The sisters were dead.

"Oh shit. Shit . . ."

Trembling, he closed his eyes and struggled to concentrate through the ringing in his ears, the pain, the fear of what Azral would do to him.

Two speedsuit agents appeared outside the door, cracking the smoked-glass pane with their armored fists. Evan pressed his fingers to his temples and yelled in desperate torment. His skin tingled with bubbles as the clock of his life spun back forty-nine seconds.

Now he found himself once again standing at the reception desk, the cool .38 back in his hand. He looked to Hannah—unmurdered, unsilenced. She continued to rail at him in all her gorgeous fury.

"Right. Hannah Banana, Always-Needs-a-Man-a. Except that man was never you. You stopped trying a long time ago, but you never . . . you never . . ."

Hannah trailed off, thrown by the sudden change in Evan's demeanor. A moment ago, he looked ready to bare her throat with his teeth. Then his head snapped back as if he'd woken up from a nap. Now his face was white with inexplicable terror. Gemma Sunder, a girl who shared Evan's talent but not his impression of it, would have said that he was being possessed by a future self.

To Hannah, it looked the very opposite of possession. It appeared the devil inside Evan Rander had finally fled.

He dropped his gun and raised his palms in trembling acquiescence.

"Okay. Okay, look, we're all good here. I went too far, but it's all right now. You're okay."

"What the hell are you talking about?"

"You'll be fine. You and . . ." He suddenly remembered Amanda and nervously jumped away. His unstabbed leg screamed with phantom pain. He didn't want a repeat of the real injury.

Hannah eyed him incredulously as he limped across the room. "You're insane."

Evan crowed a grim and broken laugh. "Maybe. I don't know. I've seen the world end fifty-five times. At the very least, it's made me cynical."

"Then hate the universe, not me."

"I hate the universe through you," he told her, with a sorrowful shrug. "It's just the way it is."

A round white portal opened up on the northern wall, stretching from rug to roof. Evan's stomach dropped. His pants trickled with urine. He'd been carrying a ray of hope that his transgression would go unnoticed. Of course not. Of course they knew.

He kneeled on the ground, raising stretched and shaky fingers. "I'm sorry. I'm sorry. I screwed up. I know it. But look, they're fine! They're both alive! I undid it!"

The portal continued to ripple with the quiet serenity of a spring pond. Evan's eyes darted around in frantic thought.

"All right, listen, listen, I'll leave them alone. I promise. Not even a phone call. I'll . . . I'll go to one of your facilities. Breed with whoever you want me to breed with. Just give me a chance to make things right. I've helped you before! You said so!"

The sisters stared at the portal with the same white horror as Evan. No one was coming out.

"Azral?"

A colossal hand of tempis burst through the surface with terrifying speed. Amanda and Hannah screamed as the man-size fingers engulfed Evan like a chess rook. As quick as it arrived, the monster arm retreated, pulling its shrieking victim into the shimmering white depths.

The portal shrank closed, leaving two siblings alone in devastated silence.

Soon the tempic bars of Hannah's cage flickered away. She fell to her knees and scuttled awkwardly across the rug. She ran her quivering fingers through Amanda's hair, her mind painfully perched between aching concern and the utter futility of asking her if she was okay.

As emergency lights flared outside and a speeding Dep began his thermal scan of the fifth floor, the daughters of Robert and Melanie Given wept in soft harmony. Neither of them were okay. No one was okay. Not a single damn thing in the world was okay.

THIRTY-FIVE

The tunnel was a relic of the hydroelectric age, a dank and moldy passage of steam pipes that stretched beneath the buildings of Battery Place. The last dangling bulb had burned out years ago. David lit the way with a melon-size ball of sunshine, a ghost from an even earlier era.

Mia rode piggyback on his shoulders, her thoughts swirling like drain water around her nine-hour memory hole. All she knew from David's curt summary was that she'd been mortally wounded by Rebel and then magically unwounded by Zack.

She launched a shaky glance at her wavy-haired savior, desperate for some kind of confirmation—a sigh, a squeeze, a "thank God you're okay." For a man who'd pulled a feat of Christlike proportions, Zack looked as macabre as his surroundings. He kept his tense gaze on Theo as the augur scanned the latest ladder to the surface.

"What exactly are you looking for?" Zack asked.

"A mouse."

"A mouse?"

"A dead mouse," said Theo. "Our exit has one at the base of the ladder."

Theo knew how crazy he sounded. Though the miracle in the magazine office had granted him fresh credibility with David, his latest plan threw Zack into the role of the angry doubter.

"Goddamn it, Theo . . ."

"I told you. We'll get them."

"How? By leaving them behind? By moving in the opposite direction from where they are?"

"They'll be all right in the short term."

"Then why did David hear one of them screaming?"

Theo's fingers twitched with stress as the cartoonist's wrath echoed down the tunnel. If Zack knew the sisters were at the mercy of Evan, he'd make a hot dash back to the building. The decision would not end well for him.

"I care about them as much as you do, Zack."

"I'm not doubting your motives. I just don't understand what's happening with you. Eight minutes ago, you were barely lucid. Now you're floating around like a Level Ten deity."

"No deity," Theo insisted. "Just a Level Two augur. I'll explain when we have time."

He stopped at the next ladder and noticed a dead brown mouse on the floor. There it was, just as he'd seen in the God's Eye. He glanced up at the square metal cover.

"Okay. This is the one. It's welded shut. You'll have to do your thing again."

Zack moved to the ladder and launched his temporis upward. In the dim light of the tunnel, his friends could see the otherworldly glow in his skin and hair, the mighty white beam that burst from his hand. Clearly Theo wasn't the only one who went up a level today. Mia wondered how many ascensions it would take before the people she loved started looking and acting like true gods.

They emerged into a delivery alley two blocks north of the office building, a thin and lifeless corridor full of concrete ramps and tempic pallets.

David lowered Mia from his back, then scanned the street at both ends. "Where to now?"

"Nowhere," said Theo. "We wait here."

"Won't be long before the Deps expand their search."

"We'll be gone before that happens."

Zack opened his knapsack and cursed at the sight of Mia's pink journal. He'd grabbed the wrong bag in the rush to flee the office. Every last cent of their money was back in the building.

In the light of day, Mia could see the huge patch of blood on Zack's shirt. *My blood*, she thought, with heart-pounding distress. She moved closer to look but was gripped by a sudden violent sickness. The others watched in concern as she dashed behind a truck ramp and threw up the bacon and waffles that Hannah had cooked in Quinwood.

David stroked her back. "You all right?"

She wiped her mouth, grimacing at the mess she made. "I'm okay."

While Zack pondered the side effects of his temporal healing act, Theo fell into grander worries. The Mia he'd seen in the God's Eye hadn't vomited at all. Something happened differently. Events had changed.

He checked David's watch, then fixed his restless glance on the eastern exit. "He should've been here already."

"Who?"

Theo was afraid to answer. Now that they were off the gilded string, his faith in a perfect outcome fell to rubble. Maybe their ride wouldn't show up after all. Maybe Hannah and Amanda—

"Someone's coming."

The silver van gleamed with sunlight as it sped down the alley. With each approaching yard, the vehicle looked less like a DP-9 cruiser and more like their old Royal Seeker. Were it not for the New York plates and slightly altered chassis, the group might have wondered if their beloved chariot had come to life and followed them.

Theo pressed down David's gun. "Put it away. We're good."

"Wait. Is that—"

"Yup."

"The real one?"

"Yes," Theo said, through a weary smile. "That is most definitely him."

He'd seen Peter Pendergen in enough visions to know the man by sight. Their futures were hopelessly entwined, a twisting braid of kinship and conflict, smiles and shouts. At the moment, the man was nothing short of golden. He was the first glimpse of sunshine after a very long storm.

The Seeker pulled to a halt. The window rolled down. Now the others could see why Rebel cast Bruce Byer as Peter's impersonator. The two men could have been siblings, with their hero's jaws, their boxer's noses, their feathered brown hair and rugged lines of experience. There was a marked difference in the eyes, however, a deep blue soulfulness that Bruce lacked and Peter had in spades.

He shined a handsome smile at Theo, both cheery and glib.

"Don't tell me I'm late 'cause I already know."

"Just glad as hell to see you."

"Likewise, Theo Maranan. You have no idea."

Peter's deep and sandy voice danced with Irish inflections. His *"T'eo Mae-rnin"* nearly chipped a daffy grin on David's face.

"How did you find us here?"

"I'll tell you everything you want to know, boy, and a few things you don't. But right now we're shy on time. Hop in."

The side doors rolled open with an electric whirr. David, Zack, and Mia clambered into the cushioned back rows while Theo took the bucket seat up front. His toes brushed against a wooden cane. He couldn't imagine it was Peter's. The man boasted a powerful build beneath his blue henley shirt. He looked like he could land a few bruises on Rebel if the need arose.

The doors closed. Peter began a convoluted series of dashboard adjustments. He caught Zack's stony glare in the rearview mirror.

"If looks were daggers, cousin, I'd be a lot shorter now."

"Just waiting for you to explain what the hell happened. We called the number you gave us. It served us right up to Rebel."

"Yeah. They pulled a fast one on me too. I'm just glad you guys are all right."

"All right? Have you bothered counting us?"

"I know exactly who's missing. We're getting them next."

Theo turned in his seat. "He's right, Zack. Trust me. They're okay. They'll be waiting for us."

"Waiting where?"

"The roof," said Peter.

"The roof," said Theo, a hair out of synch. He cast a leery glance at Peter. "You're an augur."

"Nope. Just a guy with good sources." He tilted the mirror at Mia and smiled. "By the way, darlin', it's great to finally meet you. You're not fat at all."

Mia blinked at him confusedly. "What?"

"All right. We're good to go. Strap in."

David skeptically eyed the dashboard. "Uh, this is a Royal Seeker. If they're on the roof—"

"Got it covered, son."

Technically, the van was a Royal Seeker Plus. It cost twice as much as the standard model, with one key difference.

The Silvers jumped in their seats as the vehicle emitted a steamy hiss and rose six inches off the ground. The doors locked. The tires folded inward.

They went up.

Hannah sat against the wall, cradling Amanda in her arms while they both stared catatonically out the window. It seemed like decades, not moments, since the Pelletiers yanked Evan away to God knew where. The sisters could have been elderly women by now, a pair of doddering old crones who were as white-haired as Azral and as crazy as Esis.

As the wall clock turned to 12:04, Hannah looked to Evan's handheld computer and saw several tiny figures bustling about on-screen. The tragic little creep hadn't lied about the Deps. They were all over the lobby.

"Shit." She smeared her eyes, then looked to Amanda. "We have to go."

While Hannah spent the last minute in a dull static haze, Amanda's thoughts stayed sharp as swords. She played the visceral images of the day on a savage loop—the two young Gothams gored by tempic spikes, the fierce man-demon with the six tempic arms, the giant tempic fist that pulled Evan screaming to Hell. There was no sense to this life. No God. Only cruelty and madness and tempis, tempis, tempis.

"Amanda . . ."

And that was exactly how the world would end again.

"Amanda, the Deps are coming. They'll get us if we stay here."

The widow's deep green stare briefly came into focus. She spoke in a broken whisper.

"Go."

Hannah shook her head, fighting tears. "Goddamn you. Don't."

"Run as fast as you can. They won't catch you."

"Don't do this to me. You can't give up like this."

Amanda covered her face with trembling hands, muffling her sobs and her horrible thoughts. *What does it matter, Hannah? Where will we run? Where can we possibly hide?*

"This is just what Evan wanted," Hannah cried. "He came here to break us. It's not supposed to work on you. You're supposed to be the strong one!"

"I can't go through it again."

"You think I can? You think I *will*? I'll slit my wrists before I watch the sky come down again."

"Don't . . ."

"Don't what? Don't check out early? What do you think you're doing now?" Amanda closed her eyes. "Hannah, please . . ."

"I'm not leaving without you. You either come with me or we sit here and wait for the Deps together. I can't imagine they'll be nice to us, Public Enemies Number One and Two. But hey, maybe they'll put our brains in matching jars. At least we'll finally look alike."

"Hannah, what do you want me to do? My leg's broken."

"I'll carry you."

"Where? How do you expect to get past them if you're hauling me around?" Hannah pinched her lip in busy contemplation.

"We'll go up."

"What?"

"You remember when we woke up Theo at the parade? He was all confused and thought he was picking us up from the roof. Maybe it wasn't a dream. Maybe it was a premonition."

"That's crazy. How would they pick us up?"

"I don't know. Two of them have a direct line to the future. One's a boy genius. And there's no limit to the crazy things Zack will do to get you back. He's probably already stealing a blimp."

Amanda let out a teary laugh. The maddening artist would jump into fire for her, and yet he fled for the hills at the first sign of romantic trouble. If anything, she wanted to live just to smack him.

"We don't even know if they got out of the building."

"They did," Hannah said. "I'm in the blackest mood of my life, but I know in my heart they got away. I know I want to see them again. I might even be able to handle what's coming if I had all of you with me. Can't you understand that, Amanda? Don't you feel the same way?"

Warm tears spilled down Amanda's face. She bit her lip and nodded.

"Good. So you'll quit bitching and let me carry you?"

She sniffed and nodded again. Hannah looked around.

"All right then. I guess the first step . . ."

Her eyes froze wide at the office door. A large black figure stopped just outside the clouded glass. "Oh no . . ."

The armored Dep raised his handheld thermal scanner. He snapped to alertness at the orange figures on his display.

"I have two on the fifth floor! Two on the fifth—"

His body twitched with neuroelectric mayhem as a hidden chaser from the nearby flower pot jolted him. Hannah had snatched Evan's computer from the rug and frantically mashed at the controls. She knew from Amanda's painful experience that one of the buttons remotely triggered the weapon. Apparently she'd found it.

The agent staggered forward, his mirrored black helmet crashing through the glass. He toppled back to the hallway carpet.

The other seven elites quickly converged on the fifth-floor landing. Melissa eyed the twitching agent from a distance, then motioned to three of her crew.

"Loop around and flank the other side. Make sure they—"

A small black ball the size of an apple flew out of the broken door of the law office. It bounced off a planter and rolled five yards down the hall.

The Deps watched in puzzlement as Evan's sleeping-gas grenade exploded in a swirling white cloud, far away from any living targets. Melissa caught a hint of quick movement through the smoke cover.

"It's the swifter. She's making a run for it. Go downstairs and guard all exits. Do not let her out of this building."

The agents hurried down the steps. Melissa held her breath and sped through the gas cloud. She could see the cumbersome figure on the walkway now. To her surprise, it wasn't just Hannah on the move. The Great Sisters Given were fleeing as one.

Hannah clenched her jaw, struggling to keep Amanda steady on her back. A week ago, she'd taught herself how to expand her temporal field, a trick she hoped she'd never have to use. She knew that if even a small piece of Amanda left the confines of the temporis, she'd be rifted. But with armed and armored agents running around like cheetahs, there was little choice. She had to try. She had to run faster.

Melissa bolted after them, vexed by the widening gap. Even with the burden of a 120-pound sibling, Hannah had the speed advantage. She must have been shifted at twice the suit's limit.

Before Melissa could line up a decent leg shot, Hannah ducked into the stairwell. Melissa chased her inside and crunched her brow at the heavy footsteps above her. *What the hell is she doing?*

She activated her transmitter. "Disregard my last order. The targets are ascending. Follow me in pursuit."

Amanda locked her arms around Hannah's shoulders, biting her lip to keep from screaming. Every stride was murder on her jostled ankle. Worse, she knew it'd be just a matter of moments before Hannah's legs screamed with an agony all their own. It was a seven-story climb to the roof. Hannah couldn't possibly carry her the whole way.

Halfway past the eighth floor, the actress began to stagger. Her lead on her pursuer shrank with each step. Melissa fired a quick shot as Hannah turned the ninth-floor landing. The bullet pierced the wall, missing her thigh by inches.

Hannah's calves burned with fury. Her lungs stabbed her with broken glass. Between all her dread and blinking red gauges, a cold inner voice assured her that death wouldn't be so bad. There was a Heaven, it insisted, even for mediocrities like her.

No.

She gritted her teeth and floored her inner pedal, pushing herself past 50×. The air turned ten degrees colder and three shades bluer. The sisters shot ahead of Melissa.

Amanda leered in astonishment at the strange new artifacts in her senses—the rainbow streaks of color in the corner of her vision, the distant sound of wind chimes. A large white butterfly dawdled past her, trailing arcs of light in its fluttering wake. Amanda wasn't sure if she'd lost her mind or found a strange new corner of her sister's world. It was mad and it was beautiful.

She glanced up through the indigo haze and saw the metal door to the roof. *God, she did it. She really did it.*

Hannah kicked the door open and stumbled out into the sunlight. Between all the air vents and glassy solic panels lay a sprawling gray aerolot. Every parking space was empty.

"They're not here," Hannah wheezed. "I don't see them."

Amanda caught moving shadows on the asphalt and squinted to look up. Three flashing NYPD cruisers circled above like birds of prey. They began their quick descent.

"Go to the edge," she told Hannah.

"What?"

"Go to the edge. Trust me."

Hannah staggered beyond the parking lot and stopped at the roof's southern lip. The last of her temporal energies sputtered away. The world fell back to normal speed and color.

Amanda peered over the side, all the way down to the bustle on Battery Place. She wished she could grow wings and fly them away. She wished she had more than a cruel and desperate gambit.

"Turn us around."

"M-my legs won't hold. I can barely stand."

Amanda squeezed her. "It's okay, Hannah. You did such a good job. You were amazing. Just one last move and you can rest."

As the actress spun around, Amanda cast slim white tendrils from her hands. They stretched twenty feet in each direction, forming a tight grip around air vents.

Hannah fell back into her like a sling, her muscles moaning with relief. She didn't want to think about the cagey white ropes that kept them from plummeting to their deaths.

"You sure about this, Amanda?"

"No, but it's our only leverage. I don't want to hurt any more of these people."

Neither did Hannah. She nodded darkly. "Okay. Okay."

Melissa burst through the doorway and stopped cold at Amanda's new threat. She holstered her gun and de-shifted, waving her palms at the policemen as they hopped out of their cruisers.

"Lower your weapons! Keep them down!"

One by one, the speedsuit agents made their way to the roof. Now fourteen law officers clutched their pistols at their sides as they nervously eyed the Givens.

"Don't come any closer!" Amanda yelled. "I mean it!"

Melissa removed her helmet and dropped it. She raised her voice above the whistling wind.

"All right, Amanda. It's all right. Despite all appearances, this is a very simple situation. You don't want to die and we don't want you to die. We're proving that as we speak."

"You're the one who shot at us."

"I shot at your sister's leg," Melissa replied. "Can you blame me? Last we met, she broke the spine of one of my men."

Hannah's stomach twisted. "How is he? Is he okay?"

Melissa eyed her somberly. "We got him to a reviver. He's back in Los Angeles now. Resting."

Though everything she said was technically true, Melissa omitted the fact that Ross Daley had suffered a fatal aneurysm inside the machine. Reversal was not a foolproof process, as 1.1 percent of patients learned the hard way. Ross had spun the wheel and lost. The outcome didn't bode well for Hannah, who was now on the books for murder.

"When you see him, can you please tell him I'm sorry?"

"I'll be sure to do that." Melissa looked to Amanda with concern. "Those bodies in the elevator bank . . ."

"Esis."

"That was Esis," Hannah yelled. "Amanda would never do that."

Melissa nodded eagerly. "I believe you. I do. I believe you're both good people in a bad situation, never more so than now. The way I see it, you only have two directions to go from here: forward or down. I know neither option appeals to you, but if you fall, there'll be no reviving you. At least with us, you'll have a chance."

Though their faces were half-obscured by windblown hair, Melissa found something new and dark in their expressions.

"Wouldn't you rather keep living?"

"That's all we want," said Hannah.

"That's all we ever wanted," said Amanda.

"Then you have only one choice. Now it couldn't be—"

Before Melissa could say "simpler," a new complication arose behind the sisters. Fourteen pistols swung to aim at the shiny silver aerovan that popped above the building like toast.

Zack peered through the rear passenger window, narrowing his eyes at the large assembly of men.

"David, blind the hell out of them."

"With pleasure."

Melissa spotted the boy's vengeful sneer through the window. She recalled David's flare attack on Howard and pressed her hands to her eyes.

"Everyone cover your eyes! Cover your—"

A thirty-foot cube of piercing white light enveloped all the cops and Deps on the roof. The sisters turned their wincing faces. Soon they heard the electric whirr of a sliding door behind them. Amanda felt soft young hands on her shoulders.

"It's okay," said Mia. "I got you. Let go."

With a delirious cry of relief, she released the tempis and fell back into Mia's arms. Amanda never had a chance to see the van. For all she knew, her other little sister had flown in on angel wings.

David supported Amanda's legs as Mia pulled her into the van. Hannah kept her eyes squinted shut, reeling with perplexity as someone seized her by the armpits.

"What's happening? Who's got me?"

"I do," said Zack.

The actress cracked a dizzy laugh. "Oh my God. I want to kiss you so much. Is everyone else okay? Theo?"

"I'm here," Theo said from the front. "We're all here."

"I knew it. I knew you'd find us."

He smiled exhaustedly. "I knew you'd know."

The cube of light vanished, leaving eight cops and six Deps fumbling helplessly on the concrete. Melissa uncovered her eyes and rushed to the railing. Even half-blind, she had no trouble recognizing the driver.

"Peter, don't do this. You have more to lose than they do. You have a son!"

David cast a sphere of light around Melissa's head. She fell to her knees, grimacing.

The door slid closed. Peter floored the accelerator. He bounced a baleful glare at David through the mirror.

"Goddamn it, boy. You didn't have to do that."

"She'll recover."

"I'm talking about the whole thing. What was that light you used? Was that the Cataclysm?"

"It was, in fact."

Peter pounded the wheel. "Jesus Christ! You ghost the Cataclysm on Commemoration, right on top of a goddamn building? People probably saw it for miles! They'll be talking about it for months!"

David leered at him in umbrage. "I did what I had to."

"You could've used darkness on them. You could've stunned them with noise. I know you folks are new to this world, but there are consequences—"

"Hey!" Zack shot forward in his seat, his face flushed with rage. "We almost died because of *your* instructions! You don't get to lecture him. And when your people stop trying to kill us, maybe then we'll give a shit about protecting their secrets. Until then, fuck them and fuck you."

Hannah sat between David and Zack, her hands clutched tensely on their thighs. She felt like she missed a year of plot development. She wasn't even sure who was flying the van.

Theo held up a diplomatic palm. "Look, we're all shaken up right now. Can we just—"

"Oh no!"

Everyone followed Mia's gaze out the window. Two sleek blue police cruisers flew along the Seeker's left side while another kept pace to the right. A pair of flashing aerocycles rode up the rear.

Theo's mind spun with helpless flurry. This aerial chase was a whole new wrinkle. His counterparts in the God's Eye had gotten away scot-free.

He looked to Peter. "What now?"

The Irishman aimed a tight scowl out the windshield. "It's okay. They won't get us."

"How do you know?"

"Because you haven't seen what I can do." He heaved a loud, woeful breath. "This won't be subtle either."

Seven stomachs lurched as Peter pulled the Seeker into a sharp ascent. He leveled out and looped to the left, steering them back toward the buildings of Battery Place. Despite everything her senses told her, Amanda couldn't accept the nitty-gritty, *Chitty Chitty Bang Bang* details of her current existence. She was flying. Over the city. In an automobile.

Hannah nervously scanned the police vehicles. "They're shifted. You can't outrun them."

Peter studied her in the mirror. "Which pretty sister are you?"

She narrowed her eyes suspiciously. "Hannah."

"Figured. You're already thinking like a born swifter. It's not always about speed, hon." He turned to Theo. "I'm afraid I'm gonna have to ask you for a little advance on trust."

"What do you need?"

"When I give the word, you hold the wheel and keep it steady, no matter what."

"Why? What are you—"

He steered the van on a crash course with a fifty-story skyscraper, the only conventional box tower on Battery Place. A plane of mirrored glass panels lined the front.

Peter closed his eyes and pressed his fingers to his temples. "Okay. Now. Hold it tight."

Theo leaned over and grabbed the wheel. "Wait! What are you doing?"

"Just trust me, Theo. Keep us steady."

Melissa lay on the roof, her wrist pressed over her flash-burned eyes. She listened intently to the police radio as they described the impending collision. *He wouldn't. He's not crazy.*

Theo forced the same thought while he struggled to hold the van on course. His foresight had fled him like an ejected jet pilot. He couldn't see a thing beyond the growing wall in front of them.

The Silvers kept their frozen eyes forward. Hannah locked arms with David. Amanda and Mia clasped hands. The widow threw a frantic gaze over her shoulder at Zack. He reached forward as far as he could. She closed the gap with tempis. Pink and white fingers entwined.

The van was ten feet from the building when Mia screamed and Peter's glowing eyes shot open.

A thirty-foot portal sprouted on the face of the glass.

The police cars slowed to a halt as the Seeker disappeared into the splashing depths. All witnesses in the air and on the ground stared deadfaced at the large white breach of reason, this strange new hole on the chin of Manhattan.

As quickly as it opened, the portal shrank and vanished from existence. The madness was gone, along with the Silvers.

Howard Hairston wheezed his way up the last flight of steps, then joined the rooftop gathering of beleaguered peace officers. Those who didn't dawdle in blindness kept their dazed expressions on the neighboring skyscraper, where the laws of man and nature had been so brazenly violated.

Howard found Melissa crouched at the steel-gray base of a MerryBolt rent-a-charger. Her face was half-concealed behind a curtain of messy dreads.

"Hey, boss."

She shined a feeble smile in his direction. "Hello, Howard."

"I hear you got caught in the light show."

"David was nice enough to give me my own. I see nothing but spots."

"Yeah. I've been there. Man, I really hate that kid."

"You got better. So will I."

Howard sat down beside her and studied the blinking handphone in her grip. "You got a text."

"Yes. I heard. Would you be so kind as to read it to me?"

He took the phone and scanned it in dim confusion. "It's from someone named Nameless."

"I know who it's from. What does it say?"

"'Well, hon, you did everything you could. But the foot's come down. It's Integrity's show now. God help them all.'"

Melissa rubbed her ailing eyes. She wished she'd packed some cigarettes in her armor.

"I heard two beeps, Howard. Is there—"

"Yeah. There's another one." He scrolled down her screen. "He's asking if you're free for dinner tonight. Says you two still have something to talk about."

His freckled brow rose in horror. "God. That old man isn't loving on you, is he?"

Melissa smiled softly, confident that the meal would end with nothing more than a job offer. Cedric Cain had his own plans for the six temporic fugitives, one that apparently ran counter to Integrity's. Whatever his purpose, the crafty old shade wanted them alive. That alone made him a man worth hearing out.

"Want me to respond for you?" Howard asked.

Melissa took a long moment to ponder. After all that had happened, all she had seen, she couldn't imagine going back to chasing toopers and clouders and other temporal two-bits. She didn't seem to have much of a future with the Deps anyway.

"Yes," she replied, with a heavy breath. "Tell him I'm available."

THIRTY-SIX

They emerged three and a half miles to the northeast, through the bare gray wall of an underground parking lot. The Seeker shot from the portal at sixty-four miles an hour and kissed the ground on folded tires. It scraped a sparking path across eighty-nine spaces before grinding to a halt near the elevators.

Peter puffed a winded breath, then surveyed the empty lot behind him. On any other Tuesday, their hundred-yard slide would have left a trail of dented cars, and probably a few dead mall-shoppers.

He checked the six wincing faces of his passengers. "Everyone okay?"

The Silvers were anything but. The portal jump was a new and wholly awful experience for them, like being rope-dragged through a waterfall of boiling-hot milk. One by one, they examined themselves for scald burns, finding nothing but pink and tender flesh. They looked like they'd been scrubbed from head to toe with pumice stones.

Peter clicked his tongue with empathy. "Sorry. The jaunts are always hell on first-timers. You'll be raw for a day or so." He shined a warm gaze on Mia. "You hang in there, darlin'."

He knew the poor girl had it worst of all. The moment he'd summoned the entry portal in Manhattan, Mia felt an agonizing push in her thoughts, as if someone opened an umbrella inside her head. Now she stared at her trembling hands, half-convinced that everything that happened since Quinwood was just a crazy dream.

"What just . . . what . . . ?"

"We got away," said Peter. "That's the long and short of it."

Theo studied their dark surroundings. "Where are we?"

"Hoboken, New Jersey. Watercourse Mall. First place I could think of with a big enough landing strip." He glanced through the windshield at the Seeker's smoking hood. "This thing's done for. We'll have to paw it from here."

"How far?" Hannah asked. "Amanda has a broken ankle and I can barely move my legs."

"No worries, hon. Home is just a few steps past that elevator." He unbuckled his seat belt and snatched the cane at Theo's feet. "I haven't been walking too well myself these days."

Moaning and grimacing, the Silvers extracted themselves from the van. Zack carried Amanda on his back while Mia kept her leg stabilized. Theo and David bolstered Hannah like crutches.

Peter Pendergen led the hobbling procession, moving at an impressive clip for a man with a lame left leg. He poked the call button with his cane.

"How'd you get crippled?" David asked.

Peter eyed him, stone-faced, as the doors slid open and the group boarded the elevator. He set a course for the sixth and highest floor.

"Had a cerebrovascular mishap a short while back. It's no big deal."

"You seem awfully young to be suffering strokes."

"Well, thank you. I thought the same thing. Unfortunately, these kinds of problems start early for my people. Just comes with the territory."

"Of being chronokinetic, you mean."

Peter tossed him a weak shrug. "What can I say, boy? Time always hurts the ones it loves."

The elevator fell into grim and listless silence.

"It's just temporary," Peter attested. "Few months of leg rehab and I'll be good as new." He took a bleak gander at Amanda's ankle. "Guess I won't be doing my exercises alone."

Zack kept his dark stare on the floor. Amanda rested her chin on his shoulder and studied Peter through the mirrored doors. The man was tall, well built, and ridiculously good-looking, though he carried his appeal with a preening peacock vanity that unfavorably reminded her of Derek. He'd probably charmed dozens of doe-eyed ingenues out of their tight wool sweaters. For all she knew, he was already scanning Hannah for loose threads.

And why wouldn't he? Amanda thought. *It's the end of the goddamn world. Isn't it, Peter?*

Teetering back from the edge of hysterics, she ran a soft finger near Zack's neck gash. "We'll have to disinfect that."

"We will," Peter promised. "I got everything back at the house—meds and beds, duds and suds, all an ailing body could ever hope for. You folks went through five kinds of hell to get to me. I'd say you earned some rest."

He scanned the dark reflections of his new companions, stopping at Amanda. It wasn't hard to recognize the abject despair in her lovely green eyes.

"Just wait," he told her.

Amanda looked up at him. "What?"

"Don't go losing hope just yet. Wait till you hear what I have to say."

The view from the roof was astonishing. The Silvers only had to take a few steps onto the windy lot before they saw all the way across the Hudson, to the city they'd just escaped.

From a river's distance, Manhattan was a feast for the eyes, a utopian array of artful slopes and novel curves, winding spires and colored spheres. One tower resembled a Space Needle with twenty rings. Another looked glassy to the point of translucence. Tempic tubes connected buildings at their highest levels and every street was peppered with aer traffic. For Theo, the skyline went miles beyond modernism and deep into the realm of high-budget, "holy shit," has-to-be-CGI sci-fi. Mia couldn't find the words to describe the sight. It was beautiful enough to bring her to tears.

David eyed Peter curiously as the man took a slow, wincing seat in the middle of a parking space.

"You said your home was just a few steps past the elevator."

"It is."

"Meaning we're about to take another portal."

"We are," Peter confessed, to the angry groans of Zack and Hannah. "I know. It hurts. You'll build up a tolerance. Trust me."

He tapped the ground with his cane. "Might as well sit and enjoy the fresh air, folks. I need a bit of rest before I open the next door."

While the others joined him on the concrete, Zack and Amanda stayed conjoined in their tight piggyback hug. The look of desperate solace on her sister's face prompted Hannah to lean forward and wrap her arms around

Theo, her own quasi-non-boyfriend. She traded a dismal glance with Amanda. *It's never simple for us, is it?*

Theo caressed her wrists, his vacant gaze stuck on the distant metropolis. "I can't believe we were just there a minute ago."

"I can't believe we traveled like one of Mia's notes," David said. He furrowed his brow at Peter. "Wait. We didn't jump through time, did we?"

"No. Just space. Time portals are brighter and have a strong vacuum pull. They're also quite fatal."

"Fatal?"

"A living being can't handle a trip like that," Peter explained. "I've seen folks try. It's never pretty. Me, I'm perfectly happy to stay in the present. Still plenty of places to go."

Zack eyed him sharply. "If you can jump anywhere—"

"I never said I could."

"—why did we drive twenty-five hundred miles to get to you? Why didn't you come get us?"

"There are limits to my talents, Zack. I can't leap the nation. I can't teleport someplace I've never been. If I had the power, believe me, I would've pulled you from Terra Vista before you ever met Rebel or Rander or that Dep with the funny hair."

"How do you know so much about that?" Hannah asked, in a more accusatory tone than intended. Peter smirked in good nature.

"I've had a correspondent among you all along. A pen pal, as you folks call them." He shook a stern finger at Mia. "I should've known better than to trust your self-description. I bought a whole mess of clothes for a fat girl. They're gonna hang off you like drapes."

She leered at him in bafflement. "What? When did I write you?"

"Technically, you haven't. Not yet."

Mia caught on. "You've been getting notes from my future selves."

"Dozens of them. Nice girls. Very helpful. One of them explained how to rescue Amanda and Theo from DP-9. Another told me where you'd all be today. If it wasn't for her, I'd still be sitting at home, waiting for your call."

Theo shook his head, vexed. "I don't understand. How can you get notes from her? How can she get notes from you?"

"There are only a few dozen people on Earth who can make portals like we do. We're all linked to each other, for better or worse."

"Why worse?" Amanda asked.

Peter turned somber. "I doubt any of you had the pleasure of meeting Rebel's wife, but—"

"Ivy."

He looked up at David in dull surprise. "Okay. Guess you did meet her."

"We conversed. What about her?"

"She's a traveler too. She can't jump as far as I can, but she's much more attuned to the portal network. When I sent Mia the note with my new contact number, Ivy must have tapped the link. Snatched a copy from the ether. From there, all Rebel had to do was surp my phone line and take your call in my place." He aimed a soft glance at Zack. "That's how they got the jump on you today. I underestimated their cleverness and you guys paid the price for it. I'm truly sorry."

The cartoonist shrugged with drowsy accord. With all his friends alive and breathing, he didn't have the strength to hate anyone at the moment, even Rebel.

Peter studied Zack's spooning embrace with Amanda, then cast a pensive gaze at the eastern horizon.

"We're in the halo now."

"The what?"

He swept a slow gesture from the skyline. "The Cataclysm started in Brooklyn and blew five miles in every direction, stretching all the way out here. Over sixty thousand people were caught right outside the blast, in a ring of space we call the Halo of Gotham. Those folks were considered blessed because, aside from some blindness and emotional trauma, they survived just fine. It wasn't until the pregnant women started having their babies that . . . well, some were born healthy and some weren't. And some were just born different. Those were the first of my people."

Peter jostled a loose chunk of concrete with his cane. "There are over a thousand of us in Quarter Hill, in forty-four family lines. We've lived in quiet for four generations. Now it's all coming undone."

"I am sorry for my part," David offered. "I should have been more discreet with my lumis."

"I appreciate it, son, but that wasn't what I was talking about. And even if it was, Zack's right. You don't owe my people a damn thing. It kills me to see what Rebel's doing. I don't care if you're all from another world. You're blessed and cursed in all the same ways we are. You're kin."

A large shadow enveloped them. The group looked up to see a massive metal saucer floating 150 feet in the air, casually drifting north on bright white wedges of aeris. Luminescent letters on the hub informed everyone below that Albee's Aerstraunt never closes. Ever.

While the Silvers followed the saucer's progress, Peter clambered back to his feet.

"All right. Enough jawing. I see one lovely woman in need of an ankle brace. The rest of you could use some heavy gauze and epallays." He put a hand on Mia's back. "Hold on now."

Peter closed his eyes and concentrated until a six-foot portal swirled open on the concrete wall. Mia sucked a pained breath.

"You all right?" David asked her.

"She's fine," Peter said. "All part of our connection. It'll hurt less and less each time, just like the jaunts."

Despite his assurance, nobody lined up for a second teleport. Peter exhaled glumly.

"You folks have traveled a long, hard road. I can't say your troubles are over, but I can promise you that shelter and aid are right on the other side of that door. Just a few steps more and you can finally rest. I swear it."

His new acquaintances studied him through busy eyes, caught between their desperation and their well-paved cynicism. The urge to flee was overwhelming, but they were out of steam, out of options, out of money, out of everything. A few steps were all they had left in them.

They rose to their feet and shambled toward the light like the weary souls of the departed. Two by two, limbs locked together, the Silvers disappeared into the shimmering white depths.

Only the orphans stopped at the portal. Mia held her nervous gaze at the glowing white surface.

"I—I can't. I can't."

David wrapped his arm around her. "It's all right. We'll walk through it together."

"I can't do it. It hurts."

Peter loomed behind them like a shepherd. "Go on ahead, boy. I got this."

David eyed him suspiciously. The Irishman gripped his shoulder. "I got off on a bad foot with you, son, and I will make amends. But for now I'm asking you to trust me. Please."

After a silent consultation with Mia, he squeezed her arm, then stepped through the portal. Peter watched the ripples settle.

"You weren't kidding about him. He's a lion, that one."

She lowered her head. "I'm sorry."

"You have nothing to be sorry about."

"This whole thing could have been avoided. I should have . . . *she* should have warned us not to go in that building."

He shined a droll grin. "Right. If only she had, you'd all be alive and together now."

"It's not funny."

"No, it's not," Peter admitted. "It's tragic that a girl so lovely can be so cruel to herself. I've seen the way you talk about you. I swear, there's no worse combination than adolescence and time travel."

Mia peered up at Peter. "Do you get notes from your future selves?"

"Me? Nah. I blocked those fools out years ago. One of me's enough for everyone."

"How did you do it?"

"I'll show you, Mia. I'll teach you everything you need to know." Peter jerked a thumb at the portal. "That thing over there? That's your future. You're just making keyholes now. Soon you'll be making doors."

Mia sniffed at the great white breach. To think how easily they could have escaped all their past calamities if she'd been able to rip an exit in the nearest wall. It seemed unbelievable that anyone could do such a thing.

"I still don't know how we got these powers," she confessed to Peter. "None of us were born like this."

"I can't answer that, darlin'. But it's on the list of things to find out."

He scanned the distant city, then put a hand on Mia's shoulder. "Come on. Before the boy comes back in worry."

As they moved toward the portal, Peter stroked the back of her head, a warm and fatherly gesture that made her as conflicted as the two messages she'd received about him. All at once, she wanted to hug him and run from him. She trusted him with her life and she feared he'd be the death of her. She had no idea what lay behind any of those feelings. Apparently she wasn't immune to paradox after all.

"Where does this go?" she asked him.

"Brooklyn," Peter replied, with a cheery grin. "Home."

His brownstone lay in the middle of a chain, a slender construct of red brick and glass that stood all but invisible among its siblings. Every room in the four-story building teemed with taped cardboard boxes, bulging department store bags, and hastily placed furniture. Half the lamps still had price tags dangling from the bases.

By one o'clock, all wounds were bandaged, all faces washed, all bloody garments swapped for fresh cotton loungewear. Peter secured Amanda's ankle with broken broomsticks and duct tape before leaving the house in search of better aid.

The Silvers convalesced in the hardwood living room, slouched among the mismatched chairs and sofas. Their twelve lazy feet faced one another on the circular glass coffee table like ticks on a clock dial. Only Hannah and Theo ruined the uniformity by bundling together on a recliner. While the actress wallowed in apocalyptic grief, the augur felt downright euphoric. Azral had offered him a shortcut to this very moment and Theo stubbornly insisted on forging his own path here. Now the thrill of success was incomparable, like winning two marathons at once.

Nobody moved or spoke for fifteen minutes, until Hannah retreated to the kitchen to make tea. She returned with a tray of steaming mugs, placing one on the end table near her sister.

"He doesn't have milk. I looked. Sorry."

Amanda stared ahead blankly, her senses dulled by exhaustion and painkillers. "Okay."

Theo followed the exchange with grim interest. When he'd viewed this scene with Azral, it was Mia who served the hot drinks. The girl had looked fairly healthy in that string. But this one was listless, sweaty, and jaundiced. He feared something didn't go entirely right with her reversal.

At two o'clock, Peter returned with a cartload of gifts for Amanda—a hospital-grade ankle brace, casting tape, ice packs, crutches, even a portable tomograph to gauge the extent of her bone damage. When David asked him how he managed to score such items on a major holiday, Peter merely shrugged and said he knew people.

He sat down with Amanda and pulled her legs onto his lap, peeling away her splint with the gentle grace of a lover. Zack took a forced and sudden interest in the red-leafed sycamore outside the window.

"Where in Brooklyn are we?"

"Greenpoint."

Zack gazed outside in absent marvel. "Jesus. I grew up here. The other 'here.'"

"I can show you around tomorrow, if you want."

"You think that's wise?"

Peter flicked a breezy hand. "Some hats and sunglasses and we'll be fine. It'd be awfully cruel if you folks couldn't get out once in a while."

"Wait. Didn't you tell us the Brooklyn address was compromised?"

"I said our meeting address was compromised. This place is safe. Purchased with cash through two intermediaries. No one knows I'm here. Not even my son."

Mia snapped out of her addled daze. "Where is he?"

"With my people. He's safer there. My godmother will take care of him."

"Can you call or write to him?"

"No. Too risky. I can't even see him by portal without tipping off Ivy."

Six brows curled in sympathy as the Silvers realized the extent of Peter's sacrifice. Amanda held his wrist. "I'm so sorry."

"Oh, come on now. None of that. I'll tell you exactly what I told Liam. This is just temporary. As soon as matters are straightened out with my people, I'm going home and I'm bringing you with me. Quarter Hill is where we all belong."

"What about the Deps?" Hannah asked. "They'll be looking for us there."

"They'll be looking, but they won't see. Trust me. Our town was built for secrets."

David pursed his lips, lost in thoughts of young Freddy Ballad. "You really think the other Gothams will embrace us after everything that's happened?"

"That's not . . ." Peter chuckled with forced patience. "First of all, we don't call ourselves that, ever. Secondly, yes. This whole mess started with Rebel. It'll end with him."

"You're saying we need to kill him."

"Absolutely not. If we kill him, he'll become a martyr to the cause. The clan will forever see things his way. No, we have to do something even harder than that. We have to change his mind."

Zack's face coursed with hot blood as he rediscovered his hatred. Rebel had murdered his brother and then bragged about it. He nearly shot Mia to death. Even if the man could be persuaded to abandon his jihad, Zack couldn't imagine waving hello to him at the Quarter Hill Shop & Save.

"I still don't understand why he's trying to kill us," Zack said. "I mean he's acting like we're all walking A-bombs, or future Hitlers."

Peter shook his head. "Doesn't matter. He's wrong. None of this is your fault."

"None of *what*?" David asked. "What are your people so afraid of?"

The sisters watched Peter carefully as he stared out the window, tapping his lantern jaw. The melancholy in his deep blue eyes was enough to kill their last strand of hope that Evan had lied. They covered their mouths and wept.

Theo leaned forward and rubbed Hannah's arm. "Hey. Hey. Why are you crying?"

Zack studied Amanda in ardent concern. "What happened to you back there?"

"Someone talked to them," said Peter.

"I'm asking her."

"And I'm answering for her. The moment I saw the sisters, I recognized the look on their faces. It's the same look my people have been wearing for the last ten weeks. Someone told them the bad news. Some bastard gave them the cloud without the silver lining."

"Silver lining?" Hannah cried, in a wheezing rasp. "How is there a silver lining?"

Mia tugged tissues from a box and passed them to Amanda and Hannah. On her way back to her sofa, David gently pulled her into his easy chair and locked his arms around her like a seat belt. He threw an uneasy nod at Peter.

"All right. Tell us everything."

The Irishman leaned back into the couch with a long, sorrowful sigh. He'd hoped to wait until they were better rested.

"The future's a very peculiar thing," he began. "The best prophets in the world couldn't tell you what I'll have for breakfast tomorrow, but they know for a fact that a volcano in Hawaii will erupt in four months' time. They know a small meteor will punch the Gobi desert next April and that San Francisco will fall to an earthquake in two years. It's easy as hell to see these things because they're the same across all timelines. No one can stop them from happening.

"On July 24th, the day you all arrived, the sixty-seven augurs of my clan suddenly got a peek at a whole new future. The vision hit them like acid, the single worst thing any of them had ever seen. Four of them killed themselves before the day was done. We lost a dozen more the following week. And Rebel? He used to be a reasonable guy. You'll just have to take my word for it."

The augur in the room could suddenly see where this was going. At long last, Theo understood the lingering dread that clouded the thoughts of his future selves, the same giant sword hanging over all their heads.

David reeled in bother. "I don't understand. If it's a second Cataclysm, as you implied, then why the suicidal despair? You'd have months, possibly years to evacuate."

"It's not a Cataclysm," Theo said.

The boy looked to Peter. "But when you wrote Mia—"

"I haven't written that letter yet, David. Those are the words of a future me. But I know exactly why he lied. He needed you all to get here. He didn't want you losing hope."

Zack opened and closed his mouth three times before speaking. "What . . . what . . ."

What could possibly be worse than a Cataclysm? he wanted to ask. As the words tangled in his throat, the obvious answer rolled over him like a sickness. He fell back in his chair, white-faced.

"Oh Jesus . . ."

Amanda drank him in through moist eyes. Worse than the pain of seeing Zack catch up to her was the realization that he was the only one in the room who wasn't touching or holding someone. She wanted to leap across the table and wrap herself around him, Esis be goddamned.

Peter kept his dark gaze on the two spooning teenagers, the ones who could still count their years on fingers and toes. At long last, Mia understood why a future self had urged her to come to New York in a strong state of mind, why she demanded they take a week to relax in blissful ignorance.

Now her mouth quivered in a bow, stuck on the same jagged word. "W-when?"

"No firm date," said Peter. "We know it's between four and five years, closer to five."

She fell back into David and the cruelest of math. *I'll be eighteen. He'll be twenty.*

"How?" asked the boy, in a cracked voice.

"I don't want to bog you down in the gruesome details. Just—"

"Same way," Hannah told him. That was all that needed to be said.

Peter leaned forward in fresh determination. "Okay, now that you have the bad news—"

"Why does this keep happening?"

"Mia . . ."

"Why does this keep happening?!"

All Peter could offer was a somber shrug. "I don't know the how or the why, sweetheart. My guess is that the answer's wrapped up in those Pelletiers who brought you here. I don't know any more about them than you do."

"You said there was a silver lining."

He nodded at David. "There is, but you need to bear with me while I explain it."

"Explain what, exactly?"

"Why I'm walking funny."

Their heavy brows furrowed at Peter. He blew a long breath through his knuckles, deliberating his words.

"There's a unique state of consciousness that my people occasionally achieve, a place where all the branching futures stretch out before us like a great tapestry. We call it the God's Eye, and by now one of you has become very familiar with it."

Theo nodded skittishly, unsure where Peter was going with this. "I thought it was just for augurs."

"Our blessings aren't mutually exclusive," Peter explained. "We all have a little tempis in us. A little lumis. A little foresight. We all have the chance to stumble into the God's Eye when the right or wrong wires cross in our brains. Well, on July 24th, it was my turn. I'll admit my stroke wasn't the small deal I made it out to be. It actually put me in a coma for a day."

Hannah pinched her lip in twitchy rumination. It seemed mighty odd that Theo and Peter suffered a coma at the same time, for the same duration.

"Anyway, Theo can tell you that time passes differently in the God's Eye, if it even passes at all. I don't know how long I spent there. Weeks. Months. Most of the details are lost to me now, like an old dream. All I remember is following the trail to the end of the world. I saw exactly what the augurs saw. I know why so many of them committed suicide."

Mia curled against David, fighting her tears. He held her close and stroked her hair. For a moment Amanda saw the same heavy look of rue he'd worn at the Sunday mass in Evansville.

"I also remember going beyond the end," Peter told them. "Somehow I punched through the curtain and entered this . . . I don't even know how to describe it without sounding daft. I was floating in a cold gray void. I could see the end of every timeline—a trillion trillion points of light, all lined up flat as far as the eye can see. It was a cruel and beautiful thing, like a snowdrift or a desert, or—"

"A wall," said Theo, through a dead-white face. Hannah could feel the new tension in his grip.

"You saw it?" she asked.

"Only in dreams," he replied, though he knew that would change soon. He and Peter traded a dark look of understanding before the Irishman continued.

"Now I need you all to listen to me because this is the crucial part. I saw something on that wall. And I swear to you on the life of my son that I didn't imagine it. It was truly there."

Peter's eyes grew moist. His lips quivered. He held up a single finger.

"One string. I saw one string of light that extended from the wall and just kept going. One single timeline where life continued. The moment I laid eyes on it, I knew in my heart that the end of the world wasn't like an earthquake or a meteor or an erupting volcano. It's not a fixed event. There's one string of time where someone manages to stop what's coming."

The Silvers wore the same incredulous expression for five quiet seconds.

"One string out of trillions," Hannah said.

"One is all you need, hon. I saw it. It exists. Now, I didn't have a chance to reach it before I fell out of my coma, but I know it's still there waiting for us. All someone needs to do is find it and study it. See what went right. Once we know, we'll make damn sure to repeat the process, step by step."

"Uh, when you say someone—"

"I mean one of you in particular. You know who I'm talking about."

All eyes turned to Theo. He fell inside his head, struggling to wrap his thoughts around the giant task Peter was placing on him. He'd already reverse engineered one favorable outcome, but that was just for a single hour and five friends. Now he was being asked to do the same thing on a global scale over a half decade. Assuming he could even find the string. Assuming it existed.

"Why him?" Amanda asked. "He's not the only one who can see the future."

"As of now, there are only forty augurs left in the world," Peter replied, "and Theo blows them all out of the water. He's the only one who has the power to enter the God's Eye willingly."

"I didn't."

"You will."

"I can't."

"You *will*," Peter insisted. "If you don't trust me, trust Future Mia. She's the one who told me."

Hannah wanted to cry again. Theo was only ten weeks sober. He'd just overcome a painful neurological malady. Now he'd been given a burden that no one should ever have to carry.

She glared at Peter. "You can't just dump this on him. It's not fair."

"I have a son who's fixing to die at seventeen. There's very little about this that's fair."

"I'm not worried about the fairness," said Theo. "I'm just worried you're wrong."

"I'm not."

"I'm sure Rebel feels the same way about his theory," Zack cautioned.

"Rebel's seen the string too. He knows there's a solution. He just made some terrible assumptions about the nature of it. Correcting him is our next priority, one of many. The rest of us will have plenty to do while Theo's busy."

The group sat in muddled silence for nearly a full minute. Peter leaned back and flicked a weak hand in the air.

"I don't blame you at all for your skepticism. Nobody's suffered more at the hands of the universe than you six. And yet here you are, still together, still breathing. An augur, an actress, a widow, a cartoonist, a boy, and a girl. You're the most extraordinary group of people I've ever met and I will never bet against you. Ever."

The others stayed rigidly quiet, biting their lips in tight suppression. None of them felt even a fraction as formidable as Peter made them out to be. They could only see his point when they looked around the table. There didn't seem to be a single companion without a string of miracles under their belt, even just from today.

Peter finished securing Amanda's boot, then gently swung her legs to the coffee table. He stood up and let out a stretching groan.

"I think it's well past time you folks got some rest. Should your troubled minds keep you from sleeping, as troubled minds do, remember the silver lining. We'll find the string. We'll stop what's coming. What happened to your world won't happen here."

The Silvers absently gazed ahead as Peter gathered the empty tea mugs and disappeared into the kitchen. They listened to the running faucet, the gentle clinks of spoons and ceramics.

Soon Zack rose to his feet and circled the table, extending both hands to Amanda.

"Come on. I'll take you upstairs."

While he ported her onto his back, Amanda scanned the two entwined couples on the easy chairs. Judging by their dark and dreary faces, she figured none of them would be detaching anytime soon.

Halfway up the stairs, she leaned forward and breathed a soft whisper in Zack's ear.

"Stay with me."

Though his expression remained impassive, Zack assured her in no un-certain terms that he had every intention of doing so. Every damn reason in the world.

They slumbered for hours, six weary travelers on three bare mattresses. Scant words were exchanged before their bodies succumbed to fatigue. David con-fessed to Mia that he killed a man today, and she held him. Zack told Amanda that he healed a friend today, and she held him.

Hannah had the most to say. As she clutched Theo from behind, she swore in a tender whisper that she would be there for him in any way he needed her. If she couldn't be the messiah, she could at least be the one who kept him sane. It seemed a better use of her life than singing showtunes for scale.

As the sun set on Commemoration, the Silvers woke up feeling ten years older and no more relaxed. They dissolved their sleepy unions with little fan-fare and retreated to their designated bedrooms. David and Mia set up their separate little sanctums on the second floor. Zack and Theo established their dorm-like den in the basement. Hannah wearily toiled through the clutter of boxes in the master bedroom, a huge and gorgeous chamber with a cathedral ceiling and a narrow balcony overlooking the backyard.

She caught a strange flash of light in the corner of her eye. Through the top-floor window of the neighboring brownstone, a petite young brunette pranced about in a radiant speedsuit, trailing incandescent streaks of color with every rapid gesture. The sight was both surreal and mesmerizing to Hannah, enough to knock her off her axis. Suddenly the universe seemed a dreamlike place where nothing was too far-fetched. Cartoon sparrows could fly through the window and help her make the bed. The furniture could come to life and sing a song about prudence.

"What are you looking at?"

Hannah jumped and spun around. For all the world's new possibilities, she didn't expect Amanda to be standing right behind her. Her sister had been downstairs getting her leg x-rayed, or tomographed, whatever it was called. Now she was here on the balcony, propping herself on tempic crutches, holding two paperback novels under her arm.

"Sorry," said Amanda. "Didn't mean to scare you."

"No. I'm okay. I was just . . ." Hannah took a moment to register Amanda's crude white supports. "Wow. You made your own crutches."

"Yeah. The ones Peter got me are a little too short. These will be fine."

"I thought you couldn't hold the tempis for more than a few seconds at a time."

"I thought so too. Who knows? Maybe I'm getting stronger."

Amanda briefly scanned the room, then tossed a worried look at Hannah. "Listen, I hope you're not sharing a room for my benefit. I mean if you wanted to, you know, be with Theo . . ."

"No. We're actually good the way we are, as strange as that sounds."

"That's not strange."

"Well, it's strange for me. You know how stress makes me slutty."

Amanda laughed. "I think you're working off an old image of you."

Now it was Hannah's turn to grow concerned. "What about Zack? I mean . . ."

"Oh no. We didn't. We're not—"

"I didn't think you did. I just . . ." Hannah desperately tried to find a way to express her issue without mentioning their new ticking calendar. "I just don't know why you two aren't together. Especially now."

Amanda knew, though she didn't have the strength to discuss it. At some point soon, she'd have to have a long talk with Zack about siblings and Esis. She wasn't expecting a brave response.

"It's complicated."

She dropped her books onto an end table. Hannah glimpsed armored knights on the covers. They clashed swords right above Peter Pendergen's name.

"Wow. I forgot he was an author."

"Yeah. He went out of his way to remind me."

"You don't like him?"

Amanda shrugged uncomfortably. "I don't know what to think yet."

"He seems nice, all things considered."

"He does."

"He's certainly nice to look at."

"Yes. He is that."

"You're just afraid he's wrong."

Amanda's face darkened. Hannah turned around and cast an airy sigh over the railing. "Yeah. Me too."

The crutches vanished. Amanda leaned on her sister now, resting her chin on her shoulder. They stared out at the vibrant dusk.

"I don't think we're going to die of old age," Hannah mused. "Not even in the best case."

Amanda closed her eyes. "I don't think so either."

"Mia was right, though. You and I are lucky."

"We're all lucky," Amanda insisted. "We all have family here."

"Well, they may be my siblings at heart, but you're my flesh and blood and I love you."

"I love you too, Hannah. So much. You saved my life today. You carried me."

They held each other tight, sniffling in unison. Amanda eyed her sister strangely when she broke out in a high giggle.

"What?"

"Just thinking about Mom. If she could see us right now, she'd crap a kitten."

Amanda burst with laughter. "Oh my God. She's probably running around Heaven right now, looking for a camcorder."

Hannah wiped her eyes. Amanda gave her a squeeze, then re-created her crutches.

"These painkillers are making me loopy. I need to lie down again."

"Okay. I'll come inside in a bit."

Hannah spent another ten minutes watching the young lumis dancer perform in her bedroom, twirling her array of colored lines and spirals. The actress flinched with surprise when the girl suddenly moved to the window and waved a rainbow. Hannah didn't know if she was waving at her or just continuing her routine. If the dancer wasn't so far away, Hannah might have squinted at her wrist and counted the number of watches.

With that sudden reminder, Hannah dashed inside and rooted through her jeans until she found the purple note that Ioni had slipped her at the parade. Unfolding it revealed a flyer for some rock band called the Quadrants. They were playing at a Greenwich Village bar for one night only . . . in April of next year.

She flipped the sheet over and saw a few lines of blue-ink scribble:

Hannah,

Evan Rander took a good man out of your path. I'm putting one in. Go to this event. Look around. You'll know him when you see him. He's still wearing his bracelet.

Don't lose hope, my dear Given. Don't count the hours. Whether it's four and a half years or four and a half decades, you still have a lifetime ahead of you. Enjoy as many moments as you can. Find your happy face.

Hannah leaned back against the dresser, her lips and hands trembling as she reread the note. By the third pass through, her cheeks were wet with tears and she found herself hating Ioni. The girl surely knew of the hell that awaited the Silvers in that office building, and yet she failed to warn them away. *Why the hell should I trust you?* Hannah seethed.

She dimmed the lights and then joined her sister in bed, spooning her from behind while Amanda gently snored.

After a dark and restless hour, Hannah stumbled back onto a charitable thought. Maybe Ioni had a reason for not warning Hannah. Maybe she thought the only way the six of them would survive the day was if all their enemies attacked them at once, and attacked each other in the process.

Who the hell could say? Hannah lived in a strange new world now, with temporis and speedsuits and parallel strings. It was almost too much for a poor actress to handle. All she knew was that she'd go and see the Quadrants play next April. Whether the mystery man was a Silver, a Gold, or some other glimmering color, he was one of her people. He had to be found.

As she drifted off to sleep, it occurred to her that she should probably find something nice to wear for the encounter. Maybe a sleek top over jeans. Or maybe something a little more respectable. Hannah supposed there was no rush to decide. The event was six months away. She had time.

ACKNOWLEDGMENTS

Writing this book was a three-year endeavor, one I couldn't have finished without the help and encouragement of some very fine people. They include Avi Bar-Zeev, Sara Glickstein Bar-Zeev, Mike Tunison, Craig Mertens, Mary Dalton-Hoffman, Mick Soth, Huan Nghiem, Jason Cole, D'Anna Sharon, Dustin Shaffer, Dave Bledsoe, Bill McDermott, Scott Clinkscales, and Ysabelle Pelletier. Yeah, there's a Pelletier on the list.

Extra special gratitude to my alpha testers, those patient, generous souls who guided me one rough chapter at a time—Mark Harvey, Leni Fleming, Jen Gennaco, and Gretchen Walker.

Huge thanks to David Rosenthal and his team at Blue Rider Press for taking a chance on me and helping me get the Silvers ready for prime time. All readers should be grateful to my terrific editor, Vanessa Kehren. If you think this book's fat now, you should have seen it before she got her hands on it.

No acknowledgment would be complete without mentioning the great Stuart M. Miller, my longtime agent and friend who's supported every nutty decision I've made, including the one to write a multi-part, character-driven, supernatural suspense epic.

Last but not least is Ricki Bar-Zeev, my biggest fan and toughest critic. None of this—and none of me—would have been possible without her. Thank you, Mom.

THE SILVERS SAGA WILL CONTINUE IN
BOOK TWO: THE SONG OF THE ORPHANS.

TO LEARN MORE ABOUT THE SERIES
AND TO SIGN UP TO BE NOTIFIED
WHEN NEW BOOKS ARE AVAILABLE,
VISIT WWW.DANIELPRICE.INFO.